CRIMSON SHADOWS

THE FULLY ILLUSTRATED ROBERT E. HOWARD LIBRARY
from Del Rey Books

The Coming of Conan the Cimmerian

The Savage Tales of Solomon Kane

The Bloody Crown of Conan

Bran Mak Morn: The Last King

The Conquering Sword of Conan

Kull: Exile of Atlantis

The Best of Robert E. Howard
Volume 1: Crimson Shadows

The Best of Robert E. Howard
Volume 2: Grim Lands
(forthcoming)

CRIMSON SHADOWS

THE BEST OF
ROBERT E. HOWARD

~ VOLUME ONE ~

ILLUSTRATED BY
JIM & RUTH KEEGAN

BALLANTINE BOOKS | DEL REY | NEW YORK

A Del Rey Trade Paperback Original

Copyright © 2007 by Robert E. Howard Properties, Inc.

Published in the United States by Del Rey Books,
an imprint of The Random House Publishing Group,
a division of Random House, Inc., New York.

DEL REY is a registered trademark and the Del Rey colophon
is a trademark of Random House, Inc.

ISBN 978-0-345-49018-6

Printed in the United States of America

www.delreybooks.com

2   4   6   8   9   7   5   3

Art Director: Marcelo Anciano
Typographer: Stuart Williams
Editor: Rusty Burke

To our friend Gary

You reopened trails left too long untraveled.
Thanks for showing us the way.

And to our son Rourke

You make everything we do better.

Jim & Ruth Keegan

The Shadow Kingdom
first published in *Weird Tales*, August 1929

The Ghost Kings
first published in *Weird Tales*,
December 1938

The Curse of the Golden Skull
first published in *The Howard Collector*,
Spring 1967

Red Shadows
first published in *Weird Tales*, August 1928

The One Black Stain
first published in *The Howard Collector*,
Spring 1962

The Dark Man
first published in *Weird Tales*,
December 1931

The Marching Song of Connacht
first published in *The Howard Collector*,
Spring 1972

Kings of the Night
first published in *Weird Tales*,
November 1930

Recompense
first published in *Weird Tales*,
November 1938

The Black Stone
first published in *Weird Tales*,
November 1931

The Song of a Mad Minstrel
first published in *Weird Tales*,
February-March 1931

The Fightin'est Pair
first published in *Action Stories*,
November 1931 (as *"Breed of Battle"*)

The Grey God Passes
first published in *Dark Mind, Dark Heart*,
Arkham House, 1962

The Song of the Last Briton
first published in *The Ghost Ocean*,
Gibbelins Gazette Publications, 1982

Worms of the Earth
first published in *Weird Tales*,
November 1932

An Echo from the Iron Harp
first published in *The Gold and the Grey*,
Roy A. Squires, 1974
(as *"The Gold and the Grey"*)

Lord of the Dead
first published in *Skull-Face*,
Berkley Books, 1978

Untitled
first published in *The Howard Collector*,
Summer 1964

"For the Love of Barbara Allen"
first published in *The Magazine of Fantasy
& Science Fiction*, August 1966

The Tide
first published in *Omniumgathum*,
Stygian Isle Press, 1976

The Valley of the Worm
first published in *Weird Tales*, February 1934

The Dust Dance: Selections, Version II
first published in *The Howard Collector*,
Spring 1968 (as "The Dust Dance")

The People of the Black Circle
first published in *Weird Tales*,
September, October, and November 1934

Beyond the Black River
first published in *Weird Tales*,
May and June 1935

A Word from the Outer Dark
first published in *Kadath*, No. 1, 1974

Hawk of the Hills
first published in *Top-Notch*, June 1935

Sharp's Gun Serenade
first published in *Action Stories*,
January 1937

Lines Written in the Realization That I Must Die
first published in *Weird Tales*, August 1938

Contents

Foreword

As the stories in this book will prove, Robert E. Howard was a writer who could make any genre his own, and even create a new genre when circumstance called for it. In these pages, you'll encounter stories of fantasy, horror, adventure, and humor. Taken individually, they are a real treat to illustrate. Taken as a collection, however, they present a unique challenge.

Our art director, Marcelo Anciano, made it clear that our job was to find a way to unify these stories, rather than schizophrenically shift art styles to suit the mood or character of specific tales. We had to find a common visual cue that could carry us from the ancient Hyborian kingdoms of Conan, through the Elizabethan world of Solomon Kane, to the battlefields of the American Civil War and the hills of 1930s Afghanistan. Robert E. Howard's deeply held philosophy of absolute, rugged individualism was the obvious common thread. No matter the genre, Howard wrote of individuals standing tall against the forces that would oppose them – seen and unseen, natural or otherwise – preferring to be crushed into the ground and flattened rather than to give so much as an inch.

The trick is how to express this in pictures.

Last year, on a visit to the Philadelphia Museum of Art, we saw a small painting by Thomas Eakins. It was a study of a bearded man set against a neutral background, his face and torso falling away into darkness. Despite the simplicity of presentation, the figure had a look of majesty that was nothing short of biblical. Eakins had carved out his subject in harsh light and deep shadow—a yin and yang of values combined to create elegant graphic shapes that told a complex story in one striking design.

It was this simple image that gave us our direction for the illustrations and fed nicely into our existing fascination with the streamlined poster style of the 1920s and '30s (Howard's own era). This approach was pioneered and best exemplified by the German master Ludwig Hohlwein (a devotee of the "Beggarstaffs"), whose graphic simplicity could make even an illustration for a lady's hat monumental. We tried to stay true to this artistic legacy of form and design: concise and bold with a minimum of strokes, the physical power of the individual immediately recognizable at a glance.

Of course, our efforts are not the point. We're all here for the words of Robert E. Howard. So, it's time to sit back, and prepare for REH to put steel in your arms and fire in your eyes.

Jim & Ruth Keegan
Studio City, California
January 2007

Introduction

Excitement and adventure!
That's what the readers want, and that's what I give them.

So says Robert E. Howard to Novalyne Price as they drive along beneath the Texas moon in the movie *The Whole Wide World*, and while the quotation is not attested in any written source (including Price's memoir upon which the film is based), it's hard to beat as a concise statement of what the reader will find upon first encountering the fiction of REH, as he's known to his legions of fans. As with any great writer, there is more to it than that – people don't keep reading an author's work seventy years after his death if all it offers is excitement and adventure – but Howard always lived up to the first obligation of the storyteller, which is to tell a ripping good yarn. In this volume and its forthcoming companion, you will find excitement and adventure aplenty.

Robert E. Howard (1906–1936) lived his entire life in small Texas towns, chiefly Cross Plains, far from the literary world. Yet by the time he was a teenager he had apparently decided upon a career as a writer. "It seems to me that many writers, by virtue of environments of culture, art and education, slip into writing because of their environments," he wrote to his fellow weird fictionist H. P. Lovecraft. "I became a writer in spite of my environments. Understand, I am not criticizing those environments. They were good, solid and worthy. The fact that they were not inducive to literature and art is nothing in their disfavor. Never the less, it is no light thing to enter into a profession absolutely foreign and alien to the people among which one's lot is cast; a profession which seems as dim and faraway and unreal as the shores of Europe. The people among which I lived – and yet live, mainly – made their living from cotton, wheat, cattle, oil, with the usual percentage of business men and professional men. That is most certainly not in their disfavor. But the idea of a man making his living by writing seemed, in that hardy environment, so fantastic that even today I am sometimes myself assailed by a feeling of unreality. Never the less, at the age of fifteen, having never seen a writer, a poet, a publisher or a magazine editor, and having only the vaguest ideas of procedure, I began working on the profession I had chosen."

After three years of unsuccessfully sending stories to magazines, at the age of eighteen Howard sold his first professional story to a new magazine of "the bizarre and unusual," the now legendary *Weird Tales* (which introduced the world not only to Howard, but to H. P. Lovecraft, Clark Ashton Smith, Robert Bloch, and Ray Bradbury, among many others). In a brief, twelve-year career, Howard wrote some 300 stories and more than 800 poems. His work covered a variety of genres – fantasy, boxing, westerns, horror, adventure, historical, detective, spicy, even confessions – and graced the pages of such pulp magazines as *Action Stories*, *Argosy*, *Fight Stories*, *Oriental Stories*, *Spicy Adventure*, *Sport Story*, *Strange Detective*, *Thrilling Adventure*, *Top Notch*, and a number of others. Pulp writers often found that a character who was popular with readers could be a significant meal ticket, but Howard had difficulty keeping a series going indefinitely. Once he found himself "out of contact with the conception," he was "unable to write convincingly" of that character. If he was to convince the reader, he had to be convinced himself. As Lovecraft famously noted, the thing that makes a Howard story stand out is that "he himself is in every one of them." Fortunately, characters seem to have come easily to him. He is most famous, of course, for Conan of Cimmeria, who has taken on a life of his own as "Conan the Barbarian," far removed from Howard's brilliantly original conception; herein you will find other great characters, like Kull of Atlantis, king of fabled Valusia; Solomon Kane, the swashbuckling Puritan adventurer; Bran Mak Morn, last king of an ancient race; Sailor Steve Costigan, the champion of the forecastle; Breckinridge Elkins, the man-mountain who can't seem to avoid walking into trouble; Steve Harrison, the detective who's as likely to solve the mystery with his fists as with his wits; and many others. They run the gamut from dark fantasy to broad humor, from brooding horror to gentle love story.

Given such a wealth of riches to choose from, one who has the audacity to select the "best" of a writer's work should provide some explanation as to how the stories were chosen. It must be admitted that this is, fundamentally, my personal selection of the stories and poems I think Howard's best, but with a caveat: we wanted a representative sampling of his best work, and so necessarily had to limit the number of selections for any single character. I have long wished there were a volume of Howard stories that I could hand to a friend who expressed interest in his work, a book full of great stories that illustrated the full range of his repertoire. We've ended up with a two-volume collection, rather than one, because, frankly, it was just too hard to whittle it down any further. As it is, some of my favorite stories and poems are not included, and I'm sure that there will not be many Howard fans who don't find some of their own favorites missing.

While I made the selections, I did have some assistance from a poll I conducted among long-time Howard fans, asking for their favorite stories or those they found most memorable. Of the top twenty-five stories in that poll, nineteen are included in these volumes, and five of those left out are Conan tales: to make room for other characters and stories, I made the arbitrary decision to include only two Conan stories in each volume, and the ones chosen ended up being the top four vote-getters in the poll. In most other cases, the story selected for these volumes was the highest ranking tale of its type in the poll. The top vote-getter overall was *Worms of the Earth*, followed by the Conan stories *Red Nails* (which will appear in the second volume) and *Beyond the Black River*.

The Shadow Kingdom is often cited as the first story of what has come to be known as "sword and sorcery," a genre Howard is credited with having invented, and thus is important as a milestone in the history of fantasy literature, but it is also a terrific story, one Steven Trout has called "a memorable piece of purest paranoia." Lovecraft believed that the Kull stories were the best of Howard's heroic tales, and many have agreed with his assessment, though Howard was able to sell only two stories of the series during his lifetime. *Weird Tales* editor Farnsworth Wright asked readers to name their favorite stories in each issue, and tallied the results. *The Shadow Kingdom* was the favorite of readers in the August 1929 issue, and ranked second overall that year, behind only Lovecraft's *The Dunwich Horror*.

The Curse of the Golden Skull has only the barest mention of Kull, but is included here as a fine example of Howard's prose poetry. Howard was a natural poet, often filling his letters to his friend Tevis Clyde Smith with page after page of apparently spontaneous poetry, and his friends recalled him being able to memorize long passages with only a reading or two. (He is alleged to have memorized *The Rime of the Ancient Mariner* after only two readings!) His father later recalled that Robert's mother "loved poetry. Written poetry by sheets and reams, almost books of it, were stored in her memory so that from Robert's babyhood he had heard its recital day by day." His love of poetry infuses most of his best fiction, and in prose poems like *The Curse of the Golden Skull* we find it in concentrated form.

Red Shadows, the first published story of Solomon Kane, has its supporters for the title of first sword and sorcery tale, having been published a year before *The Shadow Kingdom*. Kane is one of Howard's most fascinating, complex characters, a man who believes himself to be doing the will of God, while consorting with a witch-doctor and, in occasional moments of self-awareness, realizing that he is driven by lust for adventure. The story is an early one, written when Howard was only twenty-one, so it has a few rough patches, but it is a favorite of most REH fans and includes many memorable moments, not least Kane's vow of vengeance that sets him on the trail of Le Loup.

Lovecraft told E. Hoffmann Price, after Howard's death, "I always gasped at his profound knowledge of history . . . and admired still more his really astonishing *assimilation* and *visualisation* of it. He was almost unique in his ability to *understand* and *mentally inhabit* past ages . . ." The Solomon Kane poem *The One Black Stain* provides an outstanding example, as Howard places himself (through his Puritan adventurer) at the scene of an incident during Sir Francis Drake's circumnavigation of the globe. Another fine example herein is the poem *An Echo from the Iron Harp*, narrated by a warrior of the Cimbri who defeated Roman legions in several battles before being defeated themselves at Vercellae.

The Dark Man is one of three tales in this volume that feature Bran Mak Morn, though in this one he is a distant historical memory, living on only as a lifeless statue – or *is* it lifeless? The real protagonist of the story is the Irish outlaw Turlogh Dubh O'Brien, "Black Turlogh," whose pronouncement at the end of this savage tale seems to be all too true. So intense was Howard's interest in and admiration for the Irish that he created for himself an Irish and Celtic ancestry. Characters such as Turlogh O'Brien and Cormac Mac Art, and martial poetry like *The Marching Song of Connacht* and *The Song of the Last Briton* reflect this interest. At the time Howard was writing, the Irish war for independence from Britain and the creation of the Irish Free State were recent memories, and resentments were still raw.

Kings of the Night is quite an unusual story for Howard, in that it unites two of his characters from disparate eras, Kull of antediluvian Atlantis and Bran Mak Morn of Roman-era Britain, in a pitched battle against a Roman legion. *Weird Tales* readers voted it the best story of the November 1930 issue, and it got more votes than any other story that year.

In 1930 also Howard began corresponding with H. P. Lovecraft, and the initial exchanges apparently inspired him to try his hand at Lovecraft's style of fiction. HPL (also known to his fans by his initials) had created an artificial mythos (now widely known as the "Cthulhu mythos," after his story *The Call of Cthulhu*) which he sprinkled through his stories and those of writers whose work he was revising for publication, in order to give an impression of verisimilitude, and which he encouraged other writers to borrow from and add to. *The Black Stone* is Howard's best story of this type, featuring such contributions to the shared mythos as the German occultist Von Junzt and his hellish "Black Book," *Nameless Cults* (later dubbed, after much correspondence among the *Weird Tales* writers, *Unaussprechlichen Kulten*) and the mad poet, Justin Geoffrey (who could well have been the composer of *The Song of a Mad Minstrel*).

One of Howard's most successful series was about as far from the field of fantasy and horror fiction as one can go. An avid boxing enthusiast, Howard also had an antic sense of humor, and both of these went into the rollicking misadventures of Sailor Steve Costigan, who has a heart of gold, a head of wood, and fists of iron. An able-bodied seaman on a tramp steamer, he gets matched against the champs of other ships in exotic ports around the world, and manages to get hoodwinked by dames, cheated by shifty promoters, and victimized by misunderstandings, yet emerges (somewhat) victorious – at least in the ring. Twenty-one of the Costigan stories were published during Howard's lifetime (twenty-two if we count a story in which his name was changed to "Dennis Dorgan"), compared to seventeen Conan tales, yet Howard's boxing yarns had, until recently, gotten short shrift from fans and scholars, possibly due to the decline in popularity of the sport itself. Thanks to the work of Mark Finn and Chris Gruber, among others, these stories are again taking their rightful place in Howard's body of work, and fans are getting a chance to see the more exuberant side of REH.

In 1931, hoping to break into a magazine featuring historical fiction, Howard wrote a story called *Spears of Clontarf*, a fictionalized account of the battle in 1014 in which the Irish under Brian Boru routed the Vikings who had established themselves in Dublin. When the story was rejected, he revised it, adding a weird element in hopes of selling it to either the new magazine *Strange Tales* or his old standby *Weird Tales*. In this, too, he was unsuccessful, but not because it wasn't a fine story – it is. Farnsworth Wright, the *Weird Tales* editor, returned it with the comment that "the weird element is not as strong as I would like it to be." Possibly he had just received a letter, later published in the magazine, complaining that the story *The Dark Man* was not really weird. Fortunately, we are not required to worry about whether the story is "weird enough," and can include this fine tale of the twilight of an age.

As previously mentioned, the story most often named by Howard fans as their favorite or most memorable is the best of the Bran Mak Morn tales, *Worms of the Earth*. Here Bran swears an awful vengeance against Rome, but he pays a terrible price. No other of his fictional creations had the enduring appeal to Howard of his Picts, who appear in his fiction from 1923 to 1935, and in not only the Bran Mak Morn series, but also the Kull and Conan series, and a number of stand-alone stories. *Worms of the Earth*, though, stands out from the rest of the Pictish stories, and Howard himself explained the reason: "My interest in the Picts was always mixed with a bit of fantasy – that is, I never felt the realistic placement with them that I did with the Irish and Highland Scotch. Not that it was the less vivid; but when I came to write of them, it was still through alien eyes – thus in my first Bran Mak Morn story [*Men of the Shadows*] – which was rightfully rejected – I told the story through the person of a Gothic mercenary in the Roman army; in a long narrative rhyme which I never completed, and in which I first put Bran on paper, I told it through a Roman centurion on the Wall; in *The Lost Race* the central figure was a Briton; and in *Kings of the Night* it was a Gaelic prince. Only in my last Bran story, *The Worms of the Earth* which

Mr. Wright accepted, did I look through Pictish eyes, and speak with a Pictish tongue!"

One genre in which Howard was not entirely comfortable, and therefore not especially successful, was the detective story. Abandoning the field after about three years of trying to write them, he said, " I can't seem to get the hang of the art. Maybe it's because I don't like to write them. I'd rather write adventure stuff." There is little of "mystery" to his detective tales, but a lot of adventure, and Steve Harrison and his brethren are more likely to solve the crime with brawn than with brains. These stories have more in common with Sax Rohmer's Fu Manchu tales than with Dashiell Hammett's Continental Op. Yet, as Fred Blosser never tires of reminding me, they *are* action-packed stories, and the best of them, like the novel *Skull-Face* and the story included here, *Lord of the Dead*, can stand proudly alongside Howard's other work. I do love the over-the-top climax to this tale.

Robert E. Howard loved folk songs, and sprinkled them liberally through his fiction. At one point in the mid-1920s he corresponded with the noted folklorist Robert W. Gordon, at the time compiler of the *Adventure* magazine department "Old Songs That Men Have Sung," later the first head of the Archive of American Folk Song at the Library of Congress (where the letters he received from Howard are held). Here we have a story built around a folk song, "*For the Love of Barbara Allen.*" It shows a gentler side of Howard, not often revealed. We see it, too, in the poem *The Tide.* Fans of the movie *The Whole Wide World* may recognize two stanzas which Robert Howard, played by Vincent D'Onofrio, reads to his mother in the film. It certainly resonates with the title of Novalyne Price Ellis's memoir on which the movie was based: *One Who Walked Alone.*

Scholars are divided over whether or not REH actually believed in reincarnation, but there's no question that he used it a lot as a plot device. His James Allison stories, of which most fans consider *The Valley of the Worm* the best, probably owe something to Jack London's novel *The Star Rover*, a book which, Howard said, "I've read and reread for years, and that generally goes to my head like wine." In that book, London's protagonist, Darrell Standing, imprisoned for murder and placed in solitary confinement, escapes from the brutal reality of the present by mentally revisiting past lives. Howard apparently liked the plot device, but he made his character an invalid rather than a convict, which provides a strong contrast with the virile heroes Allison had been in his past lives. The ethnology is certainly outdated, but the story itself is timeless.

The People of the Black Circle is one of the stories people first think of when they think of Conan. It has it all, the exotic locale, the beautiful (and feisty) woman, the crafty and powerful wizards, the headlong narrative pace.

It is sword and sorcery at its best. The other Conan tale here, *Beyond the Black River*, is, as previously noted, one of only three stories named on more than half the ballots in my poll of Howard fans. It has aroused occasional controversy: some critics have claimed that, because it uses some names from Robert W. Chambers' Revolutionary War novels, the setting is probably derived from upstate New York, while others (of whom I am one) claim that it is a story of the Texas frontier, played out on Conan's Hyborian Age stage. Novalyne Price Ellis, with whom Howard discussed the story, said it was a Texas story. And we have this passage from a letter to Lovecraft: "A student of early Texas history is struck by the fact that some of the most savage battles with the Indians were fought in the territory between the Brazos and Trinity rivers.... In the old times the red-skins held the banks of the Brazos. Sometimes they drove the ever-encroaching settlers back – sometimes the white men crossed the Brazos, only to be hurled back again, sometimes clear back beyond the Trinity. But they came on again – in spite of flood, drouth, starvation and Indian massacre." Yet whatever may be its setting, this tale of conflict on the frontier is one of Howard's finest stories, and it concludes with one of his most memorable, and most often quoted, lines.

One of the earliest characters created by Robert E. Howard was Francis X. Gordon, called in the Orient "El Borak," the Swift. The author claimed to have created the character when he was only ten years old. In the surviving early El Borak stories, written when Howard was about sixteen, Gordon seems to be a relatively urbane man of the world. None of those early tales is complete, and the character apparently faded from Howard's consciousness for several years. When he started "splashing the field," though, in response to the failures of some of his markets during the Depression, he revived Gordon, but the veneer of urbanity was now gone entirely, and the former gunslinger of the Texas border had gone native in the Middle East. *Hawk of the Hills*, in addition to being a terrific story, is an interesting twist on one of the major inspirations for the El Borak series, Talbot Mundy, as Howard's character must save the hide of another who appears to be based on Mundy's Athelstan King (of *King of the Khyber Rifles*, and other stories).

By 1933, Howard's attentions were turning toward writing westerns, and when an old stand-by, *Action Stories*, returned from a year-long hiatus, he submitted a story modeled on the Steve Costigan series that had been successful in the magazine (and its sibling publication, *Fight Stories*) before it suspended publication. This time, however, his protagonist was not a battling sailor, but an enormous mountain man by the name of Breckinridge Elkins, of Bear Creek, Nevada. Breck's simple, trusting nature frequently gets him into trouble, as does his tendency to fall in love with any pretty girl he sees, but his size and indestructibility generally see him through. These are unabashed tall tales in the Texan tradition, and show off Howard's madcap humor to hilarious effect. They were so popular in *Action Stories*, appearing in every issue of that magazine between March 1934 and October 1936, that when the editor moved over to *Argosy* early in 1936, he asked Howard to supply him with stories of the same type, thus providing an opening to one of the better pulps, a market the young author had for some time been hoping to crack. Unfortunately, while Howard could have some fun with the self-destructive intent of Jack Sprague in *Sharp's Gun Serenade*, his own story did not have such a happy ending.

Here in this first of two volumes collecting the best stories from Robert E. Howard's varied repertoire, you will find plenty of thrilling action, and if you read the stories a second time, or a third, you will also find that he is, as one fan magazine put it, deeper than you think. I'll leave it to Charles Hoffman's essay to illuminate some of the great themes in these stories. For my part, I simply hope that you will find them as enthralling as I do, and will enjoy them enough to seek out other collections of his work. Turn the page, and let Robert E. Howard sweep you into his world of excitement and adventure.

Rusty Burke
2007

The Shadow Kingdom

I

A King Comes Riding

The blare of the trumpets grew louder, like a deep golden tide surge, like the soft booming of the evening tides against the silver beaches of Valusia. The throng shouted, women flung roses from the roofs as the rhythmic chiming of silver hoofs came clearer and the first of the mighty array swung into view in the broad white street that curved round the golden-spired Tower of Splendor.

First came the trumpeters, slim youths, clad in scarlet, riding with a flourish of long, slender golden trumpets; next the bowmen, tall men from the mountains; and behind these the heavily armed footmen, their broad shields clashing in unison, their long spears swaying in perfect rhythm to their stride. Behind them came the mightiest soldiery in all the world, the Red Slayers, horsemen, splendidly mounted, armed in red from helmet to spur. Proudly they sat their steeds, looking neither to right nor to left, but aware of the shouting for all that. Like bronze statues they were, and there was never a waver in the forest of spears that reared above them.

Behind those proud and terrible ranks came the motley files of the mercenaries, fierce, wild-looking warriors, men of Mu and of Kaa-u and of the hills of the east and the isles of the west. They bore spears and heavy swords, and a compact group that marched somewhat apart were the

1

bowmen of Lemuria. Then came the light foot of the nation, and more trumpeters brought up the rear.

A brave sight, and a sight which aroused a fierce thrill in the soul of Kull, king of Valusia. Not on the Topaz Throne at the front of the regal Tower of Splendor sat Kull, but in the saddle, mounted on a great stallion, a true warrior king. His mighty arm swung up in reply to the salutes as the hosts passed. His fierce eyes passed the gorgeous trumpeters with a casual glance, rested longer on the following soldiery; they blazed with a ferocious light as the Red Slayers halted in front of him with a clang of arms and a rearing of steeds, and tendered him the crown salute. They narrowed slightly as the mercenaries strode by. They saluted no one, the mercenaries. They walked with shoulders flung back, eyeing Kull boldly and straightly, albeit with a certain appreciation; fierce eyes, unblinking; savage eyes, staring from beneath shaggy manes and heavy brows.

And Kull gave back a like stare. He granted much to brave men, and there were no braver in all the world, not even among the wild tribesmen who now disowned him. But Kull was too much the savage to have any great love for these. There were too many feuds. Many were age-old enemies of Kull's nation, and though the name of Kull was now a word accursed among the mountains and valleys of his people, and though Kull had put them from his mind, yet the old hates, the ancient passions still lingered. For Kull was no Valusian but an Atlantean.

The armies swung out of sight around the gem-blazing shoulders of the Tower of Splendor and Kull reined his stallion about and started toward the palace at an easy gait, discussing the review with the commanders that rode with him, using not many words, but saying much.

"The army is like a sword," said Kull, "and must not be allowed to rust." So down the street they rode, and Kull gave no heed to any of the whispers that reached his hearing from the throngs that still swarmed the streets.

"That is Kull, see! Valka! But what a king! And what a man! Look at his arms! His shoulders!"

And an undertone of more sinister whisperings: "Kull! Ha, accursed usurper from the pagan isles" – "Aye, shame to Valusia that a barbarian sits on the Throne of Kings." . . .

Little did Kull heed. Heavy-handed had he seized the decaying throne of ancient Valusia and with a heavier hand did he hold it, a man against a nation.

After the council chamber, the social palace where Kull replied to the formal and laudatory phrases of the lords and ladies, with carefully hidden, grim amusement at such frivolities; then the lords and ladies took their formal departure and Kull leaned back upon the ermine throne and contemplated matters of state until an attendant requested permission from the great king to speak, and announced an emissary from the Pictish embassy.

Kull brought his mind back from the dim mazes of Valusian statecraft where it had been wandering, and gazed upon the Pict with little favor. The man gave back the gaze of the king without flinching. He was a lean-hipped, massive-chested warrior of middle height, dark, like all his race, and strongly built. From strong, immobile features gazed dauntless and inscrutable eyes.

"The chief of the Councilors, Ka-nu of the tribe, right hand of the king of Pictdom, sends greetings and says: 'There is a throne at the feast of the rising moon for Kull, king of kings, lord of lords, emperor of Valusia.'"

"Good," answered Kull. "Say to Ka-nu the Ancient, ambassador of the western isles, that the king of Valusia will quaff wine with him when the moon floats over the hills of Zalgara."

Still the Pict lingered. "I have a word for the king, not" – with a contemptuous flirt of his hand – "for these slaves."

Kull dismissed the attendants with a word, watching the Pict warily.

The man stepped nearer, and lowered his voice: "Come alone to feast tonight, lord king. Such was the word of my chief."

The king's eyes narrowed, gleaming like gray sword steel, coldly.

"Alone?"

"Aye."

They eyed each other silently, their mutual tribal enmity seething beneath their cloak of formality. Their mouths spoke the cultured speech, the conventional court phrases of a highly polished race, a race not their own, but from their eyes gleamed the primal traditions of the elemental savage. Kull might be the king of Valusia and the Pict might be an emissary to her courts, but there in the throne hall of kings, two tribesmen glowered at each other, fierce and wary, while ghosts of wild wars and world-ancient feuds whispered to each.

To the king was the advantage and he enjoyed it to its fullest extent. Jaw resting on hand, he eyed the Pict, who stood like an image of bronze, head flung back, eyes unflinching.

Across Kull's lips stole a smile that was more a sneer.

"And so I am to come – alone?" Civilization had taught him to speak by innuendo and the Pict's dark eyes glittered, though he made no reply. "How am I to know that you come from Ka-nu?"

"I have spoken," was the sullen response.

"And when did a Pict speak truth?" sneered Kull, fully aware that the Picts never lied, but using this means to enrage the man.

"I see your plan, king," the Pict answered imperturbably. "You wish to anger me. By Valka, you need go no further! I am angry enough. And I challenge you to meet me in single battle, spear, sword or dagger, mounted or afoot. Are you king or man?"

Kull's eyes glinted with the grudging admiration a warrior must needs give a bold foeman, but he did not fail to use the chance of further annoying his antagonist.

"A king does not accept the challenge of a nameless savage," he sneered, "nor does the emperor of Valusia break the Truce of Ambassadors. You have leave to go. Say to Ka-nu I will come alone."

The Pict's eyes flashed murderously. He fairly shook in the grasp of the primitive blood-lust; then, turning his back squarely upon the king of Valusia, he strode across the Hall of Society and vanished through the great door.

Again Kull leaned back upon the ermine throne and meditated.

So the chief of the Council of Picts wished him to come alone? But for what reason? Treachery? Grimly Kull touched the hilt of his great sword. But scarcely. The Picts valued too greatly the alliance with Valusia to break it for any feudal reason. Kull might be a warrior of Atlantis and hereditary enemy of all Picts, but too, he was king of Valusia, the most potent ally of the Men of the West.

Kull reflected long upon the strange state of affairs that made him ally of ancient foes and foe of ancient friends. He rose and paced restlessly across the hall, with the quick, noiseless tread of a lion. Chains of friendship, tribe and tradition had he broken to satisfy his ambition. And, by Valka, god of the sea and the land, he had realized that ambition! He was king of Valusia – a fading, degenerate Valusia, a Valusia living mostly in dreams of bygone glory, but still a mighty land and the greatest of the Seven Empires. Valusia – Land of Dreams, the tribesmen named it, and sometimes it seemed to Kull that he moved in a dream. Strange to him were the intrigues of court and palace, army and people. All was like a masquerade, where men and women hid their real thoughts with a smooth mask. Yet the seizing of the throne had been easy – a bold snatching of opportunity, the swift whirl of swords, the slaying of a tyrant of whom men had wearied unto death, short, crafty plotting with ambitious statesmen out of favor at court – and Kull, wandering adventurer, Atlantean exile, had swept up to the dizzy heights of his dreams: he was lord of Valusia, king of kings. Yet now it seemed that the seizing was far easier than the keeping. The sight of the Pict had brought back youthful associations to his mind, the free, wild savagery of his boyhood. And now a strange feeling of dim unrest, of unreality, stole over him as of late it had been doing. Who was he, a straightforward man of the seas and the mountain, to rule a race strangely and terribly wise with the mysticisms of antiquity? An ancient race —

"I am Kull!" said he, flinging back his head as a lion flings back his mane. "I am Kull!"

His falcon gaze swept the ancient hall. His self-confidence flowed back. . . . And in a dim nook of the hall a tapestry moved – slightly.

II
Thus Spake the Silent Halls of Valusia

The moon had not risen, and the garden was lighted with torches aglow in silver cressets when Kull sat down in the throne before the table of Ka-nu, ambassador of the western isles. At his right hand sat the ancient Pict, as much unlike an emissary of that fierce race as a man could be. Ancient was Ka-nu and wise in statecraft, grown old in the game. There was no elemental hatred in the eyes that looked at Kull appraisingly; no tribal traditions hindered his judgments. Long associations with the statesmen of the civilized nations had swept away such cobwebs. Not: who and what is this man? was the question ever foremost in Ka-nu's mind, but: can I use this man, and how? Tribal prejudices he used only to further his own schemes.

And Kull watched Ka-nu, answering his conversation briefly, wondering if civilization would make of him a thing like the Pict. For Ka-nu was soft and paunchy. Many years had stridden across the sky-rim since Ka-nu had wielded a sword. True, he was old, but Kull had seen men older than he in the forefront of battle. The Picts were a long-lived race. A beautiful girl stood at Ka-nu's elbow, refilling his goblet, and she was kept busy. Meanwhile Ka-nu kept up a running fire of jests and comments, and Kull, secretly contemptuous of his garrulity, nevertheless missed none of his shrewd humor.

At the banquet were Pictish chiefs and statesmen, the latter jovial and easy in their manner, the warriors formally courteous, but plainly hampered by their tribal affinities. Yet Kull, with a tinge of envy, was cognizant of the freedom and ease of the affair as contrasted with like affairs of the Valusian court. Such freedom prevailed in the rude camps of Atlantis – Kull shrugged his shoulders.

After all, doubtless Ka-nu, who had seemed to have forgotten he was a Pict as far as time-hoary custom and prejudice went, was right and he, Kull, would better become a Valusian in mind as in name.

At last when the moon had reached her zenith, Ka-nu, having eaten and drunk as much as any three men there, leaned back upon his divan with a comfortable sigh and said, "Now, get you gone, friends, for the king and I

5

would converse on such matters as concerns not children. Yes, you too, my pretty; yet first let me kiss those ruby lips – so; now dance away, my rose-bloom."

Ka-nu's eyes twinkled above his white beard as he surveyed Kull, who sat erect, grim and uncompromising.

"You are thinking, Kull," said the old statesman, suddenly, "that Ka-nu is a useless old reprobate, fit for nothing except to guzzle wine and kiss wenches!"

In fact, this remark was so much in line with his actual thoughts, and so plainly put, that Kull was rather startled, though he gave no sign.

Ka-nu gurgled and his paunch shook with his mirth. "Wine is red and women are soft," he remarked tolerantly. "But – ha! ha! – think not old Ka-nu allows either to interfere with business."

Again he laughed, and Kull moved restlessly. This seemed much like being made sport of, and the king's scintillant eyes began to glow with a feline light.

Ka-nu reached for the wine-pitcher, filled his beaker and glanced questioningly at Kull, who shook his head irritably.

"Aye," said Ka-nu equably, "it takes an old head to stand strong drink. I am growing old, Kull, so why should you young men begrudge me such pleasures as we oldsters must find? Ah me, I grow ancient and withered, friendless and cheerless."

But his looks and expressions failed far of bearing out his words. His rubicund countenance fairly glowed, and his eyes sparkled, so that his white beard seemed incongruous. Indeed, he looked remarkably elfin, reflected Kull, who felt vaguely resentful. The old scoundrel had lost all of the primitive virtues of his race and of Kull's race, yet he seemed more pleased in his aged days than otherwise.

"Hark ye, Kull," said Ka-nu, raising an admonitory finger, "'tis a chancy thing to laud a young man, yet I must speak my true thoughts to gain your confidence."

"If you think to gain it by flattery –"

"Tush. Who spake of flattery? I flatter only to disguard."

There was a keen sparkle in Ka-nu's eyes, a cold glimmer that did not match his lazy smile. He knew men, and he knew that to gain his end he must smite straight with this tigerish barbarian, who, like a wolf scenting a snare, would scent out unerringly any falseness in the skein of his word-web.

"You have power, Kull," said he, choosing his words with more care than he did in the council rooms of the nation, "to make yourself mightiest of all kings, and restore some of the lost glories of Valusia. So. I care little for Valusia – though the women and wine be excellent – save for the fact that the stronger Valusia is, the stronger is the Pict nation. More, with an Atlantean on the throne, eventually Atlantis will become united —"

Kull laughed in harsh mockery. Ka-nu had touched an old wound.

"Atlantis made my name accursed when I went to seek fame and fortune among the cities of the world. We — they — are age-old foes of the Seven Empires, greater foes of the allies of the Empires, as you should know."

Ka-nu tugged his beard and smiled enigmatically.

"Nay, nay. Let it pass. But I know whereof I speak. And then warfare will cease, wherein there is no gain; I see a world of peace and prosperity — man loving his fellow man — the good supreme. All this can you accomplish — *if you live!*"

"Ha!" Kull's lean hand closed on his hilt and he half rose, with a sudden movement of such dynamic speed that Ka-nu, who fancied men as some men fancy blooded horses, felt his old blood leap with a sudden thrill. Valka, what a warrior! Nerves and sinews of steel and fire, bound together with the perfect co-ordination, the fighting instinct, that makes the terrible warrior.

But none of Ka-nu's enthusiasm showed in his mildly sarcastic tone.

"Tush. Be seated. Look about you. The gardens are deserted, the seats empty, save for ourselves. You fear not *me*?"

Kull sank back, gazing about him warily.

"There speaks the savage," mused Ka-nu. "Think you if I planned treachery I would enact it here where suspicion would be sure to fall upon me? Tut. You young tribesmen have much to learn. There were my chiefs who were not at ease because you were born among the hills of Atlantis, and you despise me in your secret mind because I am a Pict. Tush. I see you as Kull, king of Valusia, not as Kull, the reckless Atlantean, leader of the raiders who harried the western isles. So you should see in me, not a Pict but an international man, a figure of the world. Now to that figure, hark! If you were slain tomorrow who would be king?"

"Kaanuub, baron of Blaal."

"Even so. I object to Kaanuub for many reasons, yet most of all for the fact that he is but a figurehead."

"How so? He was my greatest opponent, but I did not know that he championed any cause but his own."

"The night can hear," answered Ka-nu obliquely. "There are worlds within worlds. But you may trust me and you may trust Brule, the Spear-slayer. Look!" He drew from his robes a bracelet of gold representing a winged dragon coiled thrice, with three horns of ruby on the head.

"Examine it closely. Brule will wear it on his arm when he comes to you tomorrow night so that you may know him. Trust Brule as you trust yourself, and do what he tells you to. And in proof of trust, look ye!"

And with the speed of a striking hawk, the ancient snatched something from his robes, something that flung a weird green light over them, and which he replaced in an instant.

"The stolen gem!" exclaimed Kull recoiling. "The green jewel from the Temple of the Serpent! Valka! You! And why do you show it to me?"

"To save your life. To prove my trust. If I betray your trust, deal with me likewise. You hold my life in your hand. Now I could not be false to you if I would, for a word from you would be my doom."

Yet for all his words the old scoundrel beamed merrily and seemed vastly pleased with himself.

"But why do you give me this hold over you?" asked Kull, becoming more bewildered each second.

"As I told you. Now, you see that I do not intend to deal you false, and tomorrow night when Brule comes to you, you will follow his advice without fear of treachery. Enough. An escort waits outside to ride to the palace with you, lord."

Kull rose. "But you have told me nothing."

"Tush. How impatient are youths!" Ka-nu looked more like a mischievous elf than ever. "Go you and dream of thrones and power and kingdoms, while I dream of wine and soft women and roses. And fortune ride with you, King Kull."

As he left the garden, Kull glanced back to see Ka-nu still reclining lazily in his seat, a merry ancient, beaming on all the world with jovial fellowship.

A mounted warrior waited for the king just without the garden and Kull was slightly surprised to see that it was the same that had brought Ka-nu's invitation. No word was spoken as Kull swung into the saddle nor as they clattered along the empty streets.

The color and the gayety of the day had given away to the eery stillness of night. The city's antiquity was more than ever apparent beneath the bent, silver moon. The huge pillars of the mansions and palaces towered up into the stars. The broad stairways, silent and deserted, seemed to climb endlessly until they vanished in the shadowy darkness of the upper realms. Stairs to the stars, thought Kull, his imaginative mind inspired by the weird grandeur of the scene.

Clang! clang! clang! sounded the silver hoofs on the broad, moon-flooded streets, but otherwise there was no sound. The age of the city, its incredible antiquity, was almost oppressive to the king; it was as if the great silent buildings laughed at him, noiselessly, with unguessable mockery. And what secrets did they hold?

"You are young," said the palaces and the temples and the shrines, "but we are old. The world was wild with youth when we were reared. You and your tribe shall pass, but we are invincible, indestructible. We towered above a strange world, ere Atlantis and Lemuria rose from the sea; we still shall reign when the green waters sigh for many a restless fathom above the spires of Lemuria and the hills of Atlantis and when the isles of the Western Men are the mountains of a strange land.

"How many kings have we watched ride down these streets before Kull of Atlantis was even a dream in the mind of Ka, bird of Creation? Ride on, Kull of Atlantis; greater shall follow you; greater came before you. They are dust; they are forgotten; we stand; we know; we are. Ride, ride on, Kull of Atlantis; Kull the king, Kull the fool!"

And it seemed to Kull that the clashing hoofs took up the silent refrain to beat it into the night with hollow re-echoing mockery:

"Kull – the – king! Kull – the – fool!"

Glow, moon; you light a king's way! Gleam, stars; you are torches in the train of an emperor! And clang, silver-shod hoofs; you herald that Kull rides through Valusia.

Ho! Awake, Valusia! It is Kull that rides, Kull the king!

"We have known many kings," said the silent halls of Valusia.

And so in a brooding mood Kull came to the palace, where his bodyguard, men of the Red Slayers, came to take the rein of the great stallion and escort Kull to his rest. There the Pict, still sullenly speechless, wheeled his steed with a savage wrench of the rein and fled away in the dark like a phantom; Kull's heightened imagination pictured him speeding through the silent streets like a goblin out of the Elder World.

There was no sleep for Kull that night, for it was nearly dawn and he spent the rest of the night hours pacing the throneroom, and pondering over what had passed. Ka-nu had told him nothing, yet he had put himself in Kull's complete power. At what had he hinted when he had said the baron of Blaal was naught but a figurehead? And who was this Brule who was to come to him by night, wearing the mystic armlet of the dragon? And why? Above all, why had Ka-nu shown him the green gem of terror, stolen long ago from the temple of the Serpent, for which the world would rock in wars were it known to the weird and terrible keepers of that temple, and from whose vengeance not even Ka-nu's ferocious tribesmen might be able to save him? But Ka-nu knew he was safe, reflected Kull, for the statesman was too shrewd to expose himself to risk without profit. But was it to throw the king off his guard and pave the way to treachery? Would Ka-nu dare let him live now? Kull shrugged his shoulders.

III

THEY THAT WALK THE NIGHT

The moon had not risen when Kull, hand to hilt, stepped to a window. The windows opened upon the great inner gardens of the royal palace, and the breezes of the night, bearing the scents of spice trees, blew the filmy curtains about. The king looked out. The walks and groves were deserted; carefully trimmed trees were bulky shadows; fountains near by flung their slender sheen of silver in the starlight and distant fountains rippled steadily. No guards walked those gardens, for so closely were the outer walls guarded that it seemed impossible for any invader to gain access to them.

Vines curled up the walls of the palace, and even as Kull mused upon the ease with which they might be climbed, a segment of shadow detached itself from the darkness below the window and a bare, brown arm curved up over the sill. Kull's great sword hissed half-way from the sheath; then the king halted. Upon the muscular forearm gleamed the dragon armlet shown him by Ka-nu the night before.

The possessor of the arm pulled himself up over the sill and into the room with the swift, easy motion of a climbing leopard.

"You are Brule?" asked Kull, and then stopped in surprize not unmingled with annoyance and suspicion; for the man was he whom Kull had taunted in the Hall of Society; the same who had escorted him from the Pictish embassy.

"I am Brule, the Spear-slayer," answered the Pict in a guarded voice; then swiftly, gazing closely in Kull's face, he said, barely above a whisper:

"Ka nama kaa lajerama!"

Kull started. "Ha! What mean you?"

"Know you not?"

"Nay, the words are unfamiliar; they are of no language I ever heard – and yet, by Valka! – somewhere – I have heard –"

"Aye," was the Pict's only comment. His eyes swept the room, the study room of the palace. Except for a few tables, a divan or two and great shelves of books of parchment, the room was barren compared to the grandeur of the rest of the palace.

"Tell me, king, who guards the door?"

"Eighteen of the Red Slayers. But how come you, stealing through the gardens by night and scaling the walls of the palace?"

Brule sneered. "The guards of Valusia are blind buffaloes. I could steal their girls from under their noses. I stole amid them and they saw me not nor heard me. And the walls – I could scale them without the aid of vines. I have hunted tigers on the foggy beaches when the sharp east breezes blew the mist in from seaward and I have climbed the steeps of the western sea mountain. But come – nay, touch this armlet."

He held out his arm and, as Kull complied wonderingly, gave an apparent sigh of relief.

"So. Now throw off those kingly robes; for there are ahead of you this night such deeds as no Atlantean ever dreamed of."

Brule himself was clad only in a scanty loin-cloth through which was thrust a short, curved sword.

"And who are you to give me orders?" asked Kull, slightly resentful.

"Did not Ka-nu bid you follow me in all things?" asked the Pict irritably, his eyes flashing momentarily. "I have no love for you, lord, but for the moment I have put the thought of feuds from my mind. Do you likewise. But come."

Walking noiselessly, he led the way across the room to the door. A slide in the door allowed a view of the outer corridor, unseen from without, and the Pict bade Kull look.

"What see you?"

"Naught but the eighteen guardsmen."

The Pict nodded, motioned Kull to follow him across the room. At a panel in the op- posite wall Brule stopped and fumbled there a moment. Then with a light movement he stepped back, drawing his sword as he did so. Kull gave an exclamation as the panel swung silently open, revealing a dimly lighted passageway.

"A secret passage!" swore Kull softly. "And I knew nothing of it! By Valka, someone shall dance for this!"

"Silence!" hissed the Pict.

Brule was standing like a bronze statue as if straining every nerve for the slightest sound; something about his attitude made Kull's hair prickle slightly, not from fear but from some eery anticipation. Then beckoning, Brule stepped through the secret doorway which stood open behind them. The passage was bare, but not dust-covered as should have been the case with an unused secret corridor. A vague, gray light filtered through somewhere, but the source of it was not apparent. Every few feet

Kull saw doors, invisible, as he knew, from the outside, but easily apparent from within.

"The palace is a very honeycomb," he muttered.

"Aye. Night and day you are watched, king, by many eyes."

The king was impressed by Brule's manner. The Pict went forward slowly, warily, half crouching, blade held low and thrust forward. When he spoke it was in a whisper and he continually flung glances from side to side.

The corridor turned sharply and Brule warily gazed past the turn.

"Look!" he whispered. "But remember! No word! No sound – on your life!"

Kull cautiously gazed past him. The corridor changed just at the bend to a flight of steps. And then Kull recoiled. At the foot of those stairs lay the eighteen Red Slayers who were that night stationed to watch the king's study room. Brule's grip upon his mighty arm and Brule's fierce whisper at his shoulder alone kept Kull from leaping down those stairs.

"Silent, Kull! Silent, in Valka's name!" hissed the Pict. "These corridors are empty now, but I risked much in showing you, that you might then believe what I had to say. Back now to the room of study." And he retraced his steps, Kull following; his mind in a turmoil of bewilderment.

"This is treachery," muttered the king, his steel-gray eyes a-smolder, "foul and swift! Mere minutes have passed since those men stood at guard."

Again in the room of study Brule carefully closed the secret panel and motioned Kull to look again through the slit of the outer door. Kull gasped audibly. *For without stood the eighteen guardsmen!*

"This is sorcery!" he whispered, half-drawing his sword. "Do dead men guard the king?"

"*Aye!*" came Brule's scarcely audible reply; there was a strange expression in the Pict's scintillant eyes. They looked squarely into each other's eyes for an instant, Kull's brow wrinkled in a puzzled scowl as he strove to read the Pict's inscrutable face. Then Brule's lips, barely moving, formed the words:

"*The – snake – that – speaks!*"

"Silent!" whispered Kull, laying his hand over Brule's mouth. "That is death to speak! That is a name accursed!"

The Pict's fearless eyes regarded him steadily.

"Look again, King Kull. Perchance the guard was changed."

"Nay, those are the same men. In Valka's name, this is sorcery – this is insanity! I saw with my own eyes the bodies of those men, not eight minutes agone. Yet there they stand."

Brule stepped back, away from the door, Kull mechanically following.

"Kull, what know ye of the traditions of this race ye rule?"

"Much – and yet, little. Valusia is so old –"

"Aye," Brule's eyes lighted strangely, "we are but barbarians – infants compared to the Seven Empires. Not even they themselves know how old they are. Neither the memory of man nor the annals of the historians reach back far enough to tell us when the first men came up from the sea and built cities on the shore. But Kull, *men were not always ruled by men!*"

The king started. Their eyes met.

"Aye, there is a legend of my people –"

"And mine!" broke in Brule. "That was before we of the isles were allied with Valusia. Aye, in the reign of Lion-fang, seventh war chief of the Picts, so many years ago no man remembers how many. Across the sea we came, from the isles of the sunset, skirting the shores of Atlantis, and falling upon the beaches of Valusia with fire and sword. Aye, the long white beaches resounded with the clash of spears, and the night was like day from the flame of the burning castles. And the king, the king of Valusia, who died on the red sea sands that dim day –" His voice trailed off; the two stared at each other, neither speaking; then each nodded.

"Ancient is Valusia!" whispered Kull. "The hills of Atlantis and Mu were isles of the sea when Valusia was young."

The night breeze whispered through the open window. Not the free, crisp sea air such as Brule and Kull knew and reveled in, in their land, but a breath like a whisper from the past, laden with musk, scents of forgotten things, breathing secrets that were hoary when the world was young.

The tapestries rustled, and suddenly Kull felt like a naked child before the inscrutable wisdom of the mystic past. Again the sense of unreality swept upon him. At the back of his soul stole dim, gigantic phantoms, whispering monstrous things. He sensed that Brule experienced similar thoughts. The Pict's eyes were fixed upon his face with a fierce intensity. Their glances met. Kull felt warmly a sense of comradeship with this member of an enemy tribe. Like rival leopards turning at bay against hunters, these two savages made common cause against the inhuman powers of antiquity.

Brule again led the way back to the secret door. Silently they entered and silently they proceeded down the dim corridor, taking the opposite direction from that in which they had previously traversed it. After a while the Pict stopped and pressed close to one of the secret doors, bidding Kull look with him through the hidden slot.

"This opens upon a little-used stair which leads to a corridor running past the study-room door."

They gazed, and presently, mounting the stair silently, came a silent shape.

"Tu! Chief councilor!" exclaimed Kull. "By night and with bared dagger! How, what means this, Brule?"

"Murder! And foulest treachery!" hissed Brule. "Nay" – as Kull would have flung the door aside and leaped forth – "we are lost if you meet him here, for more lurk at the foot of those stairs. Come!"

Half running, they darted back along the passage. Back through the secret door Brule led, shutting it carefully behind them, then across the chamber to an opening into a room seldom used. There he swept aside some tapestries in a dim corner nook and, drawing Kull with him, stepped behind them. Minutes dragged. Kull could hear the breeze in the other room blowing the window curtains about, and it seemed to him like the murmur of ghosts. Then through the door, stealthily, came Tu, chief councilor of the king. Evidently he had come through the study room and, finding it empty, sought his victim where he was most likely to be.

He came with upraised dagger, walking silently. A moment he halted, gazing about the apparently empty room, which was lighted dimly by a single candle. Then he advanced cautiously, apparently at a loss to understand the absence of the king. He stood before the hiding place – and –

"Slay!" hissed the Pict.

Kull with a single mighty leap hurled himself into the room. Tu spun, but the blinding, tigerish speed of the attack gave him no chance for defense or counter-attack. Sword steel flashed in the dim light and grated on bone as Tu toppled backward, Kull's sword standing out between his shoulders.

Kull leaned above him, teeth bared in the killer's snarl, heavy brows a-scowl above eyes that were like the gray ice of the cold sea. Then he released the hilt and recoiled, shaken, dizzy, the hand of death at his spine.

For as he watched, Tu's face became strangely dim and unreal; the features mingled and merged in a seemingly impossible manner. Then, like a fading mask of fog, the face suddenly vanished and in its stead gaped and leered *a monstrous serpent's head!*

"Valka!" gasped Kull, sweat beading his forehead, and again: "Valka!"

Brule leaned forward, face immobile. Yet his glittering eyes mirrored something of Kull's horror.

"Regain your sword, lord king," said he. "There are yet deeds to be done."

Hesitantly Kull set his hand to the hilt. His flesh crawled as he set his foot upon the terror which lay at their feet, and as some jerk of muscular reaction caused the frightful mouth to gape suddenly, he recoiled, weak with nausea. Then, wrathful at himself, he plucked forth his sword and gazed more closely at the nameless thing that had been known as Tu, chief councilor. Save for the reptilian head, the thing was the exact counterpart of a man.

"A man with the head of a snake!" Kull murmured. "This, then, is a priest of the serpent god?"

"Aye. Tu sleeps unknowing. These fiends can take any form they will. That is, they can, by a magic charm or the like, fling a web of sorcery about their faces, as an actor dons a mask, so that they resemble anyone they wish to."

"Then the old legends were true," mused the king; "the grim old tales few dare even whisper, lest they die as blasphemers, are no fantasies. By Valka, I had thought – I had guessed – but it seems beyond the bounds of reality. Ha! The guardsmen outside the door –"

"They too are snake-men. Hold! What would you do?"

"Slay them!" said Kull between his teeth.

"Strike at the skull if at all," said Brule. "Eighteen wait without the door and perhaps a score more in the corridors. Hark ye, king, Ka-nu learned of this plot. His spies have pierced the inmost fastnesses of the snake priests and they brought hints of a plot. Long ago he discovered the secret passageways of the palace, and at his command I studied the map thereof and came here by night to aid you, lest you die as other kings of Valusia have died. I came alone for the reason that to send more would have roused suspicion. Many could not steal into the palace as I did. Some of the foul conspiracy you have seen. Snake-men guard your door, and that one, as Tu, could pass anywhere else in the palace; in the morning, if the priests failed, the real guards would be holding their places again, nothing knowing, nothing remembering; there to take the blame if the priests succeeded. But stay you here while I dispose of this carrion."

So saying, the Pict shouldered the frightful thing stolidly and vanished with it through another secret panel. Kull stood alone, his mind a-whirl. Neophytes of the mighty serpent, how many lurked among his cities? How might he tell the false from the true? Aye, how many of his trusted councilors, his generals, were men? He could be certain – of whom?

The secret panel swung inward and Brule entered.

"You were swift."

"Aye!" The warrior stepped forward, eyeing the floor. "There is gore upon the rug. See?"

Kull bent forward; from the corner of his eye he saw a blur of movement, a glint of steel. Like a loosened bow he whipped erect, thrusting upward. The warrior sagged upon the sword, his own clattering to the floor. Even at that instant Kull reflected grimly that it was appropriate that the traitor should meet his death upon the sliding, upward thrust used so much by his race. Then, as Brule slid from the sword to sprawl motionless on the floor, the face began to merge and fade, and as Kull caught his breath, his hair a-prickle, the human features vanished and there the jaws of a great snake gaped hideously, the terrible beady eyes venomous even in death.

"He was a snake priest all the time!" gasped the king. "Valka! what an elaborate plan to throw me off my guard! Ka-nu there, is he a man? Was it Ka-nu to whom I talked in the gardens? Almighty Valka!" as his flesh crawled with a horrid thought; "are the people of Valusia men or are they *all* serpents?"

Undecided he stood, idly seeing that the thing named Brule no longer wore the dragon armlet. A sound made him wheel.

Brule was coming through the secret door.

"Hold!" upon the arm upthrown to halt the king's hovering sword gleamed the dragon armlet. "Valka!" The Pict stopped short. Then a grim smile curled his lips.

"By the gods of the seas! These demons are crafty past reckoning. For it must be that that one lurked in the corridors, and seeing me go carrying the carcass of that other, took my appearance. So. I have another to do away with."

"Hold!" there was the menace of death in Kull's voice; "I have seen two men turn to serpents before my eyes. How may I know if you are a true man?"

Brule laughed. "For two reasons, King Kull. No snake-man wears this" – he indicated the dragon armlet – "nor can any say these words," and again Kull heard the strange phrase: *"Ka nama kaa lajerama."*

"Ka nama kaa lajerama," Kull repeated mechanically. "Now where, in Valka's name, have I heard that? I have not! And yet – and yet –"

"Aye, you remember, Kull," said Brule. "Through the dim corridors of memory those words lurk; though you never heard them in this life, yet in the bygone ages they were so terribly impressed upon the soul mind that never dies, that they will always strike dim chords in your memory, though you be reincarnated for a million years to come. For that phrase has come secretly down the grim and bloody eons, since when, uncounted centuries ago, those words were watchwords for the race of men who battled with the grisly beings of the Elder Universe. For none but a real man of men may speak them, whose jaws and mouth are shaped different from any other creature. Their meaning has been forgotten but not the words themselves."

"True," said Kull. "I remember the legends – Valka!" He stopped short, staring, for suddenly, like the silent swinging wide of a mystic door, misty, unfathomed reaches opened in the recesses of his consciousness and for an instant he seemed to gaze back through the vastnesses that spanned life and life; seeing through the vague and ghostly fogs dim shapes reliving dead centuries – men in combat with hideous monsters, vanquishing a planet of frightful terrors. Against a gray, ever-shifting background moved strange nightmare forms, fantasies of lunacy and fear; and man, the jest of the gods, the blind, wisdomless striver from dust to dust, following the long bloody trail of his destiny, knowing not why, bestial, blundering, like a great murderous child, yet feeling somewhere a spark of divine fire. . . . Kull drew a hand across his brow, shaken; these sudden glimpses into the abysses of memory always startled him.

"They are gone," said Brule, as if scanning his secret mind; "the bird-women, the harpies, the bat-men, the flying fiends, the wolf-people, the demons, the goblins – all save such as this being that lies at our feet, and a few of the wolf-men. Long and terrible was the war, lasting through the bloody centuries, since first the first men, risen from the mire of apedom, turned upon those who then ruled the world.

And at last mankind conquered, so long ago that naught but dim legends come to us through the ages. The snake-people were the last to go, yet at last men conquered even them and drove them forth into the waste lands of the world, there to mate with true snakes until some day, say the sages, the horrid breed shall vanish utterly. Yet the Things returned in crafty guise as men grew soft and degenerate, forgetting ancient wars. Ah, that was a grim and secret war! Among the men of the Younger Earth stole the frightful monsters of the Elder Planet, safeguarded by their horrid wisdom and mysticisms, taking all forms and shapes, doing deeds of horror secretly. No man knew who was true man and who false. No man could trust any man. Yet by means of their own craft they formed ways by which the false might be known from the true. Men took for a sign and a standard the figure of the flying dragon, the winged dinosaur, a monster of past ages, which was the greatest foe of the serpent. And men used those words which I spoke to you as a sign and symbol, for as I said, none but a true man can repeat them. So mankind triumphed. Yet again the fiends came after the years of forgetfulness had gone by – for man is still an ape in that he forgets what is not ever before his eyes. As priests they came; and for that men in their luxury and might had by then lost faith in the old religions and worships, the snake-men, in the guise of teachers of a new and truer cult, built a monstrous religion about the worship of the serpent god. Such is their power that it is now death to repeat the old legends of the snake-people, and people bow again to the serpent god in new form; and blind fools that they are, the great hosts of men see no connection between this power and the power men overthrew eons ago. As priests the snake-men are content to rule – and yet –" He stopped.

"Go on." Kull felt an unaccountable stirring of the short hair at the base of his scalp.

"Kings have reigned as true men in Valusia," the Pict whispered, "and yet, slain in battle, have died serpents – as died he who fell beneath the spear of Lion-fang on the red beaches when we of the isles harried the Seven Empires. And how can this be, Lord Kull? These kings were born of women and lived as men! This – the true kings died in secret – as you would have died tonight – and priests of the Serpent reigned in their stead, no man knowing."

Kull cursed between his teeth. "Aye, it must be. No one has ever seen a priest of the Serpent and lived, that is known. They live in utmost secrecy."

"The statecraft of the Seven Empires is a mazy, monstrous thing," said Brule. "There the true men know that among them glide the spies of the serpent, and the men who are the Serpent's allies – such as Kaanuub, baron of Blaal – yet no man dares seek to unmask a suspect lest vengeance befall him. No man trusts his fellow and the true statesmen dare not speak to each other what is in the minds of all. Could they be sure, could a snake-man or plot be unmasked before them all, then would the power of the Serpent be more than half broken; for all would then ally and make common cause, sifting out the traitors. Ka-nu alone is of sufficient shrewdness and courage to cope with them, and even Ka-nu learned only enough of their plot to tell me what would happen – what has happened up to this time. Thus far I was prepared; from now on we must trust to our luck and our craft. Here and now I think we are safe; those snake-men without the door dare not leave their post lest true men come here unexpectedly. But tomorrow they will try something else, you may be sure. Just what they will do, none can say, not even Ka-nu; but we must stay at each other's sides, King Kull, until we conquer or both be dead. Now come with me while I take this carcass to the hiding-place where I took the other being."

Kull followed the Pict with his grisly burden through the secret panel and down the dim corridor. Their feet, trained to the silence of the wilderness, made no noise. Like phantoms they glided through the ghostly light, Kull wondering that the corridors should be deserted; at every turn he expected to run full upon some frightful apparition. Suspicion surged back upon him; was this Pict leading him into ambush? He fell back a pace or two behind Brule, his ready sword hovering at the Pict's unheeding back. Brule should die first if he meant treachery. But if the Pict was aware of the king's suspicion, he showed no sign. Stolidly he tramped along, until they came to a room, dusty and long unused, where moldy tapestries hung heavy. Brule drew aside some of these and concealed the corpse behind them.

Then they turned to retrace their steps, when suddenly Brule halted with such abruptness that he was closer to death than he knew; for Kull's nerves were on edge.

"Something moving in the corridor," hissed the Pict. "Ka-nu said these ways would be empty, yet –"

He drew his sword and stole into the corridor, Kull following warily.

A short way down the corridor a strange, vague glow appeared that came toward them. Nerves a-leap, they waited, backs to the corridor wall; for what they knew not, but Kull heard Brule's breath hiss through his teeth and was reassured as to Brule's loyalty.

The glow merged into a shadowy form. A shape vaguely like a man it was, but misty and illusive, like a wisp of fog, that grew more tangible as it approached, but never fully material. A face looked at them, a pair of luminous great eyes, that seemed to hold all the tortures of a million centuries. There was no menace in that face, with its dim, worn features, but only a great pity – and that face – that face –

"Almighty gods!" breathed Kull, an icy hand at his soul; "Eallal, king of Valusia, who died a thousand years ago!"

Brule shrank back as far as he could, his narrow eyes widened in a blaze of pure horror, the sword shaking in his grip, unnerved for the first time that weird night. Erect and defiant stood Kull, instinctively holding his useless sword at the ready; flesh a-crawl, hair a-prickle, yet still a king of kings, as ready to challenge the powers of the unknown dead as the powers of the living.

The phantom came straight on, giving them no heed; Kull shrank back as it passed them, feeling an icy breath like a breeze from the arctic snow. Straight on went the shape with slow, silent footsteps, as if the chains of all the ages were upon those vague feet; vanishing about a bend of the corridor.

"Valka!" muttered the Pict, wiping the cold beads from his brow; "that was no man! That was a ghost!"

"Aye!" Kull shook his head wonderingly. "Did you not recognize the face? That was Eallal, who reigned in Valusia a thousand years ago and who was found hideously murdered in his throneroom – the room now known as the Accursed Room. Have you not seen his statue in the Fame Room of Kings?"

"Yes, I remember the tale now. Gods, Kull! that is another sign of the frightful and foul power of the snake priests – that king was slain by snake-people and thus his soul became their slave, to do their bidding throughout eternity! For the sages have ever maintained that if a man is slain by a snake-man his ghost becomes their slave."

A shudder shook Kull's gigantic frame. "Valka! But what a fate! Hark ye" – his fingers closed upon Brule's sinewy arm like steel – "hark ye! If I am wounded unto death by these foul monsters, swear that ye will smite your sword through my breast lest my soul be enslaved."

"I swear," answered Brule, his fierce eyes lighting. "And do ye the same by me, Kull."

Their strong right hands met in a silent sealing of their bloody bargain.

IV
MASKS

Kull sat upon his throne and gazed broodingly out upon the sea of faces turned toward him. A courtier was speaking in evenly modulated tones, but the king scarcely heard him. Close by, Tu, chief councilor, stood ready at Kull's command, and each time the king looked at him, Kull shuddered inwardly. The surface of court life was as the unrippled surface of the sea between tide and tide. To the musing king the affairs of the night before seemed as a dream, until his eyes dropped to the arm of his throne. A brown, sinewy hand rested there, upon the wrist of which gleamed a dragon armlet; Brule stood beside his throne and ever the Pict's fierce secret whisper brought him back from the realm of unreality in which he moved.

No, that was no dream, that monstrous interlude. As he sat upon his throne in the Hall of Society and gazed upon the courtiers, the ladies, the lords, the statesmen, he seemed to see their faces as things of illusion, things unreal, existent only as shadows and mockeries of substance. Always he had seen their faces as masks, but before he had looked on them with contemptuous tolerance, thinking to see beneath the masks shallow, puny souls, avaricious, lustful, deceitful; now there was a grim undertone, a sinister meaning, a vague horror that lurked beneath the smooth masks. While he exchanged courtesies with some nobleman or councilor he seemed to see the smiling face fade like smoke and the frightful jaws of a serpent gaping there. How many of those he looked upon were horrid, inhuman monsters, plotting his death, beneath the smooth mesmeric illusion of a human face?

Valusia – land of dreams and nightmares – a kingdom of the shadows, ruled by phantoms who glided back and forth behind the painted curtains, mocking the futile king who sat upon the throne – himself a shadow.

And like a comrade shadow Brule stood by his side, dark eyes glittering from immobile face. A real man, Brule! And Kull felt his friendship for the savage become a thing of reality and sensed that Brule felt a friendship for him beyond the mere necessity of statecraft.

And what, mused Kull, were the realities of life? Ambition, power, pride? The friendship of man, the love of women – which Kull had never known – battle, plunder, what? Was it the real Kull who sat upon the throne or was it the real Kull who had scaled the hills of Atlantis, harried the far isles of the sunset, and laughed upon the green roaring tides of the Atlantean sea? How could a man be so many different men in a lifetime? For Kull knew that there were many Kulls and he wondered which was the real Kull. After all, the priests of the Serpent merely went a step further in their magic, for all men wore masks, and many a different mask with each different man or woman; and Kull wondered if a serpent did not lurk under every mask.

So he sat and brooded in strange, mazy thought ways, and the courtiers came and went and the minor affairs of the day were completed, until at last the king and Brule sat alone in the Hall of Society save for the drowsy attendants.

Kull felt a weariness. Neither he nor Brule had slept the night before, nor had Kull slept the night before that, when in the gardens of Ka-nu he had had his first hint of the weird things to be. Last night nothing further had occurred after they had returned to the study room from the secret corridors, but they had neither dared nor cared to sleep. Kull, with the incredible vitality of a wolf, had aforetime gone for days upon days without sleep, in his wild savage days, but now his mind was edged from constant thinking and from the nerve-breaking eeriness of the past night. He needed sleep, but sleep was furthest from his mind.

And he would not have dared sleep if he had thought of it.

Another thing that had shaken him was the fact that though he and Brule had kept a close watch to see if, or when, the study-room guard was changed, yet it was changed without their knowledge; for the next morning those who stood on guard were able to repeat the magic words of Brule, but they remembered nothing out of the ordinary. They thought that they had stood at guard all night, as usual, and Kull said nothing to the contrary. He believed them true men, but Brule had advised absolute secrecy, and Kull also thought it best.

Now Brule leaned over the throne, lowering his voice so not even a lazy attendant could hear: "They will strike soon, I think, Kull. A while ago Ka-nu gave me a secret sign. The priests know that we know of their plot, of course, but they know not how much we know. We must be ready for any sort of action. Ka-nu and the Pictish chiefs will remain within hailing distance now until this is settled one way or another. Ha, Kull, if it comes to a pitched battle, the streets and the castles of Valusia will run red!"

Kull smiled grimly. He would greet any sort of action with a ferocious joy. This wandering in a labyrinth of illusion and magic was extremely irksome to his nature. He longed for the leap and clang of swords, for the joyous freedom of battle.

Then into the Hall of Society came Tu again, and the rest of the councilors.

"Lord king, the hour of the council is at hand and we stand ready to escort you to the council room."

Kull rose, and the councilors bent the knee as he passed through the way opened by them for his passage, rising behind him and following. Eyebrows were raised as the Pict strode defiantly behind the king, but no one dissented. Brule's challenging gaze swept the smooth faces of the councilors with the defiance of an intruding savage.

The group passed through the halls and came at last to the council chamber. The door was closed, as usual, and the councilors arranged themselves in the order of their rank before the dais upon which stood the king. Like a bronze statue Brule took up his stand behind Kull.

Kull swept the room with a swift stare. Surely no chance of treachery here. Seventeen councilors there were, all known to him; all of them had espoused his cause when he ascended the throne.

"Men of Valusia —" he began in the conventional manner, then halted, perplexed. The councilors had risen as a man and were moving toward him. There was no hostility in their looks, but their actions were strange for a council room. The foremost was close to him when Brule sprang forward, crouched like a leopard.

"*Ka nama kaa lajerama!*" his voice crackled through the sinister silence of the room and the foremost councilor recoiled, hand flashing to his robes; and like a spring released Brule moved and the man pitched headlong to the glint of his sword — headlong he pitched and lay still while his face faded and became the head of a mighty snake.

"Slay, Kull!" rasped the Pict's voice. "They be all serpent men!"

The rest was a scarlet maze. Kull saw the familiar faces dim like fading fog and in their places gaped horrid reptilian visages as the whole band rushed forward. His mind was dazed but his giant body faltered not.

The singing of his sword filled the room, and the onrushing flood broke in a red wave. But they surged forward again, seemingly willing to fling their lives away in order to drag down the king. Hideous jaws gaped at him; terrible eyes blazed into his unblinkingly; a frightful fetid scent pervaded the atmosphere — the serpent scent that Kull had known in southern jungles. Swords and daggers leaped at him and he was dimly aware that they wounded him. But Kull was in his element; never before had he faced such grim foes but it mattered little; they lived, their veins held blood that could be spilt and they died when his great sword cleft their skulls or drove through their bodies. Slash, thrust, thrust and swing. Yet had Kull died there but for the man who crouched at his side, parrying and thrusting. For the king was clear berserk, fighting in the terrible Atlantean way, that seeks death to deal death; he made no effort to avoid thrusts and slashes, standing straight up and ever plunging forward, no thought in his frenzied mind but to slay. Not often did Kull forget his fighting craft in his primitive fury, but now some chain had broken in his soul, flooding his mind with a red wave of slaughter-lust. He slew a foe at each blow, but they surged about him, and time and again Brule turned a thrust that would have slain, as he crouched beside Kull, parrying and warding with cold skill, slaying not as Kull slew with long slashes and plunges, but with short overhand blows and upward thrusts.

Kull laughed, a laugh of insanity. The frightful faces swirled about him in a scarlet blaze. He felt steel sink into his arm and dropped his sword in a flashing arc that cleft his foe to the breast-bone. Then the mists faded and the king saw that he and Brule stood alone above a sprawl of hideous crimson figures who lay still upon the floor.

"Valka! what a killing!" said Brule, shaking the blood from his eyes. "Kull, had these been warriors who knew how to use the steel, we had died here. These serpent priests know naught of swordcraft and die easier than any men I ever slew. Yet had there been a few more, I think the matter had ended otherwise."

Kull nodded. The wild berserker blaze had passed, leaving a mazed feeling of great weariness. Blood seeped from wounds on breast, shoulder, arm and leg. Brule, himself bleeding from a score of flesh wounds, glanced at him in some concern.

"Lord Kull, let us hasten to have your wounds dressed by the women."

Kull thrust him aside with a drunken sweep of his mighty arm.

"Nay, we'll see this through ere we cease. Go you, though, and have your wounds seen to – I command it."

The Pict laughed grimly. "Your wounds are more than mine, lord king –" he began, then stopped as a sudden thought struck him. "By Valka, Kull, this is not the council room!"

Kull looked about and suddenly other fogs seemed to fade. "Nay, this is the room where Eallal died a thousand years ago – since unused and named 'Accursed.'"

"Then by the gods, they tricked us after all!" exclaimed Brule in a fury, kicking the corpses at their feet. "They caused us to walk like fools into their ambush! By their magic they changed the appearance of all –"

"Then there is further deviltry afoot," said Kull, "for if there be true men in the councils of Valusia they should be in the real council room now. Come swiftly."

And leaving the room with its ghastly keepers they hastened through halls that seemed deserted until they came to the real council room. Then Kull halted with a ghastly shudder. *From the council room sounded a voice speaking, and the voice was his!*

23

With a hand that shook he parted the tapestries and gazed into the room. There sat the councilors, counterparts of the men he and Brule had just slain, and upon the dais stood Kull, king of Valusia.

He stepped back, his mind reeling.

"This is insanity!" he whispered. "Am I Kull? Do I stand here or is that Kull yonder in very truth and am I but a shadow, a figment of thought?"

Brule's hand clutching his shoulder, shaking him fiercely, brought him to his senses.

"Valka's name, be not a fool! Can you yet be astounded after all we have seen? See you not that those are true men bewitched by a snake-man who has taken your form, as those others took their forms? By now you should have been slain and yon monster reigning in your stead, unknown by those who bowed to you. Leap and slay swiftly or else we are undone. The Red Slayers, true men, stand close on each hand and none but you can reach and slay him. Be swift!"

Kull shook off the onrushing dizziness, flung back his head in the old, defiant gesture. He took a long, deep breath as does a strong swimmer before diving into the sea; then, sweeping back the tapestries, made the dais in a single lionlike bound. Brule had spoken truly. There stood men of the Red Slayers, guardsmen trained to move quick as the striking leopard; any but Kull had died ere he could reach the usurper. But the sight of Kull, identical with the man upon the dais, held them in their tracks, their minds stunned for an instant, and that was long enough. He upon the dais snatched for his sword, but even as his fingers closed upon the hilt, Kull's sword stood out behind his shoulders and the thing that men had thought the king pitched forward from the dais to lie silent upon the floor.

"Hold!" Kull's lifted hand and kingly voice stopped the rush that had started, and while they stood astounded he pointed to the thing which lay before them – whose face was fading into that of a snake. They recoiled, and from one door came Brule and from another came Ka-nu.

These grasped the king's bloody hand and Ka-nu spoke: "Men of Valusia, you have seen with your own eyes. This is the true Kull, the mightiest king to whom Valusia has ever bowed. The power of the Serpent is broken and ye be all true men. King Kull, have you commands?"

"Lift that carrion," said Kull, and men of the guard took up the thing.

"Now follow me," said the king, and he made his way to the Accursed Room. Brule, with a look of concern, offered the support of his arm but Kull shook him off.

The distance seemed endless to the bleeding king, but at last he stood at the door and laughed fiercely and grimly when he heard the horrified ejaculations of the councilors.

At his orders the guardsmen flung the corpse they carried beside the others, and motioning all from the room Kull stepped out last and closed the door.

A wave of dizziness left him shaken. The faces turned to him, pallid and wonderingly, swirled and mingled in a ghostly fog. He felt the blood from his wounds trickling down his limbs and he knew that what he was to do, he must do quickly or not at all.

His sword rasped from its sheath.

"Brule, are you there?"

"Aye!" Brule's face looked at him through the mist, close to his shoulder, but Brule's voice sounded leagues and eons away.

"Remember our vow, Brule. And now, bid them stand back."

His left arm cleared a space as he flung up his sword. Then with all his waning power he drove it through the door into the jamb, driving the great sword to the hilt and sealing the room forever.

Legs braced wide, he swayed drunkenly, facing the horrified councilors. "Let this room be doubly accursed. And let those rotting skeletons lie there forever as a sign of the dying might of the serpent. Here I swear that I shall hunt the serpent-men from land to land, from sea to sea, giving no rest until all be slain, that good triumph and the power of Hell be broken. This thing I swear – I – Kull – king – of – Valusia."

His knees buckled as the faces swayed and swirled. The councilors leaped forward, but ere they could reach him, Kull slumped to the floor, and lay still, face upward.

The councilors surged about the fallen king, chattering and shrieking. Ka-nu beat them back with his clenched fists, cursing savagely.

"Back, you fools! Would you stifle the little life that is yet in him? How, Brule, is he dead or will he live?" – to the warrior who bent above the prostrate Kull.

"Dead?" sneered Brule irritably. "Such a man as this is not so easily killed. Lack of sleep and loss of blood have weakened him – by Valka, he has a score of deep wounds, but none of them mortal. Yet have those gibbering fools bring the court women here at once."

Brule's eyes lighted with a fierce, proud light.

"Valka, Ka-nu, but here is such a man as I knew not existed in these degenerate days. He will be in the saddle in a few scant days and then may the serpent-men of the world beware of Kull of Valusia. Valka! but that will be a rare hunt! Ah, I see long years of prosperity for the world with such a king upon the throne of Valusia."

The Ghost Kings

The ghost kings are marching; the midnight knows their tread,
From the distant, stealthy planets of the dim, unstable dead;
There are whisperings on the night-winds and the shuddering
   stars have fled.

A ghostly trumpet echoes from a barren mountainhead;
Through the fen the wandering witch-lights gleam like phantom
   arrows sped;
There is silence in the valleys and the moon is rising red.

The ghost kings are marching down the ages' dusty maze;
The unseen feet are tramping through the moonlight's pallid haze,
Down the hollow clanging stairways of a million yesterdays.

The ghost kings are marching, where the vague moon-vapor creeps,
While the night-wind to their coming, like a thund'rous herald sweeps;
They are clad in ancient grandeur, but the world, unheeding, sleeps.

The Curse of the Golden Skull

Rotath of Lemuria was dying. Blood had ceased to flow from the deep sword gash under his heart, but the pulse in his temple hammered like kettle drums.

Rotath lay on a marble floor. Granite columns rose about him and a silver idol stared with ruby eyes at the man who lay at its feet. The bases of the columns were carved with curious monsters; above the shrine sounded a vague whispering. The trees which hemmed in and hid that mysterious fane spread long waving branches above it, and these branches were vibrant with curious leaves which rustled in the wind. From time to time great black roses scattered their dusky petals down.

Rotath lay dying and he used his fading breath in calling down curses on his slayers — on the faithless king who had betrayed him, and on that barbarian chief, Kull of Atlantis, who dealt him the death blow.

Acolyte of the nameless gods, and dying in an unknown shrine on the leafy summit of Lemuria's highest mountain — Rotath's weird inhuman eyes smoldered with a terrible cold fire. A pageant of glory and splendor passed before his mind's eye. The acclaim of worshippers, the roar of silver trumpets, the whispering shadows of mighty and mystic temples where great wings swept unseen — then the intrigues, the onslaught of the invaders — death!

Rotath cursed the king of Lemuria — the king to whom he had taught fearful and ancient mysteries and forgotten abominations. Fool that he had been to reveal his powers to a weakling who, having learned to fear him, had turned to foreign kings for aid.

How strange it seemed, that he, Rotath of the Moonstone and the Asphodel, sorcerer and magician, should be gasping out his breath on the marble floor, a victim to that most material of all threats – a keen pointed sword in a sinewy hand.

Rotath cursed the limitations of the flesh. He felt his brain crumbling and he cursed all the men of all the worlds. He cursed them by Hotath and Helgor, by Ra and Ka and Valka.

He cursed all men living and dead, and all the generations unborn for a million centuries to come, naming Vramma and Jaggta-noga and Kamma and Kulthas. He cursed humanity by the fane of the Black Gods, the tracks of the Serpent Ones, the talons of the Ape Lords and the iron bound books of Shuma Gorath.

He cursed goodness and virtue and light, speaking the names of gods forgotten even by the priests of Lemuria. He invoked the dark monstrous shadows of the older worlds, and of those black suns which lurk forever behind the stars.

He felt the shades gather about him. He was going fast. And closing about him in an ever nearing ring, he sensed the tiger taloned devils who awaited his coming. He saw their bodies of solid jet and the great red caverns of their eyes. Behind hovered the white shadows of they who had died upon his altars, in horrid torment. Like mist in the moonlight they floated, great luminous eyes fixed on him in sad accusation, a never ending host.

Rotath feared, and fearing, his curses rose louder, his blasphemies grew more terrible. With one last wild passion of fury, he placed a curse on his own bones that they might bring death and horror to the sons of men. But even as he spoke he knew that years and ages would pass and his bones turn to dust in that forgotten shrine before any man's foot disturbed its silence. So he mustered his fast waning powers for one last invocation to the dread beings he had served, one last feat of magic. He uttered a blood-freezing formula, naming a terrible name.

And soon he felt mighty elemental powers set in motion. He felt his bones growing hard and brittle. A coldness transcending earthly coldness passed over him and he lay still. The leaves whispered and the silver god laughed with cold gemmed eyes.

★★★★★★★★★★

EMERALD INTERLUDE

Years stretched into centuries, centuries became ages. The green oceans rose and wrote an epic poem in emerald and the rhythm thereof was terrible. Thrones toppled and the silver trumpets fell silent forever. The races of men passed as smoke drifts from the breast of a summer. The roaring jade green seas engulfed the lands and all mountains sank, even the highest mountain of Lemuria.

★★★★★★★★★★★★

ORCHIDS OF DEATH

A man thrust aside the trailing vines and stared. A heavy beard masked his face and mire slimed his boots. Above and about him hung the thick tropic jungle in breathless and exotic brooding. Orchids flamed and breathed about him.

Wonder was in his wide eyes. He gazed between shattered granite columns upon a crumbling marble floor. Vines twined thickly, like green serpents, among these columns and trailed their sinuous length across the floor. A curious idol, long fallen from a broken pedestal, lay upon the floor and stared up with red, unblinking eyes. The man noted the character of this corroded thing and a strong shudder shook him. He glanced unbelievingly again at the other thing which lay on the marble floor, and shrugged his shoulders.

He entered the shrine. He gazed at the carvings on the bases of the sullen columns, wondering at their unholy and indescribable appearance. Over all the scent of the orchids hung like a heavy fog.

This small, rankly grown, swampy island was once the pinnacle of a great mountain, mused the man, and he wondered what strange people had reared up this fane – and left that monstrous thing lying before the fallen idol. He thought of the fame which his discoveries should bring him – of the acclaim of mighty universities and powerful scientific societies.

He bent above the skeleton on the floor, noting the inhumanly long finger bones, the curious formation of the feet; the deep cavern-like eye-sockets, the jutting frontal bone, the general appearance of the great domed skull, which differed so horribly from mankind as he knew it.

What long dead artizan had shaped the thing with such incredible skill? He bent closer, noting the rounded ball-and-socket of the joints, the slight depressions on flat surfaces where muscles had been attached. And he started as the stupendous truth was borne on him.

This was no work of human art – that skeleton had once been clothed in flesh and had walked and spoken and lived. And this was impossible, his reeling brain told him, for the bones were of solid gold.

The orchids nodded in the shadows of the trees. The shrine lay in purple and black shade. The man brooded above the bones and wondered. How could he know of an elder world sorcery great enough to serve undying hate, by lending that hate a concrete substance, impervious to Time's destructions?

The man laid his hand on the golden skull. A sudden deathly shriek broke the silence. The man in the shrine reeled up, screaming, took a single staggering step and then fell headlong, to lie with writhing limbs on the vine-crossed marble floor.

The orchids showered down on him in a sensuous rain and his blind, clutching hands tore them into exotic fragments as he died. Silence fell and an adder crawled sluggishly from within the golden skull.

Red Shadows

I

THE COMING OF SOLOMON

The moonlight shimmered hazily, making silvery mists of illusion among the shadowy trees. A faint breeze whispered down the valley, bearing a shadow that was not of the moon-mist. A faint scent of smoke was apparent.

The man whose long, swinging strides, unhurried yet unswerving, had carried him for many a mile since sunrise, stopped suddenly. A movement in the trees had caught his attention, and he moved silently toward the shadows, a hand resting lightly on the hilt of his long, slim rapier.

Warily he advanced, his eyes striving to pierce the darkness that brooded under the trees. This was a wild and menacing country; death might be lurking under those trees. Then his hand fell away from the hilt and he leaned forward. Death indeed was there, but not in such shape as might cause him fear.

"The fires of Hades!" he murmured. "A girl! What has harmed you, child? Be not afraid of me."

The girl looked up at him, her face like a dim white rose in the dark.

"You – who are – you?" her words came in gasps.

"Naught but a wanderer, a landless man, but a friend to all in need." The gentle voice sounded somehow incongruous, coming from the man.

The girl sought to prop herself up on her elbow, and instantly he knelt and raised her to a sitting position, her head resting against his shoulder. His hand touched her breast and came away red and wet.

"Tell me." His voice was soft, soothing, as one speaks to a babe.

"Le Loup," she gasped, her voice swiftly growing weaker. "He and his men – descended upon our village – a mile up the valley. They robbed – slew – burned –"

"That, then, was the smoke I scented," muttered the man. "Go on, child."

"I ran. He, the Wolf, pursued me – and – caught me–" The words died away in a shuddering silence.

"I understand, child. Then –?"

"Then – he – he – stabbed me – with his dagger – oh, blessed saints! – mercy –"

Suddenly the slim form went limp. The man eased her to the earth, and touched her brow lightly.

"Dead!" he muttered.

Slowly he rose, mechanically wiping his hands upon his cloak. A dark scowl had settled on his somber brow. Yet he made no wild, reckless vow, swore no oath by saints or devils.

"Men shall die for this," he said coldly.

II

THE LAIR OF THE WOLF

"You are a fool!" The words came in a cold snarl that curdled the hearer's blood.

He who had just been named a fool lowered his eyes sullenly without answer.

"You and all the others I lead!" The speaker leaned forward, his fist pounding emphasis on the rude table between them. He was a tall, rangy-built man, supple as a leopard and with a lean, cruel, predatory face. His eyes danced and glittered with a kind of reckless mockery.

The fellow spoken to replied sullenly, "This Solomon Kane is a demon from Hell, I tell you."

"Faugh! Dolt! He is a man – who will die from a pistol ball or a sword thrust."

"So thought Jean, Juan and La Costa," answered the other grimly. "Where are they? Ask the mountain wolves that tore the flesh from their dead bones. Where does this Kane hide? We have searched the mountains and the valleys for leagues, and we have found no trace. I tell you, Le Loup, he comes up from hell. I knew no good would come from hanging that friar a moon ago."

The Wolf strummed impatiently upon the table. His keen face, despite lines of wild living and dissipation, was the face of a thinker. The superstitions of his followers affected him not at all.

"Faugh! I say again. The fellow has found some cavern or secret vale of which we do not know where he hides in the day."

"And at night he sallies forth and slays us," gloomily commented the other. "He hunts us down as a wolf hunts deer – by God, Le Loup, you name yourself Wolf but I think you have met at last a fiercer and more crafty wolf than yourself! The first we know of this man is when we find Jean, the most desperate bandit unhung, nailed to a tree with his own dagger through his breast, and the letters S.L.K. carved upon his dead cheeks.

"Then the Spaniard Juan is struck down, and after we find him he lives long enough to tell us that his slayer is an Englishman, Solomon Kane, who has sworn to destroy our entire band! What then? La Costa, a swordsman second only to yourself, goes forth swearing to meet this Kane. By the demons of perdition, it seems he met him! For we found his sword-pierced corpse upon a cliff. What now? Are we all to fall before this English fiend?"

"True, our best men have been done to death by him," mused the bandit chief. "Soon the rest return from that little trip to the hermit's; then we shall see. Kane can not hide forever. Then – ha, what was that?"

The two turned swiftly as a shadow fell across the table. Into the entrance of the cave that formed the bandit lair, a man staggered. His eyes were wide and staring; he reeled on buckling legs, and a dark red stain dyed his tunic. He came a few tottering steps forward, then pitched across the table, sliding off onto the floor.

"Hell's devils!" cursed the Wolf, hauling him upright and propping him in a chair. "Where are the rest, curse you?"

"Dead! All dead!"

"How? Satan's curses on you, speak!" The Wolf shook the man savagely, the other bandit gazing on in wide-eyed horror.

"We reached the hermit's hut just as the moon rose," the man muttered. "I stayed outside – to watch – the others went in – to torture the hermit – to make him reveal – the hiding place – of his gold."

"Yes, yes! Then what?" The Wolf was raging with impatience.

"Then the world turned red – the hut went up in a roar and a red rain flooded the valley – through it I saw – the hermit and a tall man clad all in black – coming from the trees–"

"Solomon Kane!" gasped the bandit. "I knew it! I –"

"Silence, fool!" snarled the chief. "Go on!"

"I fled – Kane pursued – wounded me – but I outran – him – got – here – first–"

The man slumped forward on the table.

"Saints and devils!" raged the Wolf. "What does he look like, this Kane?"

"Like – Satan –"

The voice trailed off in silence. The dead man slid from the table to lie in a red heap upon the floor.

"Like Satan!" babbled the other bandit. "I told you! 'Tis the Horned One himself! I tell you –"

He ceased as a frightened face peered in at the cave entrance.

"Kane?"

"Aye." The Wolf was too much at sea to lie. "Keep close watch, La Mon; in a moment the Rat and I will join you."

The face withdrew and Le Loup turned to the other.

"This ends the band," said he. "You, I, and that thief La Mon are all that are left. What would you suggest?"

The Rat's pallid lips barely formed the word: "Flight!"

"You are right. Let us take the gems and gold from the chests and flee, using the secret passageway."

"And La Mon?"

"He can watch until we are ready to flee. Then – why divide the treasure three ways?"

A faint smile touched the Rat's malevolent features. Then a sudden thought smote him.

"He," indicating the corpse on the floor, "said, 'I got here first.' Does that mean Kane was pursuing him here?" And as the Wolf nodded impatiently the other turned to the chests with chattering haste.

The flickering candle on the rough table lighted up a strange and wild scene. The light, uncertain and dancing, gleamed redly in the slowly widening lake of blood in which the dead man lay; it danced upon the heaps of gems and coins emptied hastily upon the floor from the brass-bound chests that ranged the walls; and it glittered in the eyes of the Wolf with the same gleam which sparkled from his sheathed dagger.

The chests were empty, their treasure lying in a shimmering mass upon the blood-stained floor. The Wolf stopped and listened. Outside was silence. There was no moon, and Le Loup's keen imagination pictured the dark slayer, Solomon Kane, gliding through the blackness, a shadow among shadows. He grinned crookedly; this time the Englishman would be foiled.

"There is a chest yet unopened," said he, pointing.

The Rat, with a muttered exclamation of surprise, bent over the chest indicated. With a single, cat-like motion, the Wolf sprang upon him, sheathing his dagger to the hilt in the Rat's back, between the shoulders. The Rat sagged to the floor without a sound.

"Why divide the treasure two ways?" murmured Le Loup, wiping his blade upon the dead man's doublet. "Now for La Mon."

He stepped toward the door; then stopped and shrank back.

At first he thought it was the shadow of a man who stood in the entrance; then he saw that it was a man himself, though so dark and still he stood that a fantastic semblance of shadow was lent him by the glittering candle.

A tall man, as tall as Le Loup he was, clad in black from head to foot, in plain, close-fitting garments that somehow suited the somber face. Long arms and broad shoulders betokened the swordsman, as plainly as the long rapier in his hand. The features of the man were saturnine and gloomy. A kind of dark pallor lent him a ghostly appearance in the uncertain light, an effect heightened by the satanic darkness of his lowering brows. Eyes, large, deep-set and unblinking, fixed their gaze upon the bandit, and looking into them, Le Loup was unable to decide what color they were. Strangely, the Mephistophelean trend of the lower features was offset by a high, broad forehead, though this was partly hidden by a featherless hat.

That forehead marked the dreamer, the idealist, the introvert, just as the eyes and the thin, straight nose betrayed the fanatic. An observer would have been struck by the eyes of the two men who stood there, facing each other. Eyes of both betokened untold deeps of power, but there the resemblance ceased.

The eyes of the bandit were hard, almost opaque, with a curious scintil-lant shallowness that reflected a thousand changing lights and gleams, like some strange gem; there was mockery in those eyes, cruelty and reckless-ness.

The eyes of the man in black, on the other hand, deep-set and staring from under prominent brows, were cold but deep; gazing into them, one had the impression of looking into countless fathoms of ice.

Now the eyes clashed, and the Wolf, who was used to being feared, felt a strange coolness on his spine. The sensation was new to him — a new thrill to one who lived for thrills, and he laughed suddenly.

"You are Solomon Kane, I suppose?" he asked, managing to make his question sound politely incurious.

"I am Solomon Kane." The voice was resonant and powerful. "Are you prepared to meet your God?"

"Why, Monsieur," Le Loup answered, bowing, "I assure you I am as ready as I ever will be. I might ask Monsieur the same question."

"No doubt I stated my inquiry wrongly," Kane said grimly. "I will change it: Are you prepared to meet your master, the Devil?"

"As to that, Monsieur" – Le Loup examined his fingernails with elaborate unconcern – "I must say that I can at present render a most satisfactory account to his Horned Excellency, though really I have no intention of so doing – for a while at least."

Le Loup did not wonder as to the fate of La Mon; Kane's presence in the cave was sufficient answer that did not need the trace of blood on his rapier to verify it.

"What I wish to know, Monsieur," said the bandit, "is why in the Devil's name have you harassed my band as you have, and how did you destroy that last set of fools?"

"Your last question is easily answered, sir," Kane replied. "I myself had the tale spread that the hermit possessed a store of gold, knowing that would draw your scum as carrion draws vultures. For days and night I have watched the hut, and tonight, when I saw your villains coming, I warned the hermit, and together we went among the trees back of the hut. Then, when the rogues were inside, I struck flint and steel to the trail I had laid, and flame ran through the trees like a red snake until it reached the powder I had placed beneath the hut floor. Then the hut and thirteen sinners went to Hell in a great roar of flame and smoke. True, one escaped, but him I had slain in the forest had not I stumbled and fallen upon a broken root, which gave him time to elude me."

"Monsieur," said Le Loup with another low bow, "I grant you the admiration I must needs bestow on a brave and shrewd foeman. Yet tell me this: Why have you followed me as a wolf follows deer?"

"Some moons ago," said Kane, his frown becoming more menacing, "you and your fiends raided a small village down the valley. You know the details better than I. There was a girl, a mere child, who, hoping to escape your lust, fled up the valley; but you, you jackal of Hell, you caught her and left her, violated and dying. I found her there, and above her dead form I made up my mind to hunt you down and kill you."

"H'm," mused the Wolf. "Yes, I remember the wench. Mon Dieu, so the softer sentiments enter into the affair! Monsieur, I had not thought you an amorous man; be not jealous, good fellow, there are many more wenches."

"Le Loup, take care!" Kane exclaimed, a terrible menace in his voice. "I have never yet done a man to death by torture, but by God, sir, you tempt me!"

The tone, and more especially the unexpected oath, coming as it did from Kane, slightly sobered Le Loup; his eyes narrowed and his hand moved toward his rapier. The air was tense for an instant; then the Wolf relaxed elaborately.

"Who was the girl?" he asked idly. "Your wife?"

"I never saw her before," answered Kane.

"Nom d'un nom!" swore the bandit. "What sort of a man are you, Monsieur, who takes up a feud of this sort merely to avenge a wench unknown to you?"

"That, sir, is my own affair; it is sufficient that I do so."

Kane could not have explained, even to himself, nor did he ever seek an explanation within himself. A true fanatic, his promptings were reasons enough for his actions.

"You are right, Monsieur." Le Loup was sparring now for time; casually he edged backward inch by inch, with such consummate acting skill that he aroused no suspicion even in the hawk who watched him. "Monsieur," said he, "possibly you will say that you are merely a noble cavalier, wandering about like a true Galahad, protecting the weaker; but you and I know different. There on the floor is the equivalent to an emperor's ransom. Let us divide it peaceably; then if you like not my company, why – nom d'un nom! – we can go our separate ways."

Kane leaned forward, a terrible brooding threat growing in his cold eyes. He seemed like a great condor about to launch himself upon his victim.

"Sir, do you assume me to be as great a villain as yourself?"

Suddenly Le Loup threw back his head, his eyes dancing and leaping with a mild mockery and a kind of insane recklessness. His shout of laughter sent the echoes flying.

"Gods of Hell! No, you fool, I do not class you with myself! Mon Dieu, Monsieur Kane, you have a task indeed if you intend to avenge all the wenches who have known my favors!"

"Shades of death! Shall I waste time in parleying with this base scoundrel!" Kane snarled in a voice suddenly blood-thirsting, and his lean frame flashed forward like a bent bow suddenly released.

At the same instant Le Loup with a wild laugh bounded backward with a movement as swift as Kane's. His timing was perfect; his back-flung hands struck the table and hurled it aside, plunging the cave into darkness as the candle toppled and went out.

Kane's rapier sang like an arrow in the dark as he thrust blindly and ferociously.

"Adieu, Monsieur Galahad!" the taunt came from somewhere in front of him, but Kane, plunging toward the sound with the savage fury of baffled wrath, caromed against a blank wall that did not yield to his blow. From somewhere seemed to come an echo of a mocking laugh.

Kane whirled, eyes fixed on the dimly outlined entrance, thinking his foe would try to slip past him and out of the cave; but no form bulked there, and when his groping hands found the candle and lighted it, the cave was empty, save for himself and the dead men on the floor.

III

THE CHANT OF THE DRUMS

Across the dusky waters the whisper came: boom, boom, boom! – a sullen reiteration. Far away and more faintly sounded a whisper of different timbre: thrum, throom, thrum! Back and forth went the vibrations as the throbbing drums spoke to each other. What tales did they carry? What monstrous secrets whispered across the sullen, shadowy reaches of the unmapped jungle?

"This, you are sure, is the bay where the Spanish ship put in?"

"Yes, Senhor; the negro swears this is the bay where the white man left the ship alone and went into the jungle."

Kane nodded grimly.

"Then put me ashore here, alone. Wait seven days; then if I have not returned and if you have no word of me, set sail wherever you will."

"Yes, Senhor."

The waves slapped lazily against the sides of the boat that carried Kane ashore. The village that he sought was on the river bank but set back from the bay shore, the jungle hiding it from sight of the ship.

Kane had adopted what seemed the most hazardous course, that of going ashore by night, for the reason that he knew, if the man he sought were in the village, he would never reach it by day. As it was, he was taking a most desperate chance in daring the nighttime jungle, but all his life he had been used to taking desperate chances. Now he gambled his life upon the slim chance of gaining the negro village under cover of darkness and unknown to the villagers.

At the beach he left the boat with a few muttered commands, and as the rowers put back to the ship which lay anchored some distance out in the bay, he turned and engulfed himself in the blackness of the jungle. Sword in one hand, dagger in the other, he stole forward, seeking to keep pointed in the direction from which the drums still muttered and grumbled.

He went with the stealth and easy movement of a leopard, feeling his way cautiously, every nerve alert and straining, but the way was not easy. Vines tripped him and slapped him in the face, impeding his progress; he was forced to grope his way between the huge boles of towering trees, and all through the underbrush about him sounded vague and menacing rustlings and shadows of movement. Thrice his foot touched something that moved beneath it and writhed away, and once he glimpsed the baleful glimmer of feline eyes among the trees. They vanished, however, as he advanced.

Thrum, thrum, thrum, came the ceaseless monotone of drums: war and death (they said); blood and lust; human sacrifice and human feast! The soul of Africa (said the drums); the spirit of the jungle; the chant of the gods of outer darkness, the gods that roar and gibber, the gods men knew when dawns were young, beast-eyed, gaping-mouthed, huge-bellied, bloody-handed, the Black Gods (sang the drums).

All this and more the drums roared and bellowed to Kane as he worked his way through the forest. Somewhere in his soul a responsive chord was smitten and answered. You too are of the night (sang the drums); there is the strength of darkness, the strength of the primitive in you; come back down the ages; let us teach you, let us teach you (chanted the drums).

Kane stepped out of the thick jungle and came upon a plainly defined trail. Beyond, through the trees came the gleam of the village fires, flames glowing through the palisades. Kane walked down the trail swiftly.

He went silently and warily, sword extended in front of him, eyes straining to catch any hint of movement in the darkness ahead, for the trees loomed like sullen giants on each hand; sometimes their great branches intertwined above the trail and he could see only a slight way ahead of him.

Like a dark ghost he moved along the shadowed trail; alertly he stared and harkened; yet no warning came first to him, as a great, vague bulk rose up out of the shadows and struck him down, silently.

IV
THE BLACK GOD

Thrum, thrum, thrum! Somewhere, with deadening monotony, a cadence was repeated, over and over, bearing out the same theme: "Fool – fool – fool!" Now it was far away, now he could stretch out his hand and almost reach it. Now it merged with the throbbing in his head until the two vibrations were as one: "Fool – fool – fool – fool –"

The fogs faded and vanished. Kane sought to raise his hand to his head, but found that he was bound hand and foot. He lay on the floor of a hut – alone? He twisted about to view the place. No, two eyes glimmered at him from the darkness. Now a form took shape, and Kane, still mazed, believed that he looked on the man who had struck him unconscious. Yet no; this man could never strike such a blow. He was lean, withered and wrinkled. The only thing that seemed alive about him were his eyes, and they seemed like the eyes of a snake.

The man squatted on the floor of the hut, near the doorway, naked save for a loin-cloth and the usual paraphernalia of bracelets, anklets and armlets. Weird fetishes of ivory, bone and hide, animal and human, adorned his arms and legs. Suddenly and unexpectedly he spoke in English.

"Ha, you wake, white man? Why you come here, eh?"

Kane asked the inevitable question, following the habit of the Caucasian. "You speak my language – how is that?"

The black man grinned.

"I slave – long time, me boy. Me, N'Longa, ju-ju man, me, great fetish. No black man like me! You white man, you hunt brother?"

Kane snarled. "I! Brother! I seek a man, yes."

The negro nodded. "Maybe so you find um, eh?"

"He dies!"

Again the negro grinned. "Me pow'rful ju-ju man," he announced apropos of nothing. He bent closer. "White man you hunt, eyes like a leopard, eh? Yes? Ha! ha! ha! ha! Listen, white man: man-with-eyes-of-a-leopard, he and Chief Songa make pow'rful palaver; they blood brothers now. Say nothing, I help you; you help me, eh?"

"Why should you help me?" asked Kane suspiciously.

The ju-ju man bent closer and whispered, "White man Songa's right-hand man; Songa more pow'rful than N'Longa. White man mighty ju-ju! N'Longa's white brother kill man-with-eyes-of-a-leopard, be blood brother to N'Longa. N'Longa be more pow'rful than Songa; palaver set."

And like a dusky ghost he floated out of the hut so swiftly that Kane was not sure but that the whole affair was a dream.

Without, Kane could see the flare of fires. The drums were still booming, but close at hand the tones merged and mingled, and the impulse-producing vibrations were lost. All seemed a barbaric clamor without rime or reason, yet there was an undertone of mockery there, savage and gloating. "Lies," thought Kane, his mind still swimming, "jungle lies like jungle women that lure a man to his doom."

Two warriors entered the hut – black giants, hideous with paint and armed with crude spears. They lifted the white man and carried him out of the hut. They bore him across an open space, leaned him upright against a post and bound him there. About him, behind him and to the side, a great semicircle of black faces leered and faded in the firelight as the flames leaped and sank. There in front of him loomed a shape hideous and obscene – a black, formless thing, a grotesque parody of a human. Still, brooding, bloodstained, like the formless soul of Africa, the horror, the Black God.

And in front and to each side, upon roughly carven thrones of teakwood, sat two men. He who sat upon the right was a black man; huge, ungainly, a gigantic and unlovely mass of dusky flesh and muscles. Small, hoglike eyes blinked out over sin-marked cheeks; huge, flabby red lips pursed in fleshy haughtiness.

The other –

"Ah, Monsieur, we meet again." The speaker was far from being the debonair villain who had taunted Kane in the cavern among the mountains. His clothes were rags; there were more lines in his face; he had sunk lower in the years that had passed. Yet his eyes still gleamed and danced with their old recklessness, and his voice held the same mocking timbre.

"The last time I heard that accursed voice," said Kane calmly, "was in a cave, in darkness, whence you fled like a hunted rat."

"Aye, under different conditions," answered Le Loup imperturbably. "What did you do after blundering about like an elephant in the dark!"

Kane hesitated, then: "I left the mountain –"

"By the front entrance? Yes? I might have known you were too stupid to find the secret door. Hoofs of the Devil, had you thrust against the chest with the golden lock, which stood against the wall, the door had opened to you and revealed the secret passageway through which I went."

"I traced you to the nearest port and there took ship and followed you to Italy, where I found you had gone," said Kane.

"Aye, by the saints, you nearly cornered me in Florence. Ho! ho! ho! I was climbing through a back window while Monsieur Galahad was battering down the front door of the tavern. And had your horse not gone lame, you would have caught up with me on the road to Rome. Again, the ship on which I left Spain had barely put out to sea when Monsieur Galahad rides up to the wharfs. Why have you followed me like this? I do not understand."

"Because you are a rogue whom it is my destiny to kill," answered Kane coldly. He did not understand. All his life he had roamed about the world aiding the weak and fighting oppression; he neither knew nor questioned why. That was his obsession, his driving force of life. Cruelty and tyranny to the weak sent a red blaze of fury, fierce and lasting, through his soul. When the full flame of his hatred was wakened and loosed, there was no rest for him until his vengeance had been fulfilled to the uttermost. If he thought of it at all, he considered himself a fulfiller of God's judgment, a vessel of wrath to be emptied upon the souls of the unrighteous. Yet in the full sense of the word Solomon Kane was not wholly a Puritan, though he thought of himself as such.

Le Loup shrugged his shoulders. "I could understand had I wronged you personally. Mon Dieu! I, too, would follow an enemy across the world, but, though I would have joyfully slain and robbed you, I never heard of you until you declared war on me."

Kane was silent, his still fury overcoming him. Though he did not realize it, the Wolf was more than merely an enemy to him; the bandit symbolized to Kane all the things against which the Puritan had fought all his life: cruelty, outrage, oppression and tyranny.

Le Loup broke in on his vengeful meditations. "What did you do with the treasure, which – gods of Hades! – took me years to accumulate? Devil take it, I had time only to snatch a handful of coins and trinkets as I ran."

"I took such as I needed to hunt you down. The rest I gave to the villages which you had looted."

"Saints and the devil!" swore Le Loup. "Monsieur, you are the greatest fool I have yet met. To throw that vast treasure – by Satan, I rage to think of it in the hands of base peasants, vile villagers! Yet, ho! ho! ho! ho! they will steal and kill each other for it. That is human nature."

"Yes, damn you!" flamed Kane suddenly, showing that his conscience had not been at rest. "Doubtless they will, being fools. Yet what could I do? Had I left it there, people might have starved and gone naked for lack of it. More, it would have been found, and theft and slaughter would have followed anyway. You are to blame, for had this treasure been left with its rightful owners, no such trouble would have ensued."

The Wolf grinned without reply. Kane not being a profane man, his rare curses had double effect and always startled his hearers, no matter how vicious or hardened they might be.

It was Kane who spoke next. "Why have you fled from me across the world? You do not really fear me."

"No, you are right. Really I do not know; perhaps flight is a habit which is difficult to break. I made my mistake when I did not kill you that night in the mountains. I am sure I could kill you in a fair fight, yet I have never even, ere now, sought to ambush you. Somehow I have not had a liking to meet you, Monsieur – a whim of mine, a mere whim. Then – mon Dieu! – mayhap I have enjoyed a new sensation – and I had thought that I had exhausted the thrills of life. And then, a man must either be the hunter or the hunted. Until now, Monsieur, I was the hunted, but I grew weary of the role – I thought I had thrown you off the trail."

"A negro slave, brought from this vicinity, told a Portuguese ship captain of a white man who landed from a Spanish ship and went into the jungle. I heard of it and hired the ship, paying the captain to bring me here."

"Monsieur, I admire you for your attempt, but you must admire me, too! Alone I came into this village, and alone among savages and cannibals I – with some slight knowledge of the language learned from a slave aboard ship – I gained the confidence of King Songa and supplanted that mummer, N'Longa. I am a braver man than you, Monsieur, for I had no ship to retreat to, and a ship is waiting for you."

"I admire your courage," said Kane, "but you are content to rule amongst cannibals – you the blackest soul of them all. I intend to return to my own people when I have slain you."

"Your confidence would be admirable were it not amusing. Ho, Gulka!"

A giant negro stalked into the space between them. He was the hugest man that Kane had ever seen, though he moved with cat-like ease and suppleness. His arms and legs were like trees, and the great, sinuous muscles rippled with each motion. His apelike head was set squarely between gigantic shoulders. His great, dusky hands were like the talons of an ape, and his brow slanted back from above bestial eyes. Flat nose and great, thick red lips completed this picture of primitive, lustful savagery.

"That is Gulka, the gorilla-slayer," said Le Loup. "He it was who lay in wait beside the trail and smote you down. You are like a wolf, yourself, Monsieur Kane, but since your ship hove in sight you have been watched by many eyes, and had you had all the powers of a leopard, you had not seen Gulka nor heard him. He hunts the most terrible and crafty of all beasts, in their native forests, far to the north, the beasts-who-walk-like-men – as that one, whom he slew some days since."

Kane, following Le Loup's fingers, made out a curious, man-like thing, dangling from a roof-pole of a hut. A jagged end thrust through the thing's body held it there. Kane could scarcely distinguish its characteristics by the firelight but there was a weird, humanlike semblance about the hideous, hairy thing.

"A female gorilla that Gulka slew and brought to the village," said Le Loup.

The giant black slouched close to Kane and stared into the Englishman's eyes. Kane returned his gaze somberly, and presently the negro's eyes dropped sullenly and he slouched back a few paces. The look in the Puritan's grim eyes had pierced the primitive hazes of the gorilla-slayer's soul, and for the first time in his life he felt fear. To throw this off, he tossed a challenging look about; then with unexpected animalness, he struck his huge chest resoundingly, grinned cavernously and flexed his mighty arms. No one spoke. Primordial bestiality had the stage, and the more highly developed types looked on with various feelings of amusement, tolerance or contempt.

Gulka glanced furtively at Kane to see if the white man was watching him, then with a sudden beastly roar, plunged forward and dragged a man from the semicircle. While the trembling victim screeched for mercy, the giant hurled him upon the crude altar before the shadowy idol. A spear rose and flashed, and the screeching ceased. The Black God looked on, his monstrous features seeming to leer in the flickering firelight. He had drunk; was the Black God pleased with the draft – with the sacrifice?

Gulka stalked back, and stopping before Kane, flourished the bloody spear before the white man's face.

Le Loup laughed. Then suddenly N'Longa appeared. He came from nowhere in particular; suddenly he was standing there, beside the post to which Kane was bound. A lifetime of study of the art of illusion had given the ju-ju man a highly technical knowledge of appearing and disappearing – which after all, consisted only in timing the audience's attention.

He waved Gulka aside with a grand gesture, and the gorilla-man slunk back, apparently to get out of N'Longa's gaze – then with incredible swiftness he turned and struck the ju-ju man a terrific blow upon the side of the head with his open hand. N'Longa went down like a felled ox, and in an instant he had been seized and bound to a post close to Kane. An uncertain murmuring rose from the tribesmen, which died out as King Songa stared angrily toward them.

Le Loup leaned back upon his throne and laughed uproariously.

"The trail ends here, Monsieur Galahad. That ancient fool thought I did not know of his plotting! I was hiding outside the hut and heard the interesting conversation you two had. Ha! ha! ha! ha! The Black God must drink, Monsieur, but I have persuaded Songa to have you two burnt; that will be much more enjoyable, though we shall have to forego the usual feast, I fear. For after the fires are lit about your feet the devil himself could not keep your carcasses from becoming charred frames of bone."

Songa shouted something imperiously, and tribesmen came bearing wood, which they piled about the feet of N'Longa and Kane. The ju-ju man had recovered consciousness, and he now shouted something in his native language. Again the murmuring arose among the shadowy throng. Songa snarled something in reply.

Kane gazed at the scene almost impersonally. Again, somewhere in his soul, dim primal deeps were stirring, age-old thought memories, veiled in the fogs of lost eons. He had been here before, thought Kane; he knew all this of old – the lurid flames beating back the sullen night, the bestial faces leering expectantly, and the god, the Black God, there in the shadows! Always the Black God, brooding back in the shadows. He had known the shouts, the frenzied chant of the worshipers, back there in the gray dawn of the world, the speech of the bellowing drums, the singing priests, the repellent, inflaming, all-pervading scent of freshly spilt blood. All this have I known, somewhere, sometime, thought Kane; now I am the main actor –

He became aware that someone was speaking to him through the roar of the drums; he had not realized that the drums had begun to boom again. The speaker was N'Longa:

"Me pow'rful ju-ju man! Watch now: I work mighty magic. Songa!" His voice rose in a screech that drowned out the wildly clamoring drums.

Songa grinned at the words N'Longa screamed at him. The chant of the drums now had dropped to a low, sinister monotone and Kane plainly heard Le Loup when he spoke:

"N'Longa says that he will now work that magic which it is death to speak, even. Never before has it been worked in the sight of living men; it is the nameless ju-ju magic. Watch closely, Monsieur; possibly we shall be further amused." The Wolf laughed lightly and sardonically.

A black man stooped, applying a torch to the wood about Kane's feet. Tiny jets of flame began to leap up and catch. Another bent to do the same with N'Longa, then hesitated. The ju-ju man sagged in his bonds; his head drooped upon his chest. He seemed dying.

Le Loup leaned forward, cursing: "Feet of the Devil! Is the scoundrel about to cheat us of our pleasure of seeing him writhe in the flames?"

The warrior gingerly touched the wizard and said something in his own language.

Le Loup laughed: "He died of fright. A great wizard, by the –"

His voice trailed off suddenly. The drums stopped as if the drummers had fallen dead simultaneously. Silence dropped like a fog upon the village and in the stillness Kane heard only the sharp crackle of the flames whose heat he was beginning to feel.

All eyes were turned upon the dead man upon the altar, for the corpse had begun to move!

First a twitching of a hand, then an aimless motion of an arm, a motion which gradually spread over the body and limbs. Slowly, with blind, uncertain gestures, the dead man turned upon his side, the trailing limbs found the earth. Then, horribly like something being born, like some frightful reptilian thing bursting the shell of nonexistence, the corpse tottered and reared upright, standing on legs wide apart and stiffly braced, arms still making useless, infantile motions. Utter silence, save somewhere a man's quick breath sounded loud in the stillness.

Kane stared, for the first time in his life smitten speechless and thoughtless. To his Puritan mind this was Satan's hand manifested.

Le Loup sat on his throne, eyes wide and staring, hand still half raised in the careless gesture he was making when frozen into silence by the unbelievable sight. Songa sat beside him, mouth and eyes wide open, fingers making curious jerky motions upon the carved arms of the throne.

Now the corpse was upright, swaying on stilt-like legs, body tilting far back until the sightless eyes seemed to stare straight into the red moon that was just rising over the black jungle. The thing tottered uncertainly in a wide, erratic half-circle, arms flung out grotesquely as if in balance, then swayed about to face the two thrones – and the Black God. A burning twig at Kane's feet cracked like the crash of a cannon in the tense silence. The horror thrust forth a foot – it took a wavering step – another. Then with stiff, jerky and automatonlike steps, legs straddled far apart, the dead man came toward the two who sat in speechless horror to each side of the Black God.

"Ah-h-h!" from somewhere came the explosive sigh, from that shadowy semicircle where crouched the terror-fascinated worshipers. Straight on stalked the grim specter. Now it was within three strides of the thrones, and Le Loup, faced by fear for the first time in his bloody life, cringed back in his chair; while Songa, with a superhuman effort breaking the chains of horror that held him helpless, shattered the night with a wild scream and, springing to his feet, lifted a spear, shrieking and gibbering in wild menace. Then as the ghastly thing halted not its frightful advance, he hurled the spear with all the power of his great, black muscles, and the spear tore through the dead man's breast with a rending of flesh and bone. Not an instant halted the thing – for the dead die not – and Songa the king stood frozen, arms outstretched as if to fend off the terror.

An instant they stood so, leaping firelight and eery moonlight etching the scene forever in the minds of the beholders. The changeless staring eyes of the corpse looked full into the bulging eyes of Songa, where were reflected all the hells of horror. Then with a jerky motion the arms of the thing went out and up. The dead hands fell on Songa's shoulders. At the first touch, the king seemed to shrink and shrivel, and with a scream that was to haunt the dreams of every watcher through all the rest of time, Songa crumpled and fell, and the dead man reeled stiffly and fell with him. Motionless lay the two at the feet of the Black God, and to Kane's dazed mind it seemed that the idol's great, inhuman eyes were fixed upon them with terrible, still laughter.

At the instant of the king's fall, a great shout went up from the blacks, and Kane, with a clarity lent his subconscious mind by the depths of his hate, looked for Le Loup and saw him spring from his throne and vanish in the darkness. Then vision was blurred by a rush of black figures who swept into the space before the god. Feet knocked aside the blazing brands whose heat Kane had forgotten, and dusky hands freed him; others loosed the wizard's body and laid it upon the earth. Kane dimly understood that the blacks believed this thing to be the work of N'Longa, and that they connected the vengeance of the wizard with himself. He bent, laid a hand on the ju-ju man's shoulder. No doubt of it: he was dead, the flesh was already cold. He glanced at the other corpses. Songa was dead, too, and the thing that had slain him lay now without movement.

Kane started to rise, then halted. Was he dreaming, or did he really feel a sudden warmth in the dead flesh he touched? Mind reeling, he again bent over the wizard's body, and slowly he felt warmness steal over the limbs and the blood begin to flow sluggishly through the veins again.

Then N'Longa opened his eyes and stared up into Kane's, with the blank expression of a new-born babe. Kane watched, flesh crawling, and saw the knowing, reptilian glitter come back, saw the wizard's thick lips part in a wide grin. N'Longa sat up, and a strange chant arose from the negroes.

Kane looked about. The blacks were all kneeling, swaying their bodies to and fro, and in their shouts Kane caught the word, "N'Longa!" repeated over and over in a kind of fearsomely ecstatic refrain of terror and worship. As the wizard rose, they all fell prostrate.

N'Longa nodded, as if in satisfaction.

"Great ju-ju – great fetish, me!" he announced to Kane. "You see? My ghost go out – kill Songa – come back to me! Great magic! Great fetish, me!"

Kane glanced at the Black God looming back in the shadows, at N'Longa, who now flung out his arms toward the idol as if in invocation.

I am everlasting (Kane thought the Black God said); I drink, no matter who rules; chiefs, slayers, wizards, they pass like the ghosts of dead men through the gray jungle; I stand, I rule; I am the soul of the jungle (said the Black God).

Suddenly Kane came back from the illusory mists in which he had been wandering. "The white man! Which way did he flee?"

N'Longa shouted something. A score of dusky hands pointed; from somewhere Kane's rapier was thrust out to him. The fogs faded and vanished; again he was the avenger, the scourge of the unrighteous; with the sudden volcanic speed of a tiger he snatched the sword and was gone.

V

THE END OF THE RED TRAIL

Limbs and vines slapped against Kane's face. The oppressive steam of the tropic night rose like mist about him. The moon, now floating high above the jungle, limned the black shadows in its white glow and patterned the jungle floor in grotesque designs. Kane knew not if the man he sought was ahead of him, but broken limbs and trampled underbrush showed that some man had gone that way, some man who fled in haste, nor halted to pick his way. Kane followed these signs unswervingly. Believing in the justice of his vengeance, he did not doubt that the dim beings who rule men's destinies would finally bring him face to face with Le Loup.

Behind him the drums boomed and muttered. What a tale they had to tell this night! of the triumph of N'Longa, the death of the black king, the overthrow of the white-man-with-eyes-like-a-leopard, and a more darksome tale, a tale to be whispered in low, muttering vibrations: the nameless ju-ju.

Was he dreaming? Kane wondered as he hurried on. Was all this part of some foul magic? He had seen a dead man rise and slay and die again; he had seen a man die and come to life again. Did N'Longa in truth send his ghost, his soul, his life essence forth into the void, dominating a corpse to do his will? Aye, N'Longa died a real death there, bound to the torture stake, and he who lay dead on the altar rose and did as N'Longa would have done had he been free. Then, the unseen force animating the dead man fading, N'Longa had lived again.

Yes, Kane thought, he must admit it as a fact. Somewhere in the darksome reaches of jungle and river, N'Longa had stumbled upon the Secret – the Secret of controlling life and death, of overcoming the shackles and limitations of the flesh. How had this dark wisdom, born in the black and blood-stained shadows of this grim land, been given to the wizard? What sacrifice had been so pleasing to the Black Gods, what ritual so monstrous, as to make them give up the knowledge of this magic? And what thoughtless, timeless journeys had N'Longa taken, when he chose to send his ego, his ghost, through the far, misty countries, reached only by death?

There is wisdom in the shadows (brooded the drums), wisdom and magic; go into the darkness for wisdom; ancient magic shuns the light; we

remember the lost ages (whispered the drums), ere man became wise and foolish; we remember the beast gods – the serpent gods and the ape gods and the nameless, the Black Gods, they who drank blood and whose voices roared through the shadowy hills, who feasted and lusted. The secrets of life and death are theirs; we remember, we remember (sang the drums).

Kane heard them as he hastened on. The tale they told to the feathered black warriors farther up the river, he could not translate; but they spoke to him in their own way, and that language was deeper, more basic.

The moon, high in the dark blue skies, lighted his way and gave him a clear vision as he came out at last into a glade and saw Le Loup standing there. The Wolf's naked blade was a long gleam of silver in the moon, and he stood with shoulders thrown back, the old, defiant smile still on his face.

"A long trail, Monsieur," said he. "It began in the mountains of France; it ends in an African jungle. I have wearied of the game at last, Monsieur – and you die. I had not fled from the village, even, save that – I admit it freely – that damnable witchcraft of N'Longa's shook my nerves. More, I saw that the whole tribe would turn against me."

Kane advanced warily, wondering what dim, forgotten tinge of chivalry in the bandit's soul had caused him thus to take his chance in the open. He half suspected treachery, but his keen eyes could detect no shadow of movement in the jungle on either side of the glade.

"Monsieur, on guard!" Le Loup's voice was crisp. "Time that we ended this fool's dance about the world. Here we are alone."

The men were now within reach of each other, and Le Loup, in the midst of his sentence, suddenly plunged forward with the speed of light, thrusting viciously. A slower man had died there, but Kane parried and sent his own blade in a silver streak that slit Le Loup's tunic as the Wolf bounded backward. Le Loup admitted the failure of his trick with a wild laugh and came in with the breath-taking speed and fury of a tiger, his blade making a white fan of steel about him.

Rapier clashed on rapier as the two swordsmen fought. They were fire and ice opposed. Le Loup fought wildly but craftily, leaving no openings, taking advantage of every opportunity. He was a living flame, bounding back, leaping in, feinting, thrusting, warding, striking – laughing like a wild man, taunting and cursing.

Kane's skill was cold, calculating, scintillant. He made no waste movement, no motion not absolutely necessary. He seemed to devote more time and effort toward defense than did Le Loup, yet there was no hesitancy in his attack, and when he thrust, his blade shot out with the speed of a striking snake.

There was little to choose between the men as to height, strength and reach. Le Loup was the swifter by a scant, flashing margin, but Kane's skill reached a finer point of perfection. The Wolf's fencing was fiery, dynamic, like the blast from a furnace. Kane was more steady – less the instinctive, more the thinking fighter, though he, too, was a born slayer, with the co-ordination that only a natural fighter possessed.

Thrust, parry, a feint, a sudden whirl of blades –

"Ha!" the Wolf sent up a shout of ferocious laughter as the blood started from a cut on Kane's cheek. As if the sight drove him to further fury, he attacked like the beast men named him. Kane was forced back before that blood-lusting onslaught, but the Puritan's expression did not alter.

Minutes flew by; the clang and clash of steel did not diminish. Now they stood squarely in the center of the glade, Le Loup untouched, Kane's garments red with the blood that oozed from wounds on cheek, breast, arm and thigh. The Wolf grinned savagely and mockingly in the moonlight, but he had begun to doubt.

His breath came hissing fast and his arm began to weary; who was this man of steel and ice who never seemed to weaken? Le Loup knew that the wounds he had inflicted on Kane were not deep, but even so, the steady flow of blood should have sapped some of the man's strength and speed by this time. But if Kane felt the ebb of his powers, it did not show. His brooding countenance did not change in expression, and he pressed the fight with as much cold fury as at the beginning.

Le Loup felt his might fading, and with one last desperate effort he rallied all his fury and strength into a single plunge. A sudden, unexpected attack too wild and swift for the eye to follow, a dynamic burst of speed and fury no man could have withstood, and Solomon Kane reeled for the first time as he felt cold steel tear through his body. He reeled back, and Le Loup with a wild shout, plunged after him, his reddened sword free, a gasping taunt on his lips.

Kane's sword, backed by the force of desperation, met Le Loup's in midair; met, held and wrenched. The Wolf's yell of triumph died on his lips as his sword flew singing from his hand.

For a fleeting instant he stopped short, arms flung wide as a crucifix, and Kane heard his wild, mocking laughter peal forth for the last time, as the Englishman's rapier made a silver line in the moonlight.

Far away came the mutter of the drums. Kane mechanically cleansed his sword on his tattered garments. The trail ended here, and Kane was conscious of a strange feeling of futility. He always felt that, after he had killed a foe. Somehow it always seemed that no real good had been wrought; as if the foe had, after all, escaped his just vengeance.

With a shrug of his shoulders Kane turned his attention to his bodily needs. Now that the heat of battle had passed, he began to feel weak and faint from the loss of blood. That last thrust had been close; had he not managed to avoid its full point by a twist of his body, the blade had transfixed him. As it was, the sword had struck glancingly, plowed along his ribs and sunk deep in the muscles beneath the shoulder-blade, inflicting a long and shallow wound.

Kane looked about him and saw that a small stream trickled through the glade at the far side. Here he made the only mistake of that kind that he ever made in his entire life. Mayhap he was dizzy from loss of blood and still mazed from the weird happenings of the night; be that as it may, he laid down his rapier and crossed, weaponless, to the stream. There he laved his wounds and bandaged them as best he could, with strips torn from his clothing.

Then he rose and was about to retrace his steps when a motion among the trees on the side of the glade where he first entered, caught his eye. A huge figure stepped out of the jungle, and Kane saw, and recognized, his doom. The man was Gulka, the gorilla-slayer. Kane remembered that he had not seen the black among those doing homage to N'Longa. How could he know the craft and hatred in that slanting skull that had led the negro, escaping the vengeance of his tribesmen, to trail down the only man he had ever feared? The Black God had been kind to his neophyte; had led him upon his victim helpless and unarmed. Now Gulka could kill his man openly – and slowly, as a leopard kills, not smiting him down from ambush as he had planned, silently and suddenly.

A wide grin split the negro's face, and he moistened his lips. Kane, watching him, was coldly and deliberately weighing his chances. Gulka had already spied the rapiers. He was closer to them than was Kane. The Englishman knew that there was no chance of his winning in a sudden race for the swords.

A slow, deadly rage surged in him – the fury of helplessness. The blood churned in his temples and his eyes smoldered with a terrible light as he eyed the negro. His fingers spread and closed like claws. They were strong, those hands; men had died in their clutch. Even Gulka's huge black column of a neck might break like a rotten branch between them – a wave of weakness made the futility of these thoughts apparent to an extent that needed not the verification of the moonlight glimmering from the spear in Gulka's black hand. Kane could not even have fled had he wished – and he had never fled from a single foe.

The gorilla-slayer moved out into the glade. Massive, terrible, he was the personification of the primitive, the Stone Age. His mouth yawned in a red cavern of a grin; he bore himself with the haughty arrogance of savage might.

Kane tensed himself for the struggle that could end but one way. He strove to rally his waning forces. Useless; he had lost too much blood. At least he would meet his death on his feet, and somehow he stiffened his buckling knees and held himself erect, though the glade shimmered before him in uncertain waves and the moonlight seemed to have become a red fog through which he dimly glimpsed the approaching black man.

Kane stooped, though the effort nearly pitched him on his face; he dipped water in his cupped hands and dashed it into his face. This revived him, and he straightened, hoping that Gulka would charge and get it over with before his weakness crumpled him to the earth.

Gulka was now about the center of the glade, moving with the slow, easy stride of a great cat stalking a victim. He was not at all in a hurry to consummate his purpose. He wanted to toy with his victim, to see fear come into those grim eyes which had looked him down, even when the possessor of those eyes had been bound to the death stake. He wanted to slay, at last, slowly, glutting his tigerish blood-lust and torture-lust to the fullest extent.

Then suddenly he halted, turned swiftly, facing another side of the glade. Kane, wondering, followed his glance.

At first it seemed like a blacker shadow among the jungle shadows. At first there was no motion, no sound, but Kane instinctively knew that some terrible menace lurked there in the darkness that masked and merged the silent trees. A sullen horror brooded there, and Kane felt as if, from that monstrous shadow, inhuman eyes seared his very soul. Yet simultaneously there came the fantastic sensation that these eyes were not directed on him. He looked at the gorilla-slayer.

The black man had apparently forgotten him; he stood, half crouching, spear lifted, eyes fixed upon that clump of blackness. Kane looked again.

Now there was motion in the shadows; they merged fantastically and moved out into the glade, much as Gulka had done. Kane blinked: was this the illusion that precedes death? The shape he looked upon was such as he had visioned dimly in wild nightmares, when the wings of sleep bore him back through lost ages.

He thought at first it was some blasphemous mockery of a man, for it went erect and was tall as a tall man. But it was inhumanly broad and thick, and its gigantic arms hung nearly to its misshapen feet. Then the moonlight smote full upon its bestial face, and Kane's mazed mind thought that the thing was the Black God coming out of the shadows, animated and blood-lusting. Then he saw that it was covered with hair, and he remembered the manlike thing dangling from the roof-pole in the native village. He looked at Gulka.

The negro was facing the gorilla, spear at the charge. He was not afraid, but his sluggish mind was wondering over the miracle that brought this beast so far from his native jungles.

The mighty ape came out into the moonlight and there was a terrible majesty about his movements. He was nearer Kane than Gulka but he did not seem to be aware of the white man. His small, blazing eyes were fixed on the black man with terrible intensity. He advanced with a curious swaying stride.

Far away the drums whispered through the night, like an accompaniment to this grim Stone Age drama. The savage crouched in the middle of the glade, but the primordial came out of the jungle with eyes bloodshot and blood-lusting. The negro was face to face with a thing more primitive then he. Again ghosts of memories whispered to Kane: you have seen such sights before (they murmured), back in the dim days, the dawn days, when beast and beast-man battled for supremacy.

Gulka moved away from the ape in a half-circle, crouching, spear ready. With all his craft he was seeking to trick the gorilla, to make a swift kill, for he had never before met such a monster as this, and though he did not fear, he had begun to doubt. The ape made no attempt to stalk or circle; he strode straight forward toward Gulka.

The black man who faced him and the white man who watched could not know the brutish love, the brutish hate that had driven the monster down from the low, forest-covered hills of the north to follow for leagues the trail of him who was the scourge of his kind – the slayer of his mate, whose body now hung from the roof-pole of the negro village.

The end came swiftly, almost like a sudden gesture. They were close, now, beast and beast-man; and suddenly, with an earth-shaking roar, the gorilla charged. A great hairy arm smote aside the thrusting spear, and the ape closed with the negro. There was a shattering sound as of many branches breaking simultaneously, and Gulka slumped silently to the earth, to lie with arms, legs and body flung in strange, unnatural positions. The ape towered an instant above him, like a statue of the primordial triumphant.

Far away Kane heard the drums murmur. The soul of the jungle, the soul of the jungle: this phrase surged through his mind with monotonous reiteration.

The three who had stood in power before the Black God that night, where were they? Back in the village where the drums rustled lay Songa – King Songa, once lord of life and death, now a shriveled corpse with a face set in a mask of horror. Stretched on his back in the middle of the glade lay he whom Kane had followed many a league by land and sea. And Gulka the gorilla-slayer lay at the feet of his killer, broken at last by the savagery which had made him a true son of this grim land which had at last overwhelmed him.

Yet the Black God still reigned, thought Kane dizzily, brooding back in the shadows of this dark country, bestial, blood-lusting, caring naught who lived or died, so that he drank.

Kane watched the mighty ape, wondering how long it would be before the huge simian spied and charged him. But the gorilla gave no evidence of having even seen him. Some dim impulse of vengeance yet unglutted prompting him, he bent and raised the negro. Then he slouched toward the jungle, Gulka's limbs trailing limply and grotesquely. As he reached the trees, the ape halted, whirling the giant form high in the air with seemingly no effort, and dashed the dead man up among the branches. There was a rending sound as a broken projecting limb tore through the body hurled so powerfully against it, and the dead gorilla-slayer dangled there hideously.

A moment the clear moon limned the great ape in its glimmer, as he stood silently gazing up at his victim; then like a dark shadow he melted noise-lessly into the jungle.

Kane walked slowly to the middle of the glade and took up his rapier. The blood had ceased to flow from his wounds, and some of his strength was returning, enough, at least, for him to reach the coast where his ship awaited him. He halted at the edge of the glade for a backward glance at Le Loup's upturned face and still form, white in the moonlight, and at the dark shadow among the trees that was Gulka, left by some bestial whim, hanging as the she-gorilla hung in the village.

Afar the drums muttered: "The wisdom of our land is ancient; the wisdom of our land is dark; whom we serve, we destroy. Flee if you would live, but you will never forget our chant. Never, never," sang the drums.

Kane turned to the trail which led to the beach and the ship waiting there.

The One Black Stain

Sir Thomas Doughty, executed at St. Julian's Bay, 1578

They carried him out on the barren sand
    where the rebel captains died;
Where the grim grey rotting gibbets stand
    as Magellan reared them on the strand,
And the gulls that haunt the lonesome land
    wail to the lonely tide.

Drake faced them all like a lion at bay,
    with his lion head upflung:
"Dare ye my word of law defy,
    to say that this traitor shall not die?"
And his captains dared not meet his eye
    but each man held his tongue.

Solomon Kane stood forth alone,
    grim man of a somber race:
"Worthy of death he well may be,
    but the court ye held was a mockery,
"Ye hid your spite in a travesty
    where Justice hid her face.

"More of the man had ye been,
    on deck your sword to cleanly draw
"In forthright fury from its sheath,
    and openly cleave him to the teeth –
"Rather than slink and hide beneath
    a hollow word of Law."

Hell rose in the eyes of Francis Drake.
    "Puritan knave!" swore he,
"Headsman, give him the axe instead!
    He shall strike off yon traitor's head!"
Solomon folded his arms and said,
    darkly and somberly:

"I am no slave for your butcher's work."
    "Bind him with triple strands!"
Drake roared in wrath and the men obeyed,
    hesitantly, as men afraid,
But Kane moved not as they took his blade
    and pinioned his iron hands.

They bent the doomed man to his knees,
    the man who was to die;
They saw his lips in a strange smile bend;
    one last long look they saw him send
At Drake, his judge and his one-time friend,
    who dared not meet his eye.

The axe flashed silver in the sun,
    a red arch slashed the sand;
A voice cried out as the head fell clear,
    and the watchers flinched in sudden fear,
Though 'twas but a sea-bird wheeling near
    above the lonely strand.

"This be every traitor's end!" Drake cried,
    and yet again;
Slowly his captains turned and went,
    and the admiral's stare was elsewhere bent
Than where cold scorn with anger blent
    in the eyes of Solomon Kane.

Night fell on the crawling waves;
    the admiral's door was closed;
Solomon lay in the stenching hold;
    his irons clashed as the ship rolled,
And his guard, grown weary and overbold,
    laid down his pike and dozed.

He woke with a hand at his corded throat
    that gripped him like a vise;
Trembling he yielded up the key,
    and the somber Puritan stood up free,
His cold eyes gleaming murderously
    with the wrath that is slow to rise.

Unseen to the admiral's cabin door
    went Solomon from the guard,
Through the night and silence of the ship,
    the guard's keen dagger in his grip;
No man of the dull crew saw him slip
    in through the door unbarred.

Drake at the table sat alone,
    his face sunk in his hands;
He looked up, as from sleeping –
    but his eyes were blank with weeping
As if he saw not, creeping,
    Death's swiftly flowing sands.

He reached no hand for gun or blade
    to halt the hand of Kane,
Nor even seemed to hear or see,
    lost in black mists of memory,
Love turned to hate and treachery,
    and bitter, cankering pain.

A moment Solomon Kane stood there,
    the dagger poised before,
As a condor stoops above a bird,
    and Francis Drake spoke not nor stirred,
And Kane went forth without a word
    and closed the cabin door.

The Dark Man

For this is the night of the drawing of swords,
And the painted tower of the heathen hordes
Leans to our hammers, fires and cords,
Leans a little and falls.

—*Chesterton*

A biting wind drifted the snow as it fell. The surf snarled along the rugged shore and farther out the long leaden combers moaned ceaselessly. Through the gray dawn that was stealing over the coast of Connacht a fisherman came trudging, a man rugged as the land that bore him. His feet were wrapped in rough cured leather; a single garment of deerskin scantily sheltered his body. He wore no other clothing. As he strode stolidly along the shore, as heedless of the bitter cold as if he were the shaggy beast he appeared at first glance, he halted. Another man loomed up out of the veil of falling snow and drifting sea-mist. Turlogh Dubh stood before him.

This man was nearly a head taller than the stocky fisherman, and he had the bearing of a fighting man. No single glance would suffice, but any man or woman whose eyes fell on Turlogh Dubh would look long. Six feet and one inch he stood, and the first impression of slimness faded on closer inspection. He was big but trimly molded; a magnificent sweep of shoulder and depth of chest. Rangy he was, but compact, combining the strength of a bull with the lithe quickness of a panther. The slightest movement he made showed that steel trap coordination that makes the super-fighter. Turlogh Dubh – Black Turlogh, once of the Clan na O'Brien.* And black he was as to hair, and dark of complexion. From under heavy black brows gleamed eyes of a hot volcanic blue. And in his clean-shaven face there was something of the somberness of dark mountains, of the ocean at midnight. Like the fisherman, he was a part of this fierce western land.

On his head he wore a plain vizorless helmet without crest or symbol. From neck to mid-thigh he was protected by a close-fitting shirt of black chain mail. The kilt he wore below his armor and which reached to his knees, was of plain drab material. His legs were wrapped with hard leather that might turn a sword edge, and the shoes on his feet were worn with much traveling.

A broad belt encircled his lean waist, holding a long dirk in a leather sheath. On his left arm he carried a small round shield of hide-covered wood, hard as iron, braced and reinforced with steel, and having a short, heavy spike in the center. An ax hung from his right wrist, and it was to this feature that the fisherman's eyes wandered. The weapon with its three-foot handle and graceful lines looked slim and light when the fisherman mentally compared it to the great axes carried by the Norsemen. Yet scarcely three years had passed, as the fisherman knew, since such axes as these had shattered the northern hosts into red defeat and broken the pagan power forever.

There was individuality about the ax as about its owner. It was not like any other the fisherman had ever seen. Single-edged it was, with a short three-edged spike on the back and another on the top of the head. Like the wielder, it was heavier than it looked. With its slightly curved shaft and the graceful artistry of the blade, it looked the weapon of an expert – swift, lethal, deadly, cobra-like. The head was of finest Irish workmanship, which meant, at that day, the finest in the world. The handle, cut from the heart of a century-old oak, specially fire-hardened and braced with steel, was as unbreakable as an iron bar.

"Who are you?" asked the fisherman with the bluntness of the west.

"Who are you to ask?" answered the other.

The fisherman's eyes roved to the single ornament the warrior wore – a heavy golden armlet on his left arm.

"Clean-shaven and close-cropped in the Norman fashion," he muttered. "And dark – you'd be Black Turlogh, the outlaw of Clan na O'Brien. You

* To avoid confusion I have used the modern terms for places and clans.—AUTHOR

range far; I heard of you last in the Wicklow hills preying off the O'Reillys and the Oastmen alike."

"A man must eat, outcast or not," growled the Dalcassian.

The fisherman shrugged his shoulders. A masterless man – it was a hard road. In those days of clans, when a man's own kin cast him out he became a son of Ishmael with a vengeance. All men's hands were against him. The fisherman had heard of Turlogh Dubh – a strange, bitter man, a terrible warrior and a crafty strategist, but one whom sudden bursts of strange madness made a marked man even in that land and age of madmen.

"It's a bitter day," said the fisherman apropos of nothing.

Turlogh stared somberly at his tangled beard and wild matted hair. "Have you a boat?"

The other nodded toward a small sheltered cove where lay snugly anchored a trim craft built with the skill of a hundred generations of men who had torn their livelihood from the stubborn sea.

"It scarce looks seaworthy," said Turlogh.

"Seaworthy? You who were born and bred on the western coast should know better. I've sailed her alone to Drumcliff Bay and back, and all the devils in the wind ripping at her."

"You can't take fish in such a sea."

"Do ye think it's only you chiefs that take sport in risking their hides? By the saints, I've sailed to Ballinskelligs in a storm – and back too – just for the fun of the thing."

"Good enough," said Turlogh. "I'll take your boat."

"Ye'll take the devil! What kind of talk is this? If you want to leave Erin, go to Dublin and take ship with your Dane friends."

A black scowl made Turlogh's face a mask of menace. "Men have died for less than that."

"Did you not intrigue with the Danes? – and is that not why your clan drove you out to starve in the heather?"

"The jealousy of a cousin and the spite of a woman," growled Turlogh. "Lies – all lies. But enough. Have you seen a long serpent beating up from the south in the last few days?"

"Aye – three days ago we sighted a dragon-beaked galley before the scud. But she didn't put in – faith, the pirates get naught from the western fishers but hard blows."

"That would be Thorfel the Fair," muttered Turlogh, swaying his ax by its wrist-strap. "I knew it."

"There has been a ship-harrying in the south?"

"A band of reavers fell by night on the castle on Kilbaha. There was a sword-quenching – and the pirates took Moira, daughter of Murtagh, a chief of the Dalcassians."

"I've heard of her," muttered the fisherman. "There'll be a whetting of swords in the south – a red sea-plowing, eh, my black jewel?"

"Her brother Dermod lies helpless from a sword-cut in the foot. The lands of her clan are harried by the MacMurroughs in the east and the O'Connors from the north. Not many men can be spared from the defense of the tribe, even to seek for Moira – the clan is fighting for its life. All Erin is rocking under the Dalcassian throne since great Brian fell. Even so, Cormac O'Brien has taken ship to hunt down her ravishers – but he follows the trail of a wild goose, for it is thought the raiders were Danes from Coningbeg. Well – we outcasts have ways of knowledge – it was Thorfel the Fair who holds the isle of Slyne, that the Norse call Helni, in the Hebrides. There he has taken her – there I follow him. Lend me your boat."

"You are mad!" cried the fisherman sharply. "What are you saying? From Connacht to the Hebrides in an open boat? In this weather? I say you are mad."

"I will essay it," answered Turlogh absently. "Will you lend me your boat?"

"No."

"I might slay you and take it," said Turlogh.

"You might," returned the fisherman stolidly.

"You crawling swine," snarled the outlaw in swift passion, "a princess of Erin languishes in grip of a red-bearded reaver of the north and you haggle like a Saxon."

"Man, I must live!" cried the fisherman as passionately. "Take my boat and I shall starve! Where can I get another like it? It is the cream of its kind!"

Turlogh reached for the armlet on his left arm. "I will pay you. Here is a torc that Brian Boru put on my arm with his own hand before Clontarf. Take it; it would buy a hundred boats. I have starved with it on my arm, but now the need is desperate."

But the fisherman shook his head, the strange illogic of the Gael burning in his eyes. "No! My hut is no place for a torc that King Brian's hands have touched. Keep it – and take the boat, in the name of the saints, if it means that much to you."

"You shall have it back when I return," promised Turlogh, "and mayhap a golden chain that now decks the bull neck of some northern rover."

The day was sad and leaden. The wind moaned and the everlasting monotone of the sea was like the sorrow that is born in the heart of man. The fisherman stood on the rocks and watched the frail craft glide and twist serpent-like among the rocks until the blast of the open sea smote it and tossed it like a feather. The wind caught the sail and the slim boat leaped and staggered, then righted herself and raced before the gale, dwindling until it was but a dancing speck in the eyes of the watcher. And then a flurry of snow hid it from his sight.

Turlogh realized something of the madness of his pilgrimage. But he was bred to hardships and peril. Cold and ice and driving sleet that would have frozen a weaker man, only spurred him to greater efforts. He was as hard and supple as a wolf. Among a race of men whose hardiness astounded even the toughest Norseman, Turlogh Dubh stood out alone. At birth he had been tossed into a snow-drift to test his right to survive. His childhood and boyhood had been spent on the mountains, coast and moors of the west. Until manhood he had never worn woven cloth upon his body; a wolf-skin had formed the apparel of this son of a Dalcassian chief. Before his outlawry he could out-tire a horse, running all day long beside it. He had never wearied at swimming. Now, since the intrigues of jealous clansmen had driven him into the wastelands and the life of the wolf, his ruggedness was such as can not be conceived by a civilized man.

The snow ceased, the weather cleared, the wind held. Turlogh necessarily hugged the coast line, avoiding the reefs against which it seemed again and again that his craft would be dashed. With tiller, sail and oar he worked tirelessly. Not one man out of a thousand of seafarers could have accomplished it, but Turlogh did. He needed no sleep; as he steered he ate from the rude provisions the fisherman had provided him. By the time he sighted Malin Head the weather had calmed wonderfully. There was still a heavy sea, but the gale had slackened to a sharp breeze that sent the little boat skipping along. Days and nights merged into each other; Turlogh drove eastward. Once he put into shore for fresh water and to snatch a few hours' sleep.

As he steered he thought of the fisherman's last words: "Why should you risk your life for a clan that's put a price on your head?"

Turlogh shrugged his shoulders. Blood was thicker than water. The mere fact that his people had booted him out to die like a hunted wolf on the moors did not alter the fact that they *were* his people. Little Moira, daughter of Murtagh na Kilbaha, had nothing to do with it. He remembered her – he had played with her when he was a boy and she a babe – he remembered the deep grayness of her eyes and the burnished sheen of her black hair, the fairness of her skin. Even as a child she had been remarkably beautiful – why, she was only a child now, for he, Turlogh, was young and he was many years her senior. Now she was speeding north to become the unwilling bride of a Norse reaver. Thorfel the Fair – the Handsome – Turlogh swore by gods that knew not the Cross. A red mist waved across his eyes so that the rolling sea swam crimson all about him. An Irish girl a captive in the skalli of a Norse pirate – with a vicious wrench Turlogh turned his bows straight for the open sea. There was a tinge of madness in his eyes.

It is a long slant from Malin Head to Helni straight out across the foaming billows, as Turlogh took it. He was aiming for a small island that lay, with many other small islands, between Mull and the Hebrides. A modern seaman with charts and compass might have difficulty in finding it. Turlogh had neither. He sailed by instinct and through knowledge. He knew these seas as a man knows his house. He had sailed them as a raider and an avenger, and once he had sailed them as a captive lashed to the deck of a Danish dragon ship. And he followed a red trail. Smoke drifting from headlands, floating pieces of wreckage, charred timbers showed that Thorfel was ravaging as he went. Turlogh growled in savage satisfaction; he was close behind the viking, in spite of the long lead. For Thorfel was burning and pillaging the shores as he went, and Turlogh's course was like an arrow's.

He was still a long way from Helni when he sighted a small island slightly off his course. He knew it of old as one uninhabited, but there he could get fresh water. So he steered for it. The Isle of Swords it was called, no man knew why. And as he neared the beach he saw a sight which he rightly interpreted. Two boats were drawn up on the shelving shore. One was a crude affair, something like the one Turlogh had, but considerably larger. The other was a long low craft – undeniably viking. Both were deserted. Turlogh listened for the clash of arms, the cry of battle, but silence reigned. Fishers, he thought, from the Scotch isles; they had been sighted by some band of rovers on ship or on some other island, and had been pursued in the long rowboat. But it had been a longer chase than they had anticipated, he was sure; else they would not have started out in an open boat. But inflamed with the murder lust, the reavers would have followed their prey across a hundred miles of rough water, in an open boat, if necessary.

Turlogh drew inshore, tossed over the stone that served for anchor and leaped upon the beach, ax ready. Then up the shore a short distance he saw a strange red huddle of forms. A few swift strides brought him face to face with mystery. Fifteen red-bearded Danes lay in their own gore in a rough circle. Not one breathed. Within this circle, mingling with the bodies of their slayers, lay other men, such as Turlogh had never seen. Short of stature they were, and very dark; their staring dead eyes were the blackest Turlogh had ever seen. They were scantily armored, and their stiff hands still gripped broken swords and daggers. Here and there lay arrows that had shattered on the corselets of the Danes, and Turlogh observed with surprize that many of them were tipped with flint.

"This was a grim fight," he muttered. "Aye, this was a rare sword-quenching. Who are these people? In all the isles I have never seen their like before. Seven – is that all? Where are their comrades who helped them slay these Danes?"

No tracks led away from the bloody spot. Turlogh's brow darkened.

"These were all – seven against fifteen – yet the slayers died with the slain. What manner of men are these who slay twice their number of vikings? They are small men – their armor is mean. Yet –"

Another thought struck him. Why did not the strangers scatter and flee, hide themselves in the woods? He believed he knew the answer. There, at the very center of the silent circle, lay a strange thing. A statue it was of some dark substance and it was in the form of a man. Some five feet long – or high – it was, carved in a semblance of life that made Turlogh start. Half over it lay the corpse of an ancient man, hacked almost beyond human semblance. One lean arm was locked about the figure; the other was outstretched, the hand gripping a flint dagger which was sheathed to the hilt in the breast of a Dane. Turlogh noted the fearful wounds that disfigured all the dark men. They had been hard to kill – they had fought until literally hacked to pieces, and dying, they had dealt death to their slayers. So much Turlogh's eyes showed him. In the dead faces of the dark strangers was a terrible desperation. He noted how their dead hands were still locked in the beards of their foes. One lay beneath the body of a huge Dane, and on this Dane Turlogh could see no wound; until he looked closer and saw the dark man's teeth were sunk, beast-like, into the bull throat of the other.

He bent and dragged the figure from among the bodies. The ancient's arm was locked about it, and he was forced to tear it away with all his strength. It was as if, even in death, the old one clung to his treasure; for Turlogh felt that it was for this image that the small dark men had died. They might have scattered and eluded their foes, but that would have meant giving up their image. They chose to die beside it. Turlogh shook his head; his hatred of the Norse, a heritage of wrongs and outrages, was a burning, living thing, almost an obsession, that at times drove him to the point of insanity. There was, in his fierce heart, no room for mercy; the sight of these Danes, lying dead at his feet, filled him with savage satisfaction. Yet he sensed here, in these silent dead men, a passion stronger than his. Here was some driving impulse deeper than his hate. Aye – and older. These little men seemed very ancient to him, not old as individuals are old, but old as a race is old. Even their corpses exuded an intangible aura of the primeval. And the image –

The Gael bent and grasped it, to lift it. He expected to encounter great weight and was astonished. It was no heavier than if it had been made of

69

light wood. He tapped it, and the sound was solid. At first he thought it was of iron; then he decided it was of stone, but such stone as he had never seen; and he felt that no such stone was to be found in the British Isles or anywhere in the world he knew. For like the little dead men it looked *old*. It was as smooth and free from corrosion as if carved yesterday, but for all that, it was a symbol of antiquity, Turlogh knew. It was the figure of a man who much resembled the small dark men who lay about it. But it differed subtly. Turlogh felt somehow that this was the image of a man who had lived long ago, for surely the unknown sculptor had had a living model. And he had contrived to breathe a touch of life into his work. There was the sweep of the shoulders, the depth of the chest, the powerfully molded arms; the strength of the features was evident. The firm jaw, the regular nose, the high forehead, all indicated a powerful intellect, a high courage, an inflexible will. Surely, thought Turlogh, this man was a king – or a god. Yet he wore no crown; his only garment was a sort of loin-cloth, wrought so cunningly that every wrinkle and fold was carved as in reality.

"This was their god," mused Turlogh, looking about him. "They fled before the Danes – but died for their god at last. Who are these people? Whence come they? Whither were they bound?"

He stood, leaning on his ax, and a strange tide rose in his soul. A sense of mighty abysses of time and space opened before; of the strange, endless tides of mankind that drift for ever; of the waves of humanity that wax and wane with the waxing and waning of the sea-tides. Life was a door opening upon two black, unknown worlds – and how many races of men with their hopes and fears, their loves and their hates, had passed through that door – on their pilgrimage from the dark to the dark? Turlogh sighed. Deep in his soul stirred the mystic sadness of the Gael.

"You were a king, once, Dark Man," he said to the silent image. "Mayhap you were a god and reigned over all the world. Your people passed – as mine are passing. Surely you were a king of the Flint People, the race whom my Celtic ancestors destroyed. Well – we have had our day and we, too, are passing. These Danes who lie at your feet – they are the conquerors now. They must have their day – but they too will pass. But you shall go with me, Dark Man, king, god or devil though you be. Aye, for it is in my mind that you will bring me luck, and luck is what I shall need when I sight Helni, Dark Man."

Turlogh bound the image securely in the bows. Again he set out for his sea-plowing. Now the skies grew gray and the snow fell in driving lances that stung and cut. The waves were gray-grained with ice and the winds bellowed and beat on the open boat. But Turlogh feared not. And his boat rode as it had never ridden before. Through the roaring gale and the driving snow it sped, and to the mind of the Dalcassian it seemed that the Dark Man lent him aid. Surely he had been lost a hundred times without supernatural assistance. With all his skill at boat-handling he wrought, and it seemed to him that there was an unseen hand on the tiller, and at the oar; that more than human skill aided him when he trimmed his sail.

And when all the world was a driving white veil in which even the Gael's sense of direction was lost, it seemed to him that he was steering in compliance with a silent voice that spoke in the dim reaches of his consciousness. Nor was he surprised when at last, when the snow had ceased and the clouds had rolled away beneath a cold silvery moon, he saw land loom up ahead and recognized it as the isle of Helni. More, he knew that just around a point of land was the bay where Thorfel's dragon ship was moored when not ranging the seas, and a hundred yards back from the bay lay Thorfel's skalli. He grinned fiercely. All the skill in the world could not have brought him to this exact spot – it was pure luck – no, it was more than luck. Here was the best place possible for him to make an approach – within half a mile of his foe's hold, yet hidden from sight of any watchers by this jutting promontory. He glanced at the Dark Man in the bows – brooding, inscrutable as the sphinx. A strange feeling stole over the Gael – that all this was his work; that he, Turlogh, was only a pawn in the game. What was this fetish? What grim secret did those carven eyes hold? Why did the dark little men fight so terribly for him?

Turlogh ran his boat inshore, into a small creek. A few yards up this he anchored and stepped out on shore. A last glance at the brooding Dark Man in the bows, and he turned and went hurriedly up the slope of the promontory, keeping to cover as much as possible. At the top of the slope he gazed down on the other side. Less than half a mile away Thorfel's dragon ship lay at anchor. And there lay Thorfel's skalli, also the long low building of rough-hewn log emitting the gleams that betokened the roaring fires within. Shouts of wassail came clearly to the listener through the sharp still air. He ground his teeth. Wassail! Aye, they were celebrating the ruin and destruction they had committed – the homes left in smoking embers – the slain men – the ravished girls. They were lords of the world, these vikings – all the southland lay helpless beneath their swords. The southland folk lived only to furnish them sport – and slaves – Turlogh shuddered violently and shook as if in a chill. The blood-sickness was on him like a physical pain, but he fought back the mists of passion that clouded his brain. He was here, not to fight but to steal away the girl they had stolen.

He took careful note of the ground, like a general going over the plan of his campaign. He noted that the trees grew thick close behind the skalli;

that the smaller houses, the storehouses and servants' huts were between the main building and the bay. A huge fire was blazing down by the shore and a few carles were roaring and drinking about it, but the fierce cold had driven most of them into the drinking-hall of the main building.

Turlogh crept down the thickly wooded slope, entering the forest which swept about in a wide curve away from the shore. He kept to the fringe of its shadows, approaching the skalli in a rather indirect route, but afraid to strike out boldly in the open lest he be seen by the watchers that Thorfel surely had out. Gods, if he only had the warriors of Clare at his back as he had of old! Then there would be no skulking like a wolf among the trees! His hand locked like iron on his ax-haft as he visualized the scene – the charge, the shouting, the blood-letting, the play of the Dalcassian axes – he sighed. He was a lone outcast; never again would he lead the swordsmen of his clan to battle.

He dropped suddenly in the snow behind a low shrub and lay still. Men were approaching from the same direction in which he had come – men who grumbled loudly and walked heavily. They came into sight – two of them, huge Norse warriors, their silver-scaled armor flashing in the moonlight. They were carrying something between them with difficulty and to Turlogh's amazement he saw it was the Dark Man. His consternation at the realization that they had found his boat was gulfed in a greater astonishment. These men were giants; their arms bulged with iron muscles. Yet they were staggering under what seemed a stupendous weight. In their hands the Dark Man seemed to weigh hundreds of pounds; yet Turlogh had lifted it lightly as a feather! He almost swore in his amazement. Surely these men were drunk. One of them spoke, and Turlogh's short neck hairs bristled at the sound of the guttural accents, as a dog will bristle at the sight of a foe.

"Let it down; Thor's death, the thing weighs a ton. Let's rest."

The other grunted a reply and they began to ease the image to the earth. Then one of them lost his hold on it; his hand slipped and the Dark Man crashed heavily into the snow. The first speaker howled.

"You clumsy fool, you dropped it on my foot! Curse you, my ankle's broken!"

"It twisted out of my hand!" cried the other. "The thing's alive, I tell you!"

"Then I'll slay it," snarled the lamed viking, and drawing his sword, he struck savagely at the prostrate figure. Fire flashed as the blade shivered into a hundred pieces, and the other Norseman howled as a flying sliver of steel gashed his cheek.

"The devil's in it!" shouted the other, throwing his hilt away. "I've not even scratched it! Here, take hold – let's get it into the ale-hall and let Thorfel deal with it."

"Let it lie," growled the second man, wiping the blood from his face. "I'm bleeding like a butchered hog. Let's go back and tell Thorfel that there's no ship stealing on the island. That's what he sent us to the point to see."

"What of the boat where we found this?" snapped the other. "Some Scotch fisher driven out of his course by the storm and hiding like a rat in the woods now, I guess. Here, bear a hand; idol or devil, we'll carry this to Thorfel."

Grunting with the effort, they lifted the image once more and went on slowly, one groaning and cursing as he limped along, the other shaking his head from time to time as the blood got into his eyes.

Turlogh rose stealthily and watched them. A touch of chilliness traveled up and down his spine. Either of these men was as strong as he, yet it was taxing their powers to the utmost to carry what he had handled easily. He shook his head and took up his way again.

At last he reached a point in the woods nearest the skalli. Now was the crucial test. Somehow he must reach that building and hide himself, unperceived. Clouds were gathering. He waited until one obscured the moon, and in the gloom that followed, ran swiftly and silently across the snow, crouching. A shadow out of the shadows he seemed. The shouts and songs from within the long building were deafening. Now he was close to its side, flattening himself against the rough-hewn logs. Vigilance was most certainly relaxed now – yet what foe should Thorfel expect, when he was friends with all northern reavers, and none else could be expected to fare forth on a night such as this had been?

A shadow among the shadows, Turlogh stole about the house. He noted a side door and slid cautiously to it. Then he drew back close against the wall. Some one within was fumbling at the latch. Then the door was flung open and a big warrior lurched out, slamming the door to behind him. Then he saw Turlogh. His bearded lips parted, but in that instant the Gael's hands shot to his throat and locked there like a wolf-trap. The threatened yell died in a gasp. One hand flew to Turlogh's wrist, the other drew a dagger and stabbed upward. But already the man was senseless; the dagger rattled feebly against the outlaw's corselet and dropped into the snow. The Norseman sagged in his slayer's grasp, his throat literally crushed by that iron grip. Turlogh flung him contemptuously into the snow and spat in his dead face before he turned again to the door.

The latch had not fastened within. The door sagged a trifle. Turlogh peered in and saw an empty room, piled with ale barrels. He entered noiselessly, shutting the door but not latching it. He thought of hiding his victim's body, but he did not know how he could do it. He must trust to luck that no one saw it in the deep snow where it lay. He crossed the room and found it let into another parallel with the outer wall. This was also a storeroom, and was empty. From this a doorway, without a door but furnished with a curtain of skins, let into the main hall, as Turlogh could tell from the sounds on the other side. He peered out cautiously.

He was looking into the drinking-hall – the great hall which served as banquet, council and living-hall of the master of the skalli. This hall, with its smoke-blackened rafters, great roaring fireplaces, and heavily laden boards, was a scene of terrific revelry tonight. Huge warriors with golden beards and savage eyes sat or lounged on the rude benches, strode about the hall or sprawled full length on the floor. They drank mightily from foaming horns and leathern jacks, and gorged themselves on great pieces of rye bread, and huge chunks of meat they cut with their daggers from whole roasted joints. It was a scene of strange incongruity, for in contrast with these barbaric men and their rough songs and shouts, the walls were hung with rare spoils that betokened civilized workmanship. Fine tapestries that Norman women had worked; richly chased weapons that princes of France and Spain had wielded; armor and silken garments from Byzantium and the Orient – for the dragon ships ranged far. With these were placed the spoils of the hunt, to show the viking's mastery of beasts as well as men.

The modern man can scarcely conceive of Turlogh O'Brien's feeling toward these men. To him they were devils – ogres who dwelt in the north only to descend on the peaceful people of the south. All the world was their prey to pick and choose, to take and spare as it pleased their barbaric whims.

His brain throbbed and burned as he gazed. As only the Gael can hate, he hated them – their magnificent arrogance, their pride and their power, their contempt for all other races, their stern, forbidding eyes – above all else he hated the eyes that looked scorn and menace on the world. The Gaels were cruel but they had strange moments of sentiment and kindness. There was no sentiment in the Norse make-up.

The sight of this revelry was like a slap in Black Turlogh's face, and only one thing was needed to make his madness complete. This was furnished. At the head of the board sat Thorfel the Fair, young, handsome, arrogant, flushed with wine and pride. He *was* handsome, was young Thorfel. In build he much resembled Turlogh himself, except that he was larger in every way, but there the resemblance ceased. As Turlogh was exceptionally dark among a dark people, Thorfel was exceptionally blond among a people essentially fair. His hair and mustache were like fine-spun gold and his light gray eyes flashed scintillant lights. By his side – Turlogh's nails bit into his palms. Moira of the O'Briens seemed greatly out of place among these huge blond men and strapping yellow-haired women. She was small, almost frail, and her hair was black with glossy bronze tints. But her skin was fair as theirs, with a delicate rose tint their most beautiful women could not boast. Her full lips were white now with fear and she shrank from the clamor and uproar. Turlogh saw her tremble as Thorfel insolently put his arm about her. The hall waved redly before Turlogh's eyes and he fought doggedly for control.

"Thorfel's brother, Osric, to his right," he muttered to himself; "on the other side Tostig, the Dane, who can cleave an ox in half with that great sword of his – they say. And there is Halfgar, and Sweyn, and Oswick, and Athelstane, the Saxon – the one *man* of a pack of sea-wolves. And name of the devil – what is this? A priest?"

A priest it was, sitting white and still in the rout, silently counting his beads, while his eyes wandered pityingly toward the slender Irish girl at the head of the board. Then Turlogh saw something else. On a smaller table to one side, a table of mahogany whose rich scrollwork showed that it was loot from the southland, stood the Dark Man. The two crippled Norsemen had brought it to the hall, after all. The sight of it brought a strange shock to Turlogh and cooled his seething brain. Only five feet tall? It seemed much larger now, somehow. It loomed above the revelry, as a god that broods on deep dark matters beyond the ken of the human insects who howl at his feet. As always when looking at the Dark Man, Turlogh felt as if a door had suddenly opened on outer space and the wind that blows among the stars. Waiting – waiting – for whom? Perhaps the carven eyes of the Dark Man looked through the skalli walls, across the snowy waste, and over the promontory. Perhaps those sightless eyes saw the five boats that even now slid silently with muffled oars, through the calm dark waters. But of this Turlogh Dubh knew nothing; nothing of the boats or their silent rowers; small, dark men with inscrutable eyes.

Thorfel's voice cut through the din: "Ho, friends!" They fell silent and turned as the young sea-king rose to his feet. "Tonight," he thundered, "I am taking a bride!"

A thunder of applause shook the smoky rafters. Turlogh cursed with sick fury.

Thorfel caught up the girl with rough gentleness and set her on the board.

"Is she not a fit bride for a viking?" he shouted. "True, she's a bit shy, but that's only natural."

"All Irish are cowards!" shouted Oswick.

"As proved by Clontarf and the scar on your jaw!" rumbled Athelstane, which gentle thrust made Oswick wince and brought a roar of rough mirth from the throng.

"'Ware her temper, Thorfel," called a bold-eyed young Juno who sat with the warriors; "Irish girls have claws like cats."

Thorfel laughed with the confidence of a man used to mastery. "I'll teach her her lessons with a stout birch switch. But enough. It grows late. Priest, marry us."

"Daughter," said the priest, unsteadily, rising, "these pagan men have brought me here by violence to perform Christian nuptials in an ungodly house. Do you marry this man willingly?"

"No! No! Oh God, no!" Moira screamed with a wild despair that brought the sweat to Turlogh's forehead. "Oh most holy master, save me from this fate! They tore me from my home – struck down the brother that would have saved me! This man bore me off as if I were a chattel – a soulless beast!"

"Be silent!" thundered Thorfel, slapping her across the mouth, lightly but with enough force to bring a trickle of blood from her delicate lips. "By Thor, you grow independent. I am determined to have a wife, and all the squeals of a puling little wench will not stop me. Why, you graceless hussy, am I not wedding you in the Christian manner, simply because of your foolish superstitions? Take care that I do not dispense with the nuptials, and take you as slave, not wife!"

"Daughter," quavered the priest, afraid, not for himself, but for her, "bethink you! This man offers you more than many a man would offer. It is at least an honorable married state."

"Aye," rumbled Athelstane, "marry him like a good wench and make the best of it. There's more than one southland woman on the cross benches of the north."

What can I do? The question tore through Turlogh's brain. There was but one thing to do – wait until the ceremony was over and Thorfel had retired with his bride. Then steal her away as best he could. After that – but he dared not look ahead. He had done and would do his best. What he did, he of necessity did alone; a masterless man had no friends, even among masterless men. There was no way to reach Moira to tell her of his presence. She must go through with the wedding without even the slim hope of deliverance that knowledge of his presence might have lent. Instinctively his eyes flashed to the Dark Man standing somber and aloof from the rout. At his feet the old quarreled with the new – the pagan with the Christian – and Turlogh even in that moment felt that the old and new were alike young to the Dark Man.

Did the carven ears of the Dark Man hear strange prows grating on the beach, the stroke of a stealthy knife in the night, the gurgle that marks the severed throat? Those in the skalli heard only their own noise and those who revelled by the fires outside sang on, unaware of the silent coils of death closing about them.

"Enough!" shouted Thorfel. "Count your beads and mutter your mummery, priest! Come here, wench, and marry!" He jerked the girl off the board and plumped her down on her feet before him. She tore loose from him with flaming eyes. All the hot Gaelic blood was roused in her.

"You yellow-haired swine!" she cried. "Do you think that a princess of Clare, with Brian Boru's blood in her veins, would sit at the cross bench of a barbarian and bear the tow-headed cubs of a northern thief? No – I'll never marry you!"

"Then I'll take you as a slave!" he roared, snatching at her wrist.

"Nor that way, either, swine!" she exclaimed, her fear forgotten in fierce triumph. With the speed of light she snatched a dagger from his girdle, and before he could seize her she drove the keen blade under her heart. The priest cried out as though he had received the wound, and springing forward, caught her in his arms as she fell.

"The curse of Almighty God on you, Thorfel!" he cried, with a voice that rang like a clarion, as he bore her to a couch near by.

Thorfel stood nonplussed. Silence reigned for an instant, and in that instant Turlogh O'Brien went mad.

"*Lamh Laidir Abu!*" the war-cry of the O'Briens ripped through the stillness like the scream of a wounded panther, and as men whirled toward the shriek, the frenzied Gael came through the doorway like the blast of a wind from hell. He was in the grip of the Celtic black fury beside which the berserk rage of the viking pales. Eyes glaring and a tinge of froth on his writhing lips, he crashed among the men who sprawled, off guard, in his path. Those terrible eyes were fixed on Thorfel at the other end of the hall, but as Turlogh rushed he smote to the right and left. His charge was the rush of a whirlwind that left a litter of dead and dying men in his wake.

Benches crashed to the floor, men yelled, ale flooded from upset casks. Swift as was the Celt's attack, two men blocked his way with drawn swords before he could reach Thorfel – Halfgar and Oswick. The scarred-faced viking went down with a cleft skull before he could lift his weapon, and Turlogh, catching Halfgar's blade on his shield, struck again like lightning and the keen ax sheared through hauberk, ribs and spine.

The hall was in a terrific uproar. Men were seizing weapons and pressing forward from all sides, and in the midst the lone Gael raged silently and terribly. Like a wounded tiger was Turlogh Dubh in his madness. His eery movement was a blur of speed, an explosion of dynamic force. Scarce had Halfgar fallen before the Gael leaped across his crumpling form at Thorfel, who had drawn his sword and stood as if bewildered. But a rush of carles swept between them. Swords rose and fell and the Dalcassian ax flashed among them like the play of summer lightning. On either hand and from before and behind a warrior drove at him. From one side Osric rushed, swinging a two-handed sword; from the other a house-carle drove in with a spear. Turlogh stooped beneath the swing of the sword and struck a double blow, forehand and back. Thorfel's brother dropped, hewed through the knee, and the carle died on his feet as the back-lash return drove the ax's back-spike through his skull. Turlogh straightened, dashing his shield into the face of the swordsman who rushed him from the front. The spike in the center of the shield made a ghastly ruin of his features; then even as the Gael wheeled cat-like to guard his rear, he felt the shadow of Death loom over him. From the corner of his eye he saw the Dane Tostig swinging his great two-handed sword, and jammed against the table, off balance, he knew that even his superhuman quickness could not save him. Then the whistling sword struck the Dark Man on the table and with a clash like thunder, shivered to a thousand blue sparks. Tostig staggered, dazedly, still holding the useless hilt, and Turlogh thrust as with a sword; the upper spike of his ax struck the Dane over the eye and crashed through to the brain.

And even at that instant, the air was filled with a strange singing and men howled. A huge carle, ax still lifted, pitched forward clumsily against the Gael, who split his skull before he saw that a flint-pointed arrow transfixed his throat. The hall seemed full of glancing beams of light that hummed like bees and carried quick death in their humming. Turlogh risked his life for a glance toward the great doorway at the other end of the hall. Through it was pouring a strange horde. Small, dark men they were, with beady black eyes and immobile faces. They were scantily armored, but they bore swords, spears and bows. Now at close range they drove their long black arrows point-blank and the carles went down in windrows.

Now a red wave of combat swept the skalli hall, a storm of strife that shattered tables, smashed the benches, tore the hangings and the trophies from the walls, and stained the floors with a red lake. There had been less of the dark strangers than vikings, but in the surprize of the attack, the first flight of arrows had evened the odds, and now at hand-grips the strange warriors showed themselves in no way inferior to their huge foes. Dazed by surprise and the ale they had drunk, with no time to arm themselves fully, the Norsemen yet fought back with all the reckless ferocity of their race. But the primitive fury of their attackers matched their own valor, and at the head of the hall, where a white-faced priest shielded a dying girl, Black Turlogh tore and ripped with a frenzy that made valor and fury alike futile.

And over all towered the Dark Man. To Turlogh's shifting glances, caught between the flash of sword and ax, it seemed that the image had grown – expanded – heightened; that it loomed giant-like over the battle; that its head rose into the smoke-filled rafters of the great hall; that it brooded like a dark cloud of death over these insects who cut each other's throats at its feet. Turlogh sensed in the lightning sword-play and the slaughter that this was the proper element of the Dark Man. Violence and fury were exuded by him. The raw scent of fresh-spilled blood was good to his nostrils and these yellow-haired corpses that rattled at his feet were as sacrifices to him.

The storm of battle rocked the mighty hall. The skalli became a shambles where men slipped in pools of blood, and slipping, died. Heads spun grinning from slumping shoulders. Barbed spears tore the heart, still beating, from the gory breast. Brains splashed and clotted the madly driving axes. Daggers lunged upward, ripping bellies and spilling entrails upon the floor. The clash and clangor of steel rose deafeningly. No quarter was asked or given. A wounded Norseman had dragged down one of the dark men, and doggedly strangled him regardless of the dagger his victim plunged again and again into his body.

One of the dark men seized a child who ran howling from an inner room, and dashed its brains out against the wall. Another gripped a Norse woman by her golden hair and hurling her to her knees, cut her throat, while she spat in his face. One listening for cries of fear or pleas for mercy would have heard none; men, women or children, they died slashing and clawing, their last gasp a sob of fury, or a snarl of quenchless hatred.

And about the table where stood the Dark Man, immovable as a mountain, washed the red waves of slaughter. Norseman and tribesman died at his feet. How many red infernos of slaughter and madness have your strange carved eyes gazed upon, Dark Man?

Shoulder to shoulder Sweyn and Thorfel fought. The Saxon Athelstane, his golden beard a-bristle with the battle-joy, had placed his back against the wall and a man fell at each sweep of his two-handed ax. Now Turlogh came in like a wave, avoiding, with a lithe twist of his upper body, the first ponderous stroke. Now the superiority of the light Irish ax was proved, for before the Saxon could shift his heavy weapon, the Dalcassian ax licked out like a striking cobra and Athelstane reeled as the edge bit through the corselet into the ribs beneath. Another stroke and he crumpled, blood gushing from his temple.

Now none barred Turlogh's way to Thorfel except Sweyn, and even as the Gael leaped like a panther toward the slashing pair, one was ahead of him. The chief of the dark men glided like a shadow under the slash of Sweyn's sword, and his own short blade thrust upward under the shirt of mail. Thorfel faced Turlogh alone. Thorfel was no coward; he even laughed with pure battle-joy as he thrust, but there was no mirth in Black Turlogh's face, only a frantic rage that writhed his lips and made his eyes coals of blue fire.

In the first whirl of steel Thorfel's sword broke. The young sea-king leaped like a tiger at his foe, thrusting with the shards of the blade. Turlogh laughed fiercely as the jagged remnant gashed his cheek, and at the same instant he cut Thorfel's left foot from under him. The Norseman fell with a heavy crash, then struggled to his knees, clawing for his dagger. His eyes were clouded.

"Make an end, curse you!" he snarled.

Turlogh laughed. "Where is your power and your glory, now?" he taunted. "You who would have for unwilling wife an Irish princess – you — "

Suddenly his hate strangled him, and with a howl like a maddened panther he swung his ax in a whistling arc that cleft the Norseman from shoulder to breast-bone. Another stroke severed the head, and with the grisly trophy in his hand he approached the couch where lay Moira O'Brien. The priest had lifted her head and held a goblet of wine to her pale lips. Her cloudy gray eyes rested with slight recognition on Turlogh – but it seemed at last she knew him and she tried to smile.

"Moira, blood of my heart," said the outlaw heavily, "you die in a strange land. But the birds in the Cullane hills will weep for you, and the heather will sigh in vain for the tread of your little feet. But you shall not be forgotten; axes shall drip for you and for you shall galleys crash and walled cities go up in flames. And that your ghost go not unassuaged into the realms of Tir-na-n-Oge, behold this token of vengeance!"

And he held forth the dripping head of Thorfel.

"In God's name, my son," said the priest, his voice husky with horror, "have done – have done. Will you do your ghastly deeds in the very presence of – see, she is dead. May God in His infinite justice have mercy on her soul, for though she took her own life, yet she died as she lived, in innocence and purity."

Turlogh dropped his ax-head to the floor and his head was bowed. All the fire of his madness had left him and there remained only a dark sadness, a deep sense of futility and weariness. Over all the hall there was no sound. No groans of the wounded were raised, for the knives of the little dark men had been at work, and save their own, there were no wounded. Turlogh sensed that the survivors had gathered about the statue on the table and now stood looking at him with inscrutable eyes. The priest mumbled over the corpse of the girl, telling his beads. Flame ate at the farther wall of the building, but none heeded it. Then from among the dead on the floor a huge form heaved up unsteadily. Athelstane the Saxon, overlooked by the killers, leaned against the wall and stared about dazedly. Blood flowed from a wound in his ribs and another in his scalp where Turlogh's ax had struck glancingly.

The Gael walked over to him. "I have no hatred for you, Saxon," said he, heavily, "but blood calls for blood and you must die."

Athelstane looked at him without an answer. His large gray eyes were serious but without fear. He too was a barbarian – more pagan than Christian; he too realized the rights of the blood-feud. But as Turlogh raised his ax, the priest sprang between, his thin hands outstretched, his eyes haggard.

"Have done! In God's name I command you! Almighty Powers, has not enough blood been shed this fearful night? In the name of the Most High, I claim this man."

Turlogh dropped his ax. "He is yours; not for your oath or your curse, not for your creed but for that you too are a man and did your best for Moira."

A touch on his arm made Turlogh turn. The chief of the strangers stood regarding him with inscrutable eyes.

"Who are you?" asked the Gael idly. He did not care; he felt only weariness.

"I am Brogar, chief of the Picts, Friend of the Dark Man."

"Why do you call me that?" asked Turlogh.

"He rode in the bows of your boat and guided you to Helni through wind and snow. He saved your life when he broke the great sword of the Dane."

Turlogh glanced at the brooding Dark One. It seemed there must be a human or superhuman intelligence behind those strange stone eyes. Was it chance alone that caused Tostig's sword to strike the image as he swung it in a death blow?

"What is this thing?" asked the Gael.

"It is the only god we have left," answered the other somberly. "It is the image of our greatest king, Bran Mak Morn, he who gathered the broken lines of the Pictish tribes into a single mighty nation, he who drove forth the Norseman and Briton and shattered the legions of Rome, centuries ago. A wizard made this statue while the great Morni yet lived and reigned, and when he died in the last great battle, his spirit entered into it. It is our god.

"Ages ago we ruled. Before the Dane, before the Gael, before the Briton, before the Roman, we reigned in the western isles. Our stone circles rose to the sun. We worked in flint and hides and were happy. Then came the Celts and drove us into the wildernesses. They held the southland. But we throve in the north and were strong. Rome broke the Britons and came against us. But there rose among us Bran Mak Morn, of the blood of Brule the Spear-slayer, the friend of King Kull of Valusia who reigned thousands of years ago before Atlantis sank. Bran became king of all Caledon. He broke the iron ranks of Rome and sent the legions cowering south behind their Wall.

"Bran Mak Morn fell in battle; the nation fell apart. Civil wars rocked it. The Gaels came and reared the kingdom of Dalriadia above the ruins of the Cruithni. When the Scot Kenneth MacAlpine broke the kingdom of Galloway, the last remnant of the Pictish empire faded like snow on the mountains. Like wolves we live now among the scattered islands, among the crags of the highlands and the dim hills of Galloway. We are a fading people. We pass. But the Dark Man remains – the Dark One, the great king, Bran Mak Morn, whose ghost dwells forever in the stone likeness of his living self."

As in a dream Turlogh saw an ancient Pict who looked much like the one in whose dead arms he had found the Dark Man, lift the image from the table. The old man's arms were thin as withered branches and his skin clung to his skull like a mummy's, but he handled with ease the image that two strong vikings had had trouble in carrying.

As if reading his thoughts Brogar spoke softly: "Only a friend may with safety touch the Dark One. We knew you to be a friend, for he rode in your boat and did you no harm."

"How know you this?"

"The Old One," pointing to the white-bearded ancient, "Gonar, high priest of the Dark One – the ghost of Bran comes to him in dreams. It was Grok, the lesser priest and his people who stole the image and took to sea in a long boat. In dreams Gonar followed; aye, as he slept he sent his spirit with the ghost of the Morni, and he saw the pursuit by the Danes, the battle and slaughter on the Isle of Swords. He saw you come and find the Dark One, and he saw that the ghost of the great king was pleased with you. Wo to the foes of the Mak Morn! But good luck shall fare the friends of him."

Turlogh came to himself as from a trance. The heat of the burning hall was in his face and the flickering flames lit and shadowed the carven face of the Dark Man as his worshippers bore him from the building, lending it a strange life. Was it, in truth, that the spirit of a long-dead king lived in that cold stone? Bran Mak Morn loved his people with a savage love; he hated their foes with a terrible hate. Was it possible to breathe into inanimate blind stone a pulsating love and hate that should outlast the centuries?

Turlogh lifted the still, slight form of the dead girl and bore her out of the flaming hall. Five long open boats lay at anchor, and scattered about the embers of the fires the carles had lit, lay the reddened corpses of the revelers who had died silently.

"How stole ye upon these undiscovered?" asked Turlogh. "And whence came you in those open boats?"

"The stealth of the panther is theirs who live by stealth," answered the Pict. "And these were drunken. We followed the path of the Dark One and we came hither from the Isle of the Altar, near the Scottish mainland, from whence Grok stole the Dark Man."

Turlogh knew no island of that name but he did realize the courage of these men in daring the seas in boats such as these. He thought of his own boat and requested Brogar to send some of his men for it. The Pict did so. While he waited for them to bring it around the point, he watched the priest bandaging the wounds of the survivors. Silent, immobile, they spoke no word either of complaint or thanks.

The fisherman's boat came scudding around the point just as the first hint of sunrise reddened the waters. The Picts were getting into their boats, lifting in the dead and wounded. Turlogh stepped into his boat and gently eased his pitiful burden down.

"She shall sleep in her own land," he said somberly. "She shall not lie in this cold foreign isle. Brogar, whither go you?"

"We take the Dark One back to his isle and his altar," said the Pict. "Through the mouth of his people he thanks you. The tie of blood is

between us, Gael, and mayhap we shall come to you again in your need, as
Bran Mak Morn, great king of Pictdom, shall come again to his people some
day in the days to come."

"And you, good Jerome? You will come with me?"

The priest shook his head and pointed to Athelstane. The wounded
Saxon reposed on a rude couch made of skins piled in the snow.

"I stay here to attend to this man. He is sorely wounded."

Turlogh looked about. The walls of the skalli had crashed into a mass
of glowing embers. Brogar's men had set fire to the storehouses and the long
galley, and the smoke and flame vied luridly with the growing morning light.

"You will freeze or starve. Come with me."

"I will find sustenance for us both. Persuade me not, my son."

"He is a pagan and a reaver."

"No matter. He is a human – a living creature. I will not leave him to die."

"So be it."

Turlogh prepared to cast off. The boats of the Picts were already
rounding the point. The rhythmic clack of their oar-locks came clearly to
him. They looked not back, bending stolidly to their work.

He glanced at the stiff corpses about the beach, at the charred embers
of the skalli and the glowing timbers of the galley. In the glare the priest
seemed unearthly in his thinness and whiteness, like a saint from some old
illuminated manuscript. In his worn pallid face was a more than human
sadness, a greater than human weariness.

"Look!" he cried suddenly, pointing seaward. "The ocean is of blood!
See how it swims red in the rising sun! Oh, my people, my people, the blood
you have spilt in anger turns the very seas to scarlet! How can you win
through?"

"I came in the snow and sleet," said Turlogh, not understanding at first.
"I go as I came."

The priest shook his head. "It is more than a mortal sea. Your hands are
red with blood and you follow a red sea-path, yet the fault is not wholly with
you. Almighty God, when will the reign of blood cease?"

Turlogh shook his head. "Not so long as the race lasts."

The morning wind caught and filled his sail. Into the west he raced like
a shadow fleeing the dawn. And so passed Turlogh Dubh O'Brien from the
sight of the priest Jerome, who stood watching, shading his weary brow with
his thin hand, until the boat was but a tiny speck far out on the tossing
wastes of the blue ocean.

The Marching Song of Connacht

The men of the East are decked in steel,
They march with a trumpet's din,
They glitter with silks and golden scales,
And high kings boast their kin —
We of the West wear the hides of wolves,
But our hearts are steel within.

They of the East ride gallant steeds,
Their spears are long and brown;
Their shields are set with sparkling stones,
And each knight wears a crown —
We fight on foot as our forebears fought,
And we drag the rider down.

We race the steed of the Saxon knight
Across the naked fen —
They of the East are full of pride,
Cubs of the Lion's den.
They boast they breed a race of kings —
But we of the West breed Men.

Kings of the Night

The Caesar lolled on his ivory throne –
  His iron legions came
To break a king in a land unknown,
  And a race without a name.
               –The Song of Bran

The dagger flashed downward. A sharp cry broke in a gasp. The form on the rough altar twitched convulsively and lay still. The jagged flint edge sawed at the crimsoned breast, and thin bony fingers, ghastly dyed, tore out the still twitching heart. Under matted white brows, sharp eyes gleamed with a ferocious intensity.

Besides the slayer, four men stood about the crude pile of stones that formed the altar of the God of Shadows. One was of medium height, lithely built, scantily clad, whose black hair was confined by a narrow iron band in the center of which gleamed a single red jewel. Of the others, two were dark like the first. But where he was lithe, they were stocky and misshapen, with knotted limbs, and tangled hair falling over sloping brows. His face denoted intelligence and implacable will; theirs merely a beast-like ferocity. The fourth man had little in common with the rest. Nearly a head taller, though his hair was black as theirs, his skin was comparatively light and he was gray-eyed. He eyed the proceedings with little favor.

And, in truth, Cormac of Connacht was little at ease. The Druids of his own isle of Erin had strange dark rites of worship, but nothing like this.

Dark trees shut in this grim scene, lit by a single torch. Through the branches moaned an eery night-wind. Cormac was alone among men of a strange race and he had just seen the heart of a man ripped from his still pulsing body. Now the ancient priest, who looked scarcely human, was glaring at the throbbing thing. Cormac shuddered, glancing at him who wore the jewel. Did Bran Mak Morn, king of the Picts, believe that this white-bearded old butcher could foretell events by scanning a bleeding human heart? The dark eyes of the king were inscrutable. There were strange depths to the man that Cormac could not fathom, nor any other man.

"The portents are good!" exclaimed the priest wildly, speaking more to the two chieftains than to Bran. "Here from the pulsing heart of a captive Roman I read – defeat for the arms of Rome! Triumph for the sons of the heather!"

The two savages murmured beneath their breath, their fierce eyes smoldering.

"Go and prepare your clans for battle," said the king, and they lumbered away with the ape-like gait assumed by such stunted giants. Paying no more heed to the priest who was examining the ghastly ruin on the altar, Bran beckoned to Cormac. The Gael followed him with alacrity. Once out of that grim grove, under the starlight, he breathed more freely. They stood on an eminence, looking out over long swelling undulations of gently waving heather. Near at hand a few fires twinkled, their fewness giving scant evidence of the hordes of tribesmen who lay close by. Beyond these were more fires and beyond these still more, which last marked the camp of Cormac's own men, hard-riding, hard-fighting Gaels, who were of that band which was just beginning to get a foothold on the western coast of Caledonia – the nucleus of what was later to become the kingdom of Dalriadia. To the left of these, other fires gleamed.

And far away to the south were more fires – mere pinpoints of light. But even at that distance the Pictish king and his Celtic ally could see that these fires were laid out in regular order.

"The fires of the legions," muttered Bran. "The fires that have lit a path around the world. The men who light those fires have trampled the races under their iron heels. And now – we of the heather have our backs at the wall. What will fall on the morrow?"

"Victory for us, says the priest," answered Cormac.

Bran made an impatient gesture. "Moonlight on the ocean. Wind in the fir tops. Do you think that I put faith in such mummery? Or that I enjoyed the butchery of a captive legionary? I must hearten my people; it was for Gron and Bocah that I let old Gonar read the portents. The warriors will fight better."

"And Gonar?"

Bran laughed. "Gonar is too old to believe – anything. He was high priest of the Shadows a score of years before I was born. He claims direct descent from that Gonar who was a wizard in the days of Brule, the Spear-slayer who was the first of my line. No man knows how old he is – sometimes I think he is the original Gonar himself!"

"At least," said a mocking voice, and Cormac started as a dim shape appeared at his side, "at least I have learned that in order to keep the faith and trust of the people, a wise man must appear to be a fool. I know secrets that would blast even your brain, Bran, should I speak them. But in order that the people may believe in me, I must descend to such things as they think proper magic – and prance and yell and rattle snakeskins, and dabble about in human blood and chicken livers."

Cormac looked at the ancient with new interest. The semi-madness of his appearance had vanished. He was no longer the charlatan, the spell-mumbling shaman. The starlight lent him a dignity which seemed to increase his very height, so that he stood like a white-bearded patriarch.

"Bran, your doubt lies there." The lean arm pointed to the fourth ring of fires.

"Aye," the king nodded gloomily. "Cormac – you know as well as I. Tomorrow's battle hinges upon that circle of fires. With the chariots of the Britons and your own Western horsemen, our success would be certain, but – surely the devil himself is in the heart of every Northman! You know how I trapped that band – how they swore to fight for me against Rome! And now that their chief, Rognar, is dead, they swear that they will be led only by a king of their own race! Else they will break their vow and go over to the Romans. Without them we are doomed, for we can not change our former plan."

"Take heart, Bran," said Gonar. "Touch the jewel in your iron crown. Mayhap it will bring you aid."

Bran laughed bitterly. "Now you talk as the people think. I am no fool to twist with empty words. What of the gem? It is a strange one, truth, and has brought me luck ere now. But I need now, no jewels, but the allegiance of three hundred fickle Northmen who are the only warriors among us who may stand the charge of the legions on foot."

"But the jewel, Bran, the jewel!" persisted Gonar.

"Well, the jewel!" cried Bran impatiently. "It is older than this world. It was old when Atlantis and Lemuria sank into the sea. It was given to Brule, the Spear-slayer, first of my line, by the Atlantean Kull, king of Valusia, in the days when the world was young. But shall that profit us now?"

"Who knows?" asked the wizard obliquely. "Time and space exist not.

There was no past, and there shall be no future. NOW is all. All things that ever were, are, or ever will be, transpire *now*. Man is forever at the center of what we call time and space. I have gone into yesterday and tomorrow and both were as real as today – which is like the dreams of ghosts! But let me sleep and talk with Gonar. Mayhap he shall aid us."

"What means he?" asked Cormac, with a slight twitching of his shoulders, as the priest strode away in the shadows.

"He has ever said that the first Gonar comes to him in his dreams and talks with him," answered Bran. "I have seen him perform deeds that seemed beyond human ken. I know not. I am but an unknown king with an iron crown, trying to lift a race of savages out of the slime into which they have sunk. Let us look to the camps."

As they walked Cormac wondered. By what strange freak of fate had such a man risen among this race of savages, survivors of a darker, grimmer age? Surely he was an atavism, an original type of the days when the Picts ruled all Europe, before their primitive empire fell before the bronze swords of the Gauls. Cormac knew how Bran, rising by his own efforts from the negligent position of the son of a Wolf clan chief, had to an extent united the tribes of the heather and now claimed kingship over all Caledon. But his rule was loose and much remained before the Pictish clans would forget their feuds and present a solid front to foreign foes. On the battle of the morrow, the first pitched battle between the Picts under their king and the Romans, hinged the future of the rising Pictish kingdom.

Bran and his ally walked through the Pictish camp where the swart warriors lay sprawled about their small fires, sleeping or gnawing half-cooked food. Cormac was impressed by their silence. A thousand men camped here, yet the only sounds were occasional low guttural intonations. The silence of the Stone Age rested in the souls of these men.

They were all short – most of them crooked of limb. Giant dwarfs; Bran Mak Morn was a tall man among them. Only the older men were bearded and they scantily, but their black hair fell about their eyes so that they peered fiercely from under the tangle. They were barefoot and clad scantily in wolfskins. Their arms consisted in short barbed swords of iron, heavy black bows, arrows tipped with flint, iron and copper, and stone-headed mallets. Defensive armor they had none, save for a crude shield of hide-covered wood; many had worked bits of metal into their tangled manes as a slight protection against sword-cuts. Some few, sons of long lines of chiefs, were smooth-limbed and lithe like Bran, but in the eyes of all gleamed the unquenchable savagery of the primeval.

These men are fully savages, thought Cormac, worse than the Gauls,

Britons and Germans. Can the old legends be true – that they reigned in a day when strange cities rose where now the sea rolls? And that they survived the flood that washed those gleaming empires under, sinking again into that savagery from which they once had risen?

Close to the encampment of the tribesmen were the fires of a group of Britons – members of fierce tribes who lived south of the Roman Wall but who dwelt in the hills and forests to the west and defied the power of Rome. Powerfully built men they were, with blazing blue eyes and shocks of tousled yellow hair, such men as had thronged the Ceanntish beaches when Caesar brought the Eagles into the Isles. These men, like the Picts, wore no armor, and were clad scantily in coarse-worked cloth and deerskin sandals. They bore small round bucklers of hard wood, braced with bronze, to be worn on the left arm, and long heavy bronze swords with blunt points. Some had bows, though the Britons were indifferent archers. Their bows were shorter than the Picts' and effective only at close range. But ranged close by their fires were the weapons that had made the name Briton a word of terror to Pict, Roman and Norse raider alike. Within the circle of firelight stood fifty bronze chariots with long cruel blades curving out from the sides. One of these blades could dismember half a dozen men at once. Tethered close by under the vigilant eyes of their guards grazed the chariot horses – big, rangy steeds, swift and powerful.

"Would that we had more of them!" mused Bran. "With a thousand chariots and my bowmen I could drive the legions into the sea."

"The free British tribes must eventually fall before Rome," said Cormac. "It would seem they would rush to join you in your war."

Bran made a helpless gesture. "The fickleness of the Celt. They can not forget old feuds. Our ancient men have told us how they would not even unite against Caesar when the Romans first came. They will not make head against a common foe together. These men came to me because of some dispute with their chief, but I can not depend on them when they are not actually fighting."

Cormac nodded. "I know; Caesar conquered Gaul by playing one tribe against another. My own people shift and change with the waxing and waning of the tides. But of all Celts, the Cymry are the most changeable, the least stable. Not many centuries ago my own Gaelic ancestors wrested Erin from the Cymric Danaans, because though they outnumbered us, they opposed us as separate tribes, rather than as a nation."

"And so these Cymric Britons face Rome," said Bran. "These will aid us on the morrow. Further I can not say. But how shall I expect loyalty from alien tribes, who am not sure of my own people? Thousands lurk in the hills, holding aloof. I am king in name only. Let me win tomorrow and they will flock to my standard; if I lose, they will scatter like birds before a cold wind."

———

A chorus of rough welcome greeted the two leaders as they entered the camp of Cormac's Gaels. Five hundred in number they were, tall rangy men, black-haired and gray-eyed mainly, with the bearing of men who lived by war alone. While there was nothing like close discipline among them, there was an air of more system and practical order than existed in the lines of the Picts and Britons. These men were of the last Celtic race to invade the Isles and their barbaric civilization was of much higher order than that of their Cymric kin. The ancestors of the Gaels had learned the arts of war on the vast plains of Scythia and at the courts of the Pharaohs where they had fought as mercenaries of Egypt, and much of what they learned they brought into Ireland with them. Excelling in metal work, they were armed, not with clumsy bronze swords, but with high-grade weapons of iron.

They were clad in well-woven kilts and leathern sandals. Each wore a light shirt of chain mail and a vizorless helmet, but this was all of their defensive armor. Celts, Gaelic or Brythonic, were prone to judge a man's valor by the amount of armor he wore. The Britons who faced Caesar deemed the Romans cowards because they cased themselves in metal, and many centuries later the Irish clans thought the same of the mail-clad Norman knights of Strongbow.

Cormac's warriors were horsemen. They neither knew nor esteemed the use of the bow. They bore the inevitable round, metal-braced buckler, dirks, long straight swords and light single-handed axes. Their tethered horses grazed not far away — big-boned animals, not so ponderous as those raised by the Britons, but swifter.

Bran's eyes lighted as the two strode through the camp. "These men are keen-beaked birds of war! See how they whet their axes and jest of the morrow! Would that the raiders in yon camp were as staunch as your men, Cormac! Then would I greet the legions with a laugh when they come up from the south tomorrow."

They were entering the circle of the Northmen fires. Three hundred men sat about gambling, whetting their weapons and drinking deep of the heather ale furnished them by their Pictish allies. These gazed upon Bran and Cormac with no great friendliness. It was striking to note the difference between them and the Picts and Celts – the difference in their cold eyes, their strong moody faces, their very bearing. Here was ferocity, and savagery, but not of the wild, upbursting fury of the Celt. Here was fierceness backed by grim determination and stolid stubbornness. The charge of the British clans was terrible, overwhelming. But they had no patience; let them be balked of immediate victory and they were likely to lose heart and scatter or fall to bickering among themselves. There was the patience of the cold blue North in these seafarers – a lasting determination that would keep them steadfast to the bitter end, once their face was set toward a definite goal.

As to personal stature, they were giants; massive yet rangy. That they did not share the ideas of the Celts regarding armor was shown by the fact that they were clad in heavy scale mail shirts that reached below mid-thigh, heavy horned helmets and hardened hide leggings, reinforced, as were their shoes, with plates of iron. Their shields were huge oval affairs of hard wood, hide and brass. As to weapons, they had long iron-headed spears, heavy iron axes, and daggers. Some had long wide-bladed swords.

Cormac scarcely felt at ease with the cold magnetic eyes of these flaxen-haired men fixed upon him. He and they were hereditary foes, even though they did chance to be fighting on the same side at present – but were they?

A man came forward, a tall gaunt warrior on whose scarred, wolfish face the flickering firelight reflected deep shadows. With his wolfskin mantle flung carelessly about his wide shoulders, and the great horns on his helmet adding to his height, he stood there in the swaying shadows, like some half-human thing, a brooding shape of the dark barbarism that was soon to engulf the world.

"Well, Wulfhere," said the Pictish king, "you have drunk the mead of council and have spoken about the fires – what is your decision?"

The Northman's eyes flashed in the gloom. "Give us a king of our own race to follow if you wish us to fight for you."

Bran flung out his hands. "Ask me to drag down the stars to gem your helmets! Will not your comrades follow you?"

"Not against the legions," answered Wulfhere sullenly. "A king led us on the viking path – a king must lead us against the Romans. And Rognar is dead."

"I am a king," said Bran. "Will you fight for me if I stand at the tip of your fight wedge?"

"A king of our own race," said Wulfhere doggedly. "We are all picked men of the North. We fight for none but a king, and a king must lead us – against the legions."

Cormac sensed a subtle threat in this repeated phrase.

"Here is a prince of Erin," said Bran. "Will you fight for the Westerner?"

"We fight under no Celt, West or East," growled the viking, and a low rumble of approval rose from the onlookers. "It is enough to fight by their side."

The hot Gaelic blood rose in Cormac's brain and he pushed past Bran, his hand on his sword. "How mean you that, pirate?"

Before Wulfhere could reply Bran interposed: "Have done! Will you fools throw away the battle before it is fought, by your madness? What of your oath, Wulfhere?"

"We swore it under Rognar; when he died from a Roman arrow we were absolved of it. We will follow only a king – against the legions."

"But your comrades will follow you – against the heather people!" snapped Bran.

"Aye," the Northman's eyes met his brazenly. "Send us a king or we join the Romans tomorrow."

Bran snarled. In his rage he dominated the scene, dwarfing the huge men who towered over him.

"Traitors! Liars! I hold your lives in my hand! Aye, draw your swords if you will – Cormac, keep your blade in its sheath. These wolves will not bite a king! Wulfhere – I spared your lives when I could have taken them.

"You came to raid the countries of the South, sweeping down from the northern sea in your galleys. You ravaged the coasts and the smoke of burning villages hung like a cloud over the shores of Caledon. I trapped you all when you were pillaging and burning – with the blood of my people on your hands. I burned your long ships and ambushed you when you followed. With thrice your number of bowmen who burned for your lives hidden in the heathered hills about you, I spared you when we could have shot you down like trapped wolves. Because I spared you, you swore to come and fight for me."

"And shall we die because the Picts fight Rome?" rumbled a bearded raider.

"Your lives are forfeit to me; you came to ravage the South. I did not promise to send you all back to your homes in the North unharmed and loaded with loot. Your vow was to fight one battle against Rome under my standard. Then I will aid your survivors to build ships and you may go where you will, with a goodly share of the plunder we take from the legions. Rognar had kept his oath. But Rognar died in a skirmish with Roman scouts and now you, Wulfhere the Dissension-breeder, you stir up your comrades to dishonor themselves by that which a Northman hates – the breaking of the sworn word."

"We break no oath," snarled the viking, and the king sensed the basic Germanic stubbornness, far harder to combat than the fickleness of the fiery Celts. "Give us a king, neither Pict, Gael nor Briton, and we will die for you. If not – then we will fight tomorrow for the greatest of all kings – the emperor of Rome!"

For a moment Cormac thought that the Pictish king, in his black rage, would draw and strike the Northman dead. The concentrated fury that blazed in Bran's dark eyes caused Wulfhere to recoil and drop a hand to his belt.

"Fool!" said Mak Morn in a low voice that vibrated with passion. "I could sweep you from the earth before the Romans are near enough to hear your death howls. Choose – fight for me on the morrow – or die tonight under a black cloud of arrows, a red storm of swords, a dark wave of chariots!"

At the mention of the chariots, the only arm of war that had ever broken the Norse shield-wall, Wulfhere changed expression, but he held his ground.

"War be it," he said doggedly. "Or a king to lead us!"

The Northmen responded with a short deep roar and a clash of swords on shields. Bran, eyes blazing, was about to speak again when a white shape glided silently into the ring of firelight.

"Soft words, soft words," said old Gonar tranquilly. "King, say no more. Wulfhere, you and your fellows will fight for us if you have a king to lead you?"

"We have sworn."

"Then be at ease," quoth the wizard; "for ere battle joins on the morrow I will send you such a king as no man on earth has followed for a hundred thousand years! A king neither Pict, Gael nor Briton, but one to whom the emperor of Rome is as but a village headman!"

While they stood undecided, Gonar took the arms of Cormac and Bran. "Come. And you, Northmen, remember your vow, and my promise which I have never broken. Sleep now, nor think to steal away in the darkness to the

95

Roman camp, for if you escaped our shafts you would not escape either my curse or the suspicions of the legionaries."

So the three walked away and Cormac, looking back, saw Wulfhere standing by the fire, fingering his golden beard, with a look of puzzled anger on his lean evil face.

The three walked silently through the waving heather under the far-away stars while the weird night wind whispered ghostly secrets about them.

"Ages ago," said the wizard suddenly, "in the days when the world was young, great lands rose where now the ocean roars. On these lands thronged mighty nations and kingdoms. Greatest of all these was Valusia – Land of Enchantment. Rome is as a village compared to the splendor of the cities of Valusia. And the greatest king was Kull, who came from the land of Atlantis to wrest the crown of Valusia from a degenerate dynasty. The Picts who dwelt in the isles which now form the mountain peaks of a strange land upon the Western Ocean, were allies of Valusia, and the greatest of all the Pictish war-chiefs was Brule the Spear-slayer, first of the line men call Mak Morn.

"Kull gave to Brule the jewel which you now wear in your iron crown, oh king, after a strange battle in a dim land, and down the long ages it has come to us, ever a sign of the Mak Morn, a symbol of former greatness. When at last the sea rose and swallowed Valusia, Atlantis and Lemuria, only the Picts survived and they were scattered and few. Yet they began again the slow climb upward, and though many of the arts of civilization were lost in the great flood, yet they progressed. The art of metal-working was lost, so they excelled in the working of flint. And they ruled all the new lands flung up by the sea and now called Europe, until down from the north came younger tribes who had scarce risen from the ape when Valusia reigned in her glory, and who, dwelling in the icy lands about the Pole, knew naught of the lost splendor of the Seven Empires and little of the flood that had swept away half a world.

"And still they have come – Aryans, Celts, Germans, swarming down from the great cradle of their race which lies near the Pole. So again was the growth of the Pictish nation checked and the race hurled into savagery. Erased from the earth, on the fringe of the world with our backs to the wall we fight. Here in Caledon is the last stand of a once mighty race. And we change. Our people have mixed with the savages of an elder age which we drove into the North when we came into the Isles, and now, save for their chieftains, such as thou, Bran, a Pict is strange and abhorrent to look upon."

"True, true," said the king impatiently, "but what has that to do – "

"Kull, king of Valusia," said the wizard imperturbably, "was a barbarian in his age as thou art in thine, though he ruled a mighty empire by the weight of his sword. Gonar, friend of Brule, your first ancestor, has been dead a hundred thousand years as we reckon time. Yet I talked with him a scant hour agone."

"You talked with his ghost —"

"Or he with mine? Did I go back a hundred thousand years, or did he come forward? If he came to me out of the past, it is not I who talked with a dead man, but he who talked with a man unborn. Past, present and future are one to a wise man. I talked to Gonar while he was alive; likewise was I alive. In a timeless, spaceless land we met and he told me many things."

The land was growing light with the birth of dawn. The heather waved and bent in long rows before the dawn wind as bowing in worship of the rising sun.

"The jewel in your crown is a magnet that draws down the eons," said Gonar. "The sun is rising — and who comes out of the sunrise?"

Cormac and the king started. The sun was just lifting a red orb above the eastern hills. And full in the glow, etched boldly against the golden rim, a man suddenly appeared. They had not seen him come. Against the golden birth of day he loomed colossal; a gigantic god from the dawn of creation. Now as he strode toward them the waking hosts saw him and sent up a sudden shout of wonder.

"Who — or what is it?" exclaimed Bran.

"Let us go to meet him, Bran," answered the wizard. "He is the king Gonar has sent to save the people of Brule."

II

I have reached these lands but newly
From an ultimate dim Thule;
From a wild weird clime that lieth sublime
Out of Space — out of Time.

—*Poe*

The army fell silent as Bran, Cormac and Gonar went toward the stranger who approached in long swinging strides. As they neared him the illusion of monstrous size vanished, but they saw he was a man of great stature. At first Cormac thought him to be a Northman but a second glance told him that nowhere before had he seen such a man. He was built much like the vikings, at once massive and lithe — tigerish. But his features were not as theirs, and his square-cut, lion-like mane of hair was as black as Bran's own. Under heavy brows glittered eyes gray as steel and cold as ice. His bronzed face, strong and inscrutable, was clean-shaven, and the broad forehead betokened a high intelligence, just as the firm jaw and thin lips showed will-power and

97

courage. But more than all, the bearing of him, the unconscious lion-like stateliness, marked him as a natural king, a ruler of men.

Sandals of curious make were on his feet and he wore a pliant coat of strangely meshed mail which came almost to his knees. A broad belt with a great golden buckle encircled his waist, supporting a long straight sword in a heavy leather scabbard. His hair was confined by a wide, heavy golden band about his head.

Such was the man who paused before the silent group. He seemed slightly puzzled, slightly amused. Recognition flickered in his eyes. He spoke in a strange archaic Pictish which Cormac scarcely understood. His voice was deep and resonant.

"Ha, Brule, Gonar did not tell me I would dream of you!"

For the first time in his life Cormac saw the Pictish king completely thrown off his balance. He gaped, speechless. The stranger continued:

"And wearing the gem I gave you, in a circlet on your head! Last night you wore it in a ring on your finger."

"Last night?" gasped Bran.

"Last night or a hundred thousand years ago – all one!" murmured Gonar in evident enjoyment of the situation.

"I am not Brule," said Bran. "Are you mad to thus speak of a man dead a hundred thousand years? He was first of my line."

The stranger laughed unexpectedly. "Well, now I know I am dreaming! This will be a tale to tell Brule when I waken on the morrow! That I went into the future and saw men claiming descent from the Spear-slayer who is, as yet, not even married. No, you are not Brule, I see now, though you have his eyes and his bearing. But he is taller and broader in the shoulders. Yet you have his jewel – oh, well – anything can happen in a dream, so I will not quarrel with you. For a time I thought I had been transported to some other land in my sleep, and was in reality awake in a strange country, for this is the clearest dream I ever dreamed. Who are you?"

"I am Bran Mak Morn, king of the Caledonian Picts. And this ancient is Gonar, a wizard, of the line of Gonar. And this warrior is Cormac na Connacht, a prince of the isle of Erin."

The stranger slowly shook his lion-like head. "These words sound strangely to me, save Gonar – and that one is not Gonar, though he too is old. What land is this?"

"Caledon, or Alba, as the Gaels call it."

"And who are those squat ape-like warriors who watch us yonder, all agape?"

"They are the Picts who own my rule."

98

"How strangely distorted folk are in dreams!" muttered the stranger. "And who are those shock-headed men about the chariots?"

"They are Britons – Cymry from south of the Wall."

"What Wall?"

"The Wall built by Rome to keep the people of the heather out of Britain."

"Britain?" the tone was curious. "I never heard of that land – and what is Rome?"

"What!" cried Bran. "You never heard of Rome, the empire that rules the world?"

"No empire rules the world," answered the other haughtily. "The mightiest kingdom on earth is that wherein I reign."

"And who are you?"

"Kull of Atlantis, king of Valusia!"

Cormac felt a coldness trickle down his spine. The cold gray eyes were unswerving – but this was incredible – monstrous – unnatural.

"Valusia!" cried Bran. "Why, man, the sea waves have rolled above the spires of Valusia for untold centuries!"

Kull laughed outright. "What a mad nightmare this is! When Gonar put on me the spell of deep sleep last night – or this night! – in the secret room of the inner palace, he told me I would dream strange things, but this is more fantastic than I reckoned. And the strangest thing is, I know I am dreaming!"

Gonar interposed as Bran would have spoken. "Question not the acts of the gods," muttered the wizard. "You are king because in the past you have seen and seized opportunities. The gods or the first Gonar have sent you this man. Let me deal with him."

Bran nodded, and while the silent army gaped in speechless wonder, just within ear-shot, Gonar spoke: "Oh great king, you dream, but is not all life a dream? How reckon you but that your former life is but a dream from which you have just awakened? Now we dream-folk have our wars and our peace, and just now a great host comes up from the south to destroy the people of Brule. Will you aid us?"

Kull grinned with pure zest. "Aye! I have fought battles in dreams ere now, have slain and been slain and was amazed when I woke from my visions. And at times, as now, dreaming I have known I dreamed. See, I pinch myself and feel it, but I know I dream for I have felt the pain of fierce wounds, in dreams. Yes, people of my dream, I will fight for you against the other dream-folk. Where are they?"

"And that you enjoy the dream more," said the wizard subtly, "forget that it is a dream and pretend that by the magic of the first Gonar, and the quality of the jewel you gave Brule, that now gleams on the crown of the

Morni, you have in truth been transported forward into another, wilder age where the people of Brule fight for their life against a stronger foe."

For a moment the man who called himself king of Valusia seemed startled; a strange look of doubt, almost of fear, clouded his eyes. Then he laughed.

"Good! Lead on, wizard."

But now Bran took charge. He had recovered himself and was at ease. Whether he thought, like Cormac, that this was all a gigantic hoax arranged by Gonar, he showed no sign.

"King Kull, see you those men yonder who lean on their long-shafted axes as they gaze upon you?"

"The tall men with the golden hair and beards?"

"Aye – our success in the coming battle hinges on them. They swear to go over to the enemy if we give them not a king to lead them – their own having been slain. Will you lead them to battle?"

Kull's eyes glowed with appreciation. "They are men such as my own Red Slayers, my picked regiment. I will lead them."

"Come then."

The small group made their way down the slope, through throngs of warriors who pushed forward eagerly to get a better view of the stranger, then pressed back as he approached. An undercurrent of tense whispering ran through the horde.

The Northmen stood apart in a compact group. Their cold eyes took in Kull and he gave back their stares, taking in every detail of their appearance.

"Wulfhere," said Bran, "we have brought you a king. I hold you to your oath."

"Let him speak to us," said the viking harshly.

"He can not speak your tongue," answered Bran, knowing that the Northmen knew nothing of the legends of his race. "He is a great king of the South – "

"He comes out of the past," broke in the wizard calmly. "He was the greatest of all kings, long ago."

"A dead man!" The vikings moved uneasily and the rest of the horde pressed forward, drinking in every word. But Wulfhere scowled: "Shall a ghost lead living men? You bring us a man you say is dead. We will not follow a corpse."

"Wulfhere," said Bran in still passion, "you are a liar and a traitor. You set us this task, thinking it impossible. You yearn to fight under the Eagles of Rome. We have brought you a king neither Pict, Gael nor Briton and you deny your vow!"

Kings of the Night

"Let him fight me, then!" howled Wulfhere in uncontrollable wrath, swinging his ax about his head in a glittering arc. "If your dead man overcomes me – then my people will follow you. If I overcome him, you shall let us depart in peace to the camp of the legions!"

"Good!" said the wizard. "Do you agree, wolves of the North?"

A fierce yell and a brandishing of swords was the answer. Bran turned to Kull, who had stood silent, understanding nothing of what was said. But the Atlantean's eyes gleamed. Cormac felt that those cold eyes had looked on too many such scenes not to understand something of what had passed.

"This warrior says you must fight him for the leadership," said Bran, and Kull, eyes glittering with growing battle-joy, nodded: "I guessed as much. Give us space."

"A shield and a helmet!" shouted Bran, but Kull shook his head.

"I need none," he growled. "Back and give us room to swing our steel!"

Men pressed back on each side, forming a solid ring about the two men, who now approached each other warily. Kull had drawn his sword and the great blade shimmered like a live thing in his hand. Wulfhere, scarred by a hundred savage fights, flung aside his wolfskin mantle and came in cautiously, fierce eyes peering over the top of his out-thrust shield, ax half lifted in his right hand.

Suddenly when the warriors were still many feet apart Kull sprang. His attack brought a gasp from men used to deeds of prowess; for like a leaping tiger he shot through the air and his sword crashed on the quickly lifted shield. Sparks flew and Wulfhere's ax hacked in, but Kull was under its sweep and as it swished viciously above his head he thrust upward and sprang out again, cat-like. His motions had been too quick for the eye to follow. The upper edge of Wulfhere's shield showed a deep cut, and there was a long rent in his mail shirt where Kull's sword had barely missed the flesh beneath.

Cormac, trembling with the terrible thrill of the fight, wondered at this sword that could thus slice through scale-mail. And the blow that gashed the shield should have shattered the blade. Yet not a notch showed in the Valusian steel! Surely this blade was forged by another people in another age!

Now the two giants leaped again to the attack and like double strokes of lightning their weapons crashed. Wulfhere's shield fell from his arm in two pieces as the Atlantean's sword sheared clear through it, and Kull staggered as the Northman's ax, driven with all the force of his great body, descended on the golden circlet about his head. That blow should have sheared through the gold like butter to split the skull beneath, but the ax rebounded, showing a great notch in the edge. The next instant the Northman was overwhelmed by a whirlwind of steel – a storm of strokes delivered with such swiftness and power that he was borne back as on the crest of a wave, unable to launch an attack of his own. With all his tried skill he sought to parry the singing steel with his ax. But he could only avert his doom for a few seconds; could only for an instant turn the whistling blade that hewed off bits of his mail, so close fell the blows. One of the horns flew from his helmet; then the ax-head itself fell away, and the same blow that severed the handle, bit through the viking's helmet into the scalp beneath. Wulfhere was dashed to his knees, a trickle of blood starting down his face.

Kull checked his second stroke, and tossing his sword to Cormac, faced the dazed Northman weaponless. The Atlantean's eyes were blazing with ferocious joy and he roared something in a strange tongue. Wulfhere gathered his legs under him and bounded up, snarling like a wolf, a dagger flashing into his hand. The watching horde gave tongue in a yell that ripped the skies as the two bodies clashed. Kull's clutching hand missed the Northman's wrist but the desperately lunging dagger snapped on the Atlantean's mail, and dropping the useless hilt, Wulfhere locked his arms about his foe in a bear-like grip that would have crushed the ribs of a lesser man. Kull grinned tigerishly and returned the grapple, and for a moment the two swayed on their feet. Slowly the black-haired warrior bent his foe backward until it seemed his spine would snap. With a howl that had nothing of the human in it, Wulfhere clawed frantically at Kull's face, trying to tear out his eyes, then turned his head and snapped his fang-like teeth into the Atlantean's arm. A yell went up as a trickle of blood started: "He bleeds! He bleeds! He is no ghost, after all, but a mortal man!"

Angered, Kull shifted his grip, shoving the frothing Wulfhere away from him, and smote him terrifically under the ear with his right hand. The viking landed on his back a dozen feet away. Then, howling like a wild man, he leaped up with a stone in his hand and flung it. Only Kull's incredible quickness saved his face; as it was, the rough edge of the missile tore his cheek and inflamed him to madness. With a lion-like roar he bounded upon his foe, enveloped him in an irresistible blast of sheer fury, whirled him high above his head as if he were a child and cast him a dozen feet away. Wulfhere pitched on his head and lay still – broken and dead.

Dazed silence reigned for an instant; then from the Gaels went up a thundering roar, and the Britons and Picts took it up, howling like wolves, until the echoes of the shouts and the clangor of sword on shield reached the ears of the marching legionaries, miles to the south.

"Men of the gray North," shouted Bran, "will you hold by your oath *now?*"

The fierce souls of the Northmen were in their eyes as their spokesman answered. Primitive, superstitious, steeped in tribal lore of fighting gods and mythical heroes, they did not doubt that the black-haired fighting man was some supernatural being sent by the fierce gods of battle.

"Aye! Such a man as this we have never seen! Dead man, ghost or devil, we will follow him, whether the trail lead to Rome or Valhalla!"

Kull understood the meaning, if not the words. Taking his sword from Cormac with a word of thanks, he turned to the waiting Northmen and silently held the blade toward them high above his head, in both hands, before he returned it to its scabbard. Without understanding, they appreciated the action. Blood-stained and disheveled, he was an impressive picture of stately, magnificent barbarism.

"Come," said Bran, touching the Atlantean's arm; "a host is marching on us and we have much to do. There is scant time to arrange our forces before they will be upon us. Come to the top of yonder slope."

There the Pict pointed. They were looking down into a valley which ran north and south, widening from a narrow gorge in the north until it debouched upon a plain to the south. The whole valley was less than a mile in length.

"Up this valley will our foes come," said the Pict, "because they have wagons loaded with supplies and on all sides of this vale the ground is too rough for such travel. Here we plan an ambush."

"I would have thought you would have had your men lying in wait long before now," said Kull. "What of the scouts the enemy is sure to send out?"

"The savages I lead would never have waited in ambush so long," said Bran with a touch of bitterness. "I could not post them until I was sure of the Northmen. Even so I had not dared to post them ere now – even yet they may take panic from the drifting of a cloud or the blowing of a leaf, and scatter like birds before a cold wind. King Kull – the fate of the Pictish nation is at stake. I am called king of the Picts, but my rule as yet is but a hollow mockery. The hills are full of wild clans who refuse to fight for me. Of the thousand bowmen now at my command, more than half are of my own clan.

"Some eighteen hundred Romans are marching against us. It is not a real invasion, but much hinges upon it. It is the beginning of an attempt to extend their boundaries. They plan to build a fortress a day's march to the north of this valley. If they do, they will build other forts, drawing bands of steel about the heart of the free people. If I win this battle and wipe out this army, I will win a double victory. Then the tribes will flock to me and the next invasion will meet a solid wall of resistance. If I lose, the clans will scatter, fleeing into the north until they can no longer flee, fighting as separate clans rather than as one strong nation.

"I have a thousand archers, five hundred horsemen, fifty chariots with their drivers and swordsmen – one hundred fifty men in all – and, thanks to you, three hundred heavily armed Northern pirates. How would you arrange your battle lines?"

"Well," said Kull, "I would have barricaded the north end of the valley – no! That would suggest a trap. But I would block it with a band of desperate men, like those you have given me to lead. Three hundred could hold the gorge for a time against any number. Then, when the enemy was engaged with these men to the narrow part of the valley, I would have my archers shoot down into them until their ranks are broken, from both sides of the vale. Then, having my horsemen concealed behind one ridge and my chariots behind the other, I would charge with both simultaneously and sweep the foe into a red ruin."

Bran's eyes glowed. "Exactly, king of Valusia. Such was my exact plan –"

"But what of the scouts?"

"My warriors are like panthers; they hide under the noses of the Romans. Those who ride into the valley will see only what we wish them to see. Those who ride over the ridge will not come back to report. An arrow is swift and silent.

"You see that the pivot of the whole thing depends on the men that hold the gorge. They must be men who can fight on foot and resist the charges of the heavy legionaries long enough for the trap to close. Outside these Northmen I had no such force of men. My naked warriors with their short swords could never stand such a charge for an instant. Nor is the armor of the Celts made for such work; moreover, they are not foot-fighters, and I need them elsewhere.

"So you see why I had such desperate need of the Northmen. Now will you stand in the gorge with them and hold back the Romans until I can spring the trap? Remember, most of you will die."

Kull smiled. "I have taken chances all my life, though Tu, chief councillor, would say my life belongs to Valusia and I have no right to so risk it –" His voice trailed off and a strange look flitted across his face. "By Valka," said he, laughing uncertainly, "sometimes I forget this is a dream! All seems so real. But it is – of course it is! Well, then, if I die I will but awaken as I have done in times past. Lead on, king of Caledon!"

Cormac, going to his warriors, wondered. Surely it was all a hoax; yet – he heard the arguments of the warriors all about him as they armed themselves and prepared to take their posts. The black-haired king was Neid himself, the Celtic war-god; he was an antediluvian king brought out of the past by Gonar; he was a mythical fighting man out of Valhalla. He was no man at all but a ghost! No, he was mortal, for he had bled. But the gods themselves bled, though they did not die. So the controversies raged. At least, thought Cormac, if it was all a hoax to inspire the warriors with the feeling of supernatural aid, it had succeeded. The belief that Kull was more than a mortal man had fired Celt, Pict and viking alike into a sort of inspired madness. And Cormac asked himself – what did he himself believe? This man was surely one from some far land – yet in his every look and action there was a vague hint of a greater difference than mere distance of space – a hint of alien Time, of misty abysses and gigantic gulfs of eons lying between the black-haired stranger and the men with whom he walked and talked. Clouds of bewilderment mazed Cormac's brain and he laughed in whimsical self-mockery.

III

> And the two wild peoples of the north
> Stood fronting in the gloam,
> And heard and knew each in his mind
> A third great sound upon the wind,
> The living walls that hedge mankind,
> The walking walls of Rome.
> —*Chesterton*

The sun slanted westward. Silence lay like an invisible mist over the valley. Cormac gathered the reins in his hand and glanced up at the ridges on both sides. The waving heather which grew rank on those steep slopes gave no evidence of the hundreds of savage warriors who lurked there. Here in the narrow gorge which widened gradually southward was the only sign of life. Between the steep walls three hundred Northmen were massed solidly in their wedge-shaped shield-wall, blocking the pass. At the tip, like the point of a spear, stood the man who called himself Kull, king of Valusia. He wore no helmet, only the great, strangely worked head-band of hard gold, but he bore on his left arm the great shield borne by the dead Rognar; and in his right hand he held the heavy iron mace wielded by the sea-king. The vikings eyed him in wonder and savage admiration. They could not understand his language, or he theirs. But no further orders were necessary. At Bran's directions they had bunched themselves in the gorge, and their only order was – hold the pass!

Bran Mak Morn stood just in front of Kull. So they faced each other, he whose kingdom was yet unborn, and he whose kingdom had been lost in the mists of Time for unguessed ages. Kings of darkness, thought Cormac, nameless kings of the night, whose realms are gulfs and shadows.

The hand of the Pictish king went out. "King Kull, you are more than king – you are a man. Both of us may fall within the next hour – but if we both live, ask what you will of me."

Kull smiled, returning the firm grip. "You too are a man after my own heart, king of the shadows. Surely you are more than a figment of my sleeping imagination. Mayhap we will meet in waking life some day."

Bran shook his head in puzzlement, swung into the saddle and rode away, climbing the eastern slope and vanishing over the ridge. Cormac hesitated: "Strange man, are you in truth of flesh and blood, or are you a ghost?"

"When we dream, we are all flesh and blood – so long as we are dreaming," Kull answered. "This is the strangest nightmare I have ever known – but you, who will soon fade into sheer nothingness as I awaken, seem as real to me *now*, as Brule, or Kananu, or Tu, or Kelkor."

Cormac shook his head as Bran had done, and with a last salute, which Kull returned with barbaric stateliness, he turned and trotted away. At the top of the western ridge he paused. Away to the south a light cloud of dust rose and the head of the marching column was in sight. Already he believed he could feel the earth vibrate slightly to the measured tread of a thousand mailed feet beating in perfect unison. He dismounted, and one of his chieftains, Domnail, took his steed and led it down the slope away from the valley, where trees grew thickly. Only an occasional vague movement among them gave evidence of the five hundred men who stood there, each at his horse's head with a ready hand to check a chance nicker.

Oh, thought Cormac, the gods themselves made this valley for Bran's ambush! The floor of the valley was treeless and the inner slopes were bare save for the waist-high heather. But at the foot of each ridge on the side facing away from the vale, where the soil long washed from the rocky slopes had accumulated, there grew enough trees to hide five hundred horsemen or fifty chariots.

At the northern end of the valley stood Kull and his three hundred vikings, in open view, flanked on each side by fifty Pictish bowmen. Hidden on the western side of the western ridge were the Gaels. Along the top of the slopes, concealed in the tall heather, lay a hundred Picts with their shafts on string. The rest of the Picts were hidden on the eastern slopes beyond which lay the Britons with their chariots in full readiness. Neither they nor the Gaels to the west could see what went on in the vale, but signals had been arranged.

Now the long column was entering the wide mouth of the valley and their scouts, light-armed men on swift horses, were spreading out between the slopes. They galloped almost within bowshot of the silent host that blocked the pass, then halted. Some whirled and raced back to the main force, while the others deployed and cantered up the slopes, seeking to see what lay beyond. This was the crucial moment. If they got any hint of the ambush, all was lost. Cormac, shrinking down into the heather, marveled at the ability of the Picts to efface themselves from view so completely. He saw a horseman pass within three feet of where he knew a bowman lay, yet the Roman saw nothing.

The scouts topped the ridges, gazed about; then most of them turned and trotted back down the slopes. Cormac wondered at their desultory manner of scouting. He had never fought Romans before, knew nothing of their arrogant self-confidence, of their incredible shrewdness in some ways, their incredible stupidity in others. These men were over-confident; a feeling radiating from their officers. It had been years since a force of Caledonians had stood before the legions. And most of these men were but newly come to Britain; part of a legion which had been quartered in Egypt. They despised their foes and suspected nothing.

But stay – three riders on the opposite ridge had turned and vanished on the other side. And now one, sitting his steed at the crest of the western ridge, not a hundred yards from where Cormac lay, looked long and narrowly down into the mass of trees at the foot of the slope. Cormac saw suspicion grow on his brown, hawk-like face. He half turned as though to call to his comrades, then instead reined his steed down the slope, leaning forward in his saddle. Cormac's heart pounded. Each moment he expected to see the man wheel and gallop back to raise the alarm. He resisted a mad impulse to leap up and charge the Roman on foot. Surely the man could feel the tenseness in the air – the hundreds of fierce eyes upon him. Now he was half-way down the slope, out of sight of the men in the valley. And now the twang of an unseen bow broke the painful stillness. With a strangled gasp the Roman flung his hands high, and as the steed reared, he pitched headlong, transfixed by a long black arrow that had flashed from the heather. A stocky dwarf sprang out of nowhere, seemingly, and seized the bridle, quieting the snorting horse, and leading it down the slope. At the fall of the Roman, short crooked men rose like a sudden flight of birds from the grass and Cormac saw the flash of a knife. Then with unreal suddenness all had subsided. Slayers and slain were unseen and only the still waving heather marked the grim deed.

The Gael looked back into the valley. The three who had ridden over the eastern ridge had not come back and Cormac knew they never would. Evidently the other scouts had borne word that only a small band of warriors was ready to dispute the passage of the legionaries. Now the head of the column was almost below him and he thrilled at the sight of these men who were doomed, swinging along with their superb arrogance. And the sight of their splendid armor, their hawk-like faces and perfect discipline awed him as much as it is possible for a Gael to be awed.

Twelve hundred men in heavy armor who marched as one so that the ground shook to their tread! Most of them were of middle height, with powerful chests and shoulders and bronzed faces – hard-bitten veterans of a hundred campaigns. Cormac noted their javelins, short keen swords and heavy shields; their gleaming armor and crested helmets, the eagles on the standards. These were the men beneath whose tread the world had shaken and empires crumbled! Not all were Latins; there were Romanized Britons among them and one century or hundred was composed of huge yellow-haired men – Gauls and Germans, who fought for Rome as fiercely as did the native-born, and hated their wilder kinsmen more savagely.

On each side was a swarm of cavalry, outriders, and the column was flanked by archers and slingers. A number of lumbering wagons carried the supplies of the army. Cormac saw the commander riding in his place – a tall man with a lean, imperious face, evident even at that distance. Marcus Sulius – the Gael knew him by repute.

A deep-throated roar rose from the legionaries as they approached their foes. Evidently they intended to slice their way through and continue without a pause, for the column moved implacably on. Whom the gods destroy they first make mad – Cormac had never heard the phrase but it came to him that the great Sulius was a fool. Roman arrogance! Marcus was used to lashing the cringing peoples of a decadent East; little he guessed of the iron in these western races.

A group of cavalry detached itself and raced into the mouth of the gorge, but it was only a gesture. With loud jeering shouts they wheeled three spears length away and cast their javelins, which rattled harmlessly on the overlapping shields of the silent Northmen. But their leader dared too much; swinging in, he leaned from his saddle and thrust at Kull's face. The great shield turned the lance and Kull struck back as a snake strikes; the ponderous mace crushed helmet and head like an eggshell, and the very steed went to its knees from the shock of that terrible blow. From the Northmen went up a short fierce roar, and the Picts beside them howled exultantly and loosed their arrows among the retreating horsemen. First blood for the people of the heather! The oncoming Romans shouted vengefully and quickened their pace as the frightened horse raced by, a ghastly travesty of a man, foot caught in the stirrup, trailing beneath the pounding hoofs.

Now the first line of the legionaries, compressed because of the narrowness of the gorge, crashed against the solid wall of shields – crashed and recoiled upon itself. The shield-wall had not shaken an inch. This was the first time the Roman legions had met with that unbreakable formation – that oldest of all Aryan battle-lines – the ancestor of the Spartan regiment – the Theban phalanx – the Macedonian formation – the English square.

Shield crashed on shield and the short Roman sword sought for an opening in that iron wall. Viking spears bristling in solid ranks above, thrust and reddened; heavy axes chopped down, shearing through iron, flesh and bone. Cormac saw Kull, looming above the stocky Romans in the forefront of the fray, dealing blows like thunderbolts. A burly centurion rushed in, shield held high, stabbing upward. The iron mace crashed terribly, shivering the sword, rending the shield apart, shattering the helmet, crushing the skull down between the shoulders – in a single blow.

The front line of the Romans bent like a steel bar about the wedge, as the legionaries sought to struggle through the gorge on each side and surround their opposers. But the pass was too narrow; crouching close against the steep walls the Picts drove their black arrows in a hail of death. At this range the heavy shafts tore through shield and corselet, transfixing the armored men. The front line of battle rolled back, red and broken, and the Northmen trod their few dead under foot to close the gaps their fall had made. Stretched the full width of their front lay a thin line of shattered forms – the red spray of the tide which had broken upon them in vain.

Cormac had leaped to his feet, waving his arms. Domnail and his men broke cover at the signal and came galloping up the slope, lining the ridge. Cormac mounted the horse brought him and glanced impatiently across the narrow vale. No sign of life appeared on the eastern ridge. Where was Bran – and the Britons?

Down in the valley, the legions, angered at the unexpected opposition of the paltry force in front of them, but not suspicious, were forming in more compact body. The wagons which had halted were lumbering on again and the whole column was once more in motion as if it intended to crash through by sheer weight. With the Gaulish century in the forefront, the legionaries were advancing again in the attack. This time, with the full force of twelve hundred men behind, the charge would batter down the resistance of Kull's warriors like a heavy ram; would stamp them down, sweep over their red ruins. Cormac's men trembled in impatience. Suddenly Marcus Sulius turned and gazed westward, where the line of horsemen was etched against the sky. Even at that distance Cormac saw his face pale. The Roman at last realized the metal of the men he faced, and that he had walked into a trap. Surely in that moment there flashed a chaotic picture through his brain – defeat – disgrace – red ruin!

It was too late to retreat – too late to form into a defensive square with the wagons for barricade. There was but one possible way out, and Marcus, crafty general in spite of his recent blunder, took it. Cormac heard his voice cut like a clarion through the din, and though he did not understand the words, he knew that the Roman was shouting for his men to smite that knot of Northmen like a blast – to hack their way through and out of the trap before it could close!

Now the legionaries, aware of their desperate plight, flung themselves headlong and terribly on their foes. The shield-wall rocked, but it gave not an inch. The wild faces of the Gauls and the hard brown Italian faces glared over locked shields into the blazing eyes of the North. Shields touching, they smote and slew and died in a red storm of slaughter, where crimsoned axes rose and fell and dripping spears broke on notched swords.

Where in God's name was Bran with his chariots? A few minutes more would spell the doom of every man who held that pass. Already they were falling fast, though they locked their ranks closer and held like iron. Those wild men of the North were dying in their tracks; and looming among their golden heads the black lion-mane of Kull shone like a symbol of slaughter, and his reddened mace showered a ghastly rain as it splashed brains and blood like water.

Something snapped in Cormac's brain.

"These men will die while we wait for Bran's signal!" he shouted. "On! Follow me into Hell, sons of Gael!"

A wild roar answered him, and loosing rein he shot down the slope with five hundred yelling riders plunging headlong after him. And even at that moment a storm of arrows swept the valley from either side like a dark cloud and the terrible clamor of the Picts split the skies. And over the eastern ridge, like a sudden burst of rolling thunder on Judgment Day, rushed the war-chariots. Headlong down the slope they roared, foam flying from the horses' distended nostrils, frantic feet scarcely seeming to touch the ground, making naught of the tall heather. In the foremost chariot, with his dark eyes blazing, crouched Bran Mak Morn, and in all of them the naked Britons were screaming and lashing as if possessed by demons. Behind the flying chariots came the Picts, howling like wolves and loosing their arrows as they ran. The heather belched them forth from all sides in a dark wave.

So much Cormac saw in chaotic glimpses during that wild ride down the slopes. A wave of cavalry swept between him and the main line of the column. Three long leaps ahead of his men, the Gaelic prince met the spears of the Roman riders. The first lance turned on his buckler, and rising in his stirrups he smote downward, cleaving his man from shoulder to breastbone. The next Roman flung a javelin that killed Domnail, but at that instant Cormac's steed crashed into his, breast to breast, and the lighter horse rolled headlong under the shock, flinging his rider beneath the pounding hoofs.

Then the whole blast of the Gaelic charge smote the Roman cavalry, shattering it, crashing and rolling it down and under. Over its red ruins Cormac's yelling demons struck the heavy Roman infantry, and the whole line reeled at the shock. Swords and axes flashed up and down and the force of their rush carried them deep into the massed ranks. Here, checked, they swayed and strove. Javelins thrust, swords flashed upward, bringing down horse and rider, and greatly outnumbered, leaguered on every side, the Gaels had perished among their foes, but at that instant, from the other side the crashing chariots smote the Roman ranks. In one long line they struck almost simultaneously, and at the moment of impact the charioteers wheeled their horses side-long and raced parallel down the ranks, shearing men down like the mowing of wheat. Hundreds died on those curving blades in that moment, and leaping from the chariots, screaming like blood-mad wildcats, the British swordsmen flung themselves upon the spears of the legionaries, hacking madly with their two-handed swords. Crouching, the Picts drove their arrows pointblank and then sprang in to slash and thrust. Maddened with the sight of victory, these wild peoples were like wounded tigers, feeling no wounds, and dying on their feet with their last gasp a snarl of fury.

But the battle was not over yet. Dazed, shattered, their formation broken and nearly half their number down already, the Romans fought back with desperate fury. Hemmed in on all sides they slashed and smote singly, or in small clumps, fought back to back, archers, slingers, horsemen and heavy legionaries mingled into a chaotic mass. The confusion was complete, but not the victory. Those bottled in the gorge still hurled themselves upon the red axes that barred their way, while the massed and serried battle thundered behind them. From one side Cormac's Gaels raged and slashed; from the other chariots swept back and forth, retiring and returning like iron whirlwinds. There was no retreat, for the Picts had flung a cordon across the way they had come, and having cut the throats of the camp followers and possessed themselves of the wagons, they sent their shafts in a storm of death into the rear of the shattered column. Those long black arrows pierced armor and bone, nailing men together. Yet the slaughter was not all on one side. Picts died beneath the lightning thrust of javelin and shortsword, Gaels pinned beneath their falling horses were hewed to pieces, and chariots, cut loose from their horses, were deluged with the blood of the charioteers.

And at the narrow head of the valley still the battle surged and eddied. Great gods – thought Cormac, glancing between lightning-like blows – do these men still hold the gorge? Aye! They held it! A tenth of their original number, dying on their feet, they still held back the frantic charges of the dwindling legionaries.

Over all the field went up the roar and the clash of arms, and birds of prey, swift-flying out of the sunset, circled above. Cormac, striving to reach Marcus Sulius through the press, saw the Roman's horse sink under him, and the rider rise alone in a waste of foes. He saw the Roman sword flash thrice, dealing a death at each blow; then from the thickest of the fray bounded a terrible figure. It was Bran Mak Morn, stained from head to foot. He cast away his broken sword as he ran, drawing a dirk. The Roman struck, but the Pictish king was under the thrust, and gripping the sword-wrist, he drove the dirk again and again through the gleaming armor.

A mighty roar went up as Marcus died, and Cormac, with a shout, rallied the remnants of his force about him and, striking in the spurs, burst through the shattered lines and rode full speed for the other end of the valley.

But as he approached he saw that he was too late. As they had lived, so had they died, those fierce sea-wolves, with their faces to the foe and their broken weapons red in their hands. In a grim and silent band they lay, even in death preserving some of the shield-wall formation. Among them, in front of them and all about them lay high-heaped the bodies of those who had sought to break them, in vain. *They had not given back a foot!* To the last man, they had died in their tracks. Nor were there any left to stride over their torn shapes; those Romans who had escaped the viking axes had been struck down by the shafts of the Picts and swords of the Gaels from behind.

Yet this part of the battle was not over. High up on the steep western slope Cormac saw the ending of that drama. A group of Gauls in the armor of Rome pressed upon a single man – a black-haired giant on whose head gleamed a golden crown. There was iron in these men, as well as in the man who had held them to their fate. They were doomed – their comrades were being slaughtered behind them – but before their turn came they would at least have the life of the black-haired chief who had led the golden-haired men of the North.

Pressing upon him from three sides they had forced him slowly back up the steep gorge wall, and the crumpled bodies that stretched along his retreat showed how fiercely every foot of the way had been contested. Here on this steep it was task enough to keep one's footing alone; yet these men at once climbed and fought. Kull's shield and the huge mace were gone, and the great sword in his right hand was dyed crimson. His mail, wrought with a forgotten art, now hung in shreds, and blood streamed from a hundred wounds on limbs, head and body. But his eyes still blazed with the battle-joy and his wearied arm still drove the mighty blade in strokes of death.

But Cormac saw that the end would come before they could reach him. Now at the very crest of the steep, a hedge of points menaced the strange king's life, and even his iron strength was ebbing. Now he split the skull of a huge warrior and the back-stroke shore through the neck-cords of another; reeling under a very rain of swords he struck again and his victim dropped at his feet, cleft to the breast-bone. Then, even as a dozen swords rose above the staggering Atlantean for the death stroke, a strange thing happened. The sun was sinking into the western sea; all the heather swam red like an ocean of blood. Etched in the dying sun, as he had first appeared, Kull stood, and then, like a mist lifting, a mighty vista opened behind the reeling king. Cormac's astounded eyes caught a fleeting gigantic glimpse of other climes and spheres – as if mirrored in summer clouds he saw, instead of the heather hills stretching away to the sea, a dim and mighty land of blue mountains and gleaming quiet lakes – the golden, purple and sapphirean spires and towering walls of a mighty city such as the earth has not known for many a drifting age.

Then like the fading of a mirage it was gone, but the Gauls on the high slope had dropped their weapons and stared like men dazed – *For the man called Kull had vanished and there was no trace of his going!*

As in a daze Cormac turned his steed and rode back across the trampled field. His horse's hoofs splashed in lakes of blood and clanged against the helmets of dead men. Across the valley the shout of victory was thundering. Yet all seemed shadowy and strange. A shape was striding across the torn corpses and Cormac was dully aware that it was Bran. The Gael swung from his horse and fronted the king. Bran was weaponless and gory; blood trickled from gashes on brow, breast and limb; what armor he had worn was clean hacked away and a cut had shorn half-way through his iron crown. But the red jewel still gleamed unblemished like a star of slaughter.

"It is in my mind to slay you," said the Gael heavily and like a man speaking in a daze, "for the blood of brave men is on your head. Had you given the signal to charge sooner, some would have lived."

Bran folded his arms; his eyes were haunted. "Strike if you will; I am sick of slaughter. It is a cold mead, this kinging it. A king must gamble with men's lives and naked swords. The lives of all my people were at stake; I sacrificed the Northmen – yes; and my heart is sore within me, for they were men! But had I given the order when you would have desired, all might have gone awry. The Romans were not yet massed in the narrow mouth of the gorge, and might have had time and space to form their ranks again and beat us off. I waited until the last moment – and the rovers died. A king belongs to his people, and can not let either his own feelings or the lives of men influence him. Now my people are saved; but my heart is cold in my breast."

Cormac wearily dropped his sword-point to the ground.

"You are a born king of men, Bran," said the Gaelic prince.

Bran's eyes roved the field. A mist of blood hovered over all, where the victorious barbarians were looting the dead, while those Romans who had escaped slaughter by throwing down their swords and now stood under guard, looked on with hot smoldering eyes.

"My kingdom – my people – are saved," said Bran wearily. "They will come from the heather by the thousands and when Rome moves against us again, she will meet a solid nation. But I am weary. What of Kull?"

"My eyes and brain were mazed with battle," answered Cormac. "I thought to see him vanish like a ghost into the sunset. I will seek his body."

"Seek not for him," said Bran. "Out of the sunrise he came – into the sunset he has gone. Out of the mists of the ages he came to us, and back into the mists of the eons has he returned – to his own kingdom."

Cormac turned away; night was gathering. Gonar stood like a white specter before him.

"To his own kingdom," echoed the wizard. "Time and Space are naught. Kull has returned to his own kingdom – his own crown – his own age."

"Then he was a ghost?"

"Did you not feel the grip of his solid hand? Did you not hear his voice – see him eat and drink, laugh and slay and bleed?"

Still Cormac stood like one in a trance.

"Then if it be possible for a man to pass from one age into one yet unborn, or come forth from a century dead and forgotten, whichever you will, with his flesh-and-blood body and his arms – then he is as mortal as he was in his own day. Is Kull dead, then?"

"He died a hundred thousand years ago, as men reckon time," answered the wizard, "but in his own age. He died not from the swords of the Gauls of this age. Have we not heard in legends how the king of Valusia traveled into a strange, timeless land of the misty future ages, and there fought in a great battle? Why, so he did! A hundred thousand years ago, or today!

"And a hundred thousand years ago – or a moment agone! – Kull, king of Valusia, roused himself on the silken couch in his secret chamber and laughing, spoke to the first Gonar, saying: 'Ha, wizard, I have in truth dreamed strangely, for I went into a far clime and a far time in my visions, and fought for the king of a strange shadow-people!' And the great sorcerer smiled and pointed silently at the red, notched sword, and the torn mail and the many wounds that the king carried. And Kull, fully woken from his 'vision' and feeling the sting and the weakness of these yet bleeding wounds, fell silent and mazed, and all life and time and space seemed like a dream of ghosts to him, and he wondered thereat all the rest of his life. For the wisdom of the Eternities is denied even unto princes and Kull could no more understand what Gonar told him than you can understand my words."

"And then Kull lived despite his many wounds," said Cormac, "and has returned to the mists of silence and the centuries. Well – he thought us a dream; we thought him a ghost. And sure, life is but a web spun of ghosts and dreams and illusion, and it is in my mind that the kingdom which has this day been born of swords and slaughter in this howling valley is a thing no more solid than the foam of the bright sea."

Recompense

I have not heard lutes beckon me, nor the brazen bugles call,
But once in the dim of a haunted lea I heard the silence fall.
I have not heard the regal drum, nor seen the flags unfurled,
But I have watched the dragons come, fire-eyed, across the world.

I have not seen the horsemen fall before the hurtling host,
But I have paced a silent hall where each step waked a ghost.
I have not kissed the tiger-feet of a strange-eyed golden god,
But I have walked a city's street where no man else had trod.

I have not raised the canopies that shelter revelling kings,
But I have fled from crimson eyes and black unearthly wings.
I have not knelt outside the door to kiss a pallid queen,
But I have seen a ghostly shore that no man else has seen.

I have not seen the standards sweep from keep and castle wall,
But I have seen a woman leap from a dragon's crimson stall,
And I have heard strange surges boom that no man heard before,
And seen a strange black city loom on a mystic night-black shore.

And I have felt the sudden blow of a nameless wind's cold breath,
And watched the grisly pilgrims go that walk the roads of Death,
And I have seen black valleys gape, abysses in the gloom,
And I have fought the deathless Ape that guards the Doors of Doom.

I have not seen the face of Pan, nor mocked the dryad's haste,
But I have trailed a dark-eyed Man across a windy waste.
I have not died as men may die, nor sinned as men have sinned,
But I have reached a misty sky upon a granite wind.

The Black Stone

They say foul beings of Old Times still lurk
In dark forgotten corners of the world,
And Gates still gape to loose, on certain nights,
Shapes pent in Hell.

                                    —*Justin Geoffrey*

I read of it first in the strange book of Von Junzt, the German eccentric who
lived so curiously and died in such grisly and mysterious fashion. It was my
fortune to have access to his *Nameless Cults* in the original edition, the so-
called Black Book, published in Düsseldorf in 1839, shortly before a hound-
ing doom overtook the author. Collectors of rare literature are familiar with
Nameless Cults mainly through the cheap and faulty translation which was
pirated in London by Bridewall in 1845, and the carefully expurgated edition
put out by the Golden Goblin Press of New York in 1909. But the volume I
stumbled upon was one of the unexpurgated German copies, with heavy
leather covers and rusty iron hasps. I doubt if there are more than half a
dozen such volumes in the entire world today, for the quantity issued was
not great, and when the manner of the author's demise was bruited about,
many possessors of the book burned their volumes in panic.

Von Junzt spent his entire life (1795–1840) delving into forbidden
subjects; he traveled in all parts of the world, gained entrance into innumer-

able secret societies, and read countless little-known and esoteric books and manuscripts in the original; and in the chapters of the Black Book, which range from startling clarity of exposition to murky ambiguity, there are statements and hints to freeze the blood of a thinking man. Reading what Von Junzt *dared* put in print arouses uneasy speculations as to what it was that he dared *not* tell. What dark matters, for instance, were contained in those closely written pages that formed the unpublished manuscript on which he worked unceasingly for months before his death, and which lay torn and scattered all over the floor of the locked and bolted chamber in which Von Junzt was found dead with the marks of taloned fingers on his throat? It will never be known, for the author's closest friend, the Frenchman Alexis Ladeau, after having spent a whole night piecing the fragments together and reading what was written, burnt them to ashes and cut his own throat with a razor.

But the contents of the published matter are shuddersome enough, even if one accepts the general view that they but represent the ravings of a madman. There among many strange things I found mention of the Black Stone, that curious, sinister monolith that broods among the mountains of Hungary, and about which so many dark legends cluster. Van Junzt did not devote much space to it – the bulk of his grim work concerns cults and objects of dark worship which he maintained existed in his day, and it would seem that the Black Stone represents some order or being lost and forgotten centuries ago. But he spoke of it as one of the *keys* – a phrase used many times by him, in various relations, and constituting one of the obscurities of his work. And he hinted briefly at curious sights to be seen about the monolith on Midsummer's Night. He mentioned Otto Dostmann's theory that this monolith was a remnant of the Hunnish invasion and had been erected to commemorate a victory of Attila over the Goths. Von Junzt contradicted this assertion without giving any refutory facts, merely remarking that to attribute the origin of the Black Stone to the Huns was as logical as assuming that William the Conqueror reared Stonehenge.

This implication of enormous antiquity piqued my interest immensely and after some difficulty I succeeded in locating a rat-eaten and moldering copy of Dostmann's *Remnants of Lost Empires* (Berlin, 1809, "Der Drachenhaus" Press). I was disappointed to find that Dostmann referred to the Black Stone even more briefly than had Von Junzt, dismissing it with a few lines as an artifact comparatively modern in contrast with the Greco-Roman ruins of Asia Minor which were his pet theme. He admitted his inability to make out the defaced characters on the monolith but pronounced them unmistakably Mongoloid. However, little as I learned from Dostmann, he did mention the name of the village adjacent to the Black Stone – Stregoicavar – an ominous name, meaning something like Witch-Town.

A close scrutiny of guide-books and travel articles gave me no further information – Stregoicavar, not on any map that I could find, lay in a wild, little-frequented region, out of the path of casual tourists. But I did find subject for thought in Dornly's *Magyar Folklore*. In his chapter on *Dream Myths* he mentions the Black Stone and tells of some curious superstitions regarding it – especially the belief that if any one sleeps in the vicinity of the monolith, that person will be haunted by monstrous nightmares for ever after; and he cited tales of the peasants regarding too-curious people who ventured to visit the Stone on Midsummer Night and who died raving mad because of *something* they saw there.

That was all I could glean from Dornly, but my interest was even more intensely roused as I sensed a distinctly sinister aura about the Stone. The suggestion of dark antiquity, the recurrent hint of unnatural events on Midsummer Night, touched some slumbering instinct in my being, as one senses, rather than hears, the flowing of some dark subterraneous river in the night.

And I suddenly saw a connection between this Stone and a certain weird and fantastic poem written by the mad poet, Justin Geoffrey: *The People of the Monolith*. Inquiries led to the information that Geoffrey had indeed written that poem while traveling in Hungary, and I could not doubt that the Black Stone was the very monolith to which he referred in his strange verse. Reading his stanzas again, I felt once more the strange dim stirrings of subconscious promptings that I had noticed when first reading of the Stone.

I had been casting about for a place to spend a short vacation and I made up my mind. I went to Stregoicavar. A train of obsolete style carried me from Temesvar to within striking distance, at least, of my objective, and a three days' ride in a jouncing coach brought me to the little village which lay in a fertile valley high up in the fir-clad mountains. The journey itself was uneventful, but during the first day we passed the old battlefield of Schomvaal where the brave Polish-Hungarian knight, Count Boris Vladinoff, made his gallant and futile stand against the victorious hosts of Suleiman the Magnificent, when the Grand Turk swept over eastern Europe in 1526.

The driver of the coach pointed out to me a great heap of crumbling stones on a hill near by, under which, he said, the bones of the brave Count lay. I remembered a passage from Larson's *Turkish Wars*: "After the skirmish" (in which the Count with his small army had beaten back the Turkish advance-guard) "the Count was standing beneath the half-ruined walls of the old castle on the hill, giving orders as to the disposition of his forces, when an aide brought to him a small lacquered case which had been taken from the body of the famous Turkish scribe and historian, Selim Bahadur, who had fallen in the fight. The Count took therefrom a roll of parchment and began to read, but he had not read far before he turned very pale and, without saying a word, replaced the parchment in the case and thrust the case into his cloak. At that very instant a hidden Turkish battery suddenly opened fire, and the balls striking the old castle, the Hungarians were horrified to see the walls crash down in ruin, completely covering the brave Count. Without a leader the gallant little army was cut to pieces, and in the war-swept years which followed, the bones of the noblemen were never recovered. Today the natives point out a huge and moldering pile of ruins near Schomvaal beneath which, they say, still rests all that the centuries have left of Count Boris Vladinoff."

I found the village of Stregoicavar a dreamy, drowsy little village that apparently belied its sinister cognomen – a forgotten back-eddy that Progress had passed by. The quaint houses and the quainter dress and manners of the people were those of an earlier century. They were

friendly, mildly curious but not inquisitive, though visitors from the outside world were extremely rare.

"Ten years ago another American came here and stayed a few days in the village," said the owner of the tavern where I had put up, "a young fellow and queer-acting – mumbled to himself – a poet, I think."

I knew he must mean Justin Geoffrey.

"Yes, he was a poet," I answered, "and he wrote a poem about a bit of scenery near this very village."

"Indeed?" Mine host's interest was aroused. "Then, since all great poets are strange in their speech and actions, he must have achieved great fame, for his actions and conversations were the strangest of any man I ever knew."

"As is usual with artists," I answered, "most of his recognition has come since his death."

"He is dead, then?"

"He died screaming in a madhouse five years ago."

"Too bad, too bad," sighed mine host sympathetically. "Poor lad – he looked too long at the Black Stone."

My heart gave a leap, but I masked my keen interest and said casually: "I have heard something of this Black Stone; somewhere near this village, is it not?"

"Nearer than Christian folk wish," he responded. "Look!" He drew me to a latticed window and pointed up at the fir-clad slopes of the brooding blue mountains. "There beyond where you see the bare face of that jutting cliff stands that accursed Stone. Would that it were ground to powder and the powder flung into the Danube to be carried to the deepest ocean! Once men tried to destroy the thing, but each man who laid hammer or maul against it came to an evil end. So now the people shun it."

"What is there so evil about it?" I asked curiously.

"It is a demon-haunted thing," he answered uneasily and with the suggestion of a shudder. "In my childhood I knew a young man who came up from below and laughed at our traditions – in his foolhardiness he went to the Stone one Midsummer Night and at dawn stumbled into the village again, stricken dumb and mad. Something had shattered his brain and sealed his lips, for until the day of his death, which came soon after, he spoke only to utter terrible blasphemies or to slaver gibberish.

"My own nephew when very small was lost in the mountains and slept in the woods near the Stone, and now in his manhood he is tortured by foul dreams, so that at times he makes the night hideous with his screams and wakes with cold sweat upon him.

"But let us talk of something else, *Herr*; it is not good to dwell upon such things."

I remarked on the evident age of the tavern and he answered with pride: "The foundations are more than four hundred years old; the original house was the only one in the village which was not burned to the ground when Suleiman's devils swept through the mountains. Here, in the house that then stood on these same foundations, it is said, the scribe Selim Bahadur had his headquarters while ravaging the country hereabouts."

I learned then that the present inhabitants of Stregoicavar are not descendants of the people who dwelt there before the Turkish raid of 1526. The victorious Moslems left no living human in the village or the vicinity thereabouts when they passed over. Men, women and children they wiped out in one red holocaust of murder, leaving a vast stretch of country silent and utterly deserted. The present people of Stregoicavar are descended from hardy settlers from the lower valleys who came into the upper levels and rebuilt the ruined village after the Turk was thrust back.

Mine host did not speak of the extermination of the original inhabitants with any great resentment and I learned that his ancestors in the lower levels had looked on the mountaineers with even more hatred and aversion than they regarded the Turks. He was rather vague regarding the causes of this feud, but said that the original inhabitants of Stregoicavar had been in the habit of making stealthy raids on the lowlands and stealing girls and children. Moreover, he said that they were not exactly of the same blood as his own people; the sturdy, original Magyar-Slavic stock had mixed and intermarried with a degraded aboriginal race until the breeds had blended, producing an unsavory amalgamation. Who these aborigines were, he had not the slightest idea, but maintained that they were "pagans" and had dwelt in the mountains since time immemorial, before the coming of the conquering peoples.

I attached little importance to this tale; seeing in it merely a parallel to the amalgamation of Celtic tribes with Mediterranean aborigines in the Galloway hills, with the resultant mixed race which, as Picts, has such an extensive part in Scotch legendry. Time has a curiously foreshortening effect on folklore, and just as tales of the Picts became intertwined with legends of an older Mongoloid race, so that eventually the Picts were ascribed the repulsive appearance of the squat primitives, whose individuality merged, in the telling, into Pictish tales, and was forgotten; so, I felt, the supposed inhuman attributes of the first villagers of Stregoicavar could be traced to older, outworn myths with invading Huns and Mongols.

The morning after my arrival I received directions from my host, who gave them worriedly, and set out to find the Black Stone. A few hours' tramp up the fir-covered slopes brought me to the face of the rugged, solid stone cliff which jutted boldly from the mountainside. A narrow trail wound up it, and mounting this, I looked out over the peaceful valley of Stregoicavar, which seemed to drowse, guarded on either hand by the great blue mountains. No huts or any sign of human tenancy showed between the cliff whereon I stood and the village. I saw numbers of scattering farms in the valley but all lay on the other side of Stregoicavar, which itself seemed to shrink from the brooding slopes which masked the Black Stone.

The summit of the cliffs proved to be a sort of thickly wooded plateau. I made my way through the dense growth for a short distance and came into a wide glade; and in the center of the glade reared a gaunt figure of black stone.

It was octagonal in shape, some sixteen feet in height and about a foot and a half thick. It had once evidently been highly polished, but now the surface was thickly dinted as if savage efforts had been made to demolish it; but the hammers had done little more than to flake off small bits of stone and mutilate the characters which once had evidently marched in a spiraling line round and round the shaft to the top. Up to ten feet from the base these characters were almost completely blotted out, so that it was very difficult to trace their direction. Higher up they were plainer, and I managed to squirm part of the way up the shaft and scan them at close range. All were more or less defaced, but I was positive that they symbolized no language now remembered on the face of the earth. I am fairly familiar with all hieroglyphics known to researchers and philologists and I can say with certainty that those characters were like nothing of which I have ever read or heard. The nearest approach to them that I ever saw were some crude scratches on a gigantic and strangely symmetrical rock in a lost valley of Yucatan. I remember that when I pointed out these marks to the archeologist who was my companion, he maintained that they either represented natural weathering or the idle scratching of some Indian. To my theory that the rock was really the base of a long-vanished column, he merely laughed, calling my attention to the dimensions of it, which suggested, if it were built with any natural rules of architectural symmetry, a column a thousand feet high. But I was not convinced.

I will not say that the characters on the Black Stone were similar to those on that colossal rock in Yucatan; but one suggested the other. As to the substance of the monolith, again I was baffled. The stone of which it was composed was a dully gleaming black, whose surface, where it was not dinted and roughened, created a curious illusion of semi-transparency.

I spent most of the morning there and came away baffled. No connection of the Stone with any other artifact in the world suggested itself to me. It was as if the monolith had been reared by alien hands, in an age distant and apart from human ken.

I returned to the village with my interest in no way abated. Now that I had seen the curious thing, my desire was still more keenly whetted to investigate the matter further and seek to learn by what strange hands and for what strange purpose the Black Stone had been reared in the long ago.

I sought out the tavern-keeper's nephew and questioned him in regard to his dreams, but he was vague, though willing to oblige. He did not mind discussing them, but was unable to describe them with any clarity. Though he dreamed the same dreams repeatedly, and though they were hideously vivid at the time, they left no distinct impression on his waking mind. He remembered them only as chaotic nightmares through which huge whirling fires shot lurid tongues of flame and a black drum bellowed incessantly. One thing only he clearly remembered—in one dream he had seen the Black Stone, not on a mountain slope but set like a spire on a colossal black castle.

As for the rest of the villagers I found them not inclined to talk about the Stone, with the exception of the schoolmaster, a man of surprizing education, who spent much more of his time out in the world than any of the rest.

He was much interested in what I told him of Von Junzt's remarks about the Stone, and warmly agreed with the German author in the alleged age of the monolith. He believed that a coven had once existed in the vicinity and that possibly all of the original villagers had been members of that fertility cult which once threatened to undermine European civilization and gave rise to the tales of witchcraft. He cited the very name of the village to prove his point; it had not been originally named Stregoicavar, he said; according to legends the builders had called it Xuthltan, which was the aboriginal name of the site on which the village had been built many centuries ago.

This fact roused again an indescribable feeling of uneasiness. The barbarous name did not suggest connection with any Scythic, Slavic or Mongolian race to which an aboriginal people of these mountains would, under natural circumstances, have belonged.

That the Magyars and Slavs of the lower valleys believed the original inhabitants of the village to be members of the witchcraft cult was evident, the schoolmaster said, by the name they gave it, which name continued to be used even after the older settlers had been massacred by the Turks, and the village rebuilt by a cleaner and more wholesome breed.

He did not believe that the members of the cult erected the monolith but he did believe that they used it as a center of their activities, and repeating vague legends which had been handed down since before the Turkish invasion, he advanced the theory that the degenerate villagers had used it as a sort of altar on which they offered human sacrifices, using as victims the girls and babies stolen from his own ancestors in the lower valleys.

He discounted the myths of weird events on Midsummer Night, as well as a curious legend of a strange deity which the witch-people of Xuthltan were said to have invoked with chants and wild rituals of flagellation and slaughter.

He had never visited the Stone on Midsummer Night, he said, but he would not fear to do so; whatever *had* existed or taken place there in the past, had been long engulfed in the mists of time and oblivion. The Black Stone had lost its meaning save as a link to a dead and dusty past.

It was while returning from a visit with this schoolmaster one night about a week after my arrival at Stregoicavar that a sudden recollection struck me – it was Midsummer Night! The very time that the legends linked with grisly implications to the Black Stone. I turned away from the tavern and strode swiftly through the village. Stregoicavar lay silent; the villagers retired early. I saw no one as I passed rapidly out of the village and up into the firs which masked the mountain slopes with whispering darkness. A broad silver moon hung above the valley, flooding the crags and slopes in a weird light and etching the shadows blackly. No wind blew through the firs, but a mysterious, intangible rustling and whispering was abroad. Surely on such nights in past centuries, my whimsical imagination told me, naked witches astride magic broomsticks had flown across this valley, pursued by jeering demoniac familiars.

I came to the cliffs and was somewhat disquieted to note that the illusive moonlight lent them a subtle appearance I had not noticed before – in the weird light they appeared less like natural cliffs and more like the ruins of cyclopean and Titan-reared battlements jutting from the mountain-slope.

Shaking off this hallucination with difficulty I came upon the plateau and hesitated a moment before I plunged into the brooding darkness of the woods. A sort of breathless tenseness hung over the shadows, like an unseen monster holding its breath lest it scare away its prey.

I shook off the sensation – a natural one, considering the eeriness of the place and its evil reputation – and made my way through the wood, experiencing a most unpleasant sensation that I was being followed, and halting once, sure that something clammy and unstable had brushed against my face in the darkness.

I came out into the glade and saw the tall monolith rearing its gaunt height above the sward. At the edge of the woods on the side toward the cliffs was a stone which formed a sort of natural seat. I sat down, reflecting that it was probably while there that the mad poet, Justin Geoffrey, had written his fantastic *People of the Monolith*. Mine host thought that it was the Stone which had caused Geoffrey's insanity, but the seeds of madness had been sown in the poet's brain long before he ever came to Stregoicavar.

A glance at my watch showed that the hour of midnight was close at hand. I leaned back, waiting whatever ghostly demonstration might appear. A thin night wind started up among the branches of the firs, with an uncanny suggestion of faint, unseen pipes whispering an eery and evil tune. The monotony of the sound and my steady gazing at the monolith produced a sort of self-hypnosis upon me; I grew drowsy. I fought this feeling, but sleep stole on me in spite of myself; the monolith seemed to sway and dance, strangely distorted to my gaze, and then I slept.

I opened my eyes and sought to rise, but lay still, as if an icy hand gripped me helpless. Cold terror stole over me. The glade was no longer deserted. It was thronged by a silent crowd of strange people, and my distended eyes took in strange barbaric details of costume which my reason told me were archaic and forgotten even in this backward land. Surely, I thought, these are villagers who have come here to hold some fantastic conclave – but another glance told me that these people were not of the folk of Stregoicavar. They were a shorter, more squat race, whose brows were lower, whose faces were broader and duller. Some had Slavic or Magyar features, but those features were degraded as from a mixture of some baser, alien strain I could not classify. Many wore the hides of wild beasts, and their whole appearance, both men and women, was one of sensual brutishness. They terrified and repelled me, but they gave me no heed. They formed in a vast half-circle in front of the monolith and began a sort of chant, flinging their arms in unison and weaving their bodies rhythmically from the waist upward. All eyes were fixed on the top of the Stone which they seemed to be invoking. But the strangest of all was the dimness of their voices; not fifty yards from me hundreds of men and women were unmistakably lifting their voices in a wild chant, yet those voices came to me as a faint indistinguishable murmur as if from across vast leagues of Space – or *time*.

Before the monolith stood a sort of brazier from which a vile, nauseous yellow smoke billowed upward, curling curiously in an undulating spiral around the black shaft, like a vast unstable serpent.

On one side of this brazier lay two figures – a young girl, stark naked and bound hand and foot, and an infant, apparently only a few months old. On the other side of the brazier squatted a hideous old hag with a queer sort of black drum on her lap; this drum she beat with slow, light blows of her open palms, but I could not hear the sound.

The rhythm of the swaying bodies grew faster and into the space between the people and the monolith sprang a naked young woman, her eyes blazing, her long black hair flying loose. Spinning dizzily on her toes, she whirled across the open space and fell prostrate before the Stone, where she lay motionless. The next instant a fantastic figure followed her – a man from whose waist hung a goatskin, and whose features were entirely hidden by a sort of mask made from a huge wolf's head, so that he looked like a monstrous, nightmare being, horribly compounded of elements both human and bestial. In his hand he held a bunch of long fir switches bound together at the larger ends, and the moonlight glinted on a chain of heavy gold looped about his neck. A smaller chain depending from it suggested a pendant of some sort, but this was missing.

The people tossed their arms violently and seemed to redouble their shouts as this grotesque creature loped across the open space with many a fantastic leap and caper. Coming to the woman who lay before the monolith, he began to lash her with the switches he bore, and she leaped up and spun into the wild mazes of the most incredible dance I have ever seen. And her tormentor danced with her, keeping the wild rhythm, matching her every whirl and bound, while incessantly raining cruel blows on her naked body. And at every blow he shouted a single word, over and over, and all the people shouted it back. I could see the working of their lips, and now the faint far-off murmur of their voices merged and blended into one distant shout, repeated over and over with slobbering ecstasy. But what that one word was, I could not make out.

In dizzy whirls spun the wild dancers, while the lookers-on, standing still in their tracks, followed the rhythm of their dance with swaying bodies and weaving arms. Madness grew in the eyes of the capering votaress and was reflected in the eyes of the watchers. Wilder and more extravagant grew the whirling frenzy of that mad dance – it became a bestial and obscene thing, while the old hag howled and battered the drum like a crazy woman, and the switches cracked out a devil's tune.

Blood trickled down the dancer's limbs but she seemed not to feel the lashing save as a stimulus for further enormities of outrageous motion; bounding into the midst of the yellow smoke which now spread out tenuous tentacles to embrace both flying figures, she seemed to merge with that foul fog and veil herself with it. Then emerging into plain view, closely followed by the beast-thing that flogged her, she shot into an indescribable, explosive burst of dynamic mad motion, and on the very crest of that mad wave, she dropped suddenly to the sward, quivering and panting as if completely overcome by her frenzied exertions. The lashing continued with unabated violence and intensity and she began to wriggle toward the monolith on her belly. The priest – or such I will call him – followed, lashing her unprotected body with all the power of his arm as she writhed along, leaving a heavy track of blood on the trampled earth. She reached the monolith, and gasping and panting, flung both arms about it and covered the cold stone with fierce hot kisses, as in frenzied and unholy adoration.

The fantastic priest bounded high in the air, flinging away the red-dabbled switches, and the worshippers, howling and foaming at the mouths, turned on each other with tooth and nail, rending one another's garments and flesh in a blind passion of bestiality. The priest swept up the infant with a long arm, and shouting again that Name, whirled the wailing babe high in the air and dashed its brains out against the monolith, leaving a ghastly stain on the black surface. Cold with horror I saw him rip the tiny body open with his bare brutish fingers and fling handfuls of blood on the shaft, then toss the red and torn shape into the brazier, extinguishing flame and smoke in a crimson rain, while the maddened brutes behind him howled over and over that Name. Then suddenly they all fell prostrate, writhing like snakes, while the priest flung wide his gory hands as in triumph. I opened my mouth to scream my horror and loathing, but only a dry rattle sounded; a huge monstrous toad-like *thing* squatted on the top of the monolith!

I saw its bloated, repulsive and unstable outline against the moonlight, and set in what would have been the face of a natural creature, its huge, blinking eyes which reflected all the lust, abysmal greed, obscene cruelty and monstrous evil that has stalked the sons of men since their ancestors mowed blind and hairless in the tree-tops. In those grisly eyes were mirrored all the unholy things and vile secrets that sleep in the cities under the sea, and that skulk from the light of day in the blackness of primordial caverns. And so that ghastly thing that the unhallowed ritual of cruelty and sadism and blood had evoked from the silence of the hills, leered and blinked down on its bestial worshippers, who groveled in abhorrent abasement before it.

Now the beast-masked priest lifted the bound and weakly writhing girl in his brutish hands and held her up toward that horror on the monolith. And as that monstrosity sucked in its breath, lustfully and slobberingly, something snapped in my brain and I fell into a merciful faint.

I opened my eyes on a still white dawn. All the events of the night rushed back on me and I sprang up, then stared about me in amazement. The monolith brooded gaunt and silent above the sward which waved, green and untrampled, in the morning breeze. A few quick strides took me across the glade; here had the dancers leaped and bounded until the ground should have been trampled bare, and here had the votaress wriggled her painful way to the Stone, streaming blood on the earth. But no drop of crimson showed on the uncrushed sward. I looked, shudderingly, at the side of the monolith against which the bestial priest had brained the stolen baby – but no dark stain nor grisly clot showed there.

A dream! It had been a wild nightmare – or else – I shrugged my shoulders. What vivid clarity for a dream!

I returned quietly to the village and entered the inn without being seen. And there I sat meditating over the strange events of the night. More and more was I prone to discard the dream-theory. That what I had seen was illusion and without material substance, was evident. But I believed that I had looked on the mirrored shadow of a deed perpetrated in ghastly actuality in bygone days. But how was I to know? What proof to show that my vision had been a gathering of foul specters rather than a mere nightmare originating in my own brain?

As if for answer a name flashed into my mind – Selim Bahadur! According to legend this man, who had been a soldier as well as a scribe, had commanded that part of Suleiman's army which had devastated Stregoicavar; it seemed logical enough; and if so, he had gone straight from the blotted-out countryside to the bloody field of Schomvaal, and his doom. I sprang up with a sudden shout – that manuscript which was taken from the Turk's body, and which Count Boris shuddered over – might it not contain some narration of what the conquering Turks found in Stregoicavar? What else could have shaken the iron nerves of the Polish adventurer? And since the bones of the Count had never been recovered, what more certain than that the lacquered case, with its mysterious contents, still lay hidden beneath the ruins that covered Boris Vladinoff? I began packing my bag with fierce haste.

Three days later found me ensconced in a little village a few miles from the old battlefield, and when the moon rose I was working with savage intensity on the great pile of crumbling stone that crowned the hill. It was back-breaking toil – looking back now I cannot see how I accomplished it, though I labored without a pause from moonrise to dawn. Just as the sun was coming up I tore aside the last tangle of stones and looked on all that was mortal of Count Boris Vladinoff – only a few pitiful fragments of crumbling bone – and among them, crushed out of all original shape, lay a case whose lacquered surface had kept it from complete decay through the centuries.

I seized it with frenzied eagerness, and piling back some of the stones on the bones I hurried away; for I did not care to be discovered by the suspicious peasants in an act of apparent desecration.

Back in my tavern chamber I opened the case and found the parchment comparatively intact; and there was something else in the case – a small squat object wrapped in silk. I was wild to plumb the secrets of those yellowed pages, but weariness forbade me. Since leaving Stregoicavar I had hardly slept at all, and the terrific exertions of the previous night combined to overcome me. In spite of myself I was forced to stretch myself on my bed, nor did I awake until sundown.

I snatched a hasty supper, and then in the light of a flickering candle, I set myself to read the neat Turkish characters that covered the parchment. It was difficult work, for I am not deeply versed in the language and the archaic style of the narrative baffled me. But as I toiled through it a word or a phrase here and there leaped at me and a dimly growing horror shook me in its grip. I bent my energies fiercely to the task, and as the tale grew clearer and took more tangible form my blood chilled in my veins, my hair stood up and my tongue clove to my mouth. All external things partook of the grisly madness of that infernal manuscript until the night sounds of insects and creatures in the woods took the form of ghastly murmurings and stealthy treadings of ghoulish horrors and the sighing of the night wind changed to tittering obscene gloating of evil over the souls of men.

At last when gray dawn was stealing through the latticed window, I laid down the manuscript and took up and unwrapped the thing in the bit of silk. Staring at it with haggard eyes I knew the truth of the matter was clinched, even had it been possible to doubt the veracity of that terrible manuscript.

And I replaced both obscene things in the case, nor did I rest or sleep or eat until that case containing them had been weighted with stones and flung into the deepest current of the Danube which, God grant, carried them back into the Hell from which they came.

It was no dream I dreamed on Midsummer Midnight in the hills above Stregoicavar. Well for Justin Geoffrey that he tarried there only in the sunlight and went his way, for had he gazed upon that ghastly conclave, his mad brain would have snapped before it did. How my own reason held, I do not know.

No – it was no dream – I gazed upon a foul rout of votaries long dead, come up from Hell to worship as of old; ghosts that bowed before a ghost.

For Hell has long claimed their hideous god. Long, long he dwelt among the hills, a brain-shattering vestige of an outworn age, but no longer his obscene talons clutch for the souls of living men, and his kingdom is a dead kingdom, peopled only by the ghosts of those who served him in his lifetime and theirs.

By what foul alchemy or godless sorcery the Gates of Hell are opened on that one eery night I do not know, but mine own eyes have seen. And I know I looked on no living thing that night, for the manuscript written in the careful hand of Selim Bahadur narrated at length what he and his raiders found in the valley of Stregoicavar; and I read, set down in detail, the blasphemous obscenities that torture wrung from the lips of screaming worshippers; and I read, too, of the lost, grim black cavern high in the hills where the horrified Turks hemmed a monstrous, bloated, wallowing toad-like being and slew it with flame and ancient steel blessed in old times by Muhammad, and with incantations that were old when Arabia was young. And even staunch old Selim's hand shook as he recorded the cataclysmic, earth-shaking death-howls of the monstrosity, which died not alone; for a half-score of his slayers perished with him, in ways that Selim would not or could not describe.

And that squat idol carved of gold and wrapped in silk was an image of *himself*, and Selim tore it from the golden chain that looped the neck of the slain high priest of the mask.

Well that the Turks swept that foul valley with torch and cleanly steel! Such sights as those brooding mountains have looked on belong to the darkness and abysses of lost eons. No – it is not fear of the toad-thing that makes me shudder in the night. He is made fast in Hell with his nauseous horde, freed only for an hour on the most weird night of the year, as I have seen. And of his worshippers, none remains.

But it is the realization that such things once crouched beast-like above the souls of men which brings cold sweat to my brow; and I fear to peer again into the leaves of Von Junzt's abomination. For now I understand his repeated phrase of *keys*! – aye! Keys to Outer Doors – links with an abhorrent past and – who knows? – of abhorrent spheres of the *present*. And I understand why the cliffs look like battlements in the moonlight and why the tavern-keeper's nightmare-haunted nephew saw in his dream, the Black Stone like a spire on a cyclopean black castle. If men ever excavate among those mountains they may find incredible things below those masking slopes. For the cave wherein the Turks trapped the – *thing* – was not truly a cavern, and I shudder to contemplate the gigantic gulf of eons which must stretch between this age and the time when the earth shook herself and reared up, like a wave, those blue mountains that, rising, enveloped unthinkable things. May no man ever seek to uproot that ghastly spire men call the Black Stone!

A Key! Aye, it is a Key, symbol of a forgotten horror. That horror has faded into the limbo from which it crawled, loathsomely, in the black dawn of the earth. But what of the other fiendish possibilities hinted at by Von Junzt – what of the monstrous hand which strangled out his life? Since reading what Selim Bahadur wrote, I can no longer doubt anything in the Black Book. Man was not always master of the earth – *and is he now?*

And the thought recurs to me – if such a monstrous entity as the Master of the Monolith somehow survived its own unspeakably distant epoch so long – *what nameless shapes may even now lurk in the dark places of the world?*

The Song of a Mad Minstrel

I am the thorn in the foot, I am the blur in the sight;
I am the worm at the root, I am the thief in the night.
I am the rat in the wall, the leper that leers at the gate;
I am the ghost in the hall, herald of horror and hate.

I am the rust on the corn, I am the smut on the wheat,
Laughing man's labor to scorn, weaving a web for his feet.
I am canker and mildew and blight, danger and death and decay;
The rot of the rain by night, the blast of the sun by day.

I warp and wither with drouth, I work in the swamp's foul yeast;
I bring the black plague from the south and the leprosy in from the east.
I rend from the hemlock boughs wine steeped in the petals of dooms;
Where the fat black serpents drowse I gather the Upas blooms.

I have plumbed the northern ice for a spell like frozen lead;
In lost gray fields of rice, I have learned from Mongol dead.
Where a bleak black mountain stands I have looted grisly caves;
I have digged in the desert sands to plunder terrible graves.

Never the sun goes forth, never the moon glows red,
But out of the south or the north, I come with the slavering dead.
I come with hideous spells, black chants and ghastly tunes;
I have looted the hidden hells and plundered the lost black moons.

There was never a king or priest to cheer me by word or look,
There was never a man or beast in the blood-black ways I took.
There were crimson gulfs unplumbed, there were black wings over a sea;
There were pits where mad things drummed, and foaming blasphemy.

There were vast ungodly tombs where slimy monsters dreamed;
There were clouds like blood-drenched plumes where unborn
   demons screamed.
There were ages dead to Time, and lands lost out of Space;
There were adders in the slime, and a dim unholy Face.

Oh, the heart in my breast turned stone, and the brain froze in my skull —
But I won through, I alone, and poured my chalice full
Of horrors and dooms and spells, black buds and bitter roots —
From the hells beneath the hells, I bring you my deathly fruits.

The Fightin'est Pair

Me and my white bulldog Mike was peaceably taking our beer in a joint on the waterfront when Porkey Straus come piling in, plumb puffing with excitement.

"Hey, Steve!" he yelped. "What you think? Joe Ritchie's in port with Terror."

"Well?" I said.

"Well, gee whiz," he said, "you mean to set there and let on like you don't know nothin' about Terror, Ritchie's fightin' brindle bull? Why, he's the pit champeen of the Asiatics. He's killed more fightin' dogs than –"

"Yeah, yeah," I said impatiently. "I know all about him. I been listenin' to what a bear-cat he is for the last year, in every Asiatic port I've touched."

"Well," said Porkey, "I'm afraid we ain't goin' to git to see him perform."

"Why not?" asked Johnnie Blinn, a shifty-eyed bar-keep.

"Well," said Porkey, "they ain't a dog in Singapore to match ag'in' him. Fritz Steinmann, which owns the pit and runs the dog fights, has scoured the port and they just ain't no canine which their owners'll risk ag'in' Terror. Just my luck. The chance of a lifetime to see the fightin'est dog of 'em all perform. And they's no first-class mutt to toss in with him. Say, Steve, why don't you let Mike fight him?"

"Not a chance," I growled. "Mike gets plenty of scrappin' on the streets. Besides, I'll tell you straight, I think dog fightin' for money is a dirty low-down game. Take a couple of fine, upstandin' dogs, full of ginger and fightin' heart, and throw 'em in a concrete pit to tear each other's throats out, just so a bunch of four-flushin' tin-horns like you, which couldn't take a punch or give one either, can make a few lousy dollars bettin' on 'em."

"But they likes to fight," argued Porkey. "It's their nature."

"It's the nature of any red-blooded critter to fight. Man or dog," I said. "Let 'em fight on the streets, for bones or for fun, or just to see which is the best dog. But pit-fightin' to the death is just too dirty for me to fool with, and I ain't goin' to get Mike into no such mess."

"Aw, let him alone, Porkey," sneered Johnnie Blinn nastily. "He's too chicken-hearted to mix in them rough games. Ain't you, Sailor?"

"Belay that," I roared. "You keep a civil tongue in your head, you wharfside rat. I never did like you nohow, and one more crack like that gets you this." I brandished my huge fist at him and he turned pale and started scrubbing the bar like he was trying for a record.

"I wantcha to know that Mike can lick this Terror mutt," I said, glaring at Porkey. "I'm fed up hearin' fellers braggin' on that brindle murderer. Mike can lick him. He can lick any dog in this lousy port, just like I can lick any man here. If Terror meets Mike on the street and gets fresh, he'll get his belly-full. But Mike ain't goin' to get mixed up in no dirty racket like Fritz Steinmann runs and you can lay to that." I made the last statement in a voice like a irritated bull, and smashed my fist down on the table so hard I splintered the wood, and made the decanters bounce on the bar.

"Sure, sure, Steve," soothed Porkey, pouring hisself a drink with a shaky hand. "No offense. No offense. Well, I gotta be goin'."

"So long," I growled, and Porkey cruised off.

Up strolled a man which had been standing by the bar. I knowed him – Philip D'Arcy, a man whose name is well known in all parts of the world. He was a tall, slim, athletic fellow, well dressed, with cold gray eyes and a steel-trap jaw. He was one of them gentleman adventurers, as they call 'em, and he'd did everything from running a revolution in South America and flying a war plane in a Balkan brawl, to exploring in the Congo. He was deadly with a six-gun, and as dangerous as a rattler when somebody crossed him.

"That's a fine dog you have, Costigan," he said. "Clean white. Not a speck of any other color about him. That means good luck for his owner."

I knowed that D'Arcy had some pet superstitions of his own, like lots of men which live by their hands and wits like him.

"Well," I said, "anyway, he's about the fightin'est dog you ever seen."

"I can tell that," he said, stooping and eying Mike close. "Powerful jaws – not too undershot – good teeth – broad between the eyes – deep chest – legs that brace like iron. Costigan, I'll give you a hundred dollars for him, just as he stands."

140

"You mean you want me to sell you Mike?" I asked kinda incredulous.
"Sure. Why not?"

"Why not!" I repeated indignantly. "Well, gee whiz, why not ask a man to sell his brother for a hundred dollars? Mike wouldn't stand for it. Anyway, I wouldn't do it."

"I need him," persisted D'Arcy. "A white dog with a dark man – it means luck. White dogs have always been lucky for me. And my luck's been running against me lately. I'll give you a hundred and fifty."

"D'Arcy," I said, "you couldst stand there and offer me money all day long and raise the ante every hand, but it wouldn't be no good. Mike ain't for sale. Him and me has knocked around the world together too long. They ain't no use talkin'."

His eyes flashed for a second. He didn't like to be crossed in any way. Then he shrugged his shoulders.

"All right. We'll forget it. I don't blame you for thinking a lot of him. Let's have a drink."

So we did and he left.

I went and got me a shave, because I was matched to fight some tramp at Ace Larnigan's Arena and I wanted to be in shape for the brawl. Well, afterwards I was walking down along the docks when I heard somebody go: "Hssst!"

I looked around and saw a yellow hand beckon me from behind a stack of crates. I sauntered over, wondering what it was all about, and there was a Chinese boy hiding there. He put his finger to his lips. Then quick he handed me a folded piece of paper, and beat it, before I couldst ask him anything.

I opened the paper and it was a note in a woman's handwriting which read: "Dear Steve, I have admired you for a long time at a distance, but have been too timid to make myself known to you. Would it be too much to ask you to give me an opportunity to tell you my emotions by word of mouth? If you care at all, I will meet you by the old Manchu House on the Tungen Road, just after dark. An affectionate admirer. P.S. Please, oh please be there! You have stole my heart away!"

"Mike," I said pensively, "ain't it plumb peculiar the strange power I got over wimmen, even them I ain't never seen? Here is a girl I don't even know the name of, even, and she has been eatin' her poor little heart out in solitude because of me. Well – " I hove a gentle sigh – "it's a fatal gift, I'm afeared."

Mike yawned. Sometimes it looks like he ain't got no romance at all about him. I went back to the barber shop and had the barber to put some ile on my hair and douse me with perfume. I always like to look genteel when I meet a feminine admirer.

Then, as the evening was waxing away, as the poets say, I set forth for the narrow winding back street just off the waterfront proper. The natives call it the Tungen Road, for no particular reason as I can see. The lamps there is few and far between and generally dirty and dim. The street's lined on both sides by lousy looking native shops and hovels. You'll come to stretches which looks clean deserted and falling to ruins.

Well, me and Mike was passing through just such a district when I heard sounds of some kind of a fracas in a dark alley-way we was passing. Feet scruffed. They was the sound of a blow and a voice yelled in English: "Halp! Halp! These Chinese is killin' me!"

"Hold everything," I roared, jerking up my sleeves and plunging for the alley, with Mike at my heels. "Steve Costigan is on the job."

It was as dark as a stack of black cats in that alley. Plunging blind, I bumped into somebody and sunk a fist to the wrist in him. He gasped and fell away. I heard Mike roar suddenly and somebody howled bloody murder. Then wham! A blackjack or something like it smashed on my skull and I went to my knees.

"That's done yer, yer blawsted Yank," said a nasty voice in the dark.

"You're a liar," I gasped, coming up blind and groggy but hitting out wild and ferocious. One of my blind licks musta connected because I heard somebody cuss bitterly. And then wham, again come that blackjack on my dome. What little light they was, was behind me, and whoever it was slugging me, couldst see me better'n I could see him. That last smash put me down for the count, and he musta hit me again as I fell.

I couldn't of been out but a few minutes. I come to myself lying in the darkness and filth of the alley and I had a most splitting headache and dried blood was clotted on a cut in my scalp. I groped around and found a match in my pocket and struck it.

The alley was empty. The ground was all tore up and they was some blood scattered around, but neither the thugs nor Mike was nowhere to be seen. I run down the alley, but it ended in a blank stone wall. So I come back onto the Tungen Road and looked up and down but seen nobody. I went mad.

"Philip D'Arcy!" I yelled all of a sudden. "He done it. He stole Mike. He writ me that note. Unknown admirer, my eye. I been played for a sucker again. He thinks Mike'll bring him luck. I'll bring him luck, the double-crossin' son-of-a-seacook. I'll sock him so hard he'll bite hisself in the ankle. I'll bust him into so many pieces he'll go through a sieve —"

With these meditations, I was running down the street at full speed, and when I busted into a crowded thoroughfare, folks turned and looked at me in amazement. But I didn't pay no heed. I was steering my course for the European Club, a kind of ritzy place where D'Arcy generally hung out. I was still going at top-speed when I run up the broad stone steps and was stopped by a pompous looking doorman which sniffed scornfully at my appearance, with my clothes torn and dirty from laying in the alley, and my hair all touseled and dried blood on my hair and face.

"Lemme by," I gritted, "I gotta see a mutt."

"Gorblime," said the doorman. "You cawn't go in there. This is a very exclusive club, don't you know. Only gentlemen are allowed here. Cawn't have a blawsted gorilla like you bursting in on the gentlemen. My word! Get along now before I call the police."

There wasn't time to argue.

With a howl of irritation I grabbed him by the neck and heaved him into a nearby goldfish pond. Leaving him floundering and howling, I kicked the door open and rushed in. I dashed through a wide hallway and found myself in a wide room with big French winders. That seemed to be the main club room, because it was very scrumptiously furnished and had all kinds of animal heads on the walls, alongside of crossed swords and rifles in racks.

They was a number of Americans and Europeans setting around drinking whiskey-and-sodas, and playing cards. I seen Philip D'Arcy setting amongst a bunch of his club-members, evidently spinning yarns about his adventures. And I seen red.

"D'Arcy!" I yelled, striding toward him regardless of the card tables I upset. "Where's my dog?"

Philip D'Arcy sprang up with a kind of gasp and all the club men jumped up too, looked amazed.

"My word!" said a Englishman in a army officer's uniform. "Who let this boundah in? Come, come, my man, you'll have to get out of this."

"You keep your nose clear of this or I'll bend it clean outa shape," I howled, shaking my right mauler under the aforesaid nose. "This ain't none of your business. D'Arcy, what you done with my dog?"

"You're drunk, Costigan," he snapped. "I don't know what you're talking about."

"That's a lie," I screamed, crazy with rage. "You tried to buy Mike and then you had me slugged and him stole. I'm on to you, D'Arcy. You think because you're a big shot and I'm just a common sailorman, you can take what you want. But you ain't gettin' away with it. You got Mike and you're goin' to give him back or I'll tear your guts out. Where is he? Tell me before I choke it outa you."

"Costigan, you're mad," snarled D'Arcy, kind of white. "Do you know whom you're threatening? I've killed men for less than that."

"You stole my dog!" I howled, so wild I hardly knew what I was doing.

"You're a liar," he rasped. Blind mad, I roared and crashed my right to his jaw before he could move. He went down like a slaughtered ox and laid still, blood trickling from the corner of his mouth. I went for him to strangle him with my bare hands, but all the club men closed in between us.

"Grab him," they yelled. "He's killed D'Arcy. He's drunk or crazy. Hold him until we can get the police."

"Belay there," I roared, backing away with both fists cocked. "Lemme see the man that'll grab me. I'll knock his brains down his throat. When that rat comes to, tell him I ain't through with him, not by a dam' sight. I'll get him if it's the last thing I do."

And I stepped through one of them French winders and strode away cursing between my teeth. I walked for some time in a kind of red mist, forgetting all about the fight at Ace's Arena, where I was already due. Then I got a idee. I was fully intending to get ahold of D'Arcy and choke the truth outa him, but they was no use trying that now. I'd catch him outside his club some time that night. Meanwhile, I thought of something else. I went into a saloon and got a big piece of white paper and a pencil, and with much labor, I printed out what I wanted to say. Then I went out and stuck it up on a wooden lamp-post where folks couldst read it. It said:

I WILL PAY ANY MAN FIFTY DOLLARS ($50) THAT CAN FIND MY BULDOG MIKE WHICH WAS STOLE BY A LO-DOWN SCUNK.
STEVE COSTIGAN.

I was standing there reading it to see that the words was spelled right when a loafer said: "Mike stole? Too bad, Sailor. But where you goin' to git the fifty to pay the reeward? Everybody knows you ain't got no money."

"That's right," I said. So I wrote down underneath the rest:

P.S. I AM GOING TO GET FIFTY DOLLARS FOR LICKING SOME MUTT AT ACE'S AREENER THAT IS WHERE THE REWARD MONEY IS COMING FROM.
S. C.

I then went morosely along the street wondering where Mike was and if he was being mistreated or anything. I moped into the Arena and found Ace walking the floor and pulling his hair.

"Where you been?" he howled. "You realize you been keepin' the crowd waitin' a hour? Get into them ring togs."

"Let 'em wait," I said sourly, setting down and pulling off my shoes. "Ace, a yellow-livered son-of-a-skunk stole my dog."

"Yeah?" said Ace, pulling out his watch and looking at it. "That's tough,

Steve. Hustle up and get into the ring, willya? The crowd's about ready to tear the joint down."

I climbed into my trunks and bathrobe and mosied up the aisle, paying very little attention either to the hisses or cheers which greeted my appearance. I clumb into the ring and looked around for my opponent.

"Where's Grieson?" asked Ace.

"'E 'asn't showed up yet," said the referee.

"Ye gods and little fishes!" howled Ace, tearing his hair. "These bone-headed leather-pushers will drive me to a early doom. Do they think a pummoter's got nothin' else to do but set around all night and pacify a ragin' mob whilst they play around? These thugs is goin' to lynch us all if we don't start some action right away."

"Here he comes," said the referee as a bath-robed figger come hurrying down the aisle. Ace scowled bitterly and held up his hands to the frothing crowd.

"The long delayed main event," he said sourly. "Over in that corner, Sailor Costigan of the *Sea Girl*, weight 190 pounds. The mutt crawlin' through the ropes is 'Limey' Grieson, weight 189. Get goin' – and I hope you both get knocked loop-legged."

The referee called us to the center of the ring for instructions and Grieson glared at me, trying to scare me before the scrap started – the conceited jassack. But I had other things on my mind. I merely mechanically noted that he was about my height – six feet – had a nasty sneering mouth and mean black eyes, and had been in a street fight recent. He had a bruise under one ear.

We went back to our corners and I said to the second Ace had give me: "Bonehead, you ain't seen nothin' of nobody with my bulldog, have you?"

"Naw, I ain't," he said, crawling through the ropes. "And beside . . . Hey, look out."

I hadn't noticed the gong sounding and Grieson was in my corner before I knowed what was happening. I ducked a slungshot right as I turned and clinched, pushing him outa the corner before I broke. He nailed me with a hard left hook to the head and I retaliated with a left to the body, but it didn't have much enthusiasm behind it. I had something else on my mind and my heart wasn't in the fight. I kept unconsciously glancing over to my corner where Mike always set, and when he wasn't there, I felt kinda lost and sick and empty.

Limey soon seen I wasn't up to par and began forcing the fight, shooting both hands to my head. I blocked and countered very slouchily and the crowd, missing my rip-roaring attack, began to murmur. Limey got too cocky and missed a looping right that had everything he had behind it. He was wide open for a instant and I mechanically ripped a left hook under his heart that made his knees buckle, and he covered up and walked away from me in a hurry, with me following in a sluggish kind of manner.

After that he was careful, not taking many chances. He jabbed me plenty, but kept his right guard high and close in. I ignores left jabs at all times, so though he was outpointing me plenty, he wasn't hurting me none. But he finally let go his right again and started the claret from my nose. That irritated me and I woke up and doubled him over with a left hook to the guts which wowed the crowd. But they yelled with rage and amazement when I failed to foller up. To tell the truth, I was fighting very absent-mindedly.

As I walked back to my corner at the end of the first round, the crowd was growling and muttering restlessly, and the referee said: "Fight, you blasted Yank, or I'll throw you h'out of the ring." That was the first time I ever got a warning like that.

"What's the matter with you, Sailor?" said Bonehead, waving the towel industriously. "I ain't never seen you fight this way before."

"I'm worried about Mike," I said. "Bonehead, where-all does Philip D'Arcy hang out besides the European Club?"

"How should I know?" he said. "Why?"

"I wanta catch him alone some place," I growled. "I betcha —"

"There's the gong, you mutt," yelled Bonehead, pushing me out of my corner. "For cat's sake, get in there and FIGHT. I got five bucks bet on you."

I wandered out into the middle of the ring and absent-mindedly wiped Limey's chin with a right that dropped him on his all-fours. He bounced up without a count, clearly addled, but just as I was fixing to polish him off, I heard a racket at the door.

"Lemme in," somebody was squalling. "I gotta see Meest Costigan. I got one fellow dog belong along him."

"Wait a minute," I growled to Limey, and run over to the ropes, to the astounded fury of the fans, who rose and roared.

"Let him in, Bat," I yelled and the feller at the door hollered back: "Alright, Steve, here he comes."

And a Chinese kid come running up the aisle grinning like all get-out, holding up a scrawny brindle bull-pup.

"Here that one fellow dog, Mees Costigan," he yelled.

"Aw heck," I said. "That ain't Mike. Mike's white. I thought everybody in Singapore knowed Mike —"

At this moment I realized that the still groggy Grieson was harassing me from the rear, so I turned around and give him my full attention for a minute.

I had him backed up ag'in' the ropes, bombarding him with lefts and rights to the head and body, when I heard Bat yell: "Here comes another'n, Steve."

"Pardon me a minute," I snapped to the reeling Limey, and run over to the ropes just as a grinning coolie come running up the aisle with a white dog which might of had three or four drops of bulldog blood in him.

"Me catchum, boss," he chortled. "Heap fine white dawg. Me catchum fifty dolla?"

"You catchum a kick in the pants," I roared with irritation. "Blame it all, that ain't Mike."

At this moment Grieson, which had snuck up behind me, banged me behind the ear with a right hander that made me see about a million stars. This infuriated me so I turned and hit him in the belly so hard I bent his back-bone. He curled up like a worm somebody'd stepped on and while the referee was counting over him, the gong ended the round.

They dragged Limey to his corner and started working on him. Bonehead, he said to me: "What kind of a game is this, Sailor? Gee whiz, that mutt can't stand up to you a minute if you was tryin'. You shoulda stopped him in the first round. Hey, lookit there."

I glanced absent-mindedly over at the opposite corner and seen that Limey's seconds had found it necessary to take off his right glove in the process of reviving him. They was fumbling over his bare hand.

"They're up to somethin' crooked," howled Bonehead. "I'm goin' to appeal to the referee."

"Here comes some more mutts, Steve," bawled Bat and down the aisle come a Chinese coolie, a Jap sailor, and a Hindoo, each with a barking dog. The crowd had been seething with bewildered rage, but this seemed to somehow hit 'em in the funny bone and they begunst to whoop and yell and laugh like a passel of hyenas. The referee was roaming around the ring cussing to hisself and Ace was jumping up and down and tearing his hair.

"Is this a prize-fight or a dog-show," he howled. "You've rooint my business. I'll be the laughin' stock of the town. I'll sue you, Costigan."

"Catchum fine dawg, Meest' Costigan," shouted the Chinese, holding up a squirming, yowling mutt which done its best to bite me.

"You deluded heathen," I roared, "that ain't even a bull dog. That's a chow."

"You clazee," he hollered. "Him fine blull dawg."

"Don't listen," said the Jap. "Him bull dog." And he held up one of them pintsized Boston bull-terriers.

"Not so," squalled the Hindoo. "Here is thee dog for you, sahib. A pure blood Rampur hound. No dog can overtake him in thee race –"

"Ye gods!" I howled. "Is everybody crazy? I oughta knowed these heathens couldn't understand my reward poster, but I thought —"

"*Look out, sailor,*" roared the crowd.

I hadn't heard the gong. Grieson had slipped up on me from behind again, and I turned just in time to get nailed on the jaw by a sweeping right-hander he started from the canvas. Wham! The lights went out and I hit the canvas so hard it jolted some of my senses back into me again.

I knowed, even then, that no ordinary gloved fist had slammed me down that way. Limey's men hadst slipped a iron knuckle-duster on his hand when they had his glove off. The referee sprung forward with a gratified yelp and begun counting over me. I writhed around, trying to get up and kill Limey, but I felt like I was done. My head was swimming, my jaw felt dead, and all the starch was gone outa my legs. They felt like they was made outa taller.

My head reeled. And I could see stars over the horizon of dogs.

"...Four..." said the referee above the yells of the crowd and the despairing howls of Bonehead, who seen his five dollars fading away. "...Five...Six...Seven..."

"There," said Limey, stepping back with a leer. "That's done yer, yer blawsted Yank."

Snap! went something in my head. That voice. Them same words. Where'd I heard 'em before? In the black alley offa the Tungen Road. A wave of red fury washed all the grogginess outa me.

I forgot all about my taller legs. I come off the floor with a roar which made the ring lights dance, and lunged at the horrified Limey like a mad bull. He caught me with a straight left coming in, but I didn't even check a instant. His arm bent and I was on top of him and sunk my right mauler so deep into his ribs I felt his heart throb under my fist. He turned green all over and crumbled to the canvas like all his bones hadst turned to butter. The dazed referee started to count, but I ripped off my gloves and pouncing on the gasping warrior, I sunk my iron fingers into his throat.

"Where's Mike, you gutter rat?" I roared. "What'd you do with him? Tell me, or I'll tear your windpipe out."

"'Ere, 'ere," squawked the referee. "You cawn't do that. Let go of him, I say. Let go, you fiend."

He got me by the shoulders and tried to pull me off. Then, seeing I wasn't even noticing his efforts, he started kicking me in the ribs. With a wrathful beller, I rose up and caught him by the nape of the neck and the seat of the britches and threwed him clean through the ropes. Then I turned back on Limey.

"You Limehouse spawn," I bellered. "I'll choke the life outa you."

"Easy, mate, easy," he gasped, green-tinted and sick. "I'll tell yer. We stole the mutt – Fritz Steinmann wanted him –"

"Steinmann?" I howled in amazement.

"He warnted a dorg to fight Ritchie's Terror," gasped Limey. "Johnnie Blinn suggested he should 'ook your Mike. Johnnie hired me and some strong-arms to turn the trick – Johnnie's gel wrote you that note – but how'd you know I was into it –"

"I oughta thought about Blinn," I raged. "The dirty rat. He heard me and Porkey talkin' and got the idee. Where is Blinn?"

"Somewheres gettin' sewed up," gasped Grieson. "The dorg like to tore him to ribbons afore we could get the brute into the bamboo cage we had fixed."

"Where is Mike?" I roared, shaking him till his teeth rattled.

"At Steinmann's, fightin' Terror," groaned Limey. "Ow, lor' – I'm sick. I'm dyin'."

I riz up with a maddened beller and made for my corner. The referee rose up outa the tangle of busted seats and cussing fans and shook his fist at me with fire in his eye.

"Steve Costigan," he yelled. "You lose the blawsted fight on a foul."

"So's your old man," I roared, grabbing my bathrobe from the limp and gibbering Bonehead. And just at that instant a regular bedlam bust loose at the ticket-door and Bat come down the aisle like the devil was chasing him. And in behind him come a mob of natives – coolies, 'ricksha boys, beggars, shop-keepers, boatmen and I don't know what all – and every one of 'em had at least one dog and some had as many as three or four. Such a horde of chows, Pekineses, terriers, hounds and mongrels I never seen and they was all barking and howling and fighting.

"Meest' Costigan," the heathens howled, charging down the aisles. "You payum fifty dolla for dogs. We catchum."

The crowd rose and stampeded, trompling each other in their flight and I jumped outa the ring and raced down the aisle to the back exit with the whole mob about a jump behind me. I slammed the door in their faces and rushed out onto the sidewalk, where the passers-by screeched and scattered at the sight of what I reckon they thought was a huge and much battered maniac running at large in a red bathrobe. I paid no heed to 'em.

Somebody yelled at me in a familiar voice, but I rushed out into the street and made a flying leap onto the running board of a passing taxi. I ripped the door open and yelled to the horrified driver: "Fritz Steinmann's place on Kang Street – and if you ain't there within three minutes I'll break your neck."

––––––––

We went careening through the streets and purty soon the driver said: "Say, are you an escaped criminal? There's a car followin' us."

"You drive," I yelled. "I don't care if they's a thousand cars follerin' us. Likely it's a Chinaman with a pink Pomeranian he wants to sell me for a white bull dog."

The driver stepped on it and when we pulled up in front of the innocent looking building which was Steinmann's secret arena, we'd left the mysterious pursuer clean outa sight. I jumped out and raced down a short flight of stairs which led from the street down to a side entrance, clearing my decks for action by shedding my bathrobe as I went. The door was shut and a burly black-jowled thug was lounging outside. His eyes narrowed with surprise as he noted my costume, but he bulged in front of me and growled: "Wait a minute, you. Where do you think you're goin'?"

"In!" I gritted, ripping a terrible right to his unshaven jaw.

Over his prostrate carcass I launched myself bodily against the door, being in too much of a hurry to stop and see if it was unlocked. It crashed in and through its ruins I catapulted into the room.

It was a big basement. A crowd of men – the scrapings of the waterfront – was ganged about a deep pit sunk in the concrete floor from which come a low, terrible, worrying sound like dogs growling through a mask of torn flesh and bloody hair – like fighting dogs growl when they have their fangs sunk deep.

The fat Dutchman which owned the dive was just inside the door and he whirled and went white as I crashed through. He threw up his hands and screamed, just as I caught him with a clout that smashed his nose and knocked six front teeth down his throat. Somebody yelled: "Look out, boys! Here comes Costigan! He's on the kill!"

The crowd yelled and scattered like chaff before a high wind as I come ploughing through 'em like a typhoon, slugging right and left and dropping a man at each blow. I was so crazy mad I didn't care if I killed all of 'em. In a instant the brink of the pit was deserted as the crowd stormed through the exits, and I jumped down into the pit. Two dogs was there, a white one and a big brindle one, though they was both so bloody you couldn't hardly tell their original color. Both had been savagely punished, but Mike's jaws had locked in the deathhold on Terror's throat and the brindle dog's eyes was glazing.

Joe Ritchie was down on his knees working hard over them and his face was the color of paste. They's only two ways you can break a bull dog's death-grip; one is by deluging him with water till he's half drowned and opens his mouth to breathe. The other'n is by choking him off. Ritchie was trying that, but Mike had such a bull's neck, Joe was only hurting his fingers.

"For gosh sake, Costigan," he gasped. "Get this white devil off. He's killin' Terror."

"Sure I will," I grunted, stooping over the dogs. "Not for your sake, but for the sake of a good game dog." And I slapped Mike on the back and said: "Belay there, Mike; haul in your grapplin' irons."

Mike let go and grinned up at me with his bloody mouth, wagging his stump of a tail like all get-out and pricking up one ear. Terror had clawed the other'n to rags. Ritchie picked up the brindle bull

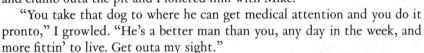

and clumb outa the pit and I follered him with Mike.

"You take that dog to where he can get medical attention and you do it pronto," I growled. "He's a better man than you, any day in the week, and more fittin' to live. Get outa my sight."

He slunk off and Steinmann come to on the floor and seen me and crawled to the door on his all-fours before he dast to get up and run, bleeding like a stuck hawg. I was looking over Mike's cuts and gashes, when I realized that a man was standing nearby, watching me.

I wheeled. It was Philip D'Arcy, with a blue bruise on his jaw where I'd socked him, and his right hand inside his coat.

"D'Arcy," I said, walking up to him. "I reckon I done made a mess of things. I just ain't got no sense when I lose my temper, and I honestly thought you'd stole Mike. I ain't much on fancy words and apologizin' won't do no good. But I always try to do what seems right in my blunderin' blame-fool way, and if you wanta, you can knock my head off and I won't raise a hand ag'in' you." And I stuck out my jaw for him to sock.

He took his hand outa his coat and in it was a cocked six-shooter.

"Costigan," he said, "no man ever struck me before and got away with it. I came to Larnigan's Arena tonight to kill you. I was waiting for you outside and when I saw you run out of the place and jump into a taxi, I followed you to do the job wherever I caught up with you. But I like you. You're a square-shooter. And a man who thinks as much of his dog as you do is my idea of the right sort. I'm putting this gun back where it belongs – and I'm willing to shake hands and call it quits, if you are."

"More'n willin'," I said heartily. "You're a real gent." And we shook. Then all at once he started laughing.

"I saw your poster," he said. "When I passed by, an Indian babu was translating it to a crowd of natives and he was certainly making a weird mess of it. The best he got out of it was that Steve Costigan was buying dogs at fifty dollars apiece. You'll be hounded by canine peddlers as long as you're in port."

"The *Sea Girl*'s due tomorrer, thank gosh," I replied. "But right now I got to sew up some cuts on Mike."

"My car's outside," said D'Arcy. "Let's take him up to my rooms. I've had quite a bit of practice at such things and we'll fix him up ship-shape."

"It's a dirty deal he's had," I growled. "And when I catch Johnnie Blinn I'm goin' kick his ears off. But," I added, swelling out my chest seven or eight inches, "I don't reckon I'll have to lick no more saps for sayin' that Ritchie's Terror is the champeen of all fightin' dogs in the Asiatics. Mike and me is the fightin'est pair of scrappers in the world."

The Grey God Passes

A voice echoed among the bleak reaches of the mountains that reared up gauntly on either hand. At the mouth of the defile that opened on a colossal crag, Conn the thrall wheeled, snarling like a wolf at bay. He was tall and massively, yet rangily, built, the fierceness of the wild dominant in his broad, sloping shoulders, his huge hairy chest and long, heavily muscled arms. His features were in keeping with his bodily aspect – a strong, stubborn jaw, low slanting forehead topped by a shock of tousled tawny hair which added to the wildness of his appearance no more than did his cold blue eyes. His only garment was a scanty loin-cloth. His own wolfish ruggedness was protection enough against the elements – for he was a slave in an age when even the masters lived lives as hard as the iron environments which bred them.

Now Conn half crouched, sword ready, a bestial snarl of menace humming in his bull-throat, and from the defile there came a tall man, wrapped in a cloak beneath which the thrall glimpsed a sheen of mail. The stranger wore a slouch hat pulled so low that from his shadowed features only one eye gleamed, cold and grim as the grey sea.

"Well, Conn, thrall of Wolfgar Snorri's son," said the stranger in a deep, powerful voice, "whither do you flee, with your master's blood on your hands?"

"I know you not," growled Conn, "nor how you know me. If you would take me, whistle up your dogs and make an end. Some of them will taste steel ere I die."

"Fool!" There was deep scorn in the reverberant tone. "I am no hunter of runaway serfs. There are wilder matters abroad. What do you smell in the sea-wind?"

Conn turned toward the sea, lapping greyly at the cliffs far below. He expanded his mighty chest, his nostrils flaring as he breathed deeply.

"I smell the tang of the salt-spume," he answered.

The stranger's voice was like the rasp of swords. "The scent of blood is on the wind – the musk of slaughter and the shouts of the slaying."

Conn shook his head, bewildered. "It is only the wind among the crags."

"There is war in your homeland," said the stranger sombrely. "The spears of the South have risen against the swords of the North and the death-fires are lighting the land like the mid-day sun."

"How can you know this?" asked the thrall uneasily. "No ship has put in to Torka for weeks. Who are you? Whence come you? How know you these things?"

"Can you not hear the skirl of the pipes, the clashing of the axes?" replied the tall stranger. "Can you not smell the war-reek the wind brings?"

"Not I," answered Conn. "It is many a long league from Torka to Erin, and I hear only the wind among the crags and the gulls screeching over the headlands. Yet if there is war, I should be among the weapon-men of my clan, though my life is forfeit to Melaghlin because I slew a man of his in a quarrel."

The stranger gave no heed, standing like a statue as he gazed far out across the reaches of hazy barren mountains and misty waves.

"It is the death-grip," he said, like one who speaks to himself. "Now comes the reaping of kings, the garnering of chiefs like a harvest. Gigantic shadows stalk red-handed across the world, and night is falling on Asgaard. I hear the cries of long-dead heroes whistling in the void, and the shouts of forgotten gods. To each being there is an appointed time, and even the gods must die..."

He stiffened suddenly with a great shout, flinging his arms seaward. Tall, rolling clouds, sailing gigantically before the gale, veiled the sea. Out of the mist came a great wind and out of the wind a whirling mass of clouds. And Conn cried out. From out the flying clouds, shadowy and horrific, swept twelve shapes. He saw, as in a nightmare, the twelve winged horses and their riders, women in flaming silver mail and winged helmets, whose golden hair floated out on the wind behind them, and whose cold eyes were fixed on some awesome goal beyond his ken.

"The Choosers of the Slain!" thundered the stranger, flinging his arms wide in a terrible gesture. "They ride in the twilight of the North! The winged hooves spurn the rolling clouds, the web of Fate is spun, the Loom and Spindle broken! Doom roars upon the gods and night falls on Asgaard! Night and the trumpets of Ragnarok!"

The cloak was blown wide in the wind, revealing the mighty, mail-clad figure; the slouch hat fell aside; the wild elf-locks blew free. And Conn shrank before the blaze of the stranger's eye. And he saw that where the other eye should have been, was but an empty socket. Thereat panic seized him, so that he turned and ran down the defile as a man flees demons. And a fearsome backward glance showed him the stranger etched against the cloud-torn sky, cloak blowing in the wind, arms flung high, and it seemed to the thrall that the man had grown monstrously in stature, that he loomed colossal among the clouds, dwarfing the mountains and the sea, and that he was suddenly grey, as with vast age.

II

Oh Masters of the North, we come with tally of remembered dead,
Of broken hearth and blazing home, and rafters crashing overhead.
A single cast of dice we throw to balance, by the leaden sea,
A hundred years of wrong and woe with one red hour of butchery.

The spring gale had blown itself out. The sky smiled blue overhead and the sea lay placid as a pool, with only a few scattered bits of driftwood along the beaches to give mute evidence of her treachery. Along the strand rode a lone horseman, his saffron cloak whipping out behind him, his yellow hair blowing about his face in the breeze.

Suddenly he reined up so short that his spirited steed reared and snorted. From among the sand dunes had risen a man, tall and powerful, of wild, shock-headed aspect, and naked but for a loin-cloth.

"Who are you," demanded the horseman, "who bear the sword of a chief, yet have the appearance of a masterless man, and wear the collar of a serf withal?"

"I am Conn, young master," answered the wanderer, "once an outlaw, once a thrall, – always a man of King Brian's, whether he will or no. And I know you. You are Dunlang O'Hartigan, friend of Murrogh, son of Brian, prince of Dal Cais. Tell me, good sir, is there war in the land?"

"Sooth to say," answered the young chief, "even now King Brian and King Malachi lie encamped at Kilmainham, before Dublin. I have but ridden from the camp this morning. From all the lands of the Vikings King Sitric of

Dublin has summoned the slayers, and Gaels and Danes are ready to join battle – and such a battle as Erin has never seen before."

Conn's eyes clouded. "By Crom!" he muttered, half to himself, "it is even as the Grey Man said – yet how could he have known? Surely it was all a dream."

"How come you here?" asked Dunlang.

"From Torka in the Orkneys in an open boat, flung down as a chip is thrown upon the tide. Of yore I slew a man of Meath, kern of Melaghlin, and King Brian's heart was hot against me because of the broken truce; so I fled. Well, the life of an outlaw is hard. Thorwald Raven, Jarl of the Hebrides, took me when I was weak from hunger and wounds, and put this collar on my neck." The kern touched the heavy copper ring encircling his bull-neck. "Then he sold me to Wolfgar Snorri's son on Torka. He was a hard master. I did the work of three men, and stood at his back and mowed down carles like wheat when he brawled with his neighbors. In return he gave me crusts from his board, a bare earth floor to sleep on, and deep scars on my back. Finally I could bear it no more, and I leaped upon him in his own skalli and crushed his skull with a log of firewood. Then I took his sword and fled to the mountains, preferring to freeze or starve there rather than die under the lash.

"There in the mountains," – again Conn's eyes clouded with doubt –" I think I dreamed," he said, "I saw a tall grey man who spoke of war in Erin, and in my dream I saw Valkyries riding southward on the clouds...

"Better to die at sea on a good venture than to starve in the Orkney mountains," he continued with more assurance, his feet on firm ground. "By chance I found a fisherman's boat, with a store of food and water, and I put to sea. By Crom! I wonder to find myself still alive! The gale took me in her fangs last night, and I know only that I fought the sea in the boat until the boat sank under my feet, and then fought her in her naked waves until my senses went from me. None could have been more surprised than I when I came to myself this dawn lying like a piece of driftwood on the beach. I have lain in the sun since, trying to warm the cold tang of the sea out of my bones."

"By the saints, Conn," said Dunlang, "I like your spirit."

"I hope King Brian likes it as well," grunted the kern.

"Attach yourself to my train," answered Dunlang. "I'll speak for you. King Brian has weightier matters on his mind than a single blood-feud. This very day the opposing hosts lie drawn up for the death-grip."

"Will the spear-shattering fall on the morrow?" asked Conn.

"Not by King Brian's will," answered Dunlang. "He is loath to shed blood on Good Friday. But who knows when the heathen will come down upon us?"

Conn laid a hand on Dunlang's stirrup-leather and strode beside him as the steed moved leisurely along.

"There is a notable gathering of weapon-men?"

"More than twenty thousand warriors on each side; the bay of Dublin is dark with the dragon-ships. From the Orkneys comes Jarl Sigurd with his raven banner. From Man comes the Viking Brodir with twenty longships. From the Danelagh in England comes Prince Amlaff, son of the King of Norway, with two thousand men. From all lands the hosts have gathered – from the Orkneys, the Shetlands, the Hebrides – from Scotland, England, Germany, and the lands of Scandinavia.

"Our spies say Sigurd and Brodir have a thousand men armed in steel mail from crown to heel, who fight in a solid wedge. The Dalcassians may be hard put to break that iron wall. Yet, God willing, we shall prevail. Then among the other chiefs and warriors there are Anrad the berserk, Hrafn the Red, Platt of Danemark, Thorstein and his comrade-in-arms Asmund, Thorleif Hordi, the Strong, Athelstane the Saxon, and Thorwald Raven, Jarl of the Hebrides."

At that name Conn grinned savagely and fingered his copper collar. "It is a great gathering if both Sigurd and Brodir come."

"That was the doing of Gormlaith," responded Dunlang.

"Word had come to the Orkneys that Brian had divorced Kormlada," said Conn, unconsciously giving the queen her Norse name.

"Aye – and her heart is black with hate against him. Strange it is that a woman so fair of form and countenance should have the soul of a demon."

"God's truth, my lord. And what of her brother, Prince Mailmora?"

"Who but he is the instigator of the whole war?" cried Dunlang angrily. "The hate between him and Murrogh, so long smoldering, has at last burst into flame, firing both kingdoms. Both were in the wrong – Murrogh perhaps more than Mailmora. Gormlaith goaded her brother on. I did not believe King Brian acted wisely when he gave honors to those against whom he had warred. It was not well he married Gormlaith and gave his daughter to Gormlaith's son, Sitric of Dublin. With Gormlaith he took the seeds of strife and hatred into his palace. She is a wanton; once she was the wife of Amlaff Cauran, the Dane; then she was wife to King Malachi of Meath, and he put her aside because of her wickedness."

"What of Melaghlin?" asked Conn.

"He seems to have forgotten the struggle in which Brian wrested Erin's crown from him. Together the two kings move against the Danes and Mailmora."

As they conversed, they passed along the bare shore until they came into a rough broken stretch of cliffs and boulders; and there they halted suddenly. On a boulder sat a girl, clad in a shimmering green garment whose pattern was so much like scales that for a bewildered instant Conn thought himself gazing on a mermaid come out of the deeps.

"Eevin!" Dunlang swung down from his horse, tossing the reins to Conn, and advanced to take her slender hands in his. "You sent for me and I have come – you've been weeping!"

Conn, holding the steed, felt an impulse to retire, prompted by superstitious qualms. Eevin, with her slender form, her wealth of shimmering golden hair, and her deep mysterious eyes, was not like any other girl he had ever seen. Her entire aspect was different from the women of the Norse-folk and of the Gaels alike, and Conn knew her to be a member of that fading mystic race which had occupied the land before the coming of his ancestors, some of whom still dwelt in caverns along the sea and deep in unfrequented forests – the De Danaans, sorcerers, the Irish said, and kin to the faeries.

"Dunlang!" The girl caught her lover in a convulsive embrace. "You must not go into battle – the weird of far-sight is on me, and I know if you go to the war, you will die! Come away with me – I'll hide you – I'll show you dim purple caverns like the castles of deep-sea kings, and shadowy forests where none save my people has set foot. Come with me and forget wars and hates and prides and ambitions, which are but shadows without reality or substance. Come and learn the dreamy splendors of far places, where fear and hate are naught, and the years seem as hours, drifting forever."

"Eevin, my love!" cried Dunlang, troubled, "you ask that which is beyond my power. When my clan moves into battle, I must be at Murrogh's side, though sure death be my portion. I love you beyond all life, but by the honor of my clan, this is an impossible thing."

"I feared as much," she answered, resigned. "You of the Tall Folk are but children – foolish, cruel, violent – slaying one another in childish quarrels. This is punishment visited on me who, alone of all my people, have loved a man of the Tall Folk. Your rough hands have bruised my soft flesh unwittingly, and your rough spirit as unwittingly bruises my heart."

"I would not hurt you, Eevin," began Dunlang, pained.

"I know," she replied, "the hands of men are not made to handle the delicate body and heart of a woman of the Dark People. It is my fate. I love and I have lost. My sight is a far sight which sees through the veil and the mists of life, behind the past and beyond the future. You will go into battle and the harps will keen for you; and Eevin of Craglea will weep until she melts in tears and the salt tears mingle with the cold salt sea."

Dunlang bowed his head, unspeaking, for her young voice vibrated with the ancient sorrow of womankind; and even the rough kern shuffled his feet uneasily.

"I have brought you a gift against the time of battle," she went on, bending lithely to lift something which caught the sun's sheen. "It may not save you, the ghosts in my soul whisper – but I hope without hope in my heart."

Dunlang stared uncertainly at what she spread before him. Conn, edging closer and craning his neck, saw a hauberk of strange workmanship and a helmet such as he had never seen before, – a heavy affair made to slip over the entire head and rest on the neckpieces of the hauberk. There was no movable vizor, merely a slit cut in the front through which to see, and the workmanship was of an earlier, more civilized age, which no man living could duplicate.

Dunlang looked at it askance, with the characteristic Celtic antipathy toward armor. The Britons who faced Caesar's legionaries fought naked, judging a man cowardly who cased himself in metal, and in later ages the Irish clans entertained the same conviction regarding Strongbow's mail-clad knights.

"Eevin," said Dunlang, "my brothers will laugh at me if I enclose myself in iron, like a Dane. How can a man have full freedom of limb, weighted by such a garment? Of all the Gaels, only Turlogh Dubh wears full mail."

"And is any man of the Gael less brave than he?" she cried passionately. "Oh, you of the Tall People are foolish! For ages the iron-clad Danes have trampled you, when you might have swept them out of the land long ago, but for your foolish pride."

"Not altogether pride, Eevin," argued Dunlang. "Of what avail is mail or plated armor against the Dalcassian ax which cuts through iron like cloth?"

"Mail would turn the swords of the Danes," she answered, "and not even an ax of the O'Briens would rend this armor. Long it has lain in the deep-sea caverns of my people, carefully protected from rust. He who wore it was a warrior of Rome in the long ago, before the legions were withdrawn from Britain. In an ancient war on the border of Wales, it fell into the hands of my people, and because its wearer was a great prince, my people treasured it. Now I beg you to wear it, if you love me."

Dunlang took it hesitantly, nor could he know that it was the armor worn by a gladiator in the days of the later Roman empire, nor wonder by what chance it had been worn by an officer in the British legion. Little of that knew Dunlang who, like most of his brother chiefs, could neither read nor write; knowledge and education were for monks and priests; a fighting man was kept too busy to cultivate the arts and sciences. He took the armor, and because he loved the strange girl, agreed to wear it – "If it will fit me."

"It will fit," she answered. "But I will see you no more alive."

She held out her white arms and he gathered her hungrily to him, while Conn looked away. Then Dunlang gently unlocked her clinging arms from about his neck, kissed her, and tore himself free.

Without a backward glance he mounted his steed and rode away, with Conn trotting easily alongside. Looking back in the gathering dusk, the kern saw Eevin standing there still, a poignant picture of despair.

III

The campfires sent up showers of sparks and illumined the land like day. In the distance loomed the grim walls of Dublin, dark and ominously silent; before the walls flickered other fires where the warriors of Leinster, under King Mailmora, whetted their axes for the coming battle. Out in the bay, the starlight glinted on myriad sails, shield-rails and arching serpent-prows. Between the city and the fires of the Irish host stretched the plain of Clontarf, bordered by Tomar's Wood, dark and rustling in the night, and the Liffey's dark, star-flecked waters.

Before his tent, the firelight playing on his white beard and glinting from his undimmed eagle eyes, sat the great King Brian Boru, among his chiefs. The king was old – seventy-three winters had passed over his lion-like head – long years crammed with fierce wars and bloody intrigues. Yet his back was straight, his arm unwithered, his voice deep and resonant. His chiefs stood about him, tall warriors with war-hardened hands and eyes whetted by the sun and the winds and the high places; tigerish princes in their rich tunics, green girdles, leathern sandals and saffron mantles caught with great golden brooches.

They were an array of war-eagles – Murrogh, Brian's eldest son, the pride of all Erin, tall and mighty, with wide blue eyes that were never placid, but danced with mirth, dulled with sadness, or blazed with fury; Murrogh's young son, Turlogh, a supple lad of fifteen with golden locks and an eager face – tense with anticipation of trying his hand for the first time in the great game of war. And there was that other Turlogh, his cousin – Turlogh

160

Dubh, who was only a few years older but who already had his full stature and was famed throughout all Erin for his berserk rages and the cunning of his deadly ax-play. And there were Meathla O'Faelan, prince of Desmond or South Munster, and his kin – the Great Stewards of Scotland – Lennox, and Donald of Mar, who had crossed the Irish Channel with their wild Highlanders – tall men, sombre and gaunt and silent. And there were Dunlang O'Hartigan and O'Hyne, chief of Connacht. But O'Kelly, brother chief of the O'Hyne, and prince of Hy Many, was in the tent of his uncle, King Malachi O'Neill, which was pitched in the camp of the Meathmen, apart from the Dalcassians, and King Brian was brooding on the matter. For since the setting of the sun, O'Kelly had been closeted with the King of Meath, and no man knew what passed between them.

Nor was Donagh, son of Brian, among the chiefs before the royal pavilion, for he was afield with a band ravaging the holdings of Mailmora of Leinster.

Now Dunlang approached the king, leading with him Conn the kern.

"My Lord," quoth Dunlang, "here is a man who was outlawed aforetime, who has spent vile durance among the Gall, and who risked his life by storm and sea to return and fight under your banner. From the Orkneys in an open boat he came, naked and alone, and the sea cast him all but lifeless on the sand."

Brian stiffened; even in small things his memory was sharp as a whetted stone. "Thou!" he cried. "Aye, I remember him. Well, Conn, you have come back – and with your red hands!"

"Aye, King Brian," answered Conn stolidly, "my hands are red, it is true, and so I look to washing off the stain in Danish blood."

"You dare stand before me, to whom your life is forfeit!"

"This alone I know, King Brian," said Conn boldly, "my father was with you at Sulcoit and the sack of Limerick, and before that followed you in your days of wandering and was one of the fifteen warriors who remained to you when King Mahon, your brother, came seeking you in the forest. And my grandsire followed Murkertagh of the Leather Cloaks, and my people have fought the Danes since the days of Thorgils. You need men who can strike strong blows, and it is my right to die in battle against my ancient enemies, rather than shamefully at the end of a rope."

King Brian nodded. "Well spoken. Take your life. Your days of outlawry are at an end. King Malachi would perhaps think otherwise, since it was a man of his you slew, but –" He paused; an old doubt ate at his soul at the thought of the King of Meath. "Let it be," he went on, "let it rest until after the battle – mayhap that will be world's end for us all."

Dunlang stepped toward Conn and laid hand on the copper collar. "Let us cut this away; you are a free man now."

But Conn shook his head. "Not until I have slain Thorwald Raven who put it there. I'll wear it into battle as a sign of no quarter."

"That is a noble sword you wear, kern," said Murrogh suddenly.

"Aye, my Lord. Murkertagh of the Leather Cloaks wielded this blade until Blacair the Dane slew him at Ardee, and it remained in the possession of the Gall until I took it from the body of Wolfgar Snorri's son."

"It is not fitting that a kern should wear the sword of a king," said Murrogh brusquely. "Let one of the chiefs take it and give him an ax instead."

Conn's fingers locked about the hilt. "He would take the sword from me had best give me the ax first," he said grimly, "and that suddenly."

Murrogh's hot temper blazed. With an oath, he strode toward Conn, who met him eye to eye and gave back not a step.

"Be at ease, my son," ordered King Brian. "Let the kern keep the blade."

Murrogh shrugged. His mood changed. "Aye, keep it and follow me into battle. We shall see if a king's sword in a kern's hands can hew as wide a path as a prince's blade."

"My lords," said Conn, "it may be God's will that I fall in the first onset — but the scars of slavery burn deep in my back this night, and I will not be backward when the spears are splintering."

IV

Therefore your doom is on you,
Is on you and your kings. . . .
—*Chesterton*

While King Brian communed with his chiefs on the plains above Clontarf, a grisly ritual was being enacted within the gloomy castle that was at once the fortress and palace of Dublin's king. With good reason did Christians fear and hate those grim walls; Dublin was a pagan city, ruled by savage heathen kings, and dark were the deeds committed therein.

In an inner chamber in the castle stood the Viking Brodir, sombrely watching a ghastly sacrifice on a grim black altar. On that monstrous stone writhed a naked, frothing thing that had been a comely youth; brutally bound and gagged, he could only twist convulsively beneath the dripping, inexorable dagger in the hands of the white-bearded wild-eyed priest of Odin.

The blade hacked through flesh and thew and bone; blood gushed, to be caught in a broad, copper bowl, which the priest, with his red-dappled beard, held high, invoking Odin in a frenzied chant. His thin, bony fingers tore the yet pulsing heart from the butchered breast, and his wild half-mad eyes scanned it with avid intensity.

"What of your divinations?" demanded Brodir impatiently.

Shadows flickered in the priest's cold eyes, and his flesh crawled with a mysterious horror. "Fifty years I have served Odin," he said – "Fifty years divined by the bleeding heart, but never such portents as these. Hark, Brodir! – If ye fight not on Good Friday, as the Christians call it, your host will be utterly routed and all your chiefs slain; if ye fight on Good Friday, King Brian will die – but he will win the day."

Brodir cursed with cold venom.

The priest shook his ancient head. "I cannot fathom the portent – and I am the last of the priests of the Flaming Circle, who learned mysteries at the feet of Thorgils. I see battle and slaughter – and yet more – shapes gigantic and terrible that stalk monstrously through the mists..."

"Enough of such mummery," snarled Brodir. "If I fall I would take Brian to Helheim with me. We go against the Gaels on the morrow, fall fair, fall foul!" He turned and strode from the room.

Brodir traversed a winding corridor and entered another, more spacious chamber, adorned, like all the Dublin king's palace, with the loot of all the world – gold-chased weapons, rare tapestries, rich rugs, divans from Byzantium and the East – plunder taken from all peoples by the roving Norsemen; for Dublin was the center of the Vikings' wide-flung world, the headquarters whence they fared forth to loot the kings of the earth.

A queenly form rose to greet him. Kormlada, whom the Gaels called Gormlaith, was indeed fair, but there was cruelty in her face and in her hard, scintillant eyes. She was of mixed Irish and Danish blood, and looked the part of a barbaric queen, with her pendant ear-rings, her golden armlets and anklets, and her silver breast-plates set with jewels. But for these breastplates, her only garments were a short silken skirt which came half way to her knees and was held in place by a wide girdle about her lithe waist, and sandals of soft red leather. Her hair was red-gold, her eyes light grey and glittering. Queen she had been, of Dublin, of Meath, and of Thomond.

And queen she was still, for she held her son Sitric and her brother Mailmora in the palm of her slim white hand. Carried off in a raid in her childhood by Amlaff Cauran, King of Dublin, she had early discovered her power over men. As the child-wife of the rough Dane, she had swayed his kingdom at will, and her ambitions increased with her power.

Now she faced Brodir with her alluring, mysterious smile, but secret uneasiness ate at her. In all the world there was but one woman she feared, and but one man. And the man was Brodir. With him she was never entirely certain of her course; she duped him as she duped all men, but it was with many misgivings, for she sensed in him an elemental savagery which, once loosed, she might not be able to control.

"What of the priest's words, Brodir?" she asked.

"If we avoid battle on the morrow we lose," the Viking answered moodily. "If we fight, Brian wins, but falls. We fight – the more because my spies tell me Donagh is away from camp with a strong band, ravaging Mailmora's lands. We have sent spies to Malachi, who has an old grudge against Brian, urging him to desert the king – or at least to stand aside and aid neither of us. We have offered him rich rewards and Brian's lands to rule. Ha! Let him step into our trap! Not gold, but a bloody sword we will give him. With Brian crushed we will turn on Malachi and tread him into the dust! But first – Brian."

She clenched her white hands in savage exultation. "Bring me his head! I'll hang it above our bridal bed."

"I have heard strange tales," said Brodir soberly. "Sigurd has boasted in his cups."

Kormlada started and scanned the inscrutable countenance. Again she felt a quiver of fear as she gazed at the sombre Viking with his tall, strong stature, his dark, menacing face, and his heavy black locks which he wore braided and caught in his sword-belt.

"What has Sigurd said?" she asked, striving to make her voice casual.

"When Sitric came to me in my skalli on the Isle of Man," said Brodir, red glints beginning to smoulder in his dark eyes, "it was his oath that if I came to his aid, I should sit on the throne of Ireland with you as my queen. Now that fool of an Orkneyman, Sigurd, boasts in his ale that *he* was promised the same reward."

She forced a laugh. "He was drunk."

Brodir burst into wild cursing as the violence of the untamed Viking surged up in him. "You lie, you wanton!" he shouted, seizing her white wrist in an iron grip. "You were born to lure men to their doom! But you will not play fast and loose with Brodir of Man!"

"You are mad!" she cried, twisting vainly in his grasp. "Release me, or I'll call my guards!"

"Call them!" he snarled, "and I'll slash the heads from their bodies. Cross me now and blood will run ankle-deep in Dublin's streets. By Thor! there will be no city left for Brian to burn! Mailmora, Sitric, Sigurd, Amlaff – I'll cut all their throats and drag you naked to my ship by your yellow hair. Dare to call out!"

She dared not. He forced her to her knees, twisting her white arm so brutally that she bit her lip to keep from screaming.

"You promised Sigurd the same thing you promised me," he went on in ill-controlled fury, "knowing neither of us would throw away his life for less!"

"No! No!" she shrieked. "I swear by the ring of Thor!" Then, as the agony grew unbearable, she dropped pretense. "Yes – yes, I promised him – oh, let me go!"

"So!" The Viking tossed her contemptuously on to a pile of silken cushions, where she lay whimpering and disheveled. "You promised me and you promised Sigurd," he said, looming menacingly above her, "but your promise to me you'll keep – else you had better never been born. The throne of Ireland is a small thing beside my desire for you – if I cannot have you, no one shall."

"But what of Sigurd?"

"He'll fall in battle – or afterward," he answered grimly.

"Good enough!" Dire indeed was the extremity in which Kormlada had not her wits about her. "It's you I love, Brodir; I promised him only because he would not aid us otherwise."

"Love!" The Viking laughed savagely. "You love Kormlada – none other. But you'll keep your vow to me or you'll rue it." And, turning on his heel, he left her chamber.

Kormlada rose, rubbing her arm where the blue marks of his fingers marred her skin. "May he fall in the first charge!" she ground between her teeth. "If either survive, may it be that tall fool, Sigurd – methinks he would be a husband easier to manage than that black-haired savage. I will perforce marry him if he survives the battle, but by Thor! he shall not long press the throne of Ireland – I'll send him to join Brian."

"You speak as though King Brian were already dead." A tranquil voice behind Kormlada brought her about to face the other person in the world she feared besides Brodir. Her eyes widened as they fell upon a slender girl clad in shimmering green, a girl whose golden hair glimmered with unearthly light in the glow of the candles. The queen recoiled, hands outstretched as if to fend her away.

"Eevin! Stand back, witch! Cast no spell on me! How came you into my palace?"

"How came the breeze through the trees?" answered the Danaan girl. "What was Brodir saying to you before I entered?"

"If you are a sorceress, you know," sullenly answered the queen.

Eevin nodded. "Aye, I know. In your own mind I read it. He had consulted the oracle of the sea-people – the blood and the torn heart," – her dainty lips curled with disgust – "and he told you he would attack tomorrow."

The queen blenched and made no reply, fearing to meet Eevin's magnetic eyes. She felt naked before the mysterious girl who could uncannily sift the contents of her mind and empty it of its secrets.

Eevin stood with bent head for a moment, then raised her head suddenly. Kormlada started, for something akin to fear shone in the were-girl's eyes.

"Who is in this castle?" she cried.

"You know as well as I," muttered Kormlada. "Sitric, Sigurd, Brodir."

"There is another!" exclaimed Eevin, paling and shuddering. "Ah, I know him of old – I feel him – he bears the cold of the North with him, the shivering tang of icy seas..."

She turned and slipped swiftly through the velvet hangings that masked a hidden doorway Kormlada had thought known only to herself and her women, leaving the queen bewildered and uneasy.

In the sacrificial chamber, the ancient priest still mumbled over the gory altar upon which lay the mutilated victim of his rite. "Fifty years I have served Odin," he maundered. "And never such portents have I read. Odin laid his mark upon me long ago in a night of horror. The years fall like withered leaves, and my age draws to a close. One by one I have seen the altars of Odin crumble. If the Christians win this battle, Odin's day is done. It comes upon me that I have offered up my last sacrifice..."

A deep, powerful voice spoke behind him. "And what more fitting than that you should accompany the soul of that last sacrifice to the realm of him you served?"

The priest wheeled, the sacrificial dagger falling from his hand. Before him stood a tall man, wrapped in a cloak beneath which shone the gleam of armor. A slouch hat was pulled low over his forehead, and when he pushed it back, a single eye, glittering and grim as the grey sea, met his horrified gaze.

Warriors who rushed into the chamber at the strangled scream that burst hideously forth, found the old priest dead beside his corpse-laden altar, unwounded, but with face and body shriveled as by some intolerable exposure, and a soul-shaking horror in his glassy eyes. Yet, save for the corpses, the chamber was empty, and none had been seen to enter it since Brodir had gone forth.

Alone in his tent with the heavily-armed gallaglachs ranged outside, King Brian was dreaming a strange dream. In his dream a tall grey giant loomed terribly above him and cried in a voice that was like thunder among the clouds, "Beware, champion of the white Christ! Though you smite my children with the sword and drive me into the dark voids of Jotunheim, yet shall I work you rue! As you smite my children with the sword, so shall I smite the son of your body, and as I go into the dark, so shall you go, likewise, when the Choosers of the Slain ride the clouds above the battle-field!"

The thunder of the giant's voice and the awesome glitter of his single eye froze the blood of the king who had never known fear, and with a strangled cry, he woke, starting up. The thick torches which burned outside illumined the interior of his tent sufficiently well for him to make out a slender form.

"Eevin!" he cried. "By my soul! it is well for kings that your people take no part in the intrigues of mortals, when you can steal under the very noses of the guards into our tents. Do you seek Dunlang?"

The girl shook her head sadly. "I see him no more alive, great king. Were I to go to him now, my own black sorrow might unman him. I will come to him among the dead tomorrow."

King Brian shivered.

"But it is not of my woes that I came to speak, My Lord," she continued wearily. "It is not the way of the Dark People to take part in the quarrels of the Tall Folk – but I love one of them. This night I talked with Gormlaith."

Brian winced at the name of his divorced queen. "And your news?" he asked.

"Brodir strikes on the morrow."

The king shook his head heavily. "It vexes my soul to spill blood on the Holy Day. But if God wills it, we will not await their onslaught – we will march at dawn to meet them. I will send a swift runner to bring back Donagh…"

Eevin shook her head once more. "Nay, great king. Let Donagh live. After the battle the Dalcassians will need strong arms to brace the sceptre."

Brian gazed fixedly at her. "I read my doom in those words. Have you cast my fate?"

Eevin spread her hands helplessly. "My Lord, not even the Dark People can rend the Veil at will. Not by the casting of fates, or the sorcery of divination, not in smoke or in blood have I read it, but a weird is upon me and I see through flame and the dim clash of battle."

"And I shall fall?"

She bowed her face in her hands.

"Well, let it fall as God wills," said King Brian tranquilly. "I have lived long and deeply. Weep not – through the darkest mists of gloom and night, dawn yet rises on the world. My clan will revere you in the long days to come. Now go, for the night wanes toward morn, and I would make my peace with God."

And Eevin of Craglea went like a shadow from the king's tent.

V

> The war was like a dream; I cannot tell
> How many heathens souls I sent to Hell.
> I only know, above the fallen ones
> I heard dark Odin shouting to his sons,
> And felt amid the battle's roar and shock
> The strife of gods that crashed in Ragnarok.
>   — Conn's Saga

Through the mist of the whitening dawn men moved like ghosts and weapons clanked eerily. Conn stretched his muscular arms, yawned cavernously, and loosened his great blade in its sheath. "This is the day the ravens drink blood, My Lord," he said, and Dunlang O'Hartigan nodded absently.

"Come hither and aid me to don this cursed cage," said the young chief. "For Eevin's sake I'll wear it; but by the saints! I had rather battle stark naked!"

The Gaels were on the move, marching from Kilmainham in the same formation in which they intended to enter battle. First came the Dalcassians, big rangy men in their saffron tunics, with a round buckler of steel-braced yew wood on the left arm, and the right hand gripping the dreaded Dalcassian ax. This ax differed greatly from the heavy weapon of the Danes; the Irish wielded it with one hand, the thumb stretched along the haft to guide the blow, and they had attained a skill at ax-fighting never before or since equalled. Hauberks they had none, neither the gallaglachs nor the kerns, though some of their chiefs, like Murrogh, wore light steel caps. But the tunics of warriors and chiefs alike had been woven with such skill and steeped in vinegar until their remarkable toughness afforded some protection against sword and arrow.

At the head of the Dalcassians strode Prince Murrogh, his fierce eyes alight, smiling as though he went to a feast instead of a slaughtering. On one side went Dunlang in his Roman corselet, closely followed by Conn, bearing the helmet, and on the other the two Turloghs — the son of Murrogh, and Turlogh Dubh, who alone of all the Dalcassians always went into battle fully armored. He looked grim enough, despite his youth, with his dark face and smoldering blue eyes, clad as he was in a full shirt of black mail, mail leggings and a steel helmet with a mail drop, and bearing a spiked buckler. Unlike the rest of the chiefs, who preferred their swords in battle, Black Turlogh fought with an ax of his own forging, and his skill with the weapon was almost uncanny.

Close behind the Dalcassians were the two companies of the Scottish, with their chiefs, the Great Stewards of Scotland, who, veterans of long wars with the Saxons, wore helmets with horsehair crests and coats of mail. With them came the men of South Munster commanded by Prince Meathla O'Faelan.

The third division consisted of the warriors of Connacht, wild men of the west, shock-headed and naked but for their wolf-skins, with their chiefs O'Kelly and O'Hyne. O'Kelly marched as a man whose soul is heavy, for the shadow of his meeting with Malachi the night before fell gauntly across him.

Somewhat apart from the three main divisions marched the tall galla-glachs and kerns of Meath, their king riding slowly before them.

And before all the host rode King Brian Boru on a white steed, his white locks blown about his ancient face and his eyes strange and fey, so that the wild kerns gazed on him with superstitious awe.

So the Gaels came before Dublin, where they saw the hosts of Leinster and Lochlann drawn up in battle array, stretching in a wide crescent from Dubhgall's Bridge to the narrow river Tolka which cuts the plain of Clontarf. Three main divisions there were – the foreign Northmen, the Vikings, with Sigurd and the grim Brodir; flanking them on the one side, the fierce Danes of Dublin, under their chief, a sombre wanderer whose name no man knew, but who was called Dubhgall, the Dark Stranger; and on the other flank the Irish of Leinster, with their king, Mailmora. The Danish fortress on the hill beyond the Liffey River bristled with armed men where King Sitric guarded the city.

There was but one way into the city from the north, the direction from which the Gaels were advancing, for in those days Dublin lay wholly south of the Liffey; that was the bridge called Dubhgall's Bridge. The Danes stood with one horn of their line guarding this entrance, their ranks curving out toward the Tolka, their backs to the sea. The Gaels advanced along the level plain which stretched between Tomar's Wood and the shore.

With little more than a bow-shot separating the hosts, the Gaels halted, and King Brian rode in front of them, holding aloft a crucifix. "Sons of Goidhel!" his voice rang like a trumpet call. "It is not given me to lead you into the fray, as I led you in days of old. But I have pitched my tent behind your lines, where you must trample me if you flee. You will not flee! Remember a hundred years of outrage and infamy! Remember your burned homes, your slaughtered kin, your ravaged women, your babes enslaved!

Before you stand your oppressors! On this day our good Lord died for you! There stand the heathen hordes which revile His Name and slay His people! I have but one command to give you – conquer or die!"

The wild hordes yelled like wolves and a forest of axes brandished on high. King Brian bowed his head and his face was grey.

"Let them lead me back to my tent," he whispered to Murrogh. "Age has withered me from the play of the axes and my doom is hard upon me. Go forth, and may God stiffen your arms to the slaying!"

Now as the king rode slowly back to his tent among his guardsmen, there was a taking up of girdles, a drawing of blades, a dressing of shields. Conn placed the Roman helmet on Dunlang's head and grinned at the result, for the young chief looked like some mythical iron monster out of Norse legendry. The hosts moved inexorably toward each other.

The Vikings had assumed their favorite wedge-shaped formation with Sigurd and Brodir at the tip. The Northmen offered a strong contrast to the loose lines of the half-naked Gaels. They moved in compact ranks, armored with horned helmets, heavy scale-mail coats reaching to their knees, and leggings of seasoned wolf-hide braced with iron plates; and they bore great kite-shaped shields of linden wood with iron rims, and long spears. The thousand warriors in the forefront wore long leggings and gauntlets of mail as well, so that from crown to heel they were steel-clad. These marched in a solid shield-wall, bucklers overlapping, and over their iron ranks floated the grim raven banner which had always brought victory to Jarl Sigurd – even if it brought death to the bearer. Now it was borne by old Rane Asgrimm's son, who felt that the hour of his death was at hand.

At the tip of the wedge, like the point of a spear, were the champions of Lochlann – Brodir in his dully glittering blue mail, which no blade had even dented; Jarl Sigurd, tall, blond-bearded, gleaming in his golden-scaled hauberk; Hrafn the Red, in whose soul lurked a mocking devil that moved him to gargantuan laughter even in the madness of battle; the tall comrades, Thorstein and Asmund; Prince Amlaff, roving son of the King of Norway; Platt of Danemark; Athelstane the Saxon; Jarl Thorwald Raven of the Hebrides; Anrad the berserk.

Toward this formidable array the Irish advanced at quick pace in more or less open formation and with scant attempt at any orderly ranks. But Malachi and his warriors wheeled suddenly and drew off to the extreme left, taking up their position on the high ground by Cabra. And when Murrogh saw this, he cursed under his breath, and Black Turlogh growled, "Who said an O'Neill forgets an old grudge? By Crom! Murrogh, we may have to guard our backs as well as our breasts before this fight be won!"

Now suddenly from the Viking ranks strode Platt of Danemark, his red hair like a crimson veil about his bare head, his silver mail gleaming. The hosts watched eagerly, for in those days few battles began without preliminary single combats.

"Donald!" shouted Platt, flinging up his naked sword so that the rising sun caught it in a sheen of silver. "Where is Donald of Mar? Are you there, Donald, as you were at Rhu Stoir, or do you skulk from the fray?"

"I am here, rogue!" answered the Scottish chief as he strode, tall and gaunt, from among his men, flinging away his scabbard.

Highlander and Dane met in the middle space between the hosts, Donald cautious as a hunting wolf, Platt leaping in reckless and headlong, eyes alight and dancing with a laughing madness. Yet it was the wary Steward's foot which slipped suddenly on a rolling pebble, and before he could regain his balance, Platt's sword lunged into him so fiercely that the keen point tore through his corselet-scales and sank deep beneath his heart. Platt's mad yell of exultation broke in a gasp. Even as he crumpled, Donald of Mar lashed out a dying stroke that split the Dane's head, and the two fell together.

Thereat a deep-toned roar went up to the heavens, and the two great hosts rolled together like a tidal wave. Then were struck the first blows of the battle. There were no maneuvers of strategy, no cavalry charges, no flights of arrows. Forty thousand men fought on foot, hand to hand, man to man, slaying and dying in red chaos. The battle broke in howling waves about the spears and axes of the warriors. The first to shock were the Dalcassians and the Vikings, and as they met, both lines rocked at the impact. The deep roar of the Norsemen mingled with the yells of the Gaels and the Northern spears splintered among the Western axes. Foremost in the fray, Murrogh's great body heaved and strained as he roared and smote right and left with a heavy sword in either hand, mowing down men like corn. Neither shield nor helmet stood beneath his terrible blows, and behind him came his warriors slashing and howling like devils. Against the compact lines of the Dublin Danes thundered the wild tribesmen of Connacht, and the men of South Munster and their Scottish allies fell vengefully upon the Irish of Leinster.

The iron lines writhed and interwove across the plain. Conn, following Dunlang, grinned savagely as he smote home with dripping blade, and his fierce eyes sought for Thorwald Raven among the spears. But in that mad sea of battle where wild faces came and went like waves, it was difficult to pick out any one man.

At first both lines held without giving an inch; feet braced, straining breast to breast, they snarled and hacked, shield jammed hard against shield. All up and down the line of battle blades shimmered and flashed like sea-spray in the sun, and the roar of battle shook the ravens that wheeled like

171

Valkyries overhead. Then, when human flesh and blood could stand no more, the serried lines began to roll forward or back. The Leinstermen flinched before the fierce onslaught of the Munster clans and their Scottish allies, giving way slowly, foot by foot, cursed by their king, who fought on foot with a sword in the forefront of the fray.

But on the other flanks, the Danes of Dublin under the redoubtable Dubhgall had held against the first blasting charge of the Western tribes, though their ranks reeled at the shock, and now the wild men in their wolf-skins were falling like garnered grain before the Danish axes.

In the center, the battle raged most fiercely; the wedge-shaped shield-wall of the Vikings held, and against its iron ranks the Dalcassians hurled their half-naked bodies in vain. A ghastly heap ringed that rim wall as Brodir and Sigurd began a slow, steady advance, the inexorable onstride of the Vikings, hacking deeper and deeper into the loose formation of the Gaels.

On the walls of Dublin Castle, King Sitric, watching the fight with Kormlada and his wife, exclaimed, "Well do the sea-kings reap the field!"

Kormlada's beautiful eyes blazed with wild exultation. "Fall, Brian!" she cried fiercely. "Fall, Murrogh! And fall too, Brodir! Let the keen ravens feed!" Her voice faltered as her eyes fell upon a tall cloaked figure standing on the battlements, apart from the people – a sombre grey giant, brooding over the battle. A cold fear stole over her and froze the words on her lips. She plucked at Sitric's cloak. "Who is he?" she whispered, pointing.

Sitric looked and shuddered. "I know not. Pay him no heed. Go not near him. When I but approached him, he spoke not or looked at me, but a cold wind blew over me and my heart shriveled. Let us rather watch the battle. The Gaels give way."

But at the foremost point of the Gaelic advance, the line held. There, like the convex center of a curving ax-blade, fought Murrogh and his chiefs. The great prince was already streaming blood from gashes on his limbs, but his heavy swords flamed in double strokes that dealt death like a harvest, and the chiefs at his side mowed down the corn of battle.

Fiercely Murrogh sought to reach Sigurd through the press. He saw the tall Jarl looming across the waves of spears and heads, striking blows like thunderstrokes, and the sight drove the Gaelic prince to madness. But he could not reach the Viking.

"The warriors are forced back," gasped Dunlang, seeking to shake the sweat from his eyes. The young chief was untouched; spears and axes alike splintered on the Roman helmet or glanced from the ancient cuirass, but, unused to armor, he felt like a chained wolf.

Murrogh spared a single swift glance; on either side of the clump of chiefs, the gallaglachs were falling back, slowly, savagely, selling each foot of ground with blood, unable to halt the irresistible advance of the mailed Northmen. These were falling, too, all along the battle-line, but they closed ranks and forced their way forward, legs braced hard, bodies strained, spears driving without cease or pause; they plowed on through a red surf of dead and dying.

"Turlogh!" gasped Murrogh, dashing the blood from his eyes. "Haste from the fray for Malachi! Bid him charge, in God's name!"

But the frenzy of slaughter was on Black Turlogh; froth flecked his lips and his eyes were those of a madman. "The Devil take Malachi!" he shouted, splitting a Dane's skull with a stroke like the slash of a tiger's paw.

"Conn!" called Murrogh, and as he spoke he gripped the big kern's shoulder and dragged him back. "Haste to Malachi – we need his support."

Conn drew reluctantly away from the mêlée, clearing his path with thunderous strokes. Across the reeling sea of blades and rocking helmets he saw the towering form of Jarl Sigurd and his lords – the billowing folds of the raven banner floated above them as their whistling swords hewed down men like wheat before the reaper.

Free of the press, the kern ran swiftly along the battle-line until he came to the higher ground of Cabra where the Meathmen thronged, tense and trembling like hunting hounds as they gripped their weapons and looked eagerly at their king. Malachi stood apart, watching the fray with moody eyes, his lion's head bowed, his fingers twined in his golden beard.

"King Melaghlin," said Conn bluntly, "Prince Murrogh urges you to charge home, for the press is great and the men of the Gael are hard beset."

The great O'Neill lifted his head and stared absently at the kern. Conn little guessed the chaotic struggle which was taking place in Malachi's soul – the red visions which thronged his brain – riches, power, the rule of all Erin, balanced against the black shame of treachery. He gazed out across the field where the banner of his nephew O'Kelly heaved among the spears. And Malachi shuddered, but shook his head.

"Nay," he said, "it is not time. I will charge – when the time comes."

For an instant king and kern looked into each others' eyes. Malachi's eyes dropped. Conn turned without a word and sped down the slope. As he went, he saw that the advance of Lennox and the men of Desmond had been checked. Mailmora, raging like a wild man, had cut down Prince Meathla O'Faelan with his own hand, a chance spear-thrust had wounded the Great Steward, and now the Leinstermen held fast against the onset of the Munster and Scottish clans. But where the Dalcassians fought, the battle was locked; the Prince of Thomond broke the onrush of the Norsemen like a jutting cliff that breaks the sea.

Conn reached Murrogh in the upheaval of slaughter. "Melaghlin says he will charge when the time comes."

"Hell to his soul!" cried Black Turlogh. "We are betrayed!"

Murrogh's blue eyes flamed. "Then in the name of God!" he roared, "*Let us charge and die!*"

The struggling men were stirred at his shout. The blind passion of the Gael surged up, bred of desperation; the lines stiffened, and a great shout shook the field that made King Sitric on his castle wall whiten and grip the parapet. He had heard such shouting before.

Now, as Murrogh leaped forward, the Gaels awoke to red fury as in men who have no hope. The nearness of doom woke frenzy in them, and, like inspired madmen, they hurled their last charge and smote the wall of shields, which reeled at the blow. No human power could stay the onslaught. Murrogh and his chiefs no longer hoped to win, or even to live, but only to glut their fury as they died, and in their despair they fought like wounded tigers – severing limbs, splitting skulls, cleaving breasts and shoulder-bones. Close at Murrogh's heels, flamed the ax of Black Turlogh and the swords of Dunlang and the chiefs; under that torrent of steel the iron line crumpled and gave, and through the breach the frenzied Gaels poured. The shield formation melted away.

At the same moment the wild men of Connacht again hurled a desperate charge against the Dublin Danes. O'Hyne and Dubhgall fell together and the Dublin men were battered backward, disputing every foot. The whole field melted into a mingled mass of slashing battlers without rank or formation. Among a heap of torn Dalcassian dead, Murrogh came at last upon Jarl Sigurd. Behind the Jarl stood grim old Rane Asgrimm's son, holding the raven banner. Murrogh slew him with a single stroke. Sigurd turned, and his sword rent Murrogh's tunic and gashed his chest, but the Irish prince smote so fiercely on the Norseman's shield that Jarl Sigurd reeled backward.

Thorleif Hordi had picked up the banner, but scarce had he lifted it when Black Turlogh, his eyes glaring, broke through and split his skull to the teeth. Sigurd, seeing his banner fallen once more, struck Murrogh with such desperate fury that his sword bit through the prince's morion and gashed his

scalp. Blood jetted down Murrogh's face, and he reeled, but before Sigurd could strike again, Black Turlogh's ax licked out like a flicker of lightning. The Jarl's warding shield fell shattered from his arm, and Sigurd gave back for an instant, daunted by the play of that deathly ax. Then a rush of warriors swept the raging chiefs apart.

"Thorstein!" shouted Sigurd. "Take up the banner!"

"Touch it not!" cried Asmund. "Who bears it, dies!" Even as he spoke, Dunlang's sword crushed his skull.

"Hrafn!" called Sigurd desperately. "Bear the banner!"

"Bear your own curse!" answered Hrafn. "This is the end of us all."

"Cowards!" roared the Jarl, snatching up the banner himself and striving to gather it under his cloak as Murrogh, face bloodied and eyes blazing, broke through to him. Sigurd flung up his sword – too late. The weapon in Murrogh's right hand splintered on his helmet, bursting the straps that held it and ripping it from his head, and Murrogh's left-hand sword, whistling in behind the first blow, shattered the Jarl's skull and felled him dead in the bloody folds of the great banner that wrapped about him as he went down.

Now a great roar went up, and the Gaels redoubled their strokes. With the formation of shields torn apart, the mail of the Vikings could not save them; for the Dalcassian axes, flashing in the sun, hewed through chain-mesh and iron plates alike, rending linden shield and horned helmet. Yet the Danes did not break.

On the high ramparts, King Sitric had turned pale, his hands trembling where he gripped the parapet. He knew that these wild men could not be beaten now, for they spilled their lives like water, hurling their naked bodies again and again into the fangs of spear and ax. Kormlada was silent, but Sitric's wife, King Brian's daughter, cried out in joy, for her heart was with her own people.

Murrogh was striving now to reach Brodir, but the black Viking had seen Sigurd die. Brodir's world was crumbling; even his vaunted mail was failing him, for though it had thus far saved his skin, it was tattered now. Never before had the Manx Viking faced the dreaded Dalcassian ax. He drew back from Murrogh's onset. In the crush, an ax shattered on Murrogh's helmet, knocking him to his knees and blinding him momentarily with its impact. Dunlang's sword wove a wheel of death above the fallen prince, and Murrogh reeled up.

The press slackened as Black Turlogh, Conn and young Turlogh drove in, hacking and stabbing, and Dunlang, frenzied by the heat of battle, tore off his helmet and flung it aside, ripping off his cuirass.

"The Devil eat such cages!" he shouted, catching at the reeling prince to support him, and even at that instant Thorstein the Dane ran in and drove his spear into Dunlang's side. The young Dalcassian staggered and fell at Murrogh's feet, and Conn leaped forward to strike Thorstein's head from his shoulders so that it whirled grinning still through the air in a shower of crimson.

Murrogh shook the darkness from his eyes. "Dunlang!" he cried in a fearful voice, falling to his knees at his friend's side and raising his head.

But Dunlang's eyes were already glazing. "Murrogh! Eevin!" Then blood gushed from his lips and he went limp in Murrogh's arms.

Murrogh leaped up with a shout of demoniac fury. He rushed into the thick of the Vikings, and his men swept in behind him.

On the hill of Cabra, Malachi cried out, flinging doubts and plots to the wind. As Brodir had plotted, so had he. He had but to stand aside until both hosts were cut to pieces, then seize Erin, tricking the Danes as they had planned to betray him. But his blood cried out against him and would not be stilled. He gripped the golden collar of Tomar about his neck, the collar he had taken so many years before from the Danish king his sword had broken, and the old fire leaped up.

"Charge and die!" he shouted, drawing his sword, and at his back the men of Meath gave tongue like a hunting pack and swarmed down into the field.

Under the shock of the Meathmen's assault, the weakened Danes staggered and broke. They tore away singly and in desperate slashing groups, seeking to gain the bay where their ships were anchored. But the Meathmen had cut off their retreat, and the ships lay far out, for the tide was at flood. All day that terrific battle had ranged, yet to Conn, snatching a startled glance at the setting sun, it seemed that scarce an hour had passed since the first lines had crashed together.

The fleeing Northmen made for the river, and the Gaels plunged in after them to drag them down. Among the fugitives and the groups of Norsemen who here and there made determined stands, the Irish chiefs were divided. The boy Turlogh was separated from Murrogh's side and vanished in the Tolka, struggling with a Dane. The clans of Leinster did not break until Black Turlogh rushed like a maddened beast into the thick of them and struck Mailmora dead in the midst of his warriors.

Murrogh, still blood-mad, but staggering from fatigue and weakened by loss of blood, came upon a band of Vikings who, back to back, resisted the conquerors. Their leader was Anrad the Berserk, who, when he saw Murrogh, rushed furiously upon him. Murrogh, too weary to parry the Dane's stroke, dropped his own sword and closed with Anrad, bearing him to the ground. The sword was wrenched from the Dane's hand as they fell. Both snatched at it, but Murrogh caught the hilt and Anrad the blade. The Gaelic prince tore it away, dragging the keen edge through the Viking's hand, severing nerve and thew; and, setting a knee on Anrad's chest, Murrogh drove the sword thrice through his body. Anrad, dying, drew a dagger, but his strength ebbed so swiftly that his arm sank. And then a mighty hand gripped his wrist and drove home the stroke he had sought to strike, so that the keen blade sank beneath Murrogh's heart. Murrogh fell back dying, and his last glance showed him a tall grey giant looming above, his cloak billowing in the wind, his one glittering eye cold and terrible. But the mazed eyes of the surrounding warriors saw only death and the dealing of death.

The Danes were all in flight now, and on the high wall King Sitric sat watching his high ambitions fade away, while Kormlada gazed wild-eyed into ruin, defeat and shame.

Conn ran among the dying and the fleeing, seeking Thorwald Raven. The kern's buckler was gone, shattered among the axes. His broad breast was gashed in half a dozen places; a sword-edge had bitten into his scalp when only his shock of tangled hair had saved him. A spear had girded into his thigh. Yet now in his heat and fury he scarcely felt these wounds.

A weakening hand caught at Conn's knee as he stumbled among dead men in wolf-skins and mailed corpses. He bent and saw O'Kelly, Malachi's nephew, and chief of the Hy Many. The chief's eyes were glazing in death. Conn lifted his head, and a smile curled the blue lips.

"I hear the war-cry of the O'Neill," he whispered. "Malachi could not betray us. He could not stand from the fray. The Red Hand – to – Victory!"

Conn rose as O'Kelly died, and caught sight of a familiar figure. Thorwald Raven had broken from the press and now fled alone and swiftly, not toward the sea or the river, where his comrades died beneath the Gaelic axes, but toward Tomar's Wood. Conn followed, spurred by his hate.

Thorwald saw him, and turned, snarling. So the thrall met his former master. As Conn rushed into close quarters, the Norseman gripped his spear-shaft with both hands and lunged fiercely, but the point glanced from the great copper collar about the kern's neck. Conn, bending low, lunged upward with all his power, so that the great blade ripped through Jarl Thorwald's tattered mail and spilled his entrails on the ground.

Turning, Conn saw that the chase had brought him almost to the king's tent, pitched behind the battle-lines. He saw King Brian Boru standing in front of the tent, his white locks flowing in the wind, and but one man attending him. Conn ran forward.

"Kern, what are your tidings?" asked the king.

"The foreigners flee," answered Conn, "but Murrogh has fallen."

"You bring evil tidings," said Brian. "Erin shall never again look on a champion like him." And age like a cold cloud closed upon him.

"Where are your guards, My Lord?" asked Conn.

"They have joined in the pursuit."

"Let me then take you to a safer place," said Conn. "The Gall fly all about us here."

King Brian shook his head. "Nay, I know I leave not this place alive, for Eevin of Craglea told me last night I should fall this day. And what avails me to survive Murrogh and the champions of the Gael? Let me lie at Armagh, in the peace of God."

Now the attendant cried out, "My king, we are undone! Men blue and naked are upon us."

"The armored Danes," cried Conn, wheeling.

King Brian drew his heavy sword.

A group of blood-stained Vikings were approaching, led by Brodir and Prince Amlaff. Their vaunted mail hung in shreds; their swords were notched and dripping. Brodir had marked the king's tent from afar, and was bent on murder, for his soul raged with shame and fury and he was beset by visions in which Brian, Sigurd, and Kormlada spun in a hellish dance. He had lost the battle, Ireland, Kormlada — now he was ready to give up his life in a dying stroke of vengeance.

Brodir rushed upon the king, Prince Amlaff at his heels. Conn sprang to bar their way. But Brodir swerved aside and left the kern to Amlaff, as he fell upon the king. Conn took Amlaff's blade in his left arm and smote a single terrible blow that rent the prince's hauberk like paper and shattered his spine. Then the kern sprang back to guard King Brian.

Then even as he turned, Conn saw Brodir parry Brian's stroke and drive his sword through the ancient king's breast. Brian went down, but even as he fell he caught himself on one knee and thrust his keen blade through flesh and bone, cutting both Brodir's legs from under him. The Viking's scream of triumph broke in a ghastly groan as he toppled in a widening pool of crimson. There he struggled convulsively and lay still.

Conn stood looking dazedly around him. Brodir's company of men had fled, and the Gaels were converging on Brian's tent. The sound of the keening for the heroes already rose to mingle with the screams and shouts that still came from the struggling hordes along the river. They were bringing Murrogh's body to the king's tent, walking slowly — weary, bloody men, with bowed heads. Behind the litter that bore the prince's body came others — laden with the bodies of Turlogh, Murrogh's son; of Donald, Steward of Mar; of O'Kelly and O'Hyne, the western chiefs; of Prince Meathla O'Faelan; of Dunlang O'Hartigan, beside whose litter walked Eevin of Craglea, her golden head sunk on her breast.

The warriors set down the litters and gathered silently and wearily about the corpse of King Brian Boru. They gazed unspeaking, their minds dulled from the agony of strife. Eevin lay motionless beside the body of her lover, as if she herself were dead; no tears stood in her eyes, no cry or moan escaped her pallid lips.

The clamor of battle was dying as the setting sun bathed the trampled field in its roseate light. The fugitives, tattered and slashed, were limping into the gates of Dublin, and the warriors of King Sitric were preparing to stand siege. But the Irish were in no condition to besiege the city. Four thousand warriors and chieftains had fallen, and nearly all the champions of the Gael were dead. But more than seven thousand Danes and Leinstermen lay stretched on the blood-soaked earth, and the power of the Vikings was broken. On Clontarf their iron reign was ended.

Conn walked toward the river, feeling now the ache of his stiffening wounds. He met Turlogh Dubh. The madness of battle was gone from Black Turlogh, and his dark face was inscrutable. From head to foot he was splattered with crimson.

"My Lord," said Conn, fingering the great copper ring about his neck, "I have slain the man who put this thrall-mark on me. I would be free of it."

Black Turlogh took his red-stained ax-head in his hands and, pressing it against the ring, drove the keen edge through the softer metal. The ax gashed Conn's shoulder, but neither heeded.

"Now I am truly free," said Conn, flexing his mighty arms. "My heart is heavy for the chiefs who have fallen, but my mind is mazed with wonder and glory. When will ever such a battle be fought again? Truly, it was a feast of the ravens, a sea of slaughter..."

His voice trailed off, and he stood like a statue, head flung back, eyes staring into the clouded heavens. The sun was sinking in a dark-ocean of scarlet. Great clouds rolled and tumbled, piled mountainously against the smouldering red of the sunset. A wind blew out of them, biting, cold, and, borne on the wind, etched shadowy against the clouds, a vague, gigantic form went flying, beard and wild locks streaming in the gale, cloak billowing out like great wings – speeding into the mysterious blue mists that pulsed and shimmered in the brooding North.

"Look up there – in the sky!" cried Conn. "The grey man! It is he! The grey man with the single terrible eye. I saw him in the mountains of Torka. I glimpsed him brooding on the walls of Dublin while the battle raged. I saw him looming above Prince Murrogh as he died. Look! He rides the wind and races among the tall clouds. He dwindles. He fades into the void! He vanishes!"

"It is Odin, god of the sea-people," said Turlogh sombrely. "His children are broken, his altars crumble, and his worshippers fallen before the swords of the South. He flees the new gods and their children, and returns to the blue gulfs of the North which gave him birth. No more will helpless victims howl beneath the daggers of his priests — no more will he stalk the black clouds." He shook his head darkly. "The Grey God passes, and we too are passing, though we have conquered. The days of the twilight come on amain, and a strange feeling is upon me as of a waning age. What are we all, too, but ghosts waning into the night?"

And he went on into the dusk, leaving Conn to his freedom — from thralldom and cruelty, as both he and all the Gaels were now free of the shadow of the Grey God and his ruthless worshippers.

The Song of the Last Briton

The sea is grey in the death of day,
    Behind me lifts the night.
I'll flee no more from the ancient shore
    Where first I saw the light.

The Saxons come and the Saxons go
    With the ebb and flow of the tide;
Their galleys loom, grim shapes of doom,
    But here shall I abide.

My castles rust in crimson dust,
    Red ruin tossed in the drift –
But the sea is grey, and the wolf's at bay,
    And the ravens circle swift.

Come from the mists of the Northern Sea
    Where the smoke blue hazes melt.
Your dead shall lie where here I die,
    The last unconquered Celt.

Worms of the Earth

"Strike in the nails, soldiers, and let our guest see the reality of our good Roman justice!"

The speaker wrapped his purple cloak closer about his powerful frame and settled back into his official chair, much as he might have settled back in his seat at the Circus Maximus to enjoy the clash of gladiatorial swords. Realization of power colored his every move. Whetted pride was necessary to Roman satisfaction, and Titus Sulla was justly proud; for he was military governor of Eboracum and answerable only to the emperor of Rome. He was a strongly built man of medium height, with the hawk-like features of the pure-bred Roman. Now a mocking smile curved his full lips, increasing the arrogance of his haughty aspect. Distinctly military in appearance, he wore the golden-scaled corselet and chased breastplate of his rank, with the short stabbing sword at his belt, and he held on his knee the silvered helmet with its plumed crest. Behind him stood a clump of impassive soldiers with shield and spear – blond titans from the Rhineland.

Before him was taking place the scene which apparently gave him so much real gratification – a scene common enough wherever stretched the far-flung boundaries of Rome. A rude cross lay flat upon the barren earth and on it was bound a man – half naked, wild of aspect with his corded limbs, glaring eyes and shock of tangled hair. His executioners were Roman soldiers, and with heavy hammers they prepared to pin the victim's hands and feet to the wood with iron spikes.

Only a small group of men watched this ghastly scene, in the dread place of execution beyond the city walls: the governor and his watchful guards; a few young Roman officers; the man to whom Sulla had referred as "guest" and who stood like a bronze image, unspeaking. Beside the gleaming splendor of the Roman, the quiet garb of this man seemed drab, almost somber.

He was dark, but he did not resemble the Latins around him. There was about him none of the warm, almost Oriental sensuality of the Mediterranean which colored their features. The blond barbarians behind Sulla's chair were less unlike the man in facial outline than were the Romans. Not his were the full curving red lips, nor the rich waving locks suggestive of the Greek. Nor was his dark complexion the rich olive of the south; rather it was the bleak darkness of the north. The whole aspect of the man vaguely suggested the shadowed mists, the gloom, the cold and the icy winds of the naked northern lands. Even his black eyes were savagely cold, like black fires burning through fathoms of ice.

His height was only medium but there was something about him which transcended mere physical bulk – a certain fierce innate vitality, comparable only to that of a wolf or a panther. In every line of his supple, compact body, as well as in his coarse straight hair and thin lips, this was evident – in the hawk-like set of the head on the corded neck, in the broad square shoulders, in the deep chest, the lean loins, the narrow feet. Built with the savage economy of a panther, he was an image of dynamic potentialities, pent in with iron self-control.

At his feet crouched one like him in complexion – but there the resemblance ended. This other was a stunted giant, with gnarly limbs, thick body, a low sloping brow and an expression of dull ferocity, now clearly mixed with fear. If the man on the cross resembled, in a tribal way, the man Titus Sulla called guest, he far more resembled the stunted crouching giant.

"Well, Partha Mac Othna," said the governor with studied effrontery, "when you return to your tribe, you will have a tale to tell of the justice of Rome, who rules the south."

"I will have a tale," answered the other in a voice which betrayed no emotion, just as his dark face, schooled to immobility, showed no evidence of the maelstrom in his soul.

"Justice to all under the rule of Rome," said Sulla. "Pax Romana! Reward for virtue, punishment for wrong!" He laughed inwardly at his own black hypocrisy, then continued: "You see, emissary of Pictland, how swiftly Rome punishes the transgressor."

"I see," answered the Pict in a voice which strongly-curbed anger made deep with menace, "that the subject of a foreign king is dealt with as though he were a Roman slave."

"He has been tried and condemned in an unbiased court," retorted Sulla.

"Aye! and the accuser was a Roman, the witnesses Roman, the judge Roman! He committed murder? In a moment of fury he struck down a Roman merchant who cheated, tricked and robbed him, and to injury added insult – aye, and a blow! Is his king but a dog, that Rome crucifies his subjects at will, condemned by Roman courts? Is his king too weak or foolish to do justice, were he informed and formal charges brought against the offender?"

"Well," said Sulla cynically, "you may inform Bran Mak Morn yourself. Rome, my friend, makes no account of her actions to barbarian kings. When savages come among us, let them act with discretion or suffer the consequences."

The Pict shut his iron jaws with a snap that told Sulla further badgering would elicit no reply. The Roman made a gesture to the executioners. One of them seized a spike and placing it against the thick wrist of the victim, smote heavily. The iron point sank deep through the flesh, crunching against the bones. The lips of the man on the cross writhed, though no moan escaped him. As a trapped wolf fights against his cage, the bound victim instinctively wrenched and struggled. The veins swelled in his temples, sweat beaded his low forehead, the muscles in arms and legs writhed and knotted. The hammers fell in inexorable strokes, driving the cruel points deeper and deeper, through wrists and ankles; blood flowed in a black river over the hands that held the spikes, staining the wood of the cross, and the splintering of bones was distinctly heard. Yet the sufferer made no outcry, though his blackened lips writhed back until the gums were visible, and his shaggy head jerked involuntarily from side to side.

The man called Partha Mac Othna stood like an iron image, eyes burning from an inscrutable face, his whole body hard as iron from the tension of his control. At his feet crouched his misshapen servant, hiding his face from the grim sight, his arms locked about his master's knees. Those arms gripped like steel and under his breath the fellow mumbled ceaselessly as if in invocation.

The last stroke fell; the cords were cut from arm and leg, so that the man would hang supported by the nails alone. He had ceased his struggling that only twisted the spikes in his agonizing wounds. His bright black eyes, unglazed, had not left the face of the man called Partha Mac Othna; in them lingered a desperate shadow of hope. Now the soldiers lifted the cross and set the end of it in the hole prepared, stamped the dirt about it to hold it erect. The Pict hung in midair, suspended by the nails in his flesh, but still no sound escaped his lips. His eyes still hung on the somber face of the emissary, but the shadow of hope was fading.

"He'll live for days!" said Sulla cheerfully. "These Picts are harder than cats to kill! I'll keep a guard of ten soldiers watching night and day to see that no one takes him down before he dies. Ho, there, Valerius, in honor of our esteemed neighbor, King Bran Mak Morn, give him a cup of wine!"

With a laugh the young officer came forward, holding a brimming wine-cup, and rising on his toes, lifted it to the parched lips of the sufferer. In the black eyes flared a red wave of unquenchable hatred; writhing his head aside to avoid even touching the cup, he spat full into the young Roman's eyes. With a curse Valerius dashed the cup to the ground, and before any could halt him, wrenched out his sword and sheathed it in the man's body.

Sulla rose with an imperious exclamation of anger; the man called Partha Mac Othna had started violently, but he bit his lip and said nothing. Valerius seemed somewhat surprized at himself, as he sullenly cleansed his sword. The act had been instinctive, following the insult to Roman pride, the one thing unbearable.

"Give up your sword, young sir!" exclaimed Sulla. "Centurion Publius, place him under arrest. A few days in a cell with stale bread and water will teach you to curb your patrician pride, in matters dealing with the will of the empire. What, you young fool, do you not realize that you could not have made the dog a more kindly gift? Who would not rather desire a quick death on the sword than the slow agony on the cross? Take him away. And you, centurion, see that guards remain at the cross so that the body is not cut down until the ravens pick bare the bones. Partha Mac Othna, I go to a banquet at the house of Demetrius – will you not accompany me?"

The emissary shook his head, his eyes fixed on the limp form which sagged on the black-stained cross. He made no reply. Sulla smiled sardonically, then rose and strode away, followed by his secretary who bore the gilded chair ceremoniously, and by the stolid soldiers, with whom walked Valerius, head sunken.

The man called Partha Mac Othna flung a wide fold of his cloak about his shoulder, halted a moment to gaze at the grim cross with its burden, darkly etched against the crimson sky, where the clouds of night were gathering. Then he stalked away, followed by his silent servant.

II

In an inner chamber of Eboracum, the man called Partha Mac Othna paced tigerishly to and fro. His sandalled feet made no sound on the marble tiles.

"Grom!" he turned to the gnarled servant, "well I know why you held my knees so tightly – why you muttered aid of the Moon-Woman – you feared I would lose my self-control and make a mad attempt to succor that poor wretch. By the gods, I believe that was what the dog Roman wished – his iron-cased watch-dogs watched me narrowly, I know, and his baiting was harder to bear than ordinarily.

"Gods black and white, dark and light!" he shook his clenched fists above his head in the black gust of his passion. "That I should stand by and see a man of mine butchered on a Roman cross – without justice and with no more trial than that farce! Black gods of R'lyeh, even you would I invoke to the ruin and destruction of those butchers! I swear by the Nameless Ones, men shall die howling for that deed, and Rome shall cry out as a woman in the dark who treads upon an adder!"

"He knew you, master," said Grom.

The other dropped his head and covered his eyes with a gesture of savage pain.

"His eyes will haunt me when I lie dying. Aye, he knew me, and almost until the last, I read in his eyes the hope that I might aid him. Gods and devils, is Rome to butcher my people beneath my very eyes? Then I am not king but dog!"

"Not so loud, in the name of all the gods!" exclaimed Grom in affright. "Did these Romans suspect you were Bran Mak Morn, they would nail you on a cross beside that other."

"They will know it ere long," grimly answered the king. "Too long I have lingered here in the guise of an emissary, spying upon mine enemies. They have thought to play with me, these Romans, masking their contempt and scorn only under polished satire. Rome is courteous to barbarian ambassadors, they give us fine houses to live in, offer us slaves, pander to our lusts with women and gold and wine and games, but all the while they laugh at us; their very courtesy is an insult, and sometimes – as today – their contempt discards all veneer. Bah! I've seen through their baitings – have remained imperturbably serene and swallowed their studied insults. But this – by the fiends of Hell, this is beyond human endurance! My people look to me; if I fail them – if I fail even one – even the lowest of my people, who will aid them? To whom shall they turn? By the gods, I'll answer the gibes of these Roman dogs with black shaft and trenchant steel!"

"And the chief with the plumes?" Grom meant the governor and his gutturals thrummed with the blood-lust. "He dies?" He flicked out a length of steel.

Bran scowled. "Easier said than done. He dies – but how may I reach him? By day his German guards keep at his back; by night they stand at door and window. He has many enemies, Romans as well as barbarians. Many a Briton would gladly slit his throat."

Grom seized Bran's garment, stammering as fierce eagerness broke the bonds of his inarticulate nature.

"Let me go, master! My life is worth nothing. I will cut him down in the midst of his warriors!"

Bran smiled fiercely and clapped his hand on the stunted giant's shoulder with a force that would have felled a lesser man.

"Nay, old war-dog, I have too much need of thee! You shall not throw your life away uselessly. Sulla would read the intent in your eyes, besides, and the javelins of his Teutons would be through you ere you could reach him. Not by the dagger in the dark will we strike this Roman, not by the venom in the cup nor the shaft from the ambush."

The king turned and paced the floor a moment, his head bent in thought. Slowly his eyes grew murky with a thought so fearful he did not speak it aloud to the waiting warrior.

"I have become somewhat familiar with the maze of Roman politics during my stay in this accursed waste of mud and marble," said he. "During a war on the Wall, Titus Sulla, as governor of this province, is supposed to hasten thither with his centuries. But this Sulla does not do; he is no coward, but the bravest avoid certain things – to each man, however bold, his own particular fear. So he sends in his place Caius Camillus, who in times of peace patrols the fens of the west, lest the Britons break over the border. And Sulla takes his place in the Tower of Trajan. Ha!"

He whirled and gripped Grom with steely fingers.

"Grom, take the red stallion and ride north! Let no grass grow under the stallion's hoofs! Ride to Cormac na Connacht and tell him to sweep the frontier with sword and torch! Let his wild Gaels feast their fill of slaughter. After a time I will be with him. But for a time I have affairs in the west."

Grom's black eyes gleamed and he made a passionate gesture with his crooked hand – an instinctive move of savagery.

Bran drew a heavy bronze seal from beneath his tunic.

"This is my safe-conduct as an emissary to Roman courts," he said grimly. "It will open all gates between this house and Baal-dor. If any official questions you too closely – here!"

Lifting the lid of an iron-bound chest, Bran took out a small, heavy leather bag which he gave into the hands of the warrior.

"When all keys fail at a gate," said he, "try a golden key. Go now!"

There were no ceremonious farewells between the barbarian king and his barbarian vassal. Grom flung up his arm in a gesture of salute; then turning, he hurried out.

Bran stepped to a barred window and gazed out into the moonlit streets.

"Wait until the moon sets," he muttered grimly. "Then I'll take the road to – Hell! But before I go I have a debt to pay."

The stealthy clink of a hoof on the flags reached him.

"With the safe-conduct and gold, not even Rome can hold a Pictish reaver," muttered the king. "Now I'll sleep until the moon sets."

With a snarl at the marble frieze-work and fluted columns, as symbols of Rome, he flung himself down on a couch, from which he had long since impatiently torn the cushions and silk stuffs, as too soft for his hard body. Hate and the black passion of vengeance seethed in him, yet he went instantly to sleep. The first lesson he had learned in his bitter hard life was to snatch sleep any time he could, like a wolf that snatches sleep on the hunting trail. Generally his slumber was as light and dreamless as a panther's, but tonight it was otherwise.

He sank into fleecy gray fathoms of slumber and in a timeless, misty realm of shadows he met the tall, lean, white-bearded figure of old Gonar, the priest of the Moon, high counsellor to the king. And Bran stood aghast, for Gonar's face was white as driven snow and he shook as with ague. Well might Bran stand appalled, for in all the years of his life he had never before seen Gonar the Wise show any sign of fear.

"What now, old one?" asked the king. "Goes all well in Baal-dor?"

"All is well in Baal-dor where my body lies sleeping," answered old Gonar. "Across the void I have come to battle with you for your soul. King, are you mad, this thought you have thought in your brain?"

"Gonar," answered Bran somberly, "this day I stood still and watched a man of mine die on the cross of Rome. What his name or his rank, I do not know. I do not care. He might have been a faithful unknown warrior of mine, he might have been an outlaw. I only know that he was mine; the first scents he knew were the scents of the heather; the first light he saw was the sunrise on the Pictish hills. He belonged to me, not to Rome. If punishment was just, then none but me should have dealt it. If he were to be tried, none but me should have been his judge. The same blood flowed in our veins; the same fire maddened our brains; in infancy we listened to the same old tales, and in youth we sang the same old songs. He was bound to my heart-strings, as every man and every woman and every child of Pictland is bound. It was mine to protect him; now it is mine to avenge him."

"But in the name of the gods, Bran," expostulated the wizard, "take your vengeance in another way! Return to the heather – mass your warriors – join with Cormac and his Gaels, and spread a sea of blood and flame the length of the great Wall!"

"All that I will do," grimly answered Bran. "But now – *now* – I will have a vengeance such as no Roman ever dreamed of! Ha, what do they know of the mysteries of this ancient isle, which sheltered strange life long before Rome rose from the marshes of the Tiber?"

"Bran, there are weapons too foul to use, even against Rome!"

Bran barked short and sharp as a jackal.

"Ha! There are no weapons I would not use against Rome! My back is at the wall. By the blood of the fiends, has Rome fought me fair? Bah! I am a barbarian king with a wolfskin mantle and an iron crown, fighting with my handful of bows and broken pikes against the queen of the world. What have I? The heather hills, the wattle huts, the spears of my shock-headed tribesmen! And I fight Rome – with her armored legions, her broad fertile plains and rich seas – her mountains and her rivers and her gleaming cities – her wealth, her steel, her gold, her mastery and her wrath. By steel and fire I will fight her – and by subtlety and treachery – by the thorn in the foot, the adder in the path, the venom in the cup, the dagger in the dark; aye," his voice sank somberly, "and by the worms of the earth!"

"But it is madness!" cried Gonar. "You will perish in the attempt you plan – you will go down to Hell and you will not return! What of your people then?"

"If I can not serve them I had better die," growled the king.

"But you can not even reach the beings you seek," cried Gonar. "For untold centuries they have dwelt *apart*. There is no door by which you can come to them. Long ago they severed the bonds that bound them to the world we know."

"Long ago," answered Bran somberly, "you told me that nothing in the universe was separated from the stream of Life – a saying the truth of which I have often seen evident. No race, no form of life but is close-knit somehow, by some manner, to the rest of Life and the world. Somewhere there is a thin link connecting *those* I seek to the world I know. Somewhere there is a Door. And somewhere among the bleak fens of the west I will find it."

Stark horror flooded Gonar's eyes and he gave back crying, "Wo! Wo! Wo! to Pictdom! Wo to the unborn kingdom! Wo, black wo to the sons of men! Wo, wo, wo, wo!"

Bran awoke to a shadowed room and the starlight on the window-bars. The moon had sunk from sight though its glow was still faint above the house tops. Memory of his dream shook him and he swore beneath his breath.

Rising, he flung off cloak and mantle, donning a light shirt of black mesh-mail, and girding on sword and dirk. Going again to the iron-bound chest he lifted several compact bags and emptied the clinking contents into the leathern pouch at his girdle. Then wrapping his wide cloak about him, he silently left the house. No servants there were to spy on him – he had impatiently refused the offer of slaves which it was Rome's policy to furnish her barbarian emissaries. Gnarled Grom had attended to all Bran's simple needs.

The stables fronted on the courtyard. A moment's groping in the dark and he placed his hand over a great stallion's nose, checking the nicker of recognition. Working without a light he swiftly bridled and saddled the great brute, and went through the courtyard into a shadowy side-street, leading him. The moon was setting, the border of floating shadows widening along the western wall. Silence lay on the marble palaces and mud hovels of Eboracum under the cold stars.

Bran touched the pouch at his girdle, which was heavy with minted gold that bore the stamp of Rome. He had come to Eboracum posing as an emissary of Pictdom, to act the spy. But being a barbarian, he had not been able to play his part in aloof formality and sedate dignity. He retained a crowded memory of wild feasts where wine flowed in fountains; of white-bosomed Roman women, who, sated with civilized lovers, looked with something more than favor on a virile barbarian; of gladiatorial games; and of other games where dice clicked and spun and tall stacks of gold changed hands. He had drunk deeply and gambled recklessly, after the manner of barbarians, and he had had a remarkable run of luck, due possibly to the indifference with which he won or lost. Gold to the Pict was so much dust, flowing through his fingers. In his land there was no need of it. But he had learned its power in the boundaries of civilization.

Almost under the shadow of the northwestern wall he saw ahead of him loom the great watch-tower which was connected with and reared above the outer wall. One corner of the castle-like fortress, farthest from the wall, served as a dungeon. Bran left his horse standing in a dark alley, with the reins hanging on the ground, and stole like a prowling wolf into the shadows of the fortress.

The young officer Valerius was awakened from a light, unquiet sleep by a stealthy sound at the barred window. He sat up, cursing softly under his breath as the faint starlight which etched the window-bars fell across the bare stone floor and reminded him of his disgrace. Well, in a few days, he ruminated, he'd be well out of it; Sulla would not be too harsh on a man with such high connections; then let any man or woman gibe at him! Damn that insolent Pict! But wait, he thought suddenly, remembering: what of the sound which had roused him?

"Hsssst!" it was a voice from the window.

Why so much secrecy? It could hardly be a foe – yet, why should it be a friend? Valerius rose and crossed his cell, coming close to the window. Outside all was dim in the starlight and he made out but a shadowy form close to the window.

"Who are you?" he leaned close against the bars, straining his eyes into the gloom.

His answer was a snarl of wolfish laughter, a long flicker of steel in the starlight. Valerius reeled away from the window and crashed to the floor, clutching his throat, gurgling horribly as he tried to scream. Blood gushed through his fingers, forming about his twitching body a pool that reflected the dim starlight dully and redly.

Outside Bran glided away like a shadow, without pausing to peer into the cell. In another minute the guards would round the corner on their regular routine. Even now he heard the measured tramp of their iron-clad feet. Before they came in sight he had vanished and they clumped stolidly by the cell-windows with no intimation of the corpse that lay on the floor within.

Bran rode to the small gate in the western wall, unchallenged by the sleepy watch. What fear of foreign invasion in Eboracum? – and certain well organized thieves and women-stealers made it profitable for the watchmen not to be too vigilant. But the single guardsman at the western gate – his fellows lay drunk in a near-by brothel – lifted his spear and bawled for Bran to halt and give an account of himself. Silently the Pict reined closer. Masked in the dark cloak, he seemed dim and indistinct to the Roman, who was only aware of the glitter of his cold eyes in the gloom. But Bran held up his hand against the starlight and the soldier caught the gleam of gold; in the other hand he saw a long sheen of steel. The soldier understood, and he did not hesitate between the choice of a golden bribe or a battle to the death with this unknown rider who was apparently a barbarian of some sort. With a grunt he lowered his spear and swung the gate open. Bran rode through, casting a handful of coins to the Roman. They fell about his feet in a golden shower, clinking against the flags. He bent in greedy haste to retrieve them and Bran Mak Morn rode westward like a flying ghost in the night.

III

Into the dim fens of the west came Bran Mak Morn. A cold wind breathed across the gloomy waste and against the gray sky a few herons flapped heavily. The long reeds and marsh-grass waved in broken undulations and out across the desolation of the wastes a few still meres reflected the dull light. Here and there rose curiously regular hillocks above the general levels, and gaunt against the somber sky Bran saw a marching line of upright monoliths – menhirs, reared by what nameless hands?

A faint blue line to the west lay the foothills that beyond the horizon grew to the wild mountains of Wales where dwelt still wild Celtic tribes – fierce blue-eyed men that knew not the yoke of Rome. A row of well-garrisoned watch-towers held them in check. Even now, far away across the moors, Bran glimpsed the unassailable keep men called the Tower of Trajan.

These barren wastes seemed the dreary accomplishment of desolation, yet human life was not utterly lacking. Bran met the silent men of the fen, reticent, dark of eye and hair, speaking a strange mixed tongue whose long-blended elements had forgotten their pristine separate sources. Bran recognized a certain kinship in these people to himself, but he looked on them with the scorn of a pure-blooded patrician for men of mixed strains.

Not that the common people of Caledonia were altogether pure-blooded; they got their stocky bodies and massive limbs from a primitive Teutonic race which had found its way into the northern tip of the isle even before the Celtic conquest of Britain was completed, and had been absorbed by the Picts. But the chiefs of Bran's folk had kept their blood from foreign taint since the beginnings of time, and he himself was a pure-bred Pict of the Old Race. But these fenmen, overrun repeatedly by British, Gaelic and Roman conquerors, had assimilated blood of each, and in the process almost forgotten their original language and lineage.

For Bran came of a race that was very old, which had spread over western Europe in one vast Dark Empire, before the coming of the Aryans, when the ancestors of the Celts, the Hellenes and the Germans were one primal people, before the days of tribal splitting-off and westward drift.

Only in Caledonia, Bran brooded, had his people resisted the flood of

Aryan conquest. He had heard of a Pictish people called Basques, who in the crags of the Pyrenees called themselves an unconquered race; but he knew that they had paid tribute for centuries to the ancestors of the Gaels, before these Celtic conquerors abandoned their mountain-realm and set sail for Ireland. Only the Picts of Caledonia had remained free, and they had been scattered into small feuding tribes – he was the first acknowledged king in five hundred years – the beginning of a new dynasty – no, a revival of an ancient dynasty under a new name. In the very teeth of Rome he dreamed his dreams of empire.

He wandered through the fens, seeking a Door. Of his quest he said nothing to the dark-eyed fenmen. They told him news that drifted from mouth to mouth – a tale of war in the north, the skirl of war-pipes along the winding Wall, of gathering-fires in the heather, of flame and smoke and rapine and the glutting of Gaelic swords in the crimson sea of slaughter. The eagles of the legions were moving northward and the ancient road resounded to the measured tramp of the iron-clad feet. And Bran, in the fens of the west, laughed, well pleased.

In Eboracum Titus Sulla gave secret word to seek out the Pictish emissary with the Gaelic name who had been under suspicion, and who had vanished the night young Valerius was found dead in his cell with his throat ripped out. Sulla felt that this sudden bursting flame of war on the Wall was connected closely with his execution of a condemned Pictish criminal, and he set his spy system to work, though he felt sure that Partha Mac Othna was by this time far beyond his reach. He prepared to march from Eboracum, but he did not accompany the considerable force of legionaries which he sent north. Sulla was a brave man, but each man has his own dread, and Sulla's was Cormac na Connacht, the black-haired prince of the Gaels, who had sworn to cut out the governor's heart and eat it raw. So Sulla rode with his ever-present bodyguard, westward, where lay the Tower of Trajan with its war-like commander, Caius Camillus, who enjoyed nothing more than taking his superior's place when the red waves of war washed at the foot of the Wall. Devious politics, but the legate of Rome seldom visited this far isle, and what of his wealth and intrigues, Titus Sulla was the highest power in Britain.

And Bran, knowing all this, patiently waited his coming, in the deserted hut in which he had taken up his abode.

One gray evening he strode on foot across the moors, a stark figure, blackly etched against the dim crimson fire of the sunset. He felt the incredible antiquity of the slumbering land, as he walked like the last man on the day after the end of the world. Yet at last he saw a token of human life – a drab hut of wattle and mud, set in the reedy breast of the fen.

A woman greeted him from the open door and Bran's somber eyes narrowed with a dark suspicion. The woman was not old, yet the evil wisdom of ages was in her eyes; her garments were ragged and scanty, her black locks tangled and unkempt, lending her an aspect of wildness well in keeping with her grim surroundings. Her red lips laughed but there was no mirth in her laughter, only a hint of mockery, and under the lips her teeth showed sharp and pointed like fangs.

"Enter, master," said she, "if you do not fear to share the roof of the witch-woman of Dagon-moor!"

Bran entered silently and sat him down on a broken bench while the woman busied herself with the scanty meal cooking over an open fire on the squalid hearth. He studied her lithe, almost serpentine motions, the ears which were almost pointed, the yellow eyes which slanted curiously.

"What do you seek in the fens, my lord?" she asked, turning toward him with a supple twist of her whole body.

"I seek a Door," he answered, chin resting on his fist. "I have a song to sing to the worms of the earth!"

She started upright, a jar falling from her hands to shatter on the hearth.

"This is an ill saying, even spoken in chance," she stammered.

"I speak not by chance but by intent," he answered.

She shook her head. "I know not what you mean."

"Well you know," he returned. "Aye, you know well! My race is very old – they reigned in Britain before the nations of the Celts and the Hellenes were born out of the womb of peoples. But my people were not first in Britain. By the mottles on your skin, by the slanting of your eyes, by the taint in your veins, I speak with full knowledge and meaning."

Awhile she stood silent, her lips smiling but her face inscrutable.

"Man, are you mad?" she asked, "that in your madness you come seeking that from which strong men fled screaming in old times?"

"I seek a vengeance," he answered, "that can be accomplished only by Them I seek."

She shook her head.

"You have listened to a bird singing; you have dreamed empty dreams."

"I have heard a viper hiss," he growled, "and I do not dream. Enough of this weaving of words. I came seeking a link between two worlds; I have found it."

"I need lie to you no more, man of the North," answered the woman. "They you seek still dwell beneath the sleeping hills. They have drawn *apart*, farther and farther from the world you know."

"But they still steal forth in the night to grip women straying on the moors," said he, his gaze on her slanted eyes. She laughed wickedly.

"What would you of me?"

"That you bring me to Them."

She flung back her head with a scornful laugh. His left hand locked like iron in the breast of her scanty garment and his right closed on his hilt. She laughed in his face.

"Strike and be damned, my northern wolf! Do you think that such life as mine is so sweet that I would cling to it as a babe to the breast?"

His hand fell away.

"You are right. Threats are foolish. I will buy your aid."

"How?" the laughing voice hummed with mockery.

Bran opened his pouch and poured into his cupped palm a stream of gold.

"More wealth than the men of the fen ever dreamed of."

Again she laughed. "What is this rusty metal to me? Save it for some white-breasted Roman woman who will play the traitor for you!"

"Name me a price!" he urged. "The head of an enemy –"

"By the blood in my veins, with its heritage of ancient hate, who is mine enemy but thee?" she laughed and springing, struck cat-like. But her dagger splintered on the mail beneath his cloak and he flung her off with a loathing flirt of his wrist which tossed her sprawling across her grass-strewn bunk. Lying there she laughed up at him.

"I will name you a price, then, my wolf, and it may be in days to come you will curse the armor that broke Atla's dagger!" She rose and came close to him, her disquietingly long hands fastened fiercely into his cloak. "I will tell you, Black Bran, king of Caledon! Oh, I knew you when you came into my hut with your black hair and your cold eyes! I will lead you to the doors of Hell if you wish – and the price shall be the kisses of a king!

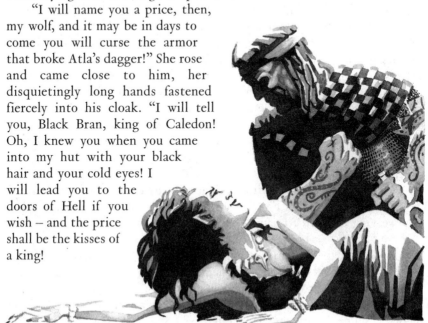

198

"What of my blasted and bitter life, I, whom mortal men loathe and fear? I have not known the love of men, the clasp of a strong arm, the sting of human kisses, I, Atla, the were-woman of the moors! What have I known but the lone winds of the fens, the dreary fire of cold sunsets, the whispering of the marsh grasses? – the faces that blink up at me in the waters of the meres, the foot-pad of night-things in the gloom, the glimmer of red eyes, the grisly murmur of nameless beings in the night!

"I am half-human, at least! Have I not known sorrow and yearning and crying wistfulness, and the drear ache of loneliness? Give to me, king – give me your fierce kisses and your hurtful barbarian's embrace. Then in the long drear years to come I shall not utterly eat out my heart in vain envy of the white-bosomed women of men; for I shall have a memory few of them can boast – the kisses of a king! One night of love, oh king, and I will guide you to the gates of Hell!"

Bran eyed her somberly; he reached forth and gripped her arm in his iron fingers. An involuntary shudder shook him at the feel of her sleek skin. He nodded slowly and drawing her close to him, forced his head down to meet her lifted lips.

IV

The cold gray mists of dawn wrapped King Bran like a clammy cloak. He turned to the woman whose slanted eyes gleamed in the gray gloom.

"Make good your part of the contract," he said roughly. "I sought a link between worlds, and in you I found it. I seek the one thing sacred to Them. It shall be the Key opening the Door that lies unseen between me and Them. Tell me how I can reach it."

"I will," the red lips smiled terribly. "Go to the mound men call Dagon's Barrow. Draw aside the stone that blocks the entrance and go under the dome of the mound. The floor of the chamber is made of seven great stones, six grouped about the seventh. Lift out the center stone – and you will see!"

"Will I find the Black Stone?" he asked.

"Dagon's Barrow is the Door to the Black Stone," she answered, "if you dare follow the Road."

"Will the symbol be well guarded?" He unconsciously loosened his blade in its sheath. The red lips curled mockingly.

"If you meet any on the Road you will die as no mortal man has died for long centuries. The Stone is not guarded, as men guard their treasures. Why should They guard what man has never sought? Perhaps They will be near, perhaps not. It is a chance you must take, if you wish the Stone. Beware, king of Pictdom! Remember it was your folk who, so long ago, cut

199

the thread that bound Them to human life. They were almost human then – they overspread the land and knew the sunlight. Now they have drawn *apart*. They know not the sunlight and they shun the light of the moon. Even the starlight they hate. Far, far apart have they drawn, who might have been men in time, but for the spears of your ancestors."

The sky was overcast with misty gray, through which the sun shone coldly yellow when Bran came to Dagon's Barrow, a round hillock overgrown with rank grass of a curious fungoid appearance. On the eastern side of the mound showed the entrance of a crudely built stone tunnel which evidently penetrated the barrow. One great stone blocked the entrance to the tomb. Bran laid hold of the sharp edges and exerted all his strength. It held fast. He drew his sword and worked the blade between the blocking stone and the sill. Using the sword as a lever, he worked carefully, and managed to loosen the great stone and wrench it out. A foul charnel-house scent flowed out of the aperture and the dim sunlight seemed less to illuminate the cavern-like opening than to be fouled by the rank darkness which clung there.

Sword in hand, ready for he knew not what, Bran groped his way into the tunnel, which was long and narrow, built up of heavy joined stones, and was too low for him to stand erect. Either his eyes became somewhat accustomed to the gloom, or the darkness was, after all, somewhat lightened by the sunlight filtering in through the entrance. At any rate he came into a round low chamber and was able to make out its general dome-like outline. Here, no doubt, in old times, had reposed the bones of him for whom the stones of the tomb had been joined and the earth heaped high above them; but now of those bones no vestige remained on the stone floor. And bending close and straining his eyes, Bran made out the strange, startlingly regular pattern of that floor: six well-cut slabs clustered about a seventh, six-sided stone.

He drove his sword-point into a crack and pried carefully. The edge of the central stone tilted slightly upward. A little work and he lifted it out and leaned it against the curving wall. Straining his eyes downward he saw only the gaping blackness of a dark well, with small, worn steps that led downward and out of sight. He did not hesitate. Though the skin between his shoulders crawled curiously, he swung himself into the abyss and felt the clinging blackness swallow him.

Groping downward, he felt his feet slip and stumble on steps too small for human feet. With one hand pressed hard against the side of the well he steadied himself, fearing a fall into unknown and unlighted depths. The steps were cut into solid rock, yet they were greatly worn away. The farther he progressed, the less like steps they became, mere bumps of worn stone.

Then the direction of the shaft changed sharply. It still led down, but at a shallow slant down which he could walk, elbows braced against the hollowed sides, head bent low beneath the curved roof. The steps had ceased altogether and the stone felt slimy to the touch, like a serpent's lair. What beings, Bran wondered, had slithered up and down this slanting shaft, for how many centuries?

The tunnel narrowed until Bran found it rather difficult to shove through. He lay on his back and pushed himself along with his hands, feet first. Still he knew he was sinking deeper and deeper into the very guts of the earth; how far below the surface he was, he dared not contemplate. Then ahead a faint witch-fire gleam tinged the abysmal blackness. He grinned savagely and without mirth. If They he sought came suddenly upon him, how could he fight in that narrow shaft? But he had put the thought of personal fear behind him when he began this hellish quest. He crawled on, thoughtless of all else but his goal.

And he came at last into a vast space where he could stand upright. He could not see the roof of the place, but he got an impression of dizzying vastness. The blackness pressed in on all sides and behind him he could see the entrance to the shaft from which he had just emerged – a black well in the darkness. But in front of him a strange grisly radiance glowed about a grim altar built of human skulls. The source of that light he could not determine, but on the altar lay a sullen night-black object – the Black Stone!

Bran wasted no time in giving thanks that the guardians of the grim relic were nowhere near. He caught up the Stone, and gripping it under his left arm, crawled into the shaft. When a man turns his back on peril its clammy menace looms more grisly than when he advances upon it. So Bran, crawling back up the nighted shaft with his grisly prize, felt the darkness turn on him and slink behind him, grinning with dripping fangs. Clammy sweat beaded his flesh and he hastened to the best of his ability, ears strained for some stealthy sound to betray that fell shapes were at his heels. Strong shudders shook him, despite himself, and the short hair on his neck prickled as if a cold wind blew at his back.

When he reached the first of the tiny steps he felt as if he had attained to the outer boundaries of the mortal world. Up them he went, stumbling and slipping, and with a deep gasp of relief, came out into the tomb, whose spectral grayness seemed like the blaze of noon in comparison to the stygian depths he had just traversed. He replaced the central stone and strode into the light of the outer day, and never was the cold yellow light of the sun more grateful, as it dispelled the shadows of black-winged nightmares of fear and madness that seemed to have ridden him up out of the black deeps. He shoved the great blocking stone back into place, and picking up the cloak he had left at the mouth of the tomb, he wrapped it about the Black Stone and hurried away, a strong revulsion and loathing shaking his soul and lending wings to his strides.

A gray silence brooded over the land. It was desolate as the blind side of the moon, yet Bran felt the potentialities of life – under his feet, in the brown earth – sleeping, but how soon to waken, and in what horrific fashion?

He came through the tall masking reeds to the still deep men called Dagon's Mere. No slightest ripple ruffled the cold blue water to give evidence of the grisly monster legend said dwelt beneath. Bran closely scanned the breathless landscape. He saw no hint of life, human or unhuman. He sought the instincts of his savage soul to know if any unseen eyes fixed their lethal gaze upon him, and found no response. He was alone as if he were the last man alive on earth.

Swiftly he unwrapped the Black Stone, and as it lay in his hands like a solid sullen block of darkness, he did not seek to learn the secret of its material nor scan the cryptic characters carved thereon. Weighing it in his hands and calculating the distance, he flung it far out, so that it fell almost exactly in the middle of the lake. A sullen splash and the waters closed over it. There was a moment of shimmering flashes on the bosom of the lake; then the blue surface stretched placid and unrippled again.

V

The were-woman turned swiftly as Bran approached her door. Her slant eyes widened.

"You! And alive! And sane!"

"I have been into Hell and I have returned," he growled. "What is more, I have that which I sought."

"The Black Stone?" she cried. "You really dared steal it? Where is it?"

"No matter; but last night my stallion screamed in his stall and I heard something crunch beneath his thundering hoofs which was not the wall of the stable – and there was blood on his hoofs when I came to see, and blood on the floor of the stall. And I have heard stealthy sounds in the night, and noises beneath my dirt floor, as if worms burrowed deep in the earth. They know I have stolen their Stone. Have you betrayed me?"

She shook her head.

"I keep your secret; they do not need my word to know you. The farther they have retreated from the world of men, the greater have grown their powers in other uncanny ways. Some dawn your hut will stand empty and if men dare investigate they will find nothing – except crumbling bits of earth on the dirt floor."

Bran smiled terribly.

"I have not planned and toiled thus far to fall prey to the talons of vermin. If They strike me down in the night, They will never know what became of their idol – or whatever it be to Them. I would speak with Them."

"Dare you come with me and meet them in the night?" she asked.

"Thunder of all gods!" he snarled. "Who are you to ask me if I dare? Lead me to Them and let me bargain for a vengeance this night. The hour of retribution draws nigh. This day I saw silvered helmets and bright shields gleam across the fens – the new commander has arrived at the Tower of Trajan and Caius Camillus has marched to the Wall."

That night the king went across the dark desolation of the moors with the silent were-woman. The night was thick and still as if the land lay in ancient slumber. The stars blinked vaguely, mere points of red struggling through the unbreathing gloom. Their gleam was dimmer than the glitter in the eyes of the woman who glided beside the king. Strange thoughts shook Bran, vague, titanic, primeval. Tonight ancestral linkings with these slumbering fens stirred in his soul and troubled him with the fantasmal, eon-veiled shapes of monstrous dreams. The vast age of his race was borne upon him; where now he walked an outlaw and an alien, dark-eyed kings in whose mold he was cast had reigned in old times. The Celtic and Roman invaders were as strangers to this ancient isle beside his people. Yet his race likewise had been invaders, and there was an older race than his – a race whose beginnings lay lost and hidden back beyond the dark oblivion of antiquity.

Ahead of them loomed a low range of hills, which formed the eastern-most extremity of those straying chains which far away climbed at last to the mountains of Wales. The woman led the way up what might have been a sheep-path, and halted before a wide black gaping cave.

"A door to those you seek, oh king!" her laughter rang hateful in the gloom. "Dare ye enter?"

His fingers closed in her tangled locks and he shook her viciously.

"Ask me but once more if I dare," he grated, "and your head and shoulders part company! Lead on."

Her laughter was like sweet deadly venom. They passed into the cave and Bran struck flint and steel. The flicker of the tinder showed him a wide dusty cavern, on the roof of which hung clusters of bats. Lighting a torch, he lifted it and scanned the shadowy recesses, seeing nothing but dust and emptiness.

"Where are They?" he growled.

She beckoned him to the back of the cave and leaned against the rough wall, as if casually. But the king's keen eyes caught the motion of her hand pressing hard against a projecting ledge. He recoiled as a round black well gaped suddenly at his feet. Again her laughter slashed him like a keen silver knife. He held the torch to the opening and again saw small worn steps leading down.

"They do not need those steps," said Atla. "Once they did, before your people drove them into the darkness. But you will need them."

She thrust the torch into a niche above the well; it shed a faint red light into the darkness below. She gestured into the well and Bran loosened his sword and stepped into the shaft. As he went down into the mystery of the darkness, the light was blotted out above him, and he thought for an instant Atla had covered the opening again. Then he realized that she was descending after him.

The descent was not a long one. Abruptly Bran felt his feet on a solid floor. Atla swung down beside him and stood in the dim circle of light that drifted down the shaft. Bran could not see the limits of the place into which he had come.

"Many caves in these hills," said Atla, her voice sounding small and strangely brittle in the vastness, "are but doors to greater caves which lie beneath, even as a man's words and deeds are but small indications of the dark caverns of murky thought lying behind and beneath."

And now Bran was aware of movement in the gloom. The darkness was filled with stealthy noises not like those made by any human foot. Abruptly sparks began to flash and float in the blackness, like flickering fireflies. Closer they came until they girdled him in a wide half-moon. And beyond the ring gleamed other sparks, a solid sea of them, fading away in the gloom until the farthest were mere tiny pin-points of light. And Bran knew they were the slanted eyes of the beings who had come upon him in such numbers that his brain reeled at the contemplation – and at the vastness of the cavern.

Now that he faced his ancient foes, Bran knew no fear. He felt the waves of terrible menace emanating from them, the grisly hate, the inhuman threat to body, mind and soul. More than a member of a less ancient race, he realized the horror of his position, but he did not fear, though he confronted the ultimate Horror of the dreams and legends of his race. His blood raced fiercely but it was with the hot excitement of the hazard, not the drive of terror.

"They know you have the Stone, oh king," said Atla, and though he knew she feared, though he felt her physical efforts to control her trembling limbs, there was no quiver of fright in her voice. "You are in deadly peril; they know your breed of old – oh, they remember the days when their ancestors were men! I can not save you; both of us will die as no human has died for ten centuries. Speak to them, if you will; they can understand your speech, though you may not understand theirs. But it will avail not – you are human – and a Pict."

Bran laughed and the closing ring of fire shrank back at the savagery in his laughter. Drawing his sword with a soul-chilling rasp of steel, he set his back against what he hoped was a solid stone wall. Facing the glittering eyes with his sword gripped in his right hand and his dirk in his left, he laughed as a blood-hungry wolf snarls.

"Aye," he growled, "I am a Pict, a son of those warriors who drove your brutish ancestors before them like chaff before the storm! – who flooded the land with your blood and heaped high your skulls for a sacrifice to the Moon-Woman! You who fled of old before my race, dare ye now snarl at your master? Roll on me like a flood, now, if ye dare! Before your viper fangs drink my life I will reap your multitudes like ripened barley – of your severed heads will I build a tower and of your mangled corpses will I rear up a wall! Dogs of the dark, vermin of Hell, worms of the earth, rush in and try my steel! When Death finds me in this dark cavern, your living will howl for the scores of your dead and your Black Stone will be lost to you for ever – for only I know where it is hidden and not all the tortures of all the Hells can wring the secret from my lips!"

Then followed a tense silence; Bran faced the fire-lit darkness, tensed like a wolf at bay, waiting the charge; at his side the woman cowered, her eyes ablaze. Then from the silent ring that hovered beyond the dim torchlight rose a vague abhorrent murmur. Bran, prepared as he was for anything, started. Gods, was *that* the speech of creatures which had once been called men?

Atla straightened, listening intently. From her lips came the same hideous soft sibilances, and Bran, though he had already known the grisly secret of her being, knew that never again could he touch her save with soul-shaken loathing.

She turned to him, a strange smile curving her red lips dimly in the ghostly light.

"They fear you, oh king! By the black secrets of R'lyeh, who are you that Hell itself quails before you? Not your steel, but the stark ferocity of your soul has driven unused fear into their strange minds. They will buy back the Black Stone at any price."

"Good," Bran sheathed his weapons. "They shall promise not to molest you because of your aid of me. And," his voice hummed like the purr of a hunting tiger, "They shall deliver into my hands Titus Sulla, governor of Eboracum, now commanding the Tower of Trajan. This They can do – how, I know not. But I know that in the old days, when my people warred with these Children of the Night, babes disappeared from guarded huts and none saw the stealers come or go. Do They understand?"

Again rose the low frightful sounds and Bran, who feared not their wrath, shuddered at their voices.

"They understand," said Atla. "Bring the Black Stone to Dagon's Ring tomorrow night when the earth is veiled with the blackness that foreruns the dawn. Lay the Stone on the altar. There They will bring Titus Sulla to you. Trust Them; They have not interfered in human affairs for many centuries, but They will keep their word."

Bran nodded and turning, climbed up the stair with Atla close behind him. At the top he turned and looked down once more. As far as he could see floated a glittering ocean of slanted yellow eyes upturned. But the owners of those eyes kept carefully beyond the dim circle of torchlight and of their bodies he could see nothing. Their low hissing speech floated up to him and he shuddered as his imagination visualized, not a throng of biped creatures, but a swarming, swaying myriad of serpents, gazing up at him with their glittering unwinking eyes.

He swung into the upper cave and Atla thrust the blocking stone back in place. It fitted into the entrance of the well with uncanny precision; Bran was unable to discern any crack in the apparently solid floor of the cavern. Atla made a motion to extinguish the torch, but the king stayed her.

"Keep it so until we are out of the cave," he grunted. "We might tread on an adder in the dark."

Atla's sweetly hateful laughter rose maddeningly in the flickering gloom.

VI

It was not long before sunset when Bran came again to the reed-grown marge of Dagon's Mere. Casting cloak and sword-belt on the ground, he stripped himself of his short leathern breeches. Then gripping his naked dirk in his teeth, he went into the water with the smooth ease of a diving seal. Swimming strongly, he gained the center of the small lake, and turning, drove himself downward.

The mere was deeper than he had thought. It seemed he would never reach the bottom, and when he did, his groping hands failed to find what he sought. A roaring in his ears warned him and he swam to the surface.

Gulping deep of the refreshing air, he dived again, and again his quest was fruitless. A third time he sought the depth, and this time his groping hands met a familiar object in the silt of the bottom. Grasping it, he swam up to the surface.

The Stone was not particularly bulky, but it was heavy. He swam leisurely, and suddenly was aware of a curious stir in the waters about him which was not caused by his own exertions. Thrusting his face below the surface, he tried to pierce the blue depths with his eyes and thought to see a dim gigantic shadow hovering there.

He swam faster, not frightened, but wary. His feet struck the shallows and he waded up on the shelving shore. Looking back he saw the waters swirl and subside. He shook his head, swearing. He had discounted the ancient legend which made Dagon's Mere the lair of a nameless water-monster, but now he had a feeling as if his escape had been narrow. The time-worn myths of the ancient land were taking form and coming to life before his eyes. What primeval shape lurked below the surface of that treacherous mere, Bran could not guess, but he felt that the fenmen had good reason for shunning the spot, after all.

Bran donned his garments, mounted the black stallion and rode across the fens in the desolate crimson of the sunset's afterglow, with the Black Stone wrapped in his cloak. He rode, not to his hut, but to the west, in the direction of the Tower of Trajan and the Ring of Dagon. As he covered the miles that lay between, the red stars winked out. Midnight passed him in the moonless night and still Bran rode on. His heart was hot for his meeting with Titus Sulla. Atla had gloated over the anticipation of watching the Roman writhe under torture, but no such thought was in the Pict's mind. The governor should have his chance with weapons – with Bran's own sword he should face the Pictish king's dirk, and live or die according to his prowess. And though Sulla was famed throughout the provinces as a swordsman, Bran felt no doubt as to the outcome.

Dagon's Ring lay some distance from the Tower – a sullen circle of tall gaunt stones planted upright, with a rough-hewn stone altar in the center. The Romans looked on these menhirs with aversion; they thought the Druids had reared them; but the Celts supposed Bran's people, the Picts, had planted them – and Bran well knew what hands reared those grim monoliths in lost ages, though for what reasons, he but dimly guessed.

The king did not ride straight to the Ring. He was consumed with curiosity as to how his grim allies intended carrying out their promise. That They could snatch Titus Sulla from the very midst of his men, he felt sure, and he believed he knew how They would do it. He felt the gnawings of a strange misgiving, as if he had tampered with powers of unknown breadth and depth, and had loosed forces which he could not control. Each time he remembered that reptilian murmur, those slanted eyes of the night before, a cold breath passed over him. They had been abhorrent enough when his people drove Them into the caverns under the hills, ages ago; what had long centuries of retrogression made of them? In their nighted, subterranean life, had They retained any of the attributes of humanity at all?

Some instinct prompted him to ride toward the Tower. He knew he was near; but for the thick darkness he could have plainly seen its stark outline tusking the horizon. Even now he should be able to make it out dimly. An obscure, shuddersome premonition shook him and he spurred the stallion into swift canter.

And suddenly Bran staggered in his saddle as from a physical impact, so stunning was the surprize of what met his gaze. The impregnable Tower of Trajan was no more! Bran's astounded gaze rested on a gigantic pile of ruins – of shattered stone and crumbled granite, from which jutted the jagged and splintered ends of broken beams. At one corner of the tumbled heap one tower rose out of the waste of crumpled masonry, and it leaned drunkenly as if its foundations had been half cut away.

Bran dismounted and walked forward, dazed by bewilderment. The moat was filled in places by fallen stones and broken pieces of mortared wall. He crossed over and came among the ruins. Where, he knew, only a few hours before the flags had resounded to the martial tramp of iron-clad feet, and the walls had echoed to the clang of shields and the blast of the loud-throated trumpets, a horrific silence reigned.

Almost under Bran's feet, a broken shape writhed and groaned. The king bent down to the legionary who lay in a sticky red pool of his own blood. A single glance showed the Pict that the man, horribly crushed and shattered, was dying.

Lifting the bloody head, Bran placed his flask to the pulped lips and the Roman instinctively drank deep, gulping through splintered teeth. In the dim starlight Bran saw his glazed eyes roll.

"The walls fell," muttered the dying man. "They crashed down like the skies falling on the day of doom. Ah Jove, the skies rained shards of granite and hailstones of marble!"

"I have felt no earthquake shock," Bran scowled, puzzled.

"It was no earthquake," muttered the Roman. "Before last dawn it began, the faint dim scratching and clawing far below the earth. We of the guard heard it – like rats burrowing, or like worms hollowing out the earth. Titus laughed at us, but all day long we heard it. Then at midnight the Tower quivered and seemed to settle – as if the foundations were being dug away –"

A shudder shook Bran Mak Morn. The worms of the earth! Thousands of vermin digging like moles far below the castle, burrowing away the foundations – gods, the land must be honeycombed with tunnels and caverns –

these creatures were even less human than he had thought – what ghastly shapes of darkness had he invoked to his aid?

"What of Titus Sulla?" he asked, again holding the flask to the legionary's lips; in that moment the dying Roman seemed to him almost like a brother.

"Even as the Tower shuddered we heard a fearful scream from the governor's chamber," muttered the soldier. "We rushed there – as we broke down the door we heard his shrieks – they seemed to recede – *into the bowels of the earth!* We rushed in; the chamber was empty. His blood-stained sword lay on the floor; in the stone flags of the floor a black hole gaped. Then – the – towers – reeled – the – roof – broke; – through – a – storm – of – crashing – walls – I – crawled –"

A strong convulsion shook the broken figure.

"Lay me down, friend," whispered the Roman. "I die."

He had ceased to breathe before Bran could comply. The Pict rose, mechanically cleansing his hands. He hastened from the spot, and as he galloped over the darkened fens, the weight of the accursed Black Stone under his cloak was as the weight of a foul nightmare on a mortal breast.

As he approached the Ring, he saw an eery glow within, so that the gaunt stones stood etched like the ribs of a skeleton in which a witch-fire burns. The stallion snorted and reared as Bran tied him to one of the menhirs. Carrying the Stone he strode into the grisly circle and saw Atla standing beside the altar, one hand on her hip, her sinuous body swaying in a serpentine manner. The altar glowed all over with ghastly light and Bran knew some one, probably Atla, had rubbed it with phosphorus from some dank swamp or quagmire.

He strode forward and whipping his cloak from about the Stone, flung the accursed thing on to the altar.

"I have fulfilled my part of the contract," he growled.

"And They, theirs," she retorted. "Look! – they come!"

He wheeled, his hand instinctively dropping to his sword. Outside the Ring the great stallion screamed savagely and reared against his tether. The night wind moaned through the waving grass and an abhorrent soft hissing mingled with it. Between the menhirs flowed a dark tide of shadows, unstable and chaotic. The Ring filled with glittering eyes which hovered beyond the dim illusive circle of illumination cast by the phosphorescent altar. Somewhere in the darkness a human voice tittered and gibbered idiotically. Bran stiffened, the shadows of a horror clawing at his soul.

He strained his eyes, trying to make out the shapes of those who ringed him. But he glimpsed only billowing masses of shadow which heaved and writhed and squirmed with almost fluid consistency.

"Let them make good their bargain!" he exclaimed angrily.

"Then see, oh king!" cried Atla in a voice of piercing mockery.

There was a stir, a seething in the writhing shadows, and from the darkness crept, like a four-legged animal, a human shape that fell down and groveled at Bran's feet and writhed and mowed, and lifting a death's-head, howled like a dying dog. In the ghastly light, Bran, soul-shaken, saw the blank glassy eyes, the bloodless features, the loose, writhing, froth-covered lips of sheer lunacy – gods, was this Titus Sulla, the proud lord of life and death in Eboracum's proud city?

Bran bared his sword.

"I had thought to give this stroke in vengeance," he said somberly. "I give it in mercy – *Vale Caesar!*"

The steel flashed in the eery light and Sulla's head rolled to the foot of the glowing altar, where it lay staring up at the shadowed sky.

"They harmed him not!" Atla's hateful laugh slashed the sick silence. "It was what he saw and came to know that broke his brain! Like all his heavy-footed race, he knew nothing of the secrets of this ancient land. This night he has been dragged through the deepest pits of Hell, where even you might have blenched!"

"Well for the Romans that they know not the secrets of this accursed land!" Bran roared, maddened, "with its monster-haunted meres, its foul witch-women, and its lost caverns and subterranean realms where spawn in the darkness shapes of Hell!"

"Are they more foul than a mortal who seeks their aid?" cried Atla with a shriek of fearful mirth. "Give them their Black Stone!"

A cataclysmic loathing shook Bran's soul with red fury.

"Aye, take your cursed Stone!" he roared, snatching it from the altar and dashing it among the shadows with such savagery that bones snapped under its impact. A hurried babel of grisly tongues rose and the shadows heaved in turmoil. One segment of the mass detached itself for an instant and Bran cried out in fierce revulsion, though he caught only a fleeting glimpse of the thing, had only a brief impression of a broad strangely flattened head, pendulous writhing lips that bared curved pointed fangs, and a hideously misshapen, dwarfish body that seemed *mottled* – all set off by those unwinking reptilian eyes. Gods! – the myths had prepared him for horror in human aspect, horror induced by bestial visage and stunted deformity – but this was the horror of nightmare and the night.

"Go back to Hell and take your idol with you!" he yelled, brandishing his clenched fists to the skies, as the thick shadows receded, flowing back and away from him like the foul waters of some black flood. "Your ancestors were men, though strange and monstrous – but gods, ye have become in ghastly fact what my people called ye in scorn! Worms of the earth, back into your holes and burrows! Ye foul the air and leave on the clean earth the slime of the serpents ye have become! Gonar was right – there are shapes too foul to use even against Rome!"

He sprang from the Ring as a man flees the touch of a coiling snake, and tore the stallion free. At his elbow Atla was shrieking with fearful laughter, all human attributes dropped from her like a cloak in the night.

"King of Pictland!" she cried, "King of fools! Do you blench at so small a thing? Stay and let me show you real fruits of the pits! Ha! ha! ha! Run, fool, run! But you are stained with the taint – you have called them forth and they will remember! And in their own time they will come to you again!"

He yelled a wordless curse and struck her savagely in the mouth with his open hand. She staggered, blood starting from her lips, but her fiendish laughter only rose higher.

Bran leaped into the saddle, wild for the clean heather and the cold blue hills of the north where he could plunge his sword into clean slaughter and his sickened soul into the red maelstrom of battle, and forget the horror which lurked below the fens of the west. He gave the frantic stallion the rein, and rode through the night like a hunted ghost, until the hellish laughter of the howling were-woman died out in the darkness behind.

An Echo from the Iron Harp

Shadows and echoes haunt my dreams
    with dim and subtle pain,
With the faded fire of a lost desire,
    like a ghost on a moonlit plain.
In the pallid mist of death-like sleep
    she comes again to me:
I see the gleam of her golden hair
    and her eyes like the deep grey sea.

———

We came from the North as the spume is blown
    when the blue tide billows down;
The kings of the South were overthrown
    in ruin of camp and town.
Shrine and temple we dashed to dust,
    and roared in the dead gods' ears;
We saw the fall of the kings of Gaul,
    and shattered the Belgae spears.

And South we rolled like a drifting cloud,
    like a wind that bends the grass,
But we smote in vain on the gates of Spain
    for our own kin held the Pass.
Then again we turned where the watch-fires burned
    to mark the lines of Rome,
And fire and tower and standard sank
    as ships that die in foam.

The legions came, hard hawk-eyed men,
    war-wise in march and fray,
But we rushed like a whirlwind on their lines
    and swept their ranks away.
Army and consul we overthrew,
    staining the trampled loam;
Horror and fear like a lifted spear
    lay hard on the walls of Rome.
Our mad desire was a flying fire
    that should burn the Appian Gate —
But our day of doom lay hard on us,
    at a toss of the dice of Fate.

There rose a man in the ranks of Rome —
    ill fall the cursed day! —
Our German allies bit the dust
    and we turned hard at bay.
And the raven came and the lean grey wolf,
    to follow the sword's red play.

Over the land like a ghostly hand
    the mists of morning lay,
We smote their horsemen in the fog
    and hacked a bloody way.
We smote their horsemen in the cloud
    and as the mists were cleared
Right through the legion massed behind
    our headlong squadron sheared.
Saddle to saddle we chained our ranks
    for naught of war we knew
But to charge in the wild old Celtic way —
    and die or slash straight through.
We left red ruin in our wake,
    dead men in ghastly ranks —
When fresh unwearied Roman arms
    smote hard upon our flanks.

Baffled and weary, red with wounds,
    leaguered on every side,
Chained to our doom we smote in vain,
    slaughtered and sank and died.
Writhing among the horses' hoofs,
    torn and slashed and gored,
Gripping still with a bloody hand,
    a notched and broken sword,
I heard the war-cry growing faint,
    drowned by the trumpet's call,
And the roar of "Marius! Marius!"
    triumphant over all.

Through the bloody dust and the swirling fog
    as I strove in vain to rise
I saw the last of the warriors fall,
    and swift as a falcon flies
The Romans rush to the barricades
    where the women watched the fight –
I heard the screams and I saw steel flash
    and naked arms toss white.
The ravisher died as he gripped his prey,
    by the dagger fiercely driven –
By the next stroke with her own hand
    the heart of the girl was riven.
Brown fingers grasped white wrists in vain –
    blood flecked the gasping loam –
The Cimbri yield no virgin-slaves
    to glut the gods of Rome!

And I saw as I crawled like a crippled snake
    to slay before I died,
Unruly golden hair that tossed
    in wild and untamed pride.
Her slim foot pressed a dead man's breast,
    her proud head back was thrown,
Matching the steel she held on high,
    her eyes in glory shone.

I saw the gleam of her golden hair
    and her eyes like the deep grey sea –
And the love in the gaze that sought me out,
    barbaric, fierce and free –
The the dagger fell and the skies fell
    and the mists closed over me.

———

Like phantoms into the ages lost
    has the Cimbrian nation passed;
Destiny shifts like summer clouds
    on Grecian hill-tops massed.
Untold centuries glide away,
    Marius long is dust;
Even eternal Rome has passed
    in days of decay and rust.
But memories live in the ghosts of dreams,
    and dreams still come to me,
And I see the gleam of her golden hair
    and her eyes like the deep grey sea.

Lord of the Dead

The onslaught was as unexpected as the stroke of an unseen cobra. One second Steve Harrison was plodding profanely but prosaically through the darkness of the alley – the next, he was fighting for his life with the snarling, mouthing fury that had fallen on him, talon and tooth. The thing was obviously a man, though in the first few dazed seconds Harrison doubted even this fact. The attacker's style of fighting was appallingly vicious and beast-like, even to Harrison who was accustomed to the foul battling of the underworld.

The detective felt the other's teeth in his flesh, and yelped profanely. But there was a knife, too; it ribboned his coat and shirt, and drew blood, and only blind chance that locked his fingers about a sinewy wrist, kept the point from his vitals. It was dark as the backdoor of Erebus. Harrison saw his assailant only as a slightly darker chunk in the blackness. The muscles under his grasping fingers were taut and steely as piano wire, and there was a terrifying suppleness about the frame writhing against his which filled Harrison with panic. The big detective had seldom met a man his equal in strength; this denizen of the dark not only was as strong as he, but was lither and quicker and tougher than a civilized man ought to be.

They rolled over into the mud of the alley, biting, kicking and slugging, and though the unseen enemy grunted each time one of Harrison's maul-like fists thudded against him, he showed no signs of weakening. His wrist was like a woven mass of steel wires, threatening momentarily to writhe out of Harrison's clutch. His flesh crawling with fear of the cold steel, the detective grasped that wrist with both his own hands, and tried to break it. A blood-thirsty howl acknowledged this futile attempt, and a voice, which had been mouthing in an unknown tongue, hissed in Harrison's ear: "Dog! You shall die in the mud, as I died in the sand! You gave my body to the vultures! I give yours to the rats of the alley! *Wellah!*"

A grimy thumb was feeling for Harrison's eye, and fired to desperation, the detective heaved his body backward, bringing up his knee with bone-crushing force. The unknown gasped and rolled clear, squalling like a cat. Harrison staggered up, lost his balance, caromed against a wall. With a scream and a rush, the other was up and at him. Harrison heard the knife whistle and chunk into the wall beside him, and he lashed out blindly with all the power of his massive shoulders. He landed solidly, felt his victim shoot off his feet backward, and heard him crash headlong into the mud. Then Steve Harrison, for the first time in his life, turned his back on a single foe and ran lumberingly but swiftly up the alley.

His breath came pantingly; his feet splashed through refuse and clanged over rusty cans. Momentarily he expected a knife in his back. "Hogan!" he bawled desperately. Behind him sounded the quick lethal patter of flying feet.

He catapulted out of the black alley mouth head on into Patrolman Hogan who had heard his urgent bellow and was coming on the run. The breath went out of the patrolman in an agonized gasp, and the two hit the sidewalk together.

Harrison did not take time to rise. Ripping the Colt .38 Special from Hogan's holster, he blazed away at a shadow that hovered for an instant in the black mouth of the alley.

Rising, he approached the dark entrance, the smoking gun in his hand. No sound came from the Stygian gloom.

"Give me your flashlight," he requested, and Hogan rose, one hand on his capacious belly, and proffered the article. The white beam showed no corpse stretched in the alley mud.

"Got away," muttered Harrison.

"Who?" demanded Hogan with some spleen. "What is this, anyway? I hear you bellowin' 'Hogan!' like the devil had you by the seat of the britches, and the next thing you ram me like a chargin' bull. What –"

"Shut up, and let's explore this alley," snapped Harrison. "I didn't mean to run into you. Something jumped me –"

"I'll say somethin' did." The patrolman surveyed his companion in the uncertain light of the distant corner lamp. Harrison's coat hung in ribbons; his shirt was slashed to pieces, revealing his broad hairy chest which heaved from his exertions. Sweat ran down his corded neck, mingling with blood from gashes on arms, shoulders and breast muscles. His hair was clotted with mud, his clothes smeared with it.

"Must have been a whole gang," decided Hogan.

"It was one man," said Harrison; "one man or one gorilla; but it talked. Are you coming?"

"I am not. Whatever it was, it'll be gone now. Shine that light up the alley. See? Nothin' in sight. It wouldn't be waitin' around for us to grab it by the tail. You better get them cuts dressed. I've warned you against short cuts through dark alleys. Plenty men have grudges against you."

"I'll go to Richard Brent's place," said Harrison. "He'll fix me up. Go along with me, will you?"

"Sure, but you better let me —"

"What ever it is, no!" growled Harrison, smarting from cuts and wounded vanity. "And listen, Hogan — don't mention this, see? I want to work it out for myself. This is no ordinary affair."

"It must not be — when *one* critter licks the tar out of Iron Man Harrison," was Hogan's biting comment; whereupon Harrison cursed under his breath.

Richard Brent's house stood just off Hogan's beat — one lone bulwark of respectability in the gradually rising tide of deterioration which was engulfing the neighborhood, but of which Brent, absorbed in his studies, was scarcely aware.

Brent was in his relic-littered study, delving into the obscure volumes which were at once his vocation and his passion. Distinctly the scholar in appearance, he contrasted strongly with his visitors. But he took charge without undue perturbation, summoning to his aid a half course of medical studies.

Hogan, having ascertained that Harrison's wounds were little more than scratches, took his departure, and presently the big detective sat opposite his host, a long whiskey glass in his massive hand.

Steve Harrison's height was above medium, but it seemed dwarfed by the breadth of his shoulders and the depth of his chest. His heavy arms hung low, and his head jutted aggressively forward. His low, broad brow, crowned with heavy black hair, suggested the man of action rather than the thinker, but his cold blue eyes reflected unexpected depths of mentality.

" '— As I died in the sand,' " he was saying. "That's what he yammered. Was he just a plain nut — or what the hell?"

Brent shook his head, absently scanning the walls, as if seeking inspiration in the weapons, antique and modern, which adorned it.

"You could not understand the language in which he spoke before?"

"Not a word. All I know is, it wasn't English and it wasn't Chinese. I do know the fellow was all steel springs and whale bone. It was like fighting a basketful of wild cats. From now on I pack a gun regular. I haven't toted one recently, things have been so quiet. Always figured I was a match for several ordinary humans with my fists, anyway. But this devil wasn't an ordinary human; more like a wild animal."

He gulped his whiskey loudly, wiped his mouth with the back of his hand, and leaned toward Brent with a curious glint in his cold eyes.

"I wouldn't be saying this to anybody but you," he said with a strange hesitancy. "And maybe you'll think I'm crazy – but – well, I've bumped off several men in my life. Do you suppose – well, the Chinese believe in vampires and ghouls and walking dead men – and with all this talk about being dead, and me killing him – do you suppose –"

"Nonsense!" exclaimed Brent with an incredulous laugh. "When a man's dead, he's dead. He can't come back."

"That's what I've always thought," muttered Harrison. "But what the devil *did* he mean about me feeding him to the vultures?"

"I will tell you!" A voice hard and merciless as a knife edge cut their conversation.

Harrison and Brent wheeled, the former starting out of his chair. At the other end of the room one of the tall shuttered windows stood open for the sake of the coolness. Before this now stood a tall rangy man whose ill-fitting garments could not conceal the dangerous suppleness of his limbs, nor the breadth of his hard shoulders. Those cheap garments, muddy and blood-stained, seemed incongruous with the fierce dark hawk-like face, the flame of the dark eyes. Harrison grunted explosively, meeting the concentrated ferocity of that glare.

"You escaped me in the darkness," muttered the stranger, rocking slightly on the balls of his feet as he crouched, catlike, a wicked curved dagger gleaming in his hand. "Fool! Did you dream I would not follow you? Here is light; you shall not escape again!"

"Who the devil are you?" demanded Harrison, standing in an unconscious attitude of defense, legs braced, fists poised.

"Poor of wit and scant of memory!" sneered the other. "You do not remember Amir Amin Izzedin, whom you slew in the Valley of the Vultures, thirty years ago! But I remember! From my cradle I remember. Before I could speak or walk, I knew that I was Amir Amin, and I remembered the Valley of Vultures. But only after deep shame and long wandering was full knowledge revealed to me. In the smoke of Shaitan I saw it! You have changed your garments of flesh, Ahmed Pasha, you Bedouin dog, but you can not escape me. By the Golden Calf!"

With a feline shriek he ran forward, dagger on high. Harrison sprang aside, surprizingly quick for a man of his bulk, and ripped an archaic spear from the wall. With a wordless yell like a warcry, he rushed, gripping it with both hands like a bayonet. Amir Amin wheeled toward him lithely, swaying his pantherish body to avoid the onrushing point. Too late Harrison realized his mistake – knew he would be spitted on the long knife as he plunged past the elusive Oriental. But he could not check his headlong impetus. And then Amir Amin's foot slipped on a sliding rug. The spear head ripped through his muddy coat, ploughed along his ribs, bringing a spurting stream of blood. Knocked off balance, he slashed wildly, and then Harrison's bull-like shoulder smashed into him, carrying them both to the floor.

Amir Amin was up first, minus his knife. As he glared wildly about for it, Brent, temporarily stunned by the unaccustomed violence, went into action. From the racks on the wall the scholar had taken a shotgun, and he wore a look of grim determination. As he lifted it, Amir Amin yelped and plunged recklessly through the nearest window. The crash of splintering glass mingled with the thunderous roar of the shotgun. Brent, rushing to the window, blinking in the powder fumes, saw a shadowy form dart across the shadowy lawn, under the trees, and vanish. He turned back into the room, where Harrison was rising, swearing luridly.

"Twice in a night is too danged much! Who is this nut, anyway? I never saw him before!"

"A Druse!" stuttered Brent. "His accent – his mention of the golden calf – his hawk-like appearance – I am sure he is a Druse."

"What the hell is a Druse?" bellowed Harrison, in a spasm of irritation. His bandages had been torn and his cuts were bleeding again.

"They live in a mountain district in Syria," answered Brent; "a tribe of fierce fighters –"

"I can tell that," snarled Harrison. "I never expected to meet anybody that could lick me in a stand-up fight, but this devil's got me buffaloed. Anyway, it's a relief to know he's a living human being. But if I don't watch my step, I won't be. I'm staying here tonight, if you've got a room where I can lock all the doors and windows. Tomorrow I'm going to see Woon Sun."

II

Few men ever traversed the modest curio shop that opened on dingy River Street and passed through the cryptic curtain-hung door at the rear of that shop, to be amazed at what lay beyond: luxury in the shape of gilt-worked velvet hangings, silken cushioned divans, tea-cups of tinted porcelain on toy-like tables of lacquered ebony, over all of which was shed a soft colored glow from electric bulbs concealed in gilded lanterns.

Steve Harrison's massive shoulders were as incongruous among those exotic surroundings as Woon Sun, short, sleek, clad in close-fitting black silk, was adapted to them.

The Chinaman smiled, but there was iron behind his suave mask.

"And so —" he suggested politely.

"And so I want your help," said Harrison abruptly. His nature was not that of a rapier, fencing for an opening, but a hammer smashing directly at its objective.

"I know that you know every Oriental in the city. I've described this bird to you. Brent says he's a Druse. You couldn't be ignorant of him. He'd stand out in any crowd. He doesn't belong with the general run of River Street gutter rats. He's a wolf."

"Indeed he is," murmured Woon Sun. "It would be useless to try to conceal from you the fact that I know this young barbarian. His name is Ali ibn Suleyman."

"He called himself something else," scowled Harrison.

"Perhaps. But he is Ali ibn Suleyman to his friends. He is, as your friend said, a Druse. His tribe live in stone cities in the Syrian mountains — particularly about the mountain called the Djebel Druse."

"Muhammadans, eh?" rumbled Harrison. "Arabs?"

"No; they are, as it were, a race apart. They worship a calf cast of gold, believe in reincarnation, and practice heathen rituals abhorred by the Moslems. First the Turks and now the French have tried to govern them, but they have never really been conquered."

"I can believe it, alright," muttered Harrison. "But why did he call me 'Ahmed Pasha'? What's he got it in for *me* for?"

Woon Sun spread his hands helplessly.

"Well, anyway," growled Harrison, "I don't want to keep on dodging knives in back alleys. I want you to fix it so I can get the drop on him. Maybe he'll talk sense, if I can get the cuffs on him. Maybe I can argue him out of this idea of killing me, whatever it is. He looks more like a fanatic than a criminal. Anyway, I want to find out just what it's all about."

"What could I do?" murmured Woon Sun, folding his hands on his round belly, malice gleaming from under his dropping lids. "I might go further and ask, *why* should I do anything for you?"

"You've stayed inside the law since coming here," said Harrison. "I know that curio shop is just a blind; you're not making any fortune out of it. But I know, too, that you're not mixed up with anything crooked. You had your dough when you came here – plenty of it – and how you got it is no concern of mine.

"But, Woon Sun," Harrison leaned forward and lowered his voice, "do you remember that young Eurasian Josef La Tour? I was the first man to reach his body, the night he was killed in Osman Pasha's gambling den. I found a note book on him, and I kept it. Woon Sun, your name was in that book!"

An electric silence impregnated the atmosphere. Woon Sun's smooth yellow features were immobile, but red points glimmered in the shoe-button blackness of his eyes.

"La Tour must have been intending to blackmail you," said Harrison. "He'd worked up a lot of interesting data. Reading that note book, I found that your name wasn't always Woon Sun; found out where you got your money, too."

The red points had faded in Woon Sun's eyes; those eyes seemed glazed; a greenish pallor overspread the yellow face.

"You've hidden yourself well, Woon Sun," muttered the detective. "But double-crossing your society and skipping with all their money was a dirty trick. If they ever find you, they'll feed you to the rats. I don't know but what it's my duty to write a letter to a mandarin in Canton, named –"

"Stop!" The Chinaman's voice was unrecognizable. "Say no more, for the love of Buddha! I will do as you ask. I have this Druse's confidence, and can arrange it easily. It is now scarcely dark. At midnight be in the alley known to the Chinese of River Street as the Alley of Silence. You know the one I mean? Good. Wait in the nook made by the angle of the walls, near the end of the alley, and soon Ali ibn Suleyman will walk past it, ignorant of your presence. Then if you dare, you can arrest him."

"I've got a gun this time," grunted Harrison. "Do this for me, and we'll forget about La Tour's note book. But no double-crossing, or –"

"You hold my life in your fingers," answered Woon Sun. "How can I double-cross you?"

Harrison grunted skeptically, but rose without further words, strode through the curtained door and through the shop, and let himself into the street. Woon Sun watched inscrutably the broad shoulders swinging aggressively through the swarms of stooped, hurrying Orientals, men and women, who thronged River Street at that hour; then he locked the shop door and hurried back through the curtained entrance into the ornate chamber behind. And there he halted, staring.

Smoke curled up in a blue spiral from a satin divan, and on that divan lounged a young woman – a slim, dark, supple creature, whose night-black hair, full red lips and scintillant eyes hinted at blood more exotic than her costly garments suggested. Those red lips curled in malicious mockery, but the glitter of her dark eyes belied any suggestion of humor, however satirical, just as their vitality belied the languor expressed in the listlessly drooping hand that held the cigaret.

"Joan!" The Chinaman's eyes narrowed to slits of suspicion. "How did you get in here?"

"Through that door over there, which opens on a passage which in turn opens on the alley that runs behind this building. Both doors were locked – but long ago I learned how to pick locks."

"But why – ?"

"I saw the brave detective come here. I have been watching him for some time now – though he does not know it." The girl's vital eyes smoldered yet more deeply for an instant.

"Have you been listening outside the door?" demanded Woon Sun, turning grey.

"I am no eavesdropper. I did not have to listen. I can guess why he came. And you promised to help him?"

"I don't know what you are talking about," answered Woon Sun, with a secret sigh of relief.

"You lie!" The girl came tensely upright on the divan, her convulsive fingers crushing her cigaret, her beautiful face momentarily contorted. Then she regained control of herself, in a cold resolution more dangerous than spitting fury. "Woon Sun," she said calmly, drawing a stubby black automatic from her mantle, "how easily, and with what good will could I kill you where you stand. But I do not wish to. We shall remain friends. See, I replace the gun. But do not tempt me, my friend. Do not try to eject me, or to use violence with me. Here, sit down and take a cigaret. We will talk this over calmly."

"I do not know what you wish to talk over," said Woon Sun, sinking down on a divan and mechanically taking the cigaret she offered, as if hypnotized by the glitter of her magnetic black eyes – and the knowledge of the hidden pistol. All his Oriental immobility could not conceal the fact that he feared this young pantheress – more than he feared Harrison. "The detective came here merely on a friendly call," he said. "I have many friends among the police. If I were found murdered they would go to much trouble to find and hang the guilty person."

"Who spoke of killing?" protested Joan, snapping a match on a pointed, henna-tinted nail, and holding the tiny flame to Woon Sun's cigaret. At the instant of contact their faces were close together, and the Chinaman drew back from the strange intensity that burned in her dark eyes. Nervously he drew on the cigaret, inhaling deeply.

"I have been your friend," he said. "You should not come here threatening me with a pistol. I am a man of no small importance on River Street. You, perhaps, are not as secure as you suppose. The time may come when you will need a friend like me —"

He was suddenly aware that the girl was not answering him, or even heeding his words. Her own cigaret smoldered unheeded in her fingers, and through the clouds of smoke her eyes burned at him with the terrible eagerness of a beast of prey. With a gasp he jerked the cigaret from his lips and held it to his nostrils.

"She-devil!" It was a shriek of pure terror. Hurling the smoking stub from him, he lurched to his feet where he swayed dizzily on legs suddenly grown numb and dead. His fingers groped toward the girl with strangling motions. "Poison — dope — the black lotos —"

She rose, thrust an open hand against the flowered breast of his silk jacket and shoved him back down on the divan. He fell sprawling and lay in a limp attitude, his eyes open, but glazed and vacant. She bent over him, tense and shuddering with the intensity of her purpose.

"You are my slave," she hissed, as a hypnotizer impels his suggestions upon his subject. "You have no will but my will. Your conscious brain is asleep, but your tongue is free to tell the truth. Only the truth remains in your drugged brain. Why did the detective Harrison come here?"

"To learn of Ali ibn Suleyman, the Druse," muttered Woon Sun in his own tongue, and in a curious lifeless sing-song.

"You promised to betray the Druse to him?"

"I promised but I lied," the monotonous voice continued. "The detective goes at midnight to the Alley of Silence, which is the Gateway to the Master. Many bodies have gone feet-first through that gateway. It is the best place to dispose of his corpse. I will tell the Master he came to spy upon him, and thus gain honor for myself, as well as ridding myself of an enemy. The white barbarian will stand in the nook between the walls, awaiting the Druse as I bade him. He does not know that a trap can be opened in the angle of the walls behind him and a hand strike with a hatchet. My secret will die with him."

Apparently Joan was indifferent as to what the secret might be, since she questioned the drugged man no further. But the expression on her beautiful face was not pleasant.

"No, my yellow friend," she murmured. "Let the white barbarian go to the Alley of Silence – aye, but it is not a yellow-belly who will come to him in the darkness. He shall have his desire. He shall meet Ali ibn Suleyman; and after him, the worms that writhe in darkness!"

Taking a tiny jade vial from her bosom, she poured wine from a porcelain jug into an amber goblet, and shook into the liquor the contents of the vial. Then she put the goblet into Woon Sun's limp fingers and sharply ordered him to drink, guiding the beaker to his lips. He gulped the wine mechanically, and immediately slumped sidewise on the divan and lay still.

"You will wield no hatchet this night," she muttered. "When you awaken many hours from now, my desire will have been accomplished – and you will need fear Harrison no longer, either – whatever may be his hold upon you." She seemed struck by a sudden thought and halted as she was turning toward the door that opened on the corridor.

"'Not as secure as I suppose' –" she muttered, half aloud. "What could he have meant by that?" A shadow, almost of apprehension, crossed her face. Then she shrugged her shoulders. "Too late to make him tell me now. No matter. The Master does not suspect – and what if he did? He's no Master of mine. I waste too much time –"

She stepped into the corridor, closing the door behind her. Then when she turned, she stopped short. Before her stood three grim figures, tall, gaunt, black-robed, their shaven vulture-like heads nodding in the dim light of the corridor.

In that instant, frozen with awful certainty, she forgot the gun in her bosom. Her mouth opened for a scream, which died in a gurgle as a bony hand was clapped over her lips.

III

The alley, nameless to white men, but known to the teeming swarms of River Street as the Alley of Silence, was as devious and cryptic as the characteristics of the race which frequented it. It did not run straight, but, slanting unobtrusively off River Street, wound through a maze of tall, gloomy structures, which, to outward seeming at least, were tenements and warehouses, and crumbling forgotten buildings apparently occupied only by rats, where boarded-up windows stared blankly.

As River Street was the heart of the Oriental quarter, so the Alley of Silence was the heart of River Street, though apparently empty and deserted. At least that was Steve Harrison's idea, though he could give no definite reason why he ascribed so much importance to a dark, dirty, crooked alley that seemed to go nowhere. The men at headquarters twitted him, telling him that he had worked so much down in the twisty mazes of rat-haunted River Street that he was getting a Chinese twist in his mind.

He thought of this, as he crouched impatiently in the angle formed by the last crook of that unsavory alley. That it was past midnight he knew from a stealthy glance at the luminous figures on his watch. Only the scurrying of rats broke the silence. He was well hidden in a cleft formed by two jutting walls, whose slanting planes came together to form a triangle opening on the alley. Alley architecture was as crazy as some of the tales which crept forth from its dank blackness. A few paces further on the alley ended abruptly at the cliff-like blankness of a wall, in which showed no windows and only a boarded-up door.

This Harrison knew only by a vague luminance which filtered greyly into the alley from above. Shadows lurked along the angles darker than the Stygian pits, and the boarded-up door was only a vague splotch in the sheer of the wall. An empty warehouse, Harrison supposed, abandoned and rotting through the years. Probably it fronted on the bank of the river, ledged by crumbling wharfs, forgotten and unused in the years since the river trade and activity had shifted into a newer part of the city.

He wondered if he had been seen ducking into the alley. He had not turned directly off River Street, with its slinking furtive shapes that drifted silently past all night long. He had come in from a wandering side street, working his way between leaning walls and jutting corners until he came out into the dark winding alley. He had not worked the Oriental quarter for so long, not to have absorbed some of the stealth and wariness of its inhabitants.

But midnight was past, and no sign of the man he hunted. Then he stiffened. Some one was coming up the alley. But the gait was a shuffling step; not the sort he would have connected with a man like Ali ibn Suleyman. A tall stooped figure loomed vaguely in the gloom and shuffled on past the detective's covert. His trained eye, even in the dimness, told Harrison that the man was not the one he sought.

The unknown went straight to the blank door and knocked three times with a long interval between the raps. Abruptly a red disk glowed in the door. Words were hissed in Chinese. The man on the outside replied in the same tongue, and his words came clearly to the tensed detective: *"Erlik Khan!"* Then the door unexpectedly opened inward, and he passed through, illumined briefly in the reddish light which streamed through the opening. Then darkness followed the closing of the door, and silence reigned again in the alley of its name.

But crouching in the shadowed angle, Harrison felt his heart pound against his ribs. He had recognized the fellow who passed through the door as a Chinese killer with a price on his head; but it was not that recognition which sent the detective's blood pumping through his veins. It was the password muttered by the evil-visaged visitant: "Erlik Khan!" It was like the materialization of a dim nightmare dream; like the confirmation of an evil legend.

For more than a year rumors had crept snakily out of the black alleys and crumbling doorways behind which the mysterious yellow people moved phantom-like and inscrutable. Scarcely rumors, either; that was a term too concrete and definite to be applied to the maunderings of dope-fiends, the ravings of madmen, the whimpers of dying men – disconnected whispers that died on the midnight wind. Yet through these disjointed mutterings had wound a dread name, fearsomely repeated, in shuddering whispers: "*Erlik Khan!*"

It was a phrase always coupled with dark deeds; it was like a black wind moaning through midnight trees; a hint, a breath, a myth, that no man could deny or affirm. None knew if it were the name of a man, a cult, a course of action, a curse, or a dream. Through its associations it became a slogan of dread: a whisper of black water lapping at rotten piles; of blood dripping on slimy stones; of death whimpers in dark corners; of stealthy feet shuffling through the haunted midnight to unknown dooms.

The men at headquarters had laughed at Harrison when he swore that he sensed a connection between various scattered crimes. They had told him, as usual, that he had worked too long among the labyrinths of the Oriental district. But that very fact made him more sensitive to furtive and subtle impressions than were his mates. And at times he had seemed almost to sense a vague and monstrous Shape that moved behind a web of illusion.

And now, like the hiss of an unseen serpent in the dark, had come to him at least as much concrete assurance as was contained in the whispered words: "*Erlik Khan!*"

Harrison stepped from his nook and went swiftly toward the boarded door. His feud with Ali ibn Suleyman was pushed into the background. The big dick was an opportunist; when chance presented itself, he seized it first and made plans later. And his instinct told him that he was on the threshold of something big.

A slow, almost imperceptible drizzle had begun. Overhead, between the towering black walls, he got a glimpse of thick grey clouds, hanging so low they seemed to merge with the lofty roofs, dully reflecting the glow of the city's myriad lights. The rumble of distant traffic came to his ears faintly and faraway. His environs seemed curiously strange, alien and aloof. He might have been stealing through the gloom of Canton, or forbidden Peking – or of Babylon, or Egyptian Memphis.

Halting before the door, he ran his hands lightly over it, and over the boards which apparently sealed it. And he discovered that some of the bolt-heads were false. It was an ingenious trick to make the door appear inaccessible to the casual glance.

Setting his teeth, with a feeling as of taking a blind plunge in the dark, Harrison rapped three times as he had heard the killer, Fang Yim, rap. Almost instantly a round hole opened in the door, level with his face, and framed dimly in a red glow he glimpsed a yellow Mongoloid visage. Sibilant Chinese hissed at him.

Harrison's hat was pulled low over his eyes, and his coat collar, turned up against the drizzle, concealed the lower part of his features. But the disguise was not needed. The man inside the door was no one Harrison had ever seen.

"Erlik Khan!" muttered the detective. No suspicion shadowed the slant eyes. Evidently white men had passed through that door before. It swung inward, and Harrison slouched through, shoulders hunched, hands thrust deep in his coat pockets, the very picture of a waterfront hoodlum. He heard the door closed behind him, and found himself in a small square chamber at the end of a narrow corridor. He noted that the door was furnished with a great steel bar, which the Chinaman was now lowering into place in the heavy iron sockets set on each side of the portal, and the hole in the center was covered by a steel disk, working on a hinge. Outside of a squatting-cushion beside the door for the doorman, the chamber was without furnishings.

All this Harrison's trained eye took in at a glance, as he slouched across the chamber. He felt that he would not be expected, as a denizen of whatever resort the place proved to be, to remain long in the room. A small red lantern, swinging from the ceiling, lighted the chamber, but the corridor seemed to be without lumination, save such as was furnished by the afore-said lantern.

Harrison slouched on down the shadowy corridor, giving no evidence of the tensity of his nerves. He noted, with sidelong glances, the firmness and newness of the walls. Obviously a great deal of work had recently been done on the interior of this supposedly deserted building.

Like the alley outside, the corridor did not run straight. Ahead of him it bent at an angle, around which shone a mellow stream of light, and beyond this bend Harrison heard a light padding step approaching. He grabbed at the nearest door, which opened silently under his hand, and closed as silently behind him. In pitch darkness he stumbled over steps, nearly falling, catching at the wall, and cursing the noise he made. He heard the padding step halt outside the door; then a hand pushed against it. But Harrison had his forearm and elbow braced against the panel. His groping fingers found a bolt and he slid it home, wincing at the faint scraping it made. A voice hissed something in Chinese, but Harrison made no answer. Turning, he groped his way hurriedly down the stairs.

Presently his feet struck a level floor, and in another instant he bumped into a door. He had a flashlight in his pocket, but he dared not use it. He fumbled at the door and found it unlocked. The edges, sill and jambs seemed to be padded. The walls, too, seemed to be specially treated, beneath his sensitive fingers. He wondered with a shiver what cries and noises those walls and padded doors were devised to drown.

Shoving open the door, he blinked in a flood of soft reddish light, and drew his gun in a panic. But no shouts or shots greeted him, and as his eyes became accustomed to the light, he saw that he was looking into a great basement-like room, empty except for three huge packing cases. There were doors at either end of the room, and along the sides, but they were all closed. Evidently he was some distance under the ground.

He approached the packing cases, which had apparently but recently been opened, their contents not yet removed. The boards of the lids lay on the floor beside them, with wads of excelsior and tow packing.

"Booze?" he muttered to himself. "Dope? Smugglers?"

He scowled down into the nearest case. A single layer of tow sacking covered the contents, and he frowned in puzzlement at the outlines under that sacking. Then suddenly, with his skin crawling, he snatched at the sacking and pulled it away – and recoiled, choking in horror. Three yellow faces, frozen and immobile, stared sightlessly up at the swinging lamp. There seemed to be another layer underneath –

Gagging and sweating, Harrison went about his grisly task of verifying what he could scarcely believe. And then he mopped away the beads of perspiration.

"Three packing cases full of dead Chinamen!" he whispered shakily. "Eighteen yellow stiffs! Great cats! Talk about wholesale murder! I thought I'd bumped into so many hellish sights that nothing could upset me. But this is piling it on *too* thick!"

It was the stealthy opening of a door which roused him from his morbid meditations. He wheeled, galvanized. Before him crouched a monstrous and brutish shape, like a creature out of a nightmare. The detective had a glimpse of a massive, half-naked torso, a bullet-like shaven head split by a toothy and slavering grin – then the brute was upon him.

Harrison was no gunman; all his instincts were of the strong-arm variety. Instead of drawing his gun, he dashed his right mauler into that toothy grin, and was rewarded by a jet of blood. The creature's head snapped back at an agonized angle, but his bony fingers had locked on the detective's lapels. Harrison drove his left wrist-deep into his assailant's midriff, causing a green tint to overspread the coppery face, but the fellow hung on, and with a wrench, pulled Harrison's coat down over his shoulders. Recognizing a trick meant to imprison his arms, Harrison did not resist the movement, but rather aided it, with a headlong heave of his powerful body that drove his lowered head hard against the yellow man's breastbone, and tore his own arms free of the clinging sleeves.

The giant staggered backward, gasping for breath, holding the futile garment like a shield before him, and Harrison, inexorable in his attack, swept him back against the wall by the sheer force of his rush, and smashed a bone-crushing left and right to his jaw. The yellow giant pitched backward, his eyes already glazed; his head struck the wall, fetching blood in streams, and he toppled face-first to the floor where he lay twitching, his shaven head in a spreading pool of blood.

"A Mongol strangler!" panted Harrison, glaring down at him. "What kind of a nightmare is this, anyway?"

It was just at that instant that a blackjack, wielded from behind, smashed down on his head; the lights went out.

IV

Some misplaced connection with his present condition caused Steve Harrison to dream fitfully of the Spanish Inquisition just before he regained consciousness. Possibly it was the clank of steel chains. Drifting back from a land of enforced dreams, his first sensation was that of an aching head, and he touched it tenderly and swore bitterly.

He was lying on a concrete floor. A steel band girdled his waist, hinged behind, and fastened before with a heavy steel lock. To that band was riveted a chain, the other end of which was made fast to a ring in the wall. A dim lantern suspended from the ceiling lighted the room, which seemed to have but one door and no window. The door was closed.

Harrison noted other objects in the room, and as he blinked and they took definite shape, he was aware of an icy premonition, too fantastic and monstrous for credit. Yet the objects at which he was staring were incredible, too.

There was an affair with levers and windlasses and chains. There was a chain suspended from the ceiling, and some objects that looked like iron fire tongs. And in one corner there was a massive, grooved block, and beside it leaned a heavy broad-edged axe. The detective shuddered in spite of himself, wondering if he were in the grip of some damnable medieval dream. He could not doubt the significance of those objects. He had seen their duplicates in museums –

Aware that the door had opened, he twisted about and glared at the figure dimly framed there – a tall, shadowy form, clad in night-black robes. This figure moved like a shadow of Doom into the chamber, and closed the door. From the shadow of a hood, two icy eyes glittered eerily, framed in a dim yellow oval of a face.

For an instant the silence held, broken suddenly by the detective's irate bellow.

"What the hell is this? Who are you? Get this chain off me!"

A scornful silence was the only answer, and under the unwinking scrutiny of those ghostly eyes, Harrison felt cold perspiration gather on his forehead and among the hairs on the backs of his hands.

"You fool!" At the peculiar hollow quality of the voice, Harrison started nervously. "You have found your doom!"

"Who are you?" demanded the detective.

"Men call me Erlik Khan, which signifies Lord of the Dead," answered the other. A trickle of ice meandered down Harrison's spine, not so much from fear, but because of the grisly thrill in the realization that at last he was face to face with the materialization of his suspicions.

"So Erlik Khan is a man, after all," grunted the detective. "I'd begun to believe that it was the name of a Chinese society."

"I am no Chinese," returned Erlik Khan. "I am a Mongol – direct descendant of Genghis Khan, the great conqueror, before whom all Asia bowed."

"Why tell me this?" growled Harrison, concealing his eagerness to hear more.

"Because you are soon to die," was the tranquil reply, "and I would have you realize that it is into the hands of no common gangster scum you have blundered.

"I was head of a lamasery in the mountains of Inner Mongolia, and, had I been able to attain my ambitions, would have rebuilt a lost empire – aye, the old empire of Genghis Khan. But I was opposed by various fools, and barely escaped with my life.

"I came to America, and here a new purpose was born in me: that of forging all secret Oriental societies into one mighty organization to do my bidding and reach unseen tentacles across the seas into hidden lands. Here, unsuspected by such blundering fools as you, have I built my castle. Already I have accomplished much. Those who oppose me die suddenly, or – you saw those fools in the packing cases in the cellar. They are members of the Yat Soy, who thought to defy me."

"Judas!" muttered Harrison. "A whole tong scuppered!"

"Not dead," corrected Erlik Khan. "Merely in a cataleptic state, induced by certain drugs introduced into their liquor by trusted servants. They were brought here in order that I might convince them of their folly in opposing me. I have a number of underground crypts like this one, wherein are implements and machines calculated to change the mind of the most stubborn."

"Torture chambers under River Street!" muttered the detective. "Damned if this isn't a nightmare!"

"You, who have puzzled so long amidst the mazes of River Street, are you surprized at the mysteries within its mysteries?" murmured Erlik Khan. "Truly, you have but touched the fringes of its secrets. Many men do my bidding – Chinese, Syrians, Mongols, Hindus, Arabs, Turks, Egyptians."

"Why?" demanded Harrison. "Why should so many men of such different and hostile religions serve you –"

"Behind all differences of religion and belief," said Erlik Khan, "lies the eternal *Oneness* that is the essence and root-stem of the East. Before Muhammad was, or Confucius, or Gautama, there were signs and symbols, ancient beyond belief, but common to all sons of the Orient. There are cults stronger and older than Islam or Buddhism – cults whose roots are lost in the blackness of the dawn ages, before Babylon was, or Atlantis sank.

"To an adept, these young religions and beliefs are but new cloaks, masking the reality beneath. Even to a dead man I can say no more. Suffice to know that I, whom men call Erlik Khan, have power above and behind the powers of Islam or of Buddha."

Harrison lay silent, meditating over the Mongol's words, and presently the latter resumed: "You have but yourself to blame for your plight. I am convinced that you did not come here tonight to spy upon me – poor, blundering, barbarian fool, who did not even guess my existence. I have learned that you came in your crude way, expecting to trap a servant of mine, the Druse Ali ibn Suleyman."

"You sent him to kill me," growled Harrison.

A scornful laugh put his teeth on edge.

"Do you fancy yourself so important? I would not turn aside to crush a blind worm. Another put the Druse on your trail – a deluded person, a miserable, egoistic fool, who even now is paying the price of folly.

"Ali ibn Suleyman is, like many of my henchmen, an outcast from his people, his life forfeit.

"Of all virtues, the Druses most greatly esteem the elementary one of physical courage. When a Druse shows cowardice, none taunts him, but when the warriors gather to drink coffee, some one spills a cup on his *abba*. That is his death-sentence. At the first opportunity, he is obliged to go forth and die as heroically as possible.

"Ali ibn Suleyman failed on a mission where success was impossible. Being young, he did not realize that his fanatical tribe would brand him as a coward because, in failing, he had not got himself killed. But the cup of shame was spilled on his robe. Ali was young; he did not wish to die. He broke a custom of a thousand years; he fled the Djebel Druse and became a wanderer over the earth.

"Within the past year he joined my followers, and I welcomed his desperate courage and terrible fighting ability. But recently the foolish person I mentioned decided to use him to further a private feud, in no way connected with my affairs. That was unwise. My followers live but to serve me, whether they realize it or not.

"Ali goes often to a certain house to smoke opium, and this person caused him to be drugged with the dust of the black lotos, which produces a hypnotic condition, during which the subject is amenable to suggestions, which, if continually repeated, carry over into the victim's waking hours.

"The Druses believe that when a Druse dies, his soul is instantly reincarnated in a Druse baby. The great Druse hero, Amir Amin Izzedin, was killed by the Arab shaykh Ahmed Pasha, the night Ali ibn Suleyman was born. Ali has always believed himself to be the reincarnated soul of Amir Amin, and mourned because he could not revenge his former self on Ahmed Pasha, who was killed a few days after he slew the Druse chief.

"All this the *person* ascertained, and by means of the black lotos, known as the Smoke of Shaitan, convinced the Druse that you, detective Harrison, were the reincarnation of his old enemy Shaykh Ahmed Pasha. It took time and cunning to convince him, even in his drugged condition, that an Arab shaykh could be reincarnated in an American detective, but the *person* was very clever, and so at last Ali was convinced, and disobeyed my orders – which were never to molest the police, unless they got in my way, and then only according to my directions. For I do not woo publicity. He must be taught a lesson.

"Now I must go. I have spent too much time with you already. Soon one will come who will lighten you of your earthly burdens. Be consoled by the realization that the foolish person who brought you to this pass is expiating her crime likewise. In fact, separated from you but by that padded partition. Listen!"

From somewhere near rose a feminine voice, incoherent but urgent.

"The foolish one realizes her mistake," smiled Erlik Khan benevolently. "Even through these walls pierce her lamentations. Well, she is not the first to regret foolish actions in these crypts. And now I must begone. Those foolish Yat Soys will soon begin to awaken."

"Wait, you devil!" roared Harrison, struggling up against his chain. "What —"

"Enough, enough!" There was a touch of impatience in the Mongol's tone. "You weary me. Get you to your meditations, for your time is short. Farewell, Mr. Harrison — *not* au revoir."

The door closed silently, and the detective was left alone with his thoughts which were far from pleasant. He cursed himself for falling into that trap; cursed his peculiar obsession for always working alone. None knew of the tryst he had tried to keep; he had divulged his plans to no one.

Beyond the partition the muffled sobs continued. Sweat began to bead Harrison's brow. His nerves, untouched by his own plight, began to throb in sympathy with that terrified voice.

Then the door opened again, and Harrison, twisting about, knew with numbing finality that he looked on his executioner. It was a tall, gaunt Mongol, clad only in sandals and a trunk-like garment of yellow silk, from the girdle of which depended a bunch of keys. He carried a great bronze bowl and some objects that looked like joss sticks. These he placed on the floor near Harrison, and squatting just out of the captive's reach, began to arrange the evil-smelling sticks in a sort of pyramidal shape in the bowl. And Harrison, glaring, remembered a half-forgotten horror among the myriad dim horrors of River Street: a corpse he had found in a sealed room where acrid fumes still hovered over a charred bronze bowl — the corpse of a Hindu, shriveled and crinkled like old leather — mummified by a lethal smoke that killed and shrunk the victim like a poisoned rat.

From the other cell came a shriek so sharp and poignant that Harrison jumped and cursed. The Mongol halted in his task, a match in his hand. His parchment-like visage split in a leer of appreciation, disclosing the withered stump of a tongue; the man was a mute.

The cries increased in intensity, seemingly more in fright than in pain, yet an element of pain was evident. The mute, rapt in his evil glee, rose and leaned nearer the wall, cocking his ear as if unwilling to miss any whimper of agony from that torture cell. Slaver dribbled from the corner of his loose mouth; he sucked his breath in eagerly, unconsciously edging nearer the wall – Harrison's foot shot out, hooked suddenly and fiercely about the lean ankle. The Mongol threw wild arms aloft, and toppled into the detective's waiting arms.

It was with no scientific wrestling hold that Harrison broke the executioner's neck. His pent-up fury had swept away everything but a berserk madness to grip and rend and tear in primitive passion. Like a grizzly he grappled and twisted, and felt the vertebrae give way like rotten twigs.

Dizzy with glutted fury he struggled up, still gripping the limp shape, gasping incoherent blasphemy. His fingers closed on the keys dangling at the dead man's belt, and ripping them free, he hurled the corpse savagely to the floor in a paroxysm of excess ferocity. The thing struck loosely and lay without twitching, the sightless face grinning hideously back over the yellow shoulder.

Harrison mechanically tried the keys in the lock at his waist. An instant later, freed of his shackles, he staggered in the middle of the cell, almost overcome by the wild rush of emotion – hope, exultation, and the realization of freedom. He snatched up the grim axe that leaned against the darkly stained block, and could have yelled with bloodthirsty joy as he felt the perfect balance of the weighty weapon, and saw the dim light gleaming on its flaring razor-edge.

An instant's fumbling with the keys at the lock, and the door opened. He looked out into a narrow corridor, dimly lighted, lined with closed doors. From one next to his, the distressing cries were coming, muffled by the padded door and the specially treated walls.

In his berserk wrath he wasted no time in trying his keys on that door. Heaving up the sturdy axe with both hands, he swung it crashing against the panels, heedless of the noise, mindful only of his frenzied urge to violent action. Under his flailing strokes the door burst inward and through its splintered ruins he lunged, eyes glaring, lips asnarl.

He had come into a cell much like the one he had just quitted. There was a rack – a veritable medieval devil-machine – and in its cruel grip writhed a pitiful white figure – a girl, clad only in a scanty chemise. A gaunt Mongol bent over the handles, turning them slowly. Another was engaged in heating a pointed iron over a small brazier.

This he saw at a glance, as the girl rolled her head toward him and cried out in agony. Then the Mongol with the iron ran at him silently, the glowing, white-hot steel thrust forward like a spear. In the grip of red fury though he

238

was, Harrison did not lose his head. A wolfish grin twisting his thin lips, he side stepped, and split the torturer's head as a melon is split. Then as the corpse tumbled down, spilling blood and brains, he wheeled catlike to meet the onslaught of the other.

The attack of this one was silent as that of the other. They too were mutes. He did not lunge in so recklessly as his mate, but his caution availed him little as Harrison swung his dripping axe. The Mongol threw up his left arm, and the curved edge sheared through muscle and bone, leaving the limb hanging by a shred of flesh. Like a dying panther the torturer sprang in turn, driving in his knife with the fury of desperation. At the same instant the bloody axe flailed down. The thrusting knife point tore through Harrison's shirt, ploughed through the flesh over his breastbone, and as he flinched involuntarily, the axe turned in his hand and struck flat, crushing the Mongol's skull like an egg shell.

Swearing like a pirate, the detective wheeled this way and that, glaring for new foes. Then he remembered the girl on the rack.

And then he recognized her at last. "Joan La Tour! What in the name –"

"Let me go!" she wailed. "Oh, for God's sake, let me go!"

The mechanism of the devilish machine balked him. But he saw that she was tied by heavy cords on wrists and ankles, and cutting them, he lifted her free. He set his teeth at the thought of the ruptures, dislocated joints and torn sinews that she might have suffered, but evidently the torture had not progressed far enough for permanent injury. Joan seemed none the worse, physically, for her experience, but she was almost hysterical. As he looked at the cowering, sobbing figure, shivering in her scanty garment, and remembered the perfectly poised, sophisticated, and self-sufficient beauty as he had known her, he shook his head in amazement. Certainly Erlik Khan knew how to bend his victims to his despotic will.

"Let us go," she pleaded between sobs. "They'll be back – they will have heard the noise –"

"Alright," he grunted; "but where the devil are we?"

"I don't know," she whimpered. "Somewhere in the house of Erlik Khan. His Mongol mutes brought me here earlier tonight, through passages and tunnels connecting various parts of the city with this place."

"Well, come on," said he. "We might as well go somewhere."

Taking her hand he led her out into the corridor, and glaring about uncertainly, he spied a narrow stair winding upward. Up this they went, to be halted soon by a padded door, which was not locked. This he closed behind him, and tried to lock, but without success. None of his keys would fit the lock.

"I don't know whether our racket was heard or not," he grunted, "unless somebody was nearby. This building is fixed to drown noise. We're in some part of the basement, I reckon."

"We'll never get out alive," whimpered the girl. "You're wounded – I saw blood on your shirt –"

"Nothing but a scratch," grunted the big detective, stealthily investigating with his fingers the ugly ragged gash that was soaking his torn shirt and waist-band with steadily seeping blood. Now that his fury was beginning to cool, he felt the pain of it.

Abandoning the door, he groped upward in thick darkness, guiding the girl of whose presence he was aware only by the contact of a soft little hand trembling in his. Then he heard her sobbing convulsively.

"This is all my fault! I got you into this! The Druse, Ali ibn Suleyman –"

"I know," he grunted; "Erlik Khan told me. But I never suspected that you were the one who put this crazy heathen up to knifing me. Was Erlik Khan lying?"

"No," she whimpered. "My brother – Josef. Until tonight I thought you killed him."

He started convulsively.

"*Me?* I didn't do it! I don't know who did. Somebody shot him over my shoulder – aiming at me, I reckon, during that raid on Osman Pasha's joint."

"I know, now," she muttered. "But I'd always believed you lied about it. I thought you killed him, yourself. Lots of people think that, you know. I wanted revenge. I hit on what looked like a sure scheme. The Druse doesn't know me. He's never seen me, awake. I bribed the owner of the opium-joint that Ali ibn Suleyman frequents, to drug him with the black lotos. Then I would do my work on him. It's much like hypnotism.

"The owner of the joint must have talked. Anyway, Erlik Khan learned how I'd been using Ali ibn Suleyman, and he decided to punish me. Maybe he was afraid the Druse talked too much while he was drugged.

"I know too much, too, for one not sworn to obey Erlik Khan. I'm part Oriental and I've played in the fringe of River Street affairs until I've got myself tangled up in them. Josef played with fire, too, just as I've been doing, and it cost him his life. Erlik Khan told me tonight who the real murderer was. It was Osman Pasha. He wasn't aiming at you. He intended to kill Josef.

"I've been a fool, and now my life is forfeit. Erlik Khan is the king of River Street."

"He won't be long," growled the detective. "We're going to get out of here some how, and then I'm coming back with a squad and clean out this damned rat hole. I'll show Erlik Khan that this is America, not Mongolia. When I get through with him –"

He broke off short as Joan's fingers closed on his convulsively. From somewhere below them sounded a confused muttering. What lay above, he had no idea, but his skin crawled at the thought of being trapped on that dark twisting stair. He hurried, almost dragging the girl, and presently encountered a door that did not seem to be locked.

Even as he did so, a light flared below, and a shrill yelp galvanized him. Far below he saw a cluster of dim shapes in a red glow of a torch or lantern. Rolling eyeballs flashed whitely, steel glimmered.

Darting through the door and slamming it behind them, he sought for a frenzied instant for a key that would fit the lock and not finding it, seized Joan's wrist and ran down the corridor that wound among black velvet hangings. Where it led he did not know. He had lost all sense of direction. But he did know that death grim and relentless was on their heels.

Looking back, he saw a hideous crew swarm up into the corridor: yellow men in silk jackets and baggy trousers, grasping knives. Ahead of him loomed a curtain-hung door. Tearing aside the heavy satin hangings, he hurled the door open and leaped through, drawing Joan after him, slamming the door behind them. And stopped dead, an icy despair gripping at his heart.

V

They had come into a vast hall-like chamber, such as he had never dreamed existed under the prosaic roofs of any Western city.

Gilded lanterns, on which writhed fantastic carven dragons, hung from the fretted ceiling, shedding a golden lustre over velvet hangings that hid the walls. Across these black expanses other dragons twisted, worked in silver, gold and scarlet. In an alcove near the door reared a squat idol, bulky, taller than a man, half hidden by a heavy lacquer screen, an obscene, brutish travesty of nature, that only a Mongolian brain could conceive. Before it stood a low altar, whence curled up a spiral of incense smoke.

But Harrison at the moment gave little heed to the idol. His attention was riveted on the robed and hooded form which sat cross-legged on a velvet divan at the other end of the hall – they had blundered full into the web of the spider. About Erlik Khan in subordinate attitudes sat a group of Orientals, Chinese, Syrians and Turks.

The paralysis of surprize that held both groups was broken by a peculiarly menacing cry from Erlik Khan, who reared erect, his hand flying to his girdle. The others sprang up, yelling and fumbling for weapons. Behind him, Harrison heard the clamor of their pursuers just beyond the door. And in that instant he recognized and accepted the one desperate alternative to instant capture. He sprang for the idol, thrust Joan into the alcove behind it, and squeezed after her. Then he turned at bay. It was the last stand – trail's end.

He did not hope to escape; his motive was merely that of a wounded wolf which drags itself into a corner where its killers must come at it from in front.

The green stone bulk of the idol blocked the entrance of the alcove save for one side, where there was a narrow space between its misshapen hip and shoulder, and the corner of the wall. The space on the other side was too narrow for a cat to have squeezed through, and the lacquer screen stood before it. Looking through the interstices of this screen, Harrison could see the whole room, into which the pursuers were now storming. The detective recognized their leader as Fang Yim, the hatchet-man.

A furious babble rose, dominated by Erlik Khan's voice, speaking English, the one common language of those mixed breeds.

"They hide behind the god; drag them forth."

"Let us rather fire a volley," protested a dark-skinned powerfully built man whom Harrison recognized – Ak Bogha, a Turk, his fez contrasting with his full dress suit. "We risk our lives, standing here in full view; he can shoot through that screen."

"Fool!" The Mongol's voice rasped with anger. "He would have fired already if he had a gun. Let no man pull a trigger. They can crouch behind the idol, and it would take many shots to smoke them out. We are not now in the Crypts of Silence. A volley would make too much noise; one shot might not be heard in the streets. But one shot will not suffice. He has but an axe; rush in and cut him down!"

Without hesitation Ak Bogha ran forward, followed by the others. Harrison shifted his grip on his axe haft. Only one man could come at him at a time –

Ak Bogha was in the narrow strait between idol and wall before Harrison moved from behind the great green bulk. The Turk yelped in fierce triumph and lunged, lifting his knife. He blocked the entrance; the men crowding behind him had only a glimpse, over his straining shoulder, of Harrison's grim face and blazing eyes.

Full into Ak Bogha's face Harrison thrust the axe head, smashing nose, lips and teeth. The Turk reeled, gasping and choking with blood, and half blinded, but struck again, like the slash of a dying panther. The keen edge sliced Harrison's face from temple to jaw, and then the flailing axe crushed in Ak Bogha's breastbone and sent him reeling backward, to fall dying.

The men behind him gave back suddenly. Harrison, bleeding like a stuck hog, again drew back behind the idol. They could not see the white giant who lurked at bay in the shadow of the god, but they saw Ak Bogha gasping his life out on the bloody floor before the idol, like a gory sacrifice, and the sight shook the nerve of the fiercest.

And now, as matters hovered at a deadlock, and the Lord of the Dead

seemed himself uncertain, a new factor introduced itself into the tense drama. A door opened and a fantastic figure swaggered through. Behind him Harrison heard Joan gasp incredulously.

It was Ali ibn Suleyman who strode down the hall as if he trod his own castle in the mysterious Djebel Druse. No longer the garments of western civilization clothed him. On his head he wore a silken *kafiyeh* bound about the temples with a broad gilded band. Beneath his voluminous, girdled *abba* showed silver-heeled boots, ornately stitched. His eye-lids were painted with *kohl*, causing his eyes to glitter even more lethally than ordinarily. In his hand was a long curved scimitar.

Harrison mopped the blood from his face and shrugged his shoulders. Nothing in the house of Erlik Khan could surprize him any more, not even this picturesque shape which might have just swaggered out of an opium dream of the East.

The attention of all was centered on the Druse as he strode down the hall, looking even bigger and more formidable in his native costume than he had in western garments. He showed no more awe of the Lord of the Dead than he showed of Harrison. He halted directly in front of Erlik Khan, and spoke without meekness.

"Why was it not told me that mine enemy was a prisoner in the house?" he demanded in English, evidently the one language he knew in common with the Mongol.

"You were not here," Erlik Khan answered brusquely, evidently liking little the Druse's manner.

"Nay, I but recently returned, and learned that the dog who was once Ahmed Pasha stood at

bay in this chamber. I have donned my proper garb for this occasion."
Turning his back full on the Lord of the Dead, Ali ibn Suleyman strode
before the idol.

"Oh, infidel!" he called, "come forth and meet my steel! Instead of the
dog's death which is your due, I offer you honorable battle – your axe against
my sword. Come forth, ere I hale you thence by your beard!"

"I haven't any beard," grunted the detective. "Come in and get me!"

"Nay," scowled Ali ibn Suleyman; "when you were Ahmed Pasha, you
were a man. Come forth, where we can have room to wield our weapons. If
you slay me, you shall go free. I swear by the Golden Calf!"

"Could I dare trust him?" muttered Harrison.

"A Druse keeps his word," whispered Joan. "But there is Erlik Khan –"

"Who are you to make promises?" called Harrison. "Erlik Khan is master
here."

"Not in the matter of my private feud!" was the arrogant reply. "I swear
by my honor that no hand but mine shall be lifted against you, and that if
you slay me, you shall go free. Is it not so, Erlik Khan?"

"Let it be as you wish," answered the Mongol, spreading his hands in a
gesture of resignation.

Joan grasped Harrison's arm convulsively, whispering urgently: "Don't
trust him! He won't keep his word! He'll betray you and Ali both! He's never
intended that the Druse should kill you – it's his way of punishing Ali, by
having some one else kill you! Don't – don't –"

"We're finished anyway," muttered Harrison, shaking the sweat and
blood out of his eyes. "I might as well take the chance. If I don't they'll rush
us again, and I'm bleeding so that I'll soon be too weak to fight. Watch your
chance, girl, and try to get away while everybody's watching Ali and me."
Aloud he called: "I have a woman here, Ali. Let her go before we start
fighting."

"To summon the police to your rescue?" demanded Ali. "No! She stands
or falls with you. Will you come forth?"

"I'm coming," gritted Harrison. Grasping his axe, he moved out of the
alcove, a grim and ghastly figure, blood masking his face and soaking his torn
garments. He saw Ali ibn Suleyman gliding toward him, half crouching, the
scimitar in his hand a broad curved glimmer of blue light. He lifted his axe,
fighting down a sudden wave of weakness – there came a muffled dull report,
and at the same instant he felt a paralyzing impact against his head. He was
not aware of falling, but realized that he was lying on the floor, conscious but
unable to speak or move.

A wild cry rang in his dulled ears and Joan La Tour, a flying white figure,
threw herself down beside him, her fingers frantically fluttering over him.

"Oh, you dogs, dogs!" she was sobbing. "You've killed him!" She lifted her head to scream: "Where is your honor now, Ali ibn Suleyman?"

From where he lay Harrison could see Ali standing over him, scimitar still poised, eyes flaring, mouth gaping, an image of horror and surprize. And beyond the Druse the detective saw the silent group clustered about Erlik Khan; and Fang Yim was holding an automatic with a strangely misshapen barrel — a Maxim silencer. One muffled shot would not be noticed from the street.

A fierce and frantic cry burst from Ali ibn Suleyman.

"Aie, my honor! My pledged word! My oath on the Golden Calf! You have broken it! You have shamed me to an infidel! You robbed me both of vengeance and honor! Am I a dog, to be dealt with thus! *Ya Maruf!*"

His voice soared to a feline screech, and wheeling, he moved like a blinding blur of light. Fang Yim's scream was cut short horribly in a ghastly gurgle, as the scimitar cut the air in a blue flame. The Chinaman's head shot from his shoulders on a jetting fountain of blood and thudded on the floor, grinning awfully in the golden light. With a yell of terrible exultation, Ali ibn Suleyman leapt straight toward the hooded shape on the divan. Fezzed and turbaned figures ran in between. Steel flashed, showering sparks, blood spurted, and men screamed. Harrison saw the Druse scimitar flame bluely through the lamplight full on Erlik Khan's coifed head. The hood fell in halves, and the Lord of the Dead rolled to the floor, his fingers convulsively clenching and unclenching.

The others swarmed about the maddened Druse, hacking and stabbing. The figure in the wide-sleeved *abba* was the center of a score of licking blades, of a gasping, blaspheming, clutching knot of straining bodies. And still the dripping scimitar flashed and flamed, shearing through flesh, sinew and bone, while under the stamping feet of the living rolled mutilated corpses. Under the impact of struggling bodies, the altar was overthrown, the smoldering incense scattered over the rugs. The next instant flame was licking at the hangings. With a rising roar and a rush the fire enveloped one whole side of the room, but the battlers heeded it not.

Harrison was aware that someone was pulling and tugging at him, someone who sobbed and gasped, but did not slacken their effort. A pair of slender hands were locked in his tattered shirt, and he was being dragged bodily through billowing smoke that blinded and half strangled him. The tugging hands grew weaker, but did not release their hold, as their owner fought on in a heart-breaking struggle. Then suddenly the detective felt a rush of clean wind, and was aware of concrete instead of carpeted wood under his shoulders.

He was lying in a slow drizzle on a sidewalk, while above him towered a wall reddened in a mounting glare. On the other side loomed broken docks, and beyond them the lurid glow was reflected on water. He heard the screams of fire sirens, and felt the gathering of a chattering, shouting crowd about him.

Life and movement slowly seeping back into his numbed veins, he lifted his head feebly, and saw Joan La Tour crouched beside him, oblivious to the rain as to her scanty attire. Tears were streaming down her face, and she cried out as she saw him move: "Oh, you're not dead – I thought I felt life in you, but I dared not let *them* know –"

"Just creased my scalp," he mumbled thickly. "Knocked me out for a few minutes – seen it happen that way before – you dragged me out –"

"While they were fighting. I thought I'd never find an outer door – here come the firemen at last!"

"The Yat Soys!" he gasped, trying to rise. "Eighteen Chinamen in that basement – my God, they'll be roasted!"

"We can't help it!" panted Joan La Tour. "We were fortunate to save ourselves. Oh!"

The crowd surged back, yelling, as the roof began to cave in, showering sparks. And through the crumpling walls, by some miracle, reeled an awful figure – Ali ibn Suleyman. His clothing hung in smoldering, bloody ribbons, revealing the ghastly wounds beneath. He had been slashed almost to pieces. His head-cloth was gone, his hair crisped, his skin singed and blackened where it was not blood-smeared. His scimitar was gone, and blood streamed down his arm over the fingers that gripped a dripping dagger.

"Aie!" he cried in a ghastly croak. "I see you, Ahmed Pasha, through the fire and mist! You live, in spite of Mongol treachery! That is well! Only by the hand of Ali ibn Suleyman, who was Amir Amin Izzedin, shall you die! I have washed my honor in blood, and it is spotless!

> *"I am a son of Maruf,*
> *Of the mountain of sanctuary;*
> *When my sword is rusty*
> *I make it bright*
> *With the blood of my enemies!"*

Reeling, he pitched face first, stabbing at Harrison's feet as he fell; then rolling on his back he lay motionless, staring sightlessly up at the flame-lurid skies.

Untitled

You have built a world of paper and wood,
    Culture and cult and lies;
Has the cobra altered beneath his hood,
    Or the fire in the tiger's eyes?

You have turned from valley and hill and flood,
    You have set yourselves apart,
Forgetting the earth that feeds the blood
    And the talon that finds the heart.

You boast you have stilled the lustful call
    Of the black ancestral ape,
But Life, the tigress that bore you all,
    Has never changed her shape.

And a strange shape comes to your faery mead,
    With a fixed black simian frown,
But you will not know and you will not heed
    Till your towers come tumbling down.

"For the Love of Barbara Allen"

"'Twas in the merry month of May,
    When all sweet buds were swellin',
Sweet William on his death-bed lay
    For the love of Barbara Allen."

My grandfather sighed and thumped wearily on his guitar, then laid it aside, the song unfinished.

"My voice is too old and cracked," he said, leaning back in his cushion-seated chair and fumbling in the pockets of his sagging old vest for cob-pipe and tobacco. "Reminds me of my brother Joel. The way he could sing that song. It was his favorite. Makes me think of poor old Rachel Ormond, who loved him. She's dyin', her nephew Jim Ormond told me yesterday. She's old; older'n I am. You never saw her, did you?"

I shook my head.

"She was a real beauty when she was young, and Joel was alive and lovin' her. He had a fine voice, Joel, and he loved to play his guitar and sing. He'd sing as he rode along. He was singin' 'Barbara Allen' when he met Rachel Ormond. She heard him singin' and came out of the laurel beside the road to listen. When Joel saw her standin' there with the mornin' sun behind her makin' jewels out of the dew on the bushes, he stopped dead and just stared like a fool. He told me it seemed as if she was standin' in a white blaze of light.

"It was mornin' in the mountains and they were both young. You never saw a mornin' in spring, in the Cumberlands?"

"I never was in Tennessee," I answered.

"No, you don't know anything about it," he retorted, in the half humorous, half petulant mood of the old. "You're a post oak gopher. You never saw anything but sand drifts and dry shinnery ridges. What do you know about mountain sides covered with birch and laurel, and cold clear streams windin' through the cool shadows and tinklin' over the rocks? What do you know about upland forests with the blue haze of the Cumberlands hangin' over them?"

"Nothing," I answered, yet even as I spoke, there leaped crystal clear into my mind with startling clarity the very image of the things of which he spoke, so vivid that my external faculties seemed almost to sense it – I could almost smell the dogwood blossoms and the cool lush of the deep woods, and hear the tinkle of hidden streams over the stones.

"You couldn't know," he sighed. "It's not your fault, and I wouldn't go back, myself, but Joel loved it. He never knew anything else, till the war came up. That's where you'd have been born if it hadn't been for the war. That tore everything up. Things didn't seem the same afterwards. I came west, like so many Tennessee folks did. I've done well in Texas – better'n I'd ever done in Tennessee. But as I get old I get to dreamin'."

His gaze was fixed on nothing, and he sighed deeply, wandering somewhat in his mind as the very old are likely to do at times.

"Four years behind Bedford Forrest," he said at last. "There never was a cavalry leader like him. Ride all day, shootin' and fightin', bed down in the snow – up before midnight, 'Boots and Saddles', and we were off again.

"Forrest never hung back. He was always in front of his men, fightin' like any three. His saber was too heavy for the average man to use, and it carried a razor edge. I remember the skirmish where Joel was killed. We come suddenly out of a defile between low hills and there was a Yankee wagon train movin' down the valley, guarded by a detachment of cavalry. We hit that cavalry like a thunder-bolt and ripped it apart.

"I can see Forrest now, standin' up in his stirrups, swingin' that big sword of his, yellin' "*Charge!* Holler, boys, holler!" And we hollered like wild men as we went in, and none of us cared if we lived or died, so long as Forrest was leadin' us.

"We tore that detachment in pieces and stomped and chased the pieces all up and down the valley. When the fight was over, Forrest reined up with his officers and said, "Gentlemen, one of my stirrups seems to have been shot away!" He had only one foot in a stirrup. But when he looked, he saw that somehow his left foot had come out of the stirrup, and the stirrup had flopped up over the saddle. He'd been sittin' on the stirrup leather, and hadn't noticed, in the excitement of the charge.

"I was right near him at the time, because my horse had fell, with a bullet through its head, and I was pullin' my saddle off. Just then my brother Joel came up on foot, smilin', with the morning sun behind him. But he was dazed with the fightin' because he had a strange look on his face, and when he saw me he stopped short, as if I was a stranger. Then he said the strangest thing: 'Why, granddad!' he said, 'You're young again! You're younger'n I am!' Then the next second a bullet from some skulkin' sniper knocked him down dead at my feet."

Again my grandfather sighed and took up his guitar.

"Rachel Ormond nearly died," he said. "She never married, never looked at any other man. When the Ormonds came to Texas, she came with 'em. Now she's dyin', up there in their house in the hills. That's what they say; I know she died years ago, when news of Joel's death came to her."

He began to thrum his guitar and sing in the curious wailing chant of the hill people.

> "They sent to the east, they sent to the west,
> To the place where she was dwellin',
> Sweet William's sick, and he sends for you,
> For the love of Barbara Allen."

My father called to me from his room on the other side of the house.

"Go out and stop those horses from fighting. I can hear them kicking the sides out of the barn."

My grandfather's voice followed me out of the house and into the stables. It was a clear still day and his voice carried far, the only sound besides the squealing and kicking of the horses in the stables, the crowing of a distant cock, and the clamor of sparrows among the mesquites.

Barbara Allen! An echo of a distant and forgotten homeland among the post-oak covered ridges of a barren land. In my mind I saw the settlers forging westward from the Piedmont, over the Alleghenies and along the Cumberland River – on foot, in lumbering wagons drawn by slow-footed oxen, on horse-back – men in broadcloth and men in buckskin. The guitars and the banjoes clinked by the fires at night, in the lonely log cabins, by the stretches of river black in the starlight, up on the long ridges where the owls hooted. Barbara Allen – a tie to the past, a link between today and the dim yesterdays.

I opened the stall and went in. My mustang Pedro, vicious as the land which bred him, had broken his halter and was assaulting the bay horse with squeals of rage, wicked teeth bared, eyes flashing, and ears laid back. I caught his mane, jerked him around, slapping him sharply on the nose when he snapped at me, and drove him from the stall. He lashed out wickedly at me with his heels as he dashed out, but I was watching for that and stepped back.

I had forgotten the bay horse. Stung to frenzy by the mustang's attack, he was ready to kill anything that came within his reach. His steel shod hoof barely grazed my skull, but that was enough to dash me into utter oblivion.

My first sensation was of movement. I was shaken up and down, up and down. Then a hand gripped my shoulder and shook me, and a voice bawled in an accent which was familiar, yet strangely unfamiliar: "Hyuh, you, Joel, yuh goin' to sleep in yo' saddle!"

I awoke with a jerk. The motion was that of the gaunt horse under me. All about me were men, gaunt and haggard in appearance, in worn grey uniforms. We were riding between two low hills, thickly timbered. I could not see what lay ahead of us because of the mass of men and horses. It was dawn, a grey unsteady dawn that made me shiver.

"Sun soon be up now," drawled one of the men, mistaking my feeling. "We'll have fightin' enough to warm our blood purty soon. Old Bedford ain't marched us all night just for fun. I heah theah's a wagon-train comin' down the valley ahaid of us."

I was still struggling feebly in a web of illusion. There was a sense of familiarity about all this, yet it was strange and alien, too. There was something I was striving to remember. I slipped a hand into my inside pocket, as if by instinct, and drew out a photograph, an old-fashioned picture. A girl smiled bravely at me, a beautiful girl with tender lips and brave eyes. I replaced it, shaking my head dazedly.

Ahead of us a low roar went up. We were riding out of the defile, and a broad valley lay spread out before us. Along this valley moved a train of clumsy, lumbering wagons. I saw men on horseback – men in blue, whose appearance and whose horses were fresher than ours. The rest is dim and confused.

I remember a bugle blown. I saw a tall rangy man on a great horse at the head of our column draw his sword and stand up in his stirrups, and his voice rang above the blast of the bugle: "*Charge!* Holler, boys, holler!"

Then there was a shout that rent the skies apart and we stormed out of the defile and down into the valley like a mountain torrent. I was like two men – one that rode and shouted and slashed right and left with a reddened saber, and one who sat wondering and fumbling for something illusive that he could not grasp. But the conviction was growing that I had experienced all this before; it was like living an episode forewarned in a dream.

The blue line held for a few minutes, then it broke in pieces before our irresistible onslaught, and we hunted them up and down the valley. The battle resolved itself into a hundred combats, where men in blue and men in grey circled each other on stamping, rearing horses, with bright blades glittering in the rising sun.

My gaunt horse stumbled and went down, and I pulled myself free. In my daze I did not take off his saddle. I walked toward a group of officers and men who were clustered about the tall man who had led the charge. As I approached, I heard him say: "Gentlemen, it seems the enemy have shot off one of my stirrups."

Then before I could hear anything else, I came face to face with a man I recognized at last. Yet like all else he was subtly altered. I gasped: "Why, granddad! You're young again! You're younger than I am!" And in that flash I *knew*; and I clenched my fists and stood dumbly waiting, frozen, paralyzed, unable to speak or stir. Then something crashed against my head and with the impact a great blaze of light lighted universal darkness for an instant, and then all was oblivion.

> "– Sweet William, he has died of grief,
>   And I shall die of sorrow!"

My grandfather's voice still wailed in my ears, faint with the distance, as I staggered to my feet, pressing my hand to the gash the bay's hoof had laid open in my scalp. I was sick and nauseated and my head swam dizzyingly. My grandfather was still singing. Less than seconds had elapsed since the bay's hoof felled me senseless on the littered stable floor. Yet in those brief seconds I had travelled through the eternities and back. I knew at last my true cosmic identity, and the reason for those dreams of wooded mountains and gurgling rivers, and of a brave sweet face that had haunted my dreams since childhood.

Going out into the corral I caught the mustang and saddled him, without bothering to dress my scalp-wound. It had quit bleeding and my head was clearing. I rode down the valley and up the hill until I came to the Ormond house, perched in gaunt poverty on a sandy hill-side, limned against the brown post-oak thickets behind it. The paint on the warped boards had long ago been worn away by rain and sun, both equally fierce in the hills of the Divide.

I dismounted and entered the yard with its barbed-wire fence. Chickens pecking on the porch scampered squawking out of the way, and a gaunt hound bayed at me. The door opened to my knock and Jim Ormond stood framed in it, a gaunt, stooped man with sunken cheeks and lacklustre eyes and gnarled hands.

He looked at me in dull surprize, for we were only acquaintances.

253

"Is Miss Rachel —" I began. "Is she — has she —" I halted in some confusion. He shook his bushy head.

"She's dyin'. Doc Blaine's with her. I reckon her time's come. She don't want to live, noway. She keeps callin' for Joel Grimes, pore old soul."

"May I come in?" I asked. "I want to see Doc Blaine." Even the dead can not intrude uninvited on the dying.

"Come in," he drew aside and I went into the miserably bare room. A frowsy-headed woman was moving about listlessly, and cotton-headed children looked timidly at me from other doorways. Doc Blaine came out from an inner room and stared at me.

"What the devil are you doing here?"

The Ormonds had lost interest in me. They went wearily about their tasks. I came close to Doc Blaine and said in a low voice: "Rachel! I must see her!" He stared at the insistence of my tone; but he is a man who instinctively grasps sometimes things that his conscious mind does not understand.

He led me into a room and I saw an old, old woman lying on a bed. Even in her old age her vitality was apparent, though that was waning fast. She lent a new atmosphere even to the miserable surroundings. And I knew her and stood transfixed. Yes, I knew her, beyond all the years and the changes they had wrought.

She stirred and murmured: "Joel! Joel! I've waited for you so long! I knew you'd come." She stretched out withered arms, and I went without a word and seated myself beside her bed. Recognition came into her glazing eyes. Her bony fingers closed on mine caressingly, and her touch was that of a young girl.

"I knew you'd come before I died," she whispered. "Death couldn't keep you away. Oh, the cruel wound on your head, Joel! But you're past suffering, just as I'll be in a few minutes. You never forgot me, Joel?"

"I never forgot you, Rachel," I answered, and I felt Doc Blaine's start behind me, and knew that my voice was not that of the John Grimes he knew, but another, different voice, whispering down the ages. I did not see him go, but I knew he tip-toed out.

"Sing to me, Joel," she whispered. "There's your guitar hanging on the wall. I've kept it always. Sing the song you sang when we met that day beside the Cumberland River. I always loved it."

I took up the ancient guitar, and though I never played one before, I had no doubts. I struck the worn strings and sang, and my voice was weird and golden. The dying woman's hands were on my arm, and as I looked, I saw and recognized the picture I had seen in the defile of the dawn. I saw youth, and love everlasting and understanding.

"Sweet William lies in the upper churchyard,
  And by his side, his lover,
  And on his grave grew a lily-white rose,
  And on hers grew a briar.
  They grew, they grew to the church-steeple-top,
  And there they grew no higher,
  They tied themselves in a true lover's knot,
  And there remained for ever."

The string snapped loudly. Rachel Ormond was lying still and her lips were smiling. I disengaged my arm gently from her dead fingers and went out. Doc Blaine met me at the door.

"Dead?"

"She died years ago," I said heavily. "She waited long for him; now she must wait somewhere else. That's the hell of war; it upsets the balance of things and throws lives into confusion that eternity can not make right."

The Tide

Thus in my mood I love you
In the drum of my heart's fast beat,
In the lure of the skies above you
And the earth beneath your feet.

Now I can lift and crown you
With the moon's white empery,
Now I can crush and drown you
In my passion's misty sea.

I can swing you high and higher
Than any man of earth,
Draw you through stars and fire
To lands of the ultimate birth.

Were I like this forever
You'd only too little to give,
But here tonight we sever
For life loves life to live.

And the higher a man may travel
The lower may he fall
And the skein that I must unravel
It was never meant for all.

And what do you know of glory,
Of the heights that I have trod,
Of the shadows grim and hoary
That hide my face from God!

Would you understand my story,
My torments and my hopes,
Or the red dark Purgatory
Where my soul in horror gropes!

Now I am man and lover
Rising with you at side
To peaks where the splendors hover –
But drifting with the tide.

And the tide? It is mine to shake it,
To battle the winds and spray,
To batter the tide and break it
Or batter my heart away.

So I leave you – that you never
The grim day have to face
When I would be gone forever
And a stranger in my place.
Tonight, tonight we sever
For my race is my own race.

The Valley of the Worm

I will tell you of Niord and the Worm. You have heard the tale before in many guises wherein the hero was named Tyr, or Perseus, or Siegfried, or Beowulf, or Saint George. But it was Niord who met the loathly demoniac thing that crawled hideously up from hell, and from which meeting sprang the cycle of hero-tales that revolves down the ages until the very substance of the truth is lost and passes into the limbo of all forgotten legends. I know whereof I speak, for I was Niord.

As I lie here awaiting death, which creeps slowly upon me like a blind slug, my dreams are filled with glittering visions and the pageantry of glory. It is not of the drab, disease-racked life of James Allison I dream, but all the gleaming figures of the mighty pageantry that have passed before, and shall come after; for I have faintly glimpsed, not merely the shapes that trail out behind, but shapes that come after, as a man in a long parade glimpses, far ahead, the line of figures that precede him winding over a distant hill, etched shadow-like against the sky. I am one and all the pageantry of shapes and guises and masks which have been, are, and shall be the visible manifestations of that illusive, intangible, but vitally existent spirit now promenading under the brief and temporary name of James Allison.

Each man on earth, each woman, is part and all of a similar caravan of shapes and beings. But they can not remember – their minds can not bridge the brief, awful gulfs of blackness which lie between those unstable shapes, and which the spirit, soul or ego, in spanning, shakes off its fleshy masks. I remember. Why I can remember is the strangest tale of all; but as I lie here with death's black wings slowly unfolding over me, all the dim folds of my previous lives are shaken out before my eyes, and I see myself in many forms and guises — braggart, swaggering, fearful, loving, foolish, all that men have been or will be.

I have been Man in many lands and many conditions; yet — and here is another strange thing — my line of reincarnation runs straight down one unerring channel. I have never been any but a man of that restless race men once called Nordheimr and later Aryans, and today name by many names and designations. Their history is my history, from the first mewling wail of a hairless white ape cub in the wastes of the arctic, to the death-cry of the last degenerate product of ultimate civilization, in some dim and unguessed future age.

My name has been Hialmar, Tyr, Bragi, Bran, Horsa, Eric, and John. I strode red-handed through the deserted streets of Rome behind the yellow-maned Brennus; I wandered through the violated plantations with Alaric and his Goths when the flame of burning villas lit the land like day and an empire was gasping its last under our sandalled feet; I waded sword in hand through the foaming surf from Hengist's galley to lay the foundations of England in blood and pillage; when Leif the Lucky sighted the broad white beaches of an unguessed world, I stood beside him in the bows of the dragon-ship, my golden beard blowing in the wind; and when Godfrey of Bouillon led his Crusaders over the walls of Jerusalem, I was among them in steel cap and brigandine.

But it is of none of these things I would speak. I would take you back with me into an age beside which that of Brennus and Rome is as yesterday. I would take you back through, not merely centuries and millenniums, but epochs and dim ages unguessed by the wildest philosopher. Oh far, far and far will you fare into the nighted Past before you win beyond the boundaries of my race, blue-eyed, yellow-haired, wanderers, slayers, lovers, mighty in rapine and wayfaring.

It is the adventure of Niord Worm's-bane of which I would speak — the root-stem of a whole cycle of hero-tales which has not yet reached its end, the grisly underlying reality that lurks behind time-distorted myths of dragons, fiends and monsters.

Yet it is not alone with the mouth of Niord that I will speak. I am James Allison no less than I was Niord, and as I unfold the tale, I will interpret some of his thoughts and dreams and deeds from the mouth of the modern I, so that the saga of Niord shall not be a meaningless chaos to you. His blood is your blood, who are sons of Aryan; but wide misty gulfs of eons lie horrifically between, and the deeds and dreams of Niord seem as alien to your deeds and dreams as the primordial and lion-haunted forest seems alien to the white-walled city street.

260

———

It was a strange world in which Niord lived and loved and fought, so long ago that even my eon-spanning memory can not recognize landmarks. Since then the surface of the earth has changed, not once but a score of times; continents have risen and sunk, seas have changed their beds and rivers their courses, glaciers have waxed and waned, and the very stars and constellations have altered and shifted.

It was so long ago that the cradle-land of my race was still in Nordheim. But the epic drifts of my people had already begun, and blue-eyed, yellow-maned tribes flowed eastward and southward and westward, on century-long treks that carried them around the world and left their bones and their traces in strange lands and wild waste places. On one of these drifts I grew from infancy to manhood. My knowledge of that northern homeland was dim memories, like half-remembered dreams, of blinding white snow plains and ice fields, of great fires roaring in the circle of hide tents, of yellow manes flying in great winds, and a sun setting in a lurid wallow of crimson clouds, blazing on trampled snow where still dark forms lay in pools that were redder than the sunset.

That last memory stands out clearer than the others. It was the field of Jotunheim, I was told in later years, whereon had just been fought that terrible battle which was the Armageddon of the Æsir-folk, the subject of a cycle of hero-songs for long ages, and which still lives today in dim dreams of Ragnarok and Goetterdaemmerung. I looked on that battle as a mewling infant; so I must have lived about – but I will not name the age, for I would be called a madman, and historians and geologists alike would rise to refute me.

But my memories of Nordheim were few and dim, paled by memories of that long, long trek upon which I had spent my life. We had not kept to a straight course, but our trend had been for ever southward. Sometimes we had bided for a while in fertile upland valleys or rich river-traversed plains, but always we took up the trail again, and not always because of drouth or famine. Often we left countries teeming with game and wild grain to push into wastelands. On our trail we moved endlessly, driven only by our restless whim, yet blindly following a cosmic law, the workings of which we never guessed, any more than the wild geese guess in their flights around the world. So at last we came into the Country of the Worm.

I will take up the tale at the time when we came into jungle-clad hills reeking with rot and teeming with spawning life, where the tom-toms of a savage people pulsed incessantly through the hot breathless night. These people came forth to dispute our way – short, strongly built men, black-haired, painted, ferocious, but indisputably white men. We knew their breed of old. They were Picts, and of all alien races the fiercest. We had met their kind before in thick forests, and in upland valleys beside mountain lakes. But many moons had passed since those meetings.

I believe this particular tribe represented the easternmost drift of the race. They were the most primitive and ferocious of any I ever met. Already they were exhibiting hints of characteristics I have noted among black savages in jungle countries, though they had dwelt in these environs only a few generations. The abysmal jungle was engulfing them, was obliterating their pristine characteristics and shaping them in its own horrific mold. They were drifting into head-hunting, and cannibalism was but a step which I believe they must have taken before they became extinct. These things are natural adjuncts to the jungle; the Picts did not learn them from the black people, for then there were no blacks among those hills. In later years they came up from the south, and the Picts first enslaved and then were absorbed by them. But with that my saga of Niord is not concerned.

We came into that brutish hill country, with its squalling abysms of savagery and black primitiveness. We were a whole tribe marching on foot, old men, wolfish with their long beards and gaunt limbs, giant warriors in their prime, naked children running along the line of march, women with tousled yellow locks carrying babies which never cried – unless it were to scream from pure rage. I do not remember our numbers, except that there were some five hundred fighting-men – and by fighting-men I mean all males, from the child just strong enough to lift a bow, to the oldest of the old men. In that madly ferocious age all were fighters. Our women fought, when brought to bay, like tigresses, and I have seen a babe, not yet old enough to stammer articulate words, twist its head and sink its tiny teeth in the foot that stamped out its life.

Oh, we were fighters! Let me speak of Niord. I am proud of him, the more when I consider the paltry crippled body of James Allison, the unstable mask I now wear. Niord was tall, with great shoulders, lean hips and mighty limbs. His muscles were long and swelling, denoting endurance and speed as well as strength. He could run all day without tiring, and he possessed a co-ordination that made his movements a blur of blinding speed. If I told you his full strength, you would brand me a liar. But there is no man on earth today strong enough to bend the bow Niord handled with ease. The longest arrow-flight on record is that of a Turkish archer who sent a shaft 482 yards. There was not a stripling in my tribe who could not have bettered that flight.

As we entered the jungle country we heard the tom-toms booming across the mysterious valleys that slumbered between the brutish hills, and in a broad, open plateau we met our enemies. I do not believe these Picts knew us, even by legends, or they had never rushed so openly to the onset, though they outnumbered us. But there was no attempt at ambush. They swarmed out of the trees, dancing and singing their war-songs, yelling their barbarous threats. Our heads should hang in their idol-hut and our yellow-haired women should bear their sons. Ho! ho! ho! By Ymir, it was Niord who laughed then, not James Allison. Just so we of the Æsir laughed to hear their threats – deep thunderous laughter from broad and mighty chests. Our trail was laid in blood and embers through many lands. We were the slayers and ravishers, striding sword in hand across the world, and that these folk threatened us woke our rugged humor.

We went to meet them, naked but for our wolfhides, swinging our bronze swords, and our singing was like rolling thunder in the hills. They sent their arrows among us, and we gave back their fire. They could not match us in archery. Our arrows hissed in blinding clouds among them, dropping them like autumn leaves, until they howled and frothed like mad dogs and charged to hand-grips. And we, mad with the fighting joy, dropped our bows and ran to meet them, as a lover runs to his love.

By Ymir, it was a battle to madden and make drunken with the slaughter and the fury. The Picts were as ferocious as we, but ours was the superior physique, the keener wit, the more highly developed fighting-brain. We won because we were a superior race, but it was no easy victory. Corpses littered the blood-soaked earth; but at last they broke, and we cut them down as they ran, to the very edge of the trees. I tell of that fight in a few bald words. I can not paint the madness, the reek of sweat and blood, the panting, muscle-straining effort, the splintering of bones under mighty blows, the rending and hewing of quivering sentient flesh; above all the merciless abysmal savagery of the whole affair, in which there was neither rule nor order, each man fighting as he would or could. If I might do so, you would recoil in horror; even the modern I, cognizant of my close kinship with those times, stand aghast as I review that butchery. Mercy was yet unborn, save as some individual's whim, and rules of warfare were as yet undreamed of. It was an age in which each tribe and each human fought tooth and fang from birth to death, and neither gave nor expected mercy.

So we cut down the fleeing Picts, and our women came out on the field to brain the wounded enemies with stones, or cut their throats with copper knives. We did not torture. We were no more cruel than life demanded. The rule of life was ruthlessness, but there is more wanton cruelty today than ever we dreamed of. It was not wanton bloodthirstiness that made us butcher wounded and captive foes. It was because we knew our chances of survival increased with each enemy slain.

Yet there was occasionally a touch of individual mercy, and so it was in this fight. I had been occupied with a duel with an especially valiant enemy. His tousled thatch of black hair scarcely came above my chin, but he was a solid knot of steel-spring muscles, than which lightning scarcely moved faster. He had an iron sword and a hide-covered buckler. I had a knotty-headed bludgeon. That fight was one that glutted even my battle-lusting soul. I was bleeding from a score of flesh wounds before one of my terrible, lashing strokes smashed his shield like cardboard, and an instant later my bludgeon glanced from his unprotected head. Ymir! Even now I stop to laugh and marvel at the hardness of that Pict's skull. Men of that age were assuredly built on a rugged plan! That blow should have spattered his brains like water. It did lay his scalp open horribly, dashing him senseless to the earth, where I let him lie, supposing him to be dead, as I joined in the slaughter of the fleeing warriors.

When I returned reeking with sweat and blood, my club horridly clotted with blood and brains, I noticed that my antagonist was regaining consciousness, and that a naked tousle-headed girl was preparing to give him the finishing touch with a stone she could scarcely lift. A vagrant whim caused me to check the blow. I had enjoyed the fight, and I admired the adamantine quality of his skull.

We made camp a short distance away, burned our dead on a great pyre, and after looting the corpses of the enemy, we dragged them across the plateau and cast them down in a valley to make a feast for the hyenas, jackals and vultures which were already gathering. We kept close watch that night, but we were not attacked, though far away through the jungle we could make out the red gleam of fires, and could faintly hear, when the wind veered, the throb of tom-toms and demoniac screams and yells – keenings for the slain or mere animal squallings of fury.

Nor did they attack us in the days that followed. We bandaged our captive's wounds and quickly learned his primitive tongue, which, however, was so different from ours that I can not conceive of the two languages having ever had a common source.

His name was Grom, and he was a great hunter and fighter, he boasted. He talked freely and held no grudge, grinning broadly and showing tusk-like teeth, his beady eyes glittering from under the tangled black mane that fell over his low forehead. His limbs were almost ape-like in their thickness.

He was vastly interested in his captors, though he could never understand why he had been spared; to the end it remained an inexplicable mystery to him. The Picts obeyed the law of survival even more rigidly than did the Æsir. They were the more practical, as shown by their more settled habits. They never roamed as far or as blindly as we. Yet in every line we were the superior race.

Grom, impressed by our intelligence and fighting qualities, volunteered to go into the hills and make peace for us with his people. It was immaterial to us, but we let him go. Slavery had not yet been dreamed of.

So Grom went back to his people, and we forgot about him, except that I went a trifle more cautiously about my hunting, expecting him to be lying in wait to put an arrow through my back. Then one day we heard a rattle of tom-toms, and Grom appeared at the edge of the jungle, his face split in his gorilla-grin, with the painted, skin-clad, feather-bedecked chiefs of the clans. Our ferocity had awed them, and our sparing of Grom further impressed them. They could not understand leniency; evidently we valued them too cheaply to bother about killing one when he was in our power.

So peace was made with much powwow, and sworn to with many strange oaths and rituals – we swore only by Ymir, and an Æsir never broke that vow. But they swore by the elements, by the idol which sat in the fetish-hut where fires burned for ever and a withered crone slapped a leather-covered drum all night long, and by another being too terrible to be named.

Then we all sat around the fires and gnawed meat-bones, and drank a fiery concoction they brewed from wild grain, and the wonder is that the feast did not end in a general massacre; for that liquor had devils in it and made maggots writhe in our brains. But no harm came of our vast drunkenness, and thereafter we dwelt at peace with our barbarous neighbors. They taught us many things, and learned many more from us. But they taught us iron-workings, into which they had been forced by the lack of copper in those hills, and we quickly excelled them.

We went freely among their villages – mud-walled clusters of huts in hilltop clearings, overshadowed by giant trees – and we allowed them to come at will among our camps – straggling lines of hide tents on the plateau where the battle had been fought. Our young men cared not for their squat beady-eyed women, and our rangy clean-limbed girls with their tousled yellow heads were not drawn to the hairy-breasted savages. Familiarity over a period of years would have reduced the repulsion on either side, until the two races would have flowed together to form one hybrid people, but long before that time the Æsir rose and departed, vanishing into the mysterious hazes of the haunted south. But before that exodus there came to pass the horror of the Worm.

I hunted with Grom and he led me into brooding, uninhabited valleys and up into silence-haunted hills where no men had set foot before us. But there was one valley, off in the mazes of the southwest, into which he would not go. Stumps of shattered columns, relics of a forgotten civilization, stood among the trees on the valley floor. Grom showed them to me, as we stood on the cliffs that flanked the mysterious vale, but he would not go down into it, and he dissuaded me when I would have gone alone. He would not speak plainly of the danger that lurked there, but it was greater than that of serpent or tiger, or the trumpeting elephants which occasionally wandered up in devastating droves from the south.

Of all beasts, Grom told me in the gutturals of his tongue, the Picts feared only Satha, the great snake, and they shunned the jungle where he lived. But there was another thing they feared, and it was connected in some manner with the Valley of Broken Stones, as the Picts called the crumbling pillars. Long ago, when his ancestors had first come into the country, they had dared that grim vale, and a whole clan of them had perished, suddenly, horribly, and unexplainably. At least Grom did not explain. The horror had come up out of the earth, somehow, and it was not good to talk of it, since it was believed that It might be summoned by speaking of It – whatever It was.

But Grom was ready to hunt with me anywhere else; for he was the greatest hunter among the Picts, and many and fearful were our adventures. Once I killed, with the iron sword I had forged with my own hands, that most terrible of all beasts – old saber-tooth, which men today call a tiger because he was more like a tiger than anything else. In reality he was almost as much like a bear in build, save for his unmistakably feline head. Saber-tooth was massive-limbed, with a low-hung, great, heavy body, and he vanished from the earth because he was too terrible a fighter, even for that grim age. As his muscles and ferocity grew, his brain dwindled until at last even the instinct of self-preservation vanished. Nature, who maintains her balance in such things, destroyed him because, had his super-fighting powers been allied with an intelligent brain, he would have destroyed all other forms of life on earth. He was a freak on the road of evolution – organic development gone mad and run to fangs and talons, to slaughter and destruction.

I killed saber-tooth in a battle that would make a saga in itself, and for months afterward I lay semi-delirious with ghastly wounds that made the toughest warriors shake their heads. The Picts said that never before had a man killed a saber-tooth single-handed. Yet I recovered, to the wonder of all.

While I lay at the doors of death there was a secession from the tribe. It was a peaceful secession, such as continually occurred and contributed greatly to the peopling of the world by yellow-haired tribes. Forty-five of the young men took themselves mates simultaneously and wandered off to found a clan of their own. There was no revolt; it was a racial custom which bore fruit in all the later ages, when tribes sprung from the same roots met, after centuries of separation, and cut one another's throats with joyous abandon. The tendency of the Aryan and the pre-Aryan was always toward disunity, clans splitting off the main stem, and scattering.

So these young men, led by one Bragi, my brother-in-arms, took their girls and venturing to the southwest, took up their abode in the Valley of Broken Stones. The Picts expostulated, hinting vaguely of a monstrous doom that haunted the vale, but the Æsir laughed. We had left our own demons and weirds in the icy wastes of the far blue north, and the devils of other races did not much impress us.

When my full strength was returned, and the grisly wounds were only scars, I girt on my weapons and strode over the plateau to visit Bragi's clan. Grom did not accompany me. He had not been in the Æsir camp for several days. But I knew the way. I remembered well the valley, from the cliffs of which I had looked down and seen the lake at the upper end, the trees thickening into forest at the lower extremity. The sides of the valley were high sheer cliffs, and a steep broad ridge at either end cut it off from the surrounding country. It was toward the lower or southwestern end that the valley-floor was dotted thickly with ruined columns, some towering high among the trees, some fallen into heaps of lichen-clad stones. What race reared them none knew. But Grom had hinted fearsomely of a hairy, apish monstrosity dancing loathsomely under the moon to a demoniac piping that induced horror and madness.

I crossed the plateau whereon our camp was pitched, descended the slope, traversed a shallow vegetation-choked valley, climbed another slope, and plunged into the hills. A half-day's leisurely travel brought me to the ridge on the other side of which lay the valley of the pillars. For many miles I had seen no sign of human life. The settlements of the Picts all lay many miles to the east. I topped the ridge and looked down into the dreaming valley with its still blue lake, its brooding cliffs and its broken columns jutting among the trees. I looked for smoke. I saw none, but I saw vultures wheeling in the sky over a cluster of tents on the lake shore.

I came down the ridge warily and approached the silent camp. In it I halted, frozen with horror. I was not easily moved. I had seen death in many forms, and had fled from or taken part in red massacres that spilled blood like water and heaped the earth with corpses. But here I was confronted with an organic devastation that staggered and appalled me. Of Bragi's embryonic clan, not one remained alive, and not one corpse was whole. Some of the hide tents still stood erect. Others were mashed down and flattened out, as if crushed by some monstrous weight, so that at first I wondered if a drove of elephants had stampeded across the camp. But no elephants ever wrought such destruction as I saw strewn on the bloody ground. The camp was a shambles, littered with bits of flesh and fragments of bodies – hands, feet, heads, pieces of human debris. Weapons lay about, some of them stained with a greenish slime like that which spurts from a crushed caterpillar.

No human foe could have committed this ghastly atrocity. I looked at the lake, wondering if nameless amphibian monsters had crawled from the calm waters whose deep blue told of unfathomed depths. Then I saw a print left by the destroyer. It was a track such as a titanic worm might leave, yards broad, winding back down the valley. The grass lay flat where it ran, and bushes and small trees had been crushed down into the earth, all horribly smeared with blood and greenish slime.

With berserk fury in my soul I drew my sword and started to follow it, when a call attracted me. I wheeled, to see a stocky form approaching me from the ridge. It was Grom the Pict, and when I think of the courage it must have taken for him to have overcome all the instincts planted in him by traditional teachings and personal experience, I realize the full depths of his friendship for me.

Squatting on the lake shore, spear in his hands, his black eyes ever roving fearfully down the brooding tree-waving reaches of the valley, Grom told me of the horror that had come upon Bragi's clan under the moon. But first he told me of it, as his sires had told the tale to him.

Long ago the Picts had drifted down from the northwest on a long, long trek, finally reaching these jungle-covered hills, where, because they were weary, and because the game and fruit were plentiful and there were no hostile tribes, they halted and built their mud-walled villages.

Some of them, a whole clan of that numerous tribe, took up their abode in the Valley of the Broken Stones. They found the columns and a great ruined temple back in the trees, and in that temple there was no shrine or altar, but the mouth of a shaft that vanished deep into the black earth, and in which there were no steps such as a human being would make and use. They built their village in the valley, and in the night, under the moon, horror came upon them and left only broken walls and bits of slime-smeared flesh.

In those days the Picts feared nothing. The warriors of the other clans gathered and sang their war-songs and danced their war-dances, and followed a broad track of blood and slime to the shaft-mouth in the temple. They howled defiance and hurled down boulders which were never heard to strike bottom. Then began a thin demoniac piping, and up from the well pranced a hideous anthropomorphic figure dancing to the weird strains of a pipe it held in its monstrous hands. The horror of its aspect froze the fierce Picts with amazement, and close behind it a vast white bulk heaved up from the subterranean darkness. Out of the shaft came a slavering mad nightmare which arrows pierced but could not check, which swords carved but could not slay. It fell slobbering upon the warriors, crushing them to crimson pulp, tearing them to bits as an octopus might tear small fishes, sucking their blood from their mangled limbs and devouring them even as they screamed and struggled. The survivors fled, pursued to the very ridge, up which, apparently, the monster could not propel its quaking mountainous bulk.

After that they did not dare the silent valley. But the dead came to their shamans and old men in dreams and told them strange and terrible secrets. They spoke of an ancient, ancient race of semi-human beings which once inhabited that valley and reared those columns for their own weird inexplicable purposes. The white monster in the pits was their god, summoned up from the nighted abysses of mid-earth uncounted fathoms below the black mold, by sorcery unknown to the sons of men. The hairy anthropomorphic being was its servant, created to serve the god, a formless elemental spirit drawn up from below and cased in flesh, organic but beyond the understanding of humanity. The Old Ones had long vanished into the limbo from whence they crawled in the black dawn of the universe, but their bestial god and his inhuman slave lived on. Yet both were organic after a fashion, and could be wounded, though no human weapon had been found potent enough to slay them.

Bragi and his clan had dwelt for weeks in the valley before the horror struck. Only the night before, Grom, hunting above the cliffs, and by that token daring greatly, had been paralyzed by a high-pitched demon piping, and then by a mad clamor of human screaming. Stretched face down in the dirt, hiding his head in a tangle of grass, he had not dared to move, even when the shrieks died away in the slobbering, repulsive sounds of a hideous feast. When dawn broke he had crept shuddering to the cliffs to look down into the valley, and the sight of the devastation, even when seen from afar, had driven him in yammering flight far into the hills. But it had occurred to him, finally, that he should warn the rest of the tribe, and returning, on his way to the camp on the plateau, he had seen me entering the valley.

So spoke Grom, while I sat and brooded darkly, my chin on my mighty fist. I can not frame in modern words the clan-feeling that in those days was a living vital part of every man and woman. In a world where talon and fang were lifted on every hand, and the hands of all men raised against an individual, except those of his own clan, tribal instinct was more than the phrase it is today. It was as much a part of a man as was his heart or his right hand. This was necessary, for only thus banded together in unbreakable groups could mankind have survived in the terrible environments of the primitive world. So now the personal grief I felt for Bragi and the clean-limbed young men and laughing white-skinned girls was drowned in a deeper sea of grief and fury that was cosmic in its depth and intensity. I sat grimly, while the Pict squatted anxiously beside me, his gaze roving from me to the menacing deeps of the valley where the accursed columns loomed like broken teeth of cackling hags among the waving leafy reaches.

I, Niord, was not one to use my brain over-much. I lived in a physical world, and there were the old men of the tribe to do my thinking. But I was one of a race destined to become dominant mentally as well as physically, and I was no mere muscular animal. So as I sat there there came dimly and then clearly a thought to me that brought a short fierce laugh from my lips.

Rising, I bade Grom aid me, and we built a pyre on the lake shore of dried wood, the ridge-poles of the tents, and the broken shafts of spears. Then we collected the grisly fragments that had been parts of Bragi's band, and we laid them on the pile, and struck flint and steel to it.

The thick sad smoke crawled serpent-like into the sky, and turning to Grom, I made him guide me to the jungle where lurked that scaly horror, Satha, the great serpent. Grom gaped at me; not the greatest hunters among the Picts sought out the mighty crawling one. But my will was like a wind that swept him along my course, and at last he led the way. We left the valley by the upper end, crossing the ridge, skirting the tall cliffs, and plunged into the fastnesses of the south, which was peopled only by the grim denizens of the jungle. Deep into the jungle we went, until we came to a low-lying expanse, dank and dark beneath the great creeper-festooned trees, where our feet sank deep into the spongy silt, carpeted by rotting vegetation, and slimy moisture oozed up beneath their pressure. This, Grom told me, was the realm haunted by Satha, the great serpent.

Let me speak of Satha. There is nothing like him on earth today, nor has there been for countless ages. Like the meat-eating dinosaur, like old saber-tooth, he was too terrible to exist. Even then he was a survival of a grimmer age when life and its forms were cruder and more hideous. There were not many of his kind then, though they may have existed in great numbers in the reeking ooze of the vast jungle-tangled swamps still farther south. He was larger than any python of modern ages, and his fangs dripped with poison a thousand times more deadly than that of a king cobra.

He was never worshipped by the pure-blood Picts, though the blacks that came later deified him, and that adoration persisted in the hybrid race that sprang from the negroes and their white conquerors. But to other peoples he was the nadir of evil horror, and tales of him became twisted into demonology; so in later ages Satha became the veritable devil of the white races, and the Stygians first worshipped, and then, when they became Egyptians, abhorred him under the name of Set, the Old Serpent, while to the Semites he became Leviathan and Satan. He was terrible enough to be a god, for he was a crawling death. I had seen a bull elephant fall dead in his tracks from Satha's bite. I had seen him, had glimpsed him writhing his horrific way through the dense jungle, had seen him take his prey, but I had never hunted him. He was too grim, even for the slayer of old saber-tooth.

But now I hunted him, plunging farther and farther into the hot, breathless reek of his jungle, even when friendship for me could not drive Grom farther. He urged me to paint my body and sing my death-song before I advanced farther, but I pushed on unheeding.

In a natural runway that wound between the shouldering trees, I set a trap. I found a large tree, soft and spongy of fiber, but thick-boled and heavy, and I hacked through its base close to the ground with my great sword, directing its fall so that when it toppled, its top crashed into the branches of a smaller tree, leaving it leaning across the runway, one end resting on the earth, the other caught in the small tree. Then I cut away the branches on the under side, and cutting a slim tough sapling I trimmed it and stuck it upright like a prop-pole under the leaning tree. Then, cutting away the tree which supported it, I left the great trunk poised precariously on the prop-pole, to which I fastened a long vine, as thick as my wrist.

Then I went alone through that primordial twilight jungle until an overpowering fetid odor assailed my nostrils, and from the rank vegetation in front of me, Satha reared up his hideous head, swaying lethally from side to side, while his forked tongue jetted in and out, and his great yellow terrible eyes burned icily on me with all the evil wisdom of the black elder world that was when man was not. I backed away, feeling no fear, only an icy sensation along my spine, and Satha came sinuously after me, his shining eighty-foot barrel rippling over the rotting vegetation in mesmeric silence. His wedge-shaped head was bigger than the head of the hugest stallion, his trunk was thicker than a man's body, and his scales shimmered with a thousand changing scintillations. I was to Satha as a mouse is to a king cobra, but I was fanged as no mouse ever was. Quick as I was, I knew I could not avoid the lightning stroke of that great triangular head; so I dared not let him come too close. Subtly I fled down the runway, and behind me the rush of the great supple body was like the sweep of wind through the grass.

He was not far behind me when I raced beneath the dead-fall, and as the great shining length glided under the trap, I gripped the vine with both hands and jerked desperately. With a crash the great trunk fell across Satha's scaly back, some six feet back of his wedge-shaped head.

I had hoped to break his spine but I do not think it did, for the great body coiled and knotted, the mighty tail lashed and thrashed, mowing down the bushes as if with a giant flail. At the instant of the fall, the huge head had whipped about and struck the tree with a terrific impact, the mighty fangs shearing through bark and wood like simitars. Now, as if aware he fought an inanimate foe, Satha turned on me, standing out of his reach. The scaly neck writhed and arched, the mighty jaws gaped, disclosing fangs a foot in length, from which dripped venom that might have burned through solid stone.

I believe, what of his stupendous strength, that Satha would have writhed from under the trunk, but for a broken branch that had been driven deep into his side, holding him like a barb. The sound of his hissing filled the jungle and his eyes glared at me with such concentrated evil that I shook despite myself. Oh, he knew it was I who had trapped him! Now I came as close as I dared, and with a sudden powerful cast of my spear, transfixed his neck just below the gaping jaws, nailing him to the tree-trunk. Then I dared greatly, for he was far from dead, and I knew he would in an instant tear the spear from the wood and be free to strike. But in that instant I ran in, and swinging my sword with all my great power, I hewed off his terrible head.

The heavings and contortions of Satha's prisoned form in life were naught to the convulsions of his headless length in death. I retreated, dragging the gigantic head after me with a crooked pole, and at a safe distance from the lashing, flying tail, I set to work. I worked with naked death then, and no man ever toiled more gingerly than did I. For I cut out the poison sacs at the base of the great fangs, and in the terrible venom I soaked the heads of eleven arrows, being careful that only the bronze points were in the liquid, which else had corroded away the wood of the tough shafts. While I was doing this, Grom, driven by comradeship and curiosity, came stealing nervously through the jungle, and his mouth gaped as he looked on the head of Satha.

For hours I steeped the arrowheads in the poison, until they were caked with a horrible green scum, and showed tiny flecks of corrosion where the venom had eaten into the solid bronze. I wrapped them carefully in broad, thick, rubber-like leaves, and then, though night had fallen and the hunting beasts were roaring on every hand, I went back through the jungled hills, Grom with me, until at dawn we came again to the high cliffs that loomed above the Valley of Broken Stones.

At the mouth of the valley I broke my spear, and I took all the unpoisoned shafts from my quiver, and snapped them. I painted my face and limbs as the Æsir painted themselves only when they went forth to certain doom, and I sang my death-song to the sun as it rose over the cliffs, my yellow mane blowing in the morning wind.

Then I went down into the valley, bow in hand.

Grom could not drive himself to follow me. He lay on his belly in the dust and howled like a dying dog.

I passed the lake and the silent camp where the pyre-ashes still smoldered, and came under the thickening trees beyond. About me the columns loomed, mere shapeless heaps from the ravages of staggering eons. The trees grew more dense, and under their vast leafy branches the very light was dusky and evil. As in twilight shadow I saw the ruined temple, cyclopean walls staggering up from masses of decaying masonry and fallen blocks of stone. About six hundred yards in front of it a great column reared up in an open glade, eighty or ninety feet in height. It was so worn and pitted by weather and time that any child of my tribe could have climbed it, and I marked it and changed my plan.

I came to the ruins and saw huge crumbling walls upholding a domed roof from which many stones had fallen, so that it seemed like the lichen-grown ribs of some mythical monster's skeleton arching above me. Titanic columns flanked the open doorway through which ten elephants could have stalked abreast. Once there might have been inscriptions and hieroglyphics on the pillars and walls, but they were long worn away. Around the great room, on the inner side, ran columns in better state of preservation. On each of these columns was a flat pedestal, and some dim instinctive memory vaguely resurrected a shadowy scene wherein black drums roared madly, and on these pedestals monstrous beings squatted loathsomely in inexplicable rituals rooted in the black dawn of the universe.

There was no altar – only the mouth of a great well-like shaft in the stone floor, with strange obscene carvings all about the rim. I tore great pieces of stone from the rotting floor and cast them down the shaft which slanted down into utter darkness. I heard them bound along the side, but I did not hear them strike bottom. I cast down stone after stone, each with a searing curse, and at last I heard a sound that was not the dwindling rumble of the falling stones. Up from the well floated a weird demon-piping that was a symphony of madness. Far down in the darkness I glimpsed the faint fearful glimmering of a vast white bulk.

I retreated slowly as the piping grew louder, falling back through the broad doorway. I heard a scratching, scrambling noise, and up from the shaft and out of the doorway between the colossal columns came a prancing incredible figure. It went erect like a man, but it was covered with fur, that was shaggiest where its face should have been. If it had ears, nose and a mouth I did not discover them. Only a pair of staring red eyes leered from the furry mask. Its misshapen hands held a strange set of pipes, on which it blew weirdly as it pranced toward me with many a grotesque caper and leap.

Behind it I heard a repulsive obscene noise as of a quaking unstable mass heaving up out of a well. Then I nocked an arrow, drew the cord and sent the shaft singing through the furry breast of the dancing monstrosity. It went down as though struck by a thunderbolt, but to my horror the piping continued, though the pipes had fallen from the malformed hands. Then I turned and ran fleetly to the column, up which I swarmed before I looked back. When I reached the pinnacle I looked, and because of the shock and surprize of what I saw, I almost fell from my dizzy perch.

Out of the temple the monstrous dweller in the darkness had come, and I, who had expected a horror yet cast in some terrestrial mold, looked on the spawn of nightmare. From what subterranean hell it crawled in the long ago I know not, nor what black age it represented. But it was not a beast, as humanity knows beasts. I call it a worm for lack of a better term. There is no earthly language which has a name for it. I can only say that it looked somewhat more like a worm than it did an octopus, a serpent or a dinosaur.

It was white and pulpy, and drew its quaking bulk along the ground, worm-fashion. But it had wide flat tentacles, and fleshy feelers, and other adjuncts the use of which I am unable to explain. And it had a long proboscis which it curled and uncurled like an elephant's trunk. Its forty eyes, set in a horrific circle, were composed of thousands of facets of as many scintillant colors which changed and altered in never-ending transmutation. But through all interplay of hue and glint, they retained their evil intelligence – intelligence there was behind those flickering facets, not human nor yet bestial, but a night-born demoniac intelligence such as men in dreams vaguely sense throbbing titanically in the black gulfs outside our material universe. In size the monster was mountainous; its bulk would have dwarfed a mastodon.

But even as I shook with the cosmic horror of the thing, I drew a feathered shaft to my ear and arched it singing on its way. Grass and bushes were crushed flat as the monster came toward me like a moving mountain and shaft after shaft I sent with terrific force and deadly precision. I could not miss so huge a target. The arrows sank to the feathers or clear out of sight in the unstable bulk, each bearing enough poison to have stricken

The Valley of the Worm

dead a bull elephant. Yet on it came, swiftly, appallingly, apparently heedless of both the shafts and the venom in which they were steeped. And all the time the hideous music played a maddening accompaniment, whining thinly from the pipes that lay untouched on the ground.

My confidence faded; even the poison of Satha was futile against this uncanny being. I drove my last shaft almost straight downward into the quaking white mountain, so close was the monster under my perch. Then suddenly its color altered. A wave of ghastly blue surged over it, and the vast bulk heaved in earthquake-like convulsions. With a terrible plunge it struck the lower part of the column, which crashed to falling shards of stone. But even with the impact, I leaped far out and fell through the empty air full upon the monster's back.

The spongy skin yielded and gave beneath my feet, and I drove my sword hilt-deep, dragging it through the pulpy flesh, ripping a horrible yard-long wound, from which oozed a green slime. Then a flip of a cable-like tentacle flicked me from the titan's back and spun me three hundred feet through the air to crash among a cluster of giant trees.

The impact must have splintered half the bones in my frame, for when I sought to grasp my sword again and crawl anew to the combat, I could not move hand or foot, could only writhe helplessly with my broken back. But I could see the monster and I knew that I had won, even in defeat. The mountainous bulk was heaving and billowing, the tentacles were lashing madly, the antennæ writhing and knotting, and the nauseous whiteness had changed to a pale and grisly green. It turned ponderously and lurched back toward the temple, rolling like a crippled ship in a heavy swell. Trees crashed and splintered as it lumbered against them.

I wept with pure fury because I could not catch up my sword and rush in to die glutting my berserk madness in mighty strokes. But the worm-god was death-stricken and needed not my futile sword. The demon pipes on the ground kept up their infernal tune, and it was like the fiend's death-dirge. Then as the monster veered and floundered, I saw it catch up the corpse of its hairy slave. For an instant the apish form dangled in midair, gripped round by the trunk-like proboscis, then was dashed against the temple wall with a force that reduced the hairy body to a mere shapeless pulp. At that the pipes screamed out horribly, and fell silent for ever.

The titan staggered on the brink of the shaft; then another change came over it – a frightful transfiguration the nature of which I can not yet describe. Even now when I try to think of it clearly, I am only chaotically conscious of a blasphemous, unnatural transmutation of form and substance, shocking and indescribable. Then the strangely altered bulk tumbled into the shaft to roll down into the ultimate darkness from whence it came, and I knew that it was

277

dead. And as it vanished into the well, with a rending, grinding groan the ruined walls quivered from dome to base. They bent inward and buckled with deafening reverberation, the columns splintered, and with a cataclysmic crash the dome itself came thundering down. For an instant the air seemed veiled with flying debris and stone-dust, through which the treetops lashed madly as in a storm or an earthquake convulsion. Then all was clear again and I stared, shaking the blood from my eyes. Where the temple had stood there lay only a colossal pile of shattered masonry and broken stones, and every column in the valley had fallen, to lie in crumbling shards.

In the silence that followed I heard Grom wailing a dirge over me. I bade him lay my sword in my hand, and he did so, and bent close to hear what I had to say, for I was passing swiftly.

"Let my tribe remember," I said, speaking slowly. "Let the tale be told from village to village, from camp to camp, from tribe to tribe, so that men may know that not man nor beast nor devil may prey in safety on the golden-haired people of Asgard. Let them build me a cairn where I lie and lay me therein with my bow and sword at hand, to guard this valley for ever; so if the ghost of the god I slew comes up from below, my ghost will ever be ready to give it battle."

And while Grom howled and beat his hairy breast, death came to me in the Valley of the Worm.

The Dust Dance

Selections, Version II

The sin and jest of the times am I
Since destiny's dance began,
When the weary gods from the dews and sods
Made me and named me man.

Ah, it's little they knew when they molded me
For a pawn of their cosmic chess,
What a mummer wild, what an insane child
They fashioned from nothingness!

For I with the shape of my kin the ape
And the soul of a soaring hawk,
I fought my way from the jungles grey
Where the hunting creatures stalk.

I champ my tusks o'er beetles and husks,
I tear red meat for my feast;
The pulse of the earth is in my mirth
And the roar of the primal beast.

By a freak of fate through the whirling spate
Of the uncouth roaring years,
Red taloned I came from the tribal flame
And the trails beside the meres.

Back of my eyes a tiger lies,
Savage of claw and tooth;
Close at my heels the baboon steals
Barren of pity and ruth.

And, ah, I know as I bellow so
With my foolish bloody mirth,
That the soul of the tree is the soul of me
And things of the physical earth.

For I was made from the dust and the dew,
The dawns, the dusk and the rain,
The snow and the grass and when I pass
I'll fade to the dust again.

For I know that all of the platitudes
That we hear from birth to youth
Slink from the backs of the brazen facts,
The reign of talon and tooth.

From the ghostly gleam of a vagrant dream,
From the shade of a wheeling bat,
From a passion-haunted vision told
In the huts where the women sat,

I wove the skein of a Hell aflame —
And it passed from breath to breath —
And paradise beyond the skies
Against the day of my death.

I roared my glee to the sullen sea
When Abel's blood was shed;
My jeer was loud in the gory crowd
That stoned St. Stephen dead.

I laughed when Nero's minions sent
Fire-tortured souls to the sky;
Without the walls of Pilate's halls
I shouted "Crucify!"

Sin of Adam was brother to me,
My zeal is passion shod,
Bearing red brands in the heathen lands
To teach them the word of God.

Sages speak of my brother love,
No love, in truth, I lack
As I hang them free from the gallows tree
And shatter them on the rack.

Seek me not in the drawing rooms
For music and light are there,
And I cloak the lusts of my blood-red soul
With culture's gossamer.

Look for me by the gibbet tree
Where a saintly hero dies,
And the jeer of each knave that he sought to save
Goes up to the naked skies.

Seek my face in a shadowy place
Where the evil torches gleam
And flesh with flesh in Satan's mesh
Mingles in lurid dream.

Let sages speak, I know the reek
Of the battlefields of earth,
The musk of the jungle is in my breath,
The tiger roar in my mirth.

The brazen realities are mine
And I laugh at dreams and rime,
For I am a man of the primal years
And a laughing slave of Time.

The People of the Black Circle

I

DEATH STRIKES A KING

The king of Vendhya was dying. Through the hot, stifling night the temple gongs boomed and the conchs roared. Their clamor was a faint echo in the gold-domed chamber where Bunda Chand struggled on the velvet-cushioned dais. Beads of sweat glistened on his dark skin; his fingers twisted the gold-worked fabric beneath him. He was young; no spear had touched him, no poison lurked in his wine. But his veins stood out like blue cords on his temples, and his eyes dilated with the nearness of death. Trembling slave-girls knelt at the foot of the dais, and leaning down to him, watching him with passionate intensity, was his sister, the Devi Yasmina. With her was the *wazam*, a noble grown old in the royal court.

She threw up her head in a gusty gesture of wrath and despair as the thunder of the distant drums reached her ears.

"The priests and their clamor!" she exclaimed. "They are no wiser than the leeches who are helpless! Nay, he dies and none can say why. He is dying now – and I stand here helpless, who would burn the whole city and spill the blood of thousands to save him."

"Not a man of Ayodhya but would die in his place, if it might be, Devi," answered the *wazam*. "This poison –"

"I tell you it is not poison!" she cried. "Since his birth he has been guarded so closely that the cleverest poisoners of the East could not reach him. Five skulls bleaching on the Tower of the Kites can testify to attempts which were made – and which failed. As you well know, there are ten men and ten women whose sole duty is to taste his food and wine, and fifty armed warriors guard his chamber as they guard it now. No, it is not poison; it is sorcery – black, ghastly magic –"

She ceased as the king spoke; his livid lips did not move, and there was no recognition in his glassy eyes. But his voice rose in an eery call, indistinct and far away, as if he called to her from beyond vast, wind-blown gulfs.

"Yasmina! Yasmina! My sister, where are you? I can not find you. All is darkness, and the roaring of great winds!"

"Brother!" cried Yasmina, catching his limp hand in a convulsive grasp. "I am here! Do you not know me –"

Her voice died at the utter vacancy of his face. A low confused moaning waned from his mouth. The slave-girls at the foot of the dais whimpered with fear, and Yasmina beat her breast in her anguish.

In another part of the city a man stood in a latticed balcony overlooking a long street in which torches tossed luridly, smokily revealing upturned dark faces and the whites of gleaming eyes. A long-drawn wailing rose from the multitude.

The man shrugged his broad shoulders and turned back into the arabesqued chamber. He was a tall man, compactly built, and richly clad.

"The king is not yet dead, but the dirge is sounded," he said to another man who sat cross-legged on a mat in a corner. This man was clad in a brown camel-hair robe and sandals, and a green turban was on his head. His expression was tranquil, his gaze impersonal.

"The people know he will never see another dawn," this man answered.

The first speaker favored him with a long, searching stare.

"What I can not understand," he said, "is why I have had to wait so long for your masters to strike. If they have slain the king now, why could they not have slain him months ago?"

"Even the arts you call sorcery are governed by cosmic laws," answered the man in the green turban. "The stars direct these actions, as in other affairs. Not even my masters can alter the stars. Not until the heavens were in the proper order could they perform this necromancy." With a long, stained finger-nail he mapped the constellations on the marble-tiled floor. "The slant of the moon presaged evil for the king of Vendhya; the stars are in turmoil, the Serpent in the House of the Elephant. During such juxtaposition, the invisible guardians are removed from the spirit of Bhunda Chand. A path is opened in the unseen realms, and once a point of contact was established, mighty powers were put in play along that path."

"Point of contact?" inquired the other. "Do you mean that lock of Bhunda Chand's hair?"

"Yes. All discarded portions of the human body still remain part of it, attached to it by intangible connections. The priests of Asura have a dim inkling of this truth, and so all nail-trimmings, hair and other waste products of the persons of the royal family are carefully reduced to ashes and the ashes hidden. But at the urgent entreaty of the princess of Khosala, who loved Bhunda Chand vainly, he gave her a lock of his long black hair as a token of remembrance. When my masters decided upon his doom, the lock, in its golden, jewel-crusted case, was stolen from under her pillow while she slept, and another substituted, so like the first that she never knew the difference. Then the genuine lock travelled by camel-caravan up the long, long road to Peshkhauri, thence up the Zhaibar Pass, until it reached the hands of those for whom it was intended."

"Only a lock of hair," murmured the nobleman.

"By which a soul is drawn from its body and across gulfs of echoing space," returned the man on the mat.

The nobleman studied him curiously.

"I do not know if you are a man or a demon, Khemsa," he said at last. "Few of us are what we seem. I, whom the Kshatriyas know as Kerim Shah, a prince from Iranistan, am no greater a masquerader than most men. They are all traitors in one way or another, and half of them know not whom they serve. There at least I have no doubts; for I serve King Yezdigerd of Turan."

"And I the Black Seers of Yimsha," said Khemsa; "and my masters are greater than yours, for they have accomplished by their arts what Yezdigerd could not with a hundred thousand swords."

Outside, the moan of the tortured thousands shuddered up to the stars which crusted the sweating Vendhyan night, and the conchs bellowed like oxen in pain.

In the gardens of the palace the torches glinted on polished helmets and curved swords and gold-chased corselets. All the noble-born fighting-men of Ayodhya were gathered in the great palace or about it, and at each broad-arched gate and door fifty archers stood on guard, with bows in their hands. But Death stalked through the royal palace and none could stay his ghostly tread.

On the dais under the golden dome the king cried out again, racked by awful paroxysms. Again his voice came faintly and far away, and again the Devi bent to him, trembling with a fear that was darker than the terror of death.

"Yasmina!" Again that far, weirdly dreeing cry, from realms immeasurable. "Aid me! I am far from my mortal house! Wizards have drawn my soul through the wind-blown darkness. They seek to snap the silver cord that binds me to my dying body. They cluster around me; their hands are taloned, their eyes are red like flame burning in darkness. *Aie*, save me, my sister! Their fingers sear me like fire! They would slay my body and damn my soul! What is this they bring before me? – *Aie!*"

At the terror in his hopeless cry Yasmina screamed uncontrollably and threw herself bodily upon him in the abandon of her anguish. He was torn by a terrible convulsion; foam flew from his contorted lips and his writhing fingers left their marks on the girl's shoulders. But the glassy blankness passed from his eyes like smoke blown from a fire, and he looked up at his sister with recognition.

"Brother!" she sobbed. "Brother –"

"Swift!" he gasped, and his weakening voice was rational. "I know now what brings me to the pyre. I have been on a far journey and I understand. I have been ensorceled by the wizards of the Himelians. They drew my soul out of my body and far away, into a stone room. There they strove to break the silver cord of life, and thrust my soul into the body of a foul night-weird their sorcery summoned up from hell. Ah! I feel their pull upon me now! Your cry and the grip of your fingers brought me back, but I am going fast. My soul clings to my body, but its hold weakens. Quick – kill me, before they can trap my soul for ever!"

"I can not!" she wailed, smiting her naked breasts.

"Swiftly, I command you!" There was the old imperious note in his failing whisper. "You have never disobeyed me – obey my last command! Send my soul clean to Asura! Haste, lest you damn me to spend eternity as a filthy gaunt of darkness. Strike, I command you! *Strike!*"

Sobbing wildly, Yasmina plucked a jeweled dagger from her girdle and plunged it to the hilt in his breast. He stiffened and then went limp, a grim smile curving his dead lips. Yasmina hurled herself face-down on the rush-covered floor, beating the reeds with her clenched hands. Outside, the gongs and conchs brayed and thundered and the priests gashed themselves with copper knives.

II

A BARBARIAN FROM THE HILLS

Chunder Shan, governor of Peshkhauri, laid down his golden pen and carefully scanned that which he had written on parchment that bore his official seal. He had ruled Peshkhauri so long only because he weighed his every word, spoken or written. Danger breeds caution, and only a wary man lives long in that wild country where the hot Vendhyan plains meet the crags of the Himelians. An hour's ride westward or northward and one crossed the border and was among the hills where men lived by the law of the knife.

The governor was alone in his chamber, seated at his ornately-carven table of inlaid ebony. Through the wide window, open for the coolness, he could see a square of the blue Himelian night, dotted with great white stars. An adjacent parapet was a shadowy line, and further crenelles and embrasures were barely hinted at in the dim starlight. The governor's fortress was strong, and situated outside the walls of the city it guarded. The breeze that stirred the tapestries on the wall brought faint noises from the streets of Peshkhauri – occasional snatches of wailing song, or the thrum of a cithern.

The governor read what he had written, slowly, with his open hand shading his eyes from the bronze butter-lamp, his lips moving. Absently, as he read, he heard the drum of horses' hoofs outside the barbican, the sharp staccato of the guards' challenge. He did not heed, intent upon his letter. It was addressed to the *wazam* of Vendhya, at the royal court of Ayodhya, and it stated, after the customary salutations:

> "Let it be known to your excellency that I have faithfully carried out your excellency's instructions. The seven tribesmen are well guarded in their prison, and I have repeatedly sent word into the hills that their chief come in person to bargain for their release. But he has made no move, except to send word that unless they are freed he will burn Peshkhauri and cover his saddle with my hide, begging your excellency's indulgence. This he is quite capable of attempting, and I have tripled the numbers of the lance guards. The man is not a native of Ghulistan. I can not with certainty predict his next move. But since it is the wish of the Devi –"

He was out of his ivory chair and on his feet facing the arched door, all in one instant. He snatched at the curved sword lying in its ornate scabbard on the table, and then checked the movement.

It was a woman who had entered unannounced, a woman whose gossamer robes did not conceal the rich garments beneath any more than they concealed the suppleness and beauty of her tall, slender figure. A filmy veil fell below her breasts, supported by a flowing head-dress bound about with a triple gold braid and adorned with a golden crescent. Her dark eyes regarded the astonished governor over the veil, and then with an imperious gesture of her white hand, she uncovered her face.

"Devi!" The governor dropped to his knee before her, his surprise and confusion somewhat spoiling the stateliness of his obeisance. With a gesture she motioned him to rise, and he hastened to lead her to the ivory chair, all the while bowing level with his girdle. But his first words were of reproof.

"Your majesty! This was most unwise! The border is unsettled. Raids from the hills are incessant. You came with a large attendance?"

"An ample retinue followed me to Peshkhauri," she answered. "I lodged my people there and came on to the fort with my maid, Gitara."

Chunder Shan groaned in horror.

"Devi! You do not understand the peril. An hour's ride from this spot the hills swarm with barbarians who make a profession of murder and rapine. Women have been stolen and men stabbed between the fort and the city. Peshkhauri is not like your southern provinces —"

"But I am here, and unharmed," she interrupted with a trace of impatience. "I showed my signet ring to the guard at the gate, and to the one outside your door, and they admitted me unannounced, not knowing me, but supposing me to be a secret courier from Ayodhya. Let us not now waste time.

"You have received no word from the chief of the barbarians?"

"None save threats and curses, Devi. He is wary and suspicious. He deems it a trap, and perhaps he is not to be blamed. The Kshatriyas have not always kept their promises to the hill people."

"He must be brought to terms!" broke in Yasmina, the knuckles of her clenched hands showing white.

"I do not understand." The governor shook his head. "When I chanced to capture these seven hillmen, I reported their capture to the *wazam*, as is the custom, and then, before I could hang them, there came an order to hold them and communicate with their chief. This I did, but the man holds aloof, as I have said. These men are of the tribe of Afghulis, but he is a foreigner from the west, and he is called Conan. I have threatened to hang them tomorrow at dawn, if he does not come."

"Good!" exclaimed the Devi. "You have done well. And I will tell you why I have given these orders. My brother —" she faltered, choking, and the governor bowed his head, with the customary gesture of respect for a departed sovereign.

"The king of Vendhya was destroyed by magic," she said at last. "I have devoted my life to the destruction of his murderers. As he died he gave me a clue, and I have followed it. I have read the Book of Skelos, and talked with nameless hermits in the caves below Jhelai. I learned how, and by whom, he was destroyed. His enemies were the Black Seers of Mount Yimsha."

"Asura!" whispered Chunder Shan, paling.

Her eyes knifed him through. "Do you fear them?"

"Who does not, your majesty?" he replied. "They are black devils, haunting the uninhabited hills beyond the Zhaibar. But the sages say that they seldom interfere in the lives of mortal men."

"Why they slew my brother I do not know," she answered. "But I have sworn on the altar of Asura to destroy them! And I need the aid of a man beyond the border. A Kshatriya army, unaided, would never reach Yimsha."

"Aye," muttered Chunder Shan. "You speak the truth there. It would be a fight every step of the way, with hairy hillmen hurling down boulders from every height, and rushing us with their long knives in every valley. The Turanians fought their way through the Himelians once, but how many returned to Khurusun? Few of those who escaped the swords of the Kshatriyas, after the king, your brother, defeated their host on the Jhumda River, ever saw Secunderam again."

"And so I must control men across the border," she said, "men who know the way to Mount Yimsha —"

"But the tribes fear the Black Seers and shun the unholy mountain," broke in the governor.

"Does the chief, Conan, fear them?" she asked.

"Well, as to that," muttered the governor, "I doubt if there is anything that devil fears."

"So I have been told. Therefore he is the man I must deal with. He wishes the release of his seven men. Very well; their ransom shall be the heads of the Black Seers!" Her voice thrummed with hate as she uttered the last words, and her hands clenched at her sides. She looked an image of incarnate passion as she stood there with her head thrown high and her bosom heaving.

Again the governor knelt, for part of his wisdom was the knowledge that a woman in such an emotional tempest is as perilous as a blind cobra to any about her.

"It shall be as you wish, your majesty." Then as she presented a calmer aspect, he rose and ventured to drop a word of warning. "I can not predict what the chief Conan's action will be. The tribesmen are always turbulent, and I have reason to believe that emissaries from the Turanians are stirring them up to raid our borders. As your majesty knows, the Turanians have established themselves in Secunderam and other northern cities, though the hill tribes remain unconquered. King Yezdigerd has long looked southward with greedy lust and perhaps is seeking to gain by treachery what he could not win by force of arms. I have thought that Conan might well be one of his spies."

"We shall see," she answered. "If he loves his followers, he will be at the gates at dawn, to parley. I shall spend the night in the fortress. I came in disguise to Peshkhauri, and lodged my retinue at an inn instead of the palace. Besides my people, only yourself knows of my presence here."

"I shall escort you to your quarters, your majesty," said the governor, and as they emerged from the doorway, he beckoned the warrior on guard there, and the man fell in behind them, spear held at salute. The maid waited, veiled like her mistress, outside the door, and the group traversed a wide, winding corridor, lighted by smoky torches, and reached the quarters reserved for visiting notables – generals and viceroys, mostly; none of the royal family had ever honored the fortress before. Chunder Shan had a perturbed feeling that the suite was not suitable to such an exalted personage as the Devi, and though she sought to make him feel at ease in her presence, he was glad when she dismissed him and he bowed himself out. All the menials of the fort had been summoned to serve his royal guest – though he did not divulge her identity – and he stationed a squad of spearmen before her doors, among them the warrior who had guarded his own chamber. In his preoccupation he forgot to replace the man.

The governor had not been gone long from her, when Yasmina suddenly remembered something else which she had wished to discuss with him, but had forgotten until that moment. It concerned the past actions of one Kerim Shah, a nobleman from Iranistan, who had dwelt for awhile in Peshkhauri before coming on to the court at Ayodhya. A vague suspicion concerning the man had been stirred by a glimpse of him in Peshkhauri that night. She wondered if he had followed her from Ayodhya. Being a truly remarkable Devi, she did not summon the governor to her again, but hurried out into the corridor alone, and hastened toward his chamber.

Chunder Shan, entering his chamber, closed the door and went to his table. There he took the letter he had been writing and tore it to bits. Scarcely had he finished when he heard something drop softly onto the parapet adjacent to the window. He looked up to see a figure loom briefly against the stars, and then a man dropped lightly into the room. The light glinted on a long sheen of steel in his hand.

"Shhhh!" he warned. "Don't make a noise, you bastard, or I'll send the devil a henchman!"

The governor checked his motion toward the sword on the table. He was within reach of the yard-long Zhaibar knife that glittered in the intruder's fist, and he knew the desperate quickness of a hillman.

The invader was a tall man, at once strong and supple. He was dressed like a hillman, but his dark features and blazing blue eyes did not match his garb. Chunder Shan had never seen a man like him; he was not an Easterner, but some barbarian from the West. But his aspect was as untamed and formidable as any of the hairy tribesmen who haunt the hills of Ghulistan.

"You come like a thief in the night," commented the governor, recovering some of his composure, although he remembered that there was no guard within call. Still, the hillman could not know that.

"I climbed a bastion," snarled the intruder. "A guard thrust his head over the battlement in time for me to rap it with my knife hilt."

"You are Conan?"

"Who else? You sent word into the hills that you wished for me to come and parley with you. Well, by Crom, I've come! Keep away from that table or I'll gut you."

"I merely wish to seat myself," answered the governor, carefully sinking into the ivory chair, which he wheeled away from the table. Conan moved restlessly before him, glancing suspiciously at the door, thumbing the razor edge of his three-foot knife. He did not walk like an Afghuli, and was bluntly direct where the East is subtle.

"You have seven of my men," he said abruptly. "You refused the ransom I offered. What the devil do you want?"

"Let us discuss terms," answered Chunder Shan cautiously.

"Terms?" There was a timbre of dangerous anger in his voice. "What do you mean? Haven't I offered you gold?"

Chunder Shan laughed.

"Gold? There is more gold in Peshkhauri than you ever saw."

"You're a liar," retorted Conan. "I've seen the *suk* of the goldsmiths in Khurusun."

"Well – more than any Afghuli ever saw," amended Chunder Shan. "And it is but a drop of all the treasure of Vendhya. Why should we desire gold? It would be more to our advantage to hang these seven thieves."

Conan ripped out a sulphurous oath and the long blade quivered in his grip as the muscles rose in ridges on his brown arm.

"I'll split your head like a ripe melon!"

A wild blue flame flickered in the hillman's eyes, but Chunder Shan shrugged his shoulders, though keeping an eye on the keen steel.

"You can kill me easily, and probably escape over the wall afterwards. But that would not save the seven tribesmen. They would surely hang them. And these men are headmen among the Afghulis."

"I know it," snarled Conan. "The tribe is baying like wolves at my heels because I have not secured their release. Tell me in plain words what you want, because by Crom, if there's no other way, I'll raise a horde and lead it to the very gates of Peshkhauri!"

Looking at the man as he stood squarely, knife in fist and eyes glaring, Chunder Shan did not doubt that he was capable of it. The governor did not believe any hill-horde could take Peshkhauri, but he did not wish a devastated countryside.

"There is a mission you must perform," he said, choosing his words with as much care as if they had been razors. "There –"

Conan had sprung back, wheeling to face the door at the same instant, lips asnarl. His barbarian ears had caught the sound noiseless to Chunder Shan – the quick tread of soft slippers outside the door. The next instant the door was thrown open and a slim, silk-robed form entered hastily, pulling the door shut – then stopping short at the sight of the hillman.

Chunder Shan sprang up, his heart jumping into his mouth.

"Devi!" he cried involuntarily, losing his head momentarily in his fright.

"Devi!" It was like an explosive echo from the hillman's lips. Chunder Shan saw recognition and intent flame up in the fierce blue eyes. The governor shouted desperately and caught at his sword, but the hillman moved with the devastating speed of a hurricane. He sprang, knocked the governor sprawling with a savage blow of his knife hilt, swept up the astounded Devi in one brawny arm and leaped for the window. Chunder Shan, struggling frantically to his feet, saw the man poise an instant on the sill, in a flutter of silken skirts and white limbs that was his royal captive, and heard his fierce, exultant snarl: "*Now* dare to hang my men!" and then Conan leaped to the parapet and was gone. A wild scream floated back to the governor's ears.

"Guard! *Guard!*" screamed the governor, struggling up and running drunkenly to the door. He tore it open and reeled into the hall. His shouts re-echoed along the corridors and warriors came running, gaping to see the governor holding his broken head, from which the blood streamed.

"Turn out the lancers!" he roared. "There has been an abduction!" Even in his frenzy he had enough sense left to withhold the full truth. He stopped short as he heard a sudden drum of hoofs outside, a frantic scream and a wild yell of barbaric exultation.

Followed by the bewildered guardsmen, the governor raced for the stair. In the courtyard of the fort a force of lancers always stood by saddled steeds, ready to ride at an instant's notice. Chunder Shan sent this squadron flying after the fugitive, though his head swam so he had to hold with both hands to the saddle. He did not divulge the identity of the victim, but said merely that the noblewoman who had borne the royal signet-ring had been carried away by the chief of the Afghulis. The abductor was out of sight and hearing, but they knew the path he would strike – the road that runs straight to the mouth of the Zhaibar. There was no moon; peasant huts rose dimly in the starlight. Behind them fell away the grim bastion of the fort, and the towers of Peshkhauri. Ahead of them loomed the black walls of the Himelians.

III

KHEMSA USES MAGIC

In the confusion that reigned in the fortress while the guard was being turned out, no one noticed that the girl who had accompanied the Devi slipped out the great arched gate and vanished in the darkness. She ran straight for the city, her garments tucked high. She did not follow the open road, but cut straight through fields and over slopes, avoiding fences and leaping irrigation ditches as surely as if it were broad daylight, and as easily as if she were a trained masculine runner. The hoof-drum of the guardsmen had faded away up the hill road before she reached the city wall. She did not go to the great gate, beneath whose arch men leaned on spears and craned their necks into the darkness, discussing the unwonted activity about the fortress. She skirted the wall until she reached a certain point where the spire of a tower was visible above the battlements. Then she placed her hands to her mouth and voiced a low weird call that carried strangely.

Almost instantly a head appeared at an embrasure and a rope came wriggling down the wall. She seized it, placed a foot in the loop at the end, and waved her arm. Then quickly and smoothly she was drawn up the sheer stone curtain. An instant later she scrambled over the merlons and stood up on a flat roof which covered a house that was built against the wall. There was an open trap there, and a man in a camel-hair robe who silently coiled the rope, not showing in any way the strain of exertion from hauling a full-grown woman up a forty foot wall.

"Where is Kerim Shah?" she gasped, panting after her long run.

"Asleep in the house below. You have news?"

"Conan has stolen the Devi out of the fortress and carried her away into the hills!" She blurted out her news in a rush, the words stumbling over each other.

Khemsa showed no emotion, but merely nodded his turbaned head.

"Kerim Shah will be glad to hear that," he said.

"Wait!" The girl threw her supple arms about his neck. She was panting hard, but not only from exertion. Her eyes blazed like black jewels in the starlight. Her upturned face was close to Khemsa's, but though he submitted to her embrace, he did not return it.

"Do not tell the Hyrkanian!" she panted. "Let us use this knowledge ourselves! The governor has gone into the hills with his riders, but he might as well chase a ghost. He has not told anyone that it was the Devi who was kidnapped. None in Peshkhauri or the fort knows it except us!"

"But what good does it do us?" the man expostulated. "My masters sent me with Kerim Shah to aid him in every way –"

"Aid yourself!" she cried fiercely. "Shake off your yoke!"

"You mean – disobey my masters?" he gasped, and she felt his whole body turn cold under her arms.

"Aye!" she shook him in the fury of her emotion. "You too are a magician! Why will you be a slave, using your powers only to elevate others? Use your arts for yourself!"

"That is forbidden!" He was shaking as if with an ague. "I am not one of the Black Circle. Only by the command of the masters do I dare to use the knowledge they have taught me."

"But you *can* use it!" she argued passionately. "Do as I beg you! Of course Conan has taken the Devi to hold as hostage against the seven tribesmen in the governor's prison. Destroy them, so Chunder Shan can not use them to buy back the Devi. Then let us go into the mountains and take her from the Afghulis. They can not stand against your sorcery with their knives! The treasure of the Vendhyan kings will be ours as ransom – and then when we have it in our hands, we can trick them, and sell her to the king of Turan. We shall have wealth beyond our maddest dreams! With it we can buy warriors! We will take Khorbhul, oust the Turanians from the hills, and send our hosts southward; become king and queen of an empire!"

Khemsa too was panting, shaking like a leaf in her grasp; his face showed grey in the starlight, beaded with great drops of perspiration.

"I love you!" she cried fiercely, writhing her body against his, almost strangling him in her wild embrace, shaking him in her abandon. "I will make a king of you! For love of you I betrayed my mistress; for love of me betray your masters! Why fear the Black Seers? By your love for me you have broken one of their laws already! Break the rest! You are strong as they!"

A man of ice could not have withstood the searing heat of her passion and fury. With an inarticulate cry he crushed her to him, bending her backward and showering gasping kisses on her eyes, face and lips.

"I'll do it!" His voice was thick with laboring emotions. He staggered like a drunken man. "The arts they have taught me shall work for me, not for my masters. We shall be rulers of the world – of the world –"

"Come then!" Twisting lithely out of his embrace, she seized his hand and led him toward the trap-door. "First we must make sure that the governor does not exchange those seven Afghulis for the Devi."

He moved like a man in a daze, until they had descended a ladder and she paused in the chamber below. Kerim Shah lay on a couch motionless, an arm across his face as though to shield his sleeping eyes from the soft light of a brass lamp. She plucked Khemsa's arm and made a quick gesture across her own throat. Khemsa lifted his hand, then his expression changed and he drew away.

"I have eaten his salt," he muttered. "Besides he can not interfere with us." He led the girl through a door that opened on a winding stair. After their soft tread had faded into silence, the man on the couch sat up. Kerim Shah wiped the sweat from his face. A knife thrust he did not dread, but he feared Khemsa as a man fears a poisonous reptile.

"People who plot on roofs should remember to lower their voices," he muttered. "But as Khemsa has turned against his masters, and as he was my only contact with them, I can count on their aid no longer. From now on I play the game in my own way."

Rising to his feet he went quickly to a table, drew pen and parchment from his girdle and scribbled a few succinct lines.

"To Khosru Khan, governor of Secunderam: the Cimmerian Conan has carried the Devi Yasmina to the villages of the Afghulis. It is an opportunity to get the Devi into our hands, as the king has so long desired. Send three thousand horsemen at once. I will meet them in the valley of Gurashah with native guides." And he signed it with a name that was not in the least like Kerim Shah.

Then from a golden cage he drew forth a carrier pigeon, to whose leg he made fast the parchment, rolled into a tiny cylinder and secured with gold wire. Then he went quickly to a casement and tossed the bird into the night. It wavered on fluttering wings, balanced, and was gone like a flitting shadow. Catching up helmet, sword and cloak, Kerim Shah hurried out of the chamber and down the winding stair.

The prison quarters of Peshkhauri were separated from the rest of the city by a massive wall, in which was set a single iron-bound door under an arch. Over the arch burned a lurid red cresset, and beside the door stood – or squatted – a warrior with spear and shield.

This warrior, leaning on his spear, and yawning from time to time, started suddenly to his feet. He had not thought he had dozed, but a man was standing before him, a man he had not heard approach. The man wore a camel-hair robe and a green turban. In the flickering light of the cresset his features were shadowy, but a pair of lambent eyes shone surprizingly in the lurid glow.

"Who comes?" demanded the warrior, presenting his spear. "Who are you?"

The stranger did not seem perturbed, though the spear point touched his bosom. His eyes held the warrior's with strange intensity.

"What are you obliged to do?" he asked, strangely.

"To guard the gate!" The warrior spoke thickly and mechanically; he stood rigid as a statue, his eyes slowly glazing.

"You lie! You are obliged to obey me! You have looked into my eyes, and your soul is no longer your own. Open that door!"

Stiffly, with the wooden features of an image, the guard wheeled about, drew a great key from his girdle, turned it in the massive lock and swung open the door. Then he stood at attention, his unseeing stare straight ahead of him.

A woman glided from the shadows and laid an eager hand on the mesmerist's arm.

"Bid him fetch us horses, Khemsa," she whispered.

"No need of that," answered the Rakhsha. Lifting his voice slightly he spoke to the guardsman. "I have no more use for you. Kill yourself!"

Like a man in a trance the warrior thrust the butt of his spear against the base of the wall, and placed the keen head against his body, just below the ribs. Then slowly, stolidly, he leaned against it with all his weight, so that it transfixed his body and came out between his shoulders. Sliding down the shaft he lay still, the spear jutting above him its full length, like a horrible stalk growing out of his back.

The girl stared down at him in morbid fascination, until Khemsa took her arm and led her through the gate. Torches lighted a narrow space between the outer wall and a lower inner one, in which were arched doors at regular intervals. A warrior paced this enclosure, and when the gate opened he came sauntering up, so secure in his knowledge of the prison's strength that he was not suspicious until Khemsa and the girl emerged from the archway. Then it was too late. The Rakhsha did not waste time in hypnotism, though his action savored of magic to the girl. The guard lowered his spear threateningly, opening his mouth to shout an alarm that would bring spearmen swarming out of the guard-rooms at either end of the alley-way. Khemsa flicked the spear aside with his left hand, as a man might flick a straw, and his right flashed out and back, seeming gently to caress the warrior's neck in passing. And the guard pitched on his face without a sound, his head lolling on a broken neck.

Khemsa did not glance at him, but went straight to one of the arched doors and placed his open hand against the heavy bronze lock. With a rending shudder the portal buckled inward. As the girl followed him through, she saw that the thick teak wood hung in splinters, the bronze bolts were bent and twisted from their sockets, and the great hinges broken and disjointed. A thousand pound battering ram with forty men to swing it could have shattered the barrier no more completely. Khemsa was drunk with freedom and the exercise of his power, glorying in his might and flinging his strength about as a young giant exercises his thews with unnecessary vigor in the exultant pride of his prowess.

The broken door let them into a small courtyard, lit by a cresset. Opposite the door was a wide grille of iron bars. A hairy hand was visible, gripping one of these bars, and in the darkness behind them glimmered the whites of eyes.

Khemsa stood silent for a space, gazing into the shadows from which those glimmering eyes gave back his stare with burning intensity. Then his hand went into his robe and came out again, and from his opening fingers a shimmering feather of sparkling dust sifted to the flags. Instantly a flare of green fire lighted the enclosure. In the brief glare the forms of seven men, standing motionless behind the bars, were limned in vivid detail; tall, hairy men in ragged hillmen's garments. They did not speak, but in their eyes blazed the fear of death, and their hairy fingers gripped the bars.

The fire died out but the glow remained, a quivering ball of lambent green that pulsed and shimmered on the flags before Khemsa's feet. The wide gaze of the tribesmen was fixed upon it. It wavered, elongated; it turned into a luminous green smoke spiralling upward. It twisted and writhed like a great shadowy serpent, then broadened and billowed out in shining folds and whorls. It grew to a cloud moving silently over the flags – straight toward the grille. The men watched its coming with dilated eyes; the bars quivered with the grip of their desperate fingers. Bearded lips parted but no sound came forth. The green cloud rolled on the bars and blotted them from sight; like a fog it oozed through the grille and hid the men within. From the enveloping folds came a strangled gasp, as of a man plunged suddenly under the surface of water. That was all.

Khemsa touched the girl's arm, as she stood with parted lips and dilated eyes. Mechanically she turned away with him, looking back over her shoulder. Already the mist was thinning; close to the bars she saw a pair of sandalled feet, the toes turned upward – she glimpsed the indistinct outlines of seven still, prostrate shapes –

"And now for a steed swifter than the fastest horse ever bred in a mortal stable," Khemsa was saying. "We will be in Afghulistan before dawn."

IV

AN ENCOUNTER IN THE PASS

Yasmina Devi could never clearly remember the details of her abduction. The unexpectedness and violence stunned her; she had only a confused impression of a whirl of happenings – the terrifying grip of a mighty arm, the blazing eyes of her abductor, and his hot breath burning on her flesh. The leap through the window to the parapet, the mad race across battlements and roofs when the fear of falling froze her, the reckless descent of a rope bound to a merlon – he went down almost at a run, his captive folded limply over his brawny shoulder – all this was a befuddled tangle in the Devi's mind. She retained a more vivid memory of him running fleetly into the shadows of the trees, carrying her like a child, and vaulting into the saddle of a fierce Bhalkhana stallion which reared and snorted. Then there was a sensation of flying, and the racing hoofs were striking sparks of fire from the flinty road as the stallion swept up the slopes.

As the girl's mind cleared, her first sensations were furious rage and shame. She was appalled. The rulers of the golden kingdoms south of the Himelians were considered little short of divine; and she was the Devi of Vendhya! Fright was submerged in regal wrath. She cried out furiously and began struggling. She, Yasmina, to be carried on the saddle-bow of a hill chief, like a common wench of the market-place! He merely hardened his massive thews slightly against her writhings, and for the first time in her life she experienced the coercion of superior physical strength. His arms felt like iron about her slender limbs. He glanced down at her and grinned hugely. His teeth glimmered whitely in the starlight. The reins lay loose on the stallion's flowing mane, and every thew and fiber of the great beast strained as he hurtled along the boulder-strewn trail. But Conan sat easily, almost carelessly, in the saddle, riding like a centaur.

"You hill-bred dog!" she panted, quivering with the impact of shame, anger and the realization of helplessness. "You dare – you *dare*! Your life shall pay for this! Where are you taking me?"

"To the villages of Afghulistan," he answered, casting a glance over his shoulder. Behind them, beyond the slopes they had traversed, torches were tossing on the walls of the fortress and he glimpsed a flare of light that meant the great gate had been opened. And he laughed, a deep-throated boom gusty as the hill wind.

"The governor has sent his riders after us," he laughed. "By Crom, we will lead him a merry chase! What do you think, Devi – will they pay seven lives for a Kshatriya princess?"

"They will send an army to hang you and your spawn of devils," she promised him with conviction. He laughed gustily and shifted her to a more comfortable position in his arms. But she took this as a fresh outrage, and renewed her vain struggles, until she saw that her efforts were only amusing him. Besides, her light silken garments, floating on the wind, were being outrageously disarranged by her struggles. She concluded that a scornful submission was the better part of dignity, and lapsed into a smoldering quiescence.

She felt even her anger being submerged by awe as they entered the mouth of the Pass, lowering like a black well mouth in the blacker walls that rose like colossal ramparts to bar their way. It was as if a gigantic knife had cut the Zhaibar out of walls of solid rock. On either hand sheer slopes pitched up for thousands of feet, and the mouth of the Pass was dark as hate. Even Conan could not see with any accuracy, but he knew the road, even by night. And knowing that armed men were racing through the starlight after him, he did not check the stallion's speed. The great brute was not yet showing fatigue. He thundered along the road that followed the valley bed, labored up a slope, swept along a low ridge where treacherous shale on either hand lurked for the unwary, and came upon a trail that followed the lap of the left-hand wall.

Not even Conan could spy, in that darkness, an ambush set by Zhaibar tribesmen. It was as they swept past the black mouth of a gorge that opened into the Pass that a javelin swished through the air and thudded home behind the stallion's straining shoulder. The great beast let out his life in a shuddering sob and stumbled, going headlong in full mid-stride. But Conan had recognized the flight and stroke of the javelin, and he acted with spring-steel quickness.

As the horse fell he leaped clear, holding the girl aloft to guard her from striking boulders. He hit on his feet like a cat, thrust her into a cleft of rock, and wheeled toward the outer darkness, drawing his knife.

Yasmina, confused by the rapidity of events, not quite sure just what had happened, saw a vague shape rush out of the darkness, bare feet slapping softly on the rock, ragged garments whipping on the wind of his haste. She glimpsed the flicker of steel, heard the lightning crack of stroke, parry and counter-stroke, and the crunch of bone as Conan's long knife split the other's skull.

Conan sprang back, crouching in the shelter of the rocks. Out in the night men were moving and a stentorian voice roared: "What, you dogs! Do you flinch? In, curse you, and take them!"

Conan started, peered into the darkness and lifted his voice.

"Yar Afzal! Is it you?"

There sounded a startled imprecation, and the voice called warily.

"Conan? Is it you, Conan?"

"Aye!" The Cimmerian laughed. "Come forth, you old war-dog. I've slain one of your men."

There was movement among the rocks, a light flared dimly, and then a flame appeared and came bobbing toward him, and as it approached, a fierce bearded countenance grew out of the darkness. The man who carried it held it high, thrust forward, and craned his neck to peer among the boulders it lighted, the other hand gripping a great curved tulwar. Conan stepped forward, sheathing his knife, and the other roared a greeting.

"Aye, it is Conan! Come out of your rocks, dogs! It is Conan!"

Others pressed into the wavering circle of light – wild, ragged, bearded men, with eyes like wolves, and long blades in their fists. They did not see Yasmina, for she was hidden by Conan's massive body. But peeping from her covert, she knew icy fear for the first time that night. These men were more like wolves than human beings.

"What are you hunting in the Zhaibar by night, Yar Afzal?" Conan demanded of the burly chief. He grinned like a bearded ghoul.

"Who knows what might come up the Pass after dark? We Wazulis are night hawks. But what of you, Conan?"

"I have a prisoner," answered the Cimmerian. And moving aside he disclosed the cowering girl. Reaching a long arm into the crevice he drew her trembling forth. Her imperious bearing was gone. She stared timidly at the ring of bearded faces that hemmed her in, and was grateful for the strong arm that clasped her possessively. The torch was thrust close to her, and there was a sucking intake of breath about the ring.

"She is my captive," Conan warned, glancing pointedly at the feet of the man he had slain, just visible within the ring of light. "I was taking her to Afghulistan, but now you have slain my horse, and the Kshatriyas are close behind me."

"Come with us to my village," suggested Yar Afzal. "We have horses hidden in the gorge. They can never follow us in the darkness. They are close behind you, you say?"

"So close that I hear now the clink of their hoofs on the flint," answered Conan grimly. Instantly there was movement; the torch was dashed out and the ragged shapes melted like phantoms into the darkness. Conan swept up the Devi in his arms, and she did not resist. The rocky ground hurt her slim feet in their soft slippers and she felt very small and helpless in that brutish, primordial blackness among those colossal, nighted crags.

Feeling her shiver in the wind that moaned down the defiles, Conan jerked a ragged cloak from its owner's shoulders and wrapped it about her. He also hissed a warning in her ear, ordering her to make no sound. She did not hear the distant clink of shod hoofs on rock that warned the keen-eared hillmen; but she was far too frightened to disobey, in any event.

She could see nothing but a few faint stars far above, but she knew by the deepening darkness when they entered the gorge mouth. There was a stir about them, the uneasy movement of horses. A few muttered words, and Conan mounted the horse of the man he had killed, lifting the girl up in front of him. Like phantoms except for the click of their hoofs, the band swept away up the shadowy gorge. Behind them on the trail they left the dead horse and the dead man, which were found less than half an hour later by the riders from the fortress, who recognized the man as a Wazuli and drew their own conclusions accordingly.

Yasmina, snuggled warmly in her captor's arms, grew drowsy in spite of herself. The motion of the horse, though it was uneven, uphill and down, yet possessed a certain rhythm which combined with weariness and emotional exhaustion to force sleep upon her. She had lost all sense of time or direction. They moved in soft thick darkness, in which she sometimes glimpsed vaguely gigantic walls sweeping up like black ramparts, or great crags shouldering the stars; at times she sensed echoing depths beneath them, or felt the wind of dizzy heights blowing cold about her. Gradually these things faded into a dreamy unwakefulness in which the clink of hoofs and the creak of saddles were like the irrelevant sounds in a dream.

She was vaguely aware when the motion ceased and she was lifted down and carried a few steps. Then she was laid down on something soft and rustling, and something – a folded coat perhaps – was thrust under her head, and the cloak in which she was wrapped was carefully tucked about her. She heard Yar Afzal laugh.

"A rare prize, Conan; fit mate for a chief of the Afghulis."

"Not for me," came Conan's answering rumble. "This wench will buy the lives of my seven headmen, blast their souls."

That was the last she heard as she sank into dreamless slumber.

She slept while armed men rode through the dark hills, and the fate of kingdoms hung in the balance. Through the shadowy gorges and defiles that night there rang the hoofs of galloping horses, and the starlight glimmered on helmets and curved blades, until the ghoulish shapes that haunt the crags stared into the darkness from ravine and boulder and wondered what things were afoot.

A band of these sat gaunt horses in the black pit-mouth of a gorge as the hurrying hoofs swept past. Their leader, a well-built man in a helmet and gilt-braided cloak, held up his hand warningly, until the riders had sped on. Then he laughed softly.

"They must have lost the trail! Or else they have found that Conan has already reached the Afghuli villages. It will take many riders to smoke out that hive. There will be squadrons riding up the Zhaibar by dawn."

"If there is fighting in the hills there will be looting," muttered a voice behind him, in the dialect of the Irakzai.

"There will be looting," answered the man with the helmet. "But first it is our business to reach the valley of Gurashah and await the riders that will be galloping southward from Secunderam before daylight."

He lifted his reins and rode out of the defile, his men falling in behind him – thirty ragged phantoms in the starlight.

V

THE BLACK STALLION

The sun was well up when Yasmina awoke. She did not start and stare blankly, wondering where she was. She awoke with full knowledge of all that had occurred. Her supple limbs were stiff from her long ride, and her firm flesh still seemed to feel the contact of the muscular arms that had borne her so far.

She was lying on a sheepskin covering a pallet of leaves on a hard-beaten dirt floor. A folded sheepskin coat was under her head, and she was wrapped in a ragged cloak. She was in a large room, the walls of which were crudely but strongly built of uncut rocks, plastered with sun-baked mud. Heavy beams supported a roof of the same kind, in which showed a trap-door up to which led a ladder. There were no windows in the thick walls, only loopholes. There was one door, a sturdy bronze affair that must have been looted from some Vendhyan border tower. Opposite it was a wide opening in the wall, with no door, but several strong wooden bars in place. Beyond them Yasmina saw a magnificent black stallion munching a pile of dried grass. The building was fort, dwelling-place and stable in one.

At the other end of the room a girl in the vest and baggy trousers of a hillwoman squatted beside a small fire, cooking strips of meat on an iron grid laid over blocks of stone. There was a sooty cleft in the wall a few feet from the floor, and some of the smoke found its way out there. The rest floated in blue wisps about the room.

The hill-girl glanced at Yasmina over her shoulder, displaying a bold, handsome face, and then continued her cooking. Voices boomed outside, then the door was kicked open, and Conan strode in. He looked more enormous than ever with the morning sunlight behind him, and Yasmina noted some details that had escaped her the night before. His garments were clean and not ragged. The broad Bakhariot girdle that supported his knife in its ornamented scabbard would have matched the robes of a prince, and there was a glint of fine Turanian mail under his shirt.

"Your captive is awake, Conan," said the Wazuli girl, and he grunted, strode up to the fire and swept the strips of mutton off into a stone dish. The squatting girl laughed up at him, with some spicy jest, and he grinned wolfishly, and hooking a toe under her haunches, tumbled her sprawling onto the floor. She seemed to derive considerable amusement from this bit of rough horse-play, but Conan paid no more heed to her. Producing a great hunk of bread from somewhere, with a copper jug of wine, he carried the lot to Yasmina, who had risen from her pallet and was regarding him doubtfully.

"Rough fare for a Devi, girl, but our best," he grunted. "It will fill your belly, at least."

He set the platter on the floor and she was suddenly aware of a ravenous hunger. Making no comment she seated herself cross-legged on the floor, and taking the dish in her lap, she began to eat, using her fingers, which were all she had in the way of table utensils. After all, adaptability is one of the tests of true aristocracy. Conan stood looking down at her, his thumbs hooked in his girdle. He never sat cross-legged, after the Eastern fashion.

"Where am I?" she asked abruptly.

"In the hut of Yar Afzal, the chief of the Khurum Wazulis," he answered. "Afghulistan lies a good many miles further on to the west. We'll hide here awhile. The Kshatriyas are beating up the hills for you – several of their squads have been up by the tribes already."

"What are you going to do?" she asked.

"Keep you until Chunder Shan is willing to trade back my seven cow-thieves," he grunted. "Women of the Wazulis are crushing ink out of *shoki* leaves, and after awhile you can write a letter to the governor."

A touch of her old imperious wrath shook her, as she thought how maddeningly her plans had gone awry, leaving her captive of the very man she had plotted to get into her power. She flung down the dish, with the remnants of her meal, and sprang to her feet, tense with anger.

"I will not write a letter! If you do not take me back, they will hang your seven men, and a thousand more besides!"

The Wazuli girl laughed mockingly, Conan scowled, and then the door opened and Yar Afzal came swaggering in. The Wazuli chief was as tall as Conan, and of greater girth, but he looked fat and slow beside the hard compactness of the Cimmerian. He plucked his red-stained beard and stared meaningly at the Wazuli girl, and that wench rose and skurried out without delay. Then Yar Afzal turned to his guest.

"The damnable people murmur, Conan," quoth he. "They wish me to murder you and take the girl to hold for ransom. They say that anyone can tell by her garments that she is a noble lady. They say why should the Afghuli dogs profit by her, when they take the risk of guarding her?"

"Lend me your horse," said Conan. "I'll take her and go."

"Pish!" boomed Yar Afzal. "Do you think I can't handle my own people? I'll have them dancing in their shirts if they cross me! They don't love you – or any outlander – but you saved my life once, and I will not forget. Come out, though, Conan; a scout has returned."

Conan hitched at his girdle and followed the chief outside. They closed the door after them, and Yasmina peeped through a loop-hole. She looked out on a level space before the hut. At the further end of that space there was a cluster of mud and stone huts, and she saw naked children playing among the boulders, and the slim, erect women of the hills going about their tasks.

Directly before the chief's hut a circle of hairy, ragged men squatted facing the door. Conan and Yar Afzal stood a few paces before the door, and between them and the ring of warriors another man sat cross-legged. This one was addressing his chief in the harsh accents of the Wazuli which Yasmina could scarcely understand, though as part of her royal education she had been taught the languages of Iranistan and the kindred tongues of Ghulistan.

"I talked with a Dagozai who saw the riders last night," said the scout. "He was lurking near when they came to the spot where we ambushed the lord Conan. He overheard their speech. Chunder Shan was with them. They found the dead horse, and one of the men recognized it as Conan's. Then they found the man Conan slew, and knew him for a Wazuli. So it seemed to them that Conan had been slain and the girl taken by the Wazuli, so they turned aside from their purpose of following to Afghulistan. But they did not know from which village the dead man was come, and we had left no trail a Kshatriya could follow.

"So they rode to the nearest Wazuli village, which was the village of Jugra, and burnt it and slew many of the people. But the men of Khojur came upon them in darkness and slew some of them, and wounded the governor. So the survivors retired down the Zhaibar in the darkness before dawn. But they returned with reinforcements before sunrise, and there has been skirmishing and fighting in the hills all morning. It is said that a great army is being raised to sweep the hills about the Zhaibar. The tribes are whetting their knives and laying ambushes in every pass from here to Gurashah valley. Moreover, Kerim Shah has returned to the hills."

A grunt went around the circle and Yasmina leaned closer to the loophole at the name she had begun to mistrust.

"Where went he?" demanded Yar Afzal.

"The Dagozai did not know; with him were thirty Irakzai of the lower villages. They rode into the hills and disappeared."

"These Irakzai are jackals that follow a lion for crumbs," growled Yar Afzal. "They have been lapping up the coins Kerim Shah scatters among the border tribes to buy men like horses. I like him not, for all he is our kinsman from Iranistan."

"He's not even that," said Conan. "I know him of old. He's an Hyrkanian, a spy of Yezdigerd's. If I catch him I'll hang his hide to a tamarisk."

"But the Kshatriyas!" clamored the men in the semi-circle. "Are we to squat on our haunches until they smoke us out? They will learn at last in which Wazuli village the wench is held! We are not loved by the Zhaibari; they will help the Kshatriyas hunt us out."

"Let them come," grunted Yar Afzal. "We can hold the defiles against a host."

One of the men leaped up and shook his fist at Conan.

"Are we to take all the risks while he reaps the rewards?" he howled. "Are we to fight his battles for him?"

With a stride Conan reached him and bent slightly to stare full into his hairy face. The Cimmerian had not drawn his long knife, but his left hand grasped the scabbard, jutting the hilt suggestively forward.

"I ask no man to fight my battles," he said softly. "Draw your blade if you dare, you yapping dog!"

The Wazuli started back, snarling like a cat.

"Dare to touch me and here are fifty men to rend you apart!" he screeched.

"What!" roared Yar Afzal, his face purpling with wrath. His whiskers bristled, his belly swelled with his rage. "Are you chief of Khurum? Do the Wazulis take orders from Yar Afzal, or from a low-bred cur?"

The man cringed before his invincible chief, and Yar Afzal, striding up to him, seized him by the throat and choked him until his face was turning black. Then he hurled the man savagely against the ground and stood over him with his tulwar in his hand.

"Is there any who questions my authority?" he roared, and his warriors looked down sullenly as his bellicose glare swept their semi-circle. Yar Afzal grunted scornfully and sheathed his weapon with a gesture that was the apex of insult. Then he kicked the fallen agitator with a concentrated vindictiveness that brought howls from his victim.

"Get down the valley to the watchers on the heights and bring word if they have seen anything," commanded Yar Afzal, and the man went, shaking with fear and grinding his teeth with fury.

Yar Afzal then seated himself ponderously on a stone, growling in his beard. Conan stood near him, legs braced apart, thumbs hooked in his girdle, narrowly watching the assembled warriors. They stared at him sullenly, not daring to brave Yar Afzal's fury, but hating the foreigner as only a hillman can hate.

"Now listen to me, you sons of nameless dogs, while I tell you what the lord Conan and I have planned to fool the Kshatriyas —" the boom of Yar Afzal's bull-like voice followed the discomfited warrior as he slunk away from the assembly.

The man passed by the cluster of huts, where women who had seen his defeat laughed at him and called stinging comments, and hastened on along the trail that wound among spurs and rocks toward the valley head.

Just as he rounded the first turn that took him out of sight of the village, he stopped short, gaping stupidly. He had not believed it possible for a stranger to enter the valley of Khurum without being detected by the hawk-eyed watchers along the heights, yet a man sat cross-legged on a low ledge beside the path – a man in a camel-hair robe and a green turban.

The Wazuli's mouth gaped for a yell, and his hand leaped to his knife hilt. But at that instant his eyes met those of the stranger and the cry died in his throat, his fingers went limp. He stood like a statue, his own eyes glazed and vacant.

For minutes the scene held motionless, then the man on the ledge drew a cryptic symbol in the dust on the rock with his forefinger. The Wazuli did not see him place anything within the compass of that emblem, but presently something gleamed there – a round, shiny black ball that looked like polished jade. The man in the green turban took this up and tossed it to the Wazuli who mechanically caught it.

"Carry this to Yar Afzal," he said, and the Wazuli turned like an automaton and went back along the path, holding the black jade ball in his outstretched hand. He did not even turn his head to the renewed jeers of the women as he passed the huts. He did not seem to hear.

The man on the ledge gazed after him with a cryptic smile. A girl's head rose above the rim of the ledge and she looked at him with admiration and a touch of fear that had not been present the night before.

"Why did you do that?" she asked.

He ran his fingers through her dark locks caressingly.

"Are you still dizzy from your flight on the *horse-of-air* that you doubt my wisdom?" he laughed. "As long as Yar Afzal lives, Conan will bide safe among the Wazuli fighting-men. It would be easier, even for me, to trap the Cimmerian as he flees alone with the girl, than to seek to slay him and take her from among them. It takes no wizard to predict what the Wazulis will do, and what Conan will do, when my victim hands the globe of Yezud to the chief of Khurum."

Back before the hut, Yar Afzal halted in the midst of some tirade, surprized and displeased to see the man he had sent up the valley, pushing his way through the throng.

"I bade you go to the watchers!" the chief bellowed. "You have not had time to come from them!"

The other did not reply; he stood woodenly, staring vacantly into the chief's face, his palm outstretched holding the jade ball. Conan, looking over Yar Afzal's shoulder, murmured something and reached to touch the chief's arm, but as he did so, Yar Afzal, in a paroxysm of anger, struck the man with his clenched fist and felled him like an ox. As he fell the jade sphere rolled to Yar Afzal's foot and the chief, seeming to see it for the first time, bent and picked it up. The men, staring perplexedly at their senseless comrade, saw their chief bend, but they did not see what he picked up from the ground.

Yar Afzal straightened, glanced at the jade, and made a motion to thrust it into his girdle.

"Carry that fool to his hut," he growled. "He has the look of a lotus-eater. He returned me a blank stare. I – *aie!*"

In his right hand, moving toward his girdle, he had suddenly felt movement where movement should not be. His voice died away as he stood and glared at nothing; and inside his clenched right hand he felt the quivering of *change*, of *motion*, of *life*. He no longer held a smooth shining sphere in his fingers. And he dared not look; his tongue clove to the roof of his mouth, and he could not open his hand. His astonished warriors saw Yar Afzal's eyes distend, the color ebb from his face. Then suddenly a bellow of agony burst from his bearded lips; he swayed and fell as if struck by lightning, his right arm tossed out in front of him. Face down he lay, and from between his opening fingers crawled a spider – a hideous, black, hairy-legged monster whose body shone like black jade. The men yelled and gave back suddenly, and the creature scuttled into a crevice of the rocks and disappeared.

The warriors started up, glaring wildly, and a voice rose above their clamor, a far-carrying voice of command which came from none knew where. Afterwards each man there – who still lived – denied that he had shouted, but all there heard it.

"Yar Afzal is dead! Kill the outlander!"

That shout focussed their whirling minds as one. Doubt, bewilderment and fear vanished in the uproaring surge of the blood-lust. A furious yell rent the skies as the tribesmen responded instantly to the suggestion. They came headlong across the open space, cloaks flapping, eyes blazing, knives lifted.

Conan's action was as quick as theirs. As the voice shouted he sprang for the hut door. But they were closer to him than he was to the door, and with one foot on the sill he had to wheel and parry the swipe of a yard-long blade. He split the man's skull – ducked another swinging knife and gutted the wielder – felled a man with his left fist and stabbed another in the belly – and heaved back mightily against the closed door with his shoulders. Hacking blades were nicking chips out of the jambs about his ears, but the door flew open under the impact of his shoulders, and he went stumbling backward into the room. A bearded tribesman, thrusting with all his fury as Conan sprang back, over-reached and pitched head-first through the doorway. Conan stooped, grasped the slack of his garments and hauled him clear, and slammed the door in the faces of the men who came surging into it. Bones snapped under the impact, and the next instant Conan slammed the bolts into place and whirled with desperate haste to meet the man who sprang from the floor and tore into action like a madman.

Yasmina cowered in a corner, staring in horror as the two men fought back and forth across the room, almost trampling her at times; the flash and clangor of their blades filled the room, and outside the mob clamored like a wolf-pack, hacking deafeningly at the bronze door with their long knives, and dashing huge rocks against it. Somebody fetched a tree trunk, and the door began to stagger under the thunderous assault. Yasmina clasped her ears, staring wildly. Violence and fury within, cataclysmic madness without. The stallion in his stall neighed and reared, thundering with his heels against the walls. He wheeled and launched his hoofs through the bars just as the tribesman, backing away from Conan's murderous swipes, stumbled against them. His spine cracked in three places like a rotten branch and he was hurled headlong against the Cimmerian, bearing him backward so they both crashed to the beaten floor. Yasmina cried out and ran forward; to her dazed sight it seemed that both were slain. She reached them just as Conan threw aside the corpse and rose. She caught his arm, trembling from head to foot.

"Oh, you live! I thought – I thought you were dead!"

He glanced down at her quickly, into the pale, upturned face and the wide staring dark eyes.

"Why are you trembling?" he demanded. "Why should you care if I live or die?"

A vestige of her poise returned to her, and she drew away, making a rather pitiful attempt at playing the Devi.

"You are preferable to those wolves howling without," she answered, gesturing toward the door, the stone sill of which was beginning to splinter away.

"That won't hold long," he muttered, then turned and went swiftly to the stall of the stallion. Yasmina clenched her hands and caught her breath as she saw him tear aside the splintered bars and go into the stall with the maddened beast. The stallion reared above him, neighing terribly, hoofs lifted, eyes and teeth flashing and ears laid back, but Conan leaped and caught his mane and with a display of sheer strength that seemed impossible, dragged the beast down on his forelegs. The steed snorted and quivered, but stood still while the man bridled him and clapped on the gold-worked saddle, with the wide silver stirrups.

Wheeling the beast around in the stall, Conan called quickly to Yasmina, and the girl came, sidling nervously past the stallion's heels. Conan was working at the stone wall, talking swiftly as he worked.

"A secret door in the wall here, that not even the Wazuli know about. Yar Afzal showed it to me once when he was drunk. It opens out into the mouth of the ravine behind the hut. Ha!"

As he tugged at a projection that seemed casual, a whole section of the wall slid back on oiled iron runners. Looking through, the girl saw a narrow defile opening in a sheer stone wall within a few feet of the hut's back wall. Then Conan sprang into the saddle and hauled her up before him. Behind them the great door groaned like a living thing and crashed in and a yell rang to the roof as the entrance was instantly flooded with hairy faces and knives in hairy fists. And then the great stallion went through the wall like a javelin from a catapult, and thundered into the defile, running low, foam flying from the bit-rings.

That move came as an absolute surprize to the Wazulis. It was a surprize, too, to those stealing down the ravine. It happened so quickly – the hurricane-like charge of the great horse – that a man in a green turban was unable to get out of the way. He went down under the frantic hoofs, and a girl screamed. Conan got one glimpse of her as they thundered by – a slim, dark girl in silk trousers and a jeweled breast-band, flattening herself against the ravine wall. Then the black horse and his riders were gone up the gorge like the spume blown before a storm, and the men who came tumbling through the wall into the defile after them met that which changed their yells of blood-lust to shrill screams of fear and death.

VI

THE MOUNTAIN OF THE BLACK SEERS

"Where now?" Yasmina was trying to sit erect on the rocking saddle bow, clutching to her captor. She was conscious of a recognition of shame that she should not find unpleasant the feel of his muscular flesh under her fingers, but under that too was a wicked little tingle that would not be denied.

"To Afghulistan," he answered. "It's a perilous road, but the stallion will carry us easily, unless we fall in with some of your friends, or my tribal enemies. Now that Yar Afzal is dead, those damned Wazulis will be on our heels. I'm surprised we haven't sighted them behind us already."

"Who was that man you rode down?" she asked.

"I don't know. I never saw him before. He's no Ghuli, that's certain. What the devil he was doing there is more than I can say. There was a girl with him, too."

"Yes." Her gaze was shadowed. "I can not understand that. That girl was my maid, Gitara. Do you suppose she was coming to aid me? That the man was a friend? If so, the Wazulis have captured them both."

"Well," he answered, "there's nothing we can do. If we go back, they'll skin us both. I can't understand how a girl like that could get this far into the mountains with only one man – and he a robed scholar, for that's what he looked like. There's something infernally queer in all this. That fellow Yar Afzal beat and sent away – he moved like a man walking in his sleep. I've seen the priests of Zamora perform their abominable rituals in their forbidden temples, and their victims had a stare like that man. The priests looked into their eyes and muttered incantations, and then the people became like walking dead men, with glassy eyes, doing as they were ordered.

"And then I saw what the fellow had in his hand, which Yar Afzal picked up. It was like a big black jade bead, such as the temple girls of Yezud wear when they dance before the black stone spider which is their god. Yar Afzal held it in his hand, and he didn't pick up anything else. Yet when he fell dead a spider, like the god at Yezud, only smaller, ran out of his fingers. And then, when the Wazulis stood uncertain there, a voice cried out for them to kill me, and I know that voice didn't come from any of the warriors, nor from the women who watched by the huts. It seemed to come from *above*."

Yasmina did not reply. She glanced at the stark outlines of the mountains all about them and shuddered. Her soul shrank from their gaunt brutality. This was a grim, naked land where anything might happen. Age-old traditions invested it with shuddersome horror for anyone born in the hot, luxuriant southern plains.

The sun was high, beating down with fierce heat, yet the wind that blew in fitful gusts seemed to sweep off slopes of ice. Once she heard a strange rushing above them that was not the sweep of the wind, and from the way Conan looked up, she knew it was not a common sound to him, either. She thought that a strip of the cold blue sky was momentarily blurred, as if some all but invisible object had swept between it and herself, but she could not be sure. Neither made any comment, but Conan loosened his knife in his scabbard.

They were following no marked trail, but dipping down into ravines so deep the sun never struck bottom, laboring up steep slopes where loose shale threatened to slide from beneath their feet, and following knife-edge ridges with blue-hazed echoing depths on either hand.

The sun had passed its zenith when they came to a narrow trail winding among the crags. Conan reined the horse aside and followed it southward, going almost at right angles to their former course.

"A Galzai village is at one end of this trail," he explained. "Their women follow it to a well, for water. You need new garments."

Glancing down at her filmy attire, Yasmina agreed with him. Her cloth-of-gold slippers were in tatters, her robes and silken under-garments torn to shreds that scarcely held together decently. Garments meant for the streets of Peshkhauri were scarcely appropriate for the crags of the Himelians.

Coming to a crook in the trail, Conan dismounted, helped Yasmina down and waited. Presently he nodded, though she heard nothing.

"A woman coming along the trail," he remarked. In sudden panic she clutched his arm.

"You will not – not kill her?"

"I don't kill women ordinarily," he grunted; "though some of these hill women are she-wolves. No," he grinned as at a huge jest. "By Crom, I'll *pay* for her clothes! How is that?" He displayed a handful of gold coins, and replaced all but the largest. She nodded, much relieved. It was perhaps natural for men to slay and die; her flesh crawled at the thought of watching the butchery of a woman.

Presently a woman appeared around the crook of the trail – a tall, slim Galzai girl, straight as a young sapling, bearing a great empty gourd. She stopped short and the gourd fell from her hands when she saw them; she wavered as though to run, then realized that Conan was too close to her to allow her to escape, and so stood still, staring at them with an expression mixed of fear and curiosity.

Conan displayed the gold coin.

"If you will give this woman your garments," he said, "I will give you this money."

The response was instant. The girl smiled broadly with surprize and delight, and, with the disdain of a hill woman for prudish conventions, promptly yanked off her sleeveless embroidered vest, slipped down her wide trousers and stepped out of them, twitched off her wide-sleeved shirt, and kicked off her sandals. Bundling them all in a bunch, she proffered them to Conan, who handed them to the astonished Devi.

"Get behind that rock and put these on," he directed, further proving himself no native hillman. "Fold your robes up into a bundle and bring them to me when you come out."

"The money!" clamored the hill girl, stretching out her hands eagerly. "The gold you promised me!"

Conan flipped the coin to her, she caught it, bit, then thrust it into her hair, bent supplely and caught up the gourd and went on down the path, as devoid of self-consciousness as of garments. Conan waited with some impatience while the Devi, for the first time in her pampered life, dressed herself. When she stepped from behind the rock he swore in surprize, and she felt a curious rush of emotions at the unrestrained admiration burning in his fierce blue eyes. She felt shame, embarrassment, yet a stimulation of vanity she had never before experienced, and the same naughty tingling she had felt before when meeting the impact of his eyes or the grasp of his arms. He laid a heavy hand on her shoulder and turned her about, staring avidly at her from all angles.

"By Crom!" said he. "In those smoky, mystic robes you were aloof and cold and far-off as a star! Now you are a woman of warm flesh and blood! You went behind that rock as the Devi of Vendhya; you come out as a hill girl – though a thousand times more beautiful than any wench of the Zhaibar! You were a goddess – now you are real!"

He spanked her resoundingly, and she, recognizing this as merely another expression of admiration, did not feel particularly outraged. It was indeed as if the changing of her garments had wrought a change in her personality. The feelings and sensations she had suppressed rose to domination in her now, as if the queenly robes she had cast off had been material shackles and inhibitions.

But Conan, in his renewed admiration, did not forget that peril lurked all about them. The further they drew away from the region of the Zhaibar, the less likely he was to encounter any Kshatriya troops. On the other hand he had been listening all throughout their flight for sounds that would tell him the vengeful Wazulis of Khurum were on their heels.

Swinging the Devi up, he followed her into the saddle and again reined the stallion westward. The bundle of garments she had given him, he hurled over a cliff, to fall into the depths of a thousand-foot gorge.

"Why did you do that?" she asked. "Why did you not give them to the girl?"

"The riders from Peshkhauri are combing these hills," he said. "They'll be ambushed and harried at every turn, and by way of reprisal they'll destroy every village they can take. They may turn westward any time. If they found a girl wearing your garments, they'd torture her into talking, and she might put them on my trail."

"What will she do?" asked Yasmina.

"Go back to her village and tell her people that a stranger stripped her and raped her," he answered.

"She'll have them on our track, alright. But she had to go on and get the water first; if she dared go back without it, they'd whip the skin off her. That gives us a long start. They'll never catch us. By nightfall we'll cross the Afghuli border."

"There are no paths or signs of human habitation in these parts," she commented. "Even for the Himelians this region seems singularly deserted. We have not seen a trail since we left the one where we met the Galzai woman."

For answer he pointed to the northwest, where she glimpsed a peak in a notch of the crags.

"Yimsha," grunted Conan. "The tribes build their villages as far from that mountain as they can."

She was instantly rigid with attention.

"Yimsha!" she whispered. "The mountain of the Black Seers!"

"So they say," he answered. "This is as near as I ever approached it. I have swung north to avoid any Kshatriya troops that might be prowling through the hills. The regular trail from Khurum to Afghulistan lies further south.

She was staring at the distant peak with avid intentness. Her nails bit into her pink palms.

"How long would it take to reach Yimsha from this point?"

"All the rest of the day, and all night," he answered, and grinned. "Do you want to go there? By Crom, it's no place for an ordinary human, from what the hill people say."

"Why do they not gather and destroy the devils that inhabit it?" she demanded.

"Wipe out wizards with swords? Anyway, they never interfere with people, unless the people interfere with them. I never saw one of them, though I've talked with men who swore they had. They say they've glimpsed people from the tower among the crags at sunset or sunrise – tall, silent men in black robes."

"Would you be afraid to attack them?"

"I?" The idea seemed a new one to him. "Why, if they imposed upon me, it would be my life or theirs. But I have nothing to do with them. I came to these mountains to raise a following of human beings, not to war with wizards."

Yasmina did not at once reply. She stared at the peak as at a human enemy, feeling all her anger and hatred stir in her bosom anew. And another feeling began to take dim shape. She had plotted to hurl against the masters of Yimsha the man in whose arms she was now carried. Perhaps there was another way, besides the method she had planned, to accomplish her purpose.

She could not mistake the look that was beginning to dawn in this wild man's eyes as they rested on her. Kingdoms have fallen when a woman's slim white hands pulled the strings of destiny – suddenly she stiffened, pointing.

"Look!"

Just visible on the distant peak there hung a cloud of peculiar aspect. It was a frosty crimson in color, veined with sparkling gold. This cloud was in motion; it rotated, and as it whirled it contracted. It dwindled to a spinning taper that flashed in the sun. And suddenly it detached itself from the snow-tipped peak, floated out over the void like a gay-hued feather, and became invisible against the cerulean sky.

"What could that have been?" asked the girl uneasily, as a shoulder of rock shut the distant mountain from view; the phenomenon had been disturbing, even in its beauty.

"The hillmen call it Yimsha's Carpet, whatever the devil that means," answered Conan. "I've seen five hundred of them running as if the devil were at their heels, to hide themselves in caves and crags, because they saw that crimson cloud float up from the peak. What the hell!"

They had advanced through a narrow, knife-cut gash between turreted walls, and emerged upon a broad ledge, flanked by a series of rugged slopes on one hand, and a gigantic precipice on the other. The dim trail followed this ledge, bent around a shoulder and reappeared at intervals far below, working a tedious way downward. And emerging from the gut that opened upon the ledge, the black stallion halted short, snorting. Conan urged him on impatiently, and the horse snorted and threw his head up and down, quivering and straining as if against an invisible barrier.

Conan swore and swung off, lifting Yasmina down with him. He went forward, with a hand thrown out before him as if expecting to encounter unseen resistance, but there was nothing to hinder him, though when he tried to lead the horse, it neighed shrilly and jerked back. Then Yasmina cried out, and Conan wheeled, hand starting to knife hilt.

Neither of them had seen him come, but he stood there, with his arms folded, a man in a camel-hair robe and a green turban. Conan grunted with surprize to recognize the man the stallion had spurned in the ravine outside the Wazuli village.

"Who the devil are you?" he demanded.

The man did not answer. Conan noticed that his eyes were wide, fixed, and of a peculiar luminous quality. And those eyes held his like a magnet.

Khemsa's sorcery was based on hypnotism, as is the case with most Eastern magic. The way has been prepared for the hypnotist for untold centuries of generations who have lived and died in the firm conviction of the reality and power of hypnotism, building up, by mass thought and practise, a colossal though intangible atmosphere against which the individual, steeped in the traditions of the land, finds himself helpless.

But Conan was not a son of the East. Its traditions were meaningless to him; he was the product of an utterly alien atmosphere. Hypnotism was not even a myth in Cimmeria. The heritage that prepared a native of the East for submission to the mesmerist was not his.

He was aware of what Khemsa was trying to do to him; but he felt the impact of the man's uncanny power only as a vague impulsion, a tugging and pulling that he could shake off as a man shakes spider webs from his garments.

Aware of hostility and black magic, he ripped out his long knife and lunged, as quick on his feet as a mountain lion.

But hypnotism was not all of Khemsa's magic. Yasmina, watching, did not see by what roguery of movement or illusion the man in the green turban avoided the terrible disembowelling thrust. But the keen blade whickered between side and lifted arm, and to Yasmina it seemed that Khemsa merely brushed his open palm lightly against Conan's bull-neck. But the Cimmerian went down like a slain ox.

Yet Conan was not dead; breaking his fall with his left hand, he slashed at Khemsa's legs even as he went down, and the Rakhsha avoided the scythe-like swipe only by a most unwizardly bound backward. Then Yasmina cried out sharply as she saw a woman she recognized as Gitara glide out from among the rocks and come up to the man. The greeting died in the Devi's throat as she saw the malevolence in the girl's beautiful face.

Conan was rising slowly, shaken and dazed by the cruel craft of that blow which, delivered with an art forgotten of men before Atlantis sank, would have broken like a rotten twig the neck of a lesser man. Khemsa gazed at him cautiously and a trifle uncertainly. The Rakhsha had learned the full flood of his own power when he faced at bay the knives of the maddened Wazulis in the ravine behind Khurum village; but the Cimmerian's resistance had perhaps shaken his new-found confidence a trifle. Sorcery thrives on success, not on failure.

He stepped forward, lifting his hand – then halted as if frozen, head tilted back, eyes wide open, hand raised. In spite of himself Conan followed his gaze, and so did the women – the girl cowering by the trembling stallion, and the girl beside Khemsa.

Down the mountain-slopes, like a whorl of shining dust blown before the wind, a crimson, conoid cloud came dancing. Khemsa's dark face turned ashen; his hand began to tremble, then sank to his side. The girl beside him, sensing the change in him, stared at him inquiringly.

The crimson shape left the mountain-slope and came down in a long arching swoop. It struck the ledge between Conan and Khemsa, and the Rakhsha gave back with a stifled cry. He backed away, pushing the girl Gitara back with groping, fending hands.

The crimson cloud balanced like a spinning top for an instant, whirling in a dazzling sheen on its point. Then without warning it was gone, vanished as a bubble vanishes when burst. There on the ledge stood four men. It was miraculous, incredible, impossible, yet it was true. They were not ghosts or phantoms. They were four tall men, with shaven, vulture-like heads, and black robes that hid their feet. Their hands were concealed by their wide sleeves. They stood in silence, their naked heads nodding slightly in unison. They were facing Khemsa, but behind them Conan felt his own blood turning to ice in his veins. Rising he backed stealthily away, until he felt the stallion's shoulder trembling against his back, and the Devi crept into the shelter of his arm. There was no word spoken. Silence hung like a stifling pall.

All four of the men in black robes stared at Khemsa. Their vulture-like faces were immobile, their eyes introspective and contemplative. But Khemsa shook like a man in an ague. His feet were braced on the rock, his calves straining as if in physical combat. Sweat ran in streams down his dark face. His right hand locked on something under his brown robe so desperately that the blood ebbed from that hand and left it white. His left hand fell on the shoulder of Gitara and clutched in agony like the grasp of a drowning man. She did not flinch or whimper, though his fingers dug like talons into her firm flesh.

Conan had witnessed hundreds of battles in his wild life, but never one like this, wherein four diabolical wills sought to beat down one lesser but equally devilish will that opposed them. But he only faintly sensed the monstrous quality of that hideous struggle. With his back to the wall, driven to bay by his former masters, Khemsa was fighting for his life with all the dark power, all the frightful knowledge they had taught him through long, grim years of neophytism and vassalage.

He was stronger than even he had guessed, and the free exercise of his powers in his own behalf had tapped unsuspected reservoirs of forces. And he was nerved to super-energy by frantic fear and desperation. He reeled before the merciless impact of those hypnotic eyes, but he held his ground. His features were distorted into a bestial grin of agony from which dripped bloody sweat, and his limbs were twisted as in a rack. It was a war of souls, of frightful brains steeped in lore forbidden to men for a million years, of mentalities which had plumbed the abysses and explored the dark stars where spawn the shadows.

Yasmina understood this better than did Conan. And she dimly understood why Khemsa could withstand the concentrated impact of those four hellish wills which might have blasted into atoms the very rock on which he stood. The reason was the girl that he clutched with the strength of his despair. She was like an anchor to his staggering soul, battered by the waves of those psychic emanations. His weakness was now his strength. His love for the girl, violent and evil though it might be, was yet a tie that bound him to the rest of humanity, providing an earthly leverage for his will, a chain that his inhuman enemies could not break. At least not break through Khemsa.

They realized that before he did. And one of them turned his gaze from the Rakhsha full upon Gitara. There was no battle there. The girl shrank and wilted like a leaf in the drouth. Irresistibly impelled, she tore herself from her lover's arms before he realized what was happening. Then a hideous thing came to pass. She began to back toward the precipice, facing her tormentors, her eyes wide and blank as dark gleaming glass from behind which a lamp has been blown out. Khemsa groaned and staggered toward her, falling into the trap set for him. A divided mind could not maintain the unequal battle. He was beaten, a straw in their hands. The girl went backward, walking like an automaton, and Khemsa reeled drunkenly after her, hands vainly outstretched, groaning, slobbering in his pain, his feet moving heavily like dead things.

On the very brink she paused, standing stiffly, her heels on the edge, and he fell on his knees and crawled whimpering toward her, groping for her, to drag her back from destruction. And just before his clumsy fingers touched her, one of the wizards laughed, like the sudden, bronze note of a bell in hell. The girl reeled suddenly, and consummate climax of exquisite cruelty, reason and understanding flooded back into her eyes which flared with awful fear. She screamed, clutched wildly at her lover's straining hands, and then, unable to save herself, fell headlong with a moaning cry.

Khemsa hauled himself to the edge and stared over, haggardly, his lips working as he mumbled to himself. Then he turned and stared for a long minute at his torturers, with wide eyes that held no human light. And then with a cry that almost burst the rocks, he reeled up and came rushing toward them, a knife lifted in his hand.

One of the Rakhshas stepped forward and stamped his foot, and as he stamped, there came a rumbling that grew swiftly to a grinding roar. Where his foot struck, a crevice opened in the solid rock that widened instantly. Then, with a deafening crash, a whole section of the ledge gave way. There was a last glimpse of Khemsa, with arms wildly upflung, and then he vanished amidst the roar of the avalanche that thundered down into the abyss.

The four looked contemplatively at the ragged edge of rock that formed the new rim of the precipice, and then turned suddenly. Conan, thrown off his feet by the shudder of the mountain, was rising, lifting Yasmina. He seemed to move as slowly as his brain was working. He was befogged and stupid. He realized that there was desperate need for him to lift the Devi on the black stallion, and ride like the wind, but an unaccountable sluggishness weighted his every thought and action.

And now the wizards had turned toward him; they raised their arms, and to his horrified sight, he saw their outlines fading, dimming, becoming hazy and nebulous, as a crimson smoke billowed around their feet and rose about them. They were blotted out by a sudden whirling cloud – and then he realized that he too was enveloped in a blinding crimson mist – he heard Yasmina scream and the stallion cried out like a woman in pain. The Devi was torn from his arm and as he lashed out with his knife blindly, a terrific blow like a gust of storm wind knocked him sprawling against a rock. Dazedly he saw a crimson conoid cloud spinning up and over the mountain slopes. Yasmina was gone, and so were the four men in black. Only the terrified stallion shared the ledge with him.

VII
ON TO YIMSHA

As mists vanish before a strong wind, the cobwebs vanished from Conan's brain. With a searing curse he leaped into the saddle and the stallion reared neighing beneath him. He glared up the slopes, hesitated, and then turned down the trail in the direction he had been going when halted by Khemsa's trickery. But now he did not ride at a measured gait. He shook loose the reins and the stallion went like a thunder-bolt, as if frantic to lose hysteria in violent physical exertion. Across the ledge and around the crag and down the narrow trail threading the great steep they plunged at break-neck speed. The path followed a fold of rock, winding interminably down from tier to tier of striated escarpment, and once, far below, Conan got a glimpse of the ruin that had fallen – a mighty pile of broken stone and boulders at the foot of a gigantic cliff.

The valley floor was still far below him when he reached a long and lofty ridge that led out from the slope like a natural causeway. Out upon this he rode, with an almost sheer drop on either hand. He could trace ahead of him the trail he had to follow; far ahead it dropped down from the ridge, and made a great horseshoe back into the river-bed at his left hand. He cursed the necessity of traversing those miles, but it was the only way. To try to descend to the lower lap of the trail here would be to attempt the impossible. Only a bird could get to the river-bed with a whole neck.

So he urged on the wearying stallion, until a clink of hoofs reached his ears, welling up from below. Pulling up short and reining to the lip of the cliff, he stared down into the dry river-bed that wound along the foot of the ridge. Along that gorge rode a motley throng – bearded men on half-wild horses, five hundred strong, bristling with weapons. And Conan shouted suddenly, leaning over the edge of the cliff, three hundred feet above them.

At his shout they reined back, and five hundred bearded faces were tilted up toward him; a deep, clamorous roar filled the canyon. Conan did not waste words.

"I was riding for Ghor!" he roared. "I had not hoped to meet you dogs on the trail. Follow me as fast as your nags can push! I'm going to Yimsha, and –"

"*Traitor!*" The howl was like a dash of ice water in his face.

"*What?*" He glared down at them, jolted speechless. He saw wild eyes blazing up at him, faces contorted with fury, fists brandishing blades.

"Traitor!" they roared back, whole-heartedly. "Where are the seven chiefs held captive in Peshkhauri?"

"Why, in the governor's prison, I suppose," he answered.

A blood-thirsty yell from a hundred throats answered him, with such a waving of weapons and a clamor that he could not understand what they were saying. He beat down the din with a bull-like roar, and bellowed: "What devil's play is this? Let one of you speak, so I can understand what you mean!"

A gaunt old chief elected himself to this position, shook his tulwar at Conan as a preamble, and shouted accusingly: "You would not let us go raiding Peshkhauri to rescue our brothers!"

"No, you fools!" roared the exasperated Cimmerian. "Even if you'd breached the wall, which is unlikely, they'd have hanged the prisoners before you could reach them."

"And you went alone to traffic with the governor!" yelled the Afghuli, working himself into a frothing frenzy.

"Well?"

"Where are the seven chiefs?" howled the old chief, making his tulwar into a glimmering wheel of steel about his head. "Where are they? Dead!"

"What!" Conan nearly fell off his horse in his surprize.

"Aye, dead!" Five hundred blood-thirsty voices assured him. The old chief brandished his arms and got the floor again. "They were not hanged!" he screeched. "A Wazuli in another cell saw them die! The governor sent a wizard to slay them by craft!"

"That must be a lie," said Conan. "The governor would not dare. Last night I talked with him —"

The admission was unfortunate. A yell of hate and accusation split the skies.

"Aye! You went to him alone! To betray us! It is no lie. The Wazuli escaped through the doors the wizard burst in his entry, and told the tale to our scouts whom he met in the Zhaibar. They had been sent forth to search for you, when you did not return. When they heard the Wazuli's tale, they returned with all haste to Ghor, and we saddled our steeds and girt our swords!"

"And what do you fools mean to do?" demanded the Cimmerian.

"To avenge our brothers!" they howled. "Death to the Kshatriyas! Slay him, brothers, he is a traitor!"

Arrows began to rattle around him. Conan rose in his stirrups, striving to make himself heard above the tumult, and then, with a roar mingled of rage, defiance and disgust, he wheeled and galloped back up the trail. Behind him and below him the Afghulis came pelting, mouthing their rage, too furious even to remember that the only way they could reach the height whereon he rode was to traverse the river-bed in the other direction, make the broad bend and follow the twisting trail up over the ridge. When they did remember this, and turned back, their repudiated chief had almost reached the point where the ridge joined the escarpment.

At the cliff he did not take the trail by which he had descended, but turned off on another, a mere trace along a rock-fault, where the stallion scrambled for footing. He had not ridden far when the stallion snorted and shied back from something lying in the trail. Conan stared down on the travesty of a man, a broken, shredded, bloody heap that gibbered and gnashed splintered teeth.

Only the dark gods that rule over the grim destinies of wizards know how Khemsa dragged his shattered body from beneath that awful cairn of fallen rocks and up the steep slope to the trail.

Impelled by some obscure reason, Conan dismounted and stood looking down at the ghastly shape, knowing that he was witness of a thing miraculous and opposed to nature. The Rakhsha lifted his gory head and his strange eyes, glazed with agony and approaching death, rested on Conan with recognition.

"Where are they?" It was a racking croak not even remotely resembling a human voice.

"Gone back to their damnable castle on Yimsha," grunted Conan. "They took the Devi with them."

"I will go!" muttered the man. "I will follow them! They killed Gitara; I will kill them – the acolytes, the Four of the Black Circle, the Master himself! Kill – kill them all!" He strove to drag his mutilated frame along the rock, but not even his indomitable will could animate that gory mass longer, where the splintered bones hung together only by torn tissue and ruptured fiber.

"Follow them!" raved Khemsa, drooling a bloody slaver. "Follow!"

"I'm going to," growled Conan. "I went to fetch my Afghulis, but they've turned on me. I'm going on to Yimsha alone. I'll have the Devi back if I have to tear down that damned mountain with my bare hands. I didn't think the governor would dare kill my headmen, when I had the Devi, but it seems he did. I'll have his head for that. She's no use to me now as a hostage, but –"

"The curse of Yizil on them!" gasped Khemsa. "Go! I am dying. Wait – take my girdle." He tried to fumble with a mangled hand at his tatters, and Conan, understanding what he sought to convey, bent and drew from about his gory waist a girdle of curious aspect.

"Follow the golden vein through the abyss," muttered Khemsa. "Wear the girdle. I had it from a Stygian priest. It will aid you, though it failed me at last. Break the crystal globe with the four golden pomegranates. Beware of the Master's transmutations – I am going to Gitara – she is waiting for me in hell – *aie, ya Skelos yar!*" And so he died.

Conan stared down at the girdle. The hair of which it was woven was not horse-hair. He was convinced that it was woven of the thick black tresses of a woman. Set in the thick mesh were tiny jewels such as he had never seen. The buckle was strangely made, in the form of a golden serpent head, flat, wedge-shaped and scaled with curious art. A strong shudder shook Conan as he handled it, and he turned as though to cast it over the precipice; then he hesitated, and finally buckled it about his waist, under the Bakhariot girdle. Then he mounted and pushed on.

The sun had sunk behind the crags. He climbed the trail in the vast shadow of the cliffs that was thrown out like a dark blue mantle over valleys and ridges far below. He was not far from the crest when, edging around the shoulder of a jutting crag, he heard the clink of shod hoofs ahead of him. He did not turn back. Indeed, so narrow was the path that the stallion could not

have wheeled his great body upon it. He rounded the jut of the rock and
came onto a portion of the path that broadened somewhat. A chorus of
threatening yells broke on his ear, but his stallion pinned a terrified horse
hard against the rock, and Conan caught the arm of the rider in an iron grip,
checking the lifted sword in mid-air.

"Kerim Shah!" muttered Conan, red glints smoldering luridly in his eyes.
The Turanian did not struggle; they sat their horses almost breast to breast,
Conan's fingers locking the other's sword-arm. Behind Kerim Shah filed a
group of lean Irakzai on gaunt horses. They glared like wolves, fingering bows
and knives, but rendered uncertain because of the narrowness of the path and
the perilous proximity of the abyss that yawned beneath them.

"Where is the Devi?" demanded Kerim Shah.

"What's it to you, you Hyrkanian spy?" snarled Conan.

"I know you have her," answered Kerim Shah. "I was on my way
northward with some tribesmen when we were ambushed by enemies in
Shalizah Pass. Many of my men were slain, and the rest of us harried
through the hills like jackals. When we had beaten off our pursuers, we
turned westward, toward Amir Jehun Pass, and this morning we came upon
a Wazuli wandering through the hills. He was quite mad, but I learned
much from his incoherent gibberings before he died. I learned that he was
the sole survivor of a band which followed a chief of the Afghulis and a
captive Kshatriya woman into a gorge behind Khurum village. He babbled
much of a man in a green turban whom the Afghuli rode down, but who,
when attacked by the Wazulis who pursued, smote them with a nameless
doom that wiped them out as a gust of wind-driven fire wipes out a cluster
of locusts.

"How that one man escaped, I do not know, nor did he; but I knew from
his maunderings that Conan of Ghor had been in Khurum with his royal
captive. And as we made our way through the hills, we overtook a naked
Galzai girl bearing a gourd of water, who told us a tale of having been
stripped and ravished by a giant foreigner in the garb of an Afghuli chief,
who, she said, gave her garments to a Vendhyan woman who accompanied
him. She said you rode westward."

Kerim Shah did not consider it necessary to explain that he had been on
his way to keep his rendezvous with the expected troops from Secunderam
when he found his way barred by hostile tribesmen. The road to Gurashah
valley through Shalizah Pass was longer than the road that wound through
Amir Jehun Pass, but the latter traversed part of the Afghuli country, which
Kerim Shah had been anxious to avoid until he came with an army. Barred
from the Shalizah road, however, he had turned to the forbidden route, until
news that Conan had not yet reached Afghulistan with his captive had

caused him to turn southward and push on recklessly in the hope of overtaking the Cimmerian in the hills.

"So you had better tell me where the Devi is," suggested Kerim Shah. "We outnumber you – "

"Let one of your dogs nock a shaft and I'll throw you over the cliff," Conan promised. "It wouldn't do you any good to kill me, anyhow. Five hundred Afghulis are on my trail, and if they find you've cheated them, they'll flay you alive. Anyway, I haven't got the Devi. She's in the hands of the Black Seers of Yimsha."

"*Tarim!*" swore Kerim Shah softly, shaken out of his poise for the first time. "Khemsa –"

"Khemsa's dead," grunted Conan. "His masters sent him to hell on a landslide. And now get out of my way. I'd be glad to kill you if I had the time, but I'm on my way to Yimsha."

"I'll go with you," said the Turanian abruptly.

Conan laughed at him. "Do you think I'd trust you, you Hyrkanian dog?"

"I don't ask you to," returned Kerim Shah. "We both want the Devi. You know my reason; King Yezdigerd desires to add her kingdom to his empire, and herself to his seraglio. And I knew you, in the days when you were a *hetman* of the *kozak* steppes, so I know your ambition is wholesale plunder. You want to loot Vendhya, and to twist out a huge ransom for Yasmina. Well, let us for the time being, without any illusions about one another, unite our forces, and try to rescue the Devi from the Seers. If we succeed, and live, we can fight it out to see who keeps her."

Conan narrowly scrutinized the other for a moment, and then nodded, releasing the Turanian's arm. "Agreed; what about your men?"

Kerim Shah turned to the silent Irakzai and spoke briefly: "This chief and I are going to Yimsha to fight the wizards. Will you go with us, or stay here to be flayed by the Afghulis who are following this man?"

They looked at him with eyes grimly fatalistic. They were doomed and they knew it – had known it ever since the singing arrows of the ambushed Dagozai had driven them back from the pass of Shalizah. The men of the lower Zhaibar had too many reeking blood-feuds among the crag-dwellers. They were too small a band to fight their way back through the hills to the villages of the border, without the guidance of the crafty Turanian. They counted themselves as dead already, so they made the reply that only dead men would make: "We will go with thee and die on Yimsha."

"Then in Crom's name let us begone," grunted Conan, fidgeting with impatience as he stared into the blue gulfs of the deepening twilight. "My wolves were hours behind me, but we've lost a devilish lot of time."

Kerim Shah backed his steed from between the black stallion and the cliff, sheathed his sword and cautiously turned the horse. Presently the band was filing up the path as swiftly as they dared. They came out upon the crest nearly a mile east of the spot where Khemsa had halted the Cimmerian and the Devi. The path they had traversed was a perilous one, even for hillmen, and for that reason Conan had avoided it that day when carrying Yasmina, though Kerim Shah, following him, had taken it supposing the Cimmerian had done likewise. Even Conan sighed with relief when the horses scrambled up over the last rim. They moved like phantom riders through an enchanted realm of shadows. The soft creak of leather, the clink of steel marked their passing, then again the dark mountain slopes lay naked and silent in the starlight.

VIII

Yasmina Knows Stark Terror

Yasmina had time but for one scream when she felt herself enveloped in that crimson whorl and torn from her protector with appalling force. She screamed once, and then she had no breath to scream. She was blinded, deafened, rendered mute and eventually senseless by the terrific rushing of the air about her. There was a dazed consciousness of dizzy height and numbing speed, a confused impression of natural sensations gone mad, and then vertigo and oblivion.

A vestige of these sensations clung to her as she recovered consciousness so she cried out and clutched wildly as though to stay a headlong and involuntary flight. Her fingers closed on soft fabric and a relieving sense of stability pervaded her. She took cognizance of her surroundings.

She was lying on a dais covered with black velvet. This dais stood in a great, dim room whose walls were hung with dusky tapestries across which crawled dragons reproduced with repellant realism. Floating shadows merely hinted at the lofty ceiling, and gloom that lent itself to illusion lurked in the corners. There seemed to be neither windows nor doors in the walls, or else they were concealed by the nighted tapestries. Where the dim light came from, Yasmina could not determine. The great room was a realm of mysteries, of shadows, and shadowy shapes in which she could not have sworn to observe movement, yet which invaded her mind with a dim and formless terror.

But her gaze fixed itself on a tangible object. On another, smaller dais of jet, a few feet away, a man sat cross-legged, gazing contemplatively at her. His long black velvet robe, embroidered with gold thread, fell loosely about him, masking his figure. His hands were folded in his sleeves. There was a velvet cap upon his head. His face was calm, placid, not unhandsome, his eyes lambent and slightly oblique. He did not move a muscle as he sat regarding her, nor did his expression alter when he saw she was conscious.

Yasmina felt fear crawl like a trickle of ice water down her supple spine. She lifted herself on her elbows and stared apprehensively at the stranger.

"Who are you?" she demanded; her voice sounded brittle and inadequate.

"I am the Master of Yimsha." The tone was rich and resonant, like the mellow notes of a temple bell.

"Why did you bring me here?" she demanded.

"Were you not seeking me?"

"If you are one of the Black Seers – yes!" she answered recklessly, believing that he could read her thoughts anyway.

He laughed softly and chills crawled up and down her spine again.

"You would turn the wild children of the hills against the Seers of Yimsha!" he smiled. "I have read it in your mind, princess. Your weak, human mind, filled with petty dreams of hate and revenge."

"You slew my brother!" A rising tide of anger was vying with her fear; her hands were clenched, her lithe body rigid. "Why did you persecute him? He never harmed you. The priests say the Seers are above meddling in human affairs. Why did you destroy the king of Vendhya?"

"How can an ordinary human understand the motives of a Seer?" returned the Master equably. "My acolytes in the temples of Turan, who are the priests behind the priests of Tarim, urged me to bestir myself in behalf of Yezdigerd. For reasons of my own, I complied. How can I explain my mystic reasons to your puny intellect? You could not understand."

"I understand this: that my brother died!" Tears of grief and rage shook in her voice. She rose upon her knees and stared at him with wide blazing eyes, as supple and dangerous as a she-panther in that moment.

"As Yezdigerd desired," agreed the Master calmly. "For awhile it was my whim to further his ambitions."

"Is Yezdigerd your vassal?" Yasmina tried to keep the timbre of her voice unaltered. She had felt her knee pressing something hard and symmetrical under a fold of velvet. Subtly she shifted her position, moving her hand under the fold.

"Is the dog that licks up the offal in the temple yard the vassal of the god?" returned the Master. He did not seem to notice the actions she sought to dissemble. Concealed by the velvet, her fingers closed on what she knew was the golden hilt of a dagger. She bent her head to hide the light of triumph in her eyes.

"I am weary of Yezdigerd," said the Master. "I have turned to other amusements – ha!"

With a fierce cry Yasmina sprang like a jungle cat, stabbing murderously. Then she stumbled and slid to the floor, where she cowered staring up at the man on the dais. He had not moved; his cryptic smile was unchanged. Tremblingly she lifted her hand and stared at it with dilated eyes. There was no dagger in her fingers; they grasped a stalk of golden lotus, the crushed blossoms drooping on the bruised stem.

She dropped it as if it had been a viper, and scrambled away from the proximity of her tormentor. She returned to her own dais, because that was at least more dignified for a queen than grovelling on the floor at the feet of a sorcerer, and eyed him apprehensively, expecting reprisals.

But the Master made no move.

"All substance is one to him who holds the key of the cosmos," he said cryptically. "To an adept nothing is immutable. At will steel blossoms bloom in unnamed gardens, or flower-swords flash in the moonlight."

"You are a devil," she sobbed.

"Not I!" he laughed. "I was born on this planet, long ago. Once I was a common man, nor have I lost all human attributes in the numberless eons of my adept-ship. A human steeped in the dark arts is greater than a devil. I am of human origin, but I rule demons. You have seen the Lords of the Black Circle – it would blast your soul to hear from what far realm I summoned them and from what doom I guard them with ensorcelled crystal and golden serpents.

"But only I can rule them. My foolish Khemsa thought to make himself great – poor fool, bursting material doors and hurtling himself and his mistress through the air from hill to hill! Yet if he had not been destroyed his power might have grown to rival mine."

He laughed again. "And you, poor, silly thing! Plotting to send a hairy hill chief to storm Yimsha! It was such a jest that I myself could have designed, had it occurred to me, that you should fall in his hands. And I read in your childish mind an intention to seduce by your feminine wiles to attempt your purpose, anyway.

"But for all your stupidity, you are a woman fair to look upon. It is my whim to keep you for my slave."

The daughter of a thousand proud emperors gasped with shame and fury at the word.

"You dare not!"

His mocking laughter cut her like a whip across her naked shoulders.

"The king dares not trample a worm in the road! Little fool, do you not realize that your royal pride is no more to me than a straw blown on the

wind? I, who have known the kisses of the queens of Hell! You have seen how
I deal with a rebel!"

Cowed and awed, the girl crouched on the velvet-covered dais. The light
grew dimmer and more phantom-like. The features of the Master became
shadowy. His voice took on a newer tone of command.

"I will never yield to you!" Her voice trembled with fear but it carried
a ring of resolution.

"You will yield," he answered with horrible conviction. "Fear and pain
shall teach you. I will lash you with horror and agony to the last quivering
ounce of your endurance, until you become as melted wax to be bent and
molded in my hands as I desire. You shall know such discipline as no mortal
woman ever knew, until my slightest command is to you as the unalterable
will of the gods. And first, to humble your pride, you shall travel back through
the lost ages, and view all the shapes that have been you. *Aie, yil la khosa!*"

At these words the shadowy room swam before Yasmina's affrighted
gaze. The roots of her hair prickled her scalp, and her tongue clove to her
palate. Somewhere a gong sounded a deep, ominous note. The dragons on the
tapestries glowed like blue fire, and then faded out. The Master on his dais
was but a shapeless shadow. The dim light gave way to soft, thick darkness,
almost tangible, that pulsed with strange radiations. She could no longer see
the Master. She could see nothing. She had a strange sensation that the walls
and ceiling had withdrawn immensely from her.

Then somewhere in the darkness a glow began, like a firefly that
rhythmically dimmed and quickened. It grew to a golden ball, and as it
expanded its light grew more intense, flaming whitely. It burst suddenly,
showering the darkness with white sparks that did not illumine the shadows.
But like an impression left in the gloom, a faint luminance remained, and
revealed a slender dusky shaft shooting up from the shadowy floor. Under
the girl's dilated gaze it spread, took shape; stems and broad leaves appeared,
and great black poisonous blossoms that towered above her as she cringed
against the velvet. A subtle perfume pervaded the atmosphere. It was the
dread figure of the black lotus that had grown up as she watched, as it grows
in the haunted, forbidden jungles of Khitai.

The broad leaves were murmurous with evil life. The blossoms bent
toward her like sentient things, nodding serpent-like on pliant stems.
Etched against soft, impenetrable darkness it loomed over her, gigantic,
blackly visible in some mad way. Her brain reeled with the drugging scent
and she sought to crawl from the dais. Then she clung to it as it seemed to
be pitching at an impossible slant. She cried out with terror and clung to the
velvet, but she felt her fingers ruthlessly torn away. There was a sensation as
of all sanity and stability crumbling and vanishing. She was a quivering atom

of sentiency driven through a black, roaring, icy void by a thundering wind that threatened to extinguish her feeble flicker of animate life like a candle blown out in a storm.

Then there came a period of blind impulse and movement, when the atom that was she mingled and merged with myriad other atoms of spawning life in the yeasty morass of existence, molded by formative forces until she emerged again a conscious individual, whirling down an endless spiral of lives.

In a mist of terror she relived all her former existences, recognized and *was* again all the bodies that had carried her ego throughout the changing ages. She bruised her feet again over the long, long weary road of life that stretched out behind her into the immemorial Past. Back beyond the dimmest dawns of Time she crouched shuddering in primordial jungles, hunted by slavering beasts of prey. Skin-clad, she waded thigh-deep in rice-swamps, battling with squawking water-fowl for the precious grains. She labored with the oxen to drag the pointed stick through the stubborn soil, and she crouched endlessly over looms in peasant huts.

She saw walled cities burst into flame, and fled screaming before the slayers. She reeled naked and bleeding over burning sands, dragged at the slaver's stirrup, and she knew the grip of hot, fierce hands on her writhing flesh, the shame and agony of brutal lust. She screamed under the bite of the lash, and moaned on the rack; mad with terror she fought against the hands that forced her head inexorably down on the bloody block.

She knew the agonies of child-birth, and the bitterness of love betrayed. She suffered all the woes and wrongs and brutalities that man has inflicted on woman throughout the eons; and she endured all the spite and malice of woman for woman. And like the flick of a fiery whip throughout was the consciousness she retained of her Devi-ship. She was all the women she had ever been, yet in her knowing she was Yasmina. This consciousness was not lost in the throes of reincarnation. At one and the same time she was a naked slave wench grovelling under the whip, and the proud Devi of Vendhya. And she suffered not only as the slave girl suffered, but as Yasmina, to whose pride the whip was like a white hot brand.

Life merged into life in flying chaos, each with its burden of woe and shame and agony, until she dimly heard her own voice screaming unbearably, like one long-drawn cry of suffering echoing down the ages.

Then she awakened on the velvet-covered dais in the mystic room.

In a ghostly grey light she saw again the dais and the cryptic robed figure seated upon it. The hooded head was bent, the high shoulders faintly etched against the uncertain dimness. She could make out no details clearly, but the hood, where the velvet cap had been, stirred a formless uneasiness in her. As she stared, there stole over her a nameless fear that froze her tongue to her palate – a feeling that it was not the Master who sat so silently on that black dais.

Then the figure moved and rose upright, towering above her. It stooped over her and the long arms in their wide black sleeves bent about her. She fought against them in speechless fright, surprized by their lean hardness. The hooded head bent down toward her averted face. And she screamed, and screamed again in poignant fear and loathing. Bony arms gripped her lithe body, and from that hood looked forth a countenance of death and decay – features like rotting parchment on a moldering skull. She screamed again, and then, as those champing, grinning jaws bent toward her lips, she lost consciousness.

IX

THE CASTLE OF THE WIZARDS

The sun had risen over the white Himelian peaks. At the foot of a long slope a group of horsemen halted and stared upward. High above them a stone tower poised on the pitch of the mountain side. Beyond and above that gleamed the walls of a greater keep, near the line where the snow began that capped Yimsha's pinnacle. There was a touch of unreality about the whole – purple slopes pitching up to that fantastic castle, toy-like with distance, and above it the white glistening peak shouldering the cold blue.

"We'll leave the horses here," grunted Conan. "That treacherous slope is safer for a man on foot. Besides, they're done."

He swung down from the black stallion which stood with wide-braced legs and drooping head. They had pushed hard throughout the night, gnawing at scraps from saddle bags, and pausing only to give the horses the rests they had to have.

"That first tower is held by the acolytes of the Black Seers," said Conan. "Or so men say; watch dogs for their masters – lesser sorcerers. They won't sit sucking their thumbs as we climb this slope."

Kerim Shah glanced up the mountain, then back the way they had come; they were already far up on Yimsha's side, and a vast expanse of lesser peaks and crags spread out beneath them. Among those labyrinths the Turanian sought in vain for a movement of color that would betray men. Evidently the pursuing Afghulis had lost their chief's trail in the night.

"Let us go, then." They tied the weary horses in a clump of tamarisk and without further comment turned up the slope. There was no cover. It was a naked incline, strewn with boulders not big enough to conceal a man. But they did conceal something else.

The party had not gone fifty steps when a snarling shape burst from behind a rock. It was one of the gaunt savage dogs that infested the hill villages, and its eyes glared redly, its jaws dripped foam. Conan was leading, but it did not attack him. It dashed past him and leaped at Kerim Shah. The Turanian leaped aside, and the great dog flung itself upon the Irakzai behind him. The man yelled and threw up his arm, which was torn by the brute's fangs as it bore him backward, and the next instant half a dozen tulwars were hacking at the beast. Yet not until it was literally dismembered did the hideous creature cease its efforts to seize and rend its attackers.

Kerim Shah bound up the wounded warrior's gashed arm, looked at him narrowly, and then turned away without a word. He rejoined Conan and they renewed the climb in silence.

Presently Kerim Shah said: "Strange to find a village dog in this place."

"There's no offal here," grunted Conan. Both turned their heads to glance back at the wounded warrior toiling after them among his companions. Sweat glistened on his dark face and his lips were drawn back from his teeth in a grimace of pain. Then both looked again at the stone tower squatting above them.

A slumberous quiet lay over the uplands. The tower showed no sign of life, nor did the strange pyramidal structure beyond it. But the men who toiled upward went with the tenseness of men walking on the edge of a crater. Kerim Shah had unslung the powerful Turanian bow that killed at five hundred paces, and the Irakzai looked to their own lighter and less lethal bows.

But they were not within bow-shot of the tower when something shot down out of the sky without warning. It passed so close to Conan that he felt the wind of the rushing wings, but it was an Irakzai who staggered and fell, blood jetting from a severed jugular. A hawk with wings like burnished steel shot up again, blood dripping from the scimitar-beak, to reel against the sky as Kerim Shah's bow-string twanged. It dropped like a plummet, but no man saw where it struck the earth.

Conan bent over the victim of the attack, but the man was already dead. No one spoke; useless to comment on the fact that never before had a hawk been known to swoop on a man. Red rage began to vie with fatalistic lethargy in the wild souls of the Irakzai. Hairy fingers nocked arrows and men glared vengefully at the tower whose very silence mocked them.

But the next attack came swiftly and direct. They all saw it – a white puff-ball of smoke that tumbled over the tower-rim and came drifting and rolling down the slope toward them. Others followed it. They seemed harmless, mere woolly globes of cloudy foam, but Conan stepped aside to avoid contact with the first. Behind him one of the Irakzai reached out and thrust his sword into the unstable mass. Instantly a sharp report shook the mountain-side. There was a burst of blinding flame, and then the puff-ball had vanished, and of the too-curious warrior remained only a heap of charred and blackened bones. The crisped hand still gripped the ivory sword hilt, but the blade was gone – melted and destroyed by that awful heat. Yet men standing almost within reach of the victim had not suffered except to be dazzled and half-blinded by the sudden flare.

"Steel touches it off," grunted Conan. "Look out – here they come!"

The slope above them was almost covered by the billowing spheres. Kerim Shah bent his bow and sent a shaft into the mass, and those touched by the arrow burst like bubbles in spurting flame. His men followed his example and for the next few minutes it was as if a thunderstorm raged on the mountain slope, with bolts of lightning striking and bursting in showers of flame. When the barrage ceased, only a few arrows were left in the quivers of the archers.

They pushed on grimly, over soil charred and blackened, where the naked rock had in places been turned to lava by the explosion of those diabolical bombs.

Now they were within easy arrow-flight of the silent tower, and they spread their line, nerves taut, ready for any horror that might descend upon them.

On the tower appeared a single figure, lifting a ten-foot bronze horn. Its strident bellow roared out across the echoing slopes, like the blare of trumpets on Judgment Day. And it began to be fearfully answered. The ground trembled under the feet of the invaders, and rumblings and grindings welled up from subterranean depths.

The Irakzai screamed, reeling like drunken men on the shuddering slope, and Conan, eyes glaring, charged recklessly up the incline, knife in hand, straight at the door that showed in the tower-wall. Above him the great horn roared and bellowed in brutish mockery. And then Kerim Shah drew a shaft to his ear and loosed.

Only a Turanian could have made that shot. The bellowing of the horn ceased suddenly, and a high, thin scream shrilled in its place. The green-robed figure on the tower staggered, clutching at the long shaft which quivered in its bosom, and then pitched across the parapet. The great horn tumbled upon the battlement and hung precariously, and another robed figure rushed to seize it, shrieking in horror. Again the Turanian bow twanged, and again it was answered by a death-howl. The second acolyte, in falling, struck the horn with his elbow and knocked it clatteringly over the parapet to land shatteringly on the rocks far below.

At such headlong speed had Conan covered the ground, that before the clattering echoes of that fall had died away, he was hacking at the door. Warned by his savage instinct suddenly, he gave back as a tide of molten lead splashed down from above. But the next instant he was back again, attacking the panels with redoubled fury. He was galvanized by the fact that his enemies had resorted to earthly weapons. The sorcery of the acolytes was limited. Their necromantic resources might well be exhausted. Kerim Shah was hurrying up the slope, his hillmen behind him in a straggling crescent. They loosed as they ran, their arrows splintering against the walls or arching over the parapet.

The heavy teak portal gave way beneath the Cimmerian's assault, and he peered inside warily, expecting anything. He was looking into a circular chamber from which a stair wound upward. On the opposite side of the chamber a door gaped open, revealing the outer slope – and the backs of half a dozen green-robed figures in full retreat.

Conan yelled, took a step into the tower, and then native caution jerked him back, just as a great block of stone fell crashing to the floor where his foot had been an instant before. Shouting to his followers he raced around the tower.

The acolytes had evacuated their first line of defense. As Conan rounded the tower he saw their green robes twinkling up the mountain ahead of him. He gave chase, panting with earnest blood-lust, and behind him Kerim Shah and the Irakzai came pelting, the latter yelling like wolves at the flight of their enemies, their fatalism momentarily submerged by temporary triumph.

The tower stood on the lower edge of a narrow plateau whose upward slant was barely perceptible. A few hundred yards away this plateau ended abruptly in a chasm which had been invisible further down the mountain. Into this chasm the acolytes apparently leaped without checking their speed. Their pursuers saw the green robes flutter and disappear over the edge.

A few moments later they themselves were standing on the brink of the mighty moat that cut them off from the castle of the Black Seers. It was a sheer-walled ravine that extended in either direction as far as they could see, apparently girdling the mountain, some four hundred yards in width and five hundred feet deep. And in it, from rim to rim, a strange, translucent mist sparkled and shimmered.

Looking down, Conan grunted. Far below him, moving across the glimmering floor, which shone like burnished silver, he saw the forms of the green-robed acolytes. Their outline was wavering and indistinct, like figures seen under deep water. They walked single file, moving toward the opposite wall.

Kerim Shah nocked an arrow and sent it singing downward. But when it struck the mist that filled the chasm it seemed to lose momentum and direction, wandering widely from its course.

"If they went down, so can we!" grunted Conan, while Kerim Shah stared after his shaft in amazement. "I saw them last at this spot – "

Squinting down he saw something shining like a golden thread across the canyon floor far below. The acolytes seemed to be following this thread, and there suddenly came to him Khemsa's cryptic words – "Follow the golden vein!" On the brink, under his very hand as he crouched, he found it – a thin vein of sparkling gold running from an outcropping of ore to the edge and down, across the silvery floor. And he found something else, which had before been invisible to him, because of the peculiar refraction of the light. The gold vein followed a narrow ramp which slanted down into the ravine, fitted with niches for hand and foot hold.

"Here's where they went down," he grunted to Kerim Shah. "They're no adepts, to waft themselves through the air! We'll follow them –"

It was at that instant that the man who had been bitten by the mad dog cried out horribly and leaped at Kerim Shah, foaming and gnashing his teeth. The Turanian, quick as a cat on his feet, sprang aside and the madman pitched head-first over the brink. The others rushed to the edge and glared after him in amazement. The maniac did not fall plummet-like. He floated slowly down through the rosy haze like a man sinking in deep water. His limbs moved like a man trying to swim, and his features were purple and convulsed beyond the contortions of his madness. Far down at last on the shining floor his body settled and lay still.

"There's death in that chasm," muttered Kerim Shah, drawing back from the rosy mist that shimmered almost at his feet. "What now, Conan?"

"On!" answered the Cimmerian grimly. "Those acolytes are human; if the mist doesn't kill them, it won't kill me." He hitched his belt, and his hands touched the girdle Khemsa had given him; he scowled, then smiled bleakly. He had forgotten that girdle; yet thrice had death passed him by to strike another victim.

The acolytes had reached the further wall and were moving up it like great green flies. Letting himself upon the ramp he descended warily. The rosy cloud lapped about his ankles, ascending as he lowered himself. It reached his knees, his thighs, his waist, his arm-pits. He felt it as one feels a thick heavy fog on a damp night. With it lapping about his chin he hesitated, and then ducked under. Instantly his breath ceased; all air was shut off from him and he felt his ribs caving in on his vitals. With a frantic effort he heaved himself up, fighting for life. His head rose above the surface and he drank air in great gulps.

Kerim Shah leaned down toward him, spoke to him, but Conan neither heard nor heeded. Stubbornly, his mind fixed on what the dying Khemsa had told him, the Cimmerian groped for the gold vein, and found that he had moved off it in his descent. Several series of hand-holds were niched in the ramp. Placing himself directly over the thread, he began climbing down once more. The rosy mist rose about him, engulfed him. Now his head was under, but he was still drinking pure air. Above him he saw his companions staring down at him, their features blurred by the haze that shimmered over his head. He gestured for them to follow, and went down swiftly, without waiting to see whether they complied or not.

Kerim Shah sheathed his sword without comment and followed, and the Irakzai, more fearful of being left alone than of the terrors that might lurk below, scrambled after him. Each man clung to the golden thread as they saw the Cimmerian do.

Down the slanting ramp they went to the ravine floor, and moved out across the shining level, treading the gold vein like rope walkers. It was as if they walked along an invisible tunnel through which air circulated freely. They felt death pressing in on them above and on either hand, but it did not touch them.

The vein crawled up a similar ramp on the other wall up which the acolytes had disappeared, and up it they went with taut nerves, not knowing what might be waiting for them among the jutting spurs of rock that fanged the lip of the precipice.

It was the green-robed acolytes who awaited them, with knives in their hands. Perhaps they had reached the limits to which they could retreat. Perhaps the Stygian girdle about Conan's waist could have told why their necromantic spells had proven so weak and so quickly exhausted. Perhaps it was knowledge of death decreed for failure that sent them leaping from among the rocks, eyes glaring and knives glittering, resorting in their desperation to material weapons.

There among the rocky fangs on the precipice lip was no war of wizard craft. It was a whirl of blades, where real steel bit and real blood spurted, where sinewy arms dealt forthright blows that severed quivering flesh, and men went down to be trodden under foot as the fight raged over them.

One of the Irakzai bled to death among the rocks, but the acolytes were down — slashed and hacked asunder or hurled over the edge to float sluggishly down to the silver floor that shone so far below.

Then the conquerors shook blood and sweat from their eyes, and looked at each other. Conan and Kerim Shah still stood upright, and four of the Irakzai.

They stood among the rocky teeth that serrated the precipice brink and from that spot a path wound up a gentle slope to a broad stair, consisting of half a dozen steps, a hundred feet across, cut out of a green jade-like substance. They led up to a broad stage or roofless gallery of the same polished stone, and above it rose, tier upon tier, the castle of the Black Seers. It seemed to have been carved out of the sheer stone of the mountain. The architecture was faultless, but unadorned. The many casements were barred and masked with curtains within. There was no sign of life, friendly or hostile.

They went up the path in silence, and warily as men treading the lair of a serpent. The Irakzai were dumb, like men marching to a certain doom. Even Kerim Shah was silent. Only Conan seemed not aware what a monstrous dislocating and uprooting of accepted thought and action their invasion constituted, what an unprecedented violation of tradition. He was not of the East; and he came of a breed who fought devils and wizards as promptly and matter-of-factly as they battled human foes.

He strode up the shining stairs and across the wide green gallery straight toward the great golden-bound teak door that opened upon it. He cast but a single glance upward at the higher tiers of the great pyramidal structure towering above him. He reached a hand for the bronze prong that jutted like a handle from the door — then checked himself, grinning hardly. The handle was made in the shape of a serpent, head lifted on arched neck; and Conan had a suspicion that that metal head would come to grisly life under his hand.

He struck it from the door with one blow, and its bronze clink on the glassy floor did not lessen his caution. He flipped it aside with his knife point, and again turned to the door. Utter silence reigned over the towers. Far below them the mountain slopes fell away into a purple haze of distance. The sun glittered on snow-clad peaks on either hand. High above a vulture hung like a black dot in the cold blue of the sky. But for it the men before the gold-bound door were the only evidence of life, tiny figures on a green jade gallery poised on the dizzy height, with that fantastic pile of stone towering above them.

A sharp wind off the snow slashed them, whipping their tatters about. Conan's long knife splintering through the teak panels roused the startled echoes. Again and again he struck, hewing through polished wood and metal bands alike. Through the sundered ruins he glared into the interior, alert and suspicious as a wolf. He saw a broad chamber, the polished stone walls untapestried, the mosaic floor uncarpeted. Square, polished ebon stools and a stone dais formed the only furnishings. The room was empty of human life. Another door showed in the opposite wall.

"Leave a man on guard outside," grunted Conan. "I'm going in."

Kerim Shah designated a warrior for that duty, and the man fell back toward the middle of the gallery, bow in hand. Conan strode into the castle, followed by the Turanian and the three remaining Irakzai. The one outside spat, grumbled in his beard, and started suddenly as a low mocking laugh reached his ears.

He lifted his head and saw, on the tier above him, a tall, black-robed figure, naked head nodding slightly as he stared down. His whole attitude suggested mockery and malignity. Quick as a flash the Irakzai bent his bow and loosed, and the arrow streaked upward to strike full in the black-robed breast. The mocking smile did not alter. The Seer plucked out the missile and threw it back at the bowman, not as a weapon is hurled, but with a contemptuous gesture. The Irakzai dodged, instinctively throwing up his arm. His fingers closed on the revolving shaft.

Then he shrieked. In his hand the wooden shaft suddenly *writhed*. Its rigid outline became pliant, melting in his grasp. He tried to throw it from him, but it was too late. He held a twisting serpent in his naked hand and already it had coiled about his wrist and its wicked wedge-shaped head darted at his muscular arm. He screamed again and his eyes became distended, his features purple. He went to his knees shaken by an awful convulsion, and then lay still.

The men inside had wheeled at his first cry. Conan took a swift stride toward the open doorway, and then halted short, baffled. To the men behind him it seemed that he strained against empty air. But though he could see nothing, there was a slick, smooth, hard surface under his hands, and he knew that a sheet of crystal had been let down in the doorway. Through it he saw the Irakzai lying motionless on the glassy gallery, an ordinary arrow sticking in his arm. Naturally, he could not see the man on the tier below.

Conan lifted his knife and smote, and the watchers were dumbfounded to see his blow checked apparently in mid-air, with the loud clang of steel that meets an unyielding substance. He wasted no more effort. He knew that not even the legendary tulwar of Amir Khurum could shatter that invisible curtain.

In a few words he explained the matter to Kerim Shah, and the Turanian shrugged his shoulders. "Well, if our exit is barred, we must find another. In the meanwhile our way lies forward, does it not?"

With a grunt the Cimmerian turned and strode across the chamber to the opposite door, with a feeling of treading on the threshold of doom. As he lifted his knife to shatter the door, it swung silently open as if of its own accord. He strode into a great hall, flanked with tall glassy columns. A hundred feet from the door began the broad jade-green steps of a stair that tapered toward the top like the side of a pyramid. What lay beyond that stair he could not tell. But between him and its shimmering foot stood a curious altar of gleaming black jade. Four great golden serpents twined their tails about this altar and reared their wedge-shaped heads in the air, facing the four quarters of the compass like the enchanted guardians of a fabled treasure. But on the altar, between the arching necks, stood only a crystal globe filled with a cloudy smoke-like substance, in which floated four golden pomegranates.

The sight stirred some dim recollection in his mind; then Conan heeded the altar no longer, for on the lower steps of the stair stood four black-robed figures. He had not seen them come. They were simply there, tall, gaunt, their vulture-heads nodding in unison, their feet and hands hidden by their flowing garments.

One lifted his arm and the sleeve fell away revealing his hand – and it was not a hand at all. Conan halted in mid-stride, compelled against his will. He had encountered a force differing subtly from Khemsa's mesmerism, and he could not advance, though he felt it in his power to retreat if he wished. His companions had likewise halted, and they seemed even more helpless than he, unable to move in either direction.

The Seer whose arm was lifted beckoned to one of the Irakzai, and the man moved toward him like one in a trance, eyes staring and fixed, blade hanging in limp fingers. As he pushed past Conan, the Cimmerian threw an arm across his breast to arrest him. Conan was so much stronger than the Irakzai that in ordinary circumstances he could have broken his spine between his hands. But now the muscular arm was brushed aside like a straw and the Irakzai moved toward the stair, treading jerkily and mechanically. He reached the steps and knelt stiffly, proffering his blade and bending his head. The Seer took the sword. It flashed as he swung it up and down. The Irakzai's head tumbled from his shoulders and thudded heavily on the black marble floor. An arch of blood jetted from the severed arteries and the body slumped over and lay with arms spread wide.

Again a malformed hand lifted and beckoned, and another Irakzai stumbled stiffly to his doom. The ghastly drama was re-enacted and another headless form lay beside the first.

As the third tribesman clumped his way past Conan to his death, the Cimmerian, his veins bulging in his temples with his efforts to break past the unseen barrier that held him, was suddenly aware of allied forces, unseen, but waking into life about him. This realization came without warning, but so powerfully he could not doubt his instinct. His left hand slid involuntarily under his Bakhariot belt and closed on the Stygian girdle. And as he gripped it he felt new strength and power flood his numbed limbs; the will to live was a pulsing white-hot fire, matched by the intensity of his burning rage.

The third Irakzai was a decapitated corpse, and the hideous finger was lifting again when Conan felt the bursting of the invisible barrier. A fierce, involuntary cry burst from his lips as he leaped with the explosive suddenness of pent-up ferocity. His left hand gripped the sorcerer's girdle as a drowning man grips a floating log, and the long knife was a sheen of light in his right. The men on the steps did not move. They watched calmly, cynically; if they felt surprize they did not show it. Conan did not allow himself to think what might chance when he came within knife-reach of them. His blood was pounding in his temples, a mist of crimson swam before his sight. He was afire with the urge to kill – to drive his knife deep into flesh and bone, and twist the blade in blood and entrails.

Another dozen strides would carry him to the steps where the sneering demons stood. He drew his breath deep, his fury rising redly as his charge gathered momentum. He was hurtling past the altar with its golden serpents when like a levin-flash there shot across his mind again as vividly as if spoken in his external ear, the cryptic words of Khemsa: *"Break the crystal ball!"*

His reaction was almost without his own volition. Execution followed impulse so spontaneously that the greatest sorcerer of the age would not have had time to read his mind and prevent his action. Wheeling like a cat from his headlong charge, he brought his knife crashing down upon the crystal. Instantly the air vibrated with a peal of terror – whether from the stairs, the altar, or the crystal itself he could not tell. Hisses filled his ears as the golden serpents, suddenly vibrant with hideous life, writhed and smote at him. But he was fired to the speed of a maddened tiger. A whirl of steel sheared through the hideous trunks that waved toward him, and he smote the crystal sphere again and yet again. And the globe burst with a noise like a thunder-clap, raining fiery shards on the black marble, and the gold pomegranates, as if released from captivity, shot upward toward the lofty roof and were gone.

A mad screaming, bestial and ghastly, was echoing through the great hall. On the steps writhed four black-robed figures, twisting in convulsions, froth dripping from their livid mouths. Then with one frenzied crescendo of inhuman ululation they stiffened and lay still, and Conan knew they were dead. He stared down at the altar and the crystal shards. Four headless golden serpents still coiled about the altar, but no alien life now animated the dully gleaming metal.

Kerim Shah was rising slowly from his knees whither he had been dashed by some unseen force. He shook his head to clear the ringing from his ears.

"Did you hear that crash when you struck? It was as if a thousand crystal panels shattered all over the castle as that globe burst. Were the souls of the wizards imprisoned in those golden balls? – Ha!"

Conan wheeled as Kerim Shah drew his sword and pointed.

Another figure stood at the head of the stair. His robe, too, was black, but of richly embroidered velvet, and there was a velvet cap on his head. His face was calm, and not unhandsome.

"Who the devil are you?" demanded Conan, staring up at him, knife in hand.

"I am the Master of Yimsha!" His voice was like the chime of a temple bell, but a note of cruel mirth ran through it.

"Where is Yasmina?" demanded Kerim Shah.

The Master laughed down at him.

"What is that to you, dead man? Have you so quickly forgotten my strength, once lent to you, that you come armed against me, you poor fool? I think I will take your heart, Kerim Shah!"

He held out his hand as if to receive something, and the Turanian cried out sharply like a man in mortal agony. He reeled drunkenly, and then, with a splintering of bones, a rending of flesh and muscle and a snapping of mail-links, his breast *burst* outward with a shower of blood, and through the ghastly aperture something red and dripping shot through the air into the Master's outstretched hand, as a bit of steel leaps to the magnet. The Turanian slumped to the floor and lay motionless, and the Master laughed and hurled the object to fall before Conan's feet – a still quivering human heart.

With a roar and a curse Conan charged the stair. From Khemsa's girdle he felt strength and deathless hate flow into him to combat the terrible emanation of power that met him on the steps. The air filled with a shimmering steely haze through which he plunged like a swimmer through surf, head lowered, left arm bent about his face, knife gripped low in his right hand. His half-blinded eyes, glaring over the crook of his elbow, made out the hated shape of the Seer before and above him, the outline wavering as a reflection wavers in disturbed water.

He was racked and torn by forces beyond his comprehension, but he felt a driving power outside and beyond his own lifting him inexorably upward and onward, despite the wizard's strength and his own agony.

Now he had reached the head of the stairs, and the Master's face floated in the steely haze before him, and a strange fear shadowed the inscrutable eyes. Conan waded through the mist as through a surf, and his knife lunged upward like a live thing. The keen point ripped the Master's robe as he sprang back with a low cry. Then before Conan's gaze the wizard vanished – simply disappeared like a burst bubble, and something long and undulating darted up one of the smaller stairs that led up to left and right from the landing.

Conan charged after it, up the left-hand stair, uncertain as to just what he had seen whip up those steps, but in a berserk mood that drowned the nausea and horror whispering at the back of his consciousness.

He plunged out into a broad corridor whose uncarpeted floor and untapestried walls were of polished jade, and something long and swift whisked down the corridor ahead of him, and into a curtained door. From within the chamber rose a scream of urgent terror. The sound lent wings to Conan's flying feet and he hurtled through the curtains and headlong into the chamber within.

A frightful scene met his glare. Yasmina cowered on the further edge of a velvet covered dais, screaming her loathing and horror, an arm lifted as if to ward off attack, while before her swayed the hideous head of a giant serpent, shining neck arching up from dark gleaming coils. With a choked cry Conan threw his knife.

Instantly the monster whirled and was upon him like the rush of wind through tall grass. The long knife quivered in its neck, point and a foot of blade showing on one side, and the hilt and a hand's breadth of steel on the other, but it only seemed to madden the giant reptile. The great head towered above the man who faced it, and then darted down, the venom-dripping jaws gaping wide. But Conan had plucked a dagger from his girdle and he stabbed upward as the head dipped down. The point tore through the lower jaw and transfixed the upper, pinning them together. The next instant the great trunk had looped itself about the Cimmerian as the snake, unable to use its fangs, employed its remaining form of attack.

Conan's left arm was pinioned among the bone-crushing folds, but his right was free. Bracing his feet to keep upright, he stretched forth his hand, gripped the hilt of the long knife jutting from the serpent's neck, and tore it free in a shower of blood. As if divining his purpose with more than bestial intelligence, the snake writhed and knotted, seeking to cast its loops about his right arm. But with the speed of light the long knife rose and fell, shearing half-way through the reptile's giant trunk.

Before he could strike again, the great pliant loops fell from him and the monster dragged itself across the floor, gushing blood from its ghastly wounds. Conan sprang after it, knife lifted, but his vicious swipe cut empty air as the serpent writhed away from him and struck its blunt nose against a panelled screen of sandalwood. One of the panels gave inward and the long, bleeding barrel whipped through it and was gone.

Conan instantly attacked the screen. A few blows rent it apart and he glared into the dim alcove beyond. No horrific shape coiled there; there was blood on the marble floor, and bloody tracks led to a cryptic arched door. Those tracks were of a man's bare feet –

"Conan!" He wheeled back into the chamber just in time to catch the Devi of Vendhya in his arms as she rushed across the room and threw herself upon him, catching him about the neck with a frantic clasp, half hysterical with terror and gratitude and relief.

His own wild blood had been stirred to its uttermost by all that had passed. He caught her to him in a grasp that would have made her wince at another time, and crushed her lips with his. She made no resistance; the Devi was drowned in the elemental woman. She closed her eyes and drank in his fierce, hot, lawless kisses with all the abandon of passionate thirst. She was panting with his violence when he ceased for breath, and glared down at her lying limp in his mighty arms.

"I knew you'd come for me," she murmured. "You would not leave me in this den of devils."

At her words recollection of their environments came to him suddenly. He lifted his head and listened intently. Silence reigned over the castle of Yimsha, but it was a silence impregnated with menace. Peril crouched in every corner, leered invisibly from every hanging.

"We'd better go while we can," he muttered. "Those cuts were enough to kill any common beast – or *man* – but a wizard has a dozen lives. Wound one, and he writhes away like a crippled snake to soak up fresh venom from some source of sorcery."

He picked up the girl and carrying her in his arms like a child, he strode out into the gleaming jade corridor and down the stairs, nerves tautly alert for any sign or sound.

"I met the Master," she whispered, clinging to him and shuddering. "He worked his spells on me to break my will. The most awful was a moldering corpse which seized me in its arms – I fainted then and lay as one dead, I do not know how long. Shortly after I regained consciousness I heard sounds of strife below, and cries, and then that snake came slithering through the curtains – ah!" She shook at the memory of that horror. "I knew somehow that it was not an illusion, but a real serpent that sought my life."

"It was not a shadow, at least," answered Conan cryptically. "He knew he was beaten, and chose to slay you rather than let you be rescued."

"What do you mean, *he*?" she asked uneasily, and then shrank against him, crying out, and forgetting her question. She had seen the corpses at the foot of the stairs. Those of the Seers were not good to look at; as they lay twisted and contorted, their hands and feet were exposed to view, and at the sight Yasmina went livid and hid her face against Conan's powerful shoulder.

X

YASMINA AND CONAN

Conan passed through the hall quickly enough, traversed the outer chamber and approached the door that let upon the gallery with uncertainty. Then he saw the floor sprinkled with tiny, glittering shards. The crystal sheet that had covered the doorway had been shivered to bits, and he remembered the crash that had accompanied the shattering of the crystal globe. He believed that every piece of crystal in the castle had broken at that instant, and some dim instinct or memory of esoteric lore vaguely suggested the truth of the monstrous connection between the Lords of the Black Circle and the golden pomegranates. He felt the short hairs bristle chilly at the back of his neck and put the matter hastily out of his mind.

He breathed a deep sigh of relief as he stepped out upon the green jade gallery. There was still the gorge to cross, but at least he could see the white peaks glistening in the sun, and the long slopes falling away into the distant blue hazes.

The Irakzai lay where he had fallen, an ugly blotch on the glassy smoothness. As Conan strode down the winding path, he was surprized to note the position of the sun. It had not yet passed its zenith; and yet it seemed to him that hours had passed since he plunged into the castle of the Black Seers.

He felt an urge to hasten, not a mere blind panic, but an instinct of peril growing behind his back. He said nothing to Yasmina, and she seemed content to nestle her dark head against his arching breast and find content in the clasp of his iron arms. He paused an instant on the brink of the chasm, frowning down. The haze which danced in the gorge was no longer rose-hued and sparkling. It was smoky, dim, ghostly, like the life-tide that flickered thinly in a wounded man. The thought came vaguely to Conan that the spells of magicians were more closely bound to their personal beings than were the actions of common men to the actors.

But far below the floor shone like tarnished silver, and the gold thread sparkled undimmed. Conan shifted Yasmina across his shoulder where she lay docilely, and began the descent. Hurriedly he descended the ramp, and hurriedly he fled across the echoing floor. He had a conviction that they were racing with time; that their chance of survival depended upon crossing that gorge of horrors before the wounded Master of the castle should regain enough power to loose some other doom upon them.

When he toiled up the further ramp and came out upon the crest, he breathed a gusty sigh of relief, and stood Yasmina upon her feet.

"You walk from here," he told her, "it's downhill all the way."

She stole a glance at the gleaming pyramid across the chasm; it reared up against the snowy slope like the citadel of silence and immemorial evil.

"Are you a magician, that you have conquered the Black Seers of Yimsha, Conan of Ghor?" she asked, as they went down the path, with his heavy arm about her supple waist.

"It was a girdle Khemsa gave me before he died," Conan answered. "Yes, I found him on the trail. It is a curious one which I'll show you when I have time. Against some spells it was weak, but against others it was strong, and a good knife is always a hearty incantation."

"But if the girdle aided you in conquering the Master," she argued, "why did it not aid Khemsa?"

He shook his head. "Who knows? But Khemsa had been the Master's slave; perhaps that weakened its magic. He had no hold on me as he had on Khemsa. Yet I can't say that I conquered him. He retreated, but I have a feeling that we haven't seen the last of him. I want to put as many miles between us and his lair as we can."

He was further relieved to find the horses tethered among the tamarisks as he had left them. He loosed them swiftly and mounted the black stallion, swinging the girl up before him. The others followed, freshened by their rest.

"And what now?" she asked. "To Afghulistan?"

"Not just now!" He grinned hardly. "Somebody – maybe the governor – killed my seven headmen. My idiotic followers think I had something to do with it, and unless I am able to convince them otherwise, they'll hunt me like a wounded jackal."

"Then what of me? If the headmen are dead, I am useless to you as a hostage. Will you slay me, to avenge them?"

He looked down at her, with eyes fiercely aglow, and laughed at the suggestion.

"Then let us ride to the border," she said. "You'll be safe from the Afghulis there –"

"Yes, on a Vendhyan gibbet."

"I am queen of Vendhya," she reminded him with a touch of her old imperiousness. "You have saved my life and at least partly avenged my brother. You shall be rewarded."

She did not intend it as it sounded, but he growled in his throat, ill-pleased.

"Keep your bounty for your city-bred dogs, princess! If you're a queen of the plains, I'm a chief of the hills, and not one foot toward the border will I take you!"

"But you would be safe —" she began bewilderedly.

"And you'd be the Devi again," he broke in. "No, girl; I prefer you as you are now — a woman of flesh and blood, riding on my saddle bow."

"But you can't *keep* me!" she cried. "You can't —"

"Watch and see!" he advised her grimly.

"But I will pay you a vast ransom —"

"Devil take your ransom," he answered roughly, his arms hardening about her supple figure. "The kingdom of Vendhya could give me nothing I desire half as much as I desire you. I took you at the risk of my neck; if your courtiers want you back, let them come up the Zhaibar and fight for you."

"But you have no followers now!" she protested. "You are hunted! How can you preserve your own life, much less mine?"

"I still have friends in the hills," he answered. "There is a chief of the Khurakzai who will keep you safely while I bicker with the Afghulis. If they will have none of me, by Crom I will ride northward with you to the steppes of the *kozaki*. I was a *hetman* among the Free Companions before I rode southward. I'll make you a queen on the Zaporoska River!"

"But I can not!" she objected. "You must not hold me —"

"If the idea's so repulsive," he demanded, "why did you yield yourself so willingly?"

"Even a queen is human," she answered, coloring. "But because I am a queen, I must consider my kingdom. Do not carry me away into some foreign country. Come back to Vendhya with me!"

"Would you make me your king?" he asked sardonically.

"Well, there are customs —" she stammered, and he interrupted her with a hard laugh.

"Yes, civilized customs that won't let you do as you wish. You'll marry some withered old king of the plains, and I can go my way with only the memory of a few kisses snatched from your lips. Ha!"

"But I must return to my kingdom!" she repeated helplessly.

"Why?" he demanded angrily. "To chafe your rump on gold thrones, and listen to the plaudits of smirking, velvet-skirted fools? Where is the gain? Listen: I was born in the Cimmerian hills where the people are all barbarians. I have been a mercenary soldier, a corsair, a *kozak*, and a hundred other things. What king has roamed the countries, fought the battles, loved the women, and won the plunder that I have?

"I came into Ghulistan to raise a horde and plunder the kingdoms to the south – your own among them. Being chief of the Afghulis was only a start. If I can conciliate them, I'll have a dozen tribes following me within a year. But if I can't I'll ride back to the steppes and loot the Turanian borders with the *kozaki*. And you'll go with me. To the devil with your kingdom; they fended for themselves before you were born."

She lay in his arms looking up at him, and she felt a tug at her spirit, a lawless, reckless urge that matched his own and was by it called into being. But a thousand generations of sovereignship rode heavy upon her.

"I can't! I can't!" she repeated helplessly.

"You haven't any choice," he assured her. "You – what the devil!"

They had left Yimsha some miles behind them, and were riding along a high ridge that separated two deep valleys. They had just topped a steep crest where they could gaze down into the valley on their right hand. And there a running fight was in progress. A strong wind was blowing away from them, carrying the sound from their ears, but even so the clashing of steel and thunder of hoofs welled up from far below.

They saw the glint of the sun on lance-tip and spired helmet. Three thousand mailed horsemen were driving before them a ragged band of turbaned riders, who fled snarling and striking like fleeing wolves.

"Turanians!" muttered Conan. "Squadrons from Secunderam. What the devil are they doing here?"

"Who are the men they pursue?" asked Yasmina. "And why do they fall back so stubbornly? They can not stand against such odds."

"Five hundred of my mad Afghulis," he growled, scowling down into the vale. "They're in a trap, and they know it."

The valley was indeed a cul-de-sac at that end. It narrowed to a high walled gorge, opening out further into a round bowl, completely rimmed with lofty, unscalable walls.

The turbaned riders were being forced into this gorge, because there was nowhere else for them to go, and they went reluctantly, in a shower of arrows and a whirl of swords. The helmeted riders harried them, but did not press in too rashly. They knew the desperate fury of the hill tribes, and they knew too that they had their prey in a trap from which there was no escape. They had recognized the hillmen as Afghulis, and they wished to hem them in and force a surrender. They needed hostages for the purpose they had in mind.

Their emir was a man of decision and initiative. When he reached Gurashah valley, and found neither guides nor emissary waiting for him, he pushed on, trusting to his own knowledge of the country. All the way from Secunderam there had been fighting, and tribesmen were licking their wounds in many a crag-perched village. He knew there was a good chance that neither

he nor any of his helmeted spearmen would ever ride through the gates of Secunderam again, for the tribes would all be up behind him now, but he was determined to carry out his orders – which were to take Yasmina Devi from the Afghulis at all costs, and to bring her captive to Secunderam, or if confronted by impossibility, to strike off her head before he himself died.

Of all this, of course, the watchers on the ridge were not aware. But Conan fidgeted with nervousness.

"Why the devil did they get themselves trapped?" he demanded of the universe at large. "I know what they're doing in these parts – they were hunting me, the dogs! Poking into every valley – and found themselves penned in before they knew it. The damned fools! They're making a stand in the gorge, but they can't hold out for long. When the Turanians have pushed them back into the bowl, they'll slaughter them at their leisure."

The din welling up from below increased in volume and intensity. In the strait of the narrow gut the Afghulis, fighting desperately, were for the time being holding their own against the mailed riders who could not throw their whole weight against them.

Conan scowled darkly, moved restlessly, fingering his hilt, and finally spoke bluntly: "Devi, I must go down to them. I'll find a place for you to hide until I come back to you. You spoke of your kingdom – well, I don't pretend to look on those hairy devils as my children, but after all, such as they are, they're my henchmen. A chief should never desert his followers, even if they desert him first. They think they were right in kicking me out – hell, I won't be cast off! I'm still chief of the Afghulis, and I'll prove it! I can climb down on foot into the gorge."

"But what of me?" she queried. "You carried me away forcibly from *my* people; now will you leave me to die in the hills alone while you go down and sacrifice yourself uselessly?"

His veins swelled with the conflict of his emotions.

"That's right," he muttered helplessly. "Crom knows what I *can* do."

She turned her head slightly, a curious expression dawning on her beautiful face. Then –

"Listen!" she cried. "Listen!" A distant fanfare of trumpets was borne faintly to their ears. They stared into the deep valley on the left, and caught a glint of steel on the further side. A long line of lances and polished helmets moved along the vale, gleaming in the sunlight.

"The riders of Vendhya!" she cried exultingly. "Even at this distance I can not mistake them!"

"There are thousands of them!" muttered Conan. "It has been long since a Kshatriya host has ridden this far into the hills."

"They are searching for me!" she exclaimed. "Give me your horse! I will ride to my warriors! The ridge is not so precipitous on the left, and I can reach the valley floor. Go to your men and make them hold out a little longer. I will lead my horsemen into the valley at the upper end and fall upon the Turanians! We will crush them in the vise! Quick, Conan! Will you sacrifice your men to your own desire?"

The burning hunger of the steppes and the wintry forests glared out of his eyes, but he shook his head and swung off the stallion, placing the reins in her hands.

"You win!" he grunted. "Ride like the devil!"

She wheeled away down the left-hand slope and he ran swiftly along the ridge until he reached the long ragged cleft that was the defile in which the fight raged. Down the rugged wall he scrambled like an ape, clinging to projections and crevices, to fall at last, feet-first, into the melee that raged in the mouth of the gorge. Blades were whickering and clanging about him, horses rearing and stamping, helmet plumes nodding among turbans that were stained crimson.

As he hit, he yelled like a wolf, caught a gold-worked rein and dodging the sweep of a scimitar, drove his long knife upward through the rider's vitals. In another instant he was in the saddle, yelling ferocious orders to the Afghulis. They stared at him stupidly for an instant, then as they saw the havoc his steel was wreaking among their enemies, they fell to their work again, accepting him without comment. In that inferno of licking blades and spurting blood there was no time to ask or answer questions.

The riders in their spired helmets and gold-worked hauberks swarmed about the gorge mouth, thrusting and slashing, and the narrow defile was packed and jammed with horses and men, the warriors crushed breast to breast, stabbing with shortened blades, slashing murderously when there was an instant's room to swing a sword. When a man went down he did not get up from beneath the stamping, swirling hoofs. Weight and sheer strength counted heavily there, and the chief of the Afghulis did the work of ten. At such times accustomed habits sway men strongly, and the warriors who were used to seeing Conan in their vanguard, were heartened mightily, despite their distrust of him.

But superior numbers counted too. The pressure of the men behind forced the horsemen of Turan deeper and deeper into the gorge, in the teeth of the flickering tulwars. Foot by foot the Afghulis were shoved back, leaving the defile-floor carpeted with dead, on which the riders trampled. As he hacked and smote like a man possessed, Conan had time for some chilling doubts – would Yasmina keep her word? She had but to join her warriors, turn southward and leave him and his band to perish.

But at last, after what seemed centuries of desperate battling, in the valley outside there rose another sound above the clash of steel and yells of slaughter. And then with a burst of trumpets that shook the walls, and rushing thunder of hoofs, five thousand riders of Vendhya smote the hosts of Secunderam.

That stroke split the Turanian squadrons asunder, shattered, tore and rent them and scattered their fragments all over the valley. In an instant the surge had ebbed back out of the gorge; there was a chaotic, confused swirl of fighting, horsemen wheeling and smiting singly and in clusters, and then the emir went down with a Kshatriya lance through his breast, and the riders in their spired helmets turned their horses down the valley, spurring like mad and seeking to slash a way through the swarms which had come upon them from the rear. As they scattered in flight, the conquerors scattered in pursuit, and all across the valley floor, and up on the slopes near the mouth and over the crests streamed the fugitives and the pursuers. The Afghulis, those left to ride, rushed out of the gorge and joined in the harrying of their foes, accepting the unexpected alliance as unquestioningly as they had accepted the return of their repudiated chief.

The sun was sinking toward the distant crags when Conan, his garments hacked to tatters and the mail under them reeking and clotted with blood, his knife dripping and crusted to the hilt, strode over the corpses to where Yasmina Devi sat her horse among her nobles on the crest of the ridge, near a lofty precipice.

"You kept your word, Devi!" he roared. "By Crom, though, I had some bad seconds down in that gorge – *look out!*"

Down from the sky swooped a vulture of tremendous size with a thunder of wings that knocked men sprawling from their horses.

The scimitar-like beak was slashing for the Devi's soft neck, but Conan was quicker – a short run, a tigerish leap, the savage thrust of a dripping knife, and the vulture voiced a horribly human cry, pitched sideways and went tumbling down the cliffs to the rocks and river a thousand feet below. As it fell, its black wings thrashing the air, it took on the semblance, not of a bird, but of a black-robed human body that fell, arms in wide black sleeves thrown abroad.

Conan turned to Yasmina, his red knife still in his hand, his blue eyes smoldering, blood oozing from wounds on his thickly-muscled arms and thighs.

"You are the Devi again," he said, grinning fiercely at the gold-clasped gossamer robe she had donned over her hill-girl attire, and awed not at all by the imposing array of chivalry all about him. "I have you to thank for the lives of some three hundred and fifty of my rogues, who are at least convinced that I didn't betray them. You have put my hands on the reins of conquest again."

"I still owe you my ransom," she said, her dark eyes glowing as they swept over him. "Ten thousand pieces of gold I will pay you –"

He made a savage, impatient gesture, shook the blood from his knife and thrust it back in its scabbard, wiping his hands on his mail.

"I will collect your ransom in my own way, at my own time," he said. "I will collect it in your palace at Ayodhya, and I will come with fifty thousand men to see that the scales are fair."

She laughed, gathering her reins into her hands. "And I will meet you on the shores of the Jhumda with a hundred thousand!"

His eyes shone with fierce appreciation and admiration, and stepping back, he lifted his hand with a gesture that was like the assumption of kingship, indicating that her road was clear before her.

Beyond the Black River

I

CONAN LOSES HIS AXE

The stillness of the forest trail was so primeval that the tread of a soft-booted foot was a startling disturbance. At least it seemed so to the ears of the wayfarer, though he was moving along the path with the caution that must be practised by any man who ventured beyond Thunder River. He was a young man of medium height, with an open countenance and a mop of tousled tawny hair unconfined by cap or helmet. His garb was common enough for that country – a coarse tunic, belted at the waist, short leather breeches beneath, and soft buckskin boots that came short of the knee. A knife hilt jutted from one boot-top. The broad leather belt supported a short heavy sword, and a buckskin pouch. There was no perturbation in the wide eyes that scanned the green walls which fringed the trail. Though not tall, he was well built, and the arms that the short wide sleeves of the tunic left bare were thick with corded muscle.

He tramped imperturbably along although the last settler's cabin lay miles behind him, and each step was carrying him nearer the grim peril that hung like a brooding shadow over the ancient forest.

He was not making as much noise as it seemed to him, though he well knew that the faint tread of his booted feet would be like a tocsin of alarm to the fierce ears that might be lurking in the treacherous green fastness. His

353

careless attitude was not genuine; his eyes and ears were keenly alert; especially his ears, for no gaze could penetrate the leafy tangle for more than a few feet in either direction.

But it was instinct more than any warning by the external senses which brought him up suddenly, his hand on his hilt. He stood stock-still in the middle of the trail, unconsciously holding his breath, wondering what he had heard, and wondering if he had heard anything. The silence seemed absolute. Not a squirrel chattered or bird chirped. Then his gaze fixed itself on a mass of bushes beside the trail a few yards ahead of him. There was no breeze, yet he had seen a branch quiver. The short hairs on his scalp prickled, and he stood for an instant undecided, certain that a move in either direction would bring death streaking at him from the bushes.

A heavy chopping crunch sounded behind the leaves. The bushes were shaken violently, and simultaneously with the sound, an arrow arched erratically from among them and vanished among the trees along the trail. The wayfarer glimpsed its flight as he sprang frantically to cover.

Crouching behind a thick stem, his sword quivering in his fingers, he saw the bushes part, and a tall figure stepped leisurely into the trail. The traveller stared in surprize. The stranger was clad like himself in regard to boots and breeks, though the latter were of silk instead of leather. But he wore a sleeveless hauberk of dark mesh-mail in place of a tunic, and a helmet perched on his black mane. That helmet held the other's gaze; it was without a crest, but adorned by short bull's horns. No civilized hand ever forged that head-piece. Nor was the face below it that of a civilized man: dark, scarred, with smoldering blue eyes, it was a face as untamed as the primordial forest which formed its background. The man held a broadsword in his right hand, and the edge was smeared with crimson.

"Come on out!" he called, in an accent unfamiliar to the wayfarer. "All's safe now. There was only one of the dogs. Come on out."

The other emerged dubiously and stared at the stranger. He felt curiously helpless and futile as he gazed on the proportions of the forest man – the massive iron-clad breast, and the arm that bore the reddened sword, burned dark by the sun and ridged and corded with muscles. He moved with the dangerous ease of a panther; he was too fiercely supple to be a product of civilization, even of that fringe of civilization which composed the outer frontiers.

Turning, he stepped back to the bushes and pulled them apart. Still not certain just what had happened, the wayfarer from the east advanced and stared down into the bushes. A man lay there, a short, dark, thickly-muscled man, naked except for a loin cloth, a necklace of human teeth and a brass armlet. A short sword was thrust into the girdle of the loin cloth, and one hand still gripped a heavy black bow. The man had long black hair; that was about all the wayfarer could tell about his head, for his features were a mask of blood and brains. His skull had been split to the teeth.

"A Pict, by the gods!" exclaimed the wayfarer.

The burning blue eyes turned upon him.

"Are you surprized?"

"Why, they told me at Velitrium, and again at the settlers' cabins along the road that these devils sometimes sneaked across the border, but I didn't expect to meet one this far in the interior."

"You're only four miles east of Black River," the stranger informed him. "They've been shot within a mile of Velitrium. No settler between Thunder River and Fort Tuscelan is really safe. I picked up this dog's trail three miles south of the fort this morning, and I've been following him ever since. I came up behind him just as he was drawing an arrow on you. Another instant and there'd have been a stranger in Hell. But I spoiled his aim for him."

The wayfarer was staring wide-eyed at the larger man, dumbfounded by the realization that the man had actually tracked down one of the forest-devils and slain him unsuspected. That implied woodsmanship of a quality undreamed, even for Conajohara.

"You are one of the fort's garrison?" he asked.

"I'm no soldier. I draw the pay and rations of an officer of the line, but I do my work in the woods. Valannus knows I'm of more use ranging along the river than cooped up in the fort."

Casually the slayer shoved the body deeper into the thickets with his foot, pulled the bushes together and turned away down the trail. The other followed him.

"My name is Balthus," he offered. "I was at Velitrium last night. I haven't decided whether I'll take up a hide of land, or enter fort-service."

"The best land near Thunder River is already taken," grunted the slayer. "Plenty of good land between Scalp Creek – you crossed it a few miles back – and the fort, but that's getting too devilish close to the river. The Picts steal over to burn and murder – like that one did. They don't always come singly. Some day they'll try to sweep the settlers out of Conajohara. And they may succeed. Probably will succeed. This colonization business is mad, anyway. There's plenty of good land east of the Bossonian marches. If the Aquilonians would cut up some of the big estates of their barons, and plant wheat where now only deer are hunted, they wouldn't have to cross the border and take the land of the Picts away from them."

"That's queer talk from a man in the service of the Governor of Conajohara," objected Balthus.

"It's nothing to me," the other retorted. "I'm a mercenary. I sell my sword to the highest bidder. I never planted wheat and never will, so long as there are other harvests to be reaped with the sword. But you Hyborians have expanded as far as you'll be allowed to expand. You've crossed the marches, burned a few villages, exterminated a few clans and pushed back the frontier to Black River; but I doubt if you'll even be able to hold what you've conquered, and you'll never push the frontier any further westward.

"Your idiotic king doesn't understand conditions here. He won't send you enough reinforcements, and there are not enough settlers to withstand the shock of a concerted attack from across the river."

"But the Picts are divided into small clans," persisted Balthus. "They'll never unite. We can whip any single clan."

"Or any three or four clans," admitted the slayer. "But some day a man will rise and unite thirty or forty clans, just as was done among the Cimmerians, when the Gundermen tried to push the border northward, years ago. They tried to colonize the southern marches of Cimmeria: destroyed a few small clans, built a fort-town, Venarium, – you've heard the tale."

"So I have indeed," replied Balthus, wincing. The memory of that red disaster was a black blot in the chronicles of a proud and warlike people. "My uncle was at Venarium when the Cimmerians swarmed over the walls. He was one of the few who escaped that slaughter. I've heard him tell the tale, many a time. The barbarians swept out of the hills in a ravening horde, without warning, and stormed Venarium with such fury none could stand before them. Men, women and children were butchered. Venarium was reduced to a mass of charred ruins, as it is to this day. The Aquilonians were driven back across the marches, and have never since tried to colonize the Cimmerian country. But you speak of Venarium familiarly. Perhaps you were there?"

"I was," grunted the other. "I was one of the horde that swarmed over the walls. I hadn't yet seen fifteen snows, but already my name was repeated about the council fires."

Balthus involuntarily recoiled, staring. It seemed incredible that the man walking tranquilly at his side should have been one of those screeching, blood-mad devils that had poured over the walls of Venarium on that long-gone day to make her streets run crimson.

"Then you, too, are a barbarian!" he exclaimed involuntarily.

The other nodded, without taking offense.

"I am Conan, a Cimmerian."

"I've heard of you!" Fresh interest quickened Balthus' gaze. No wonder the Pict had fallen victim to his own sort of subtlety. The Cimmerians were barbarians as ferocious as the Picts, and much more intelligent. Evidently

Conan had spent much time among civilized men, though that contact had obviously not softened him, nor weakened any of his primitive instincts. Balthus' apprehension turned to admiration as he marked the easy catlike stride, the effortless silence with which the Cimmerian moved along the trail. The oiled links of his armor did not clink, and Balthus knew Conan could glide through the deepest thicket or most tangled copse as noiselessly as any naked Pict that ever lived.

"You're not a Gunderman?" It was more assertion than question.

Balthus shook his head. "I'm from the Tauran."

"I've seen good woodsmen from the Tauran. But the Bossonians have sheltered you Aquilonians from the outer wildernesses for too many centuries. You need hardening."

That was true; the Bossonian marches, with their fortified villages filled with determined bowmen, had long served Aquilonia as a buffer against the outlying barbarians. Now among the settlers beyond Thunder River there was growing up a breed of forest-men capable of meeting the barbarians at their own game, but their numbers were still scanty. Most of the frontiersmen were like Balthus – more of the settler than the woodsman type.

The sun had not set, but it was no longer in sight, hidden as it was behind the dense forest wall. The shadows were lengthening, deepening back in the woods as the companions strode on down the trail.

"It'll be dark before we reach the fort," commented Conan casually – then: *"Listen!"*

He stopped short, half crouching, sword ready, transformed into a savage figure of suspicion and menace, poised to spring and rend. Balthus had heard it too – a wild scream that broke at its highest note. It was the cry of a man in dire fear or agony.

Conan was off in an instant, racing down the trail, each stride widening the distance between him and his straining companion. Balthus puffed a curse. Among the settlements of the Tauran he was accounted a good runner, but Conan was leaving him behind with an ease which was maddening. Then Balthus forgot his exasperation as his ears were outraged by the most frightful cry he had ever heard. It was not human, this one; it was a demoniacal caterwauling of hideous triumph that seemed to exult over fallen humanity and find echo in black gulfs beyond human ken.

Balthus faltered in his stride and clammy sweat beaded his flesh. But Conan did not hesitate; he darted around a bend in the trail and disappeared, and Balthus, panicky at finding himself alone with that awful scream still shuddering through the forest in grisly echoes, put on an extra burst of speed and plunged after him.

The Aquilonian slid to a stumbling halt, almost colliding with the Cimmerian who stood in the trail over a crumpled body. But Conan was not looking at the corpse which lay there in the crimson-soaked dust. He was glaring into the deep woods on each side of the trail.

Balthus muttered a horrified oath. It was the body of a man which lay there in the trail, a short, fat man, clad in the gilt-worked boots and (despite the heat) the ermine-trimmed tunic of a wealthy merchant. His fat, pale face was set in a stare of frozen horror; his thick throat had been slashed from ear to ear as if by a razor-sharp blade. The short sword still in its scabbard seemed to indicate that he had been struck down without a chance to fight for his life.

"A Pict?" Balthus whispered, as he turned to peer into the deepening shadows of the forest.

Conan shook his head and straightened to scowl down at the dead man.

"A forest devil. This is the fourth, by Crom!"

"What do you mean?"

"Did you ever hear of a Pictish wizard called Zogar Sag?"

Balthus shook his head uneasily.

"He dwells in Gwawela, the nearest village across the river. Three months ago he hid beside this road and stole a string of pack-mules from a pack-train bound for the fort – drugged their drivers, somehow. The mules belonged to this man" – Conan casually indicated the corpse with his foot – "Tiberias, a merchant of Velitrium. They were loaded with ale kegs and old Zogar stopped to guzzle before he got across the river. A woodsman named Soractus trailed him, and led Valannus and a couple of soldiers to where he lay dead drunk in a thicket. At the importunities of Tiberias, Valannus threw Zogar Sag into a cell, which is the worst insult you can give a Pict. He managed to kill his guard and escape, and sent back word that he meant to kill Tiberias and the four men who captured him in a way that would make Aquilonians shudder for centuries to come.

"Well, Soractus and the soldiers are dead. Soractus was killed on the river, the soldiers in the very shadow of the fort. And now Tiberias is dead. No Pict killed any of them. Each victim – except Tiberias, as you see – lacked his head – which no doubt is now ornamenting the altar of Zogar Sag's particular god."

"How do you know they weren't killed by the Picts?" demanded Balthus.

Conan pointed to the corpse of the merchant.

"You think that was done with a knife or a sword? Look closer and you'll see that only a *talon* could have made a gash like that. The flesh is ripped, not cut."

"Perhaps a panther —" began Balthus, without conviction.

Conan shook his head impatiently.

"A man from the Tauran wouldn't mistake the mark of a panther's claws. No. It's a forest devil summoned by Zogar Sag to carry out his revenge. Tiberias was a fool to start for Velitrium alone, and this close to dusk. But each one of the victims seemed to be smitten with madness just before doom overtook him. Look here; the signs are plain enough. Tiberias came riding along the trail on his mule, maybe with a bundle of choice otter pelts behind his saddle to sell in Velitrium, and the *thing* sprang on him from behind that bush. See where the branches are crushed down.

"Tiberias gave one scream, and then his throat was torn open and he was selling his otter skins in Hell. The mule ran away into the woods. Listen! Even now you can hear him thrashing about under the trees. The demon didn't have time to take Tiberias' head; it took fright as we came up."

"As you came up," amended Balthus. "It must not be a very terrible creature if it flees from one armed man. But how do you know it was not a Pict with some kind of a hook that rips instead of slicing? Did you see it?"

"Tiberias was an armed man," grunted Conan. "If Zogar Sag can bring demons to aid him, he can tell them which men to kill and which to let alone. No, I didn't see it. I only saw the bushes shake as it left the trail. But if you want further proof, look here!"

The slayer had stepped into the pool of blood in which the dead man sprawled. Under the bushes at the edge of the path there was a footprint, made in blood on the hard loam.

"Did a man make that?" demanded Conan.

Balthus felt his scalp prickle. Neither man nor any beast that he had ever seen could have left that strange, monstrous three-toed print, that was curiously combined of the bird and the reptile, yet a true type of neither. He spread his fingers above the print, careful not to touch it, and grunted explosively. He could not span the mark.

"What is it?" he whispered. "I never saw a beast that left a spoor like that."

"Nor any other sane man," answered Conan grimly. "It's a swamp demon – Hell, they're thick as bats in the swamps beyond Black River. You can hear them howling like damned souls when the wind blows strong from the south on hot nights."

"What shall we do?" asked the Aquilonian, peering uneasily into the deep blue shadows. The frozen fear on the dead countenance haunted him. He wondered what hideous head the wretch had seen thrust grinning from among the leaves to chill his blood with terror.

"No use to try to follow a demon," grunted Conan, drawing a short

359

woodman's axe from his girdle. "I tried tracking him after he killed Soractus. I lost his trail within a dozen steps. He might have grown himself wings and flown away, or sunk down through the earth to Hell. I don't know. I'm not going after the mule, either. It'll either wander back to the fort, or to some settler's cabin."

As he spoke Conan was busy at the edge of the trail with his axe. With a few strokes he cut a pair of saplings nine or ten feet long, and denuded them of their branches. Then he cut a length from a serpent-like vine that crawled among the bushes near-by, and making one end fast to one of the poles, a couple of feet from the end, whipped the vine over the other sapling and interlaced it back and forth. In a few moments he had a crude but strong litter.

"The demon isn't going to get Tiberias' head if I can help it," he growled. "We'll carry the body into the fort. It isn't more than three miles. I never liked the fat bastard, but we can't have Pictish devils making so cursed free with white men's heads."

The Picts were a white race, though swarthy, but the border men never spoke of them as such.

Balthus took the rear end of the litter, onto which Conan unceremoniously dumped the unfortunate merchant, and they moved on down the trail as swiftly as possible. Conan made no more noise laden with their grim burden than he had made when unencumbered. He had made a loop with the merchant's belt at the end of the poles, and was carrying his share of the load with one hand, while the other gripped his naked broadsword, and his restless gaze roved the sinister walls about them. The shadows were thickening. A darkening blue mist seemed to blur the outlines of the foliage. The forest deepened in the twilight, became a blue haunt of mystery sheltering unguessed things.

They had covered more than a mile, and the muscles in Balthus' sturdy arms were beginning to ache a little, when a cry rang shudderingly from the woods whose blue shadows were deepening into purple.

Conan started convulsively, and Balthus almost let go the poles.

"A woman!" cried the younger man. "Great Mitra, a woman cried out then!"

"A settler's wife straying in the woods," snarled Conan, setting down his end of the litter. "Looking for a cow, probably, and – stay here!"

He dived like a hunting wolf into the leafy wall. Balthus' hair bristled.

"Stay here alone with this corpse and a devil hiding in the woods?" he yelped. "I'm coming with you!"

And suiting action to words, he plunged after the Cimmerian. Conan glanced back at him, but made no objection, though he did not moderate his pace to accommodate the shorter legs of his companion. Balthus wasted his wind in swearing as the Cimmerian drew away from him again, flitting like a phantom between the trees, and then Conan burst into a dim glade and halted crouching, lips snarling, sword lifted.

"What are we stopping for?" panted Balthus, dashing the sweat out of his eyes and gripping his short sword.

"That scream came from this glade, or near by," answered Conan. "I don't mistake the location of sounds, even in the woods. But where —"

Abruptly the sound rang out again — *behind them*; in the direction of the trail they had just quitted. It rose piercingly and pitifully, the cry of a woman in frantic terror — and then, shockingly, it changed to a yell of mocking laughter that might have burst from the lips of a fiend of lower Hell.

"What in Mitra's name —!" Balthus' face was a pale blur in the gloom.

With a scorching oath Conan wheeled and dashed back the way he had come, and the Aquilonian stumbled bewilderedly after him. He blundered into the Cimmerian as the latter stopped dead, and rebounded from his brawny shoulders as though from an iron statue. Gasping from the impact, he heard Conan's breath hiss through his teeth. The Cimmerian seemed frozen in his tracks. Looking over his shoulder, Balthus felt his hair stand up stiffly. Something was moving through the deep bushes that fringed the trail — something that neither walked nor flew, but seemed to glide like a serpent. But it was not a serpent. Its outlines were indistinct, but it was taller than a man, and not very bulky. It gave off a glimmer of weird light, like a faint blue flame. Indeed, the eery fire was the only tangible thing about it. It might have been an embodied flame moving with reason and purpose through the blackening woods.

Conan snarled a savage curse and hurled his axe with ferocious will. But the thing glided on without altering its course. Indeed it was only a few instants' fleeting glimpse they had of it — a tall, shadowy thing of misty flame floating through the thickets. Then it was gone and the forest crouched in breathless stillness.

With a snarl Conan plunged through the intervening foliage and into the trail. His profanity, as Balthus floundered after him, was lurid and impassioned. The Cimmerian was standing over the litter on which lay the body of Tiberias. And that body no longer possessed a head.

"Tricked us with its damnable caterwauling!" raved Conan, swinging his great sword about his head in his wrath. "I might have known! I might have guessed a trick! Now there'll be five heads to decorate Zogar's altar."

"But what thing is it that can cry like a woman and laugh like a devil, and shines like witch-fire as it glides through the trees?" gasped Balthus, mopping the sweat from his pale face.

"A swamp devil," responded Conan morosely. "Grab those poles. We'll take in the body, anyway. At least our load's a bit lighter."

With which grim philosophy he gripped the leather loop and stalked down the trail.

II
THE WIZARD OF GWAWELA

Fort Tuscelan stood on the eastern bank of Black River, the tides of which washed the foot of the stockade. The latter was of logs, as were all the buildings within, including the donjon, to dignify it by that appellation, in which were the governor's quarters, overlooking the stockade and the sullen river. Beyond that river lay a huge forest, which approached jungle-like density along the spongy shores. Men paced the runways along the log parapet day and night, watching that dense green wall. Seldom a menacing figure appeared, but the sentries knew that they too were watched, fiercely, hungrily, with the mercilessness of ancient hate. The forest beyond the river might seem desolate and vacant of life to the ignorant eye, but life teemed there, not alone of bird and beast and reptile, but also of men, the fiercest of all the hunting beasts.

There, at the fort, civilization ended. This was no empty phrase. Fort Tuscelan was indeed the last outpost of a civilized world; it represented the westernmost thrust of the dominant Hyborian races. Beyond the river the primitive still reigned in shadowy forests, brush-thatched huts where hung the grinning skulls of men, and mud-walled enclosures where fires flickered and drums rumbled, and spears were whetted in the hands of dark, silent men with tangled black hair and the eyes of serpents. Those eyes often glared through the bushes at the fort across the river. Once dark-skinned men had built their huts where that fort stood; yes, and their huts had risen where now stood the fields and log-cabins of fair-haired settlers, back beyond Velitrium, that raw, turbulent frontier town on the banks of Thunder River, to the shores of that other river that bounds the Bossonian marches. Traders had come, and priests of Mitra who walked with bare feet and empty hands, and died horribly, most of them; but soldiers had followed, and men with axes in their hands, and women and children in ox-drawn wains. Back to Thunder River, and still back, beyond Black River, the aborigines had been pushed, with slaughter and massacre. But the dark-skinned people did not forget that once Conajohara had been theirs.

The guard inside the eastern gate bawled a challenge. Through a barred aperture torch-light flickered, glinting on a steel head-piece and suspicious eyes beneath it.

"Open the gate," snorted Conan. "You see it's me, don't you?"

Military discipline put his teeth on edge.

The gate swung inward and Conan and his companion passed through. Balthus noted that the gate was flanked by a tower on each side, the summits of which rose above the stockade. He saw loop-holes for arrows.

The guardsmen grunted as they saw the burden borne between the men. Their pikes jangled against each other as they thrust shut the gate, chin on shoulder, and Conan asked testily: "Have you never seen a headless body before?"

The faces of the soldiers were pallid in the torchlight.

"That's Tiberias," blurted one. "I recognize that fur-trimmed tunic. Valerius here owes me five lunas. I told him Tiberias had heard the loon call when he rode through the gate on his mule, with his glassy stare. I wagered he'd come back without his head."

Conan grunted enigmatically, motioned Balthus to ease the litter to the ground, and then strode off toward the governor's quarters, with the Aquilonian at his heels. The tousle-headed youth stared about him eagerly and curiously, noting the rows of barracks along the walls, the stables, the tiny merchants' stalls, the towering blockhouse, and the other buildings, with the open square in the middle where the soldiers drilled, and where, now, fires danced and men off duty lounged. These were now hurrying to join the morbid crowd gathered about the litter at the gate. The rangy figures of Aquilonian pikemen and forest runners mingled with the shorter, stockier forms of Bossonian archers.

He was not greatly surprised that the governor received them himself. Autocratic society with its rigid caste laws lay east of the marches. Valannus was still a young man, well-knit, with a finely-chiselled countenance already carved into sober cast by toil and responsibility.

"You left the fort before daybreak, I was told," he said to Conan. "I had begun to fear that the Picts had caught you at last."

"When they smoke my head the whole river will know it," grunted Conan. "They'll hear Pictish women wailing their dead as far as Velitrium – I was on a lone scout. I couldn't sleep. I kept hearing drums talking across the river."

"They talk each night," reminded the governor, his fine eyes shadowed, as he stared closely at Conan. He had learned the unwisdom of discounting wild men's instincts.

"There was a difference last night," growled Conan. "There has been ever since Zogar Sag got back across the river."

"We should either have given him presents and sent him home, or else hanged him," sighed the governor. "You advised that, but –"

"But it's hard for you Hyborians to learn the ways of the outlands," said

Conan. "Well, it can't be helped now, but there'll be no peace on the border so long as Zogar lives and remembers the cell he sweated in. I was following a warrior who slipped over to put a few white notches on his bow. After I split his head I fell in with this lad whose name is Balthus and who's come from the Tauran to help hold the frontier."

Valannus approvingly eyed the young man's frank countenance and strongly-knit frame.

"I am glad to welcome you, young sir. I wish more of your people would come. We need men used to forest life. Many of our soldiers and some of our settlers are from the eastern provinces and know nothing of woodcraft, or even of agricultural life."

"Not many of that breed this side of Velitrium," grunted Conan. "That town's full of them, though. But listen, Valannus, we found Tiberias dead on the trail." And in a few words he related the grisly affair.

Valannus paled.

"I did not know he had left the fort. He must have been mad!"

"He was," answered Conan. "Like the other four; each one, when his time came, went mad and rushed into the woods to meet his death like a hare running down the throat of a python. *Something* called to them from the deeps of the forest, something the men call a loon, for lack of a better name, but only the doomed ones could hear it. Zogar Sag's made a magic Aquilonian civilization can't overcome."

To this thrust Valannus made no reply; he wiped his brow with a shaky hand.

"Do the soldiers know of this?"

"We left the body by the eastern gate."

"You should have concealed the fact – hidden the corpse somewhere in the woods. The soldiers are nervous enough already."

"They'd have found it out some way. If I'd hidden the body, it would have been returned to the fort as the corpse of Soractus was – tied up outside the gate for the men to find in the morning."

Valannus shuddered. Turning, he walked to a casement and stared silently out over the river, black and shiny under the glint of the stars. Beyond the river the jungle rose like an ebony wall. The distant screech of a panther broke the stillness. The night seemed pressing in, blurring the sounds of the soldiers outside the blockhouse, dimming the fires. A wind whispered through the black branches, rippling the dusky water. On its wings came a low, rhythmic pulsing, sinister as the pad of a leopard's foot.

"After all," said Valannus, as if speaking his thoughts aloud, "what do we know – what does anyone know – of the things that jungle may hide? We have dim rumors of great swamps and rivers, and a forest that stretches on and on over everlasting plains and hills to end at last on the shores of the western ocean. But what things lie between this river and that ocean we dare not even guess. No white man has ever plunged deep into that fastness and returned alive to tell us what he found. We are wise in our civilized knowledge, but our knowledge extends just so far – to the western bank of that ancient river! Who knows what shapes earthly and unearthly may lurk beyond the dim circle of light our knowledge has cast?

"Who knows what gods are worshipped under the shadows of that heathen forest, or what devils crawl out of the black ooze of the swamps? Who can be sure that all the inhabitants of that black country are natural? Zogar Sag – a sage of the eastern cities would sneer at his primitive magic-making as the mummery of a fakir; yet he has driven mad and killed five men in a manner no man can explain. I wonder if he himself is wholly human."

"If I can get within axe-throwing distance of him I'll settle that question," growled Conan, helping himself to the governor's wine and pushing a glass toward Balthus, who took it hesitatingly, and with an uncertain glance toward Valannus.

The governor turned toward Conan and stared at him thoughtfully.

"The soldiers, who do not believe in ghosts or devils," he said, "are almost in a panic of fear. You, who believe in ghosts, ghouls, goblins, and all manner of uncanny things, do not seem to fear any of the things in which you believe."

"There's nothing in the universe cold steel won't cut," answered Conan. "I threw my axe at the demon, and he took no hurt, but I might have missed, in the dusk, or a branch deflected its flight. I'm not going out of my way looking for devils; but I wouldn't step out of my path to let one go by."

Valannus lifted his head and met Conan's gaze squarely.

"Conan, more depends on you than you realize. You know the weakness of this province – a slender wedge thrust into the untamed wilderness. You know that the lives of all the people west of the marches depend on this fort. Were it to fall, red axes would be splintering the gates of Velitrium before a horseman could cross the marches. His majesty, or his majesty's advisers, have ignored my pleas that more troops be sent to hold the frontier. They know nothing of border conditions, and are averse to expending any more money in this direction. The fate of the frontier depends upon the men who now hold it."

"You know that most of the army which conquered Conajohara has been withdrawn. You know the force left me is inadequate, especially since that devil Zogar Sag managed to poison our water supply, and forty men died in one day. Many of the others are sick, or have been bitten by serpents or mauled by wild beasts which seem to swarm in increasing numbers in the vicinity of the fort. The soldiers believe Zogar's boast that he could summon the forest beasts to slay his enemies.

"I have three hundred pikemen, four hundred Bossonian archers, and perhaps fifty men, who, like yourself, are skilled in woodcraft. They are worth ten times their number of soldiers, but there are so few of them — frankly, Conan, my situation is becoming precarious. The soldiers whisper of desertion; they are low spirited, believing Zogar Sag has loosed devils on us. They fear the black plague with which he threatened us — the terrible black death of the swamplands. When I see a sick soldier I sweat with fear of seeing him turn black and shrivel and die before my eyes.

"Conan, if the plague is loosed upon us, the soldiers will desert in a body! The border will be left unguarded and nothing will check the sweep of the dark-skinned hordes to the very gates of Velitrium — maybe beyond! If we can not hold the fort, how can they hold the town?

"Conan, Zogar Sag must die, if we are to hold Conajohara! You have penetrated the unknown deeper than any other man in the fort; you know where Gwawela stands, and something of the forest trails across the river. Will you take a band of men tonight and endeavor to kill or capture him? Oh, I know it's mad. There isn't more than one chance in a thousand that any of you will come back alive. But if we don't get him, it's death for us all. You can take as many men as you wish."

"A dozen men are better for a job like that than a regiment," answered Conan. "Five hundred men couldn't fight their way to Gwawela and back. But a dozen might slip in and out again. Let me pick my men. I don't want any soldiers."

"Let me go!" eagerly exclaimed Balthus. "I've hunted deer all my life on the Tauran."

"All right. Valannus, we'll eat at the stall where the foresters gather, and I'll pick my men. We'll start within an hour, drop down the river in a boat to a point below the village and then steal upon it through the woods. If we live, we should be back by daybreak."

III

THE CRAWLERS IN THE DARK

The river was a vague trace between walls of ebony. The paddles that propelled the long boat creeping along in the dense shadow of the eastern bank dipped softly into the water making no more noise than the beak of a heron. The broad shoulders of the man in front of Balthus were a blur in the dense gloom. He knew not even the keen eyes of the man who knelt in the prow could discern anything more than a few feet ahead of them. Conan was feeling his way by instinct and an intensive familiarity with the river.

No one spoke. Balthus had had a good look at his companions in the fort before they slipped out of the stockade and down the bank into the waiting canoe. They were of a new breed growing up in the world on the raw edge of the frontier – men whom grim necessity had taught woodcraft. Aquilonians of the western provinces to a man, they had many points in common. They dressed alike – in buckskin boots, leathern breeks and deer-skin shirts, with broad girdles that held axes and short swords; and they were all gaunt and scarred and hard-eyed; sinewy and taciturn.

They were wild men, of a sort, yet there was still a wide gulf between them and the Cimmerian. They were sons of civilization, reverted to a semi-barbarism. He was a barbarian of a thousand generations of barbarians. They had acquired stealth and craft, but he had been born to these things. He excelled them even in lithe economy of motion. They were wolves, but he was a tiger.

Balthus admired them and their leader and felt a pulse of pride that he was admitted into their company. He was proud that his paddle made no more noise than did theirs. In that respect at least he was their equal, though woodcraft learned in hunts on the Tauran could never equal that ground into the souls of men on the savage border.

Below the fort the river made a wide bend. The lights of the outpost were quickly lost, but the canoe held on its way for nearly a mile, avoiding snags and floating logs with almost uncanny precision.

Then a low grunt from their leader, and they swung its head about and glided toward the opposite shore. Emerging from the black shadows of the brush that fringed the bank and coming into the open of the mid-stream created a peculiar illusion of rash exposure. But the stars gave little light, and Balthus knew that unless one were watching for it, it would be all but impossible for the keenest eye to make out the shadowy shape of the canoe crossing the river.

They swung in under the overhanging bushes of the western shore and Balthus groped for and found a projecting root which he grasped. No word was spoken. All instructions had been given before the scouting party left the fort. As silently as a great panther Conan slid over the side and vanished in the bushes. Equally noiseless, nine men followed him. To Balthus, grasping the root with his paddle across his knees, it seemed incredible that ten men should thus fade into the tangled forest with no more sound than these made.

He settled himself to wait. No word passed between him and the other man who had been left with him. Somewhere, a mile or so to the north west,

Zogar Sag's village stood girdled by the thick woods. Balthus understood his orders; he and his companion were to wait for the return of the raiding party. If Conan and his men had not returned by the first tinge of dawn, then they were to race back up the river to the fort and report that the forest had again taken its immemorial toll of the invading race.

The silence was oppressive. No sound came from the black woods, invisible beyond the ebony masses that were the overhanging bushes. Balthus no longer heard the drums. They had been silent for hours. He kept blinking, unconsciously trying to see through the deep gloom. The dank night-smells of the river and the damp forest oppressed him. Somewhere, nearby, there was a sound as if a big fish had flopped and splashed the water. Balthus thought it must have leaped so close to the canoe that it had struck the side, for a slight quiver vibrated the craft. The boat's stern began to swing slightly away from the shore. The man behind him must have let go of the projection he was gripping. Balthus twisted his head to hiss a warning, and could just make out the figure of his companion, a slightly blacker bulk in the blackness.

The man did not reply. Wondering if he had fallen asleep, Balthus reached out and grasped his shoulder. To his amazement, the man crumpled under his touch and slumped down in the canoe. Twisting his body half about Balthus groped for him, his heart shooting into his throat. His fumbling fingers slid over the man's throat – only the youth's convulsive clenching of his jaws choked back the cry that rose in his throat. His fingers encountered a gaping, oozing wound – his companion's throat had been cut from ear to ear.

In that instant of horror and panic Balthus started up – and then a muscular arm out of the darkness locked fiercely about his throat, strangling his yell. The canoe rocked wildly. Balthus' knife was in his hand, though he did not remember jerking it out of his boot, and he stabbed fiercely and blindly. He felt the blade sink deep, and a fiendish yell rang in his ear, a yell that was horribly answered. The darkness seemed to come to life about him. A bestial clamor rose on all sides, and other arms grappled him. Borne under a mass of hurtling bodies the canoe rolled sidewise, but before he went under with it, something cracked against Balthus' head and the night was briefly illuminated by a blinding burst of fire before it gave way to a blackness where not even stars shone.

IV

THE BEASTS OF ZOGAR SAG

Fires dazzled Balthus again as he slowly recovered his senses. He blinked, shook his head. Their glare hurt his eyes. A confused medley of sound rose about him, growing more distinct as his senses cleared. He lifted his head and stared stupidly about him. Black figures hemmed him in, etched against crimson tongues of flame.

Memory and understanding came in a rush. He was bound upright to a post in an open space, ringed by fierce and terrible figures. Beyond that ring fires burned, tended by naked, dark-skinned women. Beyond the fires he saw huts of mud and wattle, thatched with brush. Beyond the huts there was a stockade with a broad gate. But he saw these things only incidentally. Even the cryptic dark women with their curious coiffures were noted by him only absently. His full attention was fixed in awful fascination on the men who stood glaring at him.

Short men, broad-shouldered, deep-chested, lean-hipped. They were naked except for scanty loin clouts. The firelight brought out the play of their swelling muscles in bold relief. Their dark faces were immobile, but their narrow eyes glittered with the fire that burns in the eyes of a stalking tiger. Their tangled manes were bound back with bands of copper. Swords and axes were in their hands. Crude bandages banded the limbs of some, and smears of blood were dried on their dark skins. There had been fighting, recent and deadly.

His eyes wavered away from the steady glare of his captors, and he repressed a cry of horror. A few feet away there rose a low, hideous pyramid: it was built of gory human heads. Dead eyes glared glassily up at the black sky. Numbly he recognized the countenances which were turned toward him. They were the heads of the men who had followed Conan into the forest. He could not tell if the Cimmerian's head were among them. Only a few faces were visible to him. It looked to him as if there must be ten or eleven heads at least. A deadly sickness assailed him. He fought a desire to retch. Beyond the heads lay the bodies of half a dozen Picts, and he was aware of a fierce exultation at the sight. The forest runners had taken toll, at least.

Twisting his head away from the ghastly spectacle, he became aware that another post stood near him – a stake painted black as was the one to which he was bound. A man sagged in his bonds there, naked except for his leathern breeks, whom Balthus recognized as one of Conan's woodsmen. Blood trickled from his mouth, oozed sluggishly from a gash in his side. Lifting his head he licked his livid lips and muttered, making himself heard with difficulty above the fiendish clamor of the Picts: "So they got you, too!"

"Sneaked up in the water and cut the other fellow's throat," groaned Balthus. "We never heard them till they were on us. Mitra, how can anything move so silently?"

"They're devils," mumbled the frontiersman. "They must have been watching us from the time we left mid-stream. We walked into a trap. Arrows from all sides were ripping into us before we knew it. Most of us dropped the first fire. Three or four broke through the bushes and came to hand-grips. But there were too many. Conan might have gotten away. I haven't seen his head. Been better for you and me if they'd killed us outright. I can't blame Conan. Ordinarily we'd have gotten to the village without being discovered. They don't keep spies on the river bank as far down as we landed. We must have stumbled into a big party coming up the river from the south. Some devilment is up. Too many Picts here. These aren't all Gwaweli; men from the western tribes here and from up and down the river."

Balthus stared at the ferocious shapes. Little as he knew of Pictish ways, he was aware that the number of men clustered about them was out of proportion to the size of the village. There were not enough huts to have accommodated them all. Then he noticed that there was a difference in the barbaric tribal designs painted on their faces and breasts.

"Some kind of devilment," muttered the forest runner. "They might have gathered here to watch Zogar's magic-making. He'll make some rare magic with our carcasses. Well, a border-man doesn't expect to die in bed. But I wish we'd gone out along with the rest."

The wolfish howling of the Picts rose in volume and exultation, and from a movement in their ranks, an eager surging and crowding, Balthus deduced that someone of importance was coming. Twisting his head about he saw that the stakes were set before a long building, larger than the other huts, decorated by human skulls dangling from the eaves. Through the door of that structure now danced a fantastic figure.

"Zogar!" muttered the woodsman, his bloody countenance set in wolfish lines as he unconsciously strained at his cords. Balthus saw a lean figure of middle height, almost hidden in ostrich plumes set on a harness of leather and copper. From amidst the plumes peered a hideous and malevolent face. The plumes puzzled Balthus. He knew their source lay half the width of a world to the south. They fluttered and rustled evilly as the shaman leaped and cavorted.

With fantastic bounds and prancings he entered the ring and whirled before his bound and silent captives. With another man it would have seemed ridiculous – a foolish savage prancing meaninglessly in a whirl of feathers. But that ferocious face glaring out from the billowing mass gave the scene a grim significance. No man with a face like that could seem ridiculous or like anything except the devil he was.

Suddenly he froze to statuesque stillness; the plumes rippled once and sank about him. The howling warriors fell silent. Zogar Sag stood erect and motionless, and he seemed to increase in height – to grow and expand.

Balthus experienced the illusion that the Pict was towering above him, staring contemptuously down from a great height, though he knew the shaman was not as tall as himself. He shook off the illusion with difficulty.

The shaman was talking now, a harsh, guttural intonation that yet carried the hiss of a cobra. He thrust his head on his long neck toward the wounded man on the stake; his eyes shone red as blood in the firelight. For answer the frontiersman spat full in his face.

With a fiendish howl Zogar bounded convulsively into the air, and the warriors gave tongue to a yell that shuddered up to the stars that peered over the tops of the great trees girdling the village. They rushed toward the man on the stake, but the shaman beat them back. A snarled command sent men running to the gate. They hurled it open, turned and raced back to the circle. The ring of men split, divided with desperate haste to right and left. Balthus saw the women and naked children scurrying to the huts. They peeked out of doors and windows. A broad lane was left to the open gate beyond which loomed the black forest, crowding sullenly in upon the clearing, unlighted by the fires.

A tense silence reigned as Zogar Sag turned toward the forest, raised on his tip-toes and sent a weird inhuman call shuddering out into the night. Somewhere, far out in the black forest, a deeper cry answered him. Balthus shuddered. From the timbre of that cry he knew it never came from a human throat. He remembered what Valannus had said – that Zogar boasted that he could summon wild beasts to do his bidding. The woodsman was livid beneath his mask of blood. He licked his lips spasmodically.

The village held its breath. Zogar Sag stood still as a statue, his plumes trembling faintly about him. But suddenly the gate was no longer empty.

A shuddering gasp swept over the village and men crowded hastily back, jamming each other between the huts. Balthus felt the short hair stir on his scalp. The creature that stood in the gate was like the embodiment of nightmare legend. Its color was of a curious pale quality which made it seem ghostly and unreal in the dim light. But there was nothing unreal about the low-hung savage head, and the great curved fangs that glistened in the firelight. On noiseless padded feet it approached like a phantom out of the past. It was a survival of an older, grimmer age, the ogre of many an ancient legend – a saber-tooth tiger. No Hyborian hunter had looked upon one of those primordial brutes for centuries. Immemorial myths lent the creatures a supernatural quality, induced by their ghostly color and their fiendish ferocity.

The beast that glided toward the men on the stakes was longer and heavier than a common, striped tiger, almost as bulky as a bear. Its shoulders and forelegs were so massive and mightily muscled as to give it a curiously top-heavy look, though its hind-quarters were more powerful than those of a lion. Its jaws were massive, but its head was brutishly shaped. Its brain capacity was small. It had room for no instincts except those of destruction. It was a freak of carnivorous development; evolution run amuck in a horror of fangs and talons.

This was the monstrosity Zogar Sag had summoned out of the forest. Balthus no longer doubted the actuality of the shaman's magic. Only the black arts could establish a domination over that tiny-brained, mightily-thewed monster. Like a whisper at the back of his consciousness rose the vague memory of the name of an ancient, ancient god of darkness and primordial fear, to whom once both men and beasts bowed and whose children – men whispered – still lurked in dark corners of the world. New horror tinged the glare he fixed on Zogar Sag.

The monster moved past the heap of bodies and the pile of gory heads without appearing to notice them. He was no scavenger. He hunted only the living, in a life dedicated solely to slaughter. An awful hunger burned greenly in the wide, unwinking eyes; the hunger not alone of belly-emptiness, but the lust of death-dealing. His gaping jaws slavered. The shaman stepped back; his hand waved toward the woodsman.

The great cat sank into a crouch and Balthus numbly remembered tales of its appalling ferocity: of how it would spring upon an elephant and drive its sword-like fangs so deeply into the titan's skull that they could never be withdrawn, but would keep it nailed to its victim, to die by starvation. The shaman cried out shrilly – and with an ear-shattering roar the monster sprang.

Balthus had never dreamed of such a spring, such a hurtling of incarnated destruction embodied in that giant bulk of iron thews and ripping talons. Full on the woodsman's breast it struck, and the stake splintered and snapped at the base, crashing to the earth under the impact. Then the saber-tooth was gliding toward the gate, half dragging, half carrying a hideous crimson hulk that only faintly resembled a man. Balthus glared almost paralyzed, his brain refusing to credit what his eyes had seen.

In that leap the great beast had not only broken off the stake, it had ripped the mangled body of its victim from the post to which it was bound. The huge talons in that instant of contact had disembowelled and partially dismembered the man, and the giant fangs had torn away the whole top of his head, shearing through the skull as easily as through flesh. Stout rawhide thongs had given way like paper; where the thongs had held, flesh and bones had not. Balthus retched suddenly. He had hunted bears and panthers, but he had never dreamed the beast lived which could make such a red ruin of a human frame in the flicker of an instant.

The saber-tooth vanished through the gate and a few moments later a deep roar sounded through the forest, receding in the distance. But the Picts still shrank back against the huts, and the shaman still stood facing the gate that was like a black opening to let in the night.

Cold sweat burst suddenly out on Balthus' skin. What new horror would come through that gate to make carrion-meat of *his* body? Sick panic assailed him and he strained futilely at his thongs. The night pressed in very black and horrible outside the firelight. The fires themselves glowed lurid as the fires of hell. He felt the eyes of the Picts upon him – hundreds of hungry, cruel eyes that reflected the lust of souls utterly without humanity as he knew it. They no longer seemed men; they were devils of this black jungle, as inhuman as the creatures to which the fiend in the nodding plumes screamed through the darkness.

Zogar sent another call shuddering through the night, and it was utterly unlike the first cry. There was a hideous sibilance in it – Balthus turned cold at the implication. If a serpent could hiss that loud, it would make just such a sound.

This time there was no answer – only a period of breathless silence in which the pound of Balthus' heart strangled him; and then there sounded a swishing outside the gate, a dry rustling that sent chills down Balthus' spine. Again the fire-lit gate held a hideous occupant.

Again Balthus recognized the monster from ancient legends. He saw and knew the ancient and evil serpent which swayed there, its wedge-shaped head, huge as that of a horse, as high as a tall man's head, and its palely gleaming barrel rippling out behind it. A forked tongue darted in and out, and the firelight glittered on bared fangs.

Balthus became incapable of emotion. The horror of his fate paralyzed him. That was the reptile that the ancients called Ghost Snake, the pale, abominable terror that of old glided into huts by night to devour whole families. Like the python it crushed its victim, but unlike other constrictors its fangs bore venom that carried madness and death. It too had long been considered extinct. But Valannus had spoken truly. No white man knew what shapes haunted the great forests beyond Black River.

It came on silently, rippling over the ground, its hideous head on the same level, its neck curving back slightly for the stroke. Balthus gazed with glazed, hypnotized stare into that loathsome gullet down which he would soon be engulfed, and he was aware of no sensation except a vague nausea.

And then something that glinted in the firelight streaked from the shadows of the huts, and the great reptile whipped about and went into instant convulsions. As in a dream Balthus saw a short throwing spear transfixing the mighty neck, just below the gaping jaws; the shaft protruded from one side, the steel head from the other.

Knotting and looping hideously, the maddened reptile rolled into the circle of men who strove back from him. The spear had not severed its spine, but merely transfixed its great neck muscles. Its furiously lashing tail mowed down a dozen men and its jaws snapped convulsively, splashing others with venom that burned like liquid fire. Howling, cursing, screaming, frantic, they scattered before it, knocking each other down in their flight, trampling the fallen, bursting through the huts. The giant snake rolled into a fire, scattering sparks and brands, and the pain lashed it to more frenzied efforts. A hut wall buckled under the ram-like impact of its flailing tail, disgorging howling people.

Men stampeded through the fires, knocking the logs right and left. The flames sprang up, then sank. A reddish dim glow was all that lighted that nightmare scene where the giant reptile whipped and rolled and men clawed and shrieked in frantic flight.

Balthus felt something jerk at his wrists and then, miraculously, he was free, and a strong hand dragged him behind the post. Dazedly he saw Conan, felt the forest man's iron grip on his arm.

There was blood on the Cimmerian's mail, dried blood on the sword in his right hand; he loomed dim and gigantic in the shadowy light.

"Come on! Before they get over their panic!"

Balthus felt the haft of an axe shoved into his hand. Zogar Sag had disappeared. Conan dragged Balthus after him until the youth's numb brain awoke, and his legs began to move of their own accord. Then Conan released him and ran into the building where the skulls hung. Balthus followed him. He got a glimpse of a grim stone altar, faintly lighted by the glow outside; five human heads grinned on that altar, and there was a grisly familiarity about the features of the freshest; it was the head of the merchant Tiberias. Behind the altar was an idol, dim, indistinct, bestial, yet vaguely man-like in outline. Then fresh horror choked Balthus as the shape heaved up suddenly with a rattle of chains, lifting long misshapen arms in the gloom.

Conan's sword flailed down, crunching through flesh and bone, and then the Cimmerian was dragging Balthus around the altar, past a huddled shaggy bulk on the floor, to a door at the back of the long hut. Through this they burst, out into the enclosure again. But a few yards beyond them loomed the stockade.

It was dark behind the altar-hut. The mad stampede of the Picts had not carried them in that direction. At the wall Conan halted, gripped Balthus and heaved him at arms' length in the air as he might have lifted a child. Balthus grasped the points of the upright logs set in the sun-dried mud and scrambled up on them, ignoring the havoc done his skin. He lowered a hand to the Cimmerian, when around the corner of the altar-hut sprang a fleeing Pict. He halted short, glimpsing the man on the wall in the faint glow of the fires. Conan hurled his axe with deadly aim, but the warrior's mouth was already open for a yell of warning, and it rang loud above the din, cut short as he dropped with a shattered skull.

Blind terrors had not submerged all ingrained instincts. As that wild yell rose above the clamor, there was an instant's lull, and then a hundred throats bayed ferocious answer and warriors came leaping to repel the attack presaged by the warning.

Conan leaped high, caught, not Balthus' hand but his arm near the shoulder, and swung himself up. Balthus set his teeth against the strain, and then the Cimmerian was on the wall beside him, and the fugitives dropped down on the other side.

V

THE CHILDREN OF JHEBBAL SAG

"Which way is the river?" Balthus was confused.

"We don't dare try for the river now," grunted Conan. "The woods between the village and the river are swarming with warriors. Come on! We'll head in the last direction they'll expect us to go — west!"

Looking back as they entered the thick growth, Balthus beheld the wall dotted with black heads as the savages peered over. The Picts were bewildered. They had not gained the wall in time to see the fugitives take cover. They had rushed to the wall expecting to repel an attack in force. They had seen the body of the dead warrior. But no enemy was in sight.

Balthus realized that they did not yet know their prisoner had escaped. From other sounds he believed that the warriors, directed by the shrill voice of Zogar Sag, were destroying the wounded serpent with arrows. The monster was out of the shaman's control. A moment later the quality of the yells was altered. Screeches of rage rose in the night.

Conan laughed grimly. He was leading Balthus along a narrow trail that ran west under the black branches, stepping as swiftly and surely as if he trod a well-lighted thoroughfare. Balthus stumbled after him, guiding himself by feeling the dense wall on either hand.

"They'll be after us now. Zogar's discovered you're gone, and he knows my head wasn't in the pile before the altar-hut. The dog! If I'd had another spear I'd have thrown it through him before I struck the snake. Keep to the trail. They can't track us by torchlight, and there are a score of paths leading from the village. They'll follow those leading to the river first — throw a cordon of warriors for miles along the bank, expecting us to try to break through. We won't take to the woods until we have to. We can make better time on this trail. Now buckle down to it and run as you never ran before."

"They got over their panic cursed quick!" panted Balthus, complying with a fresh burst of speed.

"They're not afraid of anything, very long," grunted Conan.

For a space nothing was said between them. The fugitives devoted all their attention to covering distance. They were plunging deeper and deeper into the wilderness and getting further away from civilization at every step, but Balthus did not question Conan's wisdom. The Cimmerian presently took time to grunt: "When we're far enough away from the village we'll swing back to the river in a big circle. No other village within miles of Gwawela. All the Picts are gathered in that vicinity. We'll circle wide around them. They can't track us until daylight. They'll pick up our path then, but before dawn we'll leave the trail and take to the woods."

They plunged on. The yells died out behind them. Balthus' breath was whistling through his teeth. He felt a pain in his side. Running became torture. He blundered against the bushes on each side of the trail. Conan pulled up suddenly, turned and stared back down the dim path.

Somewhere the moon was rising, a dim white glow amidst a tangle of branches.

"Shall we take to the woods?" panted Balthus.

"Give me your axe," murmured Conan softly. "Something is close behind us."

"Then we'd better leave the trail!" exclaimed Balthus.

Conan shook his head and drew his companion into a dense thicket. The moon rose higher, making a dim light in the path.

"We can't fight the whole tribe!" whispered Balthus.

"No human being could have found our trail so quickly, or followed us so swiftly," muttered Conan. "Keep silent."

There followed a tense silence in which Balthus felt that his heart could be heard pounding for miles away. Then abruptly, without a sound to announce its coming, a savage head appeared in the dim path. Balthus' heart jumped into his throat; at first glance he feared to look upon the awful head of the saber-tooth. But this head was smaller, more narrow; it was a leopard which stood there, snarling silently and glaring down the trail. What wind there was was blowing toward the hiding men, concealing their scent. The beast lowered his head and snuffed the trail, then moved forward uncertainly. A chill played down Balthus' spine. The brute was undoubtedly trailing them.

And it was suspicious. It lifted its head, its eyes glowing like balls of fire, and growled low in its throat. And at that instant Conan hurled the axe.

All the weight of arm and shoulder was behind the throw, and the axe was a streak of silver in the dim moon. Almost before he realized what had happened, Balthus saw the leopard rolling on the ground in its death-throes, the handle of the axe standing up from its head. The head of the weapon had split its narrow skull.

Conan bounded from the bushes, wrenched his axe free and dragged the limp body in among the trees, concealing it from the casual glance.

"Now let's go and go fast!" he grunted, leading the way southward, away from the trail. "There'll be warriors coming after that cat. As soon as he got his wits back Zogar sent him after us. The Picts would follow him, but he'd leave them far behind. He'd circle the village until he hit our trail and then come after us like a streak. They couldn't keep up with him, but they'll have an idea as to our general direction. They'd follow, listening for his cry. Well, they won't hear that, but they'll find the blood on the trail, and look around and find the body in the brush. They'll pick up our spoor there, if they can. Walk with care."

He avoided clinging briars and low hanging branches effortlessly, gliding between trees without touching the stems and always planting his feet in the places calculated to show less evidence of his passing; but with Balthus it was slower, more laborious work.

No sound came from behind them. They had covered more than a mile when Balthus said: "Does Zogar Sag catch leopard-cubs and train them for blood-hounds?"

Conan shook his head. "That was a leopard he called out of the woods."

"But," Balthus persisted, "if he can order the beasts to do his bidding, why doesn't he rouse them all and have them after us? The forest is full of leopards; why send only one after us?"

Conan did not reply for a space, and when he did it was with a curious reticence.

"He can't command all the animals. Only such as remember Jhebbal Sag."

"Jhebbal Sag?" Balthus repeated the ancient name hesitantly. He had never heard it spoken more than three or four times in his whole life.

"Once all living things worshipped him. That was long ago, when beasts and men spoke one language. Men have forgotten him; even the beasts forget. Only a few remember. The men who remember Jhebbal Sag and the beasts who remember are brothers and speak the same tongue."

Balthus did not reply; he had strained at a Pictish stake and seen the nighted jungle give up its fanged horrors at a shaman's call.

"Civilized men laugh," said Conan. "But not one can tell me how Zogar Sag can call pythons and tigers and leopards out of the wilderness and make them do his bidding. They would say it is a lie, if they dared. That's the way with civilized men. When they can't explain something by their half-baked science, they refuse to believe it."

The people on the Tauran were closer to the primitive than most Aquilonians; superstitions persisted, whose sources were lost in antiquity. And Balthus had seen that which still prickled his flesh. He could not refute the monstrous thing which Conan's words implied.

"I've heard that there's an ancient grove sacred to Jhebbal Sag somewhere in this forest," said Conan. "I don't know. I've never seen it. But more beasts *remember* in this country than any I've ever seen."

"Then others will be on our trail?"

"They are now," was Conan's disquieting answer. "Zogar would never leave our tracking to one beast alone."

"What are we to do, then?" asked Balthus uneasily, grasping his axe as he stared at the gloomy arches above them. His flesh crawled with the momentary expectation of ripping talons and fangs leaping from the shadows.

"Wait!"

Conan turned, squatted and with his knife began scratching a curious symbol in the mold. Stooping to look at it over his shoulder, Balthus felt a crawling of the flesh along his spine, he knew not why. He felt no wind against his face, but there was a rustling of leaves above them and a weird moaning swept ghostlily through the branches. Conan glanced up inscrutably, then rose and stood staring somberly down at the symbol he had drawn.

"What is it?" whispered Balthus. It looked archaic and meaningless to him. He supposed that it was his ignorance of artistry which prevented his identifying it as one of the conventional designs of some prevailing culture.

But had he been the most erudite artist in the world, he would have been no nearer the solution.

"I saw it carved in the rock of a cave no human had visited for a million years," muttered Conan. "In the uninhabited mountains beyond the Sea of Vilayet, half a world away from this spot. Later I saw a black witch-finder of Kush scratch it in the sand of a nameless river. He told me part of its meaning – it's sacred to Jhebbal Sag and the creatures which worship him. Watch!"

They drew back among the dense foliage some yards away and waited in tense silence. To the east drums muttered and somewhere to north and west other drums answered. Balthus shivered, though he knew long miles of black forest separated him from the grim beaters of those drums whose dull pulsing was a sinister overture that set the dark stage for bloody drama.

Balthus found himself holding his breath. Then with a slight shaking of the leaves, the bushes parted and a magnificent panther came into view. The moonlight dappling through the leaves shone on its glossy coat rippling with the play of the great muscles beneath it.

With its head held low it glided toward them. It was smelling out their trail. Then it halted as if frozen, its muzzle almost touching the symbol cut in the mold. For a long space it crouched motionless; it flattened its long body and laid its head on the ground before the mark. And Balthus felt the short hairs stir on his scalp. For the attitude of the great carnivore was one of awe and adoration.

Then the panther rose and backed away carefully, belly almost to the ground. With his hind-quarters among the bushes he wheeled as if in sudden panic and was gone like a flash of dappled light.

Balthus mopped his brow with a trembling hand and glanced at Conan.

The barbarian's eyes were smoldering with fires that never lit the eyes of men bred to the ideas of civilization. In that instant he was all wild, and had forgotten the man at his side. In his burning gaze Balthus glimpsed and vaguely recognized pristine images and half-embodied memories, shadows from Life's dawn, forgotten and repudiated by sophisticated races – ancient, primeval phantasms unnamed and nameless.

Then the deeper fires were masked and Conan was silently leading the way deeper into the forest.

"We've no more to fear from the beasts," he said after awhile. "But we've left a sign for men to read. They won't follow our trail very easily, and until they find that symbol they won't know for sure we've turned south. Even then it won't be easy to smell us without the beasts to aid them. But the woods south of the trail will be full of warriors looking for us. If we keep moving after daylight, we'll be sure to run into some of them. As soon as we find a good place we'll hide and wait until another night to swing back and make the river. We've got to warn Valannus, but it won't help him any if we get ourselves killed."

"Warn Valannus?"

"Hell, the woods along the river are swarming with Picts! That's why they got us. Zogar's brewing war-magic; no mere raid this time. He's done something no Pict has done in my memory – united as many as fifteen or sixteen clans. His magic did it; they'll follow a wizard farther than they will a war-chief. You saw the mob in the village; and there were hundreds hiding along the river bank that you didn't see. More coming, from the farther villages. He'll have at least three thousand fighting men. I lay in the bushes and heard their talk as they went past. They mean to attack the fort. When, I don't know, but they won't delay long. Zogar doesn't dare. He's gathered them and whipped them into a frenzy. If he doesn't lead them into battle quickly, they'll fall to quarreling with each other. They're like blood-mad tigers.

"I don't know whether they can take the fort or not. Anyway, we've got to get back across the river and give the warning. The settlers on the Velitrium road must either get into the fort or back to Velitrium. While the Picts are besieging the fort, war-parties will range the road far to the east – might even cross Thunder River and raid the thickly settled country behind Velitrium."

As he talked he was leading the way deeper and deeper into the ancient wilderness. Presently he grunted with satisfaction. They had reached a spot where the underbrush was more scattered, and an outcropping of stone was visible, wandering off southward. Balthus felt more secure as they followed it. Not even a Pict could trail them over naked rock.

"How did you get away?" he asked presently.

Conan tapped his mail shirt and helmet.

"If more borderers would wear harness there'd be fewer skulls hanging on the altar-huts. But most men make noise if they wear armor. They were waiting on each side of the path, without moving. And when a Pict stands motionless, the very beasts of the forest pass him without seeing him. They'd seen us crossing the river and got in their places. If they'd gone into ambush after we left the bank, I'd have had some hint of it. But they were waiting and not even a leaf trembled. The devil himself couldn't have suspected anything. The first suspicion I had was when I heard a shaft rasp against a bow as it was pulled back. I dropped and yelled for the men behind me to drop, but they were too slow – taken by surprise like that.

"Most of them fell at the first volley that raked us from both sides. Some of the arrows crossed the trail and struck Picts on the other side. I heard them howl." He grinned with vicious satisfaction. "Such of us as were left plunged into the woods and closed with them. When I saw the others were all down or taken, I broke through and outfooted the painted devils through the darkness. They were all around me. I ran and crawled and sneaked and sometimes I lay on my belly under the bushes while they passed me on all sides.

"I tried for the shore and found it lined with them, waiting for just such a move. But I'd have cut my way through and taken a chance on swimming, only I heard the drums pounding in the village and knew they'd taken somebody alive.

"They were all so engrossed in Zogar's magic that I was able to climb the wall behind the altar-hut. There was a warrior supposed to be watching at that point, but he was squatting behind the hut and peering around the corner at the ceremony. I came up behind him and broke his neck with my hands before he knew what was happening. It was his spear I threw into the snake, and that's his axe you're carrying."

"But what was that – that thing you killed in the altar-hut?" asked Balthus, with a shiver at the memory of the dim-seen horror.

"One of Zogar's gods. One of Jhebbal's children that didn't remember and had to be kept chained to the altar. A bull ape. The Picts think they're sacred to the Hairy One who lives on the moon – the gorilla-god of Gullah.

"It's getting light. Here's a good place to hide until we see how close they're on our trail. Probably have to wait until night to break back to the river."

A low hill pitched upward, girdled and covered by thick trees and bushes. Near the crest Conan slid into a tangle of jutting rocks, crowned by dense bushes. Lying among them they could see the jungle below without being seen. It was a good place to hide or defend. Balthus did not believe that even a Pict could have trailed them over the rocky ground for the past four or five miles, but he was afraid of the beasts that obeyed Zogar Sag. His faith in the curious symbol wavered a little now. But Conan had dismissed the possibility of beasts tracking them.

A ghostly whiteness spread through the dense branches; the patches of sky visible altered in hue – grew from pink to blue. Balthus felt the gnawing of hunger, though he had slaked his thirst at a stream they had skirted. There was complete silence, except for an occasional chirp of a bird. The drums were no longer to be heard. Balthus' thoughts reverted to the grim scene before the altar-hut.

"Those were ostrich plumes Zogar Sag wore," he said. "I've seen them on the helmets of knights who rode from the East to visit the barons of the marches. There are no ostriches in this forest, are there?"

"They came from Kush," answered Conan. "West of here, many marches, lies the sea-shore. Ships from Zingara occasionally come and trade weapons and ornaments and wine to the coastal tribes for skins and copper ore and gold dust. Sometimes they trade ostrich plumes they got from the Stygians, who in turn got them from the black tribes of Kush, which lies south of Stygia. The Pictish shamans place great store by them. But there's much risk in such trade. The Picts are too likely to try to seize the ship. And the coast is dangerous to ships. I've sailed along it when I was with the pirates of the Barachan Isles, which lie southwest of Zingara."

Balthus looked at his companion with admiration.

"I knew you hadn't spent your life on this frontier. You've mentioned several far places. You've travelled widely?"

"I've roamed far; farther than any other man of my race ever wandered. I've seen all the great cities of the Hyborians, the Shemites, the Stygians and the Hyrkanians. I've roamed in the unknown countries south of the black kingdoms of Kush, and east of the Sea of Vilayet. I've been mercenary captain, a corsair, a *kozak*, a penniless vagabond, a general – hell, I've been everything except a king, and I may be that, before I die." The fancy pleased him, and he grinned hardly. Then he shrugged his shoulders and stretched his mighty figure on the rocks. "This is as good life as any. I don't know how long I'll stay on the frontier; a week, a month, a year. I have a roving foot. But it's as well on the border as anywhere."

Balthus set himself to watch the forest below them. Momentarily he expected to see fierce painted faces thrust through the leaves. But as the hours passed no stealthy footfall disturbed the brooding quiet. Balthus believed the Picts had missed their trail and given up the chase. Conan grew restless.

"We should have sighted parties scouring the woods for us. If they've quit the chase it's because they're after bigger game. They may be gathering to cross the river and storm the fort."

"Would they come this far south if they lost the trail?"

"They've lost the trail, all right; otherwise they'd have been on our necks before now. Under ordinary circumstances they'd scour the woods for miles in every direction. Some of them should have passed within sight of this hill. They must be preparing to cross the river. We've got to take a chance and make for the river."

Creeping down the rocks Balthus felt his flesh crawl between his shoulders as he momentarily expected a withering blast of arrows from the green masses about them. He feared that the Picts had discovered them and were lying about in ambush. But Conan was convinced no enemies were near, and the Cimmerian was right.

"We're miles to the south of the village," grunted Conan. "We'll hit straight through for the river. I don't know how far down the river they've spread. We'll hope to hit it below them."

With haste that seemed reckless to Balthus they hurried eastward. The woods seemed empty of life. Conan believed that all the Picts were gathered in the vicinity of Gwawela, if, indeed, they had not already crossed the river. He did not believe they would cross in the daytime, however.

"Some woodsman would be sure to see them and give the alarm. They'll cross above and below the fort, out of sight of the sentries. Then others will get in canoes and make straight across for the river wall. As soon as they attack, those hidden in the woods on the east shore will assail the fort from the other sides. They've tried that before, and got the guts shot and hacked out of them. But this time they've got enough men to make a real onslaught of it."

They pushed on without pausing, though Balthus gazed longingly at the squirrels flitting among the branches, which he could have brought down with a cast of his axe. With a sigh he drew up his broad belt. The everlasting silence and gloom of the primitive forest was beginning to depress him. He found himself thinking of the open oak groves and sun-dappled meadows of the Tauran, of the bluff cheer of his father's steep-thatched, diamond-paned house, of the fat cows browsing through the deep, lush grass, and the hearty fellowship of the brawny, bare-armed ploughmen and herdsmen.

He felt lonely, in spite of his companion. Conan was as much a part of this wilderness as Balthus was alien to it. The Cimmerian might have spent years among the great cities of the world; he might have walked with the rulers of civilization; he might even achieve his wild whim some day and rule as king of a civilized nation; stranger things had happened. But he was no less a barbarian. He was concerned only with the naked fundamentals of life. The warm intimacies of small, kindly things, the sentiments and delicious trivialities that make up so much of civilized men's lives were meaningless to him. A wolf was no less a wolf because a whim of chance caused him to run with the watch-dogs. Bloodshed and violence and savagery were the natural elements of the life Conan knew; he could not, and would never understand the little things that are so dear to the souls of civilized men and women.

The shadows were lengthening when they reached the river and peered through the masking bushes. They could see up and down the river for about a mile each way. The sullen stream lay bare and empty. Conan scowled across at the other shore.

"We've got to take another chance here. We've got to skirt the river. We don't know whether they've crossed or not. The woods over there may be alive with them. We've got to risk it. We're about six miles south of Gwawela."

He wheeled and ducked as a bowstring twanged. Something like a white flash of light streaked through the bushes. Balthus knew it was an arrow. Then with a tigerish bound Conan was through the bushes. Balthus caught the gleam of steel as he whirled his sword, and heard a death scream. The next instant he had broken through the bushes after the Cimmerian.

A Pict with a shattered skull lay face-down on the ground, his fingers spasmodically clawing at the grass. Half a dozen others were swarming about Conan, swords and axes lifted. They had cast away their bows, useless at such deadly close quarters. Their lower jaws were painted white contrasting vividly with their dark faces, and the designs on their muscular breasts differed from any Balthus had ever seen.

One of them hurled his axe at Balthus and rushed after it with lifted knife. Balthus ducked and then caught the wrist that drove the knife licking at his throat. They went to the ground together, rolling over and over. The Pict was like a wild beast, his muscles hard as steel strings.

Balthus was striving to maintain his hold on the wild man's wrist and bring his own axe into play, but so fast and furious was the struggle that each attempt to strike was blocked. The Pict was wrenching furiously to free his knife hand, was clutching at Balthus' axe, and driving his knees at the youth's groin. Suddenly he attempted to shift his knife to his free hand, and in that instant Balthus, struggling up on one knee, split the painted head with a desperate blow of his axe.

He sprang up and glared wildly about for his companion, expecting to see him overwhelmed by numbers. Then he realized the full strength and ferocity of the Cimmerian. Conan bestrode two of his attackers, shorn half asunder by that terrible broadsword. As Balthus looked he saw the Cimmerian beat down a thrusting short sword, avoid the stroke of an axe with a cat-like sidewise spring which brought him within arm's length of a squat savage stooping for a bow. Before the Pict could straighten the red sword flailed down and clove him from shoulder to mid-breastbone where the blade stuck. The remaining warriors rushed in, one from each side. Balthus hurled his axe with an accuracy that reduced the attackers to one, and Conan, abandoning his efforts to free his sword, wheeled and met the remaining Pict with his bare hands. The stocky warrior, a head shorter than his tall enemy, leaped in striking with his axe, at the same time stabbing murderously with his knife. The knife broke on the Cimmerian's mail, and the axe checked in mid-air as Conan's fingers locked like iron on the descending arm. A bone snapped loudly, and Balthus saw the Pict wince and falter. The next instant he was swept off his feet, lifted high above the Cimmerian's head – he writhed in mid-air for an instant, kicking and thrashing, and then was dashed headlong to the earth with such force that he rebounded, and then lay still, his limp posture telling of splintered limbs and a broken spine.

"Come on!" Conan wrenched his sword free and snatched up an axe. "Grab a bow and a handful of arrows, and hurry! We've got to trust to our heels again. That yell was heard. They'll be here in no time. If we tried to swim across now, they'd feather us with arrows before we reached mid-stream!"

Up the river sounded a fierce howling. Balthus shuddered to think that it came from human mouths. Grasping the weapons he had snatched he followed Conan who plunged into the thickets away from the bank, and ran like a flying shadow.

VI
RED AXES OF THE BORDER

Conan did not plunge deeply into the forest. A few hundred yards from the river, he altered his slanting course and ran parallel with it. Balthus recognized a grim determination not to be hunted away from the river which they must cross if they were to warn the men in the fort. Behind them rose more loudly the yells of the forest men. Balthus believed the Picts had reached the glade where the bodies of the slain men lay. Then further yells seemed to indicate that the savages were streaming into the woods in pursuit. They had left a trail any Pict could follow.

Conan increased his speed and Balthus grimly set his teeth and kept on his heels, though he felt he might collapse any time. It seemed centuries since he had eaten last. He kept going more by an effort of will than anything else. His blood was pounding so furiously in his ear drums that he was not aware when the yells died out behind them.

Conan halted suddenly. Balthus leaned against a tree and panted.

"They've quit!" grunted the Cimmerian, scowling.

"Sneaking – up – on – us!" gasped Balthus. Conan shook his head.

"A short chase like this they'd yell every step of the way. No. They've gone back. I thought I heard somebody yelling behind them a few seconds before the noise began to get dimmer. They've been recalled. And that's good for us, but damned bad for the men in the fort. It means the warriors are being summoned out of the woods for the attack. Those men we ran into were warriors from a tribe down the river. They were undoubtedly headed for Gwawela to join in the assault on the fort. Damn it, we're further away than ever, now. We've *got* to get across the river."

Turning east he hurried through the thickets with no attempt at concealment. Balthus followed him, for the first time feeling the sting of lacerations on his breast and shoulder where the Pict's savage teeth had scored him. He was pushing through the thick bushes that fringed the bank when Conan pulled him back. Then he heard a rhythmic splashing and peering through the leaves, saw a dug-out canoe coming up the river, its single occupant paddling hard against the current. He was a strongly built Pict with a white heron feather thrust in a copper band that confined his square-cut mane.

"That's a Gwawela man," muttered Conan. "Emissary from Zogar. White plume shows that. He's carried a peace talk to the tribes down the river and now he's trying to get back and take a hand in the slaughter."

The lone ambassador was now almost even with their hiding place, and suddenly Balthus almost jumped out of his skin. At his very ear had sounded the harsh gutturals of a Pict. Then he realized that Conan had called to the paddler in his own tongue. The man started, scanned the bushes and called back something. Then cast a startled glance across the river, bent low and sent the canoe shooting in toward the western bank. Not understanding, Balthus saw Conan take from his hand the bow he had picked up in the glade, and notch an arrow.

The Pict had run his canoe in close to the shore, and staring up into the bushes, called out something. His answer came in the twang of the bowstring, the streaking flight of the arrow that sank to the feathers in his broad breast. With a choking gasp he slumped sidewise and rolled into the shallow water. In an instant Conan was down the bank and wading into the water to grasp the drifting canoe. Balthus stumbled after him, somewhat dazedly crawled into the canoe. Conan scrambled in, seized the paddle and sent the craft shooting toward the eastern shore. Balthus noted with envious admiration the play of the great muscles beneath the sun-burnt skin. The Cimmerian seemed an iron man, who never knew fatigue.

"What did you say to the Pict?" asked Balthus.

"Told him to pull into shore; said there was a white forest runner on the other bank who was trying to get a shot at him."

"That doesn't seem fair," Balthus objected. "He thought a friend was speaking to him. You mimicked a Pict perfectly —"

"We needed his boat," grunted Conan, not pausing in his exertions. "Only way to lure him to the bank. Which is worse — to betray a Pict who'd enjoy skinning us both alive, or betray the men across the river whose lives depend on our getting over?"

Balthus mulled over this delicate ethical question for a moment, then shrugged his shoulder and asked: "How far are we from the fort?"

Conan pointed to a creek which flowed into Black River from the east, a few hundred yards below them.

"That's South Creek; it's ten miles from its mouth to the fort. It's the southern boundary of Conajohara. Marshes miles wide south of it. No danger of a raid from across them. Nine miles above the fort North Creek forms the other boundary. Marshes beyond that, too. That's why an attack must come from the west, across Black River. Conajohara's just like a spear, with a point nineteen miles wide, thrust into the Pictish wilderness."

"Why don't we keep to the canoe and make the trip by water?"

"Because, considering the current we've got to brace, and the bends in the river, we can go faster afoot. Besides, remember Gwawela is south of the fort; if the Picts are crossing the river we'd run right into them."

Dusk was gathering as they stepped upon the eastern bank. Without pause Conan pushed on northward, at a pace that made Balthus' sturdy legs ache.

"Valannus wanted a fort built at the mouths of North and South Creeks," grunted the Cimmerian. "Then the river could be patrolled constantly. But the government wouldn't do it.

"Soft bellied fools sitting on velvet cushions with naked girls offering them iced wine on their knees – I know the breed. They can't see any further than their palace wall. Diplomacy – hell! They'd fight Picts with theories of territorial expansion. Valannus and men like him have to obey the orders of a set of damned fools. They'll never grab any more Pictish land, any more than they'll ever rebuild Venarium. The time may come when they'll see the barbarians swarming over the walls of the Eastern cities!"

A week before Balthus would have laughed at any such preposterous suggestion. Now he made no reply. He had seen the unconquerable ferocity of the men who dwelt beyond the frontiers.

He shivered, casting glances at the sullen river, just visible through the bushes, at the arches of the trees which crowded close to its banks. He kept remembering that the Picts might have crossed the river and be lying in ambush between them and the fort. It was growing dark fast.

A slight sound ahead of them jumped his heart into his throat and Conan's sword gleamed in the air. He lowered it when a dog, a great, gaunt, scarred beast, slunk out of the bushes and stood staring at them.

"That dog belonged to a settler who tried to build his cabin on the bank of the river a few miles south of the fort," grunted Conan. "The Picts slipped over and killed him, of course, and burned his cabin. We found him dead among the embers, and the dog lying senseless among three Picts he'd killed. He was almost cut to pieces. We took him to the fort and dressed his wounds, but after he recovered he took to the woods and turned wild. What now, Slasher, are you hunting the men who killed your master?"

The massive head swung from side to side and his eyes glowed greenly. He did not growl or bark. Silently as a phantom he slid in behind them.

"Let him come," muttered Conan. "He can smell the devils before we can see them."

Balthus smiled and laid his hand caressingly on the dog's head. The lips involuntarily writhed back to display the gleaming fangs, then the great beast bent his head sheepishly, and his tail moved with jerky uncertainty, as if the owner had almost forgotten the emotions of friendliness. Balthus mentally compared the great gaunt hard body with the fat sleek hounds tumbling vociferously over one another in his father's kennel yard. He sighed. The frontier was no less hard for beasts than for men. This dog had almost forgotten the meaning of kindness and friendliness.

Slasher glided ahead and Conan let him take the lead. The last tinge of dusk faded into stark darkness. The miles fell away under their steady feet. Slasher seemed voiceless. Suddenly he halted, tense, ears lifted. An instant later the men heard it – a demoniac yelling up the river ahead of them, faint as a whisper.

Conan swore like a madman.

"They've attacked the fort! We're too late! Come on!"

He increased his pace, trusting to the dog to smell out ambushes ahead. In a flood of tense excitement Balthus forgot his hunger and weariness. The yells grew louder as they advanced, and above the devilish screaming they could hear the deep shouts of the soldiers. Just as Balthus began to fear they would run into the savages who seemed to be howling just ahead of them, Conan swung away from the river in a wide semi-circle that carried them to a low rise from which they could look over the forest. They saw the fort, lighted with torches thrust over the parapets on long poles. These cast a flickering uncertain light over the clearing, and in that light they saw throngs of naked, painted figures along the fringe of the clearing. The river swarmed with canoes. The Picts had the fort completely surrounded.

An incessant hail of arrows rained against the stockade from the woods and the river. The deep twanging of the bow-strings rose above the howling. Yelling like wolves several hundred naked warriors with axes in their hands ran from under the trees and raced toward the eastern gate. They were within a hundred and fifty yards of their objective when a withering blast of arrows from the wall littered the ground with corpses and sent the survivors fleeing back to the trees. The men in the canoes rushed their boats toward the river-wall, and were met by another shower of cloth-yard shafts and a volley from the small balistas mounted on towers on that side of the stockade. Stones and logs whirled through the air and splintered and sank half a dozen canoes, killing their occupants, and the other boats drew back out of range. A deep roar of triumph rose from the walls of the fort, answered by bestial howling from all quarters.

"Shall we try to break through?" asked Balthus, trembling with eagerness.

Conan shook his head. He stood with his arms folded, his head slightly bent, a somber and brooding figure.

"The fort's doomed. The Picts are blood-mad, and won't stop until they're all killed. And there are too many of them for the men in the fort to kill. We couldn't break through, and if we did, we could do nothing but die with Valannus."

"There's nothing we can do but save our own hides, then?"

"Yes. We've got to warn the settlers. Do you know why the Picts are not trying to burn the fort with fire-arrows? Because they don't want a flame that might warn the people to the east. They plan to stamp out the fort, and then sweep east before anyone knows of its fall. They may cross Thunder River and take Velitrium before the people know what's happened. At least they'll destroy every living thing between the fort and Thunder River.

"We've failed to warn the fort, and I see now it would have done no good if we hadn't. The fort's too poorly manned. A few more charges and the Picts will be over the walls and breaking down the gates. But we can start the settlers toward Velitrium. Come on! We're outside the circle the Picts have thrown around the fort. We'll keep clear of it."

They swung out in a wide arc, hearing the rising and falling of the volume of the yells, marking each charge and repulse. The men in the fort were holding their own; but the shrieks of the Picts did not diminish in savagery. They vibrated with a timbre that held assurance of ultimate victory.

Before Balthus realized they were close to it, they broke into the road leading east.

"Now run!" grunted Conan. Balthus set his teeth. It was nineteen miles to Velitrium, a good five to Scalp Creek beyond which began the settlements. It seemed to the Aquilonian that they had been fighting and running for centuries. But the nervous excitement that rioted through his blood stimulated him to superhuman efforts.

Slasher ran ahead of them, his head to the ground, snarling low, the first sound they had heard.

"Picts ahead of us!" snarled Conan, dropping to one knee and scanning the ground in the starlight. He shook his head, baffled. "I can't tell how many. Probably only a small party. Some that couldn't wait to take the fort. They've gone ahead to butcher the settlers in their beds! Come on!"

Ahead of them presently they saw a small blaze through the trees, and heard a wild and ferocious chanting. The trail bent there, and leaving it, they cut across the bend, through the thickets. A few moments later they were looking on a hideous sight. An ox wain stood in the road piled with meager household furnishings; it was burning; the oxen lay near with their throats cut. A man and a woman lay in the road, stripped and mutilated. Five Picts were dancing about them with fantastic leaps and bounds, waving bloody axes; one of them brandished the woman's red-smeared gown.

At the sight a red haze swam before Balthus. Lifting his bow he lined the prancing figure, black against the fire, and loosed. The slayer leaped convulsively and fell dead with the arrow through his heart. Then the two white men and the dog were upon the startled survivors. Conan was animated merely by his fighting spirit and an old, old racial hate, but Balthus was afire with new-kindled wrath.

He met the first Pict to oppose him with a ferocious swipe that split the painted skull, and sprang over his falling body to grapple with the others. But Conan had already killed one of the two he had chosen, and the leap of the Aquilonian was a second late. The warrior was down with the long sword through him even as Balthus' axe was lifted. Turning toward the remaining Pict, Balthus saw Slasher rise from his victim, his great jaws dripping blood.

Balthus said nothing as he looked down at the pitiful forms in the road beside the burning wain. Both were young, the woman little more than a girl. By some whim of chance the Picts had left her face unmarred, and even in the agonies of an awful death it was beautiful. But her soft young body had been hideously slashed with many knives – a mist clouded Balthus' eyes and he swallowed chokingly. The tragedy momentarily overcame him. He felt like falling upon the ground and weeping and biting the earth.

"Some young couple just hitting out on their own," Conan was saying as he wiped his sword unemotionally. "On their way to the fort when the Picts met them. Maybe the boy was going to enter the service; maybe take up land on the river. Well, that's what will happen to every man, woman and child this side of Thunder River if we don't get them into Velitrium in a hurry."

His knees trembled with nausea as Balthus followed Conan. There was no hint of weakness in the long easy stride of the Cimmerian. There was a kinship between him and the great gaunt brute that glided beside him. Slasher no longer growled with his head to the trail. The way was clear before them. The yelling on the river came faintly to them, but Balthus believed the fort was still holding. Conan halted suddenly, with an oath.

He showed Balthus a trail that led north from the road. It was an old trail, partly grown with new young growth, and this growth had recently been broken down. Balthus realized this fact more by feel than sight, though Conan seemed to see like a cat in the dark. The Cimmerian showed him where broad wagon tracks turned off the main trail, deeply indented in the forest mold.

"Settlers going to the licks after salt," he grunted. "They're at the edges of the marsh, about nine miles from here. Blast it! They'll be cut off and butchered to a man! Listen! One man can warn the people on the road. Go ahead and wake them up and herd them into Velitrium. I'll go and get the men gathering the salt. They'll be camped by the licks. We won't come back to the road. We'll head straight through the woods."

With no further comment Conan turned off the trail and hurried down the dim path, and Balthus, after staring after him for a few moments, set down along the road. The dog had remained with him, and glided softly at his heels. When Balthus had gone a few rods he heard the animal growl. Whirling, he glared back the way he had come, and was startled to see a vague ghostly glow vanishing into the forest in the direction Conan had taken. Slasher rumbled deep in his throat, his hackles stiff and his eyes balls of green fire. Balthus remembered the grim apparition that had taken the head of the merchant Tiberias not far from that spot, and he hesitated. The thing must be following Conan. But the giant Cimmerian had repeatedly demonstrated his ability to take care of himself, and Balthus felt his duty lay toward the helpless settlers who slumbered in the path of the red hurricane. The horror of the fiery phantom was overshadowed by the horror of those limp, violated bodies beside the burning ox wain.

He hurried down the road, crossed Scalp Creek and came in sight of the first settlers' cabin – a long, low structure of axe-hewn logs. In an instant he was pounding on the door. A sleepy voice inquired his pleasure.

"Get up! The Picts are over the river!"

That brought instant response. A low cry echoed his words and then the door was thrown open by a woman in a scanty shift. Her hair hung over her bare shoulders in disorder; she held a candle in one hand and an axe in the other. Her face was colorless, her eyes wide with terror.

"Come in!" she begged. "We'll hold the cabin."

"No. We must make for Velitrium. The fort can't hold them back. It may have fallen already. Don't stop to dress. Get your children and come on."

"But my man's gone with the others after salt!" she wailed, wringing her hands. Behind her peered three tousled youngsters, blinking and bewildered.

"Conan's gone after them. He'll fetch them through safe. We must hurry up the road to warn the other cabins."

Relief flooded her countenance.

"Mitra be thanked!" she cried. "If the Cimmerian's gone after them, they're safe if mortal man can save them!"

In a whirlwind of activity she snatched up the smallest child and herded the others through the door ahead of her. Balthus took the candle and ground it out under his heel. He listened an instant. No sound came up the dark road.

"Have you got a horse?"

"In the stable," she groaned. "Oh, hurry!"

He pushed her aside as she fumbled with shaking hands at the bars. He led the horse out and lifted the children on its back, telling them to hold to its mane and to each other. They stared at him seriously, making no outcry. The woman took the horse's halter and set out up the road. She still gripped her axe and Balthus knew that if cornered she would fight with the desperate courage of a she-panther.

He held behind, listening. He was oppressed by the belief that the fort had been stormed and taken; that the dark-skinned hordes were already streaming up the road toward Velitrium, drunken on slaughter and mad for blood. They would come with the speed of starving wolves.

Presently they saw another cabin looming ahead. The woman started to shriek a warning, but Balthus stopped her. He hurried to the door and knocked. A woman's voice answered him. He repeated his warning, and soon the cabin disgorged its occupants – an old woman, two young women and four children. Like the other woman's husband, their men had gone to the salt licks the day before, unsuspecting of any danger. One of the young women seemed dazed, the other prone to hysteria. But the old woman, a stern old veteran of the frontier, quieted them harshly; she helped Balthus get out the two horses that were stabled in a pen behind the cabin and put the children on them. Balthus urged that she herself mount with them, but she shook her head and made one of the younger women ride.

"She's with child," grunted the old woman. "I can walk – and fight, too, if it comes to that."

As they set out one of the young women said: "A young couple passed along the road about dusk; we advised them to spend the night at our cabin, but they were anxious to make the fort tonight – did – did –"

"They met the Picts," answered Balthus briefly; the woman sobbed in horror.

They were scarcely out of sight of the cabin when some distance behind them quavered a long high-pitched yell.

"A wolf!" exclaimed one of the women.

"A painted wolf with an axe in his hand," muttered Balthus. "Go! Rouse the other settlers along the road and take them with you. I'll scout along behind."

Without a word the old woman herded her charges ahead of her. As they faded into the darkness, Balthus could see the pale ovals that were the faces of the children twisted back over their shoulders to stare toward him. He remembered his own people on the Tauran and a moment's giddy sickness swam over him. With momentary weakness he groaned and sank down in the road; his muscular arm fell over Slasher's massive neck and he felt the dog's warm moist tongue touch his face.

He lifted his head and grinned with a painful effort.

"Come on, boy," he mumbled, rising. "We've got work to do."

A red glow suddenly became evident through the trees. The Picts had fired the last hut. He grinned. How Zogar Sag would froth if he knew his warriors had let their destructive natures get the better of them. The fire would warn the people further up the road. They would be awake and alert when the fugitives reached them. But his face grew grim. The women were travelling slowly, on foot and on the overloaded horses. The swift-footed Picts would run them down within a mile, unless – he took his position behind a tangle of fallen logs beside the trail. The road west of him was lighted by the burning cabin, and when the Picts came he saw them first – black, furtive figures etched against the distant glare.

Drawing a shaft to the head he loosed and one of the figures crumpled. The rest melted into the woods on either side of the road. Slasher whimpered with the killing lust beside him. Suddenly a figure appeared at the fringe of the trail, under the trees, and began gliding toward the fallen timbers. Balthus' bow-string twanged and the Pict yelped, staggered and fell into the shadows with the arrow through his thigh. Slasher cleared the timbers with a bound and leaped into the bushes. They were violently shaken and then the dog slunk back to Balthus' side, his jaws crimson.

No more appeared in the trail; Balthus began to fear they were stealing past his position through the woods, and when he heard a faint sound to his left he loosed blindly. He cursed as he heard the shaft splinter against a tree, but Slasher glided away as silently as a phantom, and presently Balthus heard a thrashing and a gurgling, and then Slasher came like a ghost through the bushes, snuggling his great, crimson-stained head against Balthus' arm. Blood oozed from a wound in his shoulder, but the sounds in the wood had ceased forever.

The men lurking on the edges of the road evidently sensed the fate of their companion, and decided that an open charge was preferable to being dragged down in the dark by a devil-beast they could not see nor hear. Perhaps they realized that only one man lay behind the logs. They came with a sudden rush, breaking cover from both sides of the trail. Three dropped with arrows through them – and the remaining pair hesitated. One turned and ran back down the road, but the other lunged over the breastwork, his eyes and teeth gleaming in the dim light, his axe lifted. Balthus' foot slipped as he sprang up, but the slip saved his life. The descending axe shaved a lock of hair from his head and the Pict rolled down the logs from the force of his wasted blow. Before he could regain his feet Slasher tore his throat out.

Then followed a tense period of waiting, in which time Balthus wondered if the man who had fled had been the only survivor of the party. Obviously it had been a small band who had either left the fighting at the fort, or was scouting ahead of the main body. Each moment that passed increased the chances for safety of the women and children hurrying toward Velitrium.

Then without warning a shower of arrows whistled over his retreat. A wild howling rose from the woods along the trail. Either the survivor had gone after aid, or another party had joined the first. The burning cabin still smoldered, lending a little light. Then they were after him, gliding through the trees beside the trail. He shot three arrows and threw the bow away. As if sensing his plight, they came on, not yelling now, but in deadly silence except for a swift pad of many feet.

He fiercely hugged the head of the great dog growling at his side, muttered: "All right, boy, give 'em hell!" and sprang to his feet, drawing his axe. Then the dark figures flooded over the breastworks and closed in a storm of flailing axes, stabbing knives and ripping fangs.

VII

THE DEVIL IN THE FIRE

When Conan turned from the Velitrium road he expected a run of some nine miles and set himself to the task. But he had not gone four when he heard the sounds of a party of men ahead of him. From the noise they were making in their progress he knew they were not Picts. He hailed them.

"Who's there?" challenged a harsh voice. "Stand where you are until we know you, or you'll get an arrow through you."

"You couldn't hit an elephant in this darkness," answered Conan impatiently. "Come on, fool; it's me – Conan. The Picts are over the river."

"We suspected as much," answered the leader of the men, as they strode forward – tall, rangy men, stern-faced, with bows in their hands. "One of our party wounded an antelope and tracked it nearly to Black River. He heard them yelling down the river and ran back to our camp. We left the salt and the wagons, turned the oxen loose and came as swiftly as we could. If the Picts are besieging the fort, war-parties will be ranging up the road toward our cabins."

"Your families are safe," grunted Conan. "My companion went ahead to take them to Velitrium. If we go back to the main road we may run into the whole horde. We'll strike southeast, through the timber. Go ahead. I'll scout behind."

A few moments later the whole band was hurrying southeastward. Conan followed more slowly, keeping just within ear-shot. He cursed the noise they were making; that many Picts or Cimmerians would have moved through the woods with no more noise than the wind makes as it blows through the black branches.

He had just crossed a small glade when he wheeled, answering the conviction of his primitive instincts that he was being followed. Standing motionless among the bushes he heard the sounds of the retreating settlers fade away. Then a voice called faintly back along the way he had come: "Conan! Conan! Wait for me, Conan!"

"Balthus!" he swore bewilderedly. Cautiously he called: "Here I am!"

"Wait for me, Conan!" the voice came more distinctly.

Conan moved out of the shadows, scowling. "What the devil are you doing here – *Crom!*"

He half crouched, the flesh prickling along his spine. It was not Balthus who was emerging from the other side of the glade. A weird glow burned through the trees. It moved toward him, shimmering weirdly – a green witch-fire that moved with purpose and intent.

It halted some feet away and Conan glared at it, trying to distinguish its fire-misted outlines. The quivering flame had a solid core; the flame was but a green garment that masked some animate and evil entity; but the Cimmerian was unable to make out its shape or likeness. Then, shockingly, a voice spoke to him from amidst the fiery column.

"Why do you stand like a sheep waiting for the butcher, Conan?"

The voice was human but carried strange vibrations that were not human.

"Sheep?" Conan's wrath got the best of his momentary awe. "Do you think I'm afraid of a damned Pictish swamp devil? A friend called me."

"I called in his voice," answered the other. "The men you follow belong to my brother; I would not rob his knife of their blood. But you are mine. Oh, fool, you have come from the far grey hills of Cimmeria to meet your doom in the forests of Conajohara."

"You've had your chance at me before now," snorted Conan. "Why didn't you kill me then, if you could?"

"My brother had not painted a skull black for you and hurled it into the fire that burns for ever on Gullah's black altar. He had not whispered your name to the black ghosts that haunt the uplands of the Dark Land. But a bat has flown over the Mountains of the Dead and drawn your image in blood on the white tiger's hide that hangs before the long hut where sleep the Four Brothers of the Night. The great serpents coil about their feet and the stars burn like fire-flies in their hair."

"Why have the gods of darkness doomed me to death?" growled Conan.

Something – a hand, foot or talon, he could not tell which, thrust out from the fire and marked swiftly on the mold. A symbol blazed there, marked with fire, and faded, but not before he recognized it.

"You dared make the sign which only a priest of Jhebbal Sag dare make.

Thunder rumbled through the black Mountains of the Dead and the altar-hut of Gullah was thrown down by a wind from the Gulf of Ghosts. The loon which is messenger to the Four Brothers of the Night flew swiftly and whispered your name in my ear. Your race is run. You are a dead man already. Your head will hang in the altar-hut of my brother. Your body will be eaten by the black-winged, sharp-beaked Children of Jhil."

"Who the devil is your brother?" demanded Conan. His sword was naked in his hand, and he was subtly loosening the axe in his belt.

"Zogar Sag; a child of Jhebbal Sag who still visits his sacred groves at times. A woman of Gwawela slept in a grove holy to Jhebbal Sag. Her babe was Zogar Sag. I too am a son of Jhebbal Sag, out of a fire-being of a far realm. Zogar Sag summoned me out of the Misty Lands. With incantations and sorcery and his own blood he materialized me in the flesh of his own planet. We are one, tied together by invisible threads. His thoughts are my thoughts; if he is struck, I am bruised. If I am cut, he bleeds. But I have talked enough. Soon your ghost will talk with the ghosts of the Dark Land, and they will tell you of the old gods which are not dead, but sleep in the outer abysses, and from time to time awake."

"I'd like to see what you look like," muttered Conan, working his axe free; "you who leave a track like a bird, who burn like a flame and yet speak with a human voice."

"You shall see," answered the voice from the flame; "see, and carry the knowledge with you into the Dark Land."

The flames leaped and sank, dwindling and dimming. A face began to take shadowy form; at first Conan thought it was Zogar Sag himself who stood wrapped in green fire. But the face was higher than his own, and there was a demoniac aspect about it – Conan had noted various abnormalities about Zogar Sag's features – an obliqueness of the eyes, a sharpness of the ears, a wolfish thinness of the lips in the apparition which swayed before him. The eyes were red as coals of living fire.

More details came into view: a slender torso, covered with snaky scales, which was yet manlike in shape, with man-like arms, from the waist upward; below, long crane-like legs ended in splay, three-toed feet like those of some huge bird. Along the monstrous limbs the green fire fluttered and ran. He saw it as through a glistening mist.

Then suddenly it was towering over him, though he had not seen it move toward him. A long arm, which for the first time he noticed was armed with curving, sickle-like talons, swung high and swept down at his neck. With a fierce cry he broke the spell and bounded aside, hurling his axe. The demon avoided the cast with an unbelievably quick movement of its narrow head and was on him again with a hissing rush of leaping flames.

But fear had fought for it when it slew its other victims, and Conan was not afraid. He knew that any being clothed in material flesh can be slain by material weapons, however grisly its form may be.

One flailing talon-armed limb knocked his helmet from his head. A little lower and it would have decapitated him. But fierce joy surged through him as his savagely driven sword sank deep in the monster's groin. He bounded backward from a flailing stroke, tearing his sword free as he leaped. The talons raked his breast, ripping through mail-links as if they had been cloth. But his return spring was like that of a starving wolf. He was inside the lashing arms and driving his sword deep in the monster's belly – felt the arms lock about him and the talons ripping the mail from his back as they sought his vitals – he was lapped and dazzled by blue flame that was chill as ice – then he had torn fiercely away from the weakening arms and his sword cut the air in a tremendous swipe.

The demon staggered and fell sprawling sidewise, its head hanging only by a shred of flesh. The fires that veiled it leaped fiercely upward, now red as gushing blood, hiding the figure from view. A scent of burning flesh filled Conan's nostrils. Shaking the blood and sweat from his eyes, he wheeled and ran staggeringly through the woods. Blood trickled down his limbs. Somewhere, miles to the south, he saw the faint glow of flames that might mark a burning cabin. Behind him, toward the road, rose a distant howling that spurred him to greater efforts.

VIII
Conajohara No More

There had been fighting on Thunder River; fierce fighting before the walls of Velitrium; axe and torch had been plied up and down the bank, and many a settler's cabin lay in ashes before the painted horde was rolled back.

A strange quiet followed the storm, in which people gathered and talked in hushed voices, and men with red-stained bandages drank their ale silently in the taverns along the river bank.

There, to Conan the Cimmerian, moodily quaffing from a leathern jack, came a gaunt forester with a bandage about his head and his arm in a sling. He was the one survivor of Fort Tuscelan.

"You went with the soldiers to the ruins of the fort?"

Conan nodded.

"I wasn't able," murmured the other. "There was no fighting?"

"The Picts had fallen back across Black River. Something must have broken their nerve, though only the Devil who made them knows what."

The woodsman glanced at his bandaged arm and sighed.

"They say there were no bodies worth disposing of."

Conan shook his head. "Ashes. The Picts had piled them in the fort and set fire to the fort before they crossed the river. Their own dead and the men of Valannus."

"Valannus was killed among the last – in the hand-to-hand fighting when they broke the barriers. They tried to take him alive, but he made them kill him. They took ten of the rest of us prisoners when we were so weak from fighting we could fight no more. They butchered nine of us then and there. It was when Zogar Sag died that I got my chance to break free and run for it."

"Zogar Sag's dead?" ejaculated Conan.

"Aye. I saw him die. That's why the Picts didn't press the fight against Velitrium as fiercely as they did against the fort. It was strange. He took no wounds in battle. He was dancing among the slain, waving an axe with which he'd just brained the last of my comrades. He came at me, howling like a wolf – and then he staggered and dropped the axe, and began to reel in a circle screaming as I never heard a man or beast scream before. He fell between me and the fire they'd built to roast me, gagging and frothing at the mouth, and all at once he went rigid and the Picts shouted that he was dead. It was during the confusion that I slipped my cords and ran for the woods."

He hesitated, leaned closer to Conan and lowered his voice.

"I saw him lying in the firelight. No weapon had touched him. Yet there were red marks like the wounds of a sword in groin, belly and neck – the last as if his head had been almost severed from his body. What do you make of that?"

Conan made no reply, and the forester, aware of the reticence of barbarians on certain matters, continued: "He lived by magic, and somehow, he died by magic. It was the mystery of his death that took the heart out of the Picts. Not a man who saw it was in the fighting before Velitrium. They hurried back across Black River. Those that struck Thunder River were warriors who had come on before Zogar Sag died. They were not enough to take the city by themselves.

"I came along the road, behind their main force, and I know none followed me from the fort. I sneaked through their lines and got into the town. You brought the settlers through all right, but their women and children got into Velitrium just ahead of those painted devils. If the youth Balthus and old Slasher hadn't held them up awhile, they'd have butchered every woman and child in Conajohara. I passed the place where Balthus and the dog made their last stand. They were lying amid a heap of dead Picts – I counted seven, brained by his axe, or disembowelled by the dog's fangs, and there were others in the road with arrows sticking in them. Gods, what a fight that must have been."

"He was a man," said Conan. "I drink to his shade, and to the shade of the dog, who knew no fear." He quaffed part of the wine, then emptied the rest upon the floor, with a curious heathen gesture, and smashed the goblet. "The heads of ten Picts shall pay for his, and seven heads for the dog, who was a better warrior than many a man."

And the forester, staring into the moody, smoldering blue eyes knew the barbaric oath would be kept.

"They'll not rebuild the fort."

"No; Conajohara is lost to Aquilonia. The frontier has been pushed back. Thunder River will be the new border."

The woodsman sighed and stared at his calloused hand, worn from contact with axe haft and sword hilt. Conan reached his long arm for the wine jug. The forester stared at him, comparing him with the men about them, the men who had died along the lost river; comparing him with those other wild men over that river. Conan did not seem aware of his gaze.

"Barbarism is the natural state of mankind," the borderer said, still staring somberly at the Cimmerian. "Civilization is unnatural. It is a whim of circumstance. And barbarism must always ultimately triumph."

A Word from the Outer Dark

My ruthless hands still clutch at life —
    Still like a shoreless sea
My soul beats on in rage and strife.
    You may not shackle me.

My leopard eyes are still untamed,
    They hold a darksome light —
A fierce and brooding gleam unnamed
    That pierced primeval night.

Rear mighty temples to your god —
    I lurk where shadows sway,
Till, when your drowsy guards shall nod
    To leap and rend and slay.

For I would hurl your cities down
    And I would break your shrines
And give the site of every town
    To thistles and to vines.

Higher the walls of Nineveh
    And prouder Babel's spires —
I bellowed from the desert way —
    They crumbled in my fires.

For all the works of cultured man
    Must fare and fade and fall.
I am the Dark Barbarian
    That towers over all.

Hawk of the Hills

I

To a man standing in the gorge below, the man clinging to the sloping cliff would have been invisible, hidden from sight by the jutting ledges that looked like irregular stone steps from a distance. From a distance, also, the rugged wall looked easy to climb; but there were heartbreaking spaces between those ledges – stretches of treacherous shale, and steep pitches where clawing fingers and groping toes scarcely found a grip.

One misstep, one handhold lost and the climber would have pitched backward in a headlong, rolling fall three hundred feet to the rocky canyon bed. But the man on the cliff was Francis Xavier Gordon, and it was not his destiny to dash out his brains on the floor of a Himalayan gorge.

He was reaching the end of his climb. The rim of the wall was only a few feet above him, but the intervening space was the most dangerous he had yet covered. He paused to shake the sweat from his eyes, drew a deep breath through his nostrils, and once more matched eye and muscle against the brute treachery of the gigantic barrier. Faint yells welled up from below, vibrant with hate and edged with blood lust. He did not look down. His upper lip lifted in a silent snarl, as a panther might snarl at the sound of his hunters' voices. That was all.

His fingers clawed at the stone until blood oozed from under his broken nails. Rivulets of gravel started beneath his boots and streamed down the ledges. He was almost there – but under his toe a jutting stone began to give way. With an explosive expansion of energy that brought a tortured gasp from him, he lunged upward, just as his foothold tore from the soil that had held it. For one sickening instant he felt eternity yawn beneath him – then his upflung fingers hooked over the rim of the crest. For an instant he hung there, suspended, while pebbles and stones went rattling down the face of the cliff in a miniature avalanche. Then with a powerful knotting and contracting of iron biceps, he lifted his weight and an instant later climbed over the rim and stared down.

He could make out nothing in the gorge below, beyond the glimpse of a tangle of thickets. The jutting ledges obstructed the view from above as well as from below. But he knew his pursuers were ranging those thickets down there, the men whose knives were still reeking with the blood of his friends. He heard their voices, edged with the hysteria of murder, dwindling westward. They were following a blind lead and a false trail.

Gordon stood up on the rim of the gigantic wall, the one atom of visible life among monstrous pillars and abutments of stone; they rose on all sides, dwarfing him, brown insensible giants shouldering the sky. But Gordon gave no thought to the somber magnificence of his surroundings, or of his own comparative insignificance.

Scenery, however awesome, is but a background for the human drama in its varying phases. Gordon's soul was a maelstrom of wrath, and the distant, dwindling shouts below him drove crimson waves of murder surging through his brain. He drew from his boot the long knife he had placed there when he began his desperate climb. Half-dried blood stained the sharp steel, and the sight of it gave him a fierce satisfaction. There were dead men back there in the valley into which the gorge ran, and not all of them were Gordon's Afridi friends. Some were Orakzai, the henchmen of the traitor Afdal Khan – the treacherous dogs who had sat down in seeming amity with Yusef Shah, the Afridi chief, his three headmen and his American ally, and who had turned the friendly conference suddenly into a holocaust of murder.

Gordon's shirt was in ribbons, revealing a shallow sword cut across the thick muscles of his breast, from which blood oozed slowly. His black hair was plastered with sweat, the scabbards at his hips empty. He might have been a statue on the cliffs, he stood so motionless, except for the steady rise and fall of his arching chest as he breathed deep through expanded nostrils. In his black eyes grew a flame like fire on deep black water. His body grew rigid; muscles swelled in knotted cords on his arms, and the veins of his temples stood out.

Treachery and murder! He was still bewildered, seeking a motive. His actions until this moment had been largely instinctive, reflexes responding to peril and the threat of destruction. The episode had been so unexpected – so totally lacking in apparent reason. One moment a hum of friendly conversation, men sitting cross-legged about a fire while tea boiled and meat roasted; the next instant knives sinking home, guns crashing, men falling in the smoke – Afridi men, his friends, struck down about him, with their rifles laid aside, their knives in their scabbards.

Only his steel-trap coordination had saved him – that instant, primitive reaction to danger that is not dependent upon reason or any logical thought process. Even before his conscious mind grasped what was happening, Gordon was on his feet with both guns blazing. And then there was no time for consecutive thinking, nothing but desperate hand-to-hand fighting, and flight on foot—a long run and a hard climb. But for the thicket-choked mouth of a narrow gorge they would have had him, in spite of everything.

Now, temporarily safe, he could pause and apply reasoning to the problem of why Afdal Khan, chief of the Khoruk Orakzai, plotted thus foully to slay the four chiefs of his neighbors, the Afridis of Kurram, and their *Feringhi* friend. But no motive presented itself. The massacre seemed utterly wanton and reasonless. At the moment Gordon did not greatly care. It was enough to know that his friends were dead, and to know who had killed them.

Another tier of rock rose some yards behind him, broken by a narrow, twisting cleft. Into this he moved. He did not expect to meet an enemy; they would all be down there in the gorge, beating up the thickets for him; but he carried the long knife in his hand, just in case.

It was purely an instinctive gesture, like the unsheathing of a panther's claws. His dark face was like iron; his black eyes burned redly; as he strode along the narrow defile he was more dangerous than any wounded panther. An urge painful in its intensity beat at his brain like a hammer that would not cease: revenge! revenge! revenge! All the depths of his being responded to the reverberation. The thin veneer of civilization had been swept away by a red tidal wave. Gordon had gone back a million years into the red dawn of man's beginning; he was as starkly primitive as the colossal stones that rose about him.

Ahead of him the defile twisted about a jutting shoulder to come, as he knew, out upon a winding mountain path. That path would lead him out of the country of his enemies, and he had no reason to expect to meet any of them upon it. So it was a shocking surprise to him when he rounded the granite shoulder and came face to face with a tall man who lolled against a rock, with a pistol in his hand.

That pistol was leveled at the American's breast. Gordon stood motionless, a dozen feet separating the two men. Beyond the tall man stood a finely caparisoned Kabuli stallion, tied to a tamarisk.

"Ali Bahadur!" muttered Gordon, the red flame in his black eyes.

"Aye!" Ali Bahadur was clad in Pathan elegance. His boots were stitched with gilt thread, his turban was of rose-colored silk, and his girdled *khalat* was gaudily striped. He was a handsome man, with an aquiline face and dark, alert eyes, which just now were lighted with cruel triumph. He laughed mockingly.

"I was not mistaken, El Borak. When you fled into the thicket-choked mouth of the gorge, I did not follow you as the others did. They ran headlong into the copse, on foot, bawling like bulls. Not I. I did not think you would flee on down the gorge until my men cornered you. I believed that as soon as you got out of their sight you would climb the wall, though no man ever has climbed it before. I knew you would climb out on this side, for not even Shaitan the Dammed could scale those sheer precipices on the other side of the gorge.

"So I galloped back up the valley to where, a mile north of the spot where we camped, another gorge opens and runs westward. This path leads up out of that gorge and crosses the ridge and here turns southwesterly – as I knew you knew. My steed is swift! I knew this point was the only one at which you could reach this trail, and when I arrived, there were no boot prints in the dust to tell me you had reached it and passed on ahead of me. Nay, hardly had I paused when I heard stones rattling down the cliff, so I dismounted and awaited your coming! For only through that cleft could you reach the path."

"You came alone," said Gordon, never taking his eyes from the Orakzai. "You have more guts than I thought."

"I knew you had no guns," answered Ali Bahadur. "I saw you empty them and throw them away and draw your knife as you fought your way through my warriors. Courage? Any fool can have courage. I have wits, which is better."

"You talk like a Persian," muttered Gordon. He was caught fairly, his scabbards empty, his knife arm hanging at his side. He knew Ali would shoot at the slightest motion.

"My brother Afdal Khan will praise me when I bring him your head!" taunted the Orakzai. His Oriental vanity could not resist making a grandiose gesture out of his triumph. Like many of his race, swaggering dramatics were his weakness; if he had simply hidden behind a rock and shot Gordon when he first appeared, Ali Bahadur might be alive today.

"Why did Afdal Khan invite us to a feast and then murder my friends?" Gordon demanded. "There has been peace between the clans for years."

"My brother has ambitions," answered Ali Bahadur. "The Afridis stood in his way, though they knew it not. Why should my brother waste men in a long war to remove them? Only a fool gives warning before he strikes."

"And only a dog turns traitor," retorted Gordon.

"The salt had not been eaten," reminded Ali. "The men of Kurram were fools, and thou with them!" He was enjoying his triumph to the utmost, prolonging the scene as greatly as he dared. He knew he should have shot already.

There was a tense readiness about Gordon's posture that made his flesh crawl, and Gordon's eyes were red flame when the sun struck them. But it glutted Ali's vanity deliriously to know that El Borak, the grimmest fighter in all the North, was in his power — held at pistol muzzle, poised on the brink of Jehannum into which he would topple at the pressure of a finger on the trigger. Ali Bahadur knew Gordon's deadly quickness, how he could spring and kill in the flicker of an eyelid. But no human thews could cross the intervening yards quicker than lead spitting from a pistol muzzle. And at the first hint of movement, Ali would bring the gratifying scene to a sudden close.

Gordon opened his mouth as if to speak, then closed it. The suspicious Pathan was instantly tense. Gordon's eyes flickered past him, then back instantly, and fixed on his face with an increased intensity. To all appearances Gordon had seen something behind Ali — something he did not wish Ali to see, and was doing all in his power to conceal the fact that he had seen something, to keep Ali from turning his head. And turn his head Ali did; he did it involuntarily, in spite of himself. He had not completed the motion before he sensed the trick and jerked his head back, firing as he did so, even as he caught the blur that was the lightninglike motion of Gordon's right arm.

Motion and shot were practically simultaneous. Ali went to his knees as if struck by sudden paralysis, and flopped over on his side. Gurgling and choking he struggled to his elbows, eyes starting from his head, lips drawn back in a ghastly grin, his chin held up by the hilt of Gordon's knife that jutted from his throat. With a dying effort he lifted the pistol with both hands, trying to cock it with fumbling thumbs. Then blood gushed from his blue lips and the pistol slipped from his hands. His fingers clawed briefly at the earth, then spread and stiffened, and his head sank down on his extended arms.

Gordon had not moved from his tracks. Blood oozed slowly from a round blue hole in his left shoulder. He did not seem to be aware of the wound. Not until Ali Bahadur's brief, spasmodic twitchings had ceased did he move. He snarled, the thick, blood-glutted snarl of a jungle cat, and spat toward the prostrate Orakzai.

He made no move to recover the knife he had thrown with such deadly force and aim, nor did he pick up the smoking pistol. He strode to the stallion which snorted and trembled at the reek of spilt blood, untied him and swung into the gilt-stitched saddle.

As he reined away up the winding hill path he turned in the saddle and shook his fist in the direction of his enemies – a threat and a ferocious promise; the game had just begun; the first blood had been shed in a feud that was to litter the hills with charred villages and the bodies of dead men, and trouble the dreams of kings and viceroys.

II

Geoffrey Willoughby shifted himself in his saddle and glanced at the gaunt ridges and bare stone crags that rose about him, mentally comparing the members of his escort with the features of the landscape.

Physical environment inescapably molded its inhabitants. With one exception his companions were as sullen, hard, barbarous and somber as the huge brown rocks that frowned about them. The one exception was Suleiman, a Punjabi Moslem, ostensibly his servant, actually a valuable member of the English secret service.

Willoughby himself was not a member of that service. His status was unique; he was one of those ubiquitous Englishmen who steadily build the empire, moving obscurely behind the scenes, and letting other men take the credit – men in bemedaled uniforms, or loud-voiced men with top hats and titles.

Few knew just what Willoughby's commission was, or what niche he filled in the official structure, but the epitome of the man and his career was once embodied in the request of a harried deputy commissioner: "Hell on the border; send Willoughby!" Because of his unadvertised activities, troops did not march and cannons did not boom on more occasions than the general public ever realized. So it was not really surprising – except to those die-hards who refuse to believe that maintaining peace on the Afghan Border is fundamentally different from keeping order in Trafalgar Square – that Willoughby should be riding forth in the company of hairy cutthroats to arbitrate a bloody hill feud at the request of an Oriental despot.

Willoughby was of medium height and stockily, almost chubbily, built, though there were unexpected muscles under his ruddy skin. His hair was taffy-colored, his eyes blue, wide and deceptively ingenuous. He wore civilian khakis and a huge sun helmet. If he was armed the fact was not apparent. His frank, faintly freckled face was not unpleasant, but it displayed little evidence of the razor-sharp brain that worked behind it.

He jogged along as placidly as if he were ambling down a lane in his native Suffolk, and he was more at ease than the ruffians who accompanied him – four wild-looking, ragged tribesmen under the command of a patriarch whose stately carriage and gray-shot pointed beard did not conceal the innate savagery reflected in his truculent visage. Baber Ali, uncle of Afdal Khan, was old, but his back was straight as a trooper's, and his gaunt frame was wolfishly hard. He was his nephew's right-hand man, possessing all Afdal Khan's ferocity, but little of his subtlety and cunning.

They were following a trail that looped down a steep slope which fell away for a thousand feet into a labyrinth of gorges. In a valley a mile to the south, Willoughby sighted a huddle of charred and blackened ruins.

"A village, Baber?" he asked.

Baber snarled like an old wolf.

"Aye! That was Khuttak! El Borak and his devils burned it and slew every man able to bear arms."

Willoughby looked with new interest. It was such things as that he had come to stop, and it was El Borak he was now riding to see.

"El Borak is a son of Shaitan," growled old Baber. "Not a village of Afdal Khan's remains unburned save only Khoruk itself. And of the outlying towers, only my *sangar* remains, which lies between this spot and Khoruk. Now he has seized the cavern called Akbar's Castle, and that is in Orakzai territory. By Allah, for an hour we have been riding in country claimed by us Orakzai, but now it has become a no man's land, a border strewn with corpses and burned villages, where no man's life is safe. At any moment we may be fired upon."

"Gordon has given his word," reminded Willoughby.

"His word is not wind," admitted the old ruffian grudgingly.

They had dropped down from the heights and were traversing a narrow plateau that broke into a series of gorges at the other end. Willoughby thought of the letter in his pocket, which had come to him by devious ways. He had memorized it, recognizing its dramatic value as a historical document.

GEOFFREY WILLOUGHBY,
Ghazrael Fort:
If you want to parley, come to Shaitan's Minaret, alone. Let your escort stop outside the mouth of the gorge. They won't be molested, but if any Orakzai follows you into the gorge, he'll be shot.
FRANCIS X. GORDON.

Concise and to the point. Parley, eh? The man had assumed the role of a general carrying on a regular war, and left no doubt that he considered

Willoughby, not a disinterested arbiter, but a diplomat working in the interests of the opposing side.

"We should be near the Gorge of the Minaret," said Willoughby.

Baber Ali pointed. "There is its mouth."

"Await me here."

Suleiman dismounted and eased his steed's girths. The Pathans climbed down uneasily, hugging their rifles and scanning the escarpments. Somewhere down that winding gorge Gordon was lurking with his vengeful warriors. The Orakzai were afraid. They were miles from Khoruk, in the midst of a region that had become a bloody debatable ground through slaughter on both sides. They instinctively looked toward the southwest where, miles away, lay the crag-built village of Kurram.

Baber twisted his beard and gnawed the corner of his lip. He seemed devoured by an inward fire of anger and suspicion which would not let him rest.

"You will go forward from this point alone, *sahib*?"

Willoughby nodded, gathering up his reins.

"He will kill you!"

"I think not."

Willoughby knew very well that Baber Ali would never have thus placed himself within Gordon's reach unless he placed full confidence in the American's promise of safety.

"Then make the dog agree to a truce!" snarled Baber, his savage arrogance submerging his grudging civility. "By Allah, this feud is a thorn in the side of Afdal Khan – and of me!"

"We'll see." Willoughby nudged his mount with his heels and jogged on down the gorge, not an impressive figure at all as he slumped carelessly in his saddle, his cork helmet bobbing with each step of the horse. Behind him the Pathans watched eagerly until he passed out of sight around a bend of the canyon.

Willoughby's tranquility was partly, though not altogether, assumed. He was not afraid, nor was he excited. But he would have been more than human had not the anticipation of meeting El Borak stirred his imagination to a certain extent and roused speculations.

The name of El Borak was woven in the tales told in all the *caravanserais* and *bazaars* from Teheran to Bombay. For three years rumors had drifted down the Khyber of intrigues and grim battles fought among the lonely hills, where a hard-eyed white man was hewing out a place of power among the wild tribesmen.

The British had not cared to interfere until this latest stone cast by

Gordon into the pool of Afghan politics threatened to spread ripples that might lap at the doors of foreign palaces. Hence Willoughby, jogging down the winding Gorge of the Minaret. Queer sort of renegade, Willoughby reflected. Most white men who went native were despised by the people among whom they cast their lot. But even Gordon's enemies respected him, and it did not seem to be on account of his celebrated fighting ability alone. Gordon, Willoughby vaguely understood, had grown up on the southwestern frontier of the United States, and had a formidable reputation as a gun fanner before he ever drifted East.

Willoughby had covered a mile from the mouth of the gorge before he rounded a bend in the rocky wall and saw the Minaret looming up before him – a tall, tapering spirelike crag, detached, except at the base, from the canyon wall. No one was in sight. Willoughby tied his horse in the shade of the cliff and walked toward the base of the Minaret where he halted and stood gently fanning himself with his helmet, and idly wondering how many rifles were aimed at him from vantage points invisible to himself. Abruptly Gordon was before him.

It was a startling experience, even to a man whose nerves were under as perfect control as Willoughby's. The Englishman indeed stopped fanning himself and stood motionless, holding the helmet tilted. There had been no sound, not even the crunch of rubble under a boot heel to warn him. One instant the space before him was empty, the next it was filled by a figure vibrant with dynamic life. Boulders strewn at the foot of the wall offered plenty of cover for a stealthy advance, but the miracle of that advance – to Willoughby, who had never fought Yaqui Indians in their own country – was the silence with which Gordon had accomplished it.

"You're Willoughby, of course." The Southern accent was faint, but unmistakable.

Willoughby nodded, absorbed in his scrutiny of the man before him. Gordon was not a large man, but he was remarkably compact, with a squareness of shoulders and a thickness of chest that reflected unusual strength and vitality. Willoughby noted the black butts of the heavy pistols jutting from his hips, the knife hilt projecting from his right boot. He sought the hard bronzed face in vain for marks of weakness or degeneracy. There was a gleam in the black eyes such as Willoughby had never before seen in any man of the so-called civilized races.

No, this man was not degenerate; his plunging into native feuds and brawls indicated no retrogression. It was simply the response of a primitive nature seeking its most natural environment. Willoughby felt that the man before him must look exactly as an untamed, pre-civilization Anglo-Saxon must have looked some ten thousand years before.

"I'm Willoughby," he said. "Glad you found it convenient to meet me. Shall we sit down in the shade?"

"No. There's no need of taking up that much time. Word came to me that you were at Ghazrael, trying to get in touch with me. I sent you my answer by a Tajik trader. You got it, or you wouldn't be here. All right; here I am. Tell me what you've got to say and I'll answer you."

Willoughby discarded the plan he had partly formulated. The sort of diplomacy he'd had in mind wouldn't work here. This man was no dull bully, with a dominance acquired by brute strength alone, nor was he a self-seeking adventurer of the politician type, lying and bluffing his way through. He could not be bought off, nor frightened by a bluff. He was as real and vital and dangerous as a panther, though Willoughby felt no personal fear.

"All right, Gordon," he answered candidly. "My say is soon said. I'm here at the request of the Amir, and the *Raj.* I came to Fort Ghazrael to try to get in touch with you, as you know. My companion Suleiman helped. An escort of Orakzai met me at Ghazrael, to conduct me to Khoruk, but when I got your letter I saw no reason to go to Khoruk. They're waiting at the mouth of the gorge to conduct me back to Ghazrael when my job's done. I've talked with Afdal Khan only once, at Ghazrael. He's ready for peace. In fact it was at his request that the Amir sent me out here to try to settle this feud between you and him."

"It's none of the Amir's business," retorted Gordon. "Since when did he begin interfering with tribal feuds?"

"In this case one of the parties appealed to him," answered Willoughby. "Then the feud affects him personally. It's needless for me to remind you that one of the main caravan roads from Persia traverses this region, and since the feud began, the caravans avoid it and turn up into Turkestan. The trade that ordinarily passes through Kabul, by which the Amir acquires much rich revenue, is being deflected out of his territory."

"And he's dickering with the Russians to get it back." Gordon laughed mirthlessly. "He's tried to keep that secret, because English guns are all that keep him on his throne. But the Russians are offering him a lot of tempting bait, and he's playing with fire – and the British are afraid he'll scorch his fingers – and theirs!"

Willoughby blinked. Still, he might have known that Gordon would know the inside of Afghan politics at least as well as himself.

"But Afdal Khan has expressed himself, both to the Amir and to me, as desiring to end this feud," argued Willoughby. "He swears he's been acting on the defensive all along. If you don't agree to at least a truce, the Amir will take a hand himself. As soon as I return to Kabul and tell him you refuse to submit to arbitration, he'll declare you an outlaw, and every ruffian in the hills will be whetting his knife for your head. Be reasonable, man. Doubtless you feel you had provocation for your attacks on Afdal Khan. But you've done enough damage. Forget what's passed –"

"Forget!"

Willoughby involuntarily stepped back as the pupils of Gordon's eyes contracted like those of an angry leopard.

"Forget!" he repeated thickly. "You ask me to forget the blood of my friends! You've heard only one side of this thing. Not that I give a damn what you think, but you'll hear my side, for once. Afdal Khan has friends at court. I haven't. I don't want any."

So a wild Highland chief might have cast his defiance in the teeth of the king's emissary, thought Willoughby, fascinated by the play of passion in the dark face before him.

"Afdal Khan invited my friends to a feast and cut them down in cold blood – Yusef Shah, and his three chiefs – all sworn friends of mine, do you understand? And you ask me to forget them, as you might ask me to throw aside a worn-out scabbard! And why? So the Amir can grab his taxes off the fat Persian traders; so the Russians won't have a chance to inveigle him into some treaty the British wouldn't approve of; so the English can keep their claws sunk in on this side of the border, too!

"Well, here's my answer: You and the Amir and the *Raj* can all go to hell together. Go back to the Amir and tell him to put a price on my head. Let him send his Uzbek guards to help the Orakzai—and as many Russians and Britishers and whatever else he's able to get. This feud will end when I kill Afdal Khan. Not before."

"You're sacrificing the welfare of the many to avenge the blood of the few," protested Willoughby.

"Who says I am? Afdal Khan? He's the Amir's worst enemy, if the Amir only knew it, getting him embroiled in a war that's none of his business. In another month I'll have Afdal Khan's head, and the caravans will pass freely over this road again. If Afdal Khan should win – Why did this feud begin in the first place? I'll tell you! Afdal wants full control of the wells in this region, wells which command the caravan route, and which have been in the hands of the Afridis for centuries. Let him get possession of them and he'll fleece the merchants before they ever get to Kabul. Yes, and turn the trade permanently into Russian territory."

"He wouldn't dare –"

"He dares anything. He's got backing you don't even guess. Ask him how it is that his men are all armed with Russian rifles! Hell! Afdal's howling for help because I've taken Akbar's Castle and he can't dislodge me. He asked you to make me agree to give up the Castle, didn't he? Yes, I thought so. And if I were fool enough to do it, he'd ambush me and my men as we marched back to Kurram. You'd hardly have time to get back to Kabul before a rider would be at your heels, to tell the Amir how I'd treacherously attacked Afdal Khan and been killed in self-defense, and how Afdal had been forced to attack and burn Kurram! He's trying to gain by outside intervention what he's lost in battle, and to catch me off my guard and murder me as he did Yusef Shah. He's making monkeys out of the Amir and you. And you want me to let him make a monkey out of me – and a corpse too – just because a little dirty trade is being deflected from Kabul!"

"You needn't feel so hostile to the British –" Willoughby began.

"I don't; nor to the Persians, nor the Russians either. I just want all hands to attend to their own business and leave mine alone."

"But this blood-feud madness isn't the proper thing for a white man," pleaded Willoughby. "You're not an Afghan. You're an Englishman, by descent, at least –"

"I'm Highland Scotch and black Irish by descent," grunted Gordon. "That's got nothing to do with it. I've had my say. Go back and tell the Amir the feud will end – when I've killed Afdal Khan."

And turning on his heel he vanished as noiselessly as he had appeared.

Willoughby started after him helplessly. Damn it all, he'd handled this matter like an amateur! Reviewing his arguments he felt like kicking himself; but any arguments seemed puerile against the primitive determination of El Borak. Debating with him was like arguing with a wind, or a flood, or a forest fire, or some other elemental fact. The man didn't fit into any ordered classification; he was as untamed as any barbarian who trod the Himalayas, yet there was nothing rudimentary or underdeveloped about his mentality.

Well, there was nothing to do at present but return to Fort Ghazrael and send a rider to Kabul, reporting failure. But the game was not played out. Willoughby's own stubborn determination was roused. The affair began to take on a personal aspect utterly lacking in most of his campaigns; he began to look upon it not only as a diplomatic problem, but also as a contest of wits between Gordon and himself. As he mounted his horse and headed back up the gorge, he swore he would terminate that feud, and that it would be terminated his way, and not Gordon's.

There was probably much truth in Gordon's assertions. Of course, he and the Amir had heard only Afdal Khan's side of the matter; and of course Afdal Khan was a rogue. But he could not believe that the chief's ambitions were as sweeping and sinister as Gordon maintained. He could not believe they embraced more than a seizing of local power in this isolated hill district. Petty exactions on the caravans, now levied by the Afridis; that was all.

Anyway, Gordon had no business allowing his private wishes to interfere with official aims, which, faulty as they might be, nevertheless had the welfare of the people in view. Willoughby would never have let his personal feelings stand in the way of policy, and he considered that to do so was reprehensible in others. It was Gordon's duty to forget the murder of his friends – again Willoughby experienced that sensation of helplessness. Gordon would never do that. To expect him to violate his instincts was as sensible as expecting a hungry wolf to turn away from raw meat.

Willoughby had returned up the gorge as leisurely as he had ridden down it. Now he emerged from the mouth and saw Suleiman and the Pathans standing in a tense group, staring eagerly at him. Baber Ali's eyes burned like a wolf's. Willoughby felt a slight shock of surprise as he met the fierce intensity in the old chief's eyes. Why should Baber so savagely desire the success of his emissary? The Orakzai had been getting the worst of the war, but they were not whipped, by any means. Was there, after all, something behind the visible surface – some deep-laid obscure element or plot that involved Willoughby's mission? Was there truth in Gordon's accusations of foreign entanglements and veiled motives?

Baber took three steps forward, and his beard quivered with his eagerness. "Well?" His voice was harsh as the rasp of a sword against its scabbard. "Will the dog make peace?"

Willoughby shook his head. "He swears the feud will end only when he has slain Afdal Khan."

"Thou hast failed!"

The passion in Baber's voice startled Willoughby. For an instant he thought the chief would draw his long knife and leap upon him. Then Baber Ali deliberately turned his back on the Englishman and strode to his horse. Freeing it with a savage jerk he swung into the saddle and galloped away without a backward glance. And he did not take the trail Willoughby must follow on his return to Fort Ghazrael; he rode north, in the direction of Khoruk. The implication was unmistakable; he was abandoning Willoughby to his own resources, repudiating all responsibility for him.

Suleiman bent his head as he fumbled at his mount's girths, to hide the tinge of gray that crept under his brown skin. Willoughby turned from staring after the departing chief, to see the eyes of the four tribesmen fixed unwinkingly upon him – hard, murky eyes from under shocks of tangled hair.

He felt a slight chill crawl down his spine. These men were savages, hardly above the mental level of wild beasts. They would act unthinkingly, blindly following the instincts implanted in them and their kind throughout long centuries of merciless Himalayan existence. Their instincts were to murder and plunder all men not of their own clan. He was an alien. The protection spread over him and his companion by their chief had been removed.

By turning his back and riding away as he had, Baber Ali had tacitly given permission for the *Feringhi* to be slain. Baber Ali was himself far more of a savage than was Afdal Khan; he was governed by his untamed emotions, and prone to do childish and horrible things in moments of passion. Infuriated by Willoughby's failure to bring about a truce, it was characteristic of him to vent his rage and disappointment on the Englishman.

Willoughby calmly reviewed the situation in the time he took to gather up his reins. He could never get back to Ghazrael without an escort. If he and Suleiman tried to ride away from these ruffians, they would undoubtedly be shot in the back. There was nothing else to do but try and bluff it out. They had been given their orders to escort him to the Gorge of the Minaret and back again to Fort Ghazrael. Those orders had not been revoked in actual words. The tribesmen might hesitate to act on their own initiative, without positive orders.

He glanced at the low-hanging sun, nudged his horse.

"Let's be on our way. We have far to ride."

He pushed straight at the cluster of men who divided sullenly to let him through. Suleiman followed him. Neither looked to right nor left, nor showed by any sign that they expected the men to do other than follow them. Silently the Pathans swung upon their horses and trailed after them, rifle butts resting on thighs, muzzles pointing upward.

Willoughby slouched in his saddle, jogging easily along. He did not look back, but he felt four pair of beady eyes fixed on his broad back in sullen indecision. His matter-of-fact manner baffled them, exerted a certain dominance over their slow minds. But he knew that if either he or Suleiman showed the slightest sign of fear or doubt, they would be shot down instantly. He whistled tunelessly between his teeth, whimsically feeling as if he were riding along the edge of a volcano which might erupt at any instant.

They pushed eastward, following trails that wandered down into valleys and up over rugged slants. The sun dipped behind a thousand-foot ridge and the valleys were filled with purple shadows. They reached the spot where, as they passed it earlier in the day, Baber Ali had indicated that they would camp that night. There was a well there. The Pathans drew rein without orders from Willoughby. He would rather have pushed on, but to argue would have roused suspicions of fear on his part.

The well stood near a cliff, on a broad shelf flanked by steep slopes and ravine-cut walls. The horses were unsaddled, and Suleiman spread Willoughby's blanket rolls at the foot of the wall. The Pathans, stealthy and silent as wild things, began gathering dead tamarisk for a fire. Willoughby sat down on a rock near a cleft in the wall, and began tracing a likeness of Gordon in a small notebook, straining his eyes in the last of the twilight. He had a knack in that line, and the habit had proved valuable in the past, in the matter of uncovering disguises and identifying wanted men.

He believed that his calm acceptance of obedience as a matter of course had reduced the Pathans to a state of uncertainty, if not actual awe. As long as they were uncertain, they would not attack him.

The men moved about the small camp, performing various duties. Suleiman bent over the tiny fire, and on the other side of it a Pathan was unpacking a bundle of food. Another tribesman approached the fire from behind the Punjabi, bringing more wood.

Some instinct caused Willoughby to look up, just as the Pathan with the arm load of wood came up behind Suleiman. The Punjabi had not heard the man's approach; he did not look around. His first intimation that there was any one behind him was when the tribesman drew a knife and sank it between his shoulders.

It was done too quickly for Willoughby to shout a warning. He caught the glint of the firelight on the blade as it was driven into Suleiman's back. The Punjabi cried out and fell to his knees, and the man on the other side of the fire snatched a flint-lock pistol from among his rags and shot him through the body. Suleiman drew his revolver and fired once, and the tribesman fell into the fire, shot through the head. Suleiman slipped down in a pool of his own blood, and lay still.

It all happened while Willoughby was springing to his feet. He was unarmed. He stood frozen for an instant, helpless. One of the men picked up a rifle and fired at him point-blank. He heard the bullet smash on a rock behind him. Stung out of his paralysis he turned and sprang into the cleft of the wall. An instant later he was running as fleetly down the narrow gap as his build would allow, his heels winged by the wild howls of triumph behind him.

Willoughby would have cursed himself as he ran, could he have spared the breath. The sudden attack had been brutish, blundering, without plan or premeditation. The tribesman had unexpectedly found himself behind Suleiman and had reacted to his natural instincts. Willoughby realized that if he had had a revolver he could probably have defeated the attack, at least upon his own life. He had never needed one before; had always believed diplomacy a better weapon than a firearm. But twice today diplomacy had failed miserably. All the faults and weaknesses of his system seemed to be coming to light at once. He had made a pretty hash of this business from the start.

419

But he had an idea that he would soon be beyond self-censure or official blame. Those bloodthirsty yells, drawing nearer behind him, assured him of that.

Suddenly Willoughby was afraid, horribly afraid. His tongue seemed frozen to his palate and a clammy sweat beaded his skin. He ran on down the dark defile like a man running in a nightmare, his ears straining for the expected sound of sandaled feet pattering behind him, the skin between his shoulders crawling in expectation of a plunging knife. It was dark. He caromed into boulders, tripped over loose stones, tearing the skin of his hands on the shale.

Abruptly he was out of the defile, and a knife-edge ridge loomed ahead of him like the steep roof of a house, black against the blue-black star-dotted sky. He struggled up it, his breath coming in racking gasps. He knew they were close behind him, although he could see nothing in the dark.

But keen eyes saw the dim bulk of him outlined against the stars when he crawled over the crest. Tongues of red flame licked in the darkness below him; reports banged flatly against the rocky walls. Frantically he hauled himself over and rolled down the slope on the other side. But not all the way. Almost immediately he brought up against something hard yet yielding. Vaguely, half blind from sweat and exhaustion, he saw a figure looming over him, some object lifted in menace outlined against the stars. He threw up an arm but it did not check the swinging rifle stock. Fire burst in glittering sparks about him, and he did not hear the crackling of the rifles that ran along the crest of the ridge.

III

It was the smashing reverberation of gunfire, reechoing between narrow walls, which first impressed itself on Willoughby's sluggishly reviving consciousness. Then he was aware of his throbbing head. Lifting a hand to it, he discovered it had been efficiently bandaged. He was lying on what felt like a sheepskin coat, and he felt bare, cold rock under it. He struggled to his elbows and shook his head violently, setting his teeth against the shooting pain that resulted.

He lay in darkness, yet, some yards away, a white curtain shimmered dazzlingly before him. He swore and batted his eyes, and as his blurred sight cleared, things about him assumed their proper aspect. He was in a cave, and that white curtain was the mouth, with moonlight streaming across it. He started to rise and a rough hand grabbed him and jerked him down again, just as a rifle cracked somewhere outside and a bullet whined into the cave and smacked viciously on the stone wall.

"Keep down, *sahib!*" growled a voice in *Pashtu*. The Englishman was aware of men in the cave with him. Their eyes shone in the dark as they turned their heads toward him.

His groggy brain was functioning now, and he could understand what he saw. The cave was not a large one, and it opened upon a narrow plateau, bathed in vivid moonlight and flanked by rugged slopes. For about a hundred yards before the cave mouth the plain lay level and almost bare of rocks, but beyond that it was strewn with boulders and cut by gullies. And from those boulders and ravines white puffs bloomed from time to time, accompanied by sharp reports. Lead smacked and spattered about the entrance and whined venomously into the cavern. Somewhere a man was breathing in panting gasps that told Willoughby he was badly wounded. The moon hung at such an angle that it drove a white bar down the middle of the cave for some fifteen feet; and death lurked in that narrow strip, for the men in the cave.

They lay close to the walls on either side, hidden from the view of the besiegers and partially sheltered by broken rocks. They were not returning the fire. They lay still, hugging their rifles, the whites of their eyes gleaming in the darkness as they turned their heads from time to time.

Willoughby was about to speak, when on the plain outside a *kalpak* was poked cautiously around one end of a boulder. There was no response from the cave. The defenders knew that in all probability that sheepskin cap was stuck on a gun muzzle instead of a human head.

"Do you see the dog, *sahib?*" whispered a voice in the gloom, and Willoughby started as the answer came. For though it was framed in almost accentless *Pashtu*, it was the voice of a white man – the unmistakable voice of Francis Xavier Gordon.

"I see him. He's peeking around the other end of that boulder – trying to get a better shot at us, while his mate distracts our attention with that hat. See? Close to the ground, there – just about a hand's breadth of his head. Ready? All right – now!"

Six rifles cracked in a stuttering detonation, and instantly a white-clad figure rolled from behind the boulder, flopped convulsively and lay still, a sprawl of twisted limbs in the moonlight. That, considered Willoughby, was damned good shooting, if no more than one of the six bullets hit the exposed head. The men in the cave had phosphorous rubbed on their sights, and they were not wasting ammunition.

The success of the fusillade was answered by a chorus of wrathful yells from outside, and a storm of lead burst against the cave. Plenty of it found its way inside, and hot metal splashing from a glancing slug stung Willoughby's arm through the sleeve. But the marksmen were aiming too high to do any damage, unwilling as they were to expose themselves to the fire from the cavern. Gordon's men were grimly silent; they neither wasted lead on unseen enemies, nor indulged in the jeers and taunts so dear to the Afghan fighting man.

When the storm subsided to a period of vengeful waiting, Willoughby called in a low voice: "Gordon! Oh, I say there, Gordon!"

An instant later a dim form crawled to his side.

"Coming to at last, Willoughby? Here, take a swig of this."

A whisky flask was pressed into the Englishman's hand.

"No thanks, old chap. I think you have a man who needs it worse than I." Even as he spoke he was aware that he no longer heard the stertorous breathing of the wounded man.

"That was Ahmed Khan," said Gordon. "He's gone; died while they were shooting in here a moment ago. Shot through the body as we were making for this cave."

"That's the Orakzai out there?" asked Willoughby.

"Who else?"

The throbbing in his head irritated the Englishman; his right forearm was painfully bruised, and he was thirsty.

"Let me get this straight, Gordon – am I a prisoner?"

"That depends on the way you look at it. Just now we're all hemmed up in this cave. Sorry about your broken head. But the fellow who hit you didn't know but what you were an Orakzai. It was dark."

"What the devil happened, anyway?" demanded Willoughby. "I remember them killing Suleiman, and chasing me – then I got that clout on the head and went out. I must have been unconscious for hours."

"You were. Six of my men trailed you all the way from the mouth of the Gorge of the Minaret. I didn't trust Baber Ali, though it didn't occur to me that he'd try to kill you. I was well on my way back to Akbar's Castle when one of the men caught up with me and told me that Baber Ali had ridden off in the direction of his *sangar* and left you with his four tribesmen. I believed they intended murdering you on the road to Ghazrael, and laying it onto me. So I started after you myself.

"When you pitched camp by Jehungir's Well my men were watching from a distance, and I wasn't far away, riding hard to catch up with you before your escort killed you. Naturally I wasn't following the open trail you followed. I was coming up from the south. My men saw the Orakzai kill Suleiman, but they weren't close enough to do anything about it.

"When you ran into the defile with the Orakzai pelting after you, my men lost sight of you all in the darkness and were trying to locate you when you bumped into them. Khoda Khan knocked you stiff before he recognized you. They fired on the three men who were chasing you, and those fellows took to their heels. I heard the firing, and so did somebody else; we arrived on the scene just about the same time."

"Eh? What's that? Who?"

"Your friend, Baber Ali, with thirty horsemen! We slung you on a horse, and it was a running fight until moonrise. We were trying to get back to Akbar's Castle, but they had fresher horses and they ran us down. They got us hemmed out there on that plain and the only thing we could do was to duck in here and make our stand. So here we are, and out there he is, with thirty men – not including the three ruffians who killed your servant. He shot them in their tracks. I heard the shots and their death howls as we rode for the hills."

"I guess the old villain repented of his temper," said Willoughby. "What a cursed pity he didn't arrive a few minutes earlier. It would have saved Suleiman, poor devil. Thanks for pulling me out of a nasty mess, old fellow. And now, if you don't mind, I'll be going."

"Where?"

"Why, out there! To Ghazrael. First to Baber Ali, naturally. I've got a few things to tell that old devil."

"Willoughby, are you a fool?" Gordon demanded harshly.

"To think you'd let me go? Well, perhaps I am. I'd forgotten that as soon as I return to Kabul, you'll be declared an outlaw, won't you? But you can't keep me here forever, you know –"

"I don't intend to try," answered Gordon with a hint of anger. "If your skull wasn't already cracked I'd feel inclined to bash your head for accusing me of imprisoning you. Shake the cobwebs out of your brain. If you're an example of a British diplomat, Heaven help the empire!

"Don't you know you'd instantly be filled with lead if you stepped out there? Don't you know that Baber Ali wants your head right now more than he does mine?

"Why do you think he hasn't sent a man riding a horse to death to tell Afdal Khan he's got El Borak trapped in a cave miles from Akbar's Castle? I'll tell you: Baber Ali doesn't want Afdal to know what a mess he's made of things.

"It was characteristic of the old devil to ride off and leave you to be murdered by his ruffians; but when he cooled off a little, he realized that he'd be held responsible. He must have gotten clear to his *sangar* before he realized that. Then he took a band of horsemen and came pelting after you to save you, in the interest of his own skin, of course, but he got there too late – too late to keep them from killing Suleiman, and too late to kill you."

"But what –"

"Look at it from his viewpoint, man! If he'd gotten there in time to keep any one from being killed, it would have been all right. But with Suleiman killed by his men, he dares not leave you alive. He knows the English will hold him responsible for Suleiman's death, if they learn the true circumstances. And he knows what it means to murder a British subject – especially one as important in the secret service as I happen to know Suleiman was. But if he could put you out of the way, he could swear I killed you and Suleiman. Those men out there are all Baber's personal following – hard-bitten old wolves who'll cut any throat and swear any lie he orders. If you go back to Kabul and tell your story, Baber will be in bad with the Amir, the British, and Afdal Khan. So he's determined to shut your mouth, for good and all."

Willoughby was silent for a moment; presently he said frankly: "Gordon, if I didn't have such a high respect for your wits, I'd believe you. It all sounds reasonable and logical. But damn it, man, I don't know whether I'm recognizing logic or simply being twisted up in a web of clever lies. You're too dangerously subtle, Gordon, for me to allow myself to believe anything you say, without proof."

"Proof?" retorted Gordon grimly. "Listen!"

Wriggling toward the cave mouth he took shelter behind a broken rock and shouted in *Pashtu*: "Ohai, Baber Ali!"

The scattered firing ceased instantly, and the moonlit night seemed to hold its breath. Baber Ali's voice came back, edged with suspicion.

"Speak, El Borak! I hearken."

"If I give you the Englishman will you let me and my men go in peace?" Gordon called.

"Aye, by the beard of Allah!" came the eager answer.

"But I fear he will return to Kabul and poison the Amir against me!"

"Then kill him and throw his head out," answered Baber Ali with an oath. "By Allah, it is no more than I will do for him, the prying dog!"

In the cave Willoughby murmured: "I apologize, Gordon!"

"Well?" The old Pathan was growing impatient. "Are you playing with me, El Borak? Give me the Englishman!"

"Nay, Baber Ali, I dare not trust your promise," replied Gordon.

A bloodthirsty yell and a burst of frenzied firing marked the conclusion of the brief parley, and Gordon hugged the shelter of the shattered boulders until the spasm subsided. Then he crawled back to Willoughby.

"You see?"

"I see! It looks like I'm in this thing to the hilt with you! But why Baber Ali should have been so enraged because I failed to arrange a truce —"

"He and Afdal intended taking advantage of any truce you arranged, to trap me, just as I warned you. They were using you as a cat's-paw. They know they're licked, unless they resort to something of the sort."

There followed a period of silence, in which Willoughby was moved to inquire: "What now? Are we to stay here until they starve us out? The moon will set before many hours. They'll rush us in the dark."

"I never walk into a trap I can't get out of," answered Gordon. "I'm just waiting for the moon to dip behind that crag and get its light out of the cave. There's an exit I don't believe the Orakzai know about. Just a narrow crack at the back of the cave. I enlarged it with a hunting knife and a rifle barrel before you recovered consciousness. It's big enough for a man to slip through now. It leads out onto a ledge fifty feet above a ravine. Some of the Orakzai may be down there watching the ledge, but I doubt it. From the plain out there it would be a long, hard climb around to the back of the mountain. We'll go down on a rope made of turbans and belts, and head for Akbar's Castle. We'll have to go on foot. It's only a few miles away, but the way we'll have to go is over the mountains, and a devil's own climb."

Slowly the moon moved behind the crag, and the silver sword no longer glimmered along the rocky floor. The men in the cavern could move about without being seen by the men outside, who waited the setting of the moon with the grim patience of gray wolves.

"All right, let's go," muttered Gordon. "Khoda Khan, lead the way. I'll follow when you're all through the cleft. If anything happens to me, take the *sahib* to Akbar's Castle. Go over the ridges; there may be ambushes already planted in the valleys."

"Give me a gun," requested Willoughby. The rifle of the dead Ahmed Khan was pressed into his hand. He followed the shadowy, all-but-invisible file of Afridis as they glided into the deeper darkness in the recesses of the tunnellike cavern. Their sandals made no noise on the rocky floor, but the crunch of his boots seemed loud to the Englishman. Behind them Gordon lay near the entrance, and once he fired a shot at the boulders on the plain.

Within fifty feet the cavern floor began to narrow and pitch upward. Above them a star shone in utter blackness, marking the crevice in the rock. It seemed to Willoughby that they mounted the slanting incline for a long way; the firing outside sounded muffled, and the patch of moonlight that was the cave mouth looked small with distance. The pitch became steeper, mounting up until the taller of the Afridis bent their heads to avoid the rocky roof. An instant later they reached the wall that marked the end of the cavern and glimpsed the sky through the narrow slit.

One by one they squeezed through, Willoughby last. He came out on a ledge in the starlight that overhung a ravine which was a mass of black shadows. Above them the great black crags loomed, shutting off the moonlight; everything on that side of the mountain was in shadow.

His companions clustered at the rim of the shelf as they swiftly and deftly knotted together girdles and unwound turbans to make a rope. One end was tossed over the ledge and man after man went down swiftly and silently, vanishing into the black ravine below. Willoughby helped a stalwart tribesman called Muhammad hold the rope as Khoda Khan went down. Before he went, Khoda Khan thrust his head back through the cleft and whistled softly, a signal to carry only to El Borak's alert ears.

Khoda Khan vanished into the darkness below, and Muhammad signified that he could hold the rope alone while Willoughby descended. Behind them an occasional muffled shot seemed to indicate that the Orakzai were yet unaware that their prey was escaping them.

Willoughby let himself over the ledge, hooked a leg about the rope and went down, considerably slower and more cautiously than the men who had preceded him. Above him the huge Afridi braced his legs and held the rope as firmly as though it were bound to a tree.

Willoughby was halfway down when he heard a murmur of voices on the ledge above which indicated that Gordon had come out of the cave and joined Muhammad. The Englishman looked down and made out the dim figures of the others standing below him on the ravine floor. His feet were a yard above the earth when a rifle cracked in the shadows and a red tongue of flame spat upward. An explosive grunt sounded above him and the rope went slack in his hands. He hit the ground, lost his footing and fell headlong, rolling aside as Muhammad came tumbling down. The giant struck the earth with a thud, wrapped about with the rope he had carried with him in his fall. He never moved after he landed.

Willoughby struggled up, breathless, as his companions charged past him. Knives were flickering in the shadows, dim figures reeling in locked combat. So the Orakzai had known of this possible exit! Men were fighting all around him. Gordon sprang to the rim of the ledge and fired downward without apparent aim, but a man grunted and fell, his rifle striking against Willoughby's boot. A dim, bearded face boomed out of the darkness, snarling like a ghoul. Willoughby caught a swinging tulwar on his rifle barrel, wincing at the jolt that ran through his fingers, and fired full into the bearded face.

"El Borak!" howled Khoda Khan, hacking and slashing at something that snarled and gasped like a wild beast.

"Take the *sahib* and go!" yelled Gordon.

Willoughby realized that the fall of Muhammad with the rope had trapped Gordon on the ledge fifty feet above them.

"Nay!" shrieked Khoda Khan. "We will cast the rope up to thee –"

"Go, blast you!" roared Gordon. "The whole horde will be on your necks any minute! Go!"

The next instant Willoughby was seized under each arm and hustled at a stumbling run down the dark gorge. Men panted on each side of him, and the dripping tulwars in their hands smeared his breeches. He had a vague glimpse of three figures sprawling at the foot of the cliff, one horribly mangled. No one barred their path as they fled; Gordon's Afridis were obeying his command; but they had left their leader behind, and they sobbed curses through their teeth as they ran.

IV

Gordon wasted no time. He knew he could not escape from the ledge without a rope, by climbing either up or down, and he did not believe his enemies could reach the ledge from the ravine. He squirmed back through the cleft and ran down the slant of the cavern, expecting any instant to see his besiegers pouring into the moonlit mouth. But it stood empty, and the rifles outside kept up their irregular monotone. Obviously Baber Ali did not realize that his victims had attempted an escape by the rear. The muffled shots he must surely have heard had imparted no meaning to him, or perhaps he considered they but constituted some trickery of El Borak's. Knowledge that an opponent is full of dangerous ruses is often a handicap, instilling an undue amount of caution.

Anyway, Baber Ali had neither rushed the cavern nor sent any appreciable number of men to reenforce the lurkers on the other side of the mountain, for the volume of his firing was undiminished. That meant he did not know of the presence of his men behind the cave. Gordon was inclined to believe that what he had taken for a strategically placed force had been merely a few restless individuals skulking along the ravine, scouting on their own initiative. He had actually seen only three men, had merely assumed the presence of others. The attack, too, had been ill-timed and poorly executed. It had neither trapped them all on the ledge nor in the ravine. The shot that killed Muhammad had doubtless been aimed at himself.

Gordon admitted his mistake; confused in the darkness as to the true state of things, he had ordered instant flight when his companions might safely have lingered long enough to tie a stone to the end of the rope and cast it back up to him. He was neatly trapped and it was largely his own fault.

But he had one advantage: Baber did not know he was alone in the cavern. And there was every reason to believe that Willoughby would reach Akbar's Castle unpursued. He fired a shot into the plain and settled himself comfortably behind the rocks near the cave mouth, his rifle at his shoulder.

The moonlit plateau showed no evidence of the attackers beyond the puffs of grayish-white smoke that bloomed in woolly whorls from behind the boulders. But there was a tense expectancy in the very air. The moon was visible below the overhanging crag; it rested a red, bent horn on the solid black mass of a mountain wall. In a few moments the plain would be plunged in darkness and then it was inevitable that Baber would rush the cavern.

Yet Baber would know that in the darkness following the setting of the moon the captives might be expected to make a break for liberty. It was certain that he already had a wide cordon spread across the plain, and the line would converge quickly on the cave mouth. The longer Gordon waited after moonset, the harder it would be to slip through the closing semicircle.

He began wrenching bullets out of cartridges with his fingers and teeth and emptying the powder into his rifle barrel, even while he studied the terrain by the last light of the sinking moon. The plateau was roughly fan-shaped, widening rapidly from the cliff-flanked wall in which opened the cave mouth. Perhaps a quarter of a mile across the plain showed the dark mouth of a gorge, in which he knew were tethered the horses of the Orakzai. Probably at least one man was guarding them.

The plain ran level and bare for nearly a hundred yards before the cavern mouth, but some fifty feet away, on the right, there was a deep narrow gully which began abruptly in the midst of the plain and meandered away toward the right-hand cliffs. No shot had been fired from this ravine. If an Orakzai was hidden there he had gone into it while Gordon and his men were at the back of the cavern. It had been too close to the cave for the besiegers to reach it under the guns of the defenders.

As soon as the moon set Gordon intended to emerge and try to work his way across the plain, avoiding the Orakzai as they rushed toward the cave. It would be touch and go, the success depending on accurate timing and a good bit of luck. But there was no other alternative. He would have a chance, once he got among the rocks and gullies. His biggest risk would be that of getting shot as he ran from the cavern, with thirty rifles trained upon the black mouth. And he was providing against that when he filled his rifle barrel to the muzzle with loose powder from the broken cartridges and plugged the muzzle solidly with a huge misshapen slug he found on the cave floor.

He knew as soon as the moon vanished they would come wriggling like snakes from every direction, to cover the last few yards in a desperate rush – they would not fire until they could empty their guns point-blank into the cavern and storm in after their volley with naked steel. But thirty pairs of keen eyes would be fixed on the entrance and a volley would meet any shadowy figure seen darting from it.

The moon sank, plunging the plateau into darkness, relieved but little by the dim light of the stars. Out on the plateau Gordon heard sounds that only razor-keen ears could have caught, much less translated: the scruff of leather on stone, the faint clink of steel, the rattle of a pebble underfoot.

Rising in the black cave mouth he cocked his rifle, and poising himself for an instant, hurled it, butt first, as far to the left as he could throw it. The clash of the steel-shod butt on stone was drowned by a blinding flash of fire and a deafening detonation as the pent-up charge burst the heavy barrel asunder and in the intensified darkness that followed the flash Gordon was out of the cave and racing for the ravine on his right.

No bullet followed him, though rifles banged on the heels of that amazing report. As he had planned, the surprising explosion from an unexpected quarter had confused his enemies, wrenched their attention away from the cave mouth and the dim figure that flitted from it. Men howled with amazement and fired blindly and unreasoningly in the direction of the flash and roar. While they howled and fired, Gordon reached the gully and plunged into it almost without checking his stride – to collide with a shadowy figure which grunted and grappled with him.

In an instant Gordon's hands locked on a hairy throat, stifling the betraying yell. They went down together, and a rifle, useless in such desperate close quarters, fell from the Pathan's hand. Out on the plain pandemonium had burst, but Gordon was occupied with the blood-crazy savage beneath him.

The man was taller and heavier than himself and his sinews were like rawhide strands, but the advantage was with the tigerish white man. As they rolled on the gully floor the Pathan strove in vain with both hands to tear away the fingers that were crushing the life from his corded throat, then still clawing at Gordon's wrist with his left hand, began to grope in his girdle for a knife. Gordon released his throat with his left hand, and with it caught the other's right wrist just as the knife came clear.

The Pathan heaved and bucked like a wild man, straining his wolfish muscles to the utmost, but in vain. He could not free his knife wrist from Gordon's grasp nor tear from his throat the fingers that were bending his neck back until his bearded chin jutted upward. Desperately he threw himself sidewise, trying to bring his knee up to the American's groin, but his shift in position gave Gordon the leverage he had been seeking.

Instantly El Borak twisted the Pathan's wrist with such savage strength that a bone cracked and the knife fell from the numb fingers. Gordon released the broken wrist, snatched a knife from his own boot and ripped upward – again, again, and yet again.

Not until the convulsive struggles ceased and the body went limp beneath him did Gordon release the hairy throat. He crouched above his victim, listening. The fight had been swift, fierce and silent, enduring only a matter of seconds.

The unexpected explosion had loosed hysteria in the attackers. The Orakzai were rushing the cave, not in stealth and silence, but yelling so loudly and shooting so wildly they did not seem to realize that no shots were answering them.

Nerves hung on hair triggers can be snapped by an untoward occurrence. The rush of the warriors across the plain sounded like the stampede of cattle. A man bounded up the ravine a few yards from where Gordon crouched, without seeing the American in the pitlike blackness. Howling, cursing, shooting blindly, the hillmen stormed to the cave mouth, too crazy with excitement and confused by the darkness to see the dim figure that glided out of the gully behind them and raced silently away toward the mouth of the distant gorge.

V

Willoughby always remembered that flight over the mountains as a sort of nightmare in which he was hustled along by ragged goblins through black defiles, up tendon-straining slopes and along knife-edge ridges which fell away on either hand into depths that turned him faint with nausea. Protests, exhortations and fervent profanity did not serve to ease the flying pace at which his escort was trundling him, and presently he had no breath for protests. He did not even have time to be grateful that the expected pursuit did not seem to be materializing.

He gasped like a dying fish and tried not to look down. He had an uncomfortable feeling that the Afridis blamed him for Gordon's plight and would gladly have heaved him off a ridge but for their leader's parting command.

But Willoughby felt that he was just as effectually being killed by overexertion. He had never realized that human beings could traverse such a path – or rather such a pathless track – as he was being dragged over. When the moon sank the going was even harder, but he was grateful, for the abysses they seemed to be continually skirting were but floating gulfs of blackness beneath them, which did not induce the sick giddiness resulting from yawning chasms disclosed by the merciless moonlight.

His respect for Gordon's physical abilities increased to a kind of frantic awe, for he knew the American was known to be superior in stamina and endurance even to these long-legged, barrel-chested, iron-muscled mountaineers who seemed built of some substance that was tireless. Willoughby wished they would tire. They hauled him along with a man at each arm, and one to pull, and another to push when necessary, but even so the exertion was killing him. Sweat bathed him, drenching his garments. His thighs trembled and the calves of his legs were tied into agonizing knots.

He reflected in dizzy fragments that Gordon deserved whatever domination he had achieved over these iron-jawed barbarians. But mostly he did not think at all. His faculties were all occupied in keeping his feet and gulping air. The veins in his temples were nearly bursting and things were swimming in a bloody haze about him when he realized his escort, or captors – or torturers – had slowed to a walk. He voiced an incoherent croak of gratitude and shaking the sweat out of his dilated eyes, he saw that they were treading a path that ran over a natural rock bridge which spanned a deep gorge. Ahead of him, looming above a cluster of broken peaks, he saw a great black bulk heaving up against the stars like a misshapen castle.

The sharp challenge of a rifleman rang staccato from the other end of the span and was answered by Khoda Khan's bull-like bellow. The path led upon a jutting ledge and half a dozen ragged, bearded specters with rifles in their hands rose from behind a rampart of heaped-up boulders.

Willoughby was in a state of collapse, able only to realize that the killing grind was over. The Afridis half carried, half dragged him within the semicircular rampart and he saw a bronze door standing open and a doorway cut in solid rock that glowed luridly. It required an effort to realize that the glow came from a fire burning somewhere in the cavern into which the doorway led.

This, then, was Akbar's Castle. With each arm across a pair of brawny shoulders Willoughby tottered through the cleft and down a short narrow tunnel, to emerge into a broad natural chamber lighted by smoky torches and a small fire over which tea was brewing and meat cooking. Half a dozen men sat about the fire, and some forty more slept on the stone floor, wrapped in their sheepskin coats. Doorways opened from the huge main chamber, openings of other tunnels or cell-like niches, and at the other end there were stalls occupied by horses, a surprising number of them. Saddles, blanket rolls, bridles and other equipage, with stands of rifles and stacks of ammunition cases, littered the floor near the walls.

The men about the fire rose to their feet looking inquiringly at the Englishman and his escort, and the men on the floor awoke and sat up blinking like ghouls surprised by daylight. A tall broad-shouldered swashbuckler came striding out of the widest doorway opening into the cavern. He paused before the group, towering half a head taller than any other man there, hooked his thumbs in his girdle and glared balefully.

"Who is this *Feringhi*?" he snarled suspiciously. "Where is El Borak?"

Three of the escort backed away apprehensively, but Khoda Khan held his ground and answered: "This is the *sahib* Willoughby, whom El Borak met at the Minaret of Shaitan, Yar Ali Khan. We rescued him from Baber Ali, who would have slain him. We were at bay in the cave where Yar Muhammad shot the gray wolf three summers ago. We stole out by a cleft, but the rope fell and left El Borak on a ledge fifty feet above us, and —"

"Allah!" It was a blood-curdling yell from Yar Ali Khan who seemed transformed into a maniac. "Dogs! You left him to die! Accursed ones! Forgotten of God! I'll —"

"He commanded us to bring this Englishman to Akbar's Castle," maintained Khoda Khan doggedly. "We tore our beards and wept, but we obeyed!"

"Allah!" Yar Ali Khan became a whirlwind of energy. He snatched up rifle, bandoleer and bridle. "Bring out the horses and saddle them!" he roared and a score of men scurried. "Hasten! Forty men with me to rescue El Borak! The rest hold the Castle. I leave Khoda Khan in command."

"Leave the devil in command of hell," quoth Khoda Khan profanely. "I ride with you to rescue El Borak – or I empty my rifle into your belly."

His three comrades expressed similar intentions at the top of their voices – after fighting and running all night, they were wild as starving wolves to plunge back into hazard in behalf of their chief.

"Go or stay, I care not!" howled Yar Ali Khan, tearing out a fistful of his beard in his passion. "If El Borak is slain I will requite thee, by the prophet's beard and my feet! Allah rot me if I ram not a rifle stock down thy accursed gullets – dogs, jackals, noseless abominations, hasten with the horses!"

"Yar Ali Khan!" It was a yell from beyond the arch whence the tall Afridi had first emerged. "One comes riding hard up the valley!"

Yar Ali Khan yelled bloodthirstily and rushed into the tunnel, brandishing his rifle, with everybody pelting after him except the men detailed to saddle the horses.

Willoughby had been forgotten by the Pathans in the madhouse brewed by Gordon's lieutenant. He limped after them, remembering tales told of this gaunt giant and his berserk rages. The tunnel down which the ragged horde was streaming ran for less than a hundred feet when it widened to a mouth through which the gray light of dawn was stealing. Through this the Afridis were pouring, and Willoughby, following them, came out upon a broad ledge a hundred feet wide and fifty deep, like a gallery before a house.

Around its semicircular rim ran a massive man-made wall, shoulder-high, pierced with loopholes slanting down. There was an arched opening in the wall, closed by a heavy bronze door, and from that door, which now stood open, a row of broad shallow steps niched in solid stone led down to a trail which in turn looped down a three-hundred-foot slope to the floor of a broad valley.

The cliffs in which the cave set closed the western end of the valley, which opened to the east. Mists hung in the valley and out of them a horseman came flying, growing ghostlike out of the dimness of the dawn – a man on a great white horse, riding like the wind.

Yar Ali Khan glared wildly for an instant, then started forward with a convulsive leap of his whole body, flinging his rifle high above his head.

"El Borak!" he roared.

Electrified by his yell, the men surged to the wall and those saddling the mounts inside abandoned their task and rushed out onto the ledge. In an instant the wall was lined with tense figures, gripping their rifles and glaring into the white mists rolling beyond the fleeing rider, from which they momentarily expected pursuers to appear.

Willoughby, standing to one side like a spectator of a drama, felt a tingle in his veins at the sight and sound of the wild rejoicing with which these wild men greeted the man who had won their allegiance. Gordon was no bluffing adventurer; he was a real chief of men; and that, Willoughby realized, was going to make his own job that much harder.

No pursuers materialized out of the thinning mists. Gordon urged his mount up the trail, up the broad steps, and as he rode through the gate, bending his head under the arch, the roar of acclaim that went up would have stirred the blood of a king. The Pathans swarmed around him, catching at his hands, his garments, shouting praise to Allah that he was alive and whole. He grinned down at them, swung off and threw his reins to the nearest man, from whom Yar Ali Khan instantly snatched them jealously, with a ferocious glare at the offending warrior.

Willoughby stepped forward. He knew he looked like a scarecrow in his stained and torn garments, but Gordon looked like a butcher, with blood dried on his shirt and smeared on his breeches where he had wiped his hands. But he did not seem to be wounded. He smiled at Willoughby for the first time.

"Tough trip, eh?"

"We've been here only a matter of minutes," Willoughby acknowledged.

"You took a short cut. I came the long way, but I made good time on Baber Ali's horse," said Gordon.

"You mentioned possible ambushes in the valleys —"

"Yes. But on horseback I could take that risk. I was shot at once, but they missed me. It's hard to aim straight in the early-morning mists."

"How did you get away?"

"Waited until the moon went down, then made a break for it. Had to kill a man in the gully before the cave. We were all twisted together when I let him have the knife and that's where this blood came from. I stole Baber's horse while the Orakzai were storming the empty cave. Stampeded the herd down a canyon. Had to shoot the fellow guarding it. Baber'll guess where I went, of course. He'll be after me as quickly as he and his men can catch their horses. I suspect they'll lay siege to the Castle, but they'll only waste their time."

Willoughby stared about him in the growing light of dawn, impressed by the strength of the stronghold. One rifleman could hold the entrance through which he had been brought. To try to advance along that narrow bridge that spanned the chasm behind the Castle would be suicide for an enemy. And no force on earth could march up the valley on this side and climb that stair in the teeth of Gordon's rifles. The mountain which contained the cave rose up like a huge stone citadel above the surrounding heights. The cliffs which flanked the valley were lower than the fortified ledge; men crawling along them would be exposed to a raking fire from above. Attack could come from no other direction.

"This is really in Afdal Khan's territory," said Gordon. "It used to be a Mogul outpost, as the name implies. It was first fortified by Akbar himself. Afdal Khan held it before I took it. It's my best safeguard for Kurram.

"After the outlying villages were burned on both sides, all my people took refuge in Kurram, just as Afdal's did in Khoruk. To attack Kurram, Afdal would have to pass Akbar's Castle and leave me in his rear. He doesn't dare do that. That's why he wanted a truce – to get me out of the Castle. With me ambushed and killed, or hemmed up in Kurram, he'd be free to strike at Kurram with all his force, without being afraid I'd burn Khoruk behind him or ambush him in my country.

"He's too cautious of his own skin. I've repeatedly challenged him to fight me man to man, but he pays no attention. He hasn't stirred out of Khoruk since the feud started, unless he had at least a hundred men with him – as many as I have in my entire force, counting these here and those guarding the women and children in Kurram."

"You've done a terrible amount of damage with so small a band," said Willoughby.

"Not difficult if you know the country, have men who trust you, and keep moving. Geronimo almost whipped an army with a handful of Apaches, and I was raised in his country. I've simply adopted his tactics. The possession of this Castle was all I needed to assure my ultimate victory. If Afdal had the guts to meet me, the feud would be over. He's the chief; the others just follow him. As it is I may have to wipe out the entire Khoruk clan. But I'll get him."

The dark flame flickered in Gordon's eyes as he spoke, and again Willoughby felt the impact of an inexorable determination, elemental in its foundations. And again he swore mentally that he would end the feud himself, in his own way, with Afdal Khan alive; though how, he had not the faintest idea at present.

Gordon glanced at him closely and advised: "Better get some sleep. If I know Baber Ali, he'll come straight to the Castle after me. He knows he can't take it, but he'll try, anyway. He has at least a hundred men who follow him and take orders from nobody else – not even Afdal Khan. After the shooting starts there won't be much chance for sleeping. You look a bit done up."

Willoughby realized the truth of Gordon's comment. Sight of the white streak of dawn stealing over the ash-hued peaks weighted his eyelids with an irresistible drowsiness. He was barely able to stumble into the cave, and the smell of frying mutton exercised no charm to keep him awake. Somebody steered him to a heap of blankets and he was asleep before he was actually stretched upon them.

Gordon stood looking down at the sleeping man enigmatically and Yar Ali Khan came up as noiselessly and calmly as a gaunt gray wolf; it would have been hard to believe he was the same hurricane of emotional upset which had stormed all over the cavern a short hour before.

"Is he a friend, *sahib*?"

"A better friend than he realizes," was Gordon's grim, cryptic reply. "I think Afdal Khan's friends will come to curse the day Geoffrey Willoughby ever came into the hills."

VI

Again it was the spiteful cracking of rifles which awakened Willoughby. He sat up, momentarily confused and unable to remember where he was or how he came there. Then he recalled the events of the night; he was in the stronghold of an outlaw chief, and those detonations must mean the siege Gordon had predicted. He was alone in the great cavern, except for the horses munching fodder beyond the bars at the other end. Among them he recognized the big white stallion that had belonged to Baber Ali.

The fire had died to a heap of coals and the daylight that stole through a couple of arches, which were the openings of tunnels connecting with the outer air, was augmented by half a dozen antique-looking bronze lamps.

A pot of mutton stew simmered over the coals and a dish full of *chupatties* stood near it. Willoughby was aware of a ravenous hunger and he set to without delay. Having eaten his fill and drunk deeply from a huge gourd which hung near by, full of sweet, cool water, he rose and started toward the tunnel through which he had first entered the Castle.

Near the mouth he almost stumbled over an incongruous object – a large telescope mounted on a tripod, and obviously modern and expensive. A glance out on the ledge showed him only half a dozen warriors sitting against the rampart, their rifles across their knees. He glanced at the ribbon of stone that spanned the deep gorge and shivered as he remembered how he had crossed it in the darkness. It looked scarcely a foot wide in places. He turned back, crossed the cavern and traversed the other tunnel.

He halted in the outer mouth. The wall that rimmed the ledge was lined with Afridis, kneeling or lying at the loopholes. They were not firing. Gordon leaned idly against the bronze door, his head in plain sight of any one who might be in the valley below. He nodded a greeting as Willoughby advanced and joined him at the door. Again the Englishman found himself a member of a besieged force, but this time the advantage was all with the defenders.

Down in the valley, out of effectual rifle range, a long skirmish line of men was advancing very slowly on foot, firing as they came, and taking advantage of every bit of cover. Farther back, small in the distance, a large herd of horses grazed, watched by men who sat cross-legged in the shade of the cliff. The position of the sun indicated that the day was well along toward the middle of the afternoon.

"I've slept longer than I thought," Willoughby remarked. "How long has this firing been going on?"

"Ever since noon. They're wasting Russian cartridges scandalously. But you slept like a dead man. Baber Ali didn't get here as quickly as I thought he would. He evidently stopped to round up more men. There are at least a hundred down there."

To Willoughby the attack seemed glaringly futile. The men on the ledge were too well protected to suffer from the long-range firing. And before the attackers could get near enough to pick out the loopholes, the bullets of the Afridis would be knocking them over like tenpins. He glimpsed men crawling among the boulders on the cliffs, but they were at the same disadvantage as the men in the valley below – Gordon's riflemen had a vantage point above them.

"What can Baber Ali hope for?" he asked.

"He's desperate. He knows you're up here with me and he's taking a thousand-to-one chance. But he's wasting his time. I have enough ammunition and food to stand a six-month siege; there's a spring in the cavern."

"Why hasn't Afdal Khan kept you hemmed up here with part of his men while he stormed Kurram with the rest of his force?"

"Because it would take his whole force to storm Kurram; its defenses are almost as strong as these. Then he has a dread of having me at his back. Too big a risk that his men couldn't keep me cooped up. He's got to reduce Akbar's Castle before he can strike at Kurram."

"The devil!" said Willoughby irritably, brought back to his own situation. "I came to arbitrate this feud and now I find myself a prisoner. I've got to get out of here – got to get back to Ghazrael."

"I'm as anxious to get you out as you are to go," answered Gordon. "If you're killed I'm sure to be blamed for it. I don't mind being outlawed for the things I have done, but I don't care to shoulder something I didn't do."

"Couldn't I slip out of here tonight? By way of the bridge –"

"There are men on the other side of the gorge, watching for just such a move. Baber Ali means to close your mouth if human means can do it."

"If Afdal Khan knew what's going on he'd come and drag the old ruffian off my neck," growled Willoughby. "Afdal knows he can't afford to let his clan kill an Englishman. But Baber will take good care Afdal doesn't know, of course. If I could get a letter to him – but of course that's impossible."

"We can try it, though," returned Gordon. "You write the note. Afdal knows your handwriting, doesn't he? Good! Tonight I'll sneak out and take it to his nearest outpost. He keeps a line of patrols among the hills a few miles beyond Jehungir's Well."

"But if I can't slip out, how can you —"

"I can do it all right, alone. No offense, but you Englishmen sound like a herd of longhorn steers at your stealthiest. The Orakzai are among the crags on the other side of the Gorge of Mekram. I won't cross the bridge. My men will let me down on a rope ladder into the gorge tonight before moonrise. I'll slip up to the camp of the nearest outpost, wrap the note around a pebble and throw it among them. Being Afdal's men and not Baber's, they'll take it to him. I'll come back the way I went, after moonset. It'll be safe enough."

"But how safe will it be for Afdal Khan when he comes for me?"

"You can tell Afdal Khan he won't be harmed if he plays fair," Gordon answered. "But you'd better make some arrangements so you can see him and know he's there before you trust yourself outside this cave. And there's the pinch, because Afdal won't dare show himself for fear I'd shoot him. He's broken so many pacts himself he can't believe anybody would keep one. Not where his hide is concerned. He trusted me to keep my word in regard to Baber and your escort, but would he trust himself to my promise?"

Willoughby scowled, cramming the bowl of his pipe. "Wait!" he said suddenly. "I saw a big telescope in the cavern, mounted on a tripod – is it in working order?"

"I should say it is. I imported that from Germany by the way of Turkey and Persia. That's one reason Akbar's Castle has never been surprised. It carries for miles."

"Does Afdal Khan know of it?"

"I'm sure he does."

"Good!"

Seating himself on the ledge, Willoughby drew forth pencil and notebook, propped the latter against his knee, and wrote in his clear concise hand:

AFDAL KHAN: I am at Akbar's Castle, now being besieged by your uncle, Baber Ali. Baber was so unreasonably incensed at my failure to effect a truce that he allowed my servant Suleiman to be murdered, and now intends murdering me, to stop my mouth.

I don't have to remind you how fatal it would be to the interests of your party for this to occur. I want you to come to Akbar's Castle and get me out of this. Gordon assures me you will not be molested if you play fair, but here is a way by which you need not feel you are taking any chances: Gordon has a large telescope through which I can identify you while you are still out of rifle range. In the Gorge of Mekram, and southwest of the Castle, there is a mass of boulders split off from the right wall and well out of rifle range from the Castle. If you were to come and stand on those boulders, I could identify you easily.

    Naturally, I will not leave the Castle until I know you are present to protect me from your uncle. As soon as I have identified you, I will come down the gorge alone. You can watch me all the way and assure yourself that no treachery is intended. No one but myself will leave the Castle. On your part I do not wish any of your men to advance beyond the boulders and I will not answer for their safety if they should, as I intend to safeguard Gordon in this matter as well as yourself.

                    GEOFFREY WILLOUGHBY.

He handed the letter over for Gordon to read.

    The American nodded. "That may bring him. I don't know. He's kept out of my sight ever since the feud started."

    Then ensued a period of waiting, in which the sun seemed sluggishly to crawl toward the western peaks. Down in the valley and on the cliffs the Orakzai kept up their fruitless firing with a persistency that convinced Willoughby of the truth of Gordon's assertion that ammunition was being supplied them by some European power.

    The Afridis were not perturbed. They lounged at ease by the wall, laughed, joked, chewed jerked mutton and fired through the slanting loopholes when the Orakzai crept too close. Three still white-clad forms in the valley and one on the cliffs testified to their accuracy. Willoughby realized that Gordon was right when he said the clan which held Akbar's Castle was certain to win the war eventually. Only a desperate old savage like Baber Ali would waste time and men trying to take it. Yet the Orakzai had originally held it. How Gordon had gained possession of it Willoughby could not imagine.

    The sun dipped at last; the Himalayan twilight deepened into black-velvet, star-veined dusk. Gordon rose, a vague figure in the starlight.

    "Time for me to be going."

    He had laid aside his rifle and buckled a tulwar to his hip. Willoughby followed him into the great cavern, now dim and shadowy in the light of the bronze lamps, and through the narrow tunnel and the bronze door.

    Yar Ali Khan, Khoda Khan, and half a dozen others followed them. The light from the cavern stole through the tunnel, vaguely etching the moving figures of the men. Then the bronze door was closed softly and Willoughby's companions were shapeless blurs in the thick soft darkness around him. The gorge below was a floating river of blackness. The bridge was a dark streak that ran into the unknown and vanished. Not even the keenest eyes of the hills, watching from beyond the gorge, could have even discerned the jut of the ledge under the black bulk of the Castle, much less the movements of the men upon it.

The voices of the men working at the rim of the ledge were low and murmurous as the whispering of the night breezes. Willoughby sensed rather than saw that they were lowering the rope ladder – a hundred and fifty feet of it – into the gorge. Gordon's face was a light blur in the darkness. Willoughby groped for his hand and found him already swinging over the rampart onto the ladder, one end of which was made fast to a great iron ring set in the stone of the ledge.

"Gordon, I feel like a bounder, letting you take this risk for me. Suppose some of those devils are down there in the gorge?"

"Not much chance. They don't know we have this way of coming and going. If I can steal a horse, I'll be back in the Castle before dawn. If I can't, and have to make the whole trip there and back on foot, I may have to hide out in the hills tomorrow and get back into the Castle the next night. Don't worry about me. They'll never see me. Yar Ali Khan, watch for a rush before the moon rises."

"Aye, *sahib*." The bearded giant's undisturbed manner reassured Willoughby.

The next instant Gordon began to melt into the gloom below. Before he had climbed down five rungs the men crouching on the rampart could no longer see him. He made no sound in his descent. Khoda Khan knelt with a hand on the ropes, and as soon as he felt them go slack, he began to haul the ladder up. Willoughby leaned over the edge, straining his ears to catch some sound from below – scruff of leather, rattle of shale – he heard nothing.

Yar Ali Khan muttered, his beard brushing Willoughby's ear: "Nay, *sahib*, if such ears as yours could hear him, every Orakzai on this side of the mountain would know a man stole down the gorge! You will not hear him – nor will they. There are Lifters of the Khyber who can steal rifles out of the tents of the British soldiers, but they are blundering cattle compared to El Borak. Before dawn a wolf will howl in the gorge, and we will know El Borak has returned and will let down the ladder for him."

But like the others, the huge Afridi leaned over the rampart listening intently for some fifteen minutes after the ladder had been drawn up. Then with a gesture to the others he turned and opened the bronze door a crack. They stole through hurriedly. Somewhere in the blackness across the gorge a rifle cracked flatly and lead spanged a foot or so above the lintel. In spite of the rampart some quick eye among the crags had caught the glow of the opened door. But it was blind shooting. The sentries left on the ledge did not reply.

Back on the ledge that overlooked the valley, Willoughby noted an air of expectancy among the warriors at the loopholes. They were momentarily expecting the attack of which Gordon had warned them.

"How did Gordon take Akbar's Castle?" Willoughby asked Khoda Khan, who seemed more ready to answer questions than any of the other taciturn warriors.

The Afridi squatted beside him near the open bronze gate, rifle in hand, the butt resting on the ledge. Over them was the blue-black bowl of the Himalayan night, flecked with clusters of frosty silver.

"He sent Yar Ali Khan with forty horsemen to make a feint at Baber Ali's *sangar*," answered Khodan Khan promptly. "Thinking to trap us, Afdal drew all his men out of Akbar's Castle except three. Afdal believed three men could hold it against an army, and so they could – against an army. Not against El Borak. While Baber Ali and Afdal were striving to pin Yar Ali Khan and us forty riders between them, and were leading the dogs a merry chase over the hills, El Borak rode alone down this valley. He came disguised as a Persian trader, with his turban awry and his rich garments dusty and rent. He fled down the valley shouting that thieves had looted his caravan and were pursuing him to take from him his purse of gold and his pouch of jewels.

"The accursed ones left to guard the Castle were greedy, and they saw only a rich and helpless merchant, to be looted. So they bade him take refuge in the cavern and opened the gate to him. He rode into Akbar's Castle crying praise to Allah – with empty hands, but a knife and pistol under his *khalat*. Then the accursed ones mocked him and set on him to strip him of his riches – by Allah, they found they had caught a tiger in the guise of a lamb! One he slew with the knife, the other two he shot. Alone he took the stronghold against which armies have thundered in vain! When we forty-one horsemen evaded the Orakzai and doubled back, as it had been planned, lo! the bronze gate was open to us and we were lords of Akbar's Castle! Ha! The forgotten of God charge the stair!"

From the shadows below there welled up the sudden, swift drum of hoofs and Willoughby glimpsed movement in the darkness of the valley. The blurred masses resolved themselves into dim figures racing up the looping trail. At the same time a rattle of rifle fire burst out behind the Castle, from beyond the Gorge of Mekram. The Afridis displayed no excitement. Khoda Khan did not even close the bronze gate. They held their fire until the hoofs of the foremost horses were ringing on the lower steps of the stair. Then a burst of flame crowned the wall, and in its flash Willoughby saw wild bearded faces, horses tossing heads and manes.

In the darkness following the volley there rose screams of agony from men and beasts, mingled with the thrashing and kicking of wounded horses

443

and the grating of shod hoofs on stone as some of the beasts slid backward down the stair. Dead and dying piled in a heaving, agonized mass, and the stairs became a shambles as again and yet again the rippling volleys crashed.

Willoughby wiped a damp brow with a shaking hand, grateful that the hoofbeats were receding down the valley. The gasps and moans and cries which welled up from the ghastly heap at the foot of the stairs sickened him.

"They are fools," said Khoda Khan, levering fresh cartridges into his rifle. "Thrice in past attacks have they charged the stair by darkness, and thrice have we broken them. Baber Ali is a bull rushing blindly to his destruction."

Rifles began to flash and crack down in the valley as the baffled besiegers vented their wrath in blind discharges. Bullets smacked along the wall of the cliff, and Khoda Khan closed the bronze gate.

"Why don't they attack by way of the bridge?" Willoughby wondered.

"Doubtless they did. Did you not hear the shots? But the path is narrow and one man behind the rampart could keep it clear. And there are six men there, all skilled marksmen."

Willoughby nodded, remembering the narrow ribbon of rock flanked on either hand by echoing depths.

"Look, sahib, the moon rises."

Over the eastern peaks a glow began which grew to a soft golden fire against which the peaks stood blackly outlined. Then the moon rose, not the mellow gold globe promised by the forerunning luster, but a gaunt, red, savage moon, the moon of the high Himalayas.

Khoda Khan opened the bronze gate and peered down the stair, grunting softly in gratification. Willoughby, looking over his shoulder, shuddered. The heap at the foot of the stairs was no longer a merciful blur, for the moon outlined it in pitiless detail. Dead horses and dead men lay in a tangled gory mound with rifles and sword blades thrust out of the pile like weeds growing out of a scrap heap. There must have been at least a dozen horses, and almost as many men in that shambles.

"A shame to waste good horses thus," muttered Khoda Khan. "Baber Ali is a fool." He closed the gate.

Willoughby leaned back against the wall, drawing a heavy sheepskin coat about him. He felt sick and futile. The men down in the valley must feel the same way, for the firing was falling off, becoming spasmodic. Even Baber Ali must realize the futility of the siege by this time. Willoughby smiled bitterly to himself. He had come to arbitrate a hill feud – and down there men lay dead in heaps. But the game was not yet played out. The thought of Gordon stealing through those black mountains out there somewhere discouraged sleep. Yet he did slumber at last, despite himself.

It was Khoda Khan who shook him awake. Willoughby looked up blinking. Dawn was just whitening the peaks. Only a dozen men squatted at the loopholes. From the cavern stole the reek of coffee and frying meat.

"Your letter has been safely delivered, *sahib*."

"Eh? What's that? Gordon's returned?"

Willoughby rose stiffly, relieved that Gordon had not suffered on his account. He glanced over the wall. Down the valley the camp of the raiders was veiled by the morning mists, but several strands of smoke oozed toward the sky. He did not look down the stair; he did not wish to see the cold faces of the dead in the white dawn light.

He followed Khoda Khan into the great chamber where some of the warriors were sleeping and some preparing breakfast. The Afridi gestured toward a cell-like niche where a man lay. He had his back to the door, but the black, close-cropped hair and dusty khakis were unmistakable.

"He is weary," said Khoda Khan. "He sleeps."

Willoughby nodded. He had begun to wonder if Gordon ever found it necessary to rest and sleep like ordinary men.

"It were well to go upon the ledge and watch for Afdal Khan," said Khoda Khan. "We have mounted the telescope there, *sahib*. One shall bring your breakfast to you there. We have no way of knowing when Afdal will come."

Out on the ledge the telescope stood on its tripod, projecting like a cannon over the rampart. He trained it on the mass of boulders down the ravine. The Gorge of Mekram ran from the north to the southwest. The boulders, called the Rocks, were more than a mile to the southwest of the Castle. Just beyond them the gorge bent sharply. A man could reach the Rocks from the southwest without being spied from the Castle, but he could not approach beyond them without being seen. Nor could any one leave the Castle from that side and approach the Rocks without being seen by any one hiding there.

The Rocks were simply a litter of huge boulders which had broken off from the canyon wall. Just now, as Willoughby looked, the mist floated about them, making them hazy and indistinct. Yet as he watched them they became more sharply outlined, growing out of the thinning mist. And on the tallest rock there stood a motionless figure. The telescope brought it out in vivid clarity. There was no mistaking that tall, powerful figure. It was Afdal Khan who stood there, watching the Castle with a pair of binoculars.

"He must have got the letter early in the night, or ridden hard to get here this early," muttered Willoughby. "Maybe he was at some spot nearer than Khoruk. Did Gordon say?"

"No, *sahib*."

"Well, no matter. We won't wake Gordon. No, I won't wait for breakfast.

Tell El Borak that I'm grateful for all the trouble he's taken in my behalf and I'll do what I can for him when I get back to Ghazrael. But he'd better decide to let this thing be arbitrated. I'll see that Afdal doesn't try any treachery."

"Yes, *sahib*."

They tossed the rope ladder into the gorge and it unwound swiftly as it tumbled down and dangled within a foot of the canyon floor. The Afridis showed their heads above the ramparts without hesitation, but when Willoughby mounted the rampart and stood in plain sight, he felt a peculiar crawling between his shoulders.

But no rifle spoke from the crags beyond the gorge. Of course, the sight of Afdal Khan was sufficient guarantee of his safety. Willoughby set a foot in the ladder and went down, refusing to look below him. The ladder tended to swing and spin after he had progressed a few yards and from time to time he had to steady himself with a hand against the cliff wall. But altogether it was not so bad, and presently he heaved a sigh of relief as he felt the rocky floor under his feet. He waved his arms, but the rope was already being drawn up swiftly. He glanced about him. If any bodies had fallen from the bridge in the night battle, they had been removed. He turned and walked down the gorge, toward the appointed rendezvous.

Dawn grew about him, the white mists changing to rosy pink, and swiftly dissipating. He could make out the outlines of the Rocks plainly now, without artificial aid, but he no longer saw Afdal Khan. Doubtless the suspicious chief was watching his approach from some hiding place. He kept listening for distant shots that would indicate Baber Ali was renewing the siege, but he heard none. Doubtless Baber Ali had already received orders from Afdal Khan, and he visualized Afdal's amazement and rage when he learned of his uncle's indiscretions.

He reached the Rocks – a great heap of rugged, irregular stones and broken boulders, towering thirty feet in the air in places.

He halted and called: "Afdal Khan!"

"This way, *sahib*," a voice answered. "Among the Rocks."

Willoughby advanced between a couple of jagged boulders and came into a sort of natural theater, made by the space inclosed between the overhanging cliff and the mass of detached rocks. Fifty men could have stood there without being crowded, but only one man was in sight – a tall, lusty man in early middle life, in turban and silken *khalat*. He stood with his head thrown back in unconscious arrogance, a broad tulwar in his hand.

The faint crawling between his shoulders that had accompanied Willoughby all the way down the gorge, in spite of himself, left him at the sight. When he spoke his voice was casual.

"I'm glad to see you, Afdal Khan."

"And I am glad to see you, *sahib*!" the Orakzai answered with a chill smile. He thumbed the razor-edge of his tulwar. "You have failed in the mission for which I brought you into these hills – but your death will serve me almost as well."

Had the Rocks burst into a roar about him the surprise would have been no more shocking. Willoughby literally staggered with the impact of the stunning revelation.

"What? My death? Afdal, are you mad?"

"What will the English do to Baber Ali?" demanded the chief.

"They'll demand that he be tried for the murder of Suleiman," answered Willoughby.

"And the Amir would hang him, to placate the British!" Afdal Khan laughed mirthlessly. "But if you were dead, none would ever know! Bah! Do you think I would let my uncle be hanged for slaying that Punjabi dog? Baber was a fool to let his men take the Indian's life. I would have prevented it, had I known. But now it is done and I mean to protect him. El Borak is not so wise as I thought or he would have known that I would never let Baber be punished."

"It means ruin for you if you murder me," reminded Willoughby – through dry lips, for he read the murderous gleam in the Orakzai's eyes.

"Where are the witnesses to accuse me? There is none this side of the Castle save you and I. I have removed my men from the crags near the bridge. I sent them all into the valley – partly because I feared lest one might fire a hasty shot and spoil my plan, partly because I do not trust my own men any farther than I have to. Sometimes a man can be bribed or persuaded to betray even his chief.

"Before dawn I sent men to comb the gorge and these Rocks, to make sure no trap had been set for me. Then I came here and sent them away and remained here alone. They do not know why I came. They shall never know.

Tonight, when the moon rises, your head will be found in a sack at the foot of the stair that leads down from Akbar's Castle and there will be a hundred men to swear it was thrown down by El Borak.

"And because they will believe it themselves, none can prove them liars. I want them to believe it themselves, because I know how shrewd you English are in discovering lies. I will send your head to Fort Ali Masjid, with fifty men to swear El Borak murdered you. The British will force the Amir to send an army up here, with field pieces, and shell El Borak out of my Castle. Who will believe him if he has the opportunity to say he did not slay you?"

"Gordon was right!" muttered Willoughby helplessly. "You are a treacherous dog. Would you mind telling me just why you forced this feud on him?"

"Not at all, since you will be dead in a few moments. I want control of the wells that dominate the caravan routes. The Russians will pay me a great deal of gold to help them smuggle rifles and ammunition down from Persia and Turkestan, into Afghanistan and Kashmir and India. I will help them, and they will help me. Some day they will make me Amir of Afghanistan."

"Gordon was right," was all Willoughby could say. "The man was right! And this truce you wanted – I suppose it was another trick?"

"Of course! I wanted to get El Borak out of my Castle."

"What a fool I've been," muttered Willoughby.

"Best make your peace with God than berate yourself, *sahib*," said Afdal Khan, beginning to swing the heavy tulwar to and fro, turning the blade so that the edge gleamed in the early light. "There are only you and I and Allah to see – and Allah hates infidels! Steel is silent and sure – one stroke, swift and deadly, and your head will be mine to use as I wish –"

He advanced with the noiseless stride of the hillman. Willoughby set his teeth and clenched his hands until the nails bit into the palms. He knew it was useless to run; the Orakzai would overtake him within half a dozen strides. It was equally futile to leap and grapple with his bare hands, but it was all he could do; death would smite him in mid-leap and there would be a rush of darkness and an end of planning and working and all things hoped for –

"Wait a minute, Afdal Khan!"

The voice was moderately pitched, but if it had been a sudden scream the effect could have been no more startling. Afdal Khan started violently and whirled about. He froze in his tracks and the tulwar slipped from his fingers. His face went ashen and slowly, like an automaton, his hands rose above his shoulders.

Gordon stood in a cleft of the cleft, and a heavy pistol, held hip-high, menaced the chief's waistline. Gordon's expression was one of faint amusement, but a hot flame leaped and smoldered in his black eyes.

"El Borak!" stammered Afdal Khan dazedly. "El Borak!" Suddenly he cried out like a madman. "You are a ghost – a devil! The Rocks were empty – my men searched them?"

"I was hiding on a ledge on the cliff above their heads," Gordon answered. "I entered the Rocks after they left. Keep your hands away from your girdle, Afdal Khan. I could have shot you any time within the last hour, but I wanted Willoughby to know you for the rogue you are."

"But I saw you in the cave," gasped Willoughby, "asleep in the cave –"

"You saw an Afridi, Ali Shah, in some of my clothes, pretending to be sleeping," answered Gordon, never taking his eyes off Afdal Khan. "I was afraid if you knew I wasn't in the Castle, you'd refuse to meet Afdal, thinking I was up to something. So after I tossed your note into the Orakzai camp, I came back to the Castle while you were asleep, gave my men their orders and hid down the gorge.

"You see I knew Afdal wouldn't let Baber be punished for killing Suleiman. He couldn't if he wanted to. Baber has too many followers in the Khoruk clan. And the only way of keeping the Amir's favor without handing Baber over for trial, would be to shut your mouth. He could always lay it onto me, then. I knew that note would bring him to meet you – and I knew he'd come prepared to kill you."

"He might have killed me," muttered Willoughby.

"I've had a gun trained on him ever since you came within range. If he'd brought men with him, I'd have shot him before you left the Castle. When I saw he meant to wait here alone, I waited for you to find out for yourself what kind of a dog he is. You've been in no danger."

"I thought he arrived early, to have come from Khoruk."

"I knew he wasn't at Khoruk when I left the Castle last night," said Gordon. "I knew when Baber found us safe in the Castle he'd make a clean breast of everything to Afdal – and that Afdal would come to help him. Afdal was camped half a mile back in the hills – surrounded by a mob of fighting men, as usual, and under cover. If I could have got a shot at him then, I wouldn't have bothered to deliver your note. But this is as good a time as any."

Again the flames leaped up in the black eyes and sweat beaded Afdal Khan's swarthy skin.

"You're not going to kill him in cold blood?" Willoughby protested.

"No. I'll give him a better chance than he gave Yusef Khan."

Gordon stepped to the silent Pathan, pressed his muzzle against his ribs and drew a knife and revolver from Afdal Khan's girdle. He tossed the weapons up among the rocks and sheathed his own pistol. Then he drew his tulwar with a soft rasp of steel against leather. When he spoke his voice was calm, but Willoughby saw the veins knot and swell on his temples.

"Pick up your blade, Afdal Khan. There is no one here save the Englishman, you, I and Allah – and Allah hates swine!"

Afdal Khan snarled like a trapped panther; he bent his knees, reaching one hand toward the weapon – he crouched there motionless for an instant eying Gordon with a wide, blank glare – then all in one motion he snatched up the tulwar and came like a Himalayan hill gust.

Willoughby caught his breath at the blinding ferocity of that onslaught. It seemed to him that Afdal's hand hardly touched the hilt before he was hacking at Gordon's head. But Gordon's head was not there. And Willoughby, expecting to see the American overwhelmed in the storm of steel that played about him began to recall tales he had heard of El Borak's prowess with the heavy, curved Himalayan blade.

Afdal Khan was taller and heavier than Gordon, and he was as quick as a famished wolf. He rained blow on blow with all the strength of his corded arm, and so swiftly Willoughby could follow the strokes only by the incessant clangor of steel on steel. But that flashing tulwar did not connect; each murderous blow rang on Gordon's blade or swished past his head as he shifted. Not that the American fought a running fight. Afdal Khan moved about much more than did Gordon. The Orakzai swayed and bent his body agilely to right and left, leaped in and out, and circled his antagonist, smiting incessantly.

Gordon moved his head frequently to avoid blows, but he seldom shifted his feet except to keep his enemy always in front of him. His stance was as firm as that of a deep-rooted rock, and his blade was never beaten down. Beneath the heaviest blows the Pathan could deal it opposed an unyielding guard.

The man's wrist and forearm must be made of iron, thought Willoughby, staring in amazement. Afdal Khan beat on El Borak's tulwar like a smith on an anvil, striving to beat the American to his knee by the sheer weight of his attack; cords of muscle stood out on Gordon's wrist as he met the attack. He did not give back a foot. His guard never weakened.

Afdal Khan was panting and perspiration streamed down his dark face. His eyes held the glare of a wild beast. Gordon was not even breathing hard. He seemed utterly unaffected by the tempest beating upon him. And desperation flooded Afdal Khan's face, as he felt his own strength waning beneath his maddened efforts to beat down that iron guard.

"Dog!" he gasped, spat in Gordon's face and lunged in terrifically, staking all on one stroke, and throwing his sword arm far back before he swung his tulwar in an arc that might have felled an oak.

Then Gordon moved, and the speed of his shift would have shamed a wounded catamount. Willoughby could not follow his motion – he only saw that Afdal Khan's mighty swipe had cleft only empty air, and Gordon's blade was a blinding flicker in the rising sun. There was a sound as of a cleaver sundering a joint of beef and Afdal Khan staggered. Gordon stepped back with a low laugh, merciless as the ring of flint, and a thread of crimson wandered down the broad blade in his hand.

Afdal Khan's face was livid; he swayed drunkenly on his feet, his eyes dilated; his left hand was pressed to his side, and blood spouted between the fingers; his right arm fought to raise the tulwar that had become an imponderable weight.

"Allah!" he croaked. "Allah –" Suddenly his knees bent and he fell as a tree falls.

Willoughby bent over him in awe.

"Good heavens, he's shorn half asunder! How could a man live even those few seconds, with a wound like that?"

"Hillmen are hard to kill," Gordon answered, shaking the red drops from his blade. The crimson glare had gone out of his eyes; the fire that had for so long burned consumingly in his soul had been quenched at last, though it had been quenched in blood.

"You can go back to Kabul and tell the Amir the feud's over," he said. "The caravans from Persia will soon be passing over the roads again."

"What about Baber Ali?"

"He pulled out last night, after his attack on the Castle failed. I saw him riding out of the valley with most of his men. He was sick of the siege. Afdal's men are still in the valley but they'll leg it for Khoruk as soon as they hear what's happened to Afdal. The Amir will make an outlaw out of Baber Ali as soon as you get back to Kabul. I've got no more to fear from the Khoruk clan; they'll be glad to agree to peace."

Willoughby glanced down at the dead man. The feud had ended as Gordon had sworn it would. Gordon had been in the right all along; but it was a new and not too pleasing experience to Willoughby to be used as a pawn in a game – as he himself had used so many men and women.

He laughed wryly. "Confound you, Gordon, you've bamboozled me all the way through! You let me believe that only Baber Ali was besieging us, and that Afdal Khan would protect me against his uncle! You set a trap to catch Afdal Khan, and you used me as bait! I've got an idea that if I hadn't thought of that letter-and-telescope combination, you'd have suggested it yourself."

"I'll give you an escort to Ghazrael when the rest of the Orakzai clear out," offered Gordon.

"Damn it, man, if you hadn't saved my life so often in the past forty-eight hours, I'd be inclined to use bad language! But Afdal Khan was a rogue and deserved what he got. I can't say that I relish your methods, but they're effective! You ought to be in the secret service. A few years at this rate and you'll be Amir of Afghanistan!"

Sharp's Gun Serenade

I was heading for War Paint, jogging along easy and comfortable, when I seen a galoot coming up the trail in a cloud of dust, jest aburning the breeze. He didn't stop to pass the time of day, he went past me so fast Cap'n Kidd missed the snap he made at his hoss, which shows he was sure hightailing it. I recognized him as Jack Sprague, a young waddy which worked on a spread not far from War Paint. His face was pale and sot in a look of desprut resolution, like a man which has jest bet his pants on a pair of deuces, and he had a rope in his hand though I couldn't see nothing he might be aiming to lasso. He went fogging on up the trail into the mountains and I looked back to see if I could see the posse. Because about the only time a outlander ever heads for the high Humbolts is when he's about three jumps and a low whoop ahead of a necktie party.

I seen another cloud of dust, all right, but it warn't big enough for more'n one man, and purty soon I seen it was Bill Glanton of War Paint. But that was good enough reason for Sprague's haste, if Bill was on the prod. Glanton is from Texas, original, and whilst he is a sentimental cuss in repose he's a ring-tailed whizzer with star-spangled wheels when his feelings is ruffled. And his feelings is ruffled tolerable easy.

As soon as he seen me he yelled, "Where'd he go?"

"Who?" I says. Us Humbolt folks ain't overflowing with casual information.

"Jack Sprague!" says he. "You must of saw him. Where'd he go?"

"He didn't say," I says.

Glanton ground his teeth slightly and says, "Don't start yore derned hillbilly stallin' with me! I ain't got time to waste the week or so it takes to git information out of a Humbolt Mountain varmint. I ain't chasin' that misguided idjit to do him injury. I'm pursooin' him to save his life! A gal in War Paint has jilted him and he's so broke up about it he's threatened to ride right over the mortal ridge. Us boys has been watchin' him and follerin' him around and takin' pistols and rat-pizen and the like away from him, but this mornin' he give us the slip and taken to the hills. It was a waitress in the Bawlin' Heifer Restawrant which put me on his trail. He told her he was goin' up in the hills where he wouldn't be interfered with and hang hisself!"

"So that was why he had the rope," I says. "Well, it's his own business, ain't it?"

"No, it ain't," says Bill sternly. "When a man is in his state he ain't responsible and it's the duty of his friends to look after him. He'll thank us in the days to come. Anyway, he owes me six bucks and if he hangs hisself I'll never git paid. Come on, dang it! He'll lynch hisself whilst we stands here jawin'."

"Well, all right," I says. "After all, I got to think about the repertation of the Humbolts. They ain't never been a suicide committed up here before."

"Quite right," says Bill. "Nobody never got a chance to kill hisself up here, somebody else always done it for him."

But I ignored this slander and reined Cap'n Kidd around jest as he was fixing to bite off Bill's hoss's ear. Jack had left the trail but he left sign a blind man could foller. He had a long start on us, but we both had better hosses than his'n and after awhile we come to where he'd tied his hoss amongst the bresh at the foot of Cougar Mountain. We tied our hosses too, and pushed through the bresh on foot, and right away we seen him. He was climbing up the slope toward a ledge which had a tree growing on it. One limb stuck out over the aidge and was jest right to make a swell gallows, as I told Bill.

But Bill was in a lather.

"He'll git to that ledge before we can ketch him!" says he. "What'll we do?"

"Shoot him in the laig," I suggested, but Bill says, "No, dern it! He'll bust hisself fallin' down the slope. And if we start after him he'll hustle up to that ledge and hang hisself before we can git to him. Look there, though –

they's a thicket growin' up the slope west of the ledge. You circle around and crawl up through it whilst I git out in the open and attracts his attention. I'll try to keep him talkin' till you can git up there and grab him from behind."

So I ducked low in the bresh and ran around the foot of the slope till I come to the thicket. Jest before I div into the tangle I seen Jack had got to the ledge and was fastening his rope to the limb which stuck out over the aidge. Then I couldn't see him no more because that thicket was so dense and full of briars it was about like crawling through a pile of fighting bobcats. But as I wormed my way up through it I heard Bill yell, "Hey, Jack, don't do that, you dern fool!"

"Lemme alone!" Jack hollered. "Don't come no closter. This here is a free country! I got a right to hang myself if I wanta!"

"But it's a damfool thing to do," wailed Bill.

"My life is rooint!" asserted Jack. "My true love has been betrayed. I'm a wilted tumble-bug – I mean tumble-weed – on the sands of Time! Destiny has slapped the Zero brand on my flank! I –"

I dunno what else he said because at that moment I stepped into something which let out a ear-splitting squall and attached itself vi'lently to my hind laig. That was jest my luck. With all the thickets they was in the Humbolts, a derned cougar had to be sleeping in that'n. And of course it had to be me which stepped on him.

Well, no cougar is a match for a Elkins in a stand-up fight, but the way to lick him (the cougar, I mean; they ain't *no* way to lick a Elkins) is to git yore lick in before he can clinch with you. But the bresh was so thick I didn't see him till he had holt of me and I was so stuck up with them derned briars I couldn't hardly move nohow. So before I had time to do anything about it he had sunk most of his tushes and claws into me and was reching for new holts as fast as he could rake. It was old Brigamer, too, the biggest, meanest and oldest cat in the Humbolts. Cougar Mountain is named for him and he's so dang tough he ain't even scairt of Cap'n Kidd, which is plumb pizen to all cat-animals.

Before I could git old Brigamer by the neck and haul him loose from me he had clawed my clothes all to pieces and likewise lacerated my hide free and generous. In fact he made me so mad that when I did git him loose I taken him by the tail and mowed down the bresh in a fifteen foot circle around me with him, till the hair wore off of his tail and it slipped out of my hands. Old Brigamer then laigged it off down the mountain squalling fit to bust yore ear-drums. He was the maddest cougar you ever seen, but not mad enough to renew the fray. He must of recognized me.

At that moment I heard Bill yelling for help up above me so I headed up the slope, swearing loudly and bleeding freely, and crashing through them bushes like a wild bull. Evidently the time for stealth and silence was past. I busted into the open and seen Bill hopping around on the aidge of the ledge trying to git holt of Jack which was kicking like a grasshopper on the end of the rope, jest out of rech.

"Whyn't you sneak up soft and easy like I said?" howled Bill. "I was jest about to argy him out of the notion. He'd tied the rope around his neck and was standin' on the aidge, when that racket bust loose in the bresh and scairt him so bad he fell offa the ledge! Do somethin'."

"Shoot the rope in two," I suggested, but Bill said, "No, you cussed fool! He'd fall down the cliff and break his neck!"

But I seen it warn't a very big tree so I went and got my arms around it and give it a heave and loosened the roots, and then kinda twisted it around so the limb that Jack was hung to was over the ledge now. I reckon I busted most of the roots in the process, jedging from the noise. Bill's eyes popped out when he seen that, and he reched up kind of dazed like and cut the rope with his bowie. Only he forgot to grab Jack before he cut it, and Jack hit the ledge with a resounding thud.

"I believe he's dead," says Bill despairingful. "I'll never git that six bucks. Look how purple he is."

"Aw," says I, biting me off a chew of terbacker, "all men which has been hung looks that way. I remember onst the Vigilantes hung Uncle Jeppard Grimes, and it taken us three hours to bring him to after we cut him down. Of course, he'd been hangin' a hour before we found him."

"Shet up and help me revive him," snarled Bill, gitting the noose off of his neck. "You seleck the damndest times to converse about the sins of yore infernal relatives — look, he's comin' to!"

Because Jack had begun to gasp and kick around, so Bill brung out a bottle and poured a snort down his gullet, and pretty soon Jack sot up and felt of his neck. His jaws wagged but didn't make no sound.

Glanton now seemed to notice my disheveled condition for the first time. "What the hell happened to you?" he ast in amazement.

"Aw, I stepped on old Brigamer," I scowled.

"Well, whyn't you hang onto him?" he demanded. "Don't you know they's a big bounty on his pelt? We could of split the dough."

"I've had a bellyfull of old Brigamer," I replied irritably. "I don't care if I never see him again. Look what he done to my best britches! If you wants that bounty, you go after it yoreself."

"And let me alone!" onexpectedly spoke up Jack, eyeing us balefully. "I'm free, white and twenty-one. I hangs myself if I wants to."

"You won't neither," says Bill sternly. "Me and yore paw is old friends and I aim to save yore wuthless life if I have to kill you to do it."

"I defies you!" squawked Jack, making a sudden dive betwixt Bill's laigs and he would of got clean away if I hadn't snagged the seat of his britches with my spur. He then displayed startling ingratitude by hitting me with a rock and, whilst we was tying him up with the hanging rope, his langwidge was scandalous.

"Did you ever see sech a idjit?" demands Bill, setting on him and fanning hisself with his Stetson. "What we goin' to do with him? We cain't keep him tied up forever."

"We got to watch him clost till he gits out of the notion of killin' hisself," I says. "He can stay at our cabin for a spell."

"Ain't you got some sisters?" says Jack.

"A whole cabin-full," I says with feeling. "You cain't hardly walk without steppin' on one. Why?"

"I won't go," says he bitterly. "I don't never want to see no woman again, not even a mountain-woman. I'm a embittered man. The honey of love has turnt to tranchler pizen. Leave me to the buzzards and cougars."

"I got it," says Bill. "We'll take him on a huntin' trip way up in the high Humbolts. They's some of that country I'd like to see myself. Reckon yo're the only white man which has ever been up there, Breck – if we was to call you a white man."

"What you mean by that there remark?" I demanded heatedly. "You know damn' well I h'ain't got nary a drop of Injun blood in me – hey, look out!"

I glimpsed a furry hide through the bresh, and thinking it was old Brigamer coming back, I pulled my pistols and started shooting at it, when a familiar voice yelled wrathfully, "Hey, you cut that out, dern it!"

The next instant a pecooliar figger hove into view – a tall ga'nt old ranny with long hair and whiskers with a club in his hand and a painter hide tied around his middle. Sprague's eyes bugged out and he says: "Who in the name uh God's that?"

"Another victim of feminine wiles," I says. "That's old Joshua Braxton, of Chawed Ear, the oldest and the toughest batchelor in South Nevada. I jedge that Miss Stark, the old maid schoolteacher, has renewed her matrimonical designs onto him. When she starts rollin' sheep's eyes at him he always dons that there grab and takes to the high *sierras*."

"It's the only way to perteck myself," snarled Joshua. "She'd marry me by force if I didn't resort to strategy. Not many folks comes up here and sech as does don't recognize me in this rig. What you varmints disturbin' my solitude for? Yore racket woke me up, over in my cave. When I seen old

Brigamer high tailin' it for distant parts I figgered Elkins was on the mountain."

"We're here to save this young idjit from his own folly," says Bill. "You come up here because a woman wants to marry you. Jack comes up here to decorate a oak limb with his own carcass because one wouldn't marry him."

"Some men never knows their luck," says old Joshua enviously. "Now me, I yearns to return to Chawed Ear which I've been away from for a month. But whilst that old mudhen of a Miss Stark is there I haunts the wilderness if it takes the rest of my life."

"Well, be at ease, Josh," says Bill. "Miss Stark ain't there no more. She pulled out for Arizona three weeks ago."

"Halleloojah!" says Joshua, throwing away his club. "Now I can return and take my place among men – Hold on!" says he, reching for his club again, "likely they'll be gittin' some other old harridan to take her place. That new-fangled schoolhouse they got at Chawed Ear is a curse and a blight. We'll never be shet of husband-huntin' 'rithmetic shooters. I better stay up here after all."

"Don't worry," says Bill. "I seen a pitcher of the gal that's comin' from the East to take Miss Stark's place and I can assure you that a gal as young and pretty as her wouldn't never try to slap her brand on no old buzzard like you."

"Young and purty you says?" I ast with sudden interest.

"As a racin' filly!" he declared. "First time I ever knowed a school-marm could be less'n forty and have a face that didn't look like the beginnin's of a long drouth. She's due into Chawed Ear on the evenin' stage, and the whole town turns out to welcome her. The mayor aims to make a speech if he's sober enough, and they've got up a band to play."

"Damn foolishness!" snorted Joshua. "I don't take no stock in eddication."

"I dunno," says I. That was before I got educated. "They's times when I wisht I could read and write. We ain't never had no school on Bear Creek."

"What would you read outside of the labels onto whiskey bottles?" snorted old Joshua.

"Funny how a purty face changes a man's viewp'int," remarked Bill. "I remember onst Miss Stark ast you how you folks up on Bear Creek would like for her to come up there and teach yore chillern, and you taken one look at her face and told her it was agen the principles of Bear Creek to have their peaceful innercence invaded by the corruptin' influences of education. You said the folks was all banded together to resist sech corruption to the last drop of blood."

"It's my duty to Bear Creek to pervide culture for the risin' generation," says I, ignoring them slanderous remarks. "I feels the urge for knowledge a-heavin' and a-surgin' in my boozum. We're goin' to have a school on Bear Creek, by golly, if I have to lick every old mossback in the Humbolts. I'll build a cabin for the schoolhouse myself."

"Where'll you git a teacher?" ast Joshua. "Chawed Ear ain't goin' to let you have their'n."

"Chawed Ear is, too," I says. "If they won't give her up peaceful I resorts to force. Bear Creek is goin' to have culture if I have to wade fetlock deep in gore to pervide it. Le's go! I'm r'arin' to open the ball for arts and letters. Air you-all with me?"

"No!" says Jack, plenty emphatic.

"What we goin' to do with him?" demands Glanton.

"Aw," I said, "we'll tie him up some place along the road and pick him up as we come back by."

"All right," says Bill, ignoring Jack's impassioned protests. "I jest as soon. My nerves is frayed ridin' herd on this young idjit and I needs a little excitement to quiet 'em. You can always be counted on for *that*. Anyway, I'd like to see that there school-marm gal myself. How about you, Joshua?"

"Yo're both crazy," growls Joshua. "But I've lived up here on nuts and jackrabbits till I ain't shore of my own sanity. Anyway, I know the only way to disagree successfully with Elkins is to kill him, and I got strong doubts of bein' able to do that. Lead on! I'll do anything within reason to help keep eddication out of Chawed Ear. T'ain't only my personal feelin's regardin' schoolteachers. It's the principle of the thing."

"Git yore clothes and le's hustle then," I says.

"This painter hide is all I got," says he.

"You cain't go down into the settlements in that rig," I says.

"I can and will," says he. "I look as civilized as you do, with yore clothes all tore to rags account of old Brigamer. I got a hoss clost by. I'll git him if old Brigamer ain't already."

So Joshua went to git his hoss and me and Bill toted Jack down the slope to where our hosses was. His conversation was plentiful and heated, but we ignored it, and was jest tying him onto his hoss when Joshua arrov with his critter. Then the trouble started. Cap'n Kidd evidently thought Joshua was some kind of a varmint because every time Joshua come nigh him he taken in after him and run him up a tree. And every time Joshua tried to come down, Cap'n Kidd busted loose from me and run him back up again.

I didn't git no help from Bill. All he done was laugh like a spotted hyener till Cap'n Kidd got irritated at them guffaws and kicked him in the belly and knocked him clean through a clump of spruces. Time I got him ontangled he looked about as disreputable as what I did because most of his clothes was tore off of him. We couldn't find his hat, neither, so I tore up what was left of my shirt and he tied the pieces around his head, like a Apache. Exceptin' Jack, we was sure a wild-looking bunch.

But I was disgusted thinking about how much time we was wasting whilst all the time Bear Creek was wallering in ignorance, so the next time Cap'n Kidd went for Joshua I took and busted him betwixt the ears with my sixshooter and that had some effect onto him – a little.

So we sot out, with Jack tied onto his hoss and cussing something terrible, and Joshua on a ga'nt old nag he rode bareback with a hackamore. I had Bill to ride betwixt him and me so's to keep that painter hide as far away from Cap'n Kidd as possible, but every time the wind shifted and blowed the smell to him, Cap'n Kidd reched over and taken a bite at Joshua, and sometimes he bit Bill's hoss by accident, and sometimes he bit Bill, and the langwidge Bill directed at that pore animal was shocking to hear.

We was aiming for the trail that runs down from Bear Creek into the Chawed Ear road, and we hit it a mile west of Bowie Knife Pass. We left Jack tied to a nice shady oak tree in the pass and told him we'd be back for him in a few hours, but some folks is never satisfied. Stead of being grateful for all the trouble we'd went to for him, he acted right nasty and called us some names I wouldn't of endured if he'd been in his right mind.

But we tied his hoss to the same tree and hustled down the trail and presently come out onto the War Paint-Chawed Ear road, some miles west of Chawed Ear. And there we sighted our first human – a feller on a pinto mare and when he seen us he give a shriek and took out down the road toward Chawed Ear like the devil had him by the britches.

"Le's ast him if the teacher's got there yet," I suggested, so we taken out after him, yelling for him to wait a minute. But he jest spurred his hoss that much harder and before we'd gone any piece, Joshua's fool hoss jostled agen Cap'n Kidd, which smelt that painter skin and got the bit betwixt his teeth and run Joshua and his hoss three miles through the bresh before I could stop him. Bill follered us, and of course, time we got back to the road, the feller on the pinto mare was out of sight long ago.

So we headed for Chawed Ear but everybody that lived along the road had run into their cabins and bolted the doors, and they shot at us through the winders as we rode by. Bill said irritably, after having his off-ear nicked by a buffalo rifle, he says, "Dern it, they must know we aim to steal their schoolteacher."

"Aw, they couldn't know that," I says. "I bet they is a war on betwixt Chawed Ear and War Paint."

"Well, what they shootin' at *me* for, then?" demanded Joshua.

"How could they recognize you in that rig?" I ast. "What's that?"

Ahead of us, away down the road, we seen a cloud of dust, and here come a gang of men on hosses, waving guns and yelling.

"Well, whatever the reason is," says Bill, "we better not stop to find out! Them gents is out for blood, and," says he as the bullets begun to knock up the dust around us, "I jedge it's *our* blood!"

"Pull into the bresh," says I. "I goes to Chawed Ear in spite of hell, high water and all the gunmen they can raise."

So we taken to the bresh, and they lit in after us, about forty or fifty of 'em, but we dodged and circled and taken short cuts old Joshua knowed about, and when we emerged into the town of Chawed Ear, our pursewers warn't nowheres in sight. In fack, they warn't nobody in sight. All the doors was closed and the shutters up on the cabins and saloons and stores and everything. It was pecooliar.

As we rode into the clearing somebody let bam at us with a shotgun from the nearest cabin, and the load combed Joshua's whiskers. This made me mad, so I rode at the cabin and pulled my foot out'n the stirrup and kicked the door in, and whilst I was doing this, the feller inside hollered and jumped out the winder, and Bill grabbed him by the neck. It was Esau Barlow, one of Chawed Ear's confirmed citizens.

"What the hell's the matter with you buzzards?" roared Bill.

"Is that you, Glanton?" gasped Esau, blinking his eyes.

"A-course it's me!" roared Bill. "Do I look like a Injun?"

"Yes – *ow!* I mean, I didn't know you in that there turban," says Esau. "Am I dreamin' or is that Josh Braxton and Breck Elkins?"

"Shore it's us," snorted Joshua. "Who you think?"

"Well," says Esau, rubbing his neck and looking sidewise at Joshua's painter skin. "I didn't know!"

"Where is everybody?" Joshua demanded.

"Well," says Esau, "a little while ago Dick Lynch rode into town with his hoss all of a lather and swore he'd jest outrun the wildest war-party that ever come down from the hills!

" 'Boys,' says Dick, 'they ain't neither Injuns nor white men! They're wild men, that's what! One of 'em's big as a grizzly b'ar, with no shirt on, and he's ridin' a hoss bigger'n a bull moose! One of the others is as ragged and ugly as him, but not so big, and wearin' a Apache headdress. T'other'n's got nothin' on but a painter's hide and a club and his hair and whiskers falls to his shoulders. When they seen me,' says Dick, 'they sot up awful yells and come for me like a gang of man-eatin' cannibals. I fogged it for town,' says Dick, 'warnin' everybody along the road to fort theirselves in their cabins.'

"Well," says Esau, "when he says that, sech men as was left in town got their hosses and guns and they taken out up the road to meet the war-party before it got into town."

"Well, of all the fools!" I says. "Say, where's the new teacher?"

"The stage ain't arriv yet," says he. "The mayor and the band rode out to meet it at the Yaller Creek crossin' and escort her in to town in honor. They'd left before Dick brung news of the war-party."

"Come on!" I says to my warriors. "We likewise meets that stage!"

So we fogged it on through the town and down the road, and purty soon we heard music blaring ahead of us, and men yipping and shooting off their pistols like they does when they're celebrating, so we jedged they'd met the stage and was escorting it in.

"What you goin' to do now?" ast Bill, and about that time a noise bust out behind us and we looked back and seen that gang of Chawed Ear maniacs which had been chasing us dusting down the road after us, waving their Winchesters. I knowed they warn't no use to try to explain to them that we warn't no war-party of cannibals. They'd salivate us before we could git clost enough to make 'em hear what we was saying. So I yelled: "Come on. If they git her into town they'll fort theirselves agen us. We takes her now! Foller me!"

So we swept down the road and around the bend and there was the stage coach coming up the road with the mayor riding alongside with his hat in his hand, and a whiskey bottle sticking out of each saddle bag and his hip pocket. He was orating at the top of his voice to make hisself heard above the racket the band was making. They was blowing horns and banging drums and twanging on Jews harps, and the hosses was skittish and shying and jumping. But we heard the mayor say, "– And so we welcomes you, Miss Devon, to our peaceful little community where life runs smooth and tranquil and men's souls is overflowin' with milk and honey –" And jest then we stormed around the bend and come tearing down on 'em with the mob right behind us yelling and cussing and shooting free and fervent.

The next minute they was the damndest mix-up you ever seen, what with the hosses bucking their riders off, and men yelling and cussing, and the hosses hitched to the stage running away and knocking the mayor off'n his hoss. We hit 'em like a cyclone and they shot at us and hit us over the head with their music horns, and right in the middle of the fray the mob behind us rounded the bend and piled up amongst us before they could check their hosses, and everybody was so confused they started fighting everybody else. Nobody knowed what it was all about but me and my warriors. But Chawed Ear's motto is: "When in doubt, shoot!"

462

So they laid into us and into each other free and hearty. And we was far from idle. Old Joshua was laying out his feller-townsmen left and right with his ellum club, saving Chawed Ear from education in spite of itself, and Glanton was beating the band over their heads with his six-shooter, and I was trompling folks in my rush for the stage.

The fool hosses had whirled around and started in the general direction of the Atlantic ocean, and the driver and the shotgun guard couldn't stop 'em. But Cap'n Kidd overtook it in maybe a dozen strides and I left the saddle in a flying leap and landed on it. The guard tried to shoot me with his shotgun so I throwed it into a alder clump and he didn't let go of it quick enough so he went along with it.

I then grabbed the ribbons out of the driver's hands and swung them fool hosses around on their hind laigs, and the stage kind of revolved on one wheel for a dizzy instant, and then settled down again and we headed back up the road lickety-split and in a instant was right amongst the fracas that was going on around Bill and Joshua.

About that time I noticed that the driver was trying to stab me with a butcher knife so I kind of tossed him off the stage and there ain't no sense in him going around threatening to have me arrested account of him landing headfirst in the bass horn so it taken seven men to pull him out. He ought to watch where he falls when he gits throwed off of a stage going at a high run.

I also feels that the mayor is prone to carry petty grudges or he wouldn't be so bitter about me accidentally running over him with all four wheels. And it ain't my fault he was stepped on by Cap'n Kidd, neither. Cap'n Kidd was jest follering the stage because he knowed I was on it. And it naturally irritates him to stumble over somebody and that's why he chawed the mayor's ear.

As for them other fellers which happened to git knocked down and run over by the stage, I didn't have nothing personal agen 'em. I was jest rescuing Joshua and Bill which was outnumbered about twenty to one. I was doing them Chawed Ear idjits a favor, if they only knowed it, because in about another minute Bill would of started using the front ends of his sixshooters instead of the butts and the fight would of turnt into a massacre. Bill has got a awful temper.

Him and Joshua had did the enemy considerable damage but the battle was going agen 'em when I arriv on the field of carnage. As the stage crashed through the mob I reched down and got Joshua by the neck and pulled him out from under about fifteen men which was beating him to death with their gun butts and pulling out his whiskers by the handfulls and I slung him up on top of the other luggage. About that time we was rushing past the dogpile which Bill was the center of and I reched down and snared him as we went by, but three of the men which had holt of him wouldn't let go, so I hauled all four of 'em up onto the stage. I then handled the team with one hand and used the other'n to pull them idjits loose from Bill like pulling ticks off'n a cow's hide, and then throwed 'em at the mob which was chasing us.

Men and hosses piled up in a stack on the road which was further messed up by Cap'n Kidd plowing through it as he come busting along after the stage, and by the time we sighted Chawed Ear again, our enemies was far behind us, though still rambunctious.

We tore through Chawed Ear in a fog of dust and the women and chillern which had ventured out of their shacks squalled and run back again, though they warn't in no danger. But Chawed Ear folks is pecooliar that way.

When we was out of sight of Chawed Ear I give the lines to Bill and swung down on the side of the stage and stuck my head in. They was one of the purtiest gals I ever seen in there, all huddled up in a corner and looking so pale and scairt I was afraid she was going to faint, which I'd heard Eastern gals has a habit of doing.

"Oh, spare me!" she begged. "Please don't scalp me!"

"Be at ease, Miss Devon," I reassured her. "I ain't no Injun, nor no wild man neither. Neither is my friends here. We wouldn't none of us hurt a flea. We're that refined and soft-hearted you wouldn't believe it —" At that instant a wheel hit a stump and the stage jumped into the air and I bit my tongue and roared in some irritation, "Bill, you condemned son of a striped polecat, stop this stage before I comes up there and breaks yore cussed neck!"

"Try, you beef headed lummox," he invites, but he pulled up the hosses and I taken off my hat and opened the door. Bill and Joshua clumb down and peered over my shoulder. Miss Devon looked tolerable sick. Maybe it was something she et.

"Miss Devon," I says, "I begs yore pardon for this here informal welcome. But you sees before you a man whose heart bleeds for the benighted state of his native community. I'm Breckinridge Elkins, of Bear Creek, where hearts is pure and motives is lofty, but culture is weak.

"You sees before you," says I, growing more enthusiastic about education the longer I looked at them big brown eyes of her'n, "a man which has growed up in ignorance. I cain't neither read nor write. Joshua here, in the painter skin, he cain't neither, and neither can Bill"

"That's a lie," says Bill. "I can read and – *ooomp!*" I'd kind of stuck my elbow in his stummick. I didn't want him to spile the effeck of my speech. Miss Devon was gitting some of her color back.

"Miss Devon," I says, "will you please ma'm come up to Bear Creek and be our schoolteacher?"

"Why," says she bewilderedly, "I came West expecting to teach at Chewed Ear, but I haven't signed any contract, and –"

"How much was them snake-hunters goin' to pay you?" I ast.

"Ninety dollars a month," says she.

"We pays you a hundred," I says. "Board and lodgin' free."

"Hell's fire," says Bill. "They never was that much hard cash money on Bear Creek."

"We all donates coon hides and corn licker," I snapped. "I sells the stuff in War Paint and hands the dough to Miss Devon. Will you keep yore snout out of my business?"

"But what will the people of Chewed Ear say?" she wonders.

"Nothin'," I told her heartily. "I'll tend to *them!*"

"It seems so strange and irregular," says she weakly. "I don't know."

"Then it's all settled!" I says. "Great! Le's go!"

"Where?" she gasped, grabbing holt of the stage as I clumb onto the seat.

"Bear Creek!" I says. "Varmints and hoss-thieves, hunt the bresh! Culture is on her way to Bear Creek!" And we went fogging it down the road as fast as the hosses could hump it. Onst I looked back at Miss Devon and seen her getting pale again, so I yelled above the clatter of the wheels, "Don't be scairt, Miss Devon! Ain't nothin' goin' to hurt you. B. Elkins is on the job to perteck you, and I aim to be at yore side from now on!"

At this she said something I didn't understand. In fack, it sounded like a low moan. And then I heard Joshua say to Bill, hollering to make hisself heard, "Eddication my eye! The big chump's lookin' for a wife, that's what! Ten to one she gives him the mitten!"

"I takes that," bawled Bill, and I bellered, "Shet up that noise! Quit discussin' my private business so dern public! I – what's that?"

It sounded like firecrackers popping back down the road. Bill yelled, "Holy smoke, it's them Chawed Ear maniacs! They're still on our trail and they're gainin' on us!"

Cussing heartily I poured leather into them fool hosses, and jest then we hit the mouth of the Bear Creek trail and I swung into it. They'd never been a wheel on that trail before, and the going was tolerable rough. It was all Bill and Joshua could do to keep from gitting throwed off, and they was seldom more'n one wheel on the ground at a time. Naturally the mob gained on us and when we roared up into Bowie Knife Pass they warn't more'n a quarter mile behind us, whooping bodacious.

I pulled up the hosses beside the tree where Jack Sprague was still tied up to. He gawped at Miss Devon and she gawped back at him.

"Listen," I says, "here's a lady in distress which we're rescuin' from teachin' school in Chawed Ear. A mob's right behind us. This ain't no time to think about yoreself. Will you postpone yore sooicide if I turn you loose, and git onto this stage and take the young lady up the trail whilst the rest of us turns back the mob?"

"I will!" says he with more enthusiasm than he'd showed since we stopped him from hanging hisself. So I cut him loose and he clumb onto the stage.

"Drive on to Kiowa Canyon," I told him as he picked up the lines. "Wait for us there. Don't be scairt, Miss Devon! I'll soon be with you! B. Elkins never fails a lady fair!"

"Gup!" says Jack, and the stage went clattering and banging up the trail and me and Joshua and Bill taken cover amongst the big rocks that was on each side of the trail. The pass was jest a narrer gorge, and a lovely place for a ambush as I remarked.

Well, here they come howling up the steep slope yelling and spurring and shooting wild, and me and Bill give 'em a salute with our pistols. The charge halted plumb sudden. They knowed they was licked. They couldn't git at us because they couldn't climb the cliffs. So after firing a volley which damaged nothing but the atmosphere, they turnt around and hightailed it back towards Chawed Ear.

"I hope that's a lesson to 'em," says I as I riz. "Come! I cain't wait to git culture started on Bear Creek!"

"You cain't wait to git to sparkin' that gal," snorted Joshua. But I ignored him and forked Cap'n Kidd and headed up the trail, and him and Bill follered, riding double on Jack Sprague's hoss.

"Why should I deny my honorable intentions?" I says presently. "Anybody can see Miss Devon is already learnin' to love me! If Jack had *my* attraction for the fair sex, he wouldn't be luggin' around a ruint life. Hey, where's the stage?" Because we'd reched Kiowa Canyon and they warn't no stage.

"Here's a note stuck on a tree," says Bill. "I'll read it – well, for Lord's sake!" he yelped, *"Lissen to this."*

> Dere boys: I've desided I ain't going to hang myself, and Miss Devon has desided she don't want to teach school at Bear Creek. Breck gives her the willies. She ain't altogther shore he's human. With me it's love at first site and she's scairt if she don't marry somebody Breck will marry her, and she says I'm the best looking prospeck she's saw so far. So we're heading for War Paint to git married.
>
> Yores trooly, Jack Sprague.

"Aw, don't take it like that," says Bill as I give a maddened howl and impulsively commenced to rip up all the saplings in rech. "You've saved his life and brung him happiness!"

"And what have I brung me?" I yelled, tearing the limbs off a oak in a effort to relieve my feelings. "Culture on Bear Creek is shot to hell and my honest love has been betrayed! Bill Glanton, the next ranny you chase up into the Humbolts to commit sooicide he don't have to worry about gittin' bumped off – I attends to it myself, personal!"

Lines Written in the Realization That I Must Die

The Black Door gapes and the Black Wall rises;
  Twilight gasps in the grip of Night.
Paper and dust are the gems man prizes –
  Torches toss in my waning sight.

Drums of glory are lost in the ages,
  Bare feet fail on a broken trail –
Let my name fade from the printed pages;
  Dreams and visions are growing pale.

Twilight gathers and none can save me.
  Well and well, for I would not stay:
Let me speak through the stone you grave me:
  He never could say what he wished to say.

Why should I shrink from the sign of leaving?
  My brain is wrapped in a darkened cloud;
Now in the Night are the Sisters weaving
  For me a shroud.

Towers shake and the stars reel under,
  Skulls are heaped in the Devil's fane;
My feet are wrapped in a rolling thunder,
  Jets of agony lance my brain.

What of the world that I leave for ever?
  Phantom forms in a fading sight –
Carry me out on the ebon river
  Into the Night.

Appendices

ROBERT E. HOWARD
Twentieth-Century Mythmaker
by Charles Hoffman

Robert E. Howard's most famous creation, the indomitable barbarian warrior Conan, was introduced in the December 1932 issue of the pulp magazine *Weird Tales*. For the first story in the series, Howard provided a brief preface that served to set the stage for Conan's debut:

> Know, oh prince, that between the years when the oceans drank Atlantis and the gleaming cities, and the years of the rise of the Sons of Aryas, there was an Age undreamed of, when shining kingdoms lay spread across the world like blue mantles beneath the stars – Nemedia, Ophir, Brythunia, Hyperborea, Zamora with its dark-haired women and towers of spider-haunted mystery, Zingara with its chivalry, Koth that bordered on the pastoral lands of Shem, Stygia with its shadow-guarded tombs, Hyrkania whose riders wore steel and silk and gold. But the proudest kingdom of the world was Aquilonia, reigning supreme in the dreaming west. Hither came Conan, the Cimmerian, black-haired, sullen-eyed, sword in hand, a thief, a reaver, a slayer, with gigantic melancholies and gigantic mirth, to tread the jeweled thrones of the Earth under his sandaled feet.

Earlier, the editor of *Weird Tales* had requested some biographical information about the young author himself. Howard's response painted a very different picture:

> Like the average man, the tale of my life would merely be a dull narration of drab monotony and toil, a grinding struggle against poverty. I have spent most of my life in the hard, barren semi-waste lands of Western Texas, and since infancy my memory holds a continuous grinding round of crop failures – sandstorms – drouths – floods – hot winds that withered the corn – hailstorms that ripped the grain to pieces – late blizzards that froze the fruit in the bud – plagues of grasshoppers and boll weevils...

> I've picked cotton, helped brand a few yearlings, hauled a little garbage, worked in a grocery store, ditto a dry-goods store, worked in a law office, jerked soda, worked up in a gas office, tried to be a

public stenographer, packed a surveyor's rod, worked up oil field news for some Texas and Oklahoma papers, etc., etc., and also etc...

Finally, Howard was moved to conclude, "And there I believe is about all the information I can give about a very humdrum and commonplace life."

Many years later Mark Schultz, illustrator of *The Coming of Conan the Cimmerian*, recalled:

> I discovered Robert E. Howard's Conan in 1969, when I was thirteen years old. I read the stories then for their incomparable high adventure and mind-blasting horror. It wasn't until much later that I realized they hit so hard and stayed so timeless because Howard's feverish, passionate writing was a crystal clear reflection of a young mind in turmoil, fighting to be free of his physical surroundings.

Howard often discussed his writing with a young schoolteacher named Novalyne Price, who had literary ambitions of her own. Late in life, Price wrote a memoir of Howard entitled *One Who Walked Alone* (subsequently adapted into a touching motion picture, *The Whole Wide World*). Price recalls mentioning to Howard that she wanted to write about "real people with real problems." Howard, however, had little interest in writing about the world he saw around him, which he once characterized as "a dreary expanse of sand drifts and post-oak thickets, checkered with sterile fields where tenant farmers toil out their hideously barren lives in fruitless labor and bitter want." In defense of his own fiction, he asserted:

> The people who read my stuff want to get away from this modern, complicated world with its hypocrisy, its cruelty, its dog-eat-dog life...The civilization we live in is a lot more sinister than the time I write about. In those days, girl, men were men and women were women. They struggled to stay alive, but the struggle was worth it.

H. P. Lovecraft, with whom Howard corresponded regularly, once noted a curious paradox. Lovecraft observed that a great deal of fiction that purports to be about everyday life is actually quite often rife with sentimental distortions. Howard himself expressed a similar view: "Nobody writes realistic realism, and if they did, nobody would read it. The writers that think they write it just give their own ideas about things they think they see. The sort of man who could write realism is the fellow who never reads or writes anything."

By way of contrast, Lovecraft defined fantasy as "an art based on the imaginative life of the human mind, *frankly recognized as such*; & in its own way as natural & scientific – as truly related to natural (even if uncommon & delicate) psychological processes as the starkest of photographic realism." In other words, fantasy fiction makes no pretense of presenting the physical world as it actually is. However, in the right hands it can vividly delineate the most intensely felt yearnings of the human heart and soul, from the deepest longings and most dreadful anxieties to the loftiest aspirations. Therefore, it could be said that fantasy need have little to do with *reality*, yet have a great deal to do with *truth*, since these are not precisely the same thing.

This is, of course, not to say that realistic fiction cannot portray weighty abstractions such as spiritual damnation and redemption, just that fantasy can often do so more excitingly and entertainingly. The *Star Wars* saga of Anakin Skywalker/Darth Vader is a perfect example: for better or worse, more people have seen the *Star Wars* movies than have read *Crime and Punishment*. Most people are more familiar with the story of *Faust* than of *A Tale of Two Cities*. Fantasy is an uncannily suitable vehicle for conveying powerful themes to a mass audience.

Novalyne Price recalled a subsequent conversation with Howard: "Bob began to talk about good and evil in life. He said that life was always a struggle between good and evil, and people like to read about that struggle...He wrote for readers who wanted evil to be something big, horrible, but still something a barbarian like Conan could overcome."

Howard's remarks to Novalyne strongly suggest that he felt that his readers benefited in some way from seeing their struggles reflected on a higher level. To that end, Robert E. Howard took the oldest type of story – the tale of heroes, gods, and monsters – and reinvented it as jolting pulp fiction. His prose, not unlike that of Raymond Chandler, was direct and hard-edged, yet lyrical. The content of his stories was edgier as well. The horrific elements, owing in part to his association with Lovecraft, were more visceral than anything found in the European fantasy of Morris and Dunsany. Well in advance of writers like Mickey Spillane and Ian Fleming, Howard was crafting sexy, violent entertainment. Unusual situations, intense moods, and heightened emotional states, prominent features of Romanticism and its Gothic subgenre, were also boldly displayed in his writing. All of which indicate that Howard understood clearly that consumers of narrative art have an innate hunger to identify with characters placed in extreme circumstances.

Howard's modern brand of fantasy has often been characterized as "sword and sorcery," but Lovecraft may have been more insightful when he deemed it "artificial legendry." Howard wrote for the American working class of the early twentieth century. His readers were widely separated by time, distance, and upheaval from the myths and legends that had enthralled their ancestors in the Old World. They lived in a world rocked by cataclysm, no less than the fictional Hyborian Age of Conan had been. In 1906, the year Howard was born, the world was ruled by kings, dukes, emperors, sultans, kaisers, and czars. Twenty years later, they were all gone. The slaughter of the First World War and the lawlessness of the Roaring Twenties were followed by the malaise of the Great Depression. The Depression was a humiliating ordeal for many Americans, and Howard's rousing tales of Conan helped to empower readers with flagging spirits. In a larger sense, however, Howard sought to resurrect the heroic saga where it had long been lost.

When America declared its independence from the Mother Country, it was also bidding farewell to Saint George and King Arthur. No comparable myths grew up to take their place. The new folk legends that appeared in the wake of the Industrial Revolution celebrated laborers and producers of goods. Today everyone has heard of Paul Bunyan, John Henry, and Casey Jones, and yet no one really cares about them. One needn't marvel that no nineteenth century publisher ever attempted to use such characters to sell dime novels. Instead, stories of gunfighters and bank robbers were dime novel mainstays. "Tall tales" of how hard some guy worked were presumably less inspiring. After all, how popular would Horatio Alger's novels have been had his protagonists simply worked but remained poor?

The dime novel was followed in the early twentieth century by the pulp magazine. At this time, radio and motion pictures were in their infancies, television yet unborn. As astonishing as it may seem today, print was the primary entertainment medium for the masses. Publishing empires were built on pulp fiction magazines that usually sold for ten cents. By the late twenties, scores of different titles were on sale at any given time. The pulp jungle proved fertile ground for a new crop of homegrown heroes: cowboys, sailors, detectives, aviators, and soldiers of fortune. Interestingly, however, such pre-eminent pulp heroes as The Shadow and Doc Savage were essentially supercops, maintainers of the status quo.

Robert E. Howard had something different in mind when he conceived of Conan. His giant barbarian is an outlaw, a sword-for-hire, basically out for himself, yet still retaining a certain knack for doing the right thing. Conan is not a preserver of order; he is a mover and shaker, the whirlwind at the center of momentous events. And though his author endowed him with a very modern hard-boiled edge, Conan remains that most immemorial of heroes, the warrior. Writing before Carl Jung was well known in America, before Joseph Campbell's work had appeared, Howard possessed an instinctive grasp of mythic, archetypal figures – king, warrior, magician, *femme fatale*. He knew that the ancient figure of the warrior would resonate on a deeper, more subconscious level than, for example, the detective, a figure in some ways emblematic of the Age of Reason.

Howard's vivid "artificial legendry" has often been dismissed as "escapism." Yet if the lot of the average man is truly one of "drab monotony and toil," as Howard believed, it falls to the *skald* and the storyteller to furnish refreshment for tired minds and nourishment for the soul. Critics like Robert McKee have theorized that it is the structure of "the story" that enables a person to see his own life as something other than a chaotic jumble of trivial incidents. In the heroic saga, scintillating vistas of human potential are glimpsed. The blinders fall away; shades of gray sharpen into vibrant color. One comes away from such visions with a sense of one's own stature enhanced. This is not escape, but liberation. Howard brought a renewed vigor and freshness to the heroic saga, making it more vital and relevant to the sort of modern reader most in need of a widened vista.

In truth, the average working adult does endure his or her fair share of drudgery. The majority of people earn a living by means of tedious jobs, not rewarding careers. Herein lies a clue to Howard's well-known resentment of "civilization," for which the author has taken so much flak. Youngsters are told they can become anything they want if they try hard enough; they are never told how many waiters the world needs for every archeologist it can support. Viewed from this perspective, civilized society is like a big lottery in which most people have to lose. Countless individuals are relegated to inane tasks that oppress the spirit, ruin the body, and dull the mind. Consider the doorman stationed in front of a luxury hotel, or the low-level office clerk hunched over paperwork for long hours in a sterile cubicle. To Howard, such individuals would be better off, spiritually if not materially, wearing loincloths and carrying spears, battling openly against man and nature.

Safe and secure but unfulfilled within the folds of civilization, the adventurous among us grow restless. Bold individuals seek out ways to test and challenge themselves. Examples of this can be found at every level of society, from the mountaineer scaling a peak "because it is there" to the teenage street racer. Howard once told Lovecraft:

> Despite the tinsel and show, the artificial adjuncts, and the sometimes disgusting advertisements, ballyhoo and exploitation attendant upon such sports as boxing and football, there is, in the

actual contests, something vital and real and deep-rooted in the very life-springs of the race...Football, for instance, is nothing less than war in miniature, and provides an excellent way of working off pugnacious and combative instincts, without bloodshed.

One can experience a fleeting taste of glory through some form of athletic striving, either first hand or vicariously as a spectator. One can also experience a heightened sense of meaning, purpose, and fulfillment vicariously through art. Whatever the case, a transcendental experience is sought. There is a yearning to transcend the coarseness and banality of everyday life. Championship football and soccer games are often followed by raucous partying and even rioting, owing to the fact that most of the spectators lead exceedingly humdrum lives. Ordinary day-to-day existence all too often consists largely of slogging through a morass of inane tasks, stifling worries, and petty squabbles.

Howard endeavored to offer his readers a loftier perspective. He understood that selling window blinds, or drilling holes in sheet metal all week, or working at the rent-a-car counter at the airport is not enough to fill a man's heart. That is one reason he so excelled at depicting struggles that were epic, against evils that were truly horrific. Such is the essence of adventure, and Howard has widely been lauded as a great adventure writer. The path of the adventurer leads to glory or doom, but it skirts commonplace tedium and the gradual grinding down of the human spirit by the weight of the world. In its way, the adventure story is a subversive art form in the sense that it carries within it the implicit suggestion that *everyday life is inadequate*.

There is a human tendency to invest events like holidays, graduations, and weddings with an atmosphere of pomp and grandeur. This involves the use of the creative imagination in a manner not so different from the way the storyteller weaves his tales. "There was pageantry and high illusion and vanity, and the beloved tinsel of glory without which life is not worth living," wrote Howard concerning times gone by: "All empty show and the smoke of conceit and arrogance, but what a drab thing life would be without them." For him, there is no meaning or beauty in life other than what we dream into it.

In this and other respects, Howard could be considered an early existential writer. The term "existentialism" derives from its central tenet that "existence precedes essence," a terse definition that calls for clarification. Existentialism asserts that humans do not come into being for any special or specific purpose. Instead, one determines one's own "essential nature" through one's actions. It is basically an atheistic philosophy, although some philosophers have been able to reconcile it with faith. In either case, responsibility for creating goals, values, and meaning rests on human shoulders. Meaning in life is something that must be created, rather than discovered. Many commentators chose to dwell on the negative implications of existential philosophy, making much ado about "the meaninglessness of life" and "the absurdity of human existence." There is no meaning to be found in the vast universe beyond ourselves.

Existentialism brought into sharper focus a number of themes, ideas, motifs, and subtexts that had been cropping up with increasing frequency in literature and art during the early decades of the twentieth century. These could be found in popular art as well as fine art, even if the former remained beneath the radar of most intellectuals until comparatively recently. The works of both Robert E. Howard and H. P. Lovecraft reflect some aspect of existential thought. Thomas R. Reid has duly noted that Howard and Lovecraft "write in archetypal terms, of man's struggle against chaos and destruction. Howard's primordial heroes most often win, Lovecraft's are invariably crushed or emotionally maimed. In either case the statement of man's position is the same. From a position of utter inferiority, man must deal with the degrading and degenerate manifestations of the world in which he lives." In Conan we see the consummate self-determining man, alone in a hostile universe.

SERVING TIME IN DISILLUSIONMENT

Conan's world is one of both breathtaking wonder and blood-freezing horror. There are exotic kingdoms and gleaming citadels, but also foreboding hinterlands and mysterious ruins haunted by nightmarish specters. Fabulous wealth in the form of gold and precious gemstones lies in heaps for the taking, if one is bold enough to dare the terrors that lurk in the nearby shadows. Monstrous fifty-foot serpents rear up, fangs dripping venom. Giant slavering apes snarl and lurch forward with taloned hands extended. Yet even these terrors can be overcome by the craft, audacity, sinew, and fighting prowess of a fierce barbarian warrior. And gold is not his only reward. Alluring women await; some are slave girls, some are princesses, some are warriors in their own right, but all are almost agonizing in their physical perfection.

For daring to conjure such fever dreams, Howard has at times been labeled an "arrested adolescent" by his harsher critics. However, such critics tend to be familiar with only a small portion of Howard's work. Howard lavished whatever exuberance and love of life he possessed upon his most famous creation, leaving precious little for himself or most of his other characters.

In *The Shadow Kingdom*, King Kull broods on his throne, grappling with philosophical abstractions. *Red Shadows* introduced the dour fanatic Solomon Kane. In *The Dark Man*, Black Turlogh O'Brien fatalistically smites his enemies in the grip of a berserker rage. *Worms of the Earth* tells the tragic tale of Bran Mak Morn, who consorts with dark forces in an effort to save his dying race. The crusaders of Howard's historical stories are not knights in shining armor, but brutal men in dirty chain mail vying for power over small medieval fiefdoms.

Howard himself was buffeted by severe mood swings. He took his own life at the youthful age of thirty. While only in his early twenties, he was writing poetry redolent of world-weariness, loss, and ennui. In one such poem, "Always Comes Evening," he laments, "...my road runs out in thistles and my dreams have turned to dust..." More than once, he speaks of the bone-crushing weight of age pressing upon him, even as he admits he is young in actual years: "I fling aside the cloak of Youth and limp / A withered man upon a broken staff." Far from being an "arrested adolescent," Robert E. Howard was, if anything, a premature middle-aged burnout.

Howard gave considerable credence to the doctrine of reincarnation, and this undoubtedly contributed to his view of himself as an "old soul." Possible former incarnations notwithstanding, however, he did not live out even a single normal life span. Even so, he experienced his share of strife and conflict. This was not in the form of physical combat, but instead resulted from his struggle with his surroundings. Howard confided to Lovecraft:

> It seems to me that many writers, by virtue of environments of culture, art and education, slip into writing because of their environments. I became a writer in spite of my environments. Understand I am not criticizing these environments. They were good, solid, and worthy. The fact that they were not inducive to literature and art is nothing in their disfavor. Nevertheless, it is no light thing to enter into a profession absolutely foreign and alien to the people among which one's lot is cast.

As a youngster, Howard was introverted and sensitive with a tendency to brood over real or imagined slights by others. He undertook a rigorous bodybuilding program that gained him a powerful physique as an adult. He informed his father that, "I entered in to build my body until when a scoundrel crosses me up, I can with my bare hands tear him to pieces, double him up, and break his back with my hands alone." Growing up, he became increasingly resentful of authority: "I hated school as I hate the memory of school. It wasn't the work I minded...what I hated was the confinement – the clock-like regularity of everything; the regulation of my speech and actions; most of all the idea that someone considered himself or herself in authority over me, with the right to question my actions and interfere with my thoughts." Howard took up writing as a profession in large part because it enabled him to be his own boss: "I worked in a gas office, but lost the job because I wouldn't kow-tow to my employer and 'yes' him from morning to night. That's one reason I was never very successful working for people. So many men think an employee is a kind of servant."

All these things contributed to Howard's premature burnout. Possessed of a dominant personality, he was given to butting heads with people and situations with which he felt himself at odds. Essentially, he was fighting the whole damn world, and over time this took its toll. Hence his feelings of world-weariness and futility.

In a larger sense, however, Howard's disillusionment differs from that of the average person only in degree. Everyone experiences some form of unrequited longing or thwarted ambition. Disappointment is a fact of life, an inevitability known to all. For the more sensitive, disappointment is shadowed by disillusionment. There is a vague sense of resentment that life has somehow played one false. Often this is dismissed with the commonplace observation that things aren't always what they're cracked up to be. But in Howard's prose, as well as his poetry, disillusionment has a way of becoming magnified.

From time to time, Howard writes of some glorious dream that only serves to conceal a hideous underlying reality. In such passages, he feels moved to portray disillusionment on a grand, even cosmic, scale. For Howard's heroes it is often the result of a single, sudden horrifying revelation, rather than merely stemming from the accumulation of numerous minor disappointments. Portrayed thusly, it is another example of Howard's penchant for depicting ordinary human struggle on a mythical level. All pervasive, disillusionment enfolds humanity like some form of original sin. Not even Conan can escape it.

In classic mythology, the hero's journey often entails a descent to the underworld and communion with the dead. In *The Hour of the Dragon*, Conan delves deep beneath the shadow-guarded tombs of Stygia. There he meets the Princess Akivasha, who lived ten thousand years earlier and is celebrated in myth the world over. According to her legend, she trafficked with dark forces to remain young and beautiful forever. When she attempts to seduce him, Conan learns that Akivasha is a vampire, an unclean parasitic monster. As he escapes her lair, he is nearly overwhelmed with despair:

The legend of Akivasha was so old, and among the evil tales told of her ran a thread of beauty and idealism, of everlasting youth. To so many dreamers and poets and lovers she was not alone the evil princess of Stygian legend, but the symbol of eternal youth and beauty, shining for ever in some far realm of the gods. And this was the hideous reality. This foul perversion was the truth of that everlasting life. Through his physical revulsion ran the sense of a shattered dream of man's idolatry, its gleaming gold proved slime and cosmic filth. A wave of futility swept over him, a dim fear of the falseness of all men's dreams and idolatries.

Frequently, Conan encounters beings whose capacity for evil or depravity exceeds that of mere mortals. It's all part of a heroic saga of ordeals and triumphs surpassing those to be found in the course of ordinary, everyday life. And if there is no escaping disillusionment, Conan must experience disillusionment on an epic scale.

Thomas R. Reid has pointed out that, "One does not have to search long among extant epic works to find others which parallel underlying themes in both Lovecraft and Howard. In Norse mythology, one is confronted with a cosmology in which defeat is inevitable. Man's and the gods' transitory victories are tempered by the foreknowledge of total defeat." Reid concludes that Howard's fiction expresses "the ancient and yet increasingly modern belief that man exists in a hostile world..."

"We of North Europe had gods and demons before which the pallid mythologies of the South fade to childishness," proclaims the Irish-American narrator of one of Howard's horror stories, who goes on to add, "In the southern lands the sun shines and flowers bloom; under the soft skies men laugh at demons. But in the North, who can say what elemental spirits of evil dwell in the fierce storms and the darkness?"

Howard's view of the Northern myths was shared by Edith Hamilton, who duly noted:

The world of Norse mythology is a strange world. Asgard, the home of the gods, is unlike any other heaven men have dreamed of. No radiancy of joy is in it, no assurance of bliss. It is a grave and solemn place, over which hangs the threat of an inevitable doom. The gods know that a day will come when they will be destroyed. Sometime they will meet their enemies and go down beneath them to defeat and death. Asgard will fall in ruins...Nevertheless, the gods will fight for it to the end...

This is the conception of life which underlies the Norse religion, as somber a conception as the mind of man has given birth to. The only sustaining support possible, the one pure unsullied good men can hope to attain, is heroism...

Bleakness, futility, and the inevitable passing of all things are part of the world-view of Robert E. Howard. *The Gray God Passes* was inspired by an actual historical event, the Battle of Clontarf, which Howard transformed into his personal vision of Twilight of the Gods. In it, the Celtic warrior Black Turlogh laments, "The days of the twilight come on amain, and a strange feeling is upon me as of a waning age. What are we all, too, but ghosts waning into the night?" Such somber notes give Howard's tales a resonance lacking in the works of his imitators. It could be said that many readers *come to* Robert E. Howard for the action, adventure, thrills and horror to be found in his stories, but they *stay for* the dark, turbulent undercurrent that runs just beneath their surface.

Meaning is only possible through heroic struggle. David Weber offered these cogent observations:

> ...Bran Mak Morn fights for his people's last chance for greatness and their vengeance upon their supplanters. Kull struggles to impose his own clear, barbarian's sense of *justice* in place of the decadent, bureaucratic legalisms of Valusia. Black Turlogh O'Brien, outlawed and cast out by his own clan, sets out on a suicide mission to rescue a kidnapped maiden whose family would spit upon him, if they didn't try to kill him outright. These are very human characters, with senses of honor which may be flawed but remain unbreakable, and while the irresistible force of darkness may bear down upon them, they snatch their occasional personal victories from its jaws.

In Robert E. Howard's heroic tales, the fatalism of the old Nordic sagas is tempered by modern existential thought. Purpose is not to be found *without*, in the cold hostile universe that surrounds us, but *within*. Howard himself found meaning not in "the hard, barren semi-waste lands of Western Texas" in which he walked alone, but in the dreams and visions that stirred within him. One imposes meaning on the world through one's actions, and even when one's actions are lost to time, they are never insignificant. In *The Valley of the Worm*, Niord's name and actual deeds are long since forgotten, but the significance of his triumph is celebrated in song and story the world over. Howard's own heroic deed was to take up the profession of the writer, so little understood in his time and place, and bring his visions to the world.

To understand, and perhaps realize, one's own heroic potential, one must look beyond the everyday. In times past, men sought shelter from the cold and darkness without to warm themselves at fires. In times to come, new generations of readers will warm and reinvigorate themselves with the modern myths of Robert E. Howard.

A SHORT BIOGRAPHY of ROBERT E. HOWARD
by Rusty Burke

Robert Ervin Howard (1906–1936) ranks among the greatest writers of adventure stories. The creator of Conan the Cimmerian, Kull of Atlantis, Solomon Kane, Bran Mak Morn, Francis X. Gordon ("El Borak"), Sailor Steve Costigan, Breckenridge Elkins, and many other memorable characters, Howard, during a writing career that spanned barely a dozen years, had well over a hundred stories published in the pulp magazines of his day, chiefly *Weird Tales*, but including *Action Stories, Argosy, Fight Stories, Oriental Stories, Spicy Adventure, Sport Story, Strange Detective, Thrilling Adventure, Top Notch*, and a number of others. His stories consistently proved popular with the readers, for they are powerfully vivid adventures, with colorful, larger-than-life heroes and compelling, rivetting prose that grabs the reader from the first paragraph and sweeps him along to the thrilling conclusion. So great was the appeal of Howard's storytelling that it continues to capture new generations of readers and inspire many of the finest writers of fantasy and adventure.

Robert E. Howard was born on January 22, 1906, in the "fading little ex-cowtown" of Peaster, Texas, in Parker County, just west of Fort Worth. The Howards had been living in neighboring Palo Pinto County, on the banks of Dark Valley Creek, and returned there soon after their son was born. It is not known why Dr. Isaac Mordecai Howard and his wife, Hester Jane Ervin Howard, moved to the somewhat larger community. Dr. Howard may have thought to find a practice that did not entail lengthy absences from home, or perhaps moved his wife temporarily to the larger community so that she would have readier access to medical care when her pregnancy came to term. Hester Jane Ervin Howard, Robert's mother, did not enjoy robust health, to put it mildly: there was a history of tuberculosis in her family, and Mrs. Howard was sickly for much of Robert's life. Isaac Howard was a country doctor, a profession which often meant being away from home for days at a time. Thus he may have wished to be certain that his wife of two years, experiencing her first pregnancy in her mid-thirties, would have adequate medical attention when she delivered their first, and as it happened, only child.

Isaac Howard seems to have been possessed of a combination of wanderlust and ambition that led him to move his family frequently in search of better opportunities. By the time he was eight, Robert had lived in at least seven different, widely scattered Texas towns. Finally, in 1915, the family moved to the community of Cross Cut, in Brown County, and they would live in this vicinity, with moves to Burkett (in Coleman County) in 1917 and finally to Cross Plains (Callahan County) in 1919, for the rest of Robert's and his mother's lives.

Cross Plains in the 1920s was a small town of approximately 2,000 souls, give or take a thousand, but like much of the Central West Texas region, it went through periodic oil booms. Two town-site booms, in particular, brought hundreds, perhaps thousands, of temporary inhabitants who set up camps just outside the town limits, jammed the hotels to capacity, and rented rooms or beds in private homes. The lease men, riggers, drillers, tool dressers, and roughnecks who followed the oil were followed in their turn by those who sought to exploit them for profit, from men or women who set up temporary hamburger stands to feed them, to gamblers and prostitutes who provided "recreation," to thugs, thieves and con men who simply preyed on them. An oil boom could transform a sleepy little community into a big city in no time at all, in those days: when oil was discovered in Ranger, Texas (about 40 miles from Cross Plains) in 1917, the population increased from 1,000 to 30,000 in less than a year, and similar growth was reported in nearby Breckenridge. Cross Plains never saw anything like that kind of growth, but certainly the few thousand who did come transformed it into a wilder and rowdier town than usual. One resident recalls her family driving into town on Saturday night just to watch people, hoping fights would break out. They were rarely disappointed. Of the atmosphere in a boom town, Howard wrote: "I'll say one thing about an oil boom: it will teach a kid that Life's a pretty rotten thing about as quick as anything I can think of." Just as quickly as the town grew, however, it could decline: when the oil played out, the speculators and oil-field workers and their camp-followers moved on. The influence of this boom-and-bust cycle on Howard's later ideas about the growth and decline of civilization has often been overlooked.

Bob Howard attended the local high school, where he was remembered as polite and reserved, and to make pocket money he worked at a variety of jobs, including hauling trash, picking up and delivering laundry for dry-cleaners, clerking in stores, loading freight at the train station, and other odd jobs. He had some close friends among the local boys, but there seem to have been none who shared his literary interests.

Bob's literary interests had probably been encouraged from an early age by his mother, an ardent poetry lover. He was an avid reader, claiming even to have raided schoolhouses during the summer in his quest for books. While this story is probably hyperbolic, it does give an indication of his thirst for reading material, which was a rare commodity in the communities in which the Howards lived, most of which had no libraries, much less bookstores.

Bob seems to have had an extraordinary ability to read quickly and to remember what he had read. His friends recall their astonishment at his ability to pick up a book in the library or a store or someone's house, to quickly turn the pages and run his eyes over them, faster than they thought anyone could actually be reading, and later to be able to relate to them with perfect clarity what he had read. His library, presented by his father to Howard Payne College after his death, reveals the breadth of his interests: history and fiction are dominant, but also represented are biography, sports, poetry, anthropology, Texana, and erotica. Near the end of his life he wrote to H. P. Lovecraft:

> My favorite writers are A. Conan Doyle, Jack London, Mark Twain, Sax Rohmer, Jeffery Farnol, Talbot Mundy, Harold Lamb, R. W. Chambers, Rider Haggard, Kipling, Sir Walter Scott, [Stanley] Lane-Poole, Jim Tully, Ambrose Bierce, Arthur Machen, Edgar Allan Poe, and H. P. Lovecraft. For poetry, I like Robert W. Service, Kipling, John Masefield, James Elroy Flecker, [Robert] Vansittart, Sidney Lanier, Edgar Allan Poe, the Benets — Stephen Vincent better than William Rose — Walter de la Mare, Rupert Brooke, Siegfried Sassoon, Francis Ledwedge, Omar Khayyam, Joe Moncure March, Nathalia Crane, Henry Herbert Knibbs, Lord Dunsany, G. K. Chesterton, Bret Harte, Oscar Wilde, Longfellow, Tennyson, Swinburne, [George Sylvester] Viereck, Alfred Noyes, and Lovecraft.

In addition to his reading, Bob Howard had a passion for oral storytelling. It is well attested that he frequently told his stories aloud as he typed them: his neighbors reported that they sometimes had difficulty sleeping at night because of the racket Howard was making. His youthful buddies in Cross Cut remember that he liked to have them all play out stories he made up, and the literary friends of his adulthood recall being often enthralled by the stories he would tell when they were together. He seemed never to tire of telling stories, though he generally would not relate a tale he was actually writing: he told Novalyne Price that once the story was told, he had difficulty getting it on paper. Sometimes, however, his oral stories were the inspiration or basis for the stories he would write. He loved, too, to listen to others tell stories: in his letters he relates how as a young boy he was thrilled and terrified by the ghost tales of a former slave, and those of his grandmother. Novalyne Price remembers him sitting riveted by the stories of her grandmother, and that he loved to find old-timers who could relate tales of pioneer days. It may well be the quality of the oral story, the well-spun yarn, that makes Howard's stories so enthralling.

Howard seems to have determined upon a literary career at an early age. In a letter to H. P. Lovecraft he says that his first story was written when he was "nine or ten," and a former postmistress at Burkett recalls that he began writing stories about this time and expressed an intention of becoming a writer. He submitted his first story for professional publication when he was but 15, and his first professional sale, *Spear and Fang*, was made at age 18. Howard always insisted that he chose writing as his profession simply because it gave him the freedom to be his own boss:

"I've always had a honing to make my living by writing, ever since I can remember, and while I haven't been a howling success in that line, at least I've managed for several years now to get by without grinding at some time clock-punching job. There's freedom in this game; that's the main reason I chose it."

Whatever his reasons, once Howard had determined upon his path, he kept at it.

The Cross Plains school only went through tenth grade during Bob Howard's day, but he needed to complete the eleventh grade to qualify for college admission. Therefore, in the fall of 1922 Bob and his mother moved to Brownwood, a larger town that served as the county seat for Brown County, so that he could finish high school there. It was there that he met Truett Vinson and Clyde Smith, who would remain his friends until the end of his life: they were the first of his friends to share and encourage his interest in literature and writing. Smith, in particular, shared much of Howard's literary taste, and the two encouraged each other in writing poetry. Also at Brownwood High, Howard enjoyed his first appearances as a published author: two of his stories won cash prizes and publication in the high school paper, *The Tattler*, December 22, 1922, and three more were printed during the spring term.

After his graduation from high school, Howard returned to Cross Plains. His father, in particular, wanted him to attend college, perhaps hoping that he, too, would become a physician. But Bob had little aptitude for and no interest in science. He also claimed a passionate hatred for school. As he wrote later to Lovecraft: "I hated school as I hate the memory of school. It wasn't the work I minded; I had no trouble learning the tripe they dished out in the way of lessons – except arithmetic, and I might have learned that if I'd gone to the trouble of studying it. I wasn't at the head of my classes – except in history – but I wasn't at the foot either. I generally did just enough work to keep from flunking the courses, and I don't regret the loafing I did. But what I hated was the confinement – the clock-like regularity of everything; the regulation of my speech and actions; most of all the idea that someone considered himself or herself in authority over me, with the right to question my actions and interfere with my thoughts."

Although he did eventually take courses at the Howard Payne Commercial School, these were business courses – stenography, typing, and a program in bookkeeping; despite his interest in history, anthropology, and literature, Howard never took college courses in these subjects. During the period from his high school graduation in spring of 1923 to his completion of the bookkeeping program in the spring of 1927, he continued writing. Although he finally made his first professional sale during this period, when *Weird Tales* accepted *Spear and Fang*, he also accumulated many rejection slips. Further, because most of his early sales were to *Weird Tales*, which paid upon publication, rather than acceptance, he found that the money was not coming in as he might have liked. He therefore took a variety of jobs during these years. He tried reporting oil-field news, but found he did not like interviewing people he did not know or like about a topic that did not interest him. He tried stenography, both in a law office and as an independent public stenographer, but found he was not particularly good at it and did not like it. He worked as an assistant to an oil-field geologist, and while he did enjoy the work, he one day collapsed in the fearsome Texas summer heat, which led him to fear that he had heart problems (it was later learned that his heart had a mild tendency to race under stress), so he was just as glad when the survey ended and the geologist left town. He spent several months as a soda jerk and counterman at the Cross Plains Drug Store, a job that he actively detested, and which required so much of his time that he had little left over for writing or recreation. Thus he made a pact with his father: he would take the course in bookkeeping at the Howard Payne Academy, following which he would have one year to try to make a success of his writing. If at the end of that year he was not making it, he would try to find a bookkeeping job.

During the summer of 1927, Bob Howard met Harold Preece, who would be an important friend and correspondent for the next few years. It was Preece who encouraged Bob's interest in Irish and Celtic history and legend: he had earlier shown some interest in the subject, and now, inspired by Preece's enthusiasm, it would become an active passion. He also met, the same weekend, Booth Mooney, who would become the editor of a literary circular, *The Junto*, to which Howard, Preece, Clyde Smith, Truett Vinson, and others contributed over a period of about two years.

After completing the bookkeeping course, Howard set about in earnest the business of becoming a writer. By early 1928, it was clear that he was going to be able to succeed in this, and indeed he never again worked at any other job. *Weird Tales* had published two Howard stories in 1925, one in 1926, and one (plus two poems) in 1927. In 1928 they would publish four stories (including the first Solomon Kane tale, *Red Shadows*) and five poems. From January 1928 until his death in June 1936, Howard stories or verse appeared in nearly three of every four issues of *Weird Tales*.

Several critics have noted that Howard's writing can be divided into "periods." Though they overlap to a degree, these periods, which seemed to last two to three years each, may reveal something about Howard's writing style and methods. The most well-defined periods are those during which he wrote boxing stories, culminating in the Steve Costigan series; heroic fantasy stories, culminating with Conan; oriental adventure stories, culminating with the El Borak tales; and western stories – he was still "in" this period at his death. A close reading of Howard's letters and stories, and placement of these along a timeline, reveals that he would develop an interest in a subject, read about it avidly, immerse himself in it so thoroughly that he virtually adopted a new identity (a persona, the "voice" through which a writer speaks, not to be confused with the writer's own personality), whereupon he would begin, at first tentatively and then with increasing confidence and vigor, to write about the subject in this new "voice." Although something of the pattern can be seen from his early writing, it is most vivid beginning with his "boxing" persona, Steve Costigan.

Howard's passion for boxing is attested as early as age nine. He boxed with his friends at any opportunity, and in his late teens may have occasionally assisted in promoting fights at local clubs in Cross Plains. While working at the soda fountain at the Cross Plains Drug Store, he developed a friendship with one oil-field worker who introduced him to the amateur fighters at the local ice house, and he became a frequent participant in these bouts. Between 1925 (at the latest) and 1928, he put himself through a weight and strength program, and took on really heroic proportions. He read avidly about prizefighters, and attended fights whenever and wherever he could. By early 1929 he had begun writing and submitting boxing stories, though his first efforts mingled boxing with weird themes. (This was another of his patterns: when trying out a new literary field, he would often use characters, settings or themes with which he was already comfortable.) With the first Steve Costigan story, *The Pit of the Serpent*, in the July 1929 *Fight Stories*, he had found a market that would prove as steady for him as *Weird Tales*, at least until the Depression knocked out *Fight Stories* and its companion magazine, *Action Stories*, in 1932.

The same weekend he met Harold Preece in Austin, Howard had bought a copy of G. K. Chesterton's book-length epic poem, *The Ballad of the White Horse*, which brings together Celts, Romanized Britons, and Anglo-Saxons under King Alfred in a battle of Christians against the heathen Danish and Norse invaders of the ninth century. Howard enthusiastically praised the poem in letters to Clyde Smith, sharing lengthy passages. It apparently inspired him to begin work on *The Ballad of King Geraint*, in which he brings together representatives of various Celtic peoples of early Britain in a valiant "last stand" against the invading Angles, Saxons, and Jutes. Chesterton's idea of "telescoping history," that "it is the chief value of legend to mix up the centuries while preserving the sentiment," must have appealed to Howard greatly, for this is precisely what he did in many of his fantasy adventures, particularly in his creation of Conan's Hyborian Age, in which we find represented many different historical eras and cultures, from medieval Europe (Aquilonia and Poitain) to the American frontier (the Pictish Wilderness and its borderlands), from Cossacks (the Kozaki) to Elizabethan pirates (the Free Brotherhood). Howard "mix(ed) up the centuries while preserving the sentiment": this "telescoping" allowed him to portray what he saw as universal elements of human nature and historical patterns, as well as giving him virtually all of human history for a playground.

When Howard discovered that Harold Preece shared his enthusiasm for matters Celtic, he entered into his "Celtic" phase with his customary brio. His letters to Preece and to Clyde Smith from 1928 to 1930 are full of discussions of Irish history, legend, and poetry – he even taught himself a smattering of Irish Gaelic, and began exploring his genealogy in earnest (though he had a pronounced tendency to overstate the Irishness of his ancestry). Irish and Celtic themes came to dominate his poetry, and by 1930 he was ready to try out this new persona with fiction. In keeping with his general tendency to use older work as a springboard to the new, he first introduced an Irish character into a story featuring two earlier creations – Cormac of Connacht is often overlooked as one of the *Kings of the Night*, overshadowed by the teaming up of Bran Mak Morn and King Kull, but the story is told from the Irish king's point of view. During 1930 Howard wrote a number of stories featuring Gaelic heroes, nearly all of them outlawed by clan and country.

In June 1930 Howard received a letter from Farnsworth Wright informing him that *Weird Tales* planned to launch a companion magazine dealing with oriental fiction, and asking him to contribute. This request rekindled the author's avid interest in the Orient, particularly the Middle East, and he produced some of his finest stories for the new magazine (originally titled *Oriental Stories*, later *Magic Carpet*). But while these stories were set during the Crusades, or periods of Mongol or Islamic conquests, they inevitably featured Celtic heroes.

Also in June 1930, Howard wrote to Farnsworth Wright in praise of

H. P. Lovecraft's *The Rats in the Walls*, which had just been reprinted in *Weird Tales*. In the letter, he noted the use of a phrase in Gaelic, suggesting that Lovecraft might hold to a minority view on the settling of the British Isles. Wright sent the letter on to Lovecraft, who frankly had not supposed when he wrote the story that anyone would notice the liberty he had taken with his archaic language. He wrote to Howard to set the record straight, and so began what is surely one of the great correspondence cycles in all of fantasy literature. For the next six years, Howard and Lovecraft debated the merits of civilization versus barbarism, cities and society versus the frontier, the mental versus the physical, art versus commerce, and other subjects. At first Howard was very deferential to Lovecraft, whom he (like many of his colleagues) considered the pre-eminent writer of weird fiction of the day. But gradually Howard came to assert his own views more forcefully, and eventually could even direct withering sarcasm toward Lovecraft's views, as when he noted how "civilized" Italy was in bombing Ethiopia.

These letters provide a vast store of information on Howard's travels and activities during these years, as well as his views on many subjects, and in them we see the development of the persona that would come increasingly to dominate Howard's fiction and letters in the last part of his life, "The Texican" (a term used for Texans prior to statehood). Lovecraft, and later August Derleth, with whom Howard also began corresponding, strongly encouraged Howard's growing interests in regional history and lore, as did E. Hoffmann Price, with whom Howard was already corresponding in 1930 and who was the only writer of the *Weird Tales* group to actually meet him in person. It is unfortunate that this persona did not have a chance to develop fully by the time of Howard's death. The evidence of his letters suggests that he might have become a great western writer.

Even before Howard bought his own car in 1932, he and his parents had made many trips to various parts of Texas, to visit friends and relatives, and for his mother's health, which was in serious decline. After he bought his car, he continued to travel with his parents, but made a few trips with his friends, such as Lindsey Tyson and Truett Vinson. His travels ranged from Fort Worth to the Rio Grande Valley, from the East Texas oil fields to New Mexico. His letters to Lovecraft contain a good deal of description and discussion of the geography and history of these places, and are highly entertaining in their own right, apart from being windows into Howard's life.

In 1934, a new schoolteacher arrived in Cross Plains who was to become a major force in Bob Howard's life. Bob had met Novalyne Price a little over a year previously, when introduced to her by their mutual friend Clyde Smith. Upon moving to Cross Plains, Novalyne made several attempts to call

Bob, only to be told by his mother that he could not come to the phone, or was out of town. At last tiring of these excuses, she talked her cousin into giving her a ride to the Howard home, where she was greeted stand-offishly by his father but warmly by Bob. This was the beginning of a sometimes romantic, sometimes stormy relationship. For the first time, Bob had someone locally who shared his interests – and she was a woman! But his closeness to his mother, particularly his insistence upon attending to her in her illness, which Novalyne thought he should hire a nurse to do, rankled Novalyne, as did his refusal to attend social events. Marriage often entered their minds, and was even occasionally discussed – but the two never entertained the same feelings at the same time. When she would think she was in love, he would insist he needed his freedom. When he thought he was ready for love, she saw only the differences in their attitudes toward socializing. They were two headstrong, passionate, assertive personalities, which made for an interesting relationship, but one that was impossible to sustain. Their relationship became strained when Novalyne started dating others, including Howard's friend Truett Vinson.

Through 1935 and 1936, Howard's mother's health was in rapid decline. More and more frequently Robert had to take her to sanitariums and hospitals, and even though Dr. Howard received a courtesy discount on services, the medical bills began to mount. Bob was faced with a dilemma: his need for money was more pressing than ever, but he had little time in which to write. *Weird Tales* owed him around $800, and payments were slow. Dr. Howard, his own meager savings exhausted, moved his practice to his home, so that patients came in and out all day and night. Father and son finally tried hiring women to nurse and keep house, further filling the house with people. Bob could find no time to be alone with his writing. This, and the despair he felt as his mother inexorably slid toward death, created enormous stress for the young writer. He resurrected an apparently long-standing plan not to outlive his mother.

This was no impulsive act. For years, he had told associates such as Clyde Smith that he would kill himself were it not that his mother needed him. Much of his poetry, most of it written during the 1920s and early 1930s, clearly and forcefully reflects his suicidal ideation. He was not at all enamored with life for its own sake, seeing it only as weary, gruelling toil at the behest of others, with scant chance of success and precious little freedom. A 1931 letter to Farnsworth Wright contains several statements of common Howard themes: "Like the average man, the tale of my life would merely be a dull narration of drab monotony and toil, a grinding struggle against poverty.... I'll say one thing about an oil boom; it will teach a kid that life's a pretty rotten thing about as quick as anything I can think of.... Life's not worth living if somebody thinks he's in authority over you. . . . I'm merely one of a huge army, all of whom are bucking the line one way or another for meat for their bellies. . . . Every now and then one of us finds the going too hard and blows his brains out, but it's all in the game, I reckon."

His letters frequently express the feeling that he was a misfit in a cold and hostile world: "The older I grow the more I sense the senseless unfriendly attitude of the world at large." In nearly all his fiction, the characters are misfits, outcasts, aliens in a world that is hostile to them. One wonders if the early childhood experience of being uprooted on a regular basis, as Dr. Howard gambled on one boom town after another – the Howards had at least eight different residences, scattered all over Texas, before Robert was nine years old – may have contributed to this feeling of being an outsider in an inhospitable land.

In some of his letters to Lovecraft he expressed another variation on this theme: the feeling that he was somehow born out of his proper time. He frequently bemoaned the fate that had him born too late to have participated in the taming of the frontier. "I only wish I had been born earlier – thirty years earlier, anyway. As it was I only caught the tag end of a robust era, when I was too young to realize its meaning. When I look down the vista of the years, with all the 'improvements,' 'inventions' and 'progress' that they hold, I am infinitely thankful that I am no younger. I could wish to be older, much older. Every man wants to live out his life's span. But I hardly think life in this age is worth the effort of living. I'd like to round out my youth; and perhaps the natural vitality and animal exuberance of youth will carry me to middle age. But good God, to think of living the full three score years and ten!"

Howard also seems to have had an abhorrence of the idea of growing old and infirm. A month before his death he'd written to August Derleth: "Death to the old is inevitable, and yet somehow I often feel that it is a greater tragedy than death to the young. When a man dies young he misses much suffering, but the old have only life as a possession and somehow to me the tearing of a pitiful remnant from weak fingers is more tragic than the looting of a life in its full rich prime. I don't want to live to be old. I want to die when my time comes, quickly and suddenly, in the full tide of my strength and health."

For a young man, Howard seems to have had an exaggerated sense of growing old. When he was only twenty-four he wrote to Harold Preece, "I am haunted by the realization that my best days, mental and physical, lie behind me." Novalyne Price recalls that during the time they were dating, in 1934–35, Bob often said that he was in his "sere and yellow leaf," echoing a phrase from Macbeth: "I have lived long enough, my way of life / Is fal'n into the sere, the yellow leaf..."

Also in his May 1936 letter to Derleth, Howard mentioned that "I haven't written a weird story for nearly a year, though I've been contemplating one dealing with Coronado's expedition on the Staked Plains in 1541." This suggests that *Nekht Semerkeht* may well have been the last story Howard started, and if so, it is of interest here, in that it dwells upon the idea of suicide. "The game is not worth the candle," thinks the hero, de Guzman:

> [Man] fondles his favorite delusion that *he* is guided wholly by reason, even when reason tells him it is better to die than to live. It is not the intellect he boasts that bids him live, but the blind, black, unreasoning beast-instinct.
>
> This de Guzman knew and admitted. He did not try to deceive himself into believing that there was any intellectual reason why he should not give up the agonizing struggle, place the muzzle of a pistol to his head and quit an existence whose savor had long ago become less than its pain.

And in the end, it may be that stress played an important role in his decision to take his own life. His mother's worsening illness had necessitated frequent absences from home, to take her to medical facilities in other parts of the state, and even when the Howards were home, Bob had little uninterrupted time, or peace, in which to write. He worried constantly about his mother. It may be that a complex array of forces coalesced to convince him of the futility of existence, and to impel him to take a long-contemplated course of action.

Howard planned for his death very carefully. He made arrangements with his agent, Otis Kline, for the handling of his stories in the event of his death. He carefully put together the manuscripts he had not yet submitted to *Weird Tales* or the Kline agency, with instructions on where they were to be sent. He borrowed a gun, a .380 Colt automatic, from a friend who was unaware of his plans. Dr. Howard may have hidden Bob's own guns, aware of what he might be contemplating. He said that he had seen his son make preparations on earlier occasions when it appeared Mrs. Howard might die. He said that he was trying to keep an eye on his son, but that he did not expect him to act before his mother died.

Hester Howard sank into her final coma about the 8th of June, 1936. Bob asked Dr. J. W. Dill, who had come to be with Dr. Howard during his wife's final illness, whether anyone had been known to live after being shot through the brain. Unaware of Bob's plan, the doctor told him that such an injury meant certain death.

Dr. Howard related that Robert had disarmed him of his intentions the night before, assuming "an almost cheerful attitude": "He came to me in the night, put his arm around me and said, buck up, you are equal to it, you will go through it all right." He did not know, he said, that on the morning of the 11th, Robert asked the nurse attending Mrs. Howard if she thought his mother would ever regain consciousness, and that the nurse had told him she would not.

He then left the room, and was next seen leaving the house and getting into his car. The cook he and his father had hired said later that, looking through the kitchen window, she saw him raise his hands in prayer, though what looked to her like prayer may have been holding up the gun. She heard a shot, and saw Robert slump over the steering wheel. She screamed. Dr. Howard and Dr. Dill ran out to the car and carried Bob back into the house. Both were country doctors, and they knew that no one could live with the kind of injury Bob had sustained. He had shot himself above the right ear, the bullet emerging on the left side.

Robert Howard's robust health allowed him to survive this terrible wound for almost eight hours. He died at about 4:00 in the afternoon, Thursday, June 11, 1936, without ever regaining consciousness. His mother died the following day, also without regaining consciousness. A double funeral was held on June 14, and the mother and son were transported to Brownwood for burial.

A four-line stanza was found and said to be the last thing Robert E. Howard wrote on his old Underwood:

All fled, all done
So lift me on the pyre.
The feast is over
And the lamps expire.

Notes on the Original Howard Texts

The texts for this edition were prepared by Rusty Burke, with the assistance of Lee Breakiron, Frank Coffman, David Gentzel, Paul Herman, Glenn Lord, Patrice Louinet, Saturnino Lucio, and the Cross Plains Public Library. The stories have been checked either against Howard's original manuscripts and typescripts or the first published appearance if a manuscript or typescript was unavailable. Every effort has been made to present the work of Robert E. Howard as faithfully as possible.

Deviations from the original sources are detailed in these textual notes. In the following notes, page, line, and word numbers are given as follows: 11.20.2, indicating page 11, twentieth line, second word. Story titles, chapter numbers and titles, and breaks before and after chapter headings, titles, and illustrations are not counted; in poems, only text lines are counted. The page/line number will be followed by the reading in the original source, or a statement indicating the type of change made.

We have standardized chapter numbering, titling, and headings: Howard's own practices varied, as did those of the publications in which these stories appeared. We have not noted those changes here.

The Shadow Kingdom
Text taken from *Weird Tales*, August 1929. 10.19.4: hall; 25.8.1: wounded.

The Ghost Kings
Text taken from *Weird Tales*, December 1938. No changes have been made for this edition.

The Curse of the Golden Skull
Text taken from Howard's untitled carbon, provided by Glenn Lord. The title comes from a listing of Howard's stories made by his agent after his death. The carbon runs four pages, while the agent's list indicates the original was five pages. Some questionable readings were checked against a transcript prepared by Lord. 29.7.12: which; 29.13.1: Accolyte; 30.28.11: invokation; 30.32.8: trandscending; 31.5.11: highst; 32.13.7: "to" repeated.

Red Shadows

Text taken from *Weird Tales*, August 1928. 37.17.2: mephistophelean; 39.8.7: comma after "idly"; 43.17.11: "hog-like" hyphenated at line break, similar constructions elsewhere in the story (e.g., "catlike") not hyphenated; 45.8.14: rôle; 45.9.8: omits closing quotation marks; 45.12.14: omits closing quotation marks; 47.33.10: "is" not capitalized; 48.21.1: swaying; 57.12.1: "man-like" hyphenated at line break, similar constructions elsewhere in the story (e.g., "catlike") not hyphenated.

The One Black Stain

Text taken from *The Howard Collector*, Spring 1962. 59.14.5: sombre; 59.30.3: sombrely; 60.34.3: sombre. The typescript from which *The Howard Collector* version was taken was not available; three other drafts of the poem exist and all three conform to the American spelling of "somber." We have accordingly used this spelling. Otherwise the text is identical with that in *The Howard Collector*.

The Dark Man

Text taken from *Weird Tales*, December 1931. 64 footnote: period after "AUTHOR"; 65.38.2: "wrist-strap" hyphenated at line break; 67.12.13: "wolf-skin" hyphenated at line break; 69.1.7: comma after "muttered"; 69.24.5: "beast-like" hyphenated at line break; 79.14.7: drunken.

The Marching Song of Connacht

Text taken from Glenn Lord's transcription of Howard's typescript. No changes have been made for this edition.

Kings of the Night

Text taken from *Weird Tales*, November 1930. 91.9.12: Cæsar; 91.27.3: Cæsar; 91.31.5: Cæsar; 92.16.13: Cæsar; 93.10.11: stedfast; 97.38.13: "will-power" hyphenated at line break; 98.1.12: "lion-like" hypenated at line break; 107.26.15: "half-way" hyphenated at line break; 110.10.9-10: way possible; 111.21.3: "side-long" hyphenated at line break.

Recompense

Text taken from *Weird Tales*, November 1938. No changes have been made for this edition.

The Black Stone

Text taken from *Weird Tales*, November 1931. 122.26.3: "Midsummer's Night" not capitalized here, though it is capitalized elsewhere in the story; 123.13.6:

gleam ("glean" in Howard's earlier draft of the story); 124.5.11: no comma after "and"; 124.15.8: black-eddy ("back-eddy" in Howard's earlier draft); 125.6.7: Goeffrey; 125.9.2: "mine" not capitalized; 126.24.7: aboriginies; 130.24.5: rythmically; 131.19.5: ecstacy.

The Song of a Mad Minstrel

Text taken from *Weird Tales*, February-March 1931. No changes have been made for this edition.

The Fightin'est Pair

Text taken from *Action Stories*, November 1931 (as *Breed of Battle*). 139.21.1: "low-down" hyphenated at line break; 140.11.1: "wharf-side" hyphenated at line break; 140.12.2: no closing quotation marks after "this"; 140.28.13: "steel-trap" hyphenated at line break; 141.3.4: repeatedly; 141.6.3: no comma after "him"; 142.2.8: water front; 143.19.9: yards; 143.28.14: period after "shape"; 144.18.2: "lamp-post" hyphenated at line break; 146.18.6: comma after "said"; 146.19.6: no closing quotation marks; 149.2.6: "green-tinted" hyphenated at line break; 149.24.1: "shop-keepers" hyphenated at line break; 150.20.1: no comma after "low"; 150.38.1: "death-grip" hyphenated at line break; 151.41.1: "square-shooter" hyphenated at line break; 152.15.7: open quotation marks before "But."

The Grey God Passes

Text taken from *Dark Mind, Dark Heart* (Arkham House, 1962). 160.38.5: "and" not capitalized; 162.25.1: grisley; 162.37.14: ma; 164.30.8: Skalli; 173.10.2: gallaghlachs.

The Song of the Last Briton

Text taken from Howard's typescript, provided by Glenn Lord. No changes have been made for this edition.

Worms of the Earth

Text taken from *Weird Tales*, November 1932. In a letter to H. P. Lovecraft, circa December 1932, Howard noted several errors in the magazine appearance of the story: "Concerning 'Worms of the Earth' – I must have been unusually careless when I wrote that, considering the errors – such as 'her' for 'his', 'him' for 'himself', 'loathsome' for 'loathing', etc. I'm at a loss to say why I spelled Eboracum as Ebbracum. I must investigate the matter. I know I saw it spelled that way, somewhere; it's not likely I would make such a mistake entirely of my own volition, though I do frequently make errors. Somehow, in my mind, I have a vague idea that it's connected in some way with the Gaelic 'Ebroch' – York."

185.8.3: Ebbracum; 188.15.6: him; 189.1.6: Ebbracum; 193.27.1: Ebbracum; 193.29.11: Ebbracum; 194.33.9: Ebbracum; 196.18.2: Ebbracum; 196.24.14: Ebbracum; 198.10.3: laugh; 198.19.7: her; 198.20.1: loathsome; 199.6.6: there is a dash rather than a hyphen in "night-things"; 203.22.3: comma after 'cast'; 205.40.1: Ebbracum; 210.10.1: Ebbracum's; 210.13.6: *Cæsar.*

An Echo from the Iron Harp
Text taken from Howard's original typescript, provided by Glenn Lord. Howard typed his lines across an entire sheet; we have broken these into two lines each. Lines with initial capital letters begin one of Howard's long lines, while those which begin with lowercase letters continue the line before. The only exception is "Marius" at 216.12.1, capitalized as a proper name but part of a continuing line.

Lord of the Dead
Text taken from Howard's typescript, copy provided by the Cross Plains Public Library. 219.11.3: "to" inserted in pencil by unknown hand; 220.3.1: basketfull; 221.7.11: impetuous; 221.27.10: colon rather than semicolon after "Brent," "A" capitalized; 222.2.1: street, comma after; 222.5.9: "of" not in typescript; 222.17.14: street; 223.29.6: street; 223.41.5: street; 224.4.7: no comma after "dark"; 224.8.12: lislessly: 227.7.15: street; 227.23.10 impells; 227.34.12: any; 228.16.10: no comma after "apprehension"; 228.28.2: street; 228.30.2: unobtrusedly; 228.30.5: street; 228.34.3: street; 228.35.7: street; 229.2.3: street; 229.9.14: Alley; 229.19.11: Alley; 229.20.4: street; 230.15.6: "if" not in typescript; 231.34.7: shown; 233.25.4-5: other one end; 233.35.4: broad edged; 235.17.5: street; 235.19.12: street; 235.27.4: Confucious; 237.31.8: street; 238.15.4: paroxism; 240.7.12: word obliterated between "his" and "fury," possibly "berserk"; 240.31.10: street; 240.36.2: street; 241.11.15: riection; 241.30.5: comma after "Khan."

Untitled
Text taken from a letter from Robert E. Howard to August Derleth, dated May 9, 1936, copy obtained from the State Historical Society of Wisconsin. No changes have been made for this edition.

"For the Love of Barbara Allen"
Text taken from Howard's original typescript, copy provided by Glenn Lord. The story was originally untitled; the title is Lord's. 249.1.1: T'was; 249.10.8: John; 249.12.7: Joel; 250.5.2: petulent; 250.26.7: saddles; 251.33.8: Alleghanies; 252.29.3: comma after "wagons"; 253.23.14: dizzingly; 253.25.8: stable-floor; 253.39.12: "lack-lustre" hyphenated at line break; 254.3.10: times'; 254.4.13: no closing quotation marks; 254.8.1: frowsy headed;

254.29.13: John; 254.34.4: John; 255.11.6: hand; 255.15.4: semicolon after "else," "that's" not capitalized; 255.16.12: no closing quotation marks.

The Tide
Text taken from *Night Images* (Morning Star Press, 1976). No changes have been made for this edition.

The Valley of the Worm
Text taken from *Weird Tales*, February 1934. 260.29.7: "Worm's-bane" hyphenated at line break; 265.14.7: "pow-wow" hyphenated at line break; 275.15.9: heiroglyphics; 278.5.10: "tree-tops" hyphenated at line break.

The Dust Dance: Selections, Version II
Text taken from *The Howard Collector*, Spring 1968. 279.23.7: steal.

The People of the Black Circle
Text taken from Howard's carbon copy, provided by Glenn Lord, supplemented by the text in *Weird Tales*, September, October, and November 1934. The surviving carbon copy is incomplete, lacking pages 1–9 and 92 of a 98 page typescript; the missing text (from the beginning to "she asked" (289.18) and from "so willingly" (346.25) to "repeated helplessly" (347.10) are taken from the *Weird Tales* appearance. Howard's chapters are untitled on the carbon copy; it is not known whether the titles are Howard's or *Weird Tales* editor Farnsworth Wright's. Changes from the *Weird Tales* text: 286.3.9: sap; 287.4.2: Hills; 288.5.2: Majesty; 288.37.14: Skalos; 289.1.5: Majesty; 289.8.1: "a" omitted. Changes from Howard's carbon copy: 289.36.15: b; 290.38.1: Eastern; 291.41.1: country-side; 292.5.11: Then; 292.31.10: sent led; 295.7.6: train; 295.10.8: unwanted; 295.20.12: of; 296.7.14: not of one of; 297.7.3: between; 298.37.5: excercise; 298.38.9: excercises; 300.10.9: "the" absent from typescript; 300.15.7: "star-light" hyphenated at line break; 300.18.1: no comma after "carelessly"; 300.37.1: quiesence; 301.11.4: when; 301.38.5: gripped; 302.32.1: hillsmen; 303.10.6: irrelevent; 303.12.9: liad; 304.32.12: into; 304.33.4: seem; 306.8.5: Irakzai; 308.10.12: fore-finger; 309.12.11: asonished; 309.13.3: distended; 309.30.4: "as" absent from typescript; 311.5.9: no comma after "through"; 313.27.12: profferred; 313.34.10: hit; 313.35.3: supply; 314.22.1: comma after "flight"; 315.9.7: north west; 316.13.3: "in" absent from typescript; 316.14.7: what ever; 316.38.6: hypnostism; 318.34.4: hundred; 318.40.4: neophism; 318.41.12: excercise; 319.20.2: Raksha; 320.32.12f: the top-left corner of the carbon paper is torn; "He shook" and the "l" of "loose" are missing; the missing words appear in the *Weird Tales* version and in the first draft of the story;

321.7.7: river bed; 321.40.6: traffick; 322.6.1: "chief" not in original; 323.34.8: tough; 324.37.7: comma after "than"; 325.13.11: gald; 325.20.3: herslf; 325.20.4: in; 325.26.3: scrutinised; 325.32.7: every; 326.20.7: "to" not in original; 326.36.11: loosly; 327.2.5: onlique; 327.13.4: on; 328.7.5: comma instead of semicolon after "fingers"; 329.13.6: no comma after "first"; 329.25.11: no comma after "suddenly"; 329.35.11: "stems" not in original; the word appears in the *Weird Tales* version and in the first draft; 330.13.8: "in" not in original; 331.22.11: wide braced; 332.2.13: infest; 332.20.3: "did" not in original; 333.7.4: half blinded; 333.12.13: thunder storm; 333.13.7: nightning; 334.14.3: green robed; 334.16.4: "as" not in original; 334.32.1: sheer walled; 335.40.1: "in a" in original; 337.22.4: unprecendented; 338.15.14: black robed; 338.18.13: black robed; 339.22.10: no comma after "mid-stride"; 339.40.10: reinacted; 340.12.13: suddeness; 340.15.13: "if" not in original; 340.30.11: "whether" not in original; 340.40.7: black robed; 340.40.12: no comma after "convulsions" (typed to right edge of paper); 341.27.9: "the" not in original; 341.40.10: his; 342.7.7: stars; 342.9.7: left hand; 342.39.2: half way; 343.3.4: sandal-wood; 344.6.1: He (there is no chapter transition at this point in Howard's carbon copy); 344.14.6: hair; 344.36.2: dociley; 345.7.5: to; 345.34.1: His; 345.38.1: semicolon instead of comma after "Yes"; 349.15.6: left hand; 349.30.12: "was" repeated; 349.37.7: van-guard; 350.23.1: accepting.

Beyond the Black River
Text taken from Howard's carbon copy, provided by Glenn Lord. Pages 1 and 65 of the carbon were in such bad shape that they had to be retyped by Lord, respecting Howard's layout and errors. The chapters are untitled in the carbon copy, except for the first one. A blank line below the heading for each new chapter suggests that Howard intended to add titles later; these may have been present in the typescript sent to *Weird Tales* or may have been added by editor Farnsworth Wright. 353.8.3: and a; 353.14.8: settlers'; 355.3.8: "been" not in original; 356.13.3: "and" absent from original; 360.34.4: the words "straying" and "strayed" appear on the carbon, one typed over the other, but it is not clear which was Howard's final choice; 360.41.3: accomodate; 361.4.12: "of" absent from original; 361.15.10: blunder; 364.19.7: pythong; 367.8.7: breek; 367.9.8: sword; 368.19.3: touched; 369.9.8: coifures; 370.3.7: "four of" in original; 370.14.1: accomodated; 370.19.8: of; 372.1.12: that; 372.11.9: beast; 372.26.9: thew; 373.6.6: futiley; 373.17.13: "in" unreadable due to crease in carbon copy; 373.27.8: ancient; 377.30.2: avoiding; 377.36.1: cubs (*Weird Tales* has "bloodhounds," Howard's first draft "blood-hounds"); 377.39.7: "and" absent from original; 379.22.13: carnivora; 379.40.12f: "looking for us" unreadable due to crease in carbon copy, taken from *Weird Tales* text; 380.2.6: "to" absent from original; 380.13.10: doesn' (typed to right edge of paper); 381.9.9: villave;

382.2.11: "with" after "trade" in original; 382.40.2: laying; 383.11.8: "the" absent from original; 384.6.7: "a" absent from original; 387.9.12: "yards" absent from original, taken from *Weird Tales* text; 387.20.7: furious; 387.23.5: no comma after "Cimmerian"; 388.12.8: accrosst; 388.19.1: broast; 389.24.4: glancing; 391.37.13: "and" unreadable due to crease in carbon; 392.20.3: hideous; 392.20.4: slashdd; 392.29.1: "was" instead of "no"; 392.31.4: growl; 393.21.11: pleasur (typed to right edge of paper); 395.16.8: "shoulders" absent from original, taken from *Weird Tales* text; 396.25.5: "blood" instead of "wound" in original; 396.31.7: boths; 398.34.12: slepp; 398.39.12: comma after "blazed"; 400.25.2: settlers'; 402.21.1f: the carbon is torn here and the first two words ("No; Conajohara") are unreadable; text taken from *Weird Tales*.

A Word from the Outer Dark
Text taken from Howard's original typescript, provided by Glenn Lord. No changes have been made for this edition.

Hawk of the Hills
Text taken from *Top-Notch*, June 1935. 405.4.10: "heart-breaking" hyphenated at line break: 406.30.5: "head-man" hyphenated at line break: 407.7.5: coördination; 407.11.9: hyphen between "hand" and "fighting"; 408.38.11: to-day; 410.23.5: semicolon after "structure"; 411.40.13: rôle; 415.23.5: "the" not in original; 419.39.5: fire-arm hyphenated at line break; 419.39.8: to-day; 420.25.8: reëchoing; 424.5.3: end quotation after "mine?"; 428.1.5: reënforce; 430.29.8: "pit-like" hyphenated at line break; 433.7.6: "El" not in original; 439.33.7: to-night; 440.1.7: To-night; 440.8.12: to-night; 442.17.5: to-morrow; 448.1.1: To-night.

Sharp's Gun Serenade
Text taken from *Action Stories*, January 1937. 456.28.6: too; 459.36.11: night; 465.9.11: period after "her'n"; 465.9.12: A; 465.26.4: period after "business."

Lines Written in the Realization That I Must Die
Text taken from *Weird Tales*, August 1938. No changes have been made for this edition.

Our work on this book would never have been possible without the direct and indirect aid of so many people. James Van Hise, who first introduced us to Robert E. Howard. Marcelo Anciano to whom we owe so much. Jack and Barbara Baum for their friendship and trust. Tony Swatton and the gang at Sword & Stone for their excellent armour, weapons, and expertise. M. Graham & Co. for the oils used on the cover illustration. Michael Venables for his priceless textual guidance. And Bill Sampson, for a million reasons. We would also like to express our gratitude to Mark Westermoe, Mark Schultz, Ed Waterman, Tom Gianni, Christian Svensson, Madison Mason, James Black, Eric Underwood, and Beth Kennedy. And of course big thanks to Rusty, Stuart, Patrice, David, Fredrik, and Thommy.

Jim & Ruth Keegan

Deepest thanks to Jim, Ruth, and Stuart, who came through like champs; to Marcelo, whose vision continues to inspire us; to Glenn, Paul, Patrice, David, Nino, Lee, and Frank for assistance with the texts; to Cherry Shults at the Cross Plains Library for providing copies of typescripts; to the members of the REH Inner Circle and others who responded to my polling for the best REH stories; to the members of the Robert E. Howard United Press Association, past and present, for thirty-five years of carrying the standard; and as always to Shelly, for her patience, love and support.

Rusty Burke

My thanks go once again to Marcelo and Rusty for making this an enjoyable experience, Jim and Ruth for their excellent illustrations – it was a pleasure meeting you both. Thanks also to Mandy and Emma for being even more patient with me as I did this at home on a laptop at the dining table! I'd also like to say thank you to Matthew Foster, for his friendship and our many literary debates over the years on the merits of Howard, Lovecraft, and Machen.

Stuart Williams

I'd like to thank Rusty and Stuart for their consistent and wonderful support and most of all Jim and Ruth for making it all seem so easy with their fantastic work, thanks. Thanks must also go to Graziana who makes it all worthwhile.

Marcelo Anciano